THE MASTER'S TRIAL

MICHELLE N. HAGOOD

For my older sister.

I'll never forget the first book you gave me, how it caused me to daydream. Some of those dreams ended up in this book.

I love you, Meg.

Contents

15

1

The Bucket List

I wish I could say magic had significantly improved my life. But that would be a lie.

With a scream, I sat bolt upright.

Run.

Fragments of nightmares played through my mind. A cold sweat made my hair and clothes cling tight.

Run.

Breathing hard, I spun around. I didn't know where I was, on a highway or in a haunted tower. I didn't know if there was a knife to my throat or a shadow at my back.

Run.

The fear evaporated as my surroundings came into focus. The night before, I had fallen asleep beside tall sagebrush, an ocean of grass at my back, and the crashing waves before me.

The sagebrush was gone, leaving blackened stumps jutting out of the ground. The grass was reduced to threads of char. The sand beneath me was no longer soft, but instead, as smooth as glass. The waves hardly made a sound as they lapped over the glossy surface.

Well, shit.

I thought leaving The Magisterium of Magic would solve my problems. Instead, it just gave me more.

I rubbed my knuckles over my sternum where my core sat full of magic. It ached with the phantom pressure of the magic flare. On shaky legs, I rose to see how far the damage went.

A few yards away, half a palm tree was charred while the other half rustled in the morning breeze. It wasn't as bad as the second flare, but it was bigger than the last one, which could be a problem. If they kept getting bigger, I would have to find more remote places to sleep, which meant more traveling. Which was fine, as long as no one got hurt.

Having magic was like capturing a hurricane and trapping it in a bottle. But the bottle had no cap and I had to keep it inside with just my hand pressed to the opening. I could handle it when I was awake. For the most part.

When I was asleep was another story. As my mind played with the horrors of my memories, it also pulled on my magic. It flared out of me without purpose other than to destroy, as if it could protect me. As a Royal Nine, there was a lot of magic to play with.

They're happening more frequently. Probably because I was so tired . . . I felt it in my bones, the weakness of my limbs. My very soul felt as if it had a real, crippling weight to it. But no matter how tired I was, I was never too tired to dream.

Careful not to slip, I moved slowly across the glass. Hopefully if . . . well, *when* someone found the char and glassy beach, they would think it was from a lightning strike. Or thirty.

A short distance away was a pile of sand, not a natural dune. I had stashed my backpack underneath in case my magic flared and destroyed everything. Good thing I did, the pile was covered in glass.

I slammed my heel down, shattering the top. I kicked away the shards and dug my backpack out. I did a quick check to make sure everything was intact. My light blue hoodie didn't have any new holes and my iPod still worked. I counted that as a win.

I slung the bag over my shoulder, ready to move, but my gaze was pulled back to the waves.

The ocean was everything I wanted it to be.

It wasn't the way the colors rolled together or how the sun glinted off the crest of each breaking wave. It wasn't the sound of the water thundering against the beach or the soft breath as it moved back to sea. It wasn't even the clear, salty air.

It was the horizon. Vast and untouchable. Staring across the ocean, I couldn't tell if I was breathing, or if I was even in my body. I had never been so at peace. I was convinced time didn't actually move in California. Or maybe that was just wishful thinking.

My stomach rumbled.

Time to go.

Reluctantly leaving the beach, I followed a small trail to an empty campsite about half a mile inland. The owners were probably on a hike. I rummaged through their cooler, taking a tomato, half a block of cheddar cheese, and a fourth of a chocolate bar. There wasn't much else. They were probably leaving today.

I dropped all of that and two water bottles into my backpack. Just as I was about to leave, I spotted a white t-shirt drying over a lawn chair.

The one I was wearing had been in use for a couple of days. It was a little singed from last night. Without thinking, I snatched it from the chair and started down the road.

Nibbling on the tomato and cheese, I walked until the signs for the campgrounds were marked with miles instead of arrows. By the time a town came into view, I was shuffling my feet more than walking, and I was down a water bottle.

I found shade by a crowded beach front and collapsed. My stomach whined again. I dragged my backpack off my shoulders and took out the half-eaten chocolate bar. Well, bar wasn't accurate anymore. Thanks to the heat, it was running out of the wrapper.

I didn't care. I ate it straight from the plastic, licking every crease and fold clean. I even searched under my fingernails. I got more sand than chocolate.

As I stowed the trash in my bag, I heard the familiar rustle of paper from inside. Putting the backpack between my knees, I took out a crumpled gas receipt from five months ago. Scribbled on the back in different colors of ink was my bucket list.

~~CLIMB A MOUNTAIN~~
~~SEE THE GRAND CANYON~~
TRY CHICAGO DEEP DISH PIZZA
~~STAR GAZING~~
SEE THE HOLLYWOOD SIGN
~~RIDE A ROLLERCOASTER~~
LEARN TO RIDE A BIKE
EAT NEW YORK CHEESECAKE IN NEW YORK
GO TO DISNEYLAND

SEE BLAKE
~~TRY A MANGO~~
GO TO A CONCERT
GO TO THE BEACH

My smile grew at the last item. *Another thing I never thought I would get to do.*

I dug through my bag for a pen, moving past a napkin from a restaurant I liked in Colorado, a snow globe I managed to swipe from a gas station in Oregon, a postcard from the Grand Canyon, and a cool rock I found somewhere along the road. Thinking I found one, I pulled it out.

I was holding my wand.

The summer sun gleamed across the black surface. The carved designs of flames tickled my palm. My fingers tightened around the hilt. The magic in my chest stirred restlessly, wanting to be used.

It had been five months since I used magic. Intentionally, that is. Every second of every day, I fought the urge to let it leave my core, flood down my arm, and into my hand.

But that was too dangerous. I didn't know if he could track me by my magic, and I wasn't going to chance it.

Prying my fingers from the hilt, I dropped it back into my bag and located a pen. I smoothed the receipt flat against my knee and tried to ignore the tingling in my hand left from my wand.

With a smile, I crossed off 'Go to the beach.'

My gaze moved over the scribbled out wishes. There was still so much to do. It made me excited. But it was short lived.

SEE BLAKE.

An ache I could only describe as homesickness settled into my bones. I hadn't seen him since Christmas, which felt like eight years ago, not eight months. My eyes drifted to a payphone on the boardwalk.

As if my body acted on its own, I grabbed some loose change from my bag and got to my feet. I glided across the sand and stopped before the payphone.

This is five different kinds of stupid—probably more.

Before I could talk myself out of it, I popped in a few coins and dialed.

Pressing the receiver to my ear, I jumped when it rang. *Cheese and rice, I'm actually doing it.* My heart knocked furiously against my ribcage.

"Ello, this is Blake."

Memories washed over me. Even though I hadn't seen my best friend in months I could picture him perfectly, from the black hair that curled around his grey, fraying beanie to the crinkles at the corners of his candy apple green eyes. Blake Johnson was the closest thing I had to family. He was the first person to look out for me and give me a better life. Too bad it didn't stick.

"Ello? Is anyone there?"

The homesickness intensified, choking the air out of my lungs. I opened my mouth to say hi, to tell him I was ok, to say—

The call ended.

I moved to dial again, but I couldn't get my fingers to move. What was the point? The reality was, he was better off and safer without me.

Part of me was relieved the jackass in the leather jacket hadn't touched him. The other part wished I never called. Ignorance is bliss or whatever.

Slowly, I replaced the phone. Fighting back tears I was too dehydrated to shed, I collected my change and turned.

And ran right into someone.

"I'm so—" The apology died on my tongue. The person in front of me wore all black.

2

All Black

I stumbled back into the payphone with my heart in my throat.

The machine popped and sparked. Loose change fell from my frozen fingers. The sound of the coins clinking against the asphalt could barely be heard over the blood rushing through my ears.

My eyes snapped to their reaching hands, expecting knives or a glowing wand. Instead, I found black nail polish and open palms.

Wait.

I looked up and found a face I didn't recognize. There were no scars or glares, just confusion. And there was no leather jacket. It was just a teenager wearing black.

I scooped my backpack from the sand and bolted down the boardwalk. In the busyness of the afternoon, I dissolved into the flow of strangers. I swiped a ball cap off a café table and pulled the brim low. I darted through the crowd until I found a small alley and tucked myself inside.

Hugging my bag to my chest, I watched the stream of people pass. No one rushed by. Everyone was either distracted by a friend or a phone. No one was looking around, looking for me.

He's not here.

I sagged against the building. My shaky legs barely kept me standing.

Closing my eyes, I gulped down the humid air. With my elevated heart rate and surge of fear, magic hummed through my chest like a wave of fire. If I didn't get it under control, something was actually going to be on fire.

"He's not here," I whispered as I massaged my aching sternum. "He's not here."

Slowly, my magic settled into my core and my heart calmed. The ache remained, but it was dull.

Mopping the sweat off my forehead, I righted my new hat and stepped back into the crowd. I turned my thoughts to better things, like food.

I moved across the busy boardwalk, keeping my head down and my fingers light. Bump into someone's shoulder, take their wallet. Trip over your feet, reach into a purse. Not a lot of people were carrying cash, so it took me over an hour to get enough for a hot dog and a cold drink or just a hamburger.

As I stood in line, weighing my options, I clutched my dinner money with white knuckles. I was so hungry, it felt as if my stomach was trying to eat my other organs.

The lamp post beside the food stand flickered.

It was late afternoon, but not late enough for them to turn on. I glanced at the others and found them off. A red flag shot up in my head.

Lights didn't flicker without cause. When I was angry, they brightened or shattered. When I cried, they blinked. I learned at The Magisterium of Magic that energy attracts energy and magic was the purest form. Flickering lights meant magic was around. It didn't come from me. Which meant there was another Magic User nearby.

Run.

I peeked over my shoulder at the bustling crowd. No one was standing still, no one was watching me.

I couldn't risk it. Pocketing the money, I left my place in line. I had survived this long by being paranoid. I wasn't going to stop now.

I zig-zagged across the boardwalk, making sure not to stay in anyone's sights for long. I ducked into an alley and came out on another street. Walking a couple blocks, I backtracked to the ocean side. All the while my head was on a swivel.

The shops along the boardwalk started to empty, meaning my camouflage was running out. I spied a parking lot down the beach. If I could steal a car, I could be in another state by midnight.

With my plan in place, I headed for the parking lot at a casual pace. I looked over my shoulder once more.

That's when I saw him.

Five months had desensitized my memories of him. I forgot how dark his eyes were. In the afternoon light they looked completely black, without anything to distinguish the iris from the pupil. His black hair was roughly styled, like he had been in a fistfight seconds before. His double holster peeked out from the sides of his signature leather jacket. The scar on the left side of his face, from his cheek down his jaw, only added to his dark look.

He was the one who taught me every night at the Magisterium with a condescending tone and never ending insults. He blackmailed me by threatening to cut off Blake's head if I didn't agree to help him with the Achilles Heel, a group dedicated to fighting my father, Lawrence Hart.

In short, Michael Kale was a real son of a bitch, a pure-bred jackass.

I fled toward the parking lot as fast as I could. It felt like my feet barely touched the ground.

He was looking away. Maybe he didn't see me. Maybe I can—

The wooden slats of the boardwalk suddenly rose up in front of me, creating a wall. Without time to stop, I turned my shoulder and slammed into the wood, *hard.* I pushed off to run another way, but the planks behind me had risen up too. Sand from either side of the boardwalk walled off the sides, creating a box of sand and wood.

I fought the urge to scream. I unslung my backpack and dumped everything out on the ground. In the dim light, I groped around for my wand. The moment I found it, I pushed magic down my arm, aimed at the nearest wall, and fired.

The boardwalk exploded into a shower of splinters. I dove out of the box and into the sand. Michael was at a full sprint toward me.

I reached back for my backpack, but it was nearly empty and I didn't have time to collect my things. My light blue hoodie was at the far corner, too far to reach.

Gritting my teeth, I left behind all my souvenirs from moments I had stolen, moments I was told I would never have. Tears threatened to fill my eyes, but I couldn't allow them to distort my vision.

Getting a car is going to take too long. I just need to hide and—

Standing in the middle of the boardwalk was another man dressed in a black trench coat. *Atlas?* I had met him first on a bus leaving Kansas and then at a New Year's Festival where he tried to kill me. He worked with Michael.

He raised a hand, not the one with the wand, and waved. *Smug asshole.*

I pivoted and ran off the boardwalk. *If I can just hide—*But there was someone in all black there too. A woman with a long braid. She didn't wave, nor did she move. She stood perfectly still with her wand glowing as a silent threat.

He had more help?

I pivoted back to the parking lot, but leaning against the wooden entrance was another man. Messy blonde hair fell to his shoulders. Even though he stood with his arms crossed and no wand in sight, it didn't make him any less menacing. He was in all black. He was a Hunter.

I was completely surrounded. The ocean was to my back and I had a Hunter on all sides.

I faced Michael, the only one moving toward me. He had slowed to a walk, but each step was deliberate. I could feel his rage in each controlled movement. With my heart racing, I backed away.

Reaching under his leather jacket, he took a knife from his double holster. It had a blade like a butcher's knife. He hurled it at me.

With a surge of magic, I deflected it to the sand. Before the blade sank into the boardwalk, he was throwing another, this one with a curved edge. He threw two more, each with increasing speed.

I deflected one but a little blade slipped through my defenses. It sliced across my shoulder. With a startled cry, I clapped my hand over the cut.

That was all the opening he needed. Michael Ported beside me and grabbed my wrist. Twisting my arm painfully, he pried my wand from my fingers.

No! As my panic surged, and my magic along with it, I saw Michael wince ever so slightly.

And then I remembered. When a User had a lot of magic, like a Royal Nine, it was painful for any high status User they touched. Michael had always been so careful not to touch my skin, to not even be in touching range.

I reached up and pressed my hand against his face.

Cursing wildly, he released me. I pulled on my magic, ready to Port the hell out of there, but he kicked my legs out from under me. I slammed onto the boardwalk with enough force to eject the air from my lungs.

Michael pressed his boot to my throat, pinning me against the wood. The bastard hadn't even broken a sweat. *Had he gone easy on me?*

"I'm going to lift my boot," he said calmly, as he tucked my wand in his holster. "If you try to run, I'll sever your spine. Do you understand?"

Gritting my teeth, I nodded.

He stepped back but kept his wand glowing by his side, ready to fire at a moment's notice.

Slowly, I pushed myself to my feet. Just as I rose to my full height, he grabbed me and Ported us away from prying eyes and into the parking lot. Spinning me around, he slammed me chest first into the side of the car.

"Fancy meeting you here," I said dryly.

"God, I forgot how annoying your voice is." He kicked my feet apart.

"I was thinking the same thing."

Quickly, he patted around my waist and dipped into my pockets. He checked around my ankles and under my arms. When he found no other weapons, he turned me back to face him. He pressed the tip of his wand against my throat.

A dark shadow walked around the car. "Here you go, boss." Atlas's Irish accent gave him away as he handed Michael my backpack. The sleeve of my light blue hoodie peeked out of the zipper.

Meeting my gaze, Atlas's eyes crinkled. "'Ello, love. Long time, no see."

I lifted my middle finger without a word.

"You can go," Michael spat out as he shouldered my bag. "Take Sánchez and Went with you."

Atlas's pierced brow lifted. "You sure, boss?"

Michael nodded curtly.

Putting his fingers to his lips, Atlas whistled two notes. With a mocking salute to me, he turned on his heel and vanished. In his place, was a glowing Porting circle.

Alone, Michael lowered his wand. "Do you mind telling me what was so important that you'd waste *five months* of my time?"

I leaned against the car and shrugged.

Fire lit in his eyes. The muscle in his jaw flexed. "Always a pain in the ass."

"You're one to talk."

He took half a step closer, which was six inches too close for my liking. I tilted my head back to hold his seething gaze.

"There is an easy way I can get the information from you." The tip of his wand dug into the underside of my jaw. "And there is a hard way. One I will enjoy and one you won't. It's up to you how we proceed."

I remembered the last time he dug through my mind for answers I was unwilling to verbalize. The process was painful, nauseating, and downright intrusive.

So, I decided to answer, but in the way that would piss him off the most. "I'm on vacation."

"Vacation," he repeated slowly, like he didn't understand.

"A summer vacation," I clarified.

"You're kidding."

"Were you going to give me one?"

"No."

"Then I stand by my decision."

"Listen, Hart—"

"My name is Charlie."

His wand seared my skin as he bared his teeth. "Your impromptu vacation cost me time I could've spent getting closer to your father. Time I can't get back."

"I wish I cared, truly."

"You should. We had an agreement. You help me kill your father and you get to live happily ever after with your British friend. Or did your insufficient mind forget that?"

"Nope. I just figured out it was a lie."

He opened his mouth, but I didn't let him say whatever excuse he had lined up.

"I know about your agreement with Master Lenin. You never intended for me to live after I helped you win the war."

There was a slight pause. "Where'd you hear that?"

"Blaine Willow told me. She said some bullshit about my magic status being too high to let me live, but I think it's because you can't stand who I'm related to." I stepped forward to snarl in his face, "You see, when you help someone, they usually help you back, like Blaine. That's unless it involves a back stabber like you."

"Watch your mouth."

"Is it really so hard to believe that the apple could fall far from the tree?"

"It doesn't matter how far the apple falls if it grows from a poisonous tree."

"You know nothing about me." The window behind me cracked as my magic grew hotter.

"I don't need to. All I need to know is how dangerous you are." He lifted his wand and held it beside my face. "Let's say we do win and you get to live. A survivor of the Crown captures you, takes their wand, and slips it through your sternum and into your core."

As he talked, he angled his wand to press the glowing tip to my sternum. I flinched from the sheer heat of his magic.

"Then they just toss you at the Heel. When your core breaks open it will detonate like a bomb. If I did it right now," he pressed his wand harder into my skin, "the force of your magic exploding out of you would set off the San Andreas Fault. The state would break into pieces. But most of it would just burn."

My chest rose and fell rapidly with my terrified breathing. But I didn't dare break eye contact.

"To keep you from being a threat, your magic could be drained to reduce your status, but even then, anyone could steal what was harvested. If you had children, they'd also have your status. Either way, you'd be a continuous problem."

"And let me guess." I swallowed thickly. "You're the one who gets to kill me?"

"Yes." A lethal grin crossed his lips. "It's something I'm looking forward to." His wand glowed brighter.

Magic swirled painfully in my chest. More cracks spread through the window behind me.

"I hope when you kill me and Lawrence," I struggled to get the words past my clenched teeth, "it fills whatever gaping hole is in your chest. But it won't make you better than him. From where I'm standing, you're one and the same."

"Don't you dare."

"Or what," I spat. "You don't scare me. You're nothing but an evil son of a bitch who's gone so dark he can't justify the air he breathes."

Michael lurched forward. I flinched, expecting a ward to shoot from his wand and end me right there. Instead, he slammed his fist onto the roof of the car beside my head. The windows shattered. The radio sparked and the lights burst. The tip of his wand went to my throat again.

I stood there, shaking. Magic flared uselessly down my arm, but without my wand, it couldn't go anywhere.

I kept my eyes locked on his.

Hatred clenched his jaw. Anger flushed his neck. Bloodlust hardened his gaze.

I may have lied. He did terrify me, but I was right about one thing. He wasn't a man. His lack of control proved I was right. He might not have been ready to admit that, but I had all the proof I needed. It was shattered around our feet.

Taking slow, deliberate breaths, he lowered his wand. His boots ground glass into the asphalt as he stepped back.

He glanced at the dented space beside my head. "If you're done, I'd like to leave."

"You make it sound like I have a choice."

"You don't." He grabbed my arm and, with the aid of a transporter, Ported us out of California. In the next breath, we were in the cold stairwell of The Magisterium of Magic.

3

The Gravity of Your Commitment

The final hours of sunlight streamed down from the Magisterium's glass ceiling to glitter along the gold banisters twisting around the twin spiral staircases.

Michael and I appeared at the center of the stairwell surrounded by the gold doors marking the different wings and the common areas on the first floor: the library, dining room, infirmary, and greenhouse.

Months ago, the black stone walls presented me with a new life. Now they reminded me of the inside of a coffin.

"If I were you," Michael pulled me toward the right staircase spiraling downward, "I'd keep my smart mouth shut. He hasn't been in the best mood since you jumped ship."

"If only you knew how much I didn't care."

"You should. He decides what happens to you."

As he pulled me downstairs, his long legs had me nearly jogging to keep up. The door to Master Lenin's office was open, which meant there was no reason to pause. Michael shoved me inside and slammed the door behind him.

"Look what I found."

Master Lenin's eyes jerked up from the book in front of him and widened when they saw me.

He was the School Master of the Magisterium, one of the seven School Masters in existence. The title made him a deity to most. Knowledge was currency and he was the god forsaken bank. With that much knowledge, he could create the rules and order of the magical world.

I knew him as a lying prick.

"You never cease to amaze me, Master Kale." The School Master's cold gaze of dark brown and flecks of gold took in my rumpled clothes, the glass sprinkled on my shoes, and the bloody tear in my t-shirt. "What happened?"

"Nothing she didn't ask for." Michael leaned against the wall to my left, between the door and me.

Master Lenin turned to the small mirror on the corner of his desk. He touched what looked like a button on the bottom and turned the reflection toward himself.

When the frame glowed gold, he spoke into the mirror, "She's back. Send it over when you have it." He touched the mirror again, turning off the glow, and nodded to the chair before his desk. "Take a seat, Miss Heart."

I crossed my arms and remained right where I was.

Michael moved toward me, probably to toss me into one of the seats. But the School Master halted him with a simple shake of his head.

"I'm glad you're alive." Master Lenin flipped the large book in front of him closed. I recognized the gold cover from my time in the Records Room a few months ago.

"Because you'd have to find another poor soul to die for your cause?"

Master Lenin's eyes shot to the Master Hunter. "What's she talking about?"

"It seems that Blaine Willow was doing more than haunting your North Wing. She was spying on you too," Michael answered. "Willow told her about her fate after the war."

Master Lenin slowly turned his gold flecked gaze to me.

"How were you going to do it?" I asked, acid lacing the question. "As soon as Lawrence's body hit the floor, were you just going to turn around and shoot me in the face? Or were you going to slip something into my glass of celebratory champagne?"

"That is up to Master Kale. It was his one condition for giving his time to train you."

The lights blinked rapidly all around the room. I clenched my hands so tightly that my fingernails cut into my palms.

"I would gladly let you live," Master Lenin continued, "but your magic is too dangerous. The possibility of—"

"Michael gave me the 'you'll be a continuous problem' speech already," I snapped. "Which is funny to me because the only problems I see are coming from the two of you." I pointed at Master Lenin. "You covered up the deaths of thirty-seven students so your school could keep running. And you." When I turned to Michael all I could do was clench my teeth. "I don't even know where to start."

"Miss Heart, please sit down." Master Lenin nodded to the chair again.

"No. Why do you even need me? Find Lawrence and take him out yourself. Michael's more than capable, right?"

"It's not that simple," Michael riposted.

I whipped around. "Then explain it to me."

Michael's nostrils flared.

"Even if we knew where Master Hart was," Master Lenin jumped in, "you don't kill Masters. That's the one thing every User agrees on. Society would crucify us and we'd end up just like him."

"If you can't kill him, then how are you going to win?"

"The only way to get rid of a Master is to ruin them. You get the School Masters to reject his title and when he's just a User, then you kill him. But if his title is intact, he's untouchable."

I shook my head. "That's the stupidest thing I've ever heard."

"But it's the rules our world abides by," Master Lenin said sternly.

There was a flash of gold from the corner of Master Lenin's desk. A folded handkerchief appeared on a platter. He barely spared it a glance.

I took a deep breath before my magic popped a light bulb. "What makes this side the one worth my life? I'm leaning toward Lawrence since he hasn't stabbed me in the back or made plans to kill me."

Rage colored Michael's cheeks with a bright flush.

Sensing Michael's struggle, Master Lenin answered. "We're fighting for a world where magic status doesn't determine your right to live. Your father wants to create a paradise for those he deems worthy. He'll kill every Low Common, Deficient, and anyone who isn't loyal to him. He thinks he can decide who deserves to live."

My blood pressure skyrocketed. "Isn't that what you're doing with me?"

"You deserve to live," Master Lenin stressed. "Don't mistake that, because that's not what we're saying. But the danger of your continued existence outweighs anything else. Your life could save generations from the cruelty of fatal magic prejudice."

Bullshit. I can't even save myself.

Master Lenin continued softly, "By fighting with the Achilles Heel, with us, by removing your father from his self-proclaimed throne, you fight for more than just morality. You fight for life itself."

The raging fire in my chest had gone still. Even Michael seemed to have lost some of his anger upon hearing the School Master's answer.

"Who's going to take Lawrence's place?" I asked.

Master Lenin's eyebrows pulled together. "What do you mean?"

"Once you kill him, someone takes his place, right?"

To my surprise, Master Lenin looked toward the man in the leather jacket.

"I just want Lawrence dead. Nothing more," Michael said firmly.

Master's Lenin's lips thinned but he didn't voice his thoughts. I had no problem voicing mine.

"Coward."

Master Lenin rushed on before the Master Hunter could bite my head off. "Miss Heart, in order for all of us to move forward, we need to be on the same page."

"I don't want to move forward with you," I insisted. "I want away from this shit show."

"No," Master Lenin scolded, as if he were chastising a child. "You want your friend, Blake Johnson, to live. I thought Master Kale was extremely clear that in order for that to continue, you would join the Heel and help us win. But you broke that agreement when you ran."

I didn't like the sound of that. *I heard Blake's voice. He's ok.*

"If you choose to do so again, there will be consequences." He reached across his desk to collect the rolled-up handkerchief. He dropped it in front of me and flipped away the folds to reveal something inside.

It took me a moment to realize what I was seeing.

It couldn't be. That shit only happened in movies.

But the longer I stared, the clearer the image etched itself into my mind. It was a severed human finger.

"Your friend won't be playing guitar any time soon," Master Lenin said casually, as if there wasn't a finger on his desk.

"What the fuck, Lenin?" Michael spoke each word slowly, as if he were just as shocked as me.

"That's Blake's?" I whispered, nearly choking on the horror rising in my throat.

Master Lenin nodded. "The next time you run, it won't be another finger. It'll be his head."

My eyes snapped up from the bloody finger to the man sitting behind the desk. The temperature in the office skyrocketed as all of the lights glowed nearly white. I launched myself across the desk reaching for Master Lenin's eyes.

Michael's arms looped around my middle and hauled me away before I could deliver a single scratch. I screamed a mess of nonsensical curses.

Michael twisted me away from the desk and released me. My shoulder slammed into the wall beside the door, cracking it from the baseboard to the ceiling. Photos fell from their nails and crashed to the floor. Glass flew across the carpet.

Pushing the pain aside, I spun back to the School Master. Michael stepped in my way with his wand unholstered.

"You son of a bitch!" I yelled over him.

Master Lenin was no longer calm nor seated. He stood with his chair between us. Like that would help. "You knew the rules."

"I didn't think—" I looked back at the finger and nearly threw up. "What the hell is wrong with you?"

"Lenin, we never talked about this," Michael said tightly.

"You're saying you didn't know about this?" I yelled.

Michael's jaw flexed. "Yes."

"Liar."

"He's telling the truth," Master Lenin said. "I thought his time was best spent hunting you."

Michael looked over his shoulder. "So, you ordered my team to attack a *kid?*"

"No. I asked Magee."

Michael blinked. "You're shitting me."

Robert Magee was a name I hadn't thought of in a while. He was there when I first came to the Magisterium. Sickly sweet with false charm, and double sided manners, there was something off about him. Although I had no evidence other than my gut to support that. Until now.

"Hopefully now you understand the gravity of your commitment to the Heel," Master Lenin said coolly. "Now that you are back, you will follow *every* rule at my school. If I hear you're not, you will not have the privilege to be here."

"I don't even want to be here!" I exclaimed.

"Then I'm sure we can find a cell to put you in." He paused. "By being here, you have daylight, food, and full use of the amenities of this school."

Shit, he has me there.

"Lastly, if you *ever* break into my Records Room again, I'll lock you in a hole so dark you'll forget what the sun looks like." His gaze had hardened, making the gold flecks smolder like embers. "There are things you don't need to know and what's in that room is one of them. Do I make myself clear?"

My eyes dropped to the gold book on his desk. "Clear as glass."

"Good. I expect to hear from Master Kale that you're following his instructions to the fullest. He says jump, you do it without question. I was gracious last year, Miss Heart, because you were new, but there will be no more wasting time." He turned to Michael. "Would you like to add anything?"

He shook his head.

Master Lenin pressed on. "These last weeks of summer, you're going to be spending with Master Kale catching up on the months you missed. The only advice I can give you is to do everything he says. Do you have any questions about what we expect of you?"

I shook my head. I just wanted to get out of there. But my eyes were drawn back to the finger. "How badly did you hurt him?"

"That was the extent of his injuries. I made sure of that." Master Lenin pulled out his chair and once more sat at his desk. "I'll see you at the end of the summer." He nodded to Michael before turning back to his papers.

Michael herded me through the door and into the silent hallway. I felt like I was walking toward my death. I probably was.

"Did you really not know?" I asked when we got to the stairs. My blood was still simmering.

Michael nodded once. "I'm not in the business of maiming people."

I don't believe that.

"I'm better at killing."

Now that, I do.

He grabbed my elbow and Ported. The silence of the school fell away to the rush of an evening wind. When we reappeared, a grey sky and thin pine trees greeted us. In front was a black gate. Joining the two halves was the letter K.

So, that's what the gates to hell look like . . . I tried to look past the black iron for a glimpse of the horrors that lay behind. All I could see were more evergreens, thick sage brush, and a gravel drive that wove up the hill and out of sight.

Michael placed his hands on the gate and pushed. A glimmer of golden magic ran over the black surface before the gate soundlessly swung open. He paused just beyond the threshold and looked back. His eyes narrowed at my hesitation.

Not wanting to evoke his wrath further, I stepped forward. As soon as I did, magic, like hot, bubbling honey, glazed over my skin. This place was heavily protected.

I scanned the shadows as he closed the gates behind us. They looked empty, but that didn't stop my brain from imagining monsters, hell hounds, and cages just out of sight. I thought of Blake's severed finger.

Gravel crunched under his boots as he brushed by me. My heart raced as I followed him up the drive. At the top, lights came into view. I expected a fortress of stone with a mote, gargoyles, and maybe a skeleton or two hanging from the walls.

Instead, it was just a modest white house with dark green shutters. A long porch twisted around the structure toward the back. Vines clung to the sides and a beautiful bed of flowers waved in the wind. Across the yard was a red barn.

Michael moved up the porch to the front door, but he didn't open it right away. His jaw clenched. After a few seconds, he pushed it open.

Having no choice, I followed him inside.

"Michael?"

I stopped. The feminine voice came from deep in the house. *Does he have a housekeeper? Maybe an assistant of torture?*

"It's me," he said quietly.

Footsteps sounded closer seconds before light flooded the hallway.

"What's the color of pineapple?"

Code words? I tried to peek around him.

"Green."

A relieved sigh left the woman as she stepped closer to him. "Oh, baby, it's so good to see you. You look good! A bit thin, but good. Have you not been eating?" She cupped the side of his face. Her thumb rubbed over his scar.

"Not everyone cooks like you, Mom." He pressed a kiss to her forehead.

I choked on my spit and stumbled against the door. Michael looked over his shoulder with a questioning eyebrow.

I glanced between the two, looking for similarities. I couldn't find any. Everywhere Michael was hard, she was soft. Michael had glaring lines while she had wrinkles from smiles. Sure, they were both tall, but that was hardly *proof.*

If that was his mom, that meant . . . he brought me to his home?

Cheese and rice.

4

The Ranch

"Are you insane?" I hissed.

My brain refused to process what I was seeing. Every time I looked at the woman it was like a sharp slap to the face. *His mother? HIS MOTHER?*

Michael's eyebrow rose.

I grabbed his sleeve and pulled him back a step. "Can we have a minute?"

She looked at Michael. After a quick nod from HER SON, she stepped back. "Your father is in his study. You should let him know you're here." Then she retreated down the hall and out of view.

"You've got to be kidding me," I all but yelled.

"Keep your voice down," he snapped, yanking out of my grip. "And I told you not to touch me. What's your problem?"

"This is your house."

"No. It's my parents'."

"And your parents live here."

He rolled his eyes. "Obviously."

"Why did you bring me here?" There was no way he trusted me enough to be around his family. Hell, I didn't even trust myself! "Isn't there supposed to be a quiet cabin in the woods where no one can hear me scream?"

The corner of his lips curled in amusement. "Obviously that's the better choice, but I need someone I can trust to watch you when I'm not around."

My jaw dropped. *He's planning on leaving me alone with them?* "Where are you going?"

"I'm fighting a war, not babysitting."

Cheese and rice. "Why can't Master Lenin watch me?"

"He has a job."

"What about Magee?" As soon as I said it, I regretted it. He cut off Blake's finger. Being around him was almost as bad as staying with the Kales.

Michael's eyes narrowed. "I wouldn't trust that man with a stick."

I thrust my hands into my hair. He *had* to see how stupid this was. "There has to be some other place—"

"Out of the two of us, I hate it more that you have to be here." He dropped his voice. "Do you think I enjoy the thought of putting someone as unstable as you with my family? I'm following orders, that's it."

"Michael, I can't be here." *You have no idea just how unstable I am.*

"Well, you are. So, we both have to deal with it." With that, he opened the first door on the left without knocking. Light poured into the hallway.

I looked back at the front door, thinking of the horrible things my mind did at night. My stomach coiled tighter.

Run.

I hovered in the hallway for a few seconds with my nails biting into my palms. *I need to get out of here.* But I couldn't do that with Michael on edge. As soon as he tucked me away for the night, I could bolt. In the meantime, I had to play along.

I followed him down the hall and into the well-lit room. My jaw dropped for a second time.

A man rose from behind a large desk. He stood an inch taller than Michael. His hair was the same rich black but sprinkled with grey. He even had the same golden skin and wide shoulders.

Mr. Kale gave him a hearty slap on the back. "I hardly recognized you." His voice was deep and rich.

"You're one to talk. You're letting your hair go grey."

The laugh that came from the older man's throat made my jaw drop further. Kales can *laugh*?

"I thought it was time to look my age." He put his hand on Michael's shoulder. "It's been too damn long. I'm glad you're home. Even if it's for work."

Michael's back stiffened. "I'm surprised you accepted Lenin's offer."

"I had to see my son somehow."

"This is a bit dramatic."

"It seems dramatic measures are the only way to get your attention." His father's gaze shifted to me. He took a slow, calming breath. "That's her?"

Michael nodded.

He stepped around his son toward me. For the first time, Michael wasn't the scariest person in the room.

My feet slid back until they bumped into the doorframe. He noticed the movement and kept coming.

"I thought you'd be taller." He offered me his hand. "Atticus Kale."

Pressing myself tighter against the wall, I managed to squeak out, "Nice to meet you, sir."

"It's disrespectful not to shake a man's hand when he offers it to you."

"There's a no touching policy," Michael explained. "Her status will make your arm numb for hours."

Mr. Kale kept his hand outstretched. "I'm waiting."

I shot a glance at Michael. Both of us knew what my magic would do. Yet, he clenched his jaw and nodded once.

"I'm Charlie." I placed my hand in Mr. Kale's.

Immediately, he ripped his hand away. "Son of a bitch!" He looked at me, his hand, and Michael and then back at me again. "Damn."

"Sorry." I laced my fingers behind me, glad he had taken a few steps back.

He shook and flexed his hand. "She knew nothing about magic? Even with a shock like that?"

Michael nodded. "She's rather dull."

I fought the urge to stick my tongue out at him.

Mr. Kale turned to me. "I guess I should welcome you to my home . . . I apologize if I seem reluctant. Hart's have only brought grief into this house."

I tried to smile. "I'm surprised you're not making me sleep in the yard."

"Are you giving me ideas?" Michael asked.

"I'd prefer a sewer tank if it meant I didn't have to be around you." My mouth clicked shut. I expected Mr. Kale to jump to his son's aid. Maybe even push me into the wall.

Instead, he chuckled. "Dull, huh? She seems pretty quick to me."

"Her tongue is the only quick thing about her. I've been insulted more times than I can count."

It's not like you don't deserve it, I thought dryly.

"Someone has to keep you humble. Everyone's calling you the best Hunter the Guard ever created."

"Are you saying I'm not?" For the first time, Michael's smirk wasn't malicious. If I didn't know the man to be the purest form of evil, I would've described it as playful.

"Not at all. You just need to remember that you shoveled horse shit for the first twenty-three years of your life." Mr. Kale looked back at me and the sparkle in his eyes dimmed. "Dinner will be ready in twenty minutes. We have the guest room made up for her."

Michael nodded once. Shoving past me, he walked further into the house.

"You better be right behind me," Michael snapped.

Tearing my eyes from the older Kale, I followed after him. *Seriously, how did someone like Michael Kale have such a normal looking dad?* I expected horns or at least a pitchfork.

Down the hall, Michael shot me a sideways glance. "Why are you looking at me like that?"

"I'm just getting over the shock that you have parents."

He gave me a dry look. "I do have a belly button. That implies I have parents."

"It's not like I've ever seen it."

His nose scrunched, like the thought of me ever seeing him without a shirt and his leather jacket was the grossest thing ever. I agreed.

"I always thought Satan spit on a rock and you just jumped out of the steam."

"That's not the first time I've heard something like that," he muttered. Reaching around me, he opened a door next to the kitchen. "You'll be staying in here."

I expected a cement floor with a sleeping bag thrown in the corner.

Instead, I was greeted by off-white carpet and a large bed covered in pillows and a burnt orange comforter. A set of large windows framed by yellow curtains lined the wall across the room. A door to the right led to a private bath.

"I'm surprised there are no bars over the windows," I mused sarcastically.

He dropped my backpack on the floor and crossed his arms over his chest. His tall frame filled the doorway. "Are you saying there should be?"

I rolled my eyes and shook my head.

"I need to make sure we're on the same page," Michael said. "That way you won't have any excuses when you do something stupid."

I chose not to say anything about the fact that he said 'when' and not 'if.'

"We're here for barely five minutes and you're already telling me the rules." I sat on the bed. "I'm surprised you waited this long."

His eyes narrowed. "This isn't funny."

"It is a little. All of this almost makes you seem human. Too bad I already know you don't have a soul." I showcased my best smile.

"Cute." His lip twitched with annoyance. "I see you got rid of your stupid red streak."

I touched the ends of my brown hair. On the left side, there used to be a single lock of hair as red as Kool-Aid. He may have thought it was stupid, but in Kansas, where everything was dictated and controlled, the red streak was my little rebellion.

"I didn't want to have something you could identify me by."

He grunted. "How did you stay on the run for five months? The only person who's evaded me that long is your father."

I shrugged. "I picked up some tricks from the other foster kids. Some ran away from juvie sentences, so they knew how to stay under the radar." I paused. "How did you find me?"

"You called Johnson." Now it was his turn to smile. "Your fondness for him is your biggest weakness."

"I had to make sure you hadn't killed him."

"You should have thought of that before you ran."

There was a pause. I wondered if both of us were thinking of Blake's finger.

"You won't be able to make the same move here," he went on. "Magic surrounds the entire property. You can Port anywhere within the property, but not out of it."

A cold sweat covered the back of my neck. *So that's why barred windows aren't necessary. I'm already in a cage.*

"Since you wasted five months of my time, we'll jump straight into lessons first thing tomorrow morning. They won't be over until I say so. I'm going to start by teaching you how to protect yourself without your wand. That way, if there's a rerun of the Richard While situation, you can beat the hell out of him instead of jumping out of a tower."

I fought the urge to cover the scar on my neck as his eyes dipped toward it. Clearing my throat, I looked down at my hands. "Would Helen be able to get rid of these scars?"

"No. They were inflicted with a magical object. They can't be changed."

I peeked up at him. *Is that why he still has the scar on his face?* I was told Lawrence gave it to him. I didn't know the specifics, and I wasn't going to ask.

"When you're not in lessons, you'll be here catching up on schoolwork." He pointed to the bookcase under the window. "Lenin expects a weekly report of how you're doing. So, for the love of God, pay attention."

He dropped his voice to a hostile tone. "You will keep interactions with my family to a minimum. You do not leave this room until I get you. I don't care if the house is on fire. You stay. You're not allowed to talk to them, unless they speak to you. You're not allowed to be alone with them. If it involves my family, it is off limits. I'll be staying across the hall, so don't even think about sneaking out. Got it?"

Each word felt like a punch to my gut. I felt dirty. Like I would ruin anything I touched. I looked at my scarred hands. With all the magic in them, I probably would. So I nodded.

"Good." He grabbed the door handle and started to leave. "I'll see you in—" Abruptly, his head snapped around, looking down the hall.

On the other side of the house a screen door slammed. Mumbled voices rose from curiosity to excitement. Feet clamored across the hardwood and in the next moment someone ran right into Michael, coiling their arms tightly around him.

His hands hovered by his sides like he didn't know what to do. Then he just melted. His arms wound around the small frame in front of him. He pulled her so tightly against him that her toes left the ground.

"You're going to break my ribs," she laughed, although her arms were just as tight around his neck.

"I know she's your favorite, but you can at least pretend it's not true," a deeper voice chuckled.

Michael set her back on her feet and extended his hand toward the man just out of view. "Damn, Zak, how long are you going to let your hair grow? You look like you're in a boy band." With a crooked smile, he pulled him into a bear hug.

"That's exactly what I said." The woman crossed her arms on top of her pregnant belly.

"You're one to talk." My mouth dropped as the man ruffled Michael's hair. "Do you even remember how to use a comb?"

Michael swatted his hand away with a look of annoyance, but it wasn't the kind he usually sent my way. Hints of a smile tugged at his lips.

The woman opened her mouth to join in on the playful banter when her hazel eyes caught sight of me. The reaction was immediate.

Her expression went cold. Her smile dropped. Her arms wrapped around her stomach like she was trying to shield it from me.

I could tell she was related to Michael. Not in the 'distant relative because they have the same nose' way but because she looked like mom and he looked like dad. The only difference was that she lacked the Kale black hair. Hers was the same color as dark caramel.

The other man noticed the drastic change and followed her gaze.

When our eyes met, I thought I was looking at a second Michael. It wasn't because his face resembled Michael's. On the contrary, this man's face was rounder and his hair was longer. It was still black, although not as dark, and it fell past his ears. I knew they were brothers because of the glare he was giving me.

Michael Kale had siblings. And they loathed me just as much as he did. *Run.*

"So, that's the bastard's kid." The brother rolled a toothpick across his tongue. "She doesn't look that impressive."

"Because she's not." Michael leaned against the doorframe. All three looked like they were at the zoo inspecting the newest animal.

"Dad said she was dumped in a trashcan," the brother said, without looking away.

Embarrassment flushed through my bloodstream. *Was Michael just telling that to everyone?*

Michael nodded. "As a newborn."

"What's up with the scars?" his sister asked.

I clenched my hands around the ones on my palms. My head dipped so my hair could cover the one on my neck.

"She attracts trouble like a magnet," Michael explained. "She ran into a demon a few months back."

"And she's still alive? Huh. I would've put money against her. She doesn't look like she can do anything."

"Now you see my dilemma."

His sister's disgusted expression raked over me. She picked up on the knots in my hair and the stains and tears in my shirt.

Seeing my searching gaze, Michael reluctantly answered my unasked question. "This is Zak and Meg."

I waved. "Hi."

Meg shrunk back closer to her brothers. Zak continued to roll the toothpick between his teeth like he was imagining it as one of my bones.

Mrs. Kale cleared her throat behind them. "Dinner's ready."

Zak immediately turned to the kitchen. Meg stayed only long enough to look me over once more. Then Michael pulled the door closed. His boots clomped down the hallway.

Run.

As soon as I couldn't hear him, I grabbed my bag and ran to the window. I threw it open and peered into the darkness. Just outside was a small garden with a few bushes and bundles of flowers.

Run.

Ducking through, I stepped onto the mulch and pulled the window closed. The full moon highlighted the treeline and barn roof. As my eyes adjusted to the silver light, I could just make out the road.

Tiptoeing across the gravel, I retraced my steps to the front gate. The wilderness snapped and rustled as I passed. Whether it was the wind or something else, I couldn't tell. I shot a look over my shoulder. The only thing following me was darkness.

When I reached the gate, I was nearly shaking with the need to get out of there. Grabbing the black iron, I pulled.

Golden magic flared from the space between the two sides of the gate. The flash moved high into the sky and curved like we were under a dome of glass. But the gate didn't budge. I pulled again, but this time I dug my heels into the gravel and leaned back with all my weight. It didn't even creak.

Michael wasn't kidding. I couldn't get out.

I thought about hiding in the woods. Then I could make a mad dash to the gate whenever it was opened . . . But Blake would be dead faster than I could Port to his front door.

Why did fate keep dealing me shitty cards?

When I released the gate, the golden magic dimmed, leaving me in the silver light of the moon. It felt like my life was no longer my own. Everything from here on out would be for a cause I wanted nothing to do with.

Run.

Run.

Run.

But for once, the call couldn't drive me forward. I was backed into a corner with five hateful Kales in front of me and a magical cage at my back.

With nowhere to go, I started back up the driveway. The chilly night air numbed my feet and sent the rest of me shaking.

Instead of returning to the house, I ducked into the barn. If I was going to stay here, I needed to be careful. Would one of them sneak in and try to slit my throat? Zak looked like he wanted to. The biggest threat was Michael. If I flared and hurt his family, who knows what he would do to Blake? Or me?

Horses nickered at me as I passed by. When they saw I had nothing for them, they moved back into their stalls.

Protected from the wind, the air was warmer inside. I looked around for a good hiding place. I found a tack room and a room dedicated to horse feed. But I wondered if they were visited regularly.

At the back of the barn, I scaled a ladder into the loft where towers of hay bales were stored. I squeezed between the stacks until I found a space in the back big enough for someone to curl up for the night.

Perfect.

Fighting a yawn, I moved down the ladder and back to the house. Peeling back the covers on the bed, I took off the top sheet and a patchwork quilt. I positioned the decorative pillows to look like a body before throwing the comforter over it. Just in case Michael paid me a midnight visit. I locked the door for good measure.

Grabbing the two blankets, I slipped out the window and back into the barn. I struggled up the ladder with my bundle and squeezed between the towers of hay. Tossing the blankets in the corner, I laid down and wrapped them around me.

Finally, I surrendered to my exhaustion. I was too tired to dread the next day.

5

Just a Horse with Wings

I woke up by headbutting the side of the barn.

Mumbling incoherent curses, I rubbed my forehead. Before sleep could tempt me back, I remembered where I was . . . the Kale ranch.

My eyes snapped open. *Cheese and rice.*

Beneath me, footsteps tramped against the dirt floor. Moving slowly, I rose from my hidden corner, squeezed between the rows of hay, and back to the ladder.

Peering over, I spotted Mr. Kale pushing a wheelbarrow. Grabbing a pitchfork, he heaved a section of hay into a stall. The unfed horses stood eagerly at their doors. The impatient ones pawed at the walls.

"I'm coming," Mr. Kale said gently. He tossed the pitchfork into the wheelbarrow and moved further down the row.

Picking up another section of hay, he flipped it into the stall of a tall palomino. "Since when have I not fed you? How about a little trust, huh?" He ruffled the horse's mane and continued down the line of stalls.

The fact that that man was related to Michael astounded me.

When Mr. Kale was almost at the other end of the barn, I quickly descended the ladder. Dropping behind a stack of buckets, I waited to see if I had been spotted. Leaning out of my cover, I saw that Mr. Kale had his back to me.

I bolted from the barn back to the house. I shoved open the window and pulled myself inside.

The room was filled with the smell of pancakes. I swayed a little as a wave of hunger rolled through my stomach. The clock on the bedside table said it was half past five.

Fighting back the lightheadedness, I closed the window and remade the bed. I smelled like I slept in a barn so I took a quick shower. It was a good thing I did because I had hay in my hair. Putting on the clothes I wore yesterday, I tried to run a brush through my tangles.

As soon as the clock struck six, the lock unbolted and the door opened. Michael looked a little surprised to see me awake. He wasn't as surprised as I was at the sight of him without his double holster. His Henley shirt looked incomplete without it.

"You're up."

I pulled my eyes from his shirt to meet his hard gaze. "You said lessons were first thing."

"So your ears do work." He smirked. Stepping into the hall, he waved me toward him.

Before I could cross the threshold, his arm shot in front of me, blocking my way.

His dark eyes bore into mine. "Don't mistake the fact I didn't behead you in your sleep as anything less than the fact I didn't want to get out of bed last night."

"I wouldn't dream of it." My stomach grumbled. "Are you done or do you have anything else you'd like to clear up?"

He dropped his arm, but hesitated before leading me down the hall. I knew why. He wasn't in any hurry to take me back to his family.

A low ache pounded in my chest. There was nothing I could say that would ease his mind. All I could do was stand there and wait for him to make the first move.

With his jaw clenched, he finally walked into the kitchen. Keeping my head down, I followed after him.

Mrs. Kale was flipping pancakes. Bacon sizzled on the griddle and the radio played softly in the background. Meg sat on the counter with a bowl of pancake batter in her lap.

My stomach gurgled.

"Where is everyone?" Michael asked.

"The boys are out feeding the animals." Mrs. Kale turned from the stove and froze when she saw me. "Good morning, Charlie," she said with a strained smile.

"Morning."

"Did you sleep alright?"

"Yes, ma'am."

Her smile slipped when she noticed my wrinkled clothes.

I spotted Michael's double holster slung over one of the chairs at the table. Squeezed into the slot with his wand was mine. I moved toward the chair beside it. Over the sizzling of bacon, my footsteps sounded too loud in a kitchen occupied by four people.

"Don't you fucking dare," Michael snapped as I grabbed the chair.

My hand leapt off the chair like it was a hot iron. *Was it special?* Stepping away from the table, I bumped into the railing separating the kitchen from the living room.

"Just don't touch anything," he said. His cheeks were flushed with anger. Unsure what I did to deserve such a reaction, I crossed my arms tightly over my stomach and remained still.

"She needs to eat," Mrs. Kale said softly.

"Not at the table," he responded gruffly. "She can eat on our way out."

"And for dinner?"

"I'll bring it to her." His eyes locked onto mine. "When you're done, you can put your dishes in the hall."

I nodded. A moment of silence followed, with only the sizzle of bacon to fill it.

Meg cleared her throat. "That mattress used to be mine. I never could sleep on it. I think there's a lump on the left side."

Oh no. If I had actually slept on the bed, I would know that. "I'm not a picky sleeper."

"If it does bother you . . ." She caught her brother's gaze and dropped her eyes to the bowl in her lap.

Michael stepped toward the counter, blocking her from my view.

The back door swung open and Mr. Kale came in with Zak. Mr. Kale went straight for his wife. Taking his black cowboy hat from his head, he placed a kiss on her shoulder.

"Huh." Zak's eyes locked on to me like a loaded gun. "If I had known we were letting animals eat in the house I would've brought the dog in." He tossed his gloves to the counter and started down the hall.

"Breakfast is almost ready," Mrs. Kale called after him.

"I'll eat when she's gone," Zak said without a glance back.

A heavy silence cloaked the kitchen in his wake.

Mrs. Kale took the last pancakes off the griddle and brought them to the table. "Have as much as you like," she said without looking at me. Instead of sitting down, she went to the sink and immediately began cleaning. Mr. Kale busied himself with fixing up a cup of coffee. Meg just stared at her belly.

They weren't going to eat with me around.

I was absolutely starving. The last thing I ate was that melted chocolate bar and I didn't know how long ago that was. But the knots in my stomach and the deafening silence made it hard to swallow.

Stepping closer to the table, careful not to touch the chairs or the table itself, I picked up a few of the steaming pancakes.

"Let's go." Michael snatched his holster from the chair and threaded his arms through the loops.

"When will you be done?" Mr. Kale asked. Leaning against the counter, he sipped his coffee.

"I'm hoping by dinner, but that's not up to me." Michael shot a pointed look my way.

I almost stuck my tongue out at him.

"Good luck."

Michael huffed. Turning his cold gaze to me, he gestured toward the back door.

He didn't need to tell me twice. I barely kept myself from running out of the house. I folded one pancake in half and tucked it in the pocket of my hoodie. The other I stuffed into my mouth.

Stepping off the back porch, I stopped.

When we arrived last night, darkness hid the landscape. The Kale's house was nestled in the middle of a mountain range covered in evergreens with an aspen here and there. A stoic cat surveyed the chickens clucking around the yard. Just behind the house, to the right of the barn, was a lake that stretched toward a faraway bank. Yellow flowers speckled the valley behind the barn. Horses moseyed around in fenced off pastures.

In a paddock closest to the barn, a spotted horse looked at us over the railing. Its jaw rocked back and forth, working a mouthful of hay. Seeing that we weren't very exciting, the horse shook its mane. From its back rose a pair of snow white wings.

I nearly choked on my pancake.

Michael's shoulder rammed into mine as he started across the yard. He made it nearly all the way to the barn before he realized I wasn't following.

"Now what?" he snapped, spinning back to face me.

Unable to speak, I pointed at the horse with wings.

"It's a Pegasus," he said. "So what?"

I continued to stare. It stretched its brilliant white wings overhead, before folding them against its sides.

"It's a ranch, what did you expect?"

"That's a *magical* horse," I countered. "Ranches have pigs and cows and stuff. Not that!" My eyes flew to the pastures behind the barn. I had assumed they were all horses, like a normal person, but the closer I looked I saw not all of them were.

When they kept their wings folded, they were hard to distinguish from a distance. But when they played, their wings shot out and flapped gracefully at their sides. A few took off at a run, leapt into the air and glided to another portion of the pasture. Their horse friends followed behind at a trot.

Rolling his eyes, Michael took off across the yard. "It's just a horse with wings."

Maybe to someone without a soul. I continued to look over the countryside, watching the mythical horses play.

"Stop slouching," he called over his shoulder. "Your spine looks like a question mark."

I straightened my back, coming to my full height of five-five. Instantly I wanted to shrink back—it helped me fly under the radar—but I didn't want to know what he would do if he thought I was ignoring him.

Leaving the yard and all the wonders behind, he led us into the forest. After a couple minutes, the trees opened into a meadow. The grass had been cut short and the sound of running water echoed nearby. The trees blocked the breeze, making it a little warmer.

"This is the only place you're allowed to use magic." Michael faced me with my wand in hand. "I'll give you your wand at the start of each lesson and once we leave, you give it back. Understood?"

"Yep."

He extended my wand to me. "Do we need to go over the basics?"

"I'm not an idiot." I snatched it from his hand.

"You had me fooled. Tell me what a charm is."

"The lowest cast of magic." I crossed my arms.

"And the highest?"

"Wards. Enchantments are intermediate."

He nodded to a log beside him. "Do you remember how to levitate—"

Magic surged down my arm and into my wand. Before he could punctuate his question, I sent my magic under the log and flipped it over his head, all without looking away from him. The log dropped to the ground and cracked into pieces. I tried not to wince as the sound echoed around us.

Michael's eyes narrowed. After a beat, he pulled out his wand. "I think you should start learning to deflect magic."

My heart jumped. "You'll be firing at me?"

Run.

"Only small wards." Sliding one foot back, he turned his shoulder to me and pointed his wand at my chest. "Consider this moving to the next level."

He said that like it was a good thing.

I aimed my wand and pulled on my magic. The scalding glow rolled down my shoulders and into my palm. There it waited for my command.

Magic illuminated his wand seconds before the first ward left the tip.

With a flick of my wrist, the ward swerved to the left and slammed into the ground. Dirt flew into the air and grass fluttered about like confetti.

With his next shot, I wasn't so lucky. The magic cast grazed my shoulder.

"Dammit!" I dropped my wand to grip my shoulder. A deep ache pulsed through my bones. Flexing my fingers, they moved sluggishly.

"What did I tell you about the chest?" he called.

"It's the biggest target on the body," I replied through clenched teeth.

"Then why did you expose it?" He shook his head. "You're lucky that wasn't a full blast of magic. You'd be dead if it was." He nodded to my wand. "Let's go again."

Swallowing my groan, I scooped up my wand. This time I mimicked his stance, pointing my shoulder toward him. When I aimed my wand at his chest, he nodded in approval.

Then he fired.

6

Well, That Couldn't Be Right

I spent a couple weeks dodging magic.

By the end of each day, I was covered in sweat and close calls. My body ached as if each brush of magic were a fist. I gladly chose it over being around the other Kales.

I thought I would get used to stepping into the tense kitchen every morning. Or at least grow numb to the atmosphere. But no matter how many days passed, it was hard to breathe whenever I was around them.

Training was rigorous and far more grueling than what we did during our night lessons at the Magisterium. We started at six in the morning and didn't stop until six in the evening. There were no breaks. Michael was determined to fit five months of missed training into what little time we had at the ranch. By the time dinner came around I was ravenous.

All of that, plus the brutal mixture of little sleep and constantly being on edge, began to weigh on me. My thoughts and movements were becoming slower with each passing day. But I couldn't ask for a reprieve. I wouldn't dare.

By noon, the sun was hot. My hair clung to the nape of my neck and forehead. I deflected the ward to the right. Then I dodged one, but stepped in the way of another. The blast didn't just graze my side, it hit my ribcage.

His next shot struck my shoulder. Curses spewed out of my mouth as my arm went numb and limp.

He didn't slow because he didn't care. His next ward was aimed at my other shoulder. My left arm flopped about as I tried to dodge it.

The cast of magic grazed my skin before cracking the earth open behind me. My wand almost slipped through my fingers as a spasm ran down my arm.

His phone rang, halting his next ward. He held up his hand making sure I wouldn't fire on him. He pulled out his phone before it rang a third time.

"This is Kale." He slid his wand into his holster and ran a hand through his hair.

While he was distracted, I doubled over my knees and gasped for air. The ward that hit my ribs had done something to my lungs. I couldn't hold a breath for longer than a count of three.

"I'm with Hart's kid."

"It's Charlie," I grumbled under my breath.

"Try me," he said into the phone. His eyes flickered back to me. "I can't right now." With a roll of his eyes, he nodded. "I'll be right there."

My interest piqued. *If he was leaving, did that mean we were done for the day?*

"We're heading back to the house," he said as he snatched his jacket from the grass. "You can catch up on your reading for Lenin."

Thank God.

He walked over and plucked the wand from my stiff fingers. "We'll resume when I get back."

I didn't even care at that point. As long as I got a break, I was happy.

Breathing hard, I slowly followed him to the house. It was strange walking back before sunset.

There was so much more activity in the yard. Zak was atop a Pegasus in a round corral making it run circles while Mr. Kale watched with critical eyes. Mrs. Kale was on her knees in front of the flowerbed with a pile of uprooted weeds beside her.

Michael led me to the front door. "Stay in your room." He didn't have to add a threat at the end of that. His glare promised a hundred painful consequences.

"I will." As a sign of good faith, I walked into the house without further prompting.

Breathing heavily, I stopped and leaned against the doorframe to the bedroom I hadn't used. Under the window were the books I was supposed to be studying. But there was also a beautiful, untouched bed.

My eyelids dropped. *A nap couldn't hurt, right?* I had never flared during a nap . . . though I had hardly taken naps while I was on the run. But that didn't register. I was just too tired.

"You look awful."

I jumped and spun toward the kitchen.

Meg had a couple water jugs levitating in front of her, obviously going to help her mom. "Has that bed started bothering you?"

"Nope." *Being constantly woken up by nightmares was.*

"Really? You look like you haven't slept since you got here."

"I'm just not used to waking up this early," I lied.

"If you need something . . ." she trailed off, as if remembering who I was.

I forced a smile. "I'm fine, thank you." Before she felt obligated to offer anything else, I stepped into the bedroom and closed the door behind me.

Kicking off my shoes, I crawled onto the mattress. It molded to my body like a warm hug. It was a thousand times better than the barn loft.

I brought my limp arm to my chest. Seconds after my eyes closed, I was asleep.

A knock woke me up.

My eyes snapped to the clock. It was half past two. *Crap on a cracker.* If Michael was back, he was going to be so pissed that I wasn't studying.

I stumbled off the bed and dove for the bookcase. My left arm flopped about as I pulled out a book.

"Come in!" I called as I opened to a random page.

The last person I expected peeked her head into the room. Meg, propping a laundry basket on her hip, gave me an uneasy smile.

"I hope I'm not interrupting."

"Not at all." Red flags popped up everywhere as she stepped into the room. "You shouldn't be in here . . ."

Her lips curled. *Did all the Kales smirk?* "Why not?"

"Michael won't like it."

"Yeah, well, he's never been a fan of the things I do." She set the basket on the bed. "I brought some clothes. Since I'm getting fatter," she patted her belly, "these are just taking up space in my closet. I thought you could use them."

"I'm fine."

"I searched your room so I know you don't have any other clothes." She met my astonished stare. "Relax. It was right when you got here, and it was a complete waste of time. You had nothing interesting."

I'm pretty sure that was an insult.

"I noticed you've been wearing the same two shirts for the last three weeks. Please tell me you're washing them." Meg crinkled her nose.

I nodded. "In the sink."

"That's disgusting." She offered me a t-shirt with a band album on the front that I had never heard of. "I'm doing you a favor. That shirt is going to evolve soon and no one wants to smell that."

Setting down the book, I got to my feet and took it from her. I retreated a couple steps back.

"Well, try it on." She sat on the edge of the bed with a sigh. "If they're too big I can use a charm to shrink them."

I blinked at her. She wanted me to try it on right there? My mind instantly went to the scars covering my back. I remembered her reaction to the demon scars. *What would she say about the ones I got from Denny?*

"Don't be shy. We're all girls here. Or at least I hope so." She stroked her belly with a small smile.

I didn't want to see if she shared the same philosophy of disobedience-equals-consequences that her brother had. So, I grabbed the bottom of the shirt with one arm, and struggled to pull it over my head.

"Holy shit. What happened?"

I followed her gaze to my torso, thinking she was looking at the scar I got when my magic was drained.

One side of my ribcage was deep purple, the darkest shade of thunder clouds. Rimmed with navy blue, it spread toward my back, highlighting where Michael's ward grazed my skin. Sure enough, my shoulder was painted the same horrible shade.

"Michael's teaching me how to deflect magic."

Meg's eyes widened. "You were hit with magic?"

I nodded. Quickly I tugged the collar of the clean shirt over my head, hiding the bruises from sight. The feeling of clean fabric was indescribable. Too bad I was mostly numb to get the full effect.

"And Michael didn't say anything? He can be as dense as a pile of logs sometimes." She rose to her feet. "I'll be right back." Quickly she exited the room and a couple seconds later I heard the front door bang shut.

It wasn't long before the door opened again. By the sounds of it, Meg wasn't alone. Mrs. Kale stepped into the room with a look I wasn't used to. She was concerned.

Her hands hovered in front of the hem of the shirt. "Can I see?"

More red flags. But this time it was over the fact I was now alone with Michael's mother. How would she react when she saw the bruise? I imagined it would be like a wolf seeing an injured rabbit. *Will she make it worse?*

I figured if I didn't obey, what was coming would be ten times worse. Using my good arm, I tugged the hem above the bruise on my ribs.

She reached forward. Closing my eyes tight, I prepared myself to feel pain at her touch.

"Can you feel that?"

My rising apprehension paused. Opening my eyes, I looked down to find her gently prodding the purple skin.

I shook my head. "No, ma'am."

"Is this the only place you were hit?"

"My shoulder."

She reached for my neck.

I flinched, expecting her hands to be as rough and scarred as Michael's.

Mrs. Kale stopped. She held up her hand, palm facing me to show she meant no harm. Her fingers were calloused, but not with scars. Moving slowly, she pulled the collar of the shirt away from my neck.

She hissed at the dark plum bruise covering my shoulder. "Can you feel your arm at all?"

I shook my head. "No, ma'am."

"Can you move it?"

"No, ma'am."

Disapproval pressed her lips firmly together. "I'm going to grab my kit. Meg, can you help her out of that shirt?"

"I'm fine," I blurted. "Really. I've had worse."

If anything, my statement pushed Mrs. Kale from the room faster. Her footsteps quickly beat up the stairs to the second floor.

"I doubt that." Being careful to not touch my skin, Meg helped tug my limp arm from the shirtsleeve. "Wards kill anything they touch."

I looked down at my arm. The skin was grey. My fingernails looked blue.

"Judging by the color of these marks, Michael toned down the intensity of the ward," Meg continued. "Hopefully your system's just in shock."

"And if it's not?" I squeaked.

"You'll need a new arm."

Cheese and rice.

Many times, I had seen those kinds of bruises on Michael when he came to our lessons. But they were usually gone the next day. He went for hours while his body was shutting down.

"Michael knows this. So why didn't he do anything?" Meg paused. "Better yet, why didn't you say anything?"

"I didn't know."

"As your teacher that should've been the first thing he taught you," Mrs. Kale said as she stepped back into the room. With her was a small white suitcase. She dropped it on the bed and unzipped the largest compartment.

Trays jutted out in tiers like a pop-up book. Collections of bottles were alphabetized on the spinning shelves. In separate mesh pockets were medical tools such as scalpels and syringes. In the lower half were glass jars and packages of herbs.

Mrs. Kale pulled on a pair of white latex gloves. She tore the wrapper of a syringe and grabbed a bottle filled with a familiar chunky blue potion; a healing potion. I was surprised she was helping me. Most mornings she barely looked at me.

She stuck the needle through the lid and pulled the healing potion inside. Once it was nearly filled, she brought the needle to my shoulder. I felt nothing as the needle sank into my skin.

She only injected a small amount of the potion. Then she moved the needle over a few centimeters and did the same.

As she moved around the bruise, the color broke up. The horrid plum purple color brightened to a cherry red. An itch started deep in my muscles. But I still couldn't move my arm.

Once she did the same to my side, she dropped the empty syringe to the bed and grabbed another with a larger needle. This time she selected a long thin bottle filled with a runny red liquid. She only filled the syringe a little.

She poised the needle above my shoulder. "This is going to hurt." Then she brought the needle down swiftly and stabbed the center of the bruise.

As soon as the potion entered my body, a spasm ran down my arm. Fire filled my veins and then it turned ice cold. My hand curled into a fist, but I didn't dare make a sound.

She had the needle in my side before I knew she had moved. My breathing stalled as the potion froze to my ribs. Slowly, the burning ice eased. Unfurling my hands, I touched my side and winced.

"Is there any more numbness?" Mrs. Kale asked.

I shook my head. "No, ma'am."

"Can you wiggle your fingers for me?" She gestured to my left hand.

I was relieved when I was able to do just that. My wrist and elbow did their jobs as well. My shoulder still ached where the ward hit and the skin was still red but I could move it.

"If anything goes numb, get me immediately." Mrs. Kale put the two potions back in their designated slots. With a swish of her wand, the syringes disappeared from the bed.

"How'd you learn to do that?" I pushed my arm through the sleeve and pulled the new shirt over my bruised ribs.

"I used to be a nurse." She paused just for a moment. Her eyes looked over the medical kit like she was seeing an old friend.

Meg dropped her eyes to her lap.

Clearing her throat, Mrs. Kale zipped up the case. "If those bruises don't start fading, I'll have to use something stronger." Her grip on the case tightened. "This won't happen again." She nodded firmly and left the room.

Meg pulled the laundry basket between us. "Here. Look through this. Whatever you don't want you can leave in the basket and set outside," she said as she rose to her feet.

"Thank you." I gestured to the basket. "You didn't have to do this."

She stared at me for a moment. Her hazel eyes searched my face. "You're not what I thought you'd be. The way Michael described you, I thought you'd be the antichrist. But you might be the only sane person here."

I tilted my head. "What do you mean?"

She shook her head. Just before she left, she said, "If you need anything, let me know."

I sat beside the laundry basket and stared at the closed door. *What just happened?* It almost looked like two Kales . . . were nice to me.

Well, that couldn't be right.

7

Nightmare Flares

My feet beat up the stairs.

But no matter how fast I ran, I wasn't going anywhere.

He was gaining on me.

His footsteps grew louder and louder.

The hairs on the back of my neck moved as his breath brushed across my skin.

I turned with my magic ready but there was no one there.

The stairs disappeared from under my feet. I screamed, tumbling through the blackness. In an instant, it transformed into an ocean of fire.

I wrapped my arms around my head. But the fire was everywhere. When I screamed, flames blew out of my lungs. I squeezed my eyes shut, but the fire pushed past my eyelashes. The flames dug into every pore.

My magic flared in every direction. I screamed as it tore out of my chest, wanting to protect me. That only made the flames brighter. They rushed over me, drenching me in crimson.

Then they transformed into waves of water. Cold as ice, they covered me head to toe. I sucked in a shocked breath and choked.

My eyes flew open.

The moon rippled above me in glowing ribbons. I sat up, freezing lake water poured out of my hair and off the end of my nose. I coughed and spewed water out of my lungs. Inhaling sharply, my chest split with a pain so white-hot I stopped, despite my desperate need for oxygen.

I clutched my wet shirt as the pain pressed against my lungs. I tried to calmly breathe through it but all I could do was gasp.

A hand gripped my jaw and forced my gaze upward. Following the arm to a face, my heart sank.

The hand belonged to Michael.

And his face was etched with fury.

The cloudless sky seemed to bend forward and mix into his midnight locks. His eyes were vacuums of space threatening to swallow me whole. He would've looked like a vengeful ghost highlighted by the harsh light of the moon if it weren't for the hellish glow around him. Fire light struck his face, highlighting every furious edge.

Like a moth, my eyes followed the bright light over his shoulder.

Flames rolled out of the hay loft. Smoke billowed from the blackened walls. Mr. Kale and Zak released the horses and Pegasus from the barn, coughing against the thick smoke.

Across the yard, the house also suffered. Every window facing the barn was shattered. The white paint had peeled, exposing the wood beneath. The beams of the front porch smoldered with orange embers. The flattened flowerbed held no surviving flowers.

No no no!

Michael snapped his fingers in front of my face, drawing my attention back to him. "What the hell did you do?" Michael's skin was too warm to be normal and his shirt had whiffs of smoke rolling from it. He held his other hand close to his chest. He must have pulled me out.

"I—I—" Another strike of pain split through my chest.

"Hey!" He grabbed my jaw, forcing me to look at him again. He didn't even care that he was touching me. "Answer me!"

"Michael!"

Mrs. Kale stopped at the water's edge. Everything about her was frazzled; her robe was half-tied and only one foot was sporting a slipper. She trembled when her gaze landed on me. "Get her out of the lake before she freezes."

He grabbed my elbow and yanked me from the water. Cold air assaulted me from all sides, sending me into a fit of shivers. He dragged me, soaking wet, into the house.

Glass crunched under his boots as he dragged me down the darkened hall. With small pockets of white moonlight, I could just barely make out picture frames that hung crooked or cracked on the hardwood. Around the living room, furniture was out of place, blown away from the windows. Most looked like porcupines with glass shards for quills.

He picked up an over-turned chair and tossed me into it. Then he slammed the back of the chair into the wall so the only thing I could see was him.

"What the hell just happened?" he snarled.

"I'm sorry." A hot tear slipped down my cheek. "I didn't . . ." I sucked in a sharp breath. "I didn't mean to."

"What exactly did you do?"

I swiped furiously at my cheeks. I put both hands on his chest and pushed. "Get out of my face."

He stepped back and my chair dropped back to the floor. "Explain. Or I'll find the answer myself."

I winced, remembering the last time I hadn't told him what he wanted to know. He had pressed his wand to my forehead and used magic to search through my memories. It was a painful experience I wasn't willing to go through again.

"I have nightmares." I wrapped my arms around my aching chest.

"You expect me to believe—"

"I'm in the North Tower."

He blinked. Recognition dawned on his face.

"I'm running to the top," I panted, "and I can feel him breathing . . . on the back of my neck—"

"Richard While."

My stomach turned at the mention of the demon that tried to steal my magic five months back.

"That doesn't explain the fire."

"The staircase ends . . . and I fall." My vision began to blur as my head went light. "Everything bursts into flames . . . just like that night."

"Why didn't you tell me?" he growled. "You could've killed my entire family tonight. What were you—"

I doubled over my knees.

"Charlie?"

It felt as if my lungs were shrinking. The pressure in my chest made it impossible to get more than a sip of air.

He pushed me back against the chair. His anger stilled when he heard the rasp in my chest. Jumping to his feet, he ran to the hallway. "Mom! Bring your med kit!"

He spun around, sliding on broken glass, and dropped to his knees beside me. "You need to slow your breathing." He pressed two fingers into the side of my neck. Cringing, he switched to his other hand.

"I . . . I can't," I wheezed. "My chest . . . is on fire." I couldn't make out any shapes. With all the light fixtures burned out, the darkness overwhelmed my vision.

I didn't see Mrs. Kale or Meg until they were right in front of me. Even then, they were blurs of color as my lungs continued to whine and rasp.

Mrs. Kale knocked away her son's hand. She winced as she replaced his fingers with hers. She grabbed the collar of my shirt and yanked it past my collarbone.

The center of my chest glowed.

8

This is Your Brilliant Solution?

"Meg, get back." Mrs. Kale shoved her away from the medical kit. "There's magic leaking into her chest."

"But I can help—"

"The baby shouldn't be around this much exposed magic." Mrs. Kale moved in between me and Meg. "Get back!"

Biting her tongue, Meg retreated. She crossed her arms over her belly, but she didn't leave the room.

"It doesn't make sense. That flare wasn't large enough to crack her core." Michael's eyes locked on to mine. "Has this happened since you left the Magisterium?"

I nodded.

"How many times?"

"A few," I gasped.

"I need an *exact* number."

I closed my eyes tightly as a wave of pain rushed against my ribcage. "Seven," I whispered.

Both him and Mrs. Kale cursed.

"Dammit, Charlie! Why didn't you say anything?"

"I didn't want . . . you to think . . . I was unstable."

"You sure convinced me otherwise," he snapped.

"Enough," Mrs. Kale barked. Rummaging through her kit, she removed an amber stone the size of an egg. She placed it against the center of my chest, right where the ache was the strongest. The whole stone glowed except for a small sliver near the bottom.

"There's the crack." Mrs. Kale tossed the stone toward her case. "Help me lay her down." With a wave of her wand, the glass and splintered furniture scurried across the floor leaving a patch free of debris.

"What's happening?" My head spun as Michael lifted me from the chair and laid me on the cold floor. With another wince, he pulled his other hand to his chest. His fingers were blue.

"Magic flares are uncontrolled bursts of magic. Depending on the intensity, one flare won't hurt a User. But a few of this caliber will crack the lining of your core," Mrs. Kale explained.

She took a pair of scissors and cut the t-shirt just enough to expose the glowing skin. "Magic is draining into your chest, which is shutting down your organs."

Returning to her case, she took out a silver circle. With careful fingers, she placed it right over my sternum, directly over my core. A hoarse cry left my throat as it locked onto my skin. Raising her wand, she held it over the center of the circle.

"What are you doing?" If this wasn't the perfect time to kill me, then I didn't know what was.

"I have to seal the crack before your magic collapses your lungs. So . . . please hold still." She took a deep breath and her hands steadied.

A series of crashes and curses rolled down the hall. Zak stormed into the kitchen. His wild gaze flew around the room taking in the damage and mayhem until he found me. "I'm going to kill you."

Michael jumped to his feet, placing himself between his brother and me. "Don't."

Zak's nostrils flared. "What the hell, man? She almost killed us!"

Michael glared down at me. He was still pissed. "Almost."

"Still a good enough reason to gut her." He moved to push past just as Mrs. Kale lowered her wand. The tip glowed as it stabbed into my chest.

My scream shook the walls. Mrs. Kale pinned my shoulder down with her free hand as she twisted her wrist. Her wand sank deeper.

Fire flooded my ribcage, refusing to let me breathe. My magic throbbed through my chest. Just when I thought my ribcage would char and crumble, Mrs. Kale yanked back her wand, taking the fire with it.

I sucked in a full lung of air. The suffocating ache had drained from my body, leaving me shivering from the lake water.

I jumped to my feet and staggered away from her. Glass and splintered wood poked and sliced at the soles of my feet, but I didn't care. I yanked the silver ring from my chest and threw it away.

Breathing hard, I looked down at my torn shirt. My skin wasn't glowing or punctured from Mrs. Kale's wand, just prickled with goosebumps.

"You saved her?" Zak bellowed. "No way. She doesn't get to live after what she just did!"

He shoved past Michael with his hand outstretched, fingers braced like a claw for my throat. Grasped in his other hand was a knife.

Michael grabbed him and flattened him against the wall, all with one hand. He pinned him there with his forearm. "Don't test me right now, brother."

Zak's grip tightened on the knife.

"Enough!"

I jumped and almost slipped on the wet floor. Mr. Kale stormed into the room, his heavy boots crunching on shattered glass. He pushed Michael off his brother and wrenched the knife from Zak's hand. "Don't be stupid, Zakery."

His dark brown eyes quickly took inventory of his family, moving from Meg to Mrs. Kale. When he saw no injuries, he turned to me. "Are you ok?"

"Who gives a damn if she's ok?" Zak roared. His eyes locked onto his brother. "What I want to know is how you couldn't find her for months with a flare like that!"

"Shut up," Michael spat. "They're too small to track."

Zak's eyes widened. "That was small? It blew out all the widows! And almost burned down the barn!"

"You're lucky the house is still standing." I winced when they all turned to me. I took advantage of the silence and addressed Mr. Kale. "I can help repair the barn."

"What you can do is get the hell off this ranch," Zak growled.

"Zakery." Mrs. Kale's voice whipped across the decimated kitchen. "Go get some air." He opened his mouth, but she cut him off. "Now."

Zak shot me a look of raw, unbridled anger. I could almost feel it heating my skin. He shoved past Michael and stormed out of the house, slamming the screen door.

"We'll help with repairs," Michael repeated.

His father shook his head. "Stick to your training. There's no use wasting your time."

"It could be good discipline for her."

"Good discipline?" Mr. Kale surprised me by laughing. "I think she's doing enough of that to herself." He looked at me over his son's shoulder. "Did you mean to burn my barn?"

I shook my head. "No, sir."

"Are you sorry?"

My heart squeezed painfully in my chest. "Yes, sir." *More than you know.*

"Then that's good enough for me."

"Dad—"

"Michael." He placed a hand on his son's shoulder. "Your job is to train. Mine is to take care of this ranch. Let's not get in each other's way." With that, he walked after his eldest son.

I leaned back against the wall and rubbed the goosebumps on my arms. I peeked at Michael. With his hands clasped behind his neck, he stared up at the scorched ceiling where the dining room chandelier used to hang.

The tension of his braced arms pulled the sleeve of his shirt up his bicep. Starting from the inside of his left elbow, coils of scales wrapped around his arm before slithering underneath his shirt. The ink was the purest black I had ever seen, almost darker than his eyes, if that was possible.

"What causes the flares?" Mrs. Kale asked softly.

Michael dropped his arms, concealing the tattoo from my curiosity. "Nightmares, apparently. Can you make a dreamless potion?"

"I tried sleeping pills," I said. "I even set timers to wake myself up every few hours. None of it worked."

"If those didn't work, I doubt a dreamless potion would do any better." Mrs. Kale tightened the belt on her bathrobe.

Michael rubbed a hand over his face. The kitchen dissolved into thoughtful silence.

I couldn't bring myself to look at anyone other than Michael. I was used to his hate filled eyes. Meg and Mrs. Kale were nice to me before, but now that they knew I was off my rocker, there was no way they would continue.

"Is your hand ok?" I asked. He still had it fisted over his gut. In the low lighting, it looked like his fingers were going from blue to white.

"It's fine," he answered gruffly.

Mrs. Kale didn't buy it. "Did you touch her while she was flaring?"

After a pause, Michael nodded.

My heart sank. I saw what my magic did to the house and the barn. *What did it do to his hand?*

Wordlessly, Mrs. Kale took a bottle from her bag and handed it to him.

Catching my eye, Michael nodded down the hall. "Go dry off."

Thankful for the escape, I dripped all the way to my room. In the bathroom, sheltered from the brisk night air, I tugged off my wet clothes and quickly pulled on some clothes from Meg's basket.

The soft weave soothed my cold skin. The weight of the sweater was as close to a hug as I had gotten in a while. Would Meg take back the clothes? She had to be scared of me now.

I peeked my head into the bedroom and padded across to the pile of clothes by the window. I picked out a couple sweaters and t-shirts. Tucking a pair of jeans under my arm, I closed myself back in the bathroom.

Dropping to my knees, I folded the clothes in tight bundles. I tucked them in the far back of the cupboard under the sink. I rearranged the bottles to hide them from view. Just in case.

When I closed the doors, I sat back on my heels and pushed a hand into my wet hair. *Cheese and rice, tomorrow's going to be a nightmare. Michael will destroy me for what I almost did . . .*

My eyes flooded with hot tears. Pressing the long sleeves of the sweater to my eyes, I took two slow deep breaths. *Get a grip, Charlie.* Dropping my hands, I blinked back the moisture and rose to my feet.

When I opened the door, my goosebumps came back with a prickling vengeance. Cold air rushed through the open window, filling the empty room.

Wait. Empty?

My eyes bounced from one wall to the next. The bed was gone.

I stepped further into the room and glanced around once more to make sure the shadows weren't playing tricks on me. *It was here when I came to change, right?*

As I looked around again, my gaze was pulled to the open door directly across the hall. Like a beacon of burnt orange, there was the bed, comforter and all.

Didn't Michael say his room was across the hall?

Cautiously, I walked over and stopped at the threshold. I was expecting dark walls with satanic symbols or rows of exotic animal heads. But like the rest of the house, I was surprised.

The walls were dark green. Bookcases stacked with dusty textbooks crowded the walls. Many of the titles I recognized from my classes at the Magisterium. The bed that belonged to this room, Michael's bed, was pushed as far from mine as the room would allow.

I glanced toward the kitchen and then to the front door. There was no sign of the Kales.

Turning back to the green room, my eyes landed on the sole surviving picture hanging beside the door. Captured within an antique gold frame were two people; one man and one woman.

In the dim lighting, the woman gave a dimpled smile to the camera. Her rippling black hair froze in a midsummer breeze. She had Mrs. Kale's soft features and Mr. Kale's strong nose. She was definitely a Kale . . . a cousin, maybe?

The man in the photo had his lips pressed against her cheek. A long tendril of her hair curled over his face. In the dim light, it looked like Michael. But he didn't know how to smile, let alone show affection.

"Uh . . . Michael?" I pulled my eyes away from the photo. "Why's my bed in your room?"

The bathroom door opened, and I all but dropped dead of shock. Michael was in plaid pajama bottoms and a dark long-sleeved shirt. It was the first time I had seen him in something other than his worn leather jacket. He wasn't even wearing socks.

"And you're not listening." He crossed his arms over his chest.

I blinked. "What?" *Cheese and rice, he looks so normal.*

"You're sleeping in here."

The cold water must've affected my hearing. "I'm sorry. I thought you said I was sleeping here."

"You are."

I laughed. "No."

"I wasn't asking."

Now I crossed my arms. "This is your brilliant solution to the nightmares? What are you going to do? Wake me up every time I'm having one?"

"Actually, yes."

"Do you know how little sleep you're going to get? I know what you're like in a good mood. I don't want to see you sleep deprived. How about we find a cave—"

"I don't need sleep. I've been trained to function without it."

"Then I'm going to find a cave." I turned and almost ran into him. "I *really* hate when you Port in front of me."

"And I *really* don't care." He placed his hands on either side of the door, blocking my exit. "You can get into that bed willingly, or I can tie you to it every night. Your choice."

"What if you can't wake me up?" I looked at his right hand, expecting it to still be blue. But it looked normal and healthy as ever.

"I'll drop you in the lake again." He sighed. "I don't want you to have a flare just as much as you don't. You aren't going to do anything. Not with me around, anyway."

I wanted to believe him. I wanted to fall asleep and not be afraid of what my mind would do without my permission. But that would mean I would have to trust Michael and I trusted that man as much as I trusted a rattlesnake.

Impatient as usual, he said, "It's nearly midnight. Get in bed."

"No." I pushed him out of my way and stepped into the hall. That's as far as I got.

He looped an arm around my waist, tossed me over his shoulder, and kicked the door closed.

"A graveyard would be better than sleeping here! Let me go!" I pounded my fists against his back and kicked my legs wildly. "Michael Kale, let me go!"

And he did.

He threw me onto the bed. I bounced and smacked my head against the headboard. Flipping the covers off the end, he threw them in my face. Then he moved to his own.

"I meant what I said. I will tie you down if you leave." The light clicked off and darkness claimed the room.

"I hate you."

"Goodnight to you, too."

9

Hot Chocolate

Peeking over the pillowcase, my tired eyes searched for the bedside clock but could only make out blurry shapes.

When it came into focus, I sat up and shoved the hair out of my face. *That can't be right.* I rubbed the sleep from my eyes and looked again. Sure enough, the clock read twelve-fifteen.

What was even more surprising than the time was the person sitting beside the bed.

Mrs. Kale closed her book with a soft smile. "Good afternoon, sleepy."

I had never seen her in anything but her morning robe. Today she wore a navy plaid shirt and bootcut jeans.

"What . . ." I twisted around to look at the other bed. It was empty. "What are you doing in here?"

"Michael asked me to sit with you until you woke up. Just in case you had another nightmare." She stood and walked over to the windows. "I didn't think that was going to be a problem though. You were so exhausted that when I stubbed my foot an hour ago you didn't even flinch."

"Where is he?" I looked at the door, expecting him to be brooding in the hallway.

"He left this morning."

My eyes snapped back to her earnest expression. *He left me alone after what I did last night?*

She yanked the curtains back letting sunlight spill into the room. "Did you sleep alright?"

Squinting against the new flood of light, I nodded. "Yes, ma'am."

"Oh, honey." She turned from the window with a grimace. "You can call me Eloise. I'm far too young for 'ma'am.'"

Cheese and rice. If Michael ever caught me calling her by her first name . . .

"I'm going to suggest that you jump in the shower." She nodded her head toward the bathroom. "You smell like the lake. When you come out, we'll get you something to eat." Picking up her book, she left the room.

That wasn't how I thought the morning would go. I thought for sure after last night's catastrophe, Michael would pull me out of bed and throw me into some hellish training.

A strand of hair fell in front of my face. I winced at the smell of murky lake water.

Shoving the fluffy comforter aside, I struggled to get out of bed. My head spun. A dull ache throbbed in my chest. Breathing slowly, I waited until I was sure I could walk and got to my feet.

Quickly, I slipped across the hall to my room. I grabbed clean clothes from the basket Meg brought me and jumped into the shower. The hot water did wonders to my sore muscles. But the ache in my chest remained.

By the time I was dressed, my stomach was growling. Just before leaving my room, I paused at the doorway. Michael made it very clear that I wasn't to go anywhere without him.

Mrs. Kale shuffled around the corner, drying her hands on a towel embroidered with peaches and the day of the week. "No need to lurk."

I took a tentative step out of the room. When Michael didn't pop out of the wall and drop kick me back inside, I followed her into the kitchen.

Last night might as well have been a bad dream. All the pictures were hung and straight. The furniture sat around the room without tears or shards of glass sticking out of them. Every light fixture held a fresh light bulb.

"How are you feeling?" she asked.

"Ok. My chest is a little sore and my head hurts."

Mrs. Kale nodded. "That is what I call a magical hangover. They're a side effect of magic flares, I'm afraid."

That would make sense why I was used to feeling like crap every time my nightmares set something on fire.

Slowly, like she was unsure, she stepped toward me. "Can I check your core? I want to make sure the patch I placed is holding."

She picked up her medical bag and set it on the table. Unzipping it, she turned the rotating shelves until she found the same amber stone from the night before.

Mrs. Kale patted the seat at the head of the table.

Michael told me to stay far away from his family. Promises of spilled blood colored the tone of his words, my blood.

"It'll be quick," she promised.

The ache in my chest nagged at me to sit down, just for a bit. I walked toward her and scooted back into the seat as far from her as I could.

She held up the stone and reached slowly toward the collar of my shirt. When I didn't pull away, she tugged it down to where the crack was.

"What does that thing do?" I asked. All I could think about was when she stabbed me with her wand.

Holding up the oval stone, she said, "It mimics your core. The enchantments in the stone draw magic through your skin and direct it back into your chest, reflecting an image of your core into the stone."

Tugging my shirt down again, she pressed the smooth stone to my skin. It glowed just like before, but this time there was no dark spot.

"See? Last night there was a crack here." She pointed to the bottom right corner. "But since the whole thing is lit up, that means the patch is holding." She sighed with relief. "It's been a few decades since I mended a cracked core. I kept waking up last night thinking I did something wrong."

"Why did you stop being a nurse?"

She smiled sadly. "I didn't have the nerve for it anymore. Not after . . ." She cleared her throat and leaned closer. "That's interesting. . . It looks like there's a second layer around your core."

I tucked my chin, trying to get a better look at the stone. A faint line wrapped around the perimeter. "What does that mean?"

She shook her head. "Royal statuses are hard to read. There's so much magic that it messes with the equipment."

Mrs. Kale tossed the stone into her case and pushed the shelves back inside. Jumping to her feet, she moved to the other side of the kitchen.

"Why are you being so nice to me?" I winced. I didn't mean for that to come out, but there it was.

"What do you mean?" She picked up a glass of water by the sink and took a sip.

"I almost destroyed your house and barn last night. Michael hates me and so does the rest of your family. You should too."

"You slept in the barn so you wouldn't burn down my house. The barn can be fixed. This house . . . this house is filled with memories that make it irreplaceable. You protected us the best you could and that means something to me." Sadness lowered her gaze. "As for my family, they're hurting. Your father's sins aren't yours. Give them time to see that."

My curiosity had never been more alive. A hundred questions crawled up my throat. A slight tremble in Mrs. Kale's hand froze every single one. Whatever sins Lawrence had committed against them, they weren't little crimes. They were the kind of things people went to hell for.

With that realization came even more questions.

Mrs. Kale turned her back to me. Her expression may have been hidden, but her shoulders were still low. "Would you like something to drink?"

My growling stomach thought of the perfect thing. "Do you have hot chocolate?"

"It's the middle of summer," she laughed.

"It's my favorite."

She sniffed. "Well. Then there's no reason not to make it." She started pulling open cupboards, and before I knew it, the rich smells of chocolate filled the kitchen.

"Did Michael say when he was coming back?"

"No." Mrs. Kale reached into the pantry for a bag of marshmallows. "I called him when you were in the shower, but he didn't say when."

"Did he leave any instructions for me about lessons?"

"There won't be a lesson today."

I rocked back in my seat. "What? Really?"

"Your core needs time to heal or the crack could reopen, but worse." The edge in Mrs. Kale's voice made me think she already had this conversation, trying to convince someone else.

"Did he leave any instructions?"

She dropped a handful of marshmallows into the cup of hot chocolate and set it in front of me. "To be honest, we thought you were going to sleep all day."

I picked up the steaming mug and took a sip of the best hot chocolate I had ever had. As soon as the creamy liquid slid down my throat, the ache in my chest was ignored. My stomach warmed. It might have just been the chocolate, but the sunlight seemed a little brighter.

Greedily, I swallowed nearly a fourth of the cup, scalding my throat.

Mrs. Kale chuckled. "Would you like some—"

The front door slammed open. "You're going to get it this time, Zak," Meg roared. "Mom!"

"I'm in here, honey!" Mrs. Kale moved toward the hall.

When Meg entered the kitchen, her face was flushed and her eyes sparkled with rage. "Kick Zak off the ranch. Disown him."

"Why would I do that?"

"He brought *her* here."

Mrs. Kale froze at the sound of high heels on the hardwood. Zak was the first to appear, but he refused to meet his sister's seething gaze or his mother's questioning glance. He had no issue glaring at me though.

A woman stepped around him and the infamous Kale glare settled over both Kale women's faces.

Their target was a woman cloaked in cold beauty. Her pale hair was so straight it reminded me of icicles. She wore a tight emerald dress that had gems lining the collar.

"A simple hello would be fine." Her smooth voice sent chills through my body.

"You need to leave. Michael will be home any minute and it won't be good for either of you if he sees you together." Mrs. Kale pinned her son with a stare as hard as steel.

The stranger chuckled. "Oh, please. That man hasn't stepped foot in this house in eighty years. I doubt he even remembers you're here."

"Joke's on you, bitch," Meg sneered.

"Pleasant as always, Megan." She glanced at Meg's stomach. "I see the rumors are true. Congrats. Although, I wish I could say I'm surprised."

"That's it." Meg took one step forward with her freshly painted nails raised.

Zak jumped between them just in time. "Easy tiger."

"If you don't get out of my way, you're next," Meg hissed.

"Now who is this?" The stranger's piercing blue eyes landed on me, hungrily taking in every inch.

Mrs. Kale blocked me from her calculating stare. "She's none of your business."

Again, the woman chuckled. "Zak, who's the pathetic child at the table?"

"That's Charlie."

"She's here with Michael's invitation." Meg sent a silencing look to her brother.

"Sure. And I'm a virgin." She leaned around Mrs. Kale to peer at me again. "I've seen cows that look more impressive than her."

"Are you talking about your reflection?" Meg quipped.

The woman ignored her. "Have you even graduated?" she asked me.

"Uh, this is my last year."

"Held back, huh?" She shook her head. "Damn, things have really gone to hell since I left."

Rude. "I'm sorry, who are you?"

Meg's lips curled in disgust. "This is Brandy; Michael's ex-wife and Zak's reoccurring mistake."

10

The Ex

I choked on my spit.

Ex-wife?

I looked from Meg to Mrs. Kale and then back again, waiting for one of them to burst out laughing. When no one delivered a punchline, I looked at the blonde standing beside Zak.

I tried to picture her with Michael, instead of hanging off Zak's broad frame. But no matter how hard I tried, I couldn't see him beside her, let alone kissing her. I could picture him eating a human heart easier than him loving that blonde.

The front door slammed closed.

"Why is the front door open?" Michael called.

The tension in the kitchen doubled. Zak grimaced. Brandy's lips curled up at the corners. Meg was grinning too, but with a completely different emotion.

"You're going to get it," Meg told her older brother.

Zak glared back without a word.

As Michael drew closer, Brandy flung her hair over her shoulder. As he came around the corner, Zak and Brandy parted, turning to face him.

Michael stopped dead in his tracks. An array of emotions flitted across his face. Shock. Anger. Disappointment. He settled on disgust.

"Michael." Brandy took a step forward, lifting her chest. "What has it been? A hundred years?"

"Not nearly long enough," he said in a low voice that made my blood nearly freeze. For the first time, I wasn't the most hated one in the house.

"You haven't aged a day," she purred.

"I wish I could say the same." His eyes snapped to his brother. "I see you still bring trash into the house."

"You started it." Zak jerked his chin toward me.

"You're not happy to see me?" Brandy asked with a voice as toxically sweet as arsenic.

"The only time I'll be happy to see you is when you're in a shallow grave."

Damn. I fought to keep my expression neutral.

"How are you still mad at me?" she asked. "You've clearly forgiven Zakery."

"Because he's my brother. You're just a bitch."

Her mouth curled with malice. "Careful, Michael. Your emotions are showing. I thought you abandoned them when you started your killing sprees." She fluttered her eyelashes. "What's your body count these days? Stop me when I get close. One hundred? Two hundred? Three?" Her eyebrows arched. "Four?"

"Stop talking, Brandy," he sneered. "What makes you think I won't kill you right now just to up my numbers?"

A sharp laugh shook her shoulders. "Oh, my God. You don't even know." Her glittering eyes cut back to me. "So. Who is she? Did you find some troubled youth to take off the street to redeem your soul? Or what's left of it."

"You're one to talk," Meg snapped.

"Is anyone going to answer my question? Or is she another ugly thing we're going to ignore?"

I chewed on her bitter words. '*Troubled*' and I were old acquaintances, but I hated the sound of it coming from her red lips.

"The only ugly thing we'd like to ignore is you," I said dryly.

Michael shot me a surprised look. For the first time, it wasn't filled with hate. Amusement pulled at his lips.

"She's here at my invitation, unlike you." Michael turned his bared teeth to Zak. "What the hell are you doing bringing her here?"

"Since you can bring anyone into the house, why can't I? I invited her for a drink. Dinner was implied."

"If she's eating here, I'm leaving."

"Oh." Brandy stuck out her bottom lip. "I'm not that bad."

"You're worse." Michael beckoned me into the hall. Shielding me from Brandy's curious gaze, he herded me into the garage with Meg on our heels.

Slamming the door behind him, he marched up to a black truck. He yanked open the back door and nodded for me to hop in.

"Where are we going?"

"Anywhere but here."

Before he could pick me up and toss me inside, I crawled in. He slammed the door so hard the truck shook. I slid across the whole bench to sit behind Meg, as far from Michael as the car would allow.

Michael didn't wait for seatbelts to click. He started the ignition and pulled out of the garage with a squeal of rubber. A cloud of dust billowed from the wheels as he floored it toward the front gate.

"Dammit!" He slammed his hand into the steering wheel. "Why did he have to bring *her* here?"

"Maybe because you slammed him into a wall this morning." Meg hurriedly jerked her seatbelt around her. "That's not to mention there's a couple centuries of conflict between you two. You waved the flag in front of the bull; this is what you get."

"There's nothing I could've done that would warrant *her*."

"That's not what he thinks."

"Well, he's an idiot." Michael slammed on the breaks in front of the black gate. "If he wanted to roll around with an anaconda, he should've gone to the zoo, not brought one back. Is he capable of remembering everything I've done to protect this family? Porting her here throws all of that away."

"You can't keep us in this snow globe forever." Meg's voice softened. "After Lauren . . . it's lonely here sometimes."

My ears perked up. *Who's Lauren?*

Michael rounded on her. "Why are you defending him?"

"I'm not. He's a complete ass for bringing the Wicked Bitch of the West."

"It sure sounded like you were."

"You've been away for a while, Michael. There aren't a lot of people that like Kales these days. You don't have to be an ass about it." Crossing her arms, she looked out the window at the pine trees. "You're the reason we're in exile."

The cab grew quiet.

Cheese and rice, I shouldn't be here. I shrank down in my seat, feeling like I was too close to an exposed nerve. I kept still in case any sound I made would redirect Michael's rage to me.

After a while he loosened his fingers from the wheel. "Do you want to get something to eat?"

"Never ask me that question. Always assume my answer is yes." Meg rubbed her pregnant belly. "After seeing her, I need to drown myself in cheese. Did you see her face? How many enchantments do you think she has on it?"

Michael made no comment.

He slipped out of the cab and flung open the gate. Not a word was spoken as we drove through. Magic sizzled across my skin reminding me I was leaving the magical cage I had been in for weeks.

Magic stirred in my chest. I could Port before either Michael or Meg knew what happened.

As the gates closed behind us, Michael slid his right hand under his jacket. His obsidian gaze met mine through the rearview mirror. His message was clear. If he felt any magic, I'd be splattered across the back seat.

His threat silenced my magic. I leaned against the door and stared out the window. Twenty minutes later, we entered a small town. Passing through stop signs and down one-way streets, he parked the truck outside a pink Mexican restaurant.

Turning off the ignition, Michael twisted the moaning skull ring around his index finger. When it made a full turn, magic poured from the silver metal and covered his body.

I saw him do the same at the New Year's Festival. Once the magic covered his all black, glaring exterior, it dissolved into the lanky build of an average man. With nothing outstanding about his appearance, he would be easily overlooked and easily forgotten.

Hopping out of the car, I followed the Kale siblings into the pink stucco building. Michael ordered first, growling his order to the poor girl behind the counter. After Meg ordered, she looked expectantly at me.

My stomach gurgled and whined. The hot chocolate and marshmallows had done nothing but make me hungrier. I took full advantage of the situation and ordered the biggest burrito on the menu.

Our group was silent as we collected our food and made our way to a table closest to the fire exit. Michael sat with his back to the wall where he could see the entire restaurant.

He took a bite of his quesadilla and glanced at me. Rolling his eyes, Michael wiped the melted cheese from the corner of his mouth. "Say what's on your mind."

I couldn't contain myself any longer. "Ex-wife?"

"I did have a life before I was a Hunter."

"Not much of one if you ask me." Meg avoided his fiery gaze as she selected a nacho and shoved it into her mouth.

"You couldn't have picked a fouler woman even if you held auditions."

His glare returned to me. "What's your point?"

"Why would you want to marry her?"

Meg mumbled something that sounded like, "Beats me."

When he opened his mouth, his eyes were glazed over with something that resembled a real emotion. Past memories relaxed the hard lines of his face.

"It was a long time ago. We were both different people then." He blinked and the memories were gone.

"Do you enchant your face?"

He blanched just as Meg choked on her nachos. "Of course not!" he snapped, more offended than anything else. "What the hell makes you ask that?"

"You said Brandy enchants her face. I just assumed that's how you look the way you do."

"The way that I do?" he asked. His temper was rising again.

I'm missing something. "You're over two hundred years old and you don't look it."

"And you just assumed that I enchant my face?"

"It's not like you've told me anything different," I said, matching his tone. "Or really explained anything to me that doesn't involve hurting people."

"You never asked."

"You hate when I ask questions!"

"We age slow," Meg jumped in before our conversation could get much louder. Already, we were drawing the attention of the closer tables. "Once we become adults, our magic sort of just . . . freezes us. We still get wrinkles and grey hair, but much later. Like late four hundreds for Royals and High Commons."

"Then why did Brandy enchant her face?" I kept myself from looking at Michael. "Is she a lot older?"

Meg shook her head. "No, she just wanted fuller lips, higher cheek-bones, and to look even more like a bitch than she did naturally."

Ten other questions sprang up in my mind. Before I could voice them, Michael's phone rang. He quickly tugged it from his pocket and pushed away from the table. With long strides, he headed out the door and pressed his phone to his ear.

Swallowing my curiosity, I turned back to my burrito, but stopped. I looked at Meg and saw a well of information.

She stopped mid-chew. "Why are you looking at me like that?"

"Who left who?"

She glanced at her brother through the window. He was standing with one arm crossed over his chest as he stared at the air in front of him. In other words, he wasn't paying any attention to us.

She leaned closer. "Thank God it was Michael. That bitch is bitchy enough. She does not need anything else to make her bitchier."

I smiled. I was starting to like her. "What happened?"

"You did *not* hear any of this from me." She leaned closer, or as close as her belly allowed. "It was a couple decades after they got married. Michael was studying magical arts to get a title. Brandy was mooching off him. I still have no idea what she did during the day. One night, he came home early and found her in Zak's lap—not his brightest moment. Apparently, it had been going on for a while. Anyway, the next week, Michael joined the Hunter Guard with Lawrence."

"*That's* why he became a Hunter?"

Meg shook her head. "They were talking about it for years before he applied. The whole thing always intrigued him." Meg picked up another dripping nacho. "I never understood it, but Michael was excited to be a part of something bigger and to learn more about magic. He was always a nerd about that kind of stuff."

"Huh . . ." I glanced at him through the window. "I always thought there was a different reason he became a Hunter."

"Like what?"

I shrugged. "He liked the sight of blood?"

She snorted and kept eating. "After seeing his wife straddling his brother, he didn't have anything holding him back. Plus, I bet making her a widow was too good of a 'fuck you' to pass up."

"Doesn't he have to be dead to make her a widow?" Taking a bite of my food, I watched him run a hand through his black hair.

"When you get accepted into the Hunter Guard, you get a death certificate. Legally, you're dead to the world."

Oh, right. I remember Moose telling me about that.

Michael rolled his eyes and nodded to whatever was being said on the phone. After a few minutes, he returned to our table.

"That was Sánchez." He took a bite of his quesadilla. "Apparently, you turned a warehouse to ashes in Oregon two months back."

The food in my stomach instantly turned to rocks. With great difficulty, I swallowed the bite in my mouth. "It was empty, if that matters."

"It doesn't. You said you flared seven times. Where are the others?"

Embarrassment heated my cheeks. "By the Grand Canyon and outside Las Vegas, L.A., and Portland. The others are at campsites."

He tossed his food down to the table. He picked up his phone and started typing. "So, you just set a bunch of stuff on fire for your summer break?"

Irritation flared through my chest. "That's none of your business."

"Of course not." He tossed a clump of cheese into his mouth. "Why would it be? I'm just the guy who has to send his world class Hunters to each location to clean up your mess. And if there were witnesses, I have to coordinate the process of capping those memories."

"Is capping memories your band-aid for everything?" I slammed my burrito down. The insides tumbled onto the table.

After I found Blaine Willow's diary, Master Lenin placed a cap of magic over the memories. I could recall sitting in my room at the Magisterium with the well-worn diary in my lap. But, every time I tried to remember what was on the pages, my mind went blank. The only way I would ever regain those memories was if Master Lenin unlocked them.

"I prefer not to use band-aids at all. I prefer not to clean up other people's messes." To make a point, Michael dropped his gaze to the mess of food in front of me.

Magic smoldered in my chest. It rose and stretched over my shoulders, inching toward my palm. Grinding my teeth, I shoved away from the table.

His hand latched onto my forearm, halting my retreat. "It seems like running is all you're good at. So please, go right ahead and run. I need to blow off some steam anyway."

I tried to pull out of his grip, but that just made his fingers tighten. A lightbulb popped and burned out overhead.

"Don't get mad," he said coolly. "I'm just stating facts."

"I'm already mad! I ran to get away from *you*. Because around you, I won't get a future."

"Keep your voice down." He sent a withering look to a nosy cattle rancher.

"Why should I? Do you think I give a damn what a couple Regulars think? At least most of them will get to live past the age of twenty-five!"

"Who said you won't?"

"Are you planning on letting me live that long?"

"You'll live as long as you're needed."

"What's going on?"

Michael and I turned to Meg. She had finished her mountain of nachos and glanced between the two of us with blatant curiosity.

"Your brother is going to kill me when the war is over." Ice water ran through my veins at the sight of Meg's grateful expression. "Please. Don't bother hiding your pleasure in that fact."

"Are you saying we shouldn't?" Michael yanked me closer. "Do you intentionally keep forgetting your father took everything from me, or are you really that stupid?"

"Everything? Really? By the looks of it, you have a house, parents, and two siblings. Hell, you even have an interesting job." I leaned forward. "You sure have a lot for a man who says he has nothing."

His fingers dug through the sleeve of my sweater and squeezed my bones until I thought they were going to snap. I held my breath to keep myself from making a sound.

In a low voice, he growled, "Your ignorance pisses me off so much that it's taking every ounce of my control not to break you right here."

Fire laced my veins. "Give it your best shot."

His breath rushed sharply out of his nose. His fingers tightened to the point where my eyes watered.

"Is there a problem here?"

We both looked up to see the manager of the restaurant. He held up a phone with his meaty fingers. 911 was already dialed in.

Michael released my arm. His expression waned from murderous to indifferent as he leaned back in his seat. "No. Just a disagreement."

"I wasn't asking you." The manager turned to me. "Is he bothering you, miss?"

If I said yes, this poor guy would probably end up dead behind a dumpster. I gave him a smile. "I'm fine, thank you. It's nothing I can't handle."

He hesitated before walking back to the counter. Silence fell over our table.

Meg cleared her throat. "We should go before he decides he wants to play the hero."

Michael tore his gaze from me and focused on his sister. "Brandy's probably still there."

"I doubt it. Mom probably kicked her out by now. And since Zak only brought her to piss you off, he should be gone too."

"If he isn't, I'm going to kill him." Michael backed away from the table and walked toward the door without a glance back.

As soon as Michael left the restaurant, Meg's eyes slid closed. Her lip trembled ever so slightly.

"You're afraid of him," I realized out loud. "But he's your brother."

Her eyes flew open, ready to spill a thousand and one excuses, but they all died as she watched Michael get into the truck. "That's not my brother."

She pushed herself to her feet and headed for the door. Having lost my appetite, I collected my uneaten food and tossed it in the trash.

Michael didn't say anything as I slipped into the back seat. My arm throbbed, but I didn't dare touch it. I wouldn't give him the satisfaction of knowing it was bothering me.

When we got back to the house, judging from the cold, cackling laughter coming from the back-porch, Brandy hadn't left. As soon as Michael heard the noise, he Ported from the house. Meg went upstairs without a word.

Closing myself in the now shared room, I crawled onto the bed and hugged my bruised arm to my chest. The dull throb in my bones made it into my dreams.

11

Midnight Kale Encounters

My stomach gurgled under the covers.

Rolling over, I curled around my pillow and tried to go back to sleep. My stomach let out another whimper and rumble.

Cheese and rice, what time is it?

The thick darkness of the room said it was past midnight. Another painful wave of hunger rumbled through my belly.

I twisted around and looked at the other side of the room. Michael's bed was empty and the sheets were still tucked in place.

He hadn't gone to bed.

Maybe he wasn't on the property.

Sleep faded from my mind as my stomach let out another whine. *If he's not here . . .*

I had years of practice sneaking out of my room. If I was quick, if I was quiet, I could make it into the kitchen, get a snack, and be back before my sheets were cold.

Don't be stupid. If Michael finds you out of bed, he'll lose his shit.

Be quick! My stomach coaxed with a grumble. *You can do it. For the food.*

Without making more than a rustle, I slid my legs out from the sheets and placed my feet to the cold floor. I tiptoed across the room and paused at the door.

I pressed my ear to the wood and found the house was asleep as well. Stepping into the hall, I pulled the door closed enough to make it look like it could be shut. Creeping forward, I peeked around the corner into the empty kitchen.

My mouth watered at the sight of the fridge. I darted over and popped open the door. Cool air rushed over my feet. With a shiver, I grabbed a bag of leftover chicken.

I popped open the zip lock seal. The scent of lemon pepper darted into my nose, causing my mouth to flood.

I wolfed down what was left of a chicken breast. I grabbed another piece and chewed it just enough to swallow. I only ate a little. Not so much that someone would know it was missing. I sealed the bag and grabbed the next container of leftovers, grilled green beans. I was so hungry my stomach wasn't registering it had food.

My hunger dimmed as I moved to a fruit salad. After a couple bites of the yogurt covered apples, I closed the plastic container and eased the refrigerator door closed.

Licking my fingers clean, I tiptoed down the hall. Just as I was about to slide back into the room, the picture beside the door again caught my eye.

Squinting in the dull light, I lifted the picture from the nail. The same beautiful woman with Mrs. Kale's eyes and Mr. Kale's nose grinned up from the frame. I looked at the man kissing her cheek.

Is that . . . Michael?

First off, the man in the picture was wearing a blue shirt. His lips were twisted with a suppressed smile. Michael didn't smile, at least not without malice.

"Beautiful, isn't she?"

I spun toward the front door.

A looming silhouette stretched across the hallway. His broad shoulders leaned against the wall as his legs stretched to the other side, one knee bent. A bottle of liquor glittered in the low light. The faint sugary scent of rum turned the stolen meal in my stomach.

The broad shoulders and the fact that I wasn't getting chewed out, meant it was the other Kale brother.

I nodded. "Who is she?"

"Lauren." Zak brought the bottle to his lips and took a long drink. "Her name was Lauren."

Zak lowered the bottle and met my gaze. He may have been slurring, but his eyes were sharp. They were locked on to me like an aimed rifle.

"They were twins, you know. Her and Michael." He took another swig. All the while his eyes never left mine. "Your father killed her."

Oh, my God. I felt all the blood drain from my body.

He stumbled to his feet. The blue rum sloshed from the bottle. In two quick strides, he crossed the hall, backing me against the wall. The photo slipped from my fingers and clattered to the floor.

"I don't know how Michael hasn't killed you yet. You look so much like the bastard—or your eyes do. He always had so much more self-control than I did." His eyes moved down my face to the pulse in my neck. "I would've killed you the moment I laid eyes on you."

I was very, very aware we were alone. If I screamed, would anyone come to help?

Even though the lights were off, the hall lights flickered dimly like sparks over a campfire. My heart hammered frantically against my ribs but I didn't dare let my face show it.

"I should go back to my room," I said evenly. "Before Michael comes back." I slid against the wall.

The rum shattered on the floor, soaking my bare feet. Zak pinned my shoulders to the wall.

"Everyone else can't see it. They think you're innocent. Harmless. But I know what you are. You're a Trojan horse. You're here to destroy us." As he spoke, his alcohol-heavy breath swept across my face and his empty hand encircled my neck.

"Zak. I don't know Lawrence." Fear surged recklessly through my veins. "I have never met hi—"

"I'm not a fool." His fingertips pressed deeper into my neck. "I won't let another Hart wreck this family."

Quick as lightning, the back of his hand cracked across my cheek. It happened so fast I didn't feel anything until I was on the floor in the puddle of rum. Pain pulsed through my jaw. The bitter taste of blood filled my mouth.

He pulled his wand from his pocket. "Michael will thank me for this. Everyone will. Ending your bloodline will make this piss-poor existence worth it."

He aimed his wand at my head.

12

The Wounds of the Kales

I knocked his hand away.

His ward crashed into the wall, scorching the wallpaper beside me. The blast shocked the side of my face. A sharp ringing echoed through my ear but I managed to kick his feet from under him.

Jumping up, I dove into my room and barely got the door closed before Zak threw his full weight against the wood. I pressed my back to the door, trying to keep it closed.

The whole door shook as he rammed his shoulder harder against it. A crack split up the middle.

I wildly searched the room for somewhere to hide. The bed was gone and if the bedroom door couldn't survive Zak's brute force, the bathroom door wouldn't either.

My eyes landed on the window.

Run.

Zak's fist shoved through the door. His fingers brushed the top of my head.

Run.

I lunged forward and crashed into the window. My fingers shook so hard it was difficult to flip the latch.

Run.

Throwing it open, I dove through just as Zak's hand grabbed my ankle.

I kicked back and struck him in the face. The drunk stumbled back as I hit the ground on my shoulder. The garden mulch scratched my skin as I scrambled to my feet.

I ran for the woods like I had never run before. As I was about to pass the barn, a tall body suddenly Ported in front of me.

I screamed.

"Whoa—" Strong hands grabbed my arms, jarring me to a screeching halt. It was Michael. Even though he looked like he was still pissed from our previous conversation, he was a welcome sight.

"What the hell are—" His gaze dropped to the split in my lip. "You're bleeding." He tilted my head so my throbbing jaw was in full view. "What happened?"

The back door burst open. Zak stumbled onto the front porch and down the steps. His gaze swung wildly around the yard until he saw me. He exhaled like an enraged bull. "There you are."

Michael instantly connected the dots and pulled me behind him so fast that my head spun. I managed to catch my balance and turn just in time to see Michael punch his brother in the face.

Zak stumbled, dropping his wand. Shaking the stars from his head, he lunged, going for Michael's middle.

He would have tackled him to the ground if Michael hadn't anchored his feet. Using Zak's momentum against him, Michael threw him to the side. Zak rolled a few times. Slowly, he pushed himself onto his hands and knees.

Before he could get his feet under him, Michael stalked over with gravel crunching under his boots. Then he kicked Zak squarely in the stomach.

Mr. Kale charged out of the barn. He stalled for a moment, watching in horror as one son beat the other.

I dove for the discarded wand as Michael raised his foot for the second time. As soon as I wrapped my fingers around it, I Ported between the brothers and pushed Michael back.

"Get out of my way," he growled.

Mimicking his movements, I kept him from stepping around me. "Michael, stop."

"I said, 'get out of my way.'" He reached forward to shove me aside.

I leveled the wand at his chest. "And I said '*stop.*'"

Anger darkened his eyes. "Give me the wand."

"If I do, you'll kick him again."

"Damn right, I will."

"Michael." Mr. Kale snapped out of his shock. "Calm yourself, son."

"Calm myself? He could have single-handedly doomed this war." His eyes seared into his brother.

"I don't care about your war," Zak wheezed. "She shouldn't be alive, not for what she's done."

"She hasn't done anything." Mr. Kale's voice was like a whip.

"She's *his* kid," Zak rasped. "It's only a matter of time before she does something to us."

Michael tried to move around me again. "You fucking—"

"Enough." Mr. Kale's eyes cut to me. "Charlie, hand me the wand."

With my attention pulled away from him, Michael knocked my arm aside and twisted the wand from my fingers. His other hand latched around my throat.

"Michael!" Mr. Kale rebuked.

"This is your fault," he sneered. "I gave you an order to remain in your room."

I tried to tug out of his grip, but it was pointless. "I was hungry," I croaked.

"You couldn't wait until morning? You had dinner—"

"No. *You* had dinner."

His eyebrows pulled together as if he was trying to remember what happened hours ago.

Mr. Kale Ported beside him and gripped Michael's wrists. Mr. Kale's fingers dug into his pressure points, and Michael's fingers instantly released my throat.

He shoved Michael back. Raising the wand, he shot two wards into the black sky, illuminating the barnyard with golden magic. The horses neighed uneasily in their stalls. One of the barn cats scurried into the pasture.

Just as the magic began to fade, the front door swung open. Mrs. Kale walked down the porch, tying her robe around her.

She surveyed the scene with curiosity: Zak on the ground, Michael clutching his hand, and me with a split lip. "What on earth is going on?"

"Zak went after Charlie," Michael explained. "He hit her and chased her through the window."

"Zakery Atticus Kale!" Mrs. Kale gasped. "What is the matter with you?"

"I was about to ask him the same thing before I was interrupted." Michael's eyes cut to me.

"I'm fine," I said quickly. "Really."

"Nothing about this is fine." Mr. Kale threw his hands into the air. "He hit you."

"How did he get to her?" Mrs. Kale asked. "I thought she was with you."

"I was with Dad when she snuck out of her room. She didn't eat dinner."

Confusion pulled at Mrs. Kale's eyebrows. "I thought you got dinner when you went out."

"We . . ." Michael shuffled his feet against the gravel. "We got into an argument and she didn't finish."

"So, she hasn't eaten all day?" she asked quietly.

"I thought you gave her something when she woke up," Michael said in a rush.

"I would have if Zak hadn't brought Brandy Charles into my house." It seemed to take all of Mrs. Kale's energy not to look at him. "Has this happened before?"

Michael's lips parted to answer.

"I wasn't talking to you." Crossing her arms, she turned her pointed gaze to me. "Has this happened before?"

I opened my mouth to tell her no, but that wasn't true. The night we first came to the ranch, he went into the kitchen with his siblings and I went to the hayloft without dinner. And then there were the training days where we didn't stop for lunch. My gaze slid to Michael.

"Don't look at him," Mrs. Kale said sharply. "Has this happened before?"

My nails cut sharply into my palms. I nodded.

Shock and disappointment mingled on Mrs. Kale's face as she looked between her two boys. She opened her mouth but no words came out. Her silence had more impact than anything she could have said. Both Michael and Zak winced.

Michael cleared his throat. "I was busy—"

"No. You can use that excuse for not coming home for seven decades but I will not allow you to use it here. Because this, *this* is cruel." Mrs. Kale shook her head. "Charlie, come with me."

"Mom—"

"Don't you start." She pointed an accusing finger at Michael. Even though she was wrapped in a bathrobe, she looked close to transforming into a fire breathing dragon. "There is no reason for you to treat her like this in *my* house."

"Why does everyone keep forgetting who she's related to?" Michael snarled.

"I don't give a damn who she's related to. Her father killed Lauren. She didn't. Stop treating her like she did."

"She's—"

"Michael, so help me God, not another word." She held out her hand. "Charlie, I won't ask again."

I glanced at Michael. He was seconds away from ripping me apart in the middle of the yard.

Mr. Kale walked up to me, blocking me from the simmering Hunter's view. With gentle hands, he turned me and guided me to his wife.

"Both of you will stay out here until you can work this out." She turned to her oldest son. "Before you step a foot inside my house, there won't be a single drop of alcohol in your system. And you." She shook her head at Michael. "You can come back in when you start acting like my son."

Michael flinched.

With a hand on my shoulder, Mrs. Kale steered me toward the house. I didn't dare look back.

Stepping inside, Mrs. Kale flipped on the kitchen lights. Immediately, she opened the refrigerator and took out a gallon of milk. Cabinets banged as she collected a pan and a container of oatmeal.

I slipped onto a stool at the counter. Using my sleeve, I wiped the blood from my split lip.

Mr. Kale leaned against the wall so he could still see down the hall and out the front door. He rubbed at his tired eyes.

"I'm sorry," I muttered. "I shouldn't have left my room."

"You have nothing to apologize for." Mr. Kale's eyes dropped to my throbbing jaw. With a sigh, he retrieved a pack of ice from the freezer and handed it to me. Then he returned to his post by the hall.

"None of this should have happened in this house." Mrs. Kale's motions were jerky as she poured oatmeal into a pan and filled it with water. "They're good boys and I'm so proud of them. But with each passing year, I lose a little more of them. They weren't always like this. They're both just so *angry*. I know that's not a good excuse but . . ." Her thought went unfinished.

"It's your father's fault," Mr. Kale said bitterly. "*He* corrupted them."

"No." Mrs. Kale shook her head. "Lawrence may have killed Lauren, but we did this to ourselves."

"Eloise—"

"We're broken, Atticus. And no one in this family is willing to admit it! Zak's an alcoholic. Megan is pregnant from a night she can't remember. Michael used to be human! And we haven't even gotten to us!" Mrs. Kale swiped at the tear on her cheek. "Lawrence may have delivered the blow, but we broke this family."

Mr. Kale stared at the floor, spinning his wedding ring around his finger.

In the silence, the oatmeal bubbled on the stove. Glancing over my shoulder, I looked through the front door. Zak was still on the ground with his head in his hands and Michael stood a few paces away with his arms crossed. Both were focused firmly on the gravel driveway.

"Is it true?" I asked. "Lawrence killed Lauren?"

Mrs. Kale flinched. Mr. Kale stopped fiddling with his wedding ring, going completely still.

Mrs. Kale nodded. "And Aaron, her husband. And their son, Lucas. He lined them up on the front porch and executed them in front of Michael."

13

The Sins of the Father

And just like that, everything about Michael made sense.

Why he was in charge of the Achilles Heel.

Why he hated Lawrence.

Why he hated me.

No wonder that whenever he looked me in the eyes, he seemed to want to yank out my eyeballs, roots and all. He said they were just like Lawrence's. My stomach rolled so violently I thought about running to the bathroom.

"Why?" I asked, thoroughly horrified.

"Lawrence thinks that by ridding the world of our weakest Users, we as a species, will be stronger. He's one of the twelve Royal Tens to ever be born and that put a chip on his shoulder. Because of that he was treated like a prince. His family treated weakness like a sin. So that's how he viewed Users with low statuses."

"There was more to it than that," Mr. Kale interjected quietly.

"No. His family raised him with that thinking and it poisoned him. Lawrence was twisted from the start." Mrs. Kale sniffed. "Then The Trial destroyed him and the Hunter Guard sharpened him. That's why I never wanted Michael to take that damn oath.

"Lawrence killed dozens of Deficients, adults and children. He wanted Michael to join him, to purify and rule the new age of magic. But Michael said no. Lawrence thought his family was holding him back, so in order to set him free he . . ." She stared at the wall in front of her. "Michael and Lawrence were best friends. For decades they were each other's shadow. Lauren used to joke that they were the real twins, not her and Michael.

"The night he killed Lauren, it was their birthday. He almost killed Michael too. Someone told me that we found him just in time. But Lawrence killed a part of him that night. Sometimes I'm not sure he really made it down from that mountain."

Mr. Kale closed his eyes.

The boiling oatmeal in front of Mrs. Kale was the only thing to disturb the silence. It took her a while before she moved again. Taking a bowl, she scooped in a generous amount, sprinkled the top with brown sugar, and added a splash of milk. Then she set the it in front of me.

Her eyes filled with tears at the sight of the ice pack pressed to my cheek. "I'm sorry you had to meet him like this. He was so different back then."

"We all were," Mr. Kale mumbled.

"I'll bring you food from now on," Mrs. Kale said firmly as she turned to clean up. "I'll also be checking you for bruises after your lessons."

I wasn't sure what to say to that. Wordlessly, I set down the ice pack and started in on the oatmeal. For a while, no one said a word. Mr. Kale stared at his shoes and Mrs. Kale cleaned the pot and scrubbed the stove.

Footsteps plodded up the porch. Mr. Kale straightened. The heavy thump of each footfall announced who it was before they stepped into the kitchen. Mrs. Kale turned just as Michael stopped in the doorway.

He cleared his throat. "Zak's asking for you, Mom."

Mrs. Kale dried off her hands and headed outside. Looking through the screen door, I watched her kneel beside him.

"Can I talk to Charlie?" Michael asked.

Mr. Kale's eyes slid to me. "Are you ok with that?"

I nodded.

Straightening from the wall, Mr. Kale took his time walking down the hall. He paused at the front door, offering me a chance to change my mind. I smiled, letting him know it was ok. With a curt nod, he pushed through the screen door.

My eyes dropped to Michael's red knuckles. The amount of force and the precise way he threw that punch at Zak meant his hand had to be hurting something awful. I had half the mind to let him feel all of it. But after learning about what happened between him and Lawrence . . . Taking the ice pack from the counter, I held it out to him.

His eyes snagged on my bruised forearm. There were five purple and blue ovals, his fingerprints from the day before.

Moving slowly, he took the ice from me and pressed it to his knuckles. "How's your jaw?"

"I've had worse."

His posture mimicked his father's moments before as he leaned his hip against the counter. Despite saying that he wanted to talk, he didn't speak. He just stared at the ice pack pressed to his hand.

I turned back to the counter and pulled my midnight snack closer. I twirled my spoon through a pool of melted brown sugar and scooped it into my mouth. When the bowl was nearly empty, I looked up again.

Michael hadn't moved.

My eyes strayed to the scar etched into the side of his face. "Why didn't you tell me about Lauren?"

"To be honest," he lifted the pack and glanced at his red knuckles, "I wasn't sure I could tell you without killing you."

I scooped the last bit of oatmeal into my mouth. "You should've told me."

"What good would that have done?"

I shrugged. I didn't know the answer to that either. Over his shoulder, the picture of him and Lauren caught my attention on the floor. The man in the frame and the one icing his knuckles might as well have been two different people.

"I'm sorry," I mumbled, "for what Lawrence did. I can't even imagine what that must've been like."

He looked up from the ice pack. Wariness narrowed his eyes, as if he were searching for an ulterior motive for my apology.

"I hope he rots in hell for it."

"He will." His eyes flickered over me, searching for what prompted my declaration. He wouldn't find the reason and I wasn't going to give it to him.

His gaze dropped to the bruises on my forearm again. Clearing his throat, he asked, "Do you know how to hit anything properly?"

I shook my head. "I'm usually on the receiving end in those situations."

"Would you like to change that?"

My stomach churned. "That would make me like them."

"If you injure people for your own pleasure, I'd agree. In this case, if they make the first move, you'd be able to stop them."

"I don't even want to do that."

"You need to stand up for yourself or tonight will be a common occurrence." He looked down at the ice pack. "That way, if someone grabs you, or his idiot brother comes at you in the middle of the night, you can put them in their place."

Moving away from the counter, he offered the ice pack back to me. "I'm sorry. About tonight."

Taking the ice pack, I pressed it to my cheek.

Without another word, Michael left the kitchen. His apology continued to ring in my ears. I thought he didn't know those words.

14

The Morning After

For the second day in a row, I woke up late.

With a yawn, I rolled over to look at the other side of the room. The yawn was cut short by the ache in my jaw. The split skin of my lip burned.

Oh, right. Last night was a complete disaster.

Sitting up, I found Michael's bed was empty.

Shuffling out of the covers, I carefully washed my face and took a brush to my hair. I grabbed another one of Meg's t-shirts and tugged it over my head.

A knock came at the door.

The heavy knuckles alerted me who it was before I opened it.

Michael stood in the hall with a steaming coffee mug. His eyes jumped from one bruise to the next. Bringing the mug to his lips, he took a large gulp and headed for the far side of the kitchen table.

"Morning, Charlie." Mr. Kale lowered his newspaper when I walked in. He even smiled at me.

"Morning."

"What would you like for breakfast, honey?" Mrs. Kale called from the other side of the room. "I can whip up some French toast. We also have cereal in the pantry."

My eyes jumped to Michael. *She called me 'honey.'* This was way too much interaction.

"She's not talking to me," Michael said.

Glancing toward the pantry, I tucked a stray lock of hair behind my ear. French toast sounded amazing. But the tension between the Kales was like a tightrope. I needed to get out of there before it snapped.

The pantry housed at least eight boxes of cereal, ranging from plain Cheerios to Lucky Charms. If I wasn't going to have French toast, I was going to have something with just as much sugar.

I glanced back at Michael. "Can I have Lucky Charms?"

"Of course!" Mrs. Kale patted the countertop and turned to grab a bowl. "Have a seat."

Ducking my head, I stepped into the open and claimed a stool at the counter. My shoulders tensed with the feeling of Michael's black eyes boring into my back.

Mrs. Kale paused mid-pour. Her morning cheer froze as her gaze fixated on the other side of the room. Mr. Kale's newspaper ruffled as he lowered it to the table.

I twisted around and found Zak in the doorway.

Dark shadows hung below his eyes. His tattered locks were proof he hadn't slept well last night. A slight tremor ran through his hands.

Just like Michael, he looked at my aching jaw. A strong contradiction of emotions swirled through his dark brown eyes; satisfaction, guilt, justification, and then loathing. Clearing his throat, he stepped toward me.

I shrank back, nearly falling off the stool.

He stopped a few feet back. Again, his eyes dipped to the bruise.

"I'm sorry." Zak extended his hand with bruised knuckles toward me.

I had been slapped, punched, backhanded, and kicked. But none of those people had ever apologized afterward. None of them even looked sorry. Hearing those words didn't make my jaw hurt any less, but it was appreciated.

I held up my hand, reminding him of my magic. "I don't want to hurt you."

"My arm is already numb from—" He dropped his gaze.

Dropping my feet to the floor, I grasped his forearm. Instead of pulling away, like everyone else did, he gripped back firmly.

"You punch like a cat without claws."

He blinked, taken aback.

I smiled at him. "That was a joke."

Zak did his best to return the strained smile. "Harts were always shit at telling jokes."

"Language," Mrs. Kale murmured from the other side of the island. She finished pouring the cereal and added a heavy splash of milk. As she put the bowl in front of me, Zak shuffled toward her.

I looked across the kitchen to the quiet man in black. He and his father sat on opposite sides of the table. While Mr. Kale was absorbed in the newspaper, Michael stared back at me.

I tried to smile, hoping to tell him we were moving forward, but it ended up just being a sad upturn of the lips. Ducking my head, I pulled my breakfast closer and dove into the colorful marshmallows.

"What are you going to do for lessons today?" Mr. Kale asked, flipping to another page.

Michael looked across the room to his mother. "When do you think she can use magic again?"

Mrs. Kale turned away from Zak. "Do you feel any pain in your chest?"

With my mouth full of cereal, I shook my head.

"I'd give it another day, just to be safe."

Michael nodded. "Then we can start with hand-to-hand form. That way she can hand Zak his drunken ass next time."

"There won't be a next time," Zak said firmly as his cheeks flushed pink.

Mrs. Kale handed her eldest a large mug of coffee and then turned back to me. "I'll stop by around noon with some lunch."

I stopped mid-chew to look over at Michael. Was it safe for her to come by in the middle of lessons? But he wasn't looking at me.

"Here, honey." Mrs. Kale grabbed the cereal box and poured more into my bowl. "You're too thin for my liking."

Before someone could disagree with her, I hunched over the bowl. The clink of the spoon was the only sound to disturb the tense silence. No sooner was the last marshmallow scooped into my mouth than Michael took his empty coffee mug to the sink and stopped beside me.

"Ready?"

Chewing quickly, I nodded.

"Did you get enough to eat?" Mrs. Kale asked, reaching for the bowl.

"Yes, thank you." I smiled as much as the split lip would allow. When I turned to the Master Hunter, my shoulders tensed under his black gaze. Was he going to make me pay for this?

Slipping off the stool, I headed for the back door with his heavy boots following after me.

"What did I say about your posture?" he asked as he slid the back door closed behind him.

I spun to face him, looking for any hints of anger. My shoulders pulled back bringing me to my full height. Feeling exposed, I wrapped my arms around my middle.

But he wasn't fuming. He nodded once, giving his approval, and then he started across the gravel. For the rest of the day, I waited for him to retaliate for last night. He never did.

For the rest of the summer, Mrs. Kale kept her word. Lessons halted at noon for lunch. They would stop again at three for a snack and a water break. At the end of the day, she brought dinner to our shared room and checked me over for bruises. Michael was on his best brooding behavior.

Before long, our time at the ranch ran out. I thought five weeks with the Kales would drag on forever. Or maybe I wouldn't survive it. It was just wishful thinking, a flimsy hope, that I'd never see the Magisterium again.

Surprisingly, I was sorry to leave the ranch. I loved the feeling of the house, the sounds of breakfast in the morning, and the peacefulness of the afternoon. The noise from the animals was soothing after hard lessons.

Even the Kales themselves. I enjoyed watching them interact. After the tension bled away, it was clear they actually cared for each other. In each foster home, people were forced to be there and forced to get along. Here, while there were moments of agitation, it was effortless and comfortable. Something inside my soul craved everything about it.

I had it once in a foster home I thought would be my last. I could barely remember the smooth hands of a mother rubbing my arms and the smell of pumpkin pie. The memory was chased away by the sharp sound of a belt hitting skin.

After a half day of lessons, Michael and I packed for the horrible trip back to the black stone school.

"Oh! I almost forgot." Mrs. Kale dashed out of the room and returned with a large plastic container with a red lid. Chocolate covered raisins tumbled against the sides as she stuffed it into my bag. "Michael mentioned you liked them."

I bit my lip to keep from looking like a clown. "Thank you."

"Next time you're here, it won't be as exciting. I promise." A smile lifted her lips.

I was surprised at the warmth that filled my chest at the thought of a next time.

"There won't be a next time," Michael said from the other side of the room. The look on his face reminded me I wasn't welcome here.

I stepped away from his mom. *This isn't for you, Charlie. Stray dogs don't get let into the house.*

I grabbed my bag and slipped into the bathroom. Not that I had anything to pack in there. I thought it best to be out of the way for their goodbye.

Setting my bag on the counter, I listened to the murmured conversation in the bedroom. I kept my gaze locked on the rug to keep from seeing my hideous blue-grey eyes in the mirror. After learning what Lawrence did . . . I hated them. I hated their color, their shape, the star burst pattern at the center. I hated that they were a reminder that I was his daughter.

As soon as I heard Mrs. Kale leave, I joined Michael back in the room. Pulling my bag over my shoulders, I expected him to lead me from the house and down the drive.

Instead, he reached into his back pocket and took out his wallet. He thumbed through a collection of business cards and removed a gold one with Master Lenin's name printed in black.

Bending down, he stuck the stiff paper between the wooden boards of the floor. Tugging his wand from the holster beneath his jacket, he tapped the upright card.

The gold paper absorbed his magic and started to grow. Quickly, it rose above our heads and solidified into a door. As soon as it stopped glowing, Michael pushed it open and gestured for me to go through.

The Magisterium of Magic was heavily protected by wards. No one could just Port in. The only way into the school was with a blood-coded transporter, and apparently an enchanted business card from Master Lenin.

I stepped over the threshold and into the living room of my apartment at the Magisterium.

Unlike the rest of the castle, the walls were plastered with red brick. The far wall was made entirely of glass, displaying a mountain range of thick evergreen pines. To the right was a study with a desk, a plush sitting area, and walls of bookcases. To the left was the bedroom with an attached private bathroom. In each room was a deep fireplace that warded off the cold. Right beside the door was a kitchenette with barstools.

Welcome back to hell, Charlie.

15

As is Tradition

Being back meant I wasn't under the protective bubble of the ranch.

I could Port. I could blip off the map. Before I could even consider pulling on my magic, Michael stepped into the room after me. He snatched a glint of silver off the kitchen counter and grabbed my wrist.

"Orientation is in an hour. Don't be late." Quickly, he clasped a silver bracelet around my wrist and dropped my hand. "If you are, I'll know."

Meaning, the silver chain was enchanted to track my movements around the castle. While the links were delicately made, I felt each one as if they were anchored to cement blocks.

No more running. I found it a little hard to breathe.

"The clasp will notify me when you touch it, so don't even try." Reaching into the pocket of his jacket, he took out a jar filled with a thick pasty cream. "My mother cooked this up for you. It'll hide your scars. We can't have people asking where you got them. Those marks are associated with a demon attack."

Right. Because we don't want anyone to know how much of a failure Master Lenin is.

"Do I have to remind you what happens when you touch someone?"

I folded my arms. "If they're in a high magic tier, my magic will shock them."

He nodded. "Now that I know you know, you don't have an excuse when you mess up. *Don't touch anyone,*" he stressed. "There's a transporter in your room for our lesson tonight. It will go off at ten sharp, so don't be late."

Walking over to the couch, he dropped his duffle bag on the cushions. "Just so we're clear, since I'll be sleeping here to make sure you don't level the school with a midnight flare, the living room is mine after hours. If you come into my area, I will physically harm you. Got it?"

I nodded. At least I didn't have to worry about that . . . although leveling the school didn't sound like a bad thing to me.

"Do I have to tell you not to breathe a word of your summer at the ranch?"

"No."

"Excellent. Because if you do—"

"I'll find myself with my throat slit, hanging over a cliff." I shifted my grip on my bag. Chocolate covered raisins rolled around their container. "I know."

"And anything about the tower—"

"I can't even remember most of it. So, I won't mention it. Plus, the less I think about it, the more I can trick myself into believing it never happened."

"Don't forget too much. I would hate for you to make the same mistake twice."

"Are you purposefully a jackass or can you just not not be one?" I gritted my teeth against the hot flare of magic in my chest. "It happened. I learned my lesson. Let's move on."

"That's completely up to you. If you did learn from it, this will be the last time we speak of it." Straightening his jacket, Michael headed for the enchanted door standing beside the kitchen counter. "I meant what I said at the beginning of the summer. You're out of chances. If you mess up, I will put you down."

He stepped through the magic door. It slammed behind him and disappeared with a flash of gold.

I stuck out my tongue at the space he left.

My attention was drawn to the silver bracelet around my wrist. While my blood hummed with the need to run and run far, the bracelet acted as a ball and chain. What was the point of running if Michael would be there waiting for me?

My souring mood changed when I registered the thick silence of the apartment. The last time I was here, the coffee table was smashed to bits. The hardwood floors were scratched, the furniture was flipped, and the light fixtures were blown. It was the night Richard While dragged me to the North Tower to steal my magic.

But the coffee table had been replaced. The lights were uncracked and shining bright. It was like it never happened.

My fingers nervously ran over the scar on my palm again and again.

As I unpacked, I kept glancing over my shoulder. I don't know what I was expecting, but I didn't want to stay in my room any longer than I had to. I grabbed my status pin, a number six for a Common, and stuck it through my shirt. Another one of Master Lenin's lies; I was enrolled as a Common Six, so no one knew I was a Royal Nine.

As soon as I stepped into the hall, I was crushed by a wave of excited chatter. When I reached the stairwell, I peered over the railing between the spiraling staircases to the center of the school seven floors down.

Unlike the last time I was here, it wasn't empty. In front of the dining room doors was a desk with five Users standing before a long line of noisy students. On either side of the table was a cart full of scrolls.

Registration had started.

Making my way down the stairs, I scanned the stairwell for familiar faces. Daniel, Cornelia, Nirean . . . I would even take Clarence.

Not spotting any of them, I joined the back of the line and kept my head down. We inched slowly across the stairwell and around the gaudy clock tower until I finally reached the registration table.

"Name?" a woman asked.

"Charlie Heart."

She stared up at me as if she were waiting for a punchline.

I rolled my eyes. "Heart; like the thing that beats in your chest. H-E-A—"

"I don't need you to spell it for me." She scrawled my name at the bottom of a very long list. She grabbed her wand and waved it over her head. A scroll jumped from the cart and dropped to the table beside her.

Without looking up, she handed it to me. "Sign this."

I whipped it open. Did I care what I was signing? Nope. There was nothing else they could take from me.

At the bottom of the scroll, something sliced into my thumb. Blood seeped out of the cut and absorbed into the paper before I could wipe it off.

She ripped the scroll out of my hands. "Next!"

I stuck my bleeding thumb in my mouth and walked into the dining room.

Against the back wall was a stage. Filling the room was a collection of round tables encircled by curved benches. The left side of the room was dominated by a buffet. Tall windows on either side let the winter sunlight flood the room.

I stood on my tiptoes searching for my group once again. The student body of the Magisterium was segregated based on status. Deficients, statuses one through three, sat closest to the door. Commons, statuses four through seven, took up the center of the room. That left the Royals, eight to ten, to take up the front before the stage. It was the same in every classroom, too.

Searching the middle of the room, I spotted two familiar faces.

Clarence Hardy sat in a pair of faded blue jeans and a graphic t-shirt of a zombie. With short cut black hair, he lounged against the table like he was on a beach watching the waves.

Beside him, fashionably dressed with her usual bowtie, was Nirean Knowles. Her dark skin complimented her fine pressed shirt. The sides of her hair were cut short, leaving the top curls longer.

I felt a sense of relief upon seeing them. At least I wasn't going to be alone in this black stone coffin. Weaving through the crowd, I plopped into the seat next to Clarence.

"Hey."

Clarence's scarred eyebrow rose.

Nirean scoffed. "You're kidding."

"What?" I asked, taken aback by her sharp tone.

Shaking her head, she slid off the bench and left the table without a glance back.

"What was that about?" I turned to Clarence.

But he was getting to his feet, too.

"Hey, where are you going?"

"No use sitting with liars," he responded before finding another table.

I sat there, completely dumbfounded. I raced through my memories of last semester. I couldn't think of anything that would earn me that kind of treatment. We were on good terms . . . at least Nirean and I were.

"Good afternoon, everyone!" Master Lenin's voice boomed from the front of the room. The School Master, dressed in a velvet navy suit, smiled from behind the podium. "Welcome back to The Magisterium of Magic. Please take a seat."

I slouched forward, dropping my chin into my palm.

"I hope you all had an excellent summer. For those of you who are joining us for the first time, welcome! During the five years you spend here, you will have access to world-class teachers and a plethora of ancient knowledge on the magical arts. This time will lay a foundation for the rest of your lives. If you apply yourselves, the future you want will be within your grasp.

"The castle has four wings with seven floors in each. Your apartments are located on the seventh floor—you should have gotten your room key when you checked in. On your schedule, the locations of your classes are coded by room number, floor, and wing. Any of your older classmates can assist you if you need it. Breakfast is from seven-thirty to nine. Lunch runs from eleven-thirty to one. Dinner begins at five and ends at seven. Come when your schedule allows.

"On the first floor, you have access to the library, which has the largest collection of enchanted textbooks in the world. Any of the books are yours to use as well as the stock of the greenhouse in the adjacent wing. There are two gyms, one in the South East Wing and the other in the North West Wing. The pool can be found on the second floor of the North East Wing and the sports field is in the South West. The lowest floor belongs to the teachers, where you can find their personal offices.

"In order to have a successful year, I ask that you abide by a couple of rules. All students must be in their rooms by ten o'clock. Outside the school is off limits."

Master Lenin shuffled his notes. "For those of you who are starting your final year, your future stands behind a single obstacle. Your Testing Year."

A murmur of excitement passed through the room.

"Every month you will have a final exam. After your teachers evaluate your test scores, they will be sent to specialists from across the globe. The best ranking students will be offered apprenticeships with—"

"With Masters of all trades, yes. But how about you earn a Master title for yourself instead?"

The room turned toward the interruption with murmured shock.

A towering figure stood in the doorway. He wore a thick coat lined with white fur. His head of black curls was dusted with snow.

"K—Konstantin," Master Lenin stuttered. His eyelashes fluttered with confusion. "I mean, Master Theodore. I'm in the middle of orientation. If you'll give me a moment to finish, I can—"

"Graduating students," Master Theodore called from the doorway with a thick Russian accent, "your Testing Year has been replaced. This year, The Magisterium of Magic will be hosting The Master's Trial."

The room went impossibly still.

"He has to be kidding," I heard someone whisper from the next table.

That was the only thing I heard. Every other student was so quiet that, for a moment, it seemed like no one was even breathing. Backs were straight. Knuckles went white. More than a few mouths gaped open.

I looked at the newcomer's face. He didn't look like he was joking. I wished there was someone I could ask. My heart fell at the thought of Moose. *She would have told me.*

"The Master's Trial is to take place next year," Master Lenin said evenly. "As is tradition. Every fifty years—"

"The Master of Combat Power, Master Hunter Lawrence Hart has requested that it happen this year."

My eyes snapped back to the newcomer. *Master Hart? As in Lawrence Hart?*

My question was echoed in whispers from table-to-table as Master Theodore reached into his thick coat, took out a folded letter, and held it over his head. "School Masters Loran, Aluna, Han, and myself have all agreed to his request. Majority rules."

Master Lenin spun on his heel and Ported, leaving the podium to appear beside the Russian. He was a good head shorter than the other School Master, but he still managed to rip the letter from his grasp. Turning his back to the room, he hurriedly unfolded it.

"At registration, each of you was given a scroll and you came away with a bleeding finger," Master Theodore continued loudly to the waiting students. "Your blood has been used to enter you into The Trial selection. From those scrolls, three students will be chosen based on magic status and grades. These components will be weighed against all the students in this graduating year. The three selected students will compete against three students from each of the Seven Great Magic Schools for the prize of earning a Master title.

"The graduating classes from each of the Seven Great Schools will be arriving tomorrow. The Master's Trial will start when the twenty-one Contestants are named. Good luck." He turned to leave, but Master Lenin grabbed him by the arm.

"What's going on, Konstantin?" he hissed.

Master Theodore shook off his grip. "I just said."

"I am not prepared to intake six graduating classes, let alone host—"

"Then I suggest you get to work." With that, he Ported.

As soon as he was gone, the dining room erupted. Students yanked out phones and enchanted mirrors to make calls. Questions were yelled from across the room at the School Master.

"Was he serious?"

"Master Lenin, what does this mean?"

"The Trial was supposed to happen during my year!"

"How can Master Hart move up The Trial?"

"I was studying for my Testing Year, not The Trial! I'm not prepared for this."

Still holding the letter, Master Lenin faced the room looking a little pale. He raised his hand in a silencing gesture, but the questions continued.

I shrank back against the table as the energy in the dining room only intensified. I looked at the fresh scab on my thumb. *Was I entered into . . . whatever that is?* I shook my head. *Master Lenin would never allow it.*

Master Lenin reached under his suit jacket for his wand. Pulling on his magic, he placed the glowing tip to his chin.

"Silence, please." His voice reverberated around the dining room, quieting every student. "I have just as much information as you," he said evenly. "I am going to get to the bottom of this. Enjoy the welcome-back reception that our cooking crew has prepared for you. When I have more information, I will let you know." He Ported.

The volume of the dining room doubled in his absence. Students jumped to their feet, not toward the buffet, but to confer with other students. They gathered in tight pods, discussing the news with fervor.

I had never heard so many voices in the room before. From what Moose had told me, a good chunk of the student body had transferred to other schools because of Master Lenin's involvement with Achilles Heel. Some thought it wasn't safe to be close to a School Master who allied himself with a Master Hunter like Michael. Others just didn't agree with what he was fighting for.

In that moment, the dining room sounded as if every seat was filled. Everyone had something to say about the change in testing and Trial date.

Meanwhile, I sat alone.

I had no idea what The Trial was and there was no one to ask. *Moose would tell me the significance of the switch.* Looking around the buzzing room, I felt her absence like a black hole.

I went through the buffet and loaded up a plate of spaghetti casserole. Everyone else seemed too occupied with The Trial news to eat. At the table closest to the buffet, a pair of girls were crying. A group by the door stormed out of the dining room.

I didn't want to eat in a room that reminded me so much of Moose, so I took my dinner to the second floor of the North East Wing. With everyone in the dining room, the pool was empty. Taking off my shoes, I soaked my feet and ate in silence.

When curfew rolled around, I had no choice but to go back to my room. As soon as the transporter beeped, I grabbed it.

"I'll be damned." Michael was in the middle of taking off his coat. "You're on time."

He stood in the middle of our usual training classroom. The room was covered in dust and caked in loneliness. Stacks of chairs lined the wall before an old chalkboard. A beaten-up desk was shoved in the corner.

"Just trying to keep you on your toes." I tucked the transporter into my front pocket. "Do you have my wand?"

"Of course." He tossed his jacket to the ground. "For your Testing Year, I'm going to get you a medical slip from Helen so you don't have to shake hands during your exams. Better yet, maybe I can get Lenin to pull you from it entirely."

"There is no Testing Year."

He gave me a look. "There's always a Testing Year."

"Some Master came during orientation and told everyone that it was being replaced by a trial."

Michael froze. He stared at me for so long I thought he was looking through me. "What Master?"

"Master Theodore, I think." I shrugged. "He had an accent."

"And he said *The Master's Trial* is happening?" he asked slowly. "This year?"

I nodded. "He said Lawrence wanted it early. He had signatures from other School Masters."

"Lawrence." Michael rocked back on his heels.

"What does that mean?" I asked, feeling out of the loop.

Whirling around, he scooped his jacket from the floor and headed for the door. "Go back to your room." The door slammed behind him.

16

Solution in a Trashcan

Was Michael flustered?

When he saw a severed finger on Master Lenin's desk, he was taken aback but not startled. If there was something out there that could rattle Michael Kale, I wanted a front row seat.

I flew out the door. He was moving a lot faster than I thought. He had already made it to the main stairwell. By the time I had made it there, he was already on the lower level.

Taking the stairs two at a time, I slowed near the bottom where Master Lenin's assistant's desk sat. Tessa Baker was slouched low in her desk chair with her eyes closed. A phone was nestled in the crook of her neck.

"Yes, Mrs. Hollis," she said dryly. "I hear your frustrations and I am happy to bring them to Master Lenin. But like I told you before, he is unavailable at this time. Yes, still."

Keeping low, I ducked her line of sight and rounded the corner to Master Lenin's office. Before I was even at the doorway, I could hear Michael.

"Cut the bullshit, Lenin." Michael slammed the door so hard the hinges creaked.

I pressed my ear to the door and barely heard Master Lenin's exasperated sigh. "It didn't concern you."

Footsteps echoed down the hall a second before Tessa Baker came around the curve.

Her steps faltered when she saw me, but she was on a mission. Clutched to her chest was a stack of papers.

Just as she reached the door, we both heard Michael rage through the walls. "It didn't concern me? Everything concerning Lawrence concerns me! Especially with something this big!"

She winced, but knocked anyway. The School Master called for her to enter.

"Sorry to bother you, Master Lenin . . . again," she said as she pushed open the door. "I have fifteen messages from aggravated parents. Mrs. Hollis called for a third time and there were ten calls from various Masters. I'm not sure how much longer I can hold them off. I'm worried they'll start showing up."

"I'll return their calls in the morning," Master Lenin groaned.

"Of course. Here are the messages I did take. Hi, Master Kale," she greeted him as she walked further into the office. "I apologize for the language. I just wrote down everything verbatim."

"Thank you, Tessa."

"And Miss Heart is standing in the hall."

Shit.

The door flew open to reveal Michael, knob in hand. His cheeks were slightly flushed, and he was even breathing a little heavier than normal. The intensity of his burning glare made me think it was a colossal mistake to follow him.

"I thought I told you to go back to your room," he said curtly.

"I ignored you." With confidence I didn't have, I brushed by him into the office. Sidestepping Tessa Baker as she left, I dropped into one of the chairs before Master Lenin's desk. "So, what's the big deal with this trial thing?"

Michael shook his head at the ceiling.

"The Master's Trial," Master Lenin corrected, "is the longest, most prestigious tradition in the history of magic. It happens every fifty years, like clockwork. It's never been moved. And I was going to tell you," he told Michael.

"When?" Michael snapped. "As they started congregating the schools? Or maybe when the First Trial started?"

"Please refrain from adding more drama to this situation."

I bit back a smile.

"You think I'm being dramatic? How is Theodore coming by uninvited, announcing The Trial a year early, not something you tell me immediately?"

"I understand you feel left out—"

"This isn't a childish slight, Lenin," Michael corrected harshly. "I'm not feeling left out. My feelings aren't hurt. I'm shocked you would let something of this magnitude sit for so long."

"Do you have any idea how much needs to get done to cram twelve months of work into twenty-four hours?" Master Lenin asked briskly. "I have to get the dorm floors expanded and cleaned. I need to add thirty additional classrooms on each floor of each wing, not to mention the entire North Wing needs to be renovated since it's been haunted for a few decades." He rubbed his eyes.

He dropped his hand and redirected his exhausted gaze to Michael. "Master Hart has been playing this close to his chest. Everything is ready: the judges, the Guardian selection, and even the Trial Fields. I was quite literally the last person to know. Based on your past experience of The Trial, I thought you wouldn't want anything to do with it."

Oo, I want to know more about that.

"This can't happen," Michael said in a low voice. "He'll be too close. Charlie is here for fuck's sake, and if he sees her—"

"He'll think she's just a kid. She's enrolled as a Common Six. There's no reason for him to look closely."

"She's a Royal Nine. He'll sniff her out."

I crinkled my nose. *Not a fan of that description.*

"Which is why I pulled her scroll the moment Theodore left." Master Lenin lifted the scroll I had signed during registration from his desk. "She won't be entered in The Trial. She won't be anywhere near him."

"Good." Michael ripped the scroll from his hand and hurled it across the room. It struck the wall and rebounded into the trashcan.

"Why take out my scroll?" I asked. Both men looked a little surprised that I was still there. "It's not like I could have been chosen. I don't know enough about magic."

"It's not just based on knowledge, although high grades are a contributing factor for some being selected. Your status would guarantee you a spot."

Hold the phone. I can get into The Trial? I glanced at the trashcan where my scroll peeked over the rim.

Master Theodore said that if you won The Trial, you got a Master's title. Michael and Master Lenin said it was the highest rank among Magic Users.

If I got my own title, did that mean neither Michael nor Master Lenin could kill me after the war? Lawrence was still breathing right now, because of his titles.

Better yet, could they even force me to fight for the Achilles Heel?

Hope bloomed in my chest. *Is The Trial my Get Out of Jail Free Card?* With a title, I could protect Blake. I could remove myself from this situation entirely and there would be nothing Michael or Master Lenin could do about it.

Master Heart . . . that name held power. Maybe it was because that was what everyone referred to Lawrence as. But thinking about it in regards to myself made me warm with pleasure. *No one would be able to use me ever again.*

Fate was in the habit of giving me the short end of the stick, but it looks like she may have finally slipped up. I had a way out of this mess. I had a way to get my life back.

All I had to do was get into The Trial.

"What's our next move?" Michael gripped the back of the chair.

"I'm not sure there is one." Crossing his arms, Master Lenin leaned back into his plush, leather seat. "The rules are clear; it's forbidden to interfere with The Trial and its staff. Lawrence is completely untouchable for the next year."

I would be untouchable.

"You have to get me on the inside. You have that power, right? Maybe I could be on staff—"

"Master Kale—"

"I can use an illusion disguise."

"The magic and security measures surrounding The Trial will guarantee that some time or another, you would be found out. Your title would be removed."

With a curse, Michael drove his hands into his hair.

"You realize what this is, don't you?" Master Lenin asked him. "Lawrence is making a play for the Masters. I know your views on The Trial, as does the entire magical world. He wants you to act out and, I speculate, to get you and myself discredited. If he knocks us out of the way, there's nothing stopping him from gaining the loyalty of the last few reluctant Masters."

And if he did that, he could have their titles stripped and then have them killed.

"But we also have the chance to play the same game," Master Lenin stressed. "All of the Masters will be in one place. We can sway them to our side. But that only works if we play this right. So, for the sake of the Heel and the justice you and I both seek, keep your temper in check."

You and I both seek? I squinted at Master Lenin. He didn't mention losing anything or anyone to Lawrence.

Michael nodded tightly. "Then start with LeOnie."

Master Lenin's eyebrows rose. "Why Master LeOnie?"

"Because that's who I'd start with if I were Lawrence." Michael took a slow deep breath. "What if I sent a member of my team into The Trial? They could be a Guardian."

A what?

"If they were," Michael continued, "they could tell us which of the Masters Lawrence makes a move on. Then you could make an opposing play for the others."

"Yes, but—"

"There are five Hunters left in the entire world. Three of them I have on my team. Not even Lawrence can come up with a good enough reason for them to not counsel a Contestant."

Master Lenin's eyebrow jumped as his mind weighed through Michael's argument. "Fine." Opening the top drawer, he pulled out a thick legal envelope. He leaned over the desk, extending it to Michael. "Have whoever you choose fill it out. I'll need it back by tomorrow at noon."

Michael nodded.

"In the meantime, I need your word that you will not interfere and you will stay far away from this Trial."

Michael nodded again.

Then Master Lenin turned his gold flecked eyes on me. "The same goes for you. We can't have your father getting too close."

"You got it." I kicked my feet up on the corner of his desk, tipping over a stack of letters. "Oh, sorry."

Before either man could move, I dropped to my knees to collect the mess. In the flurry of papers, I snuck my scroll out of the trashcan and slipped it into the pocket of my hoodie.

I stood with the stack of papers held to my chest, concealing the bulge of the scroll. Setting them back on the desk, I slipped my hands into the pocket and held it tight.

"Sorry," I said again, for good measure.

Michael rolled his eyes.

Master Lenin reached over to straighten the pages to his liking. "You should go to bed."

I looked between the two of them, hating that I was going to miss out on Michael freaking out. But the longer I was there with the scroll in my pocket, the more likely they would see me hiding it.

With a carefree shrug, I left the office. I kept my steps slow as I walked down the hall, in case they could read anything from my pace. Tessa was on the phone when I passed so she paid me no attention. I kept the easy pace until I was in my room with the door bolted behind me.

There, I took out the scroll. I unrolled it to see my name and the smear of blood at the end.

If I could pull this off, I could be back on the beach and, this time, I wouldn't have to hide. I could lounge. And maybe Blake would be with me.

I grinned. *Who knew I would find my solution in a trashcan?*

17

The Seven Great Magical Schools

The next day, The Trial was all anyone could talk about.

At breakfast, there was a group of girls who whispered about it in the food line. During Advanced Wand Techniques, students beside me were passing notes about it. Between classes, teachers discussed it in the hallways. But any questions about it in class were all deflected with the same answer and the same tight-lipped tension.

"I'll leave that for Master Lenin to answer."

I kept my registration scroll on me from the moment I woke up. I put it in the corner of my bag so I could reach in and assure myself it was there whenever I wanted.

I just need to find a way to get it entered without alerting Master Lenin.

I thought about giving it to Tessa Baker, but I couldn't be sure she wouldn't tell him. There had to be a way. I would shout my real magic status in front of the whole dining room if I had to.

The other schools were coming at noon. I planned to get a good spot to scope out the competition. If I got into The Trial, I wanted to see what I was going up against. In the meantime, I kept my head down and went through the day anonymous and undetected, biding my time.

"Charlie Heart with an E."

I stopped short in the doorway to the dining room. A tornado of butterflies swirled through my chest. My heart did a little jump.

Turning, I found Daniel Phillips with a dimpled grin so wide the corners of his eyes crinkled. The brown of his irises was so warm I wondered if he was the human embodiment of hot chocolate.

"Daniel, hi!"

"I thought we'd seen the last of you," he said, coming closer. His hands loosely gripped the straps of his messenger bag.

A lie slipped easily off my tongue. "I decided to try a semester at the European Academy."

"I can't blame you. After Moose." He rushed on. "If you're here, does that mean you're . . ."

"I'm staying." I reached into my bag to touch the scroll.

He clenched his fist before him with a victorious smile. "Be honest. It was the cinnamon rolls, wasn't it?"

"That was high on the list," I laughed.

"I was sad that you didn't say goodbye when you left."

Surprised, I said, "I didn't think you would care."

"Then that's on me, because I do." His grin softened. "I'm glad you're back."

For the first time in a long while, I told the truth. "It's good to see you."

His eyes brightened. "Cornelia and I were going to meet up for lunch. She's going to be so stoked that you're back."

He took my hand and pulled me into the dining room, past the buffet, and nearly halfway through the room. We stopped at a table beside the tall windows. The air was colder here, thanks to the snowy view outside. Seated at the table was the prettiest girl in the school.

"Cornelia!" Daniel called. "Look who I found."

Her whole face lit up. With a shriek of joy, she jumped to her feet and wrapped her arms around my neck. Her comforting vanilla perfume filled my lungs and warmed me just as much as her hug.

"No way!" She took a step back and clasped her hands in front of her. Her sapphire eyes lit up. "Does that mean you chose the Magisterium? You're staying?"

I nodded. "I'm here for good."

"Yay!" She wrapped me in a hug again.

I felt no such joy, but I kept my smile in place.

Michael could use them against you, I thought as my heart filled with lead. *He used Blake to trap you here. Imagine what he could do with two more anchors.*

I thought about making an exit from this cozy duo, but I couldn't bring myself to leave. *Just for a little bit and then I'll detach.*

A soft chime rang from the stairwell as the clock signaled that it was noon.

"Oh, it's almost time!" Cornelia snatched her bag and two wrapped sandwiches from the table. "If I had known you were here, I would have grabbed you lunch."

"No worries—" I started.

"I'll hop in line and grab you one," Daniel offered.

"You don't have to do that."

"I've got it. Just save me a spot on the stairs." He disappeared toward the buffet line.

Cornelia looped her arm through mine and led me out of the dining room. The whole school had the same thought. The intertwining staircases were packed with students all the way up to the sixth floor. Some were seated, some leaned against the railing. All were peering down to the main floor.

Cornelia found a part of an unoccupied banister on the third floor for us to squeeze into. Just as she was about to lean into the railing, someone shouldered her out of the way, taking her spot. Flushing bright red, she moved back.

"Hey." I tapped the guy on the shoulder. "My friend was standing there."

He looked at Cornelia and the number four pinned to her shirt. Then he looked at my pin. Wordlessly, he scooted over.

With flushed cheeks, Cornelia shifted back into her original spot.

"There's Master Lenin," someone called over the noise.

Every eye turned to the bottom of the stairs as Master Lenin came up from the lower level. And he wasn't alone.

"Wow," I muttered. "Who are they?"

Following behind him were eight Users in black armor. Each suit was rimmed with gold. At the center of the chestplate was the crest of The Magisterium of Magic; a compass rose with an owl perched on top.

"Master Lenin's personal guards," Cornelia whispered back. "I've never seen them at the school before."

"Good afternoon!" Master Lenin's voice echoed up the stairwell. "We're just getting a few things in order before we welcome the other schools."

Behind him, two guards closed the South Wing doors. Another pair moved the students on the main level so there was a path to the North Wing.

The rest spread out around the stairwell, placing themselves on either side of the doors of all of the other wings and rooms.

I thought the North Wing was closed to students.

"Master Lenin," a girl called from the floor above us. "Can Master Hart really move up The Trial?"

The din of moving students quieted as all eyes turned to Master Lenin.

The School Master looked up the twisting staircases. The stairwell was so quiet, he didn't have to use his wand to project.

"Yes, he can."

"How?" another student asked.

"He's a Trial Winner. And he got four of the seven School Masters to agree."

"But why?" This time it was a teacher questioning him.

"I'm sure there is a good reason," Master Lenin said evenly. "Is it out of character that it's happening a year early? Yes. But that just means we get to dethrone the school who won the last Trial sooner. The Magisterium deserves the title of being the best out of the Seven Great Schools. We get to prove that."

Glancing around the stairwell, some looked placated by his answer. I spotted Daniel squeezing through the crowded staircase. He offered me a wrapped sandwich and took the spot beside me.

Master Lenin pocketed his hands. "We're just about ready to welcome the graduating class from each school for the rest of the year.

"As the hosting school, it's our job to make them feel at home. You will respect them or you'll have a conversation with me." He paused. His tone hinted that it wouldn't be a fun conversation. "You have the advantage because this is your home away from home. They're coming to an unfamiliar place of strangers. Be kind and help where you can."

"Where are they going to stay?" someone yelled from a higher floor.

"Each of the apartment levels has been expanded. The North Wing will house most of them." Taking out his wand, he waved it toward the set of towering gold doors. They swung open with a deep groan, revealing a hallway of black stone with glittering chandeliers and golden doors.

A chill crept up my spine. The last time I had seen that wing, it was covered in dust. None of the lights worked.

"What about the ghost?" a teacher asked.

"That has been handled." Master Lenin's hard tone indicated that follow up questions were unwelcome.

"Did you hear anything about that?" Cornelia whispered to Daniel.

He shook his head. "Not sure how he managed to do that."

He didn't. I did.

Master Lenin's assistant, Tessa Baker, tapped the School Master's shoulder. She whispered in his ear before retreating to the wall.

He nodded to the stairwell of students and teachers. "Let's get started."

Turning to the South Wing doors, he tapped his wand against each door twice. Magic coated the gold metal, making them glow brighter.

"What are they doing?" I whispered to Daniel.

"Making a portal," he said as two guards grabbed the handles and heaved them open. A blast of cold air rushed into the room.

The students lining the stairs crowded the railing. Cornelia leaned all the way over for a better look through the enchanted doorway.

"Please welcome the students from The University for Advanced Tactical Magic."

The scene through the South Wing doors didn't belong to our school. Instead of black stone, there were walls of pale blue ice. Black iron chandeliers hung from the ceiling. Mighty torches were fused to the walls.

The first person through was the same man from the night before, Master Theodore. He grasped Master Lenin's forearm and his shoulder in greeting. Three stories up, I could see Master Lenin wince from the force of it.

Releasing Master Lenin, he strolled into the school with the same confidence as before; like he owned it.

Behind him came two guards holding a burgundy chest with black accents. Each guard wore armor of matching colors with thick fur collars.

The students had 'looking for and welcoming a fight' written all over them. Each had a thick coat over uniforms of dark athletic gear.

Seeing them gave me the first doubts over my plan of getting in The Trial. *I need to start lifting weights immediately.*

When the majority of the students had filed down the newly expanded North Wing, the South Wing doors were closed and reopened. The light fragrance of flowers on a warm breeze spread through the room.

"Please welcome The Magical Academy of the Earth." Master Lenin turned to the doorway and clapped.

The School Master came out in a white suit made of silk with bold red appliques. He stopped before Master Lenin to grasp his forearm. It was a quick exchange before he moved deeper into the school.

Following behind were two guards in white armor. Between them was a chest painted in white and red. The students that followed wore pink silk.

"I always thought that school name was ridiculous," Cornelia whispered.

"Not as stupid as their curriculum," someone said on the other side of her. "They teach that magic comes from the earth."

"What does that mean?" I asked Daniel.

"Their studies concentrate more on potions," he responded. "Very little wand magic is taught."

I pressed closer to the railing. *If that's true, maybe I'd have the upper hand.* Michael taught me nothing but magic.

When the last student in pink crossed into the North Wing, the South Wing doors were closed and opened once again. This time a rush of salty air blew through the stairwell. Sand ran across the black floor.

"Aquarius: The Undersea School of Enchantments," Master Lenin declared.

I pressed closer to the railing. "Didn't Ace transfer there?"

"Ace Navarro?" Daniel leaned over my shoulder. "I knew she left. I didn't know which school she went to."

I shivered as his breath danced across my cheek.

Their School Master limped forward with the aid of a cane. He stopped beside Master Lenin and grasped his forearm. He even smiled before slowly leading his school inside.

The chest that followed was bright blue and gold. The guards who carried it wore the same colors.

The Aquarius students looked at our black stone walls with disdain. Many looked longingly at the cloudless beach behind them. Shivering in their shorts and t-shirts, they followed their teachers further into the Magisterium.

"What do they teach?" I asked.

"Illusions and enchantments, mostly." Daniel shook his head with a little eye roll.

Illusions and enchantments . . . I didn't have a lot of experience with those. That might be an issue.

When the doors opened again, dry scorching air whipped through the stairwell.

"Welcome, Lions of Magic."

"What do they teach?" I asked Daniel.

"Uh," he thought for a moment, "it's hard to explain. It's magic on the defensive, but as brutal as possible."

A woman entered first in a tight gold dress with a collar that looked to be made of a lion's mane. She barely clasped forearms with Master Lenin before turning away. Behind her, two guards carried a chest made of wood with ivory accents. Their armor looked to be made of different shades of sandstone.

The students stood tall with perfect postures and no smiles. They were all in black suits, even the girls.

"What's in the chests?" I asked.

"The scrolls from the graduating year," Daniel said. "It's how they select the Contestants for The Trial."

Bingo.

So, I just had to find the Magisterium's chest. *Was it as simple as dropping my scroll in?*

"Where do they keep them?"

"I don't know," he said, as if he had never thought about it before. "I would imagine in the School Master's quarters until the Naming Ceremony."

I didn't see a chest in Master Lenin's office last night. That meant it was offsite. I didn't know where that would be and I couldn't leave the school to find out. So, I wouldn't be doing anything until tonight.

The doors closed. As magic gleamed over them, condensation beaded on the surface. The Magisterium guards yanked them open. The air it released was so heavy with moisture it might as well have been a wave of water.

"Please welcome The Serpentine School of Magic." A bright red parrot soared into the stairwell.

A few stairs below me, a student hissed like a snake. "Watch out for the Jungle School." Those around him laughed.

I expected them to come in wearing giant snakes or something scaly. Instead, they were dressed in plain clothes; no uniform.

If the School Master hadn't walked in first, I wouldn't have known he was anything special in his button-up and faded jeans. He walked by Master Lenin without a glance. Their guards wore forest green and their chest was painted bright yellow. The students walked in quietly, stone-faced, and left rather quickly.

I leaned over to ask Daniel what they taught, but he was a step ahead of me. "They focus on survival on the offensive," he whispered. "It's more about how to get what you want with as much force as needed. I've heard their poison curriculum is unmatched."

Poison? Cheese and rice.

"The final school to join us," Master Lenin said as his magic moved up the doors, "is The European Academy for Practical Magic."

When their School Master came into the Magisterium, he not only grabbed Master Lenin's arm, he embraced him. There was a brief moment of pleasantries, before he walked into the North Wing.

I eyed the chest painted sage green with white trim carried between the guards of matching armor. "What's practical magic?"

Daniel shrugged. "Precise, sophisticated magic, I guess."

Out of all of the schools, this one displayed the most class. The guys were dressed in three-piece suits. The girls wore dresses or pantsuits in neutral colors. They walked smoothly and held their backs straight. Wrinkles did not exist in their world.

"God," Cornelia groaned. "Can you imagine having to wear that to school every day?"

When the last arrivals had moved into the North Wing, Master Lenin smiled. "Please welcome our new students to their home for the year. The Naming Ceremony will begin at seven." Bringing his phone to his ear, he turned sharply and headed to the lower level. Tessa was a step behind him.

Daniel's phone chimed. Digging it out of his pocket, his face fell. "Miss Baker wants me in Master Lenin's office."

"Is everything ok?" I asked, fearing that maybe Master Lenin would warn him away from me. My heart twinged. *That might be for the best.*

"He probably needs extra hands for the Naming Ceremony." His thumbs flew across the screen with his response. "It usually takes place a week after everyone arrives." Pocketing his phone, his brown eyes found mine. "Will you save me a seat for the ceremony?"

My heart fluttered. Against my better judgment, I nodded. "Sure."

Grinning, he flew down the stairs. I eyed the teeming crowd of different uniforms and furs below. I never thought the school would seem crowded. That was going to work in my favor. I was invisible in a crowd. I could hunt down those chests and no one would notice I was there.

"I want to hear about the rest of your summer," Cornelia called over the din.

She'll add to my cover. "Want to walk around while we catch up? I kind of want to check out the new students too."

She looped her arm through mine. "You read my mind."

We started down the stairs, and began the hunt for my way into The Trial.

18

The Naming Ceremony

Wherever those chests were, they were hidden well.

Short of going into rooms and searching, Cornelia and I walked the full blueprint of the school. We even went down to the teacher's level after I said I needed some quiet. They were nowhere. I asked Cornelia if she knew anything about them, but she shook her head.

"Honestly, I've never been too interested in learning about The Trial. What's the point, you know?" She shrugged. "With my status, I'll never get in."

Most of the other schools had started exploring the Magisterium. Each level was flooded with students dressed in different colors and materials. We'd shuffle behind a large group of Tactical University students in thick furs only to be almost run over by a student dressed in pink silk. My toes were stepped on. I took an elbow to the kidneys.

All the while, the guards in black and gold remained motionless around the stairwell.

By the time we were supposed to be in the dining room, I was irritated, over stimulated, and near hopelessness.

Those chests have to make an appearance again. Why would they go through the drama of showing them off only to hide them away?

Hungry, Cornelia and I joined the flow of students to the dining room.

Sometime in the afternoon, the room had been expanded to accommodate more tables and another buffet line on the other side. In addition, the tables were now draped in tablecloths. Grouped in clusters, there were seven colors; blood-red, olive-green, sea-blue, canary-yellow, tan, black, and white. At the center of each was a clear vase filled with golden flowers.

For as full as it was, with the graduating classes from six other schools, the only real noise came from the shuffle of feet through the buffet line and the tight whispers around tables.

"It's like someone died in here," Cornelia whispered from the doorway.

I nodded. "This Trial is a big deal, huh?"

"Oh yeah. It's like the Super Bowl for Magic Users." She stood on her tiptoes. "I see a table near the middle with some room." She headed toward the grouping of tables dressed in black.

As we snaked through the room, I spotted a flash of electric blue. Tessa Baker entered through the side door, looking a bit frazzled and out of breath. Following behind her were the guards of each school from earlier. Each carried their own painted chest.

I almost tripped. *There they are.* My hand was already in my bag seeking out the scroll.

I traced the line of guards as they made their way to the stage. One by one, under Tessa's careful direction, the chests were placed on the platform. All of them I had seen before, except the black and gold one Tessa levitated behind her.

That has to have the Magisterium's scrolls in it.

"I'm going to use the bathroom," I told Cornelia. "I'll be right back."

I headed for the door, pretending to leave the room. When I was out of sight from Cornelia, I skirted around the far side of the dining room, moving closer and closer to the stage. I took a seat at an empty table near the cold windows and pulled my bag onto my lap. As the guards left through the side door, Tessa stayed to make sure the chests were positioned neatly, and there was no lint or dust defacing them. She even took out a handkerchief to polish a couple of the latches.

So, how do I get the scroll in?

There weren't any locks on the front. But that didn't mean they weren't sealed with magic.

I couldn't just walk up. I didn't have to look around to know that people were watching the chests intently: faculty, students, and the Magisterium guards who stayed on the edges of the room.

I only knew simple magic and even then, I was better with tricks and lies.

I sat up a little straighter. *Then let's use tricks and lies.*

Pulling out my wand, I kept it close to my leg, hidden from view. I drew on a small strand of magic and directed it toward the Magisterium's chest. A slight brush of magic caressed the seam between the lid and body. Just barely the lid moved.

Bingo! It wasn't sealed. *Probably because no one is stupid enough to try this. Or have a reason to try this.*

Next step, distraction. With my magic at the ready, I directed my attention to the opposite side of the room. A tiny spark of gold flew from my wand, zipping between tables, around moving feet, to the buffet. It collided with a stack of trays, sending them crashing to the floor.

In the quietness of the room, it sounded like a car crashed into a Lego store. Every head turned. I stood, feigning a look of interest at the noise. Others followed suit, creating a wave of curiosity through the room.

No one noticed the lid of the Magisterium's chest lift. No one noticed something zip from my bag toward the open chest. No one heard the lid close. No one looked at me as I passed by. It just looked like I was moving closer to the mess of trays. That was if anyone looked.

Biting back a grin, I rejoined Cornelia.

Master Lenin said that my status would guarantee me a spot in The Trial. Now I just had to wait and see if he was full of shit or not.

"I have never seen the dining room this full." Daniel slid into the seat beside Cornelia. He sent a dimpled smile my way. "I never thought I would use the word *small* to describe this school."

"At least they're nice," Cornelia chirped. "I talked with some girls from Aquarius. Did you know their school is actually underwater?"

"The guys from The University for Advanced Tactical Magic aren't." Daniel shook his head. "I tried to introduce myself to one and he spit at my shoes."

My nose wrinkled. "That's gross."

"At least he missed."

To keep myself from staring at the Magisterium's chest, I looked around the room at the students I might compete against.

"Which school usually wins?" I asked.

"The University, the Magisterium, and the European Academy," Daniel answered. "From what I've heard, Lions of Magic has significantly improved their curriculum. So maybe they'll make some headway this turn."

"Why do they win?"

"Because each school focuses on something different as the core of their learning. The Tactical University focuses on fighting. The Magisterium focuses on knowledge of the magical arts. The European Academy specializes in sophisticated magic—they've won second place for a while. Those skills translate better in The Trial."

"Have the other schools ever won?" Cornelia leaned into the table to pluck a gold flower from the centerpiece. "Aquarius, Serpentine . . . and the other one?"

"The Magical Academy." Daniel shook his head. "No. Although they've tried, regardless of the rules."

That sounds ominous.

"The world is changing." Daniel crossed his arms on top of the table. "What we used to value, like survival and enchantments, no longer moves the world like they used to. Knowledge and battle tactics hold the most power."

It's like the world is preparing for war.

"Who won the last Trial?" I asked.

"Victor Haltland from the University. It was brutal. Only three Contestants from the Top Seven made it out."

"Made it out." I turned to face him. "What do you mean?"

A hush fell over the room. Daniel sat up a little straighter. Following his gaze, I watched Master Lenin enter. Behind him, in single file, were each of the School Masters. Wordlessly, they made their way to the stage. The room was so silent, the thump of the cane from Aquarius' School Master was clear.

Climbing the stage, the School Masters made their way to the chest with their school colors. Once they were all in place, Master Lenin faced the room.

My heart jumped. *Here we go.*

"Good evening," Master Lenin began. "Twenty-one hundred years ago, the School Masters of the Seven Great Schools were in a disagreement. Each thought their school was the best, that they created the best Users. To settle this, they created a test and invited every Master of every trade to watch."

My eyes widened. *The magical world's most powerful would be watching? All of them?*

"From the graduating class of each school, three students were chosen to compete in three Trials. Through the years, the theme of each Trial has changed to best challenge the newest generation of Magic Users, but the core stayed the same. At the end of each Trial, one Contestant from each school was eliminated until only one from each school remained.

"If a Contestant finished a Trial well, they could catch the eye of a Master and earn an apprenticeship. It takes years to earn enough credentials to be considered by a Master. By being called into The Trial, a Contestant could jump to the front of the line and get the experience of a lifetime.

"But, if they made it into the Top Seven and outshined, outwitted, and outdid every other Contestant, if they earned first place, an apprenticeship would be an insult. Instead, the winning school got the prize of being called the best in the world. And the first place Contestant became a Master."

My heart rate increased.

"It takes decades, or for some titles, it takes centuries to be called a Master. If a User wins a Master title, they will go down in history as a Trial Winner, earning a place in Founder's Hall. That's why only the smartest, most capable, and strongest Users from this year's graduating classes will be called to participate.

"If your name is called, The Master's Trial will replace your Testing Year. Normally, students would have twelve tests to show the world what they are capable of. But if you're named for The Trial, you'll only have three, and they'll be the most difficult challenges you'll ever face."

My eyes dropped to the chest at his feet. Butterflies danced around my stomach.

"Forty-nine years ago, we watched Victor Haltland overcome giants from the north in the First Trial. He diagnosed and treated a disease inside himself within the Second Trial. And for the Third, he competed against a magical projection of himself to cross the finish line. In the end, The University for Advanced Tactical Magic was named first and Victor Haltland earned a title."

Yells and clanging silverware erupted from where the graduating class of the University was seated.

"Tonight, all of that is possible once again. Tonight, we will find out who will participate in The Master's Trial." He waved his wand and all seven chests opened in unison. "Tonight, we start a new chapter."

Here we go.

"The moment your name is called, the world turns its attention to you. Never again will you get the opportunity to have the eye of every Master upon you. Whether you choose to participate or not, your life changes to-day."

My life starts today.

Master Lenin turned and gestured to the School Master at the far end of the line. "We will start with The Magical Academy of the Earth. Master Loran, if you please."

A man in a red and white silk suit stepped closer to the chest. He was shorter than the others, but he didn't lack the strength or fierceness in his face. He took his wand from his sleeve and waved it over the chest.

Three scrolls lifted out of the pile. With a flash of gold, the scrolls burst into flames. The fire took the shape of two girls and a boy.

"Lin Cho-Hoy," Master Loran read out. "Malan Thompson, and Tala Abalos."

The room applauded as the three students walked onto the stage. The swirling fire figures bowed and disappeared back into their glowing scrolls. Each Contestant then grabbed their scroll from the air. They each grasped the forearm of their School Master before taking the place of the fire figure.

Cool.

"From Aquarius: The Undersea School of Enchantments, Master Harley Finch," Master Lenin called.

I expected someone with bleached, wind-blown hair and a deep tan. Instead, it was the Master with greying hair and a cane. He twisted off the top of his cane, revealing his wand, and waved it over the blue chest. Three scrolls burst into flames.

"Amelia Markus," he called in a booming voice. Cheers erupted from where the school was seated. "Marissa Larson and Bailey Jones."

When the Contestants were on the stage and the clapping subsided, Master Lenin continued, "From Lions of Magic, Master Aluna."

A thin, elegant woman, draped in a floor-length animal skin dress, took her wand from a chain around her neck.

"Aboiy Dlamini," she said in a cool voice. "Emeka Selasi, and Vienna Schneider."

As the three newest Contestants walked onto the stage, Master Lenin called, "From The European Academy for Practical Magic, Master Thomas Harlan."

Daniel stiffened as a tall dark-haired man in a deep green suit stepped forward. Reaching into his jacket, he removed his wand and enchanted the chest at his feet.

Three scrolls rose and transformed into flaming figures. My gaze snagged on the last one. *Why does he look familiar?*

Master Harlan cleared his throat. "Anna Clarkson, Leon Smith, and Blake Johnson."

"Did he say Blake Johnson?" I blurted.

The school stood and cheered. My knees banged against the underside of the table as I staggered to my feet. I scoured the crowd of students for something, anything. Did I want it to be true? Did I want to be wrong?

But there was no denying it.

There he was.

Walking up the stairs toward a mirror image of himself was Blake Johnson in a light grey suit. And despite the fancy get up, he wore a beanie as familiar to me as the owner was. My saving grace of Haven Avenue, my comfort on my worst days, and my best friend of five years.

I never thought I would see him again, and he was *here*. I thought I was going to explode from the sheer joy of it. I had half a mind to sprint across the room to throw my arms around him.

Blake had *magic*.

Blake was *here*.

Then my heart plummeted. If he was here, that would mean he was closer to Michael's blade. No longer would Michael have to go to Kansas to inflict a fatal wound upon my soul, now he just had to cross a building.

He can't be here.

But he was.

And he was on stage turning to face the room.

I sat down before he saw me standing with my mouth gaping open.

"From The Magisterium of Magic." The scrolls ignited and the figures straightened. I was so thoroughly rattled; I couldn't stop staring at Blake.

He can't be here.

"Daniel Phillips."

Daniel jerked in his seat. He stared widely at the stage.

Cornelia bounced in her seat. Giggling, she pulled him into a hug. Even kids from the other tables reached over to shake his forearm. Daniel smiled broadly as he pulled me into a hug.

I kept my back to the stage. My heart galloped around my chest. *What is happening?*

"Clarence Hardy," Master Lenin called. Nirean slapped him on the back as he jumped to his feet.

There was a pause.

"And Charlie Heart."

My gaze snapped to the fire figures.

Master Lenin stared right at me. As was everyone between us. Even Daniel stopped advancing to the stage to look back at our table.

"Charlie!" Cornelia squealed. Putting a hand over her smiling mouth she said with a giggle, "Oh my, God! You've been chosen!"

19

The Chosen Twenty-One

Cheese and rice, it worked.

But the victory wasn't sweet. It felt fragile, riddled with sharp edges. As I got back to my feet, my eyes were on Blake.

He was whispering to the Contestant to his left, Leon, so he hadn't seen me yet.

Daniel must have thought I was frozen in a state of shock because he stepped in front of me, blocking my view of the room and the far stage. With an easy smile, he took my hand.

"Come on, let's walk up together." He helped me step over the bench and, without releasing my hand, guided me toward the stage.

Blake turned then. His candy apple green eyes appraised Daniel as if the competition had already started. Maybe it had. And then they turned to me.

It looked like he stopped breathing. His lips parted, but no words came.

Daniel let go of my hand. We had reached the bottom of the stairs. Swallowing hard, I turned just in time to see him bow to his fire figure. I looked at mine.

She gave me such a strong look I could hardly call her me. I had never seen that amount of strength or determination on my face. Ever.

I peeked at Master Lenin and met his gaze of arctic degrees.

I quickly stepped onto the stage. The fire figure bowed, and with a rush of flames, returned to the floating scroll. My hands shook as I plucked it out of the air. As soon as I grabbed it, my left wrist burned.

The skin glowed and darkened into a black band that encircled my wrist with the number fifteen in the center. Looking down the line of students,

Daniel's wrist said thirteen and Clarence's said fourteen. The Contestants farther down the line had different descending numbers.

I faced the room to keep myself from looking down the line. To Blake.

"From The Serpentine School of Magic, Master Han," Master Lenin continued with a clipped tone.

A tall, dark-skinned gentleman in black stepped forward. Taking his wand from his pocket, he transformed the scrolls. "Marina Rafael, Thiago Luis, and Josephine Gloriana Paulo."

Once the new Contestants were on the stage, Master Lenin announced, "From The University for Advanced Tactical Magic, the last Trial's champion, Master Theodore."

The surprise visitor from the night before stepped forward with a truly arrogant grin. He took his wand from his fur coat and, with a grand flourish, enchanted the chest and the scrolls. Upon seeing the first fire figure, he threw his head back with a booming laugh.

"Dmitri Theodore!"

The school erupted. Jumping up from their seats, they rushed a student with blue hair.

Theodore . . . were they related?

"Glen Host," Master Theodore called over the noise, "and Igorek Len."

Hooting and hollering, Dmitri and Igorek embraced. Slapping each other on the back, they walked up together. Every single kid from that school stood a good four inches taller than six feet and every part of them was two times wider than I was with muscle.

I remembered each of these students had chosen the school they were now competing for. That meant they upheld the core of the school like their heart pumped blood through their bodies.

They wanted to be fighters. They knew dedication, how to fight, how to break. I had been in the magical world for less than a year and knew about as much as a grapefruit.

This might not have been my best idea.

Shut up. Think of the title. You can handle big muscles.

Master Lenin looked at the line with a broad smile. "Ladies and gentlemen, I give you the Chosen Twenty-One Trial Contestants!"

The sound the crowd made was deafening. Students stomped their feet. Others yelled or let out shrieking whistles.

When it died down enough to be heard, Master Lenin said, "Contestants, please follow Miss Baker." Then he went back to addressing the room.

I turned and followed Daniel across the stage. One by one our line moved through the side door. The guards on either side fell in behind.

Without a word, Tessa Baker led us down the hall to a door in the middle of the hallway. It led us out of the cool air of the school to a warm and sunny room; a stark contrast to the black stone of the Magisterium.

Glass took the place of walls, letting a flood of sunset colors into the room. The only things inside were two tables. If they were pushed together, they would've made the shape of a crescent moon.

"Have a seat," Tessa told us. "The Masters will join you in a moment." She firmly shut the door behind her.

"Charlie."

My heart launched into my throat. I turned toward the voice and came face to face with Blake.

I threw my arms around his neck. It was what I had wanted to do all summer. I held him tight in case it was a dream. But it wasn't. He held me just as close.

"I can't believe this." Sniffling, he tried to pull back, but I held on. "Let me see you."

Reluctantly, I stepped back and looked up into his watery eyes.

"I thought you were dead," he said. "Your bus crashed. It was all over the news."

Oh, right. I opened my mouth and the lie came so effortlessly I barely noticed. "We stopped at a gas station and the bus left without me. I wasn't on it when it crashed."

"What luck." He shook his head. "Why didn't you phone me? I would've picked you up."

"I sent a note . . ." The look on his face told me he never got it. I guess that promise was another one of Master Lenin's ploys to keep me under his thumb. "Honestly, I thought you'd be better off without me."

"You were bloody wrong about that." He pulled me back to his chest. "I can't believe you're here. And you have *magic.* Denny never said anything about sending you to a special school."

"You never mentioned your fancy overseas school was special either," I countered.

He broke into a fit of laughter and released me. "I should've guessed you had magic the moment you fell off my roof." He looked down at the pin on my sweater. "A Common Six." He grinned broadly. "Isn't that something?"

I searched for his pin and found it on the lapel of his suit jacket. He was a Common Seven.

His smile softened. "It's really good to see you."

I took his hand, ready to repeat the same thing. But his hand felt different in mine. And then I remembered.

I looked down. The little finger on his left hand was missing. Seeing the lonely knuckle, anger raged in my gut.

"What happened?" I asked tightly.

He winced. "I wish I could say I lost it heroically, but I was mugged. By Regs, if you can believe it. I forgot my wand at home like an idiot."

If I ever see Magee again, I'm going to punch him in the face.

"What was that I heard about your last name?" he asked, flipping the conversation. "Did I hear Master Lenin right? Charlie *Heart?*"

"Did you think my last name was really Doe?" Since I was found in a trashcan, the first set of foster parents named me Jane Doe.

"Kind of, yeah."

A chill raced up my spine. *How would he react when he found out who my father was?* I would have to make damn sure he never found out. I couldn't afford to lose him now that I had gotten him back.

"Relax." I waved off his concern. "It's spelled with an E. There's no relation to the other guy."

"I know that. You're nothing like the bastard. How did you get that name?"

"Just something I pulled out of a hat." I shrugged.

"You got the short stick with that one. What other surprises have you got?" he chuckled halfheartedly.

My father.

My status.

My involvement in a war.

"How exactly do you two know each other?" Clarence drawled from the tables.

"We were neighbors." Blake quickly wiped the moisture from his eyes.

"Charming." Clarence's tone indicated he felt the opposite. "So, Charlie, what lies did you spin to get into The Trial?"

I crossed my arms. "What makes you think I lied?"

He cocked his scarred eyebrow. His dark blue eyes dropped to the status pin at the front of my shirt. "You're a Common."

"Watch yourself, mate." I almost smiled at Blake's tone.

"Who are you again?" Clarence rubbed his scarred eyebrow.

"Shut up. You're giving me a headache," one of the Tactical University students, Dmitri, said with an accent as thick as his arms. The tips of his black curls were dyed ice blue.

"Oh, let them fight it out," the red head from Blake's school, Anna Clarkson, quipped. "It's the only entertainment until the old man gets back."

"Very respectful," snapped the stunning Lin Cho-Hoy from The Magical Academy of the Earth. "Are all Magisterium students like this?"

"She's not from the Magisterium," Daniel said. "And, no. We aren't."

"Speak for yourself," Clarence muttered.

"He was," I retorted.

Anna clicked her compact shut and turned in her seat to look at me. She stuck out her bottom lip and asked, "Did I hurt your feelings?"

"No, you just insulted our school," Daniel answered dryly.

She smiled. It was as warm and friendly as a python. "I would apologize if I cared. And just to clarify, I don't. You should forfeit now if you can't handle what's coming. I'm going to win and there's nothing you can do about it."

"It's a bit early for that, isn't it?" Blake arched an eyebrow.

A booming laugh came from the platinum blond beside Dmitri. Contestant Twenty-One, Igorek Len, looked at Anna with amusement. "You mean you're going to place after me, correct? You're so small. You stand no chance."

Dmitri laughed with him.

"This is a Trial for real Users. All boys and girls should go home now," Josephine Gloriana Paulo, from The Serpentine School of Magic, said in a bored tone.

"Are you planning on forfeiting then?" Blake asked with a smirk.

As if he knew a fight was about to break out, Master Lenin entered the room, followed by the other six School Masters and his guards. Blake and I sat down in the closest chairs next to Daniel. Everyone else sat up straighter.

When all the leaders were seated at the front, Master Lenin smiled. "Congratulations for making it into The Trial. I hope you're not taking this lightly. From here on out, you're representing your school.

"Before we begin, I'll introduce the School Masters of the Seven Great Schools."

My eyes flickered to the six people behind Master Lenin. Magee told me that School Masters were the most important people in the magical world. Knowledge was power and they held the most knowledge. They shaped the laws that governed our world, they chose what was taught in schools, and they could give a User a title or take it away. They were as close to royalty as any king or queen.

"Master Bia Loran, from The Magical Academy of the Earth, will host the theme party for the First Trial."

Clicking his heels together, he bowed sharply.

"Master Thomas Harlan, the Master of The European Academy for Practical Magic. He will be hosting the First Trial."

The tall, dark-haired man gave a small bow.

"From The Serpentine School of Magic, Master Markus Han will be the host of the Second Trial theme party."

The School Master nodded from where he stood.

"From Aquarius: The Undersea School of Enchantments, Master Harley Finch. He is in charge of the Second Trial."

The man with the cane gave a small wave with two fingers.

"Master Aluna from Lions of Magic. She will be hosting the theme party for the Third Trial."

She stepped forward and also bowed.

"The Master of The University for Advanced Tactical Magic, Master Konstantin Theodore, will be hosting the Final Trial."

The surprise visitor from the night before stepped forward. I could see the resemblance to Dmitri, Contestant Nineteen. Thick black hair, huge shoulders. With a thick accent and curled lips, he said, "I wish you luck against my school."

Ignoring the comment, Master Lenin went on, "And I am Master Henry Lenin, Master of The Magisterium of Magic. I am also the host of this year's

Trial. If you have anything to report about The Trial or its Contestants, you may come to me and I will present it to the judges. As you know—"

"Master Lenin, you forgot someone." Master Theodore, who had not stepped back, gestured to the door. "May I present our world's finest and a previous Trial Winner, Master of Combat Power, and Master Hunter, Lawrence Hart."

Instantly everyone jumped to their feet. I mimicked the movement, but only out of shock.

Lawrence was here?

I had only ever seen a picture of him. It did nothing to prepare me for the man who strolled into the room.

His tall, lean frame rose to meet the top of the doorframe. His dirty blond hair was groomed as neatly as the rest of him. His suit was a deep red, the color of wine.

His eyes, a cool mixture of light blue and grey, moved over the twenty-one students. My heart froze as they drew closer to me, but they drifted over without pause.

I tried to find any resemblance between us. We were different in almost every way. His nose was long and sharp while mine was small and round. His golden hair was perfect as if it were painted in place. We might have shared the same hair color, but mine had been dyed for so long that I had forgotten its natural shade.

Our eyes were an entirely different story. They were perfect mirror images. The shape, color, and even the explosion of blue around the pupil were exactly the same.

No wonder why Michael hates my eyes.

A man with grey streaked hair and cobalt blue eyes followed the Master in red into the room. The armor cinched over the guard's body clinked as he entered. Between the plates was a thick, black fabric. The armor was so dark in color it almost looked black. Only when the light reflected just right could you see its true color: red.

"Good evening, everyone."

My eyes snapped away from the lethal man in armor. This was the first time I had heard the voice of my father. I expected something deep, but it was smooth. Lawrence Hart even smiled.

I mimicked everyone else and bowed at the waist. I forced my lungs to stretch slowly with each breath to keep my magic calm. My heart wanted to race out of my chest and from the room.

"You may be seated." When we sat, Lawrence continued. "What a good crop we have this year. I'm Master Lawrence Hart. I designed the three Trials with the help of these fine men and women." He gestured to the Masters behind him. "We have an enticing Trial planned for you. Master Lenin," he turned toward the man, "you may continue."

A slight flush brushed across the older man's cheeks. "Thank you, Master Hart. As you know, there will be three Trials. Each Trial has its own color and theme. The theme for each will be announced at least a week before each Trial starts. After the conclusion of each Trial, one Contestant from each school will be eliminated.

"The judges will evaluate you on how you get to the finish line, how well you use the skills you accumulate in your classes and your training, and how you use your magic. Since your School Masters will most likely be biased towards their own Contestants, the judges will be a panel of anonymous individuals.

"Before we discuss the rules, you must choose a Guardian, someone who will train and assist you through the entire Trial." He turned and nodded to Master Harlan.

Master Harlan opened the door for the second time. A string of people walked in and lined the wall behind the School Masters. The sound of high heels preceded a woman in an emerald green pantsuit.

When I saw her face, my brain short circuited. *Was that Brandy Charles? Michael's ex?*

She filed into the room, flipped her hair over her shoulder, and leaned back against the wall.

"You're kidding me," Daniel muttered.

That was my exact thought. But he wasn't looking at her, he was looking at the doorway.

Arthur Atlas, Michael Kale's right-hand man, shot me a wink.

Facial hair lined his upper lip and the curve of his jaw. His tousled dark brown hair looked like he just rolled out of bed. On his neck was a tattoo of a sword; the handle started below his pierced ear and disappeared under the collar of his trench coat. On the hilt were two intertwining A's. The backs of both of his hands were also inked; one with an anatomical heart and the other with the curve of a spine.

"It's one of the Horsemen," Daniel whispered, following Atlas all the way across the room with his eyes. Many Contestants shifted uneasily in their seats as he leaned casually against the wall.

"Horsemen?" I asked. The name rang a bell, but I couldn't recall why.

"It's what they call Master Kale's hunting party, the Four Horsemen," he whispered back. "They do as they please, and only follow orders from Master Kale. He's the best Hunter in the world. Hell, he's practically king to most people. With him, there's nothing they can't do."

I looked down the line of Guardians and spotted another man dressed all in black. His blond hair was stiff with gel and his clothes were well-tailored. Arrogance circled him like an overpowering cologne.

"Who's that?"

Daniel shrugged. "Looks like another Hunter."

"He doesn't work with Master Kale?"

Daniel shook his head.

Once the line of Guardians had settled, Master Lenin continued. "You may choose anyone in this room. Before you do, you have the opportunity to forfeit. This is the only time you may do so. For any reason you think you cannot compete, now's your time to say so."

The door flew open.

One last man joined the room.

Michael.

20

The Guardian

"Holy shit," Blake muttered.

I was thinking the same thing.

Once more the Chosen Twenty-One rose to their feet. I quickly stood so I didn't stand out. I fully expected him to come over, grab me by the hair, and drag me from the room. But he didn't spare me a single glance.

He headed right for Lawrence.

"I've never seen any of them in person." Blake's eyes followed Michael as he slowly crossed the room. "My parents used to say if I wasn't good, the Horsemen would come after me . . . Bloody hell, I can't believe he's *here*."

"I heard he killed a hundred Users by himself with just his hands," Daniel whispered.

"My dad said he took out a man's soul and he wears it in that ring." Blake pointed to the moaning skull around Michael's index finger.

"If you want to get through this Trial, those men," Daniel gestured to Atlas and Michael, "are the ones you want for your Guardian."

"I apologize for being late," Michael said as he closed the final feet between himself and Lawrence.

I expected him to cut off Lawrence's head or stab him in the chest. *Something.* But he just handed him a large envelope.

The guard in dark red armor stepped toward Michael with unblinking cobalt eyes. Lawrence held up two fingers, wordlessly ordering him to stop. The guard stepped back.

A cold smile pulled at Lawrence's lips. "I don't recall inviting you to participate, Master Kale . . . since you never wanted to participate in the first place." He smiled at the obvious insult and took the envelope.

Curious, I leaned over to Blake. "What did he mean by that?"

Blake whispered so low I barely heard him. "When Master Kale was at the Magisterium, The Master's Trial was held. He and Master Hart were both chosen to compete, but Master Kale refused."

Shocked, I jerked my eyes to the man in the leather jacket. "Why?"

"Don't know. All I know is that people didn't take it well. Like at all. You're expected to participate when your name is called. When he didn't, people threw a fit demanding he be expelled. Master Lenin refused, only because he was a Royal, but he wasn't happy about it either."

Michael didn't bat an eyelash. "I took it upon myself to enroll."

"I didn't think you'd want to invest your time here."

"I suggest you think a little more, Lawrence."

The room shifted uncomfortably. Some of the Contestants glanced toward the door like they were wondering if they should bolt. Clarence openly glared at Michael. Dmitri too.

Lawrence kept his cool. He took out the contents of the envelope and looked them over. After a few seconds, he faced the room. "Contestants, be seated." Once we were in our seats again, he went on. "We have a last-minute sign up for a Guardian. Master Kale," he turned his blue-grey eyes back to the man in black, "please join the others."

Michael nodded toward the Contestants. Every eye was on him as he made his way to Atlas in the lineup.

Master Lenin cleared his throat. "Welcome, Master Kale. Now, to business. We'll start with the last Trial's winning school. Contestant Twenty-One, Igorek Len. You may select your Guardian first."

Igorek Len looked at the selection of Guardians carefully. His eyes weighed each one against the others. Then he said, "Master Michael Kale."

I guess what Daniel said was true. If you wanted to get through The Trial with high enough marks to win a title, Michael was the way to go.

Master Lenin looked down the line of potential Guardians. "Master Kale, do you accept?"

Michael shook his head. "No."

What? I looked at Michael. He casually stood with his hands in his pockets. He looked indifferent as usual. I glanced at the Contestant he had just rejected. Igorek was tall and strong. I looked down at myself. I was a limp noodle compared to him.

Was I supposed to choose Michael? Would he even accept if I did? I'd think he wouldn't want to draw attention to me by being my Guardian. But if he could get me closer to that title . . .

The remaining University students called on the Master Hunter, but he refused. Dmitri Theodore requested his father as his Guardian and was accepted. Blake made a disapproving sound in the back of his throat.

Once all three University Contestants had Guardians, Master Lenin started with Contestant One, Lin Cho-Hoy from The Magical Academy of the Earth.

Contestant after Contestant chose their Guardian. Everyone's first choice was Michael, who answered with the same flat "No." Even when the super fit students asked, he denied. Brandy Charles accepted to be Guardian to Anna Clarkson, which was no surprise. They could've been twins.

"Contestant Twelve, Blake Johnson, who do you choose?"

Blake pushed back his chair and stood. "Master Michael Kale." He looked at the man in black, not in his eyes, but at the space beside his head.

Michael didn't wait for Master Lenin to ask. "No."

"Worth a shot," he muttered. Clearing his throat, he tried again. "My next choice is Hunter Arthur Atlas."

The tattooed Hunter straightened from the wall with delight brightening his eyes. He examined my friend from head to toe before he nodded. "Sure, mate. Sounds like fun."

"Nicely done," Daniel whispered as Blake took his seat.

"Contestant Thirteen, Daniel Phillips," Master Lenin called.

Daniel released a shaky breath as he pushed himself to his feet. His eyes were fixated on the same spot in the lineup of Guardians.

Just barely, Michael shook his head.

Swallowing hard, Daniel looked down the selection. "Sean Fields, would you do the honor of working with me?"

The surprised man straightened from the wall. His jeweled green eyes were so wide they might as well have been large cut emeralds. "Yes! Of—of course."

Daniel nodded gratefully to the man and sat down.

"Contestant Fourteen, Clarence Hardy. You're up."

Clarence didn't bother getting to his feet. Rocking his chair back on its legs, he looked at the end of the line. "Hunter Brandon Moore."

Brandon Moore nodded once. "It would be my pleasure, Contestant Hardy."

Master Lenin kneaded his forehead. "Contestant Fifteen, Charlie Heart. Please choose your Guardian."

Upon hearing my last name out loud, my eyes jerked to the man who shared the same. Lawrence nodded, recognizing he had my attention.

I jerked my gaze away from him to his enemy. My mouth was as dry as an old cracker. A hurricane of butterflies fluttered around my stomach.

Would he say no? If he did, who else could I pick?

Looking at Michael, I rose to my feet. "Master Michael Kale."

Clarence snorted. "No chance in hell."

"Master Kale, do you accept?" In Master Lenin's tone, known only to those who were listening for it, was a hard edge.

Michael looked me over from head to toe. I had a strong feeling of déjà vu from when we first met. It was like he was taking off my skin, looking for every possible flaw, and then weighing it to see if it was worth his time to fix.

He locked eyes with me. I crossed my fingers behind my back.

"Yes."

21

What Did You Do?

For the first time since I met the bastard, I smiled at him.

He's going to help me drop him like a hot rock, and he has no clue.

"You're kidding! *Her?*" Anna Clarkson all but launched out of her chair. Everyone around the room looked like they were thinking the same thing.

Michael ignored her. "It'll be a pleasure to work with you, Contestant Heart." As soon as the words were out of his mouth, the tattoo on my wrist tingled. Two thin bands caged the original image with his initials, MGK.

Looking up, I saw Michael had a matching tattoo on his left wrist. My Contestant number and initials were inked into his skin.

"Fascinating." Lawrence Hart now looked at me with a pinch of interest, as did everyone else.

When all the Contestants chose a Guardian, Master Lenin said, "Please sit with your Guardians and go over your contracts. After they are signed, you may have some time to get to know each other before Master Hart forecasts the upcoming year."

Blake and Daniel walked over to their Guardians, leaving me alone. Michael cut through the room right toward me. On the other side of the curved table, he glowered down at me.

I waited for the insults, the lecture, the brutal verbal assault. Instead, he extended his hand toward me. "Michael Kale."

Right . . . we aren't supposed to know each other. "Charlie Heart." I gripped his forearm. "Pleasure to meet you."

"Likewise." Glancing around the room, he leaned down and braced his hands on the table, bringing us to eye level. "What the *fuck* are you doing here?"

There it is.

"I have no idea what you mean," I said nonchalantly.

"Yes, you do."

"My name was called. I answered just like everyone else."

"Bullshit," he hissed. "Your scroll was in the trash. There's no way you could have been entered."

"Well, I was."

"You're going to regret whatever you did—"

"You're the one who should be filled with regret. You should have given me a better last name." My eyes flickered to the man in the red suit over his shoulder.

His eyes flashed. He took my scroll from me and unrolled it. "Read this."

Smiling up at him, I turned it to face me and read:

THE CONTESTANT CONTRACT

Failure to arrive before the appointed time of The Trial's commencement will result in disqualification.

To ensure a fair competition, Contestants are strictly prohibited from receiving any outside assistance during The Trial, apart from the guidance of their selected Guardian and the use of pre-approved equipment. Failure to comply will lead to disqualification.

Contestants may reject their selected Guardian and appoint another if they deem the partnership unnecessary, unhelpful, or unsuitable for other justifiable reasons.

Each Contestant will receive one 'Save' at the start of The Trial to be used in one Trial. This 'Save' allows them to either exit the current Trial or introduce their selected Guardian to assist them. For the Third Trial, the 'Save' will not be available due to prior performances.

The Trial concludes when the last surviving Contestant
crosses the finish line.

Maiming or crippling another Contestant outside of The
Trial Field will result in immediate disqualification.

I choked on my spit. "*Maiming?*"

Michael shrugged. "It happens when some Contestants get overly competitive."

"Are all Magic Users barbaric by nature?" I turned my eyes to the man in black.

"It's our past. Even though the world has changed, some people can't let go of tradition." Now it was his turn to grin maliciously. "Regretting your stunt now?"

"Nope." I continued.

Assaulting another Contestant outside of The Trial
will result in the immediate revocation of the offending Contestant's Save. A second instance of such
behavior will lead to disqualification.

Killing another active Contestant outside of The
Trial will result in the immediate removal of the
offending school, including all active Contestants and
Guardians, from The Trial.

Should a Contestant be disqualified or eliminated
during the Second or Third Trials, one of the remaining two chosen Contestants will be asked to continue
in their place.

Any Contestant who engages in sabotage, including
but not limited to poisoning, stealing or damaging
equipment, harming or killing another's selected
Guardian, employing external individuals to dispose

of or forcibly restrain another Contestant, will be immediately removed from The Trial.

The judges reserve the right to disqualify any Contestant deemed to be neglecting their duties as a participant. In such instances, one of the two other Contestants from the same school may assume their place.

I,____,
acknowledge and accept these terms and pledge my dedicated participation to the fullest extent for the benefit of my school.

When I got to the end of the scroll, a pen dropped onto the tabletop. My fingers shook as I picked it up. I pressed it to the scroll but no ink came out.

"You have to sign in blood. Press it to your finger," Michael directed.

Yikes. I pressed the tip to my finger. With a sharp prick, blood rushed into the chamber. I quickly scrawled my name on the line.

It was official. I was a Contestant. *I'm going to get a title.*

"Has everyone signed their contracts?" When everyone nodded, Master Lenin smiled. "I'm going to hand it over to Master Hart, who will explain what your year is going to look like."

Michael turned and sat on the edge of the table in front of me.

Lawrence Hart stepped forward with his hands clasped loosely in front of him. "Congratulations, Contestants. This year is going to define your future. I'm excited to see where it takes us."

Me too.

"Every three months, there will be a Trial; the first in November, the second in February, and the final one in May will finish out the school year. That means you have two months to train for each. In those two months, you will learn the theme of The Trial. A week before each, you will stay onsite at the Trial Field. Don't worry about your classes during that time. Your top priority will be training.

"For the first two Trials, the only people who will watch are Masters. If you Ascend to the next Trial, and they think you're worth their time, Masters will send you feedback. This is the only time you'll get valuable suggestions from experts to improve."

Daniel leaned forward with excitement.

"If you Ascend to the Second and Third Trials, you will have opportunities to meet them. This is the only time every fifty years where Masters of every trade are brought together. So, use your time with them wisely.

"Please follow me." Lawrence walked out of the room. His red armored shadow followed after him.

As we passed through the door, leaving behind the swirling evening colors, magic rolled over my skin. We left the light filled building and entered an oversized gym.

The floors were padded. Outlining three of the walls were private training areas with glass dividers. Painted on each door was a number for each Contestant. The last wall not housing Contestant training rooms was lined with weapons. The center of the room was filled with workout equipment, from treadmills to weight lifting benches.

"You will train every day here. When you're not training, your attention should be on your classes. Each of you has your own training area, you will see them clearly marked. Up there," he pointed to the ceiling made of black glass, "is where the judges will be watching.

"They will evaluate how you use your time here, as well as how you spend your time on the Field. I'll give you a heads up; crossing the finish line first does not guarantee you a spot in the next Trial. What you do to get to the finish line will distinguish you from the others and determine if you Ascend or not.

"If you win the Final Trial, your school will be titled 'The Best in the World' for the next fifty years and you will gain the status of a Master. You will be regarded as one of the most important individuals in the world. In order to obtain that, you must first make it into the Top Seven. So, respect your School Masters, respect your Guardians, and impress the judges. I look forward to seeing who comes out on top."

I looked around at the other Contestants, at my competition. A nervous tremor shook through my fingers. *I can do this.*

"The First Trial will be on November thirtieth. Guardians, Master

Lenin has some details to discuss with you before you turn in for the night. Contestants, good luck and good night."

Lawrence bowed. The Contestants, Guardians, and School Masters applauded as he stood. Then he left with his armored guard in tow.

As the crowd broke up, Michael grabbed my elbow and steered me across the padded floor and into the training room marked with the number fifteen.

Not a second had passed before Master Lenin also stepped inside. "Bossart, Markham, secure the doors."

His two guards, both women, stationed themselves outside the training room. Placing their backs to the doors, they blocked anyone from coming in or peering through the glass.

"What did you do?" Master Lenin hissed. His gold flecked eyes were riveted on me.

"What makes you think I did anything?"

"I pulled your scroll from administration," he said, stepping closer. "It was in my office. Master Kale threw it in the trash. There is no way it could have been in that chest for selection!"

"Well, you know what they say." I took an uneasy step back. "One man's trash is another's treasure."

"Do you have any idea what you have done?" he roared. "You were supposed to remain hidden. Now Master Hart has a direct line of sight to you. He could figure this whole thing out! I thought you were on the same page with staying out of this."

"I took a little page out of your book," I snapped. "I lied. I saw a chance to get out from under your thumb, and I took it, then levitated it right where I wanted it. If I get a title, you can kiss my ass. And it looks like your threats against Blake are coming to an end since he was named for The Trial too! What a great day!"

"You won't make it past the First Trial," Michael snapped.

"And how would you know?" I rounded on him. "You never participated."

"You son of a—" Michael took a large step toward me.

Master Lenin stopped him with a hand on his shoulder. "You have no idea what you are getting yourself into. This isn't a game. Contestants die in this Trial."

Cheese and rice. I kept my face neutral. They couldn't see me waiver.

"Every Contestant who was named today has been learning and honing their skills for years. They know more magic than you. They know more casts than you. They just know more. They will crush you, and there will be nothing we can do to stop them."

"Then I guess my *Guardian*," I looked to Michael, "better do a good job training me. In order to keep me alive, you have to take me all the way to the finish line." I gave him my best Michael Kale-impression smirk. "It's not so fun being used, is it?"

"I told you," Michael said coldly. "It doesn't matter how far the apple falls from the tree."

"I learned that from *you*."

"Did you notice that Lawrence was the only Trial Winner present today? Did it cross your tiny mind to ask *why*?" He didn't let me answer. "There's something called the Winner's Curse. Whatever you do to make it to the finish line, and you will do horrible things, will haunt you. Winners inevitably kill themselves to escape that. Your father joined the Hunter Guard because of his Winner's Curse. I didn't participate because I didn't want that. If you do make it to the end, and that's a huge if, I hope your curse eats you alive."

My ignorance was biting me in the ass and he knew it.

"That's enough." Master Lenin held up a hand to both of us. "I made it very clear that I wanted you to stay away from this Trial. *Both* of you."

My eyebrows skyrocketed upward. I never heard anyone talk to Michael like that. Most people were afraid to look him in the eyes. Hell, I was most days. But I mostly did it out of spite.

Michael's cheeks took on a rosy hue. "You really expected me to just sit back and—"

"Yes, I did. Hunter Atlas was already in place. He could've stepped up to be her Guardian just as easily. She would have flown under the radar, but with you popping out of nowhere and becoming her Guardian, she'll have every eye on her."

The two Masters stared at each other, daring the other to say something.

"You should get some rest, Contestant Heart," Master Lenin said tightly. "Master Kale, we should get going. Once the Guardian orientation is over, meet me in my office."

Michael nodded with a tight jaw.

With that, Master Lenin retreated from the training room, taking the guards with him.

Michael pinched his eyes closed. His shoulders were so tense, I was surprised his jacket didn't split down the middle.

Wordlessly, he shoved passed me.

I wanted to feel smug over what I had just accomplished, but the victory felt double-edged. Everything Michael had said, Winner's Curses and Contestant deaths, lingered at the back of my mind.

22
Truce

Someone knocked on my door at the most ungodly hour of the morning. Fumbling for my wand, I rolled out of bed with every intention to kill whoever was knocking.

I cursed when the door banged against the wall.

Michael pushed his way into the room and kicked the door shut behind him. Upon seeing my wand, he smirked. "Good morning to you, too."

"What do you want?" I pushed the hair out of my face and moved back toward my bed.

"Lenin wants to talk."

"And he couldn't wait till after breakfast?" I flopped onto the bed and curled around my pillow.

"Not with you being a Trial Contestant."

Right . . . cheese and rice, that wasn't a dream. My mood brightened. *My title.* "I'll get my shoes."

He tilted his head. "That was incredibly easy. I didn't have to threaten you."

Because this is the first time I want something from you. Slipping on my shoes, I followed him into the hall.

The school was as silent as a windless graveyard. Every move we made echoed against the walls. I shook off the chills that crawled over my skin. The last time I was out, and it was this quiet was when I was going to talk to a ghost.

Walking down to the teacher's floor, the torches burst into life. Michael pushed open Master Lenin's door and motioned for me to go first. Inside, I plopped onto one of the fluffy red chairs.

"Good morning, Contestant Heart." Like usual, the School Master was behind his desk with numerous scrolls and books before him. He looked to be wearing the same suit he had on for the Naming Ceremony.

"What can I do for you?" I yawned.

"Because of your recent *honor*," he said that word sarcastically, "of becoming a Trial Contestant, people are going to pay more attention to you. In order to keep your bloodline hidden, Master Kale and I created an identity for you."

"Charlie Heart isn't enough?" I asked dryly.

"No." He held up a magazine. I was on the cover with a caption that read 'MASTER KALE'S FIRST MISTAKE?' Before I could rip it from his hands, he pulled it back. "People are going to be asking questions and we cannot afford for you to say the wrong thing."

He handed me a folder. "Here's everything you need to know. You'll need to memorize it."

Flipping it open, I scanned the pages. It had everything from a current residence to a small magic school name; Cornwall Magic High. They took everything that made me me and threw it out. The only things they kept were that I lived in Salina, Kansas, I was born in April, and had no living parents.

My magic status was the same lie it was last year, a Common Six. My blood type was B+. There were school records going all the way back to kindergarten, or what I assumed was kindergarten. There was a sheet with all my grades. Although, they were higher than the ones I usually got.

"Helen and Hunter Wentworth cooked this up for you." Master Lenin set a jar in front of me. Inside was a clear liquid with tiny pink bubbles floating through it. "If you apply this to your skin, it should keep high statuses from feeling your magic. In The Trial, it's guaranteed that you will meet Royals, and we can't have them feeling your real status."

I looked up from the jar and flipped the folder closed. "I don't understand."

Michael was the one who answered. "If anyone asks where you went to school, why you came to the Magisterium—you need to give a confident answer. If you don't, they'll ask why a nineteen-year-old—"

"Twenty," I corrected. "My birthday was in April."

With narrowed eyes, he continued, "I don't care. My point is, they will ask why someone your age never went to a magic school. That kind of suspicion will draw Lawrence's eye and then it's game over."

That made sense.

Master Lenin nodded. "Exactly. If there is trouble, you can use this." He opened the middle drawer of his desk and took out a cellphone. "Call me or Master Kale if you are in trouble. Our numbers are already programmed in."

I took the phone as laughter bubbled up my throat. "You're kidding." I looked between the two Masters. "You're the last people I would call: the jackass who wants to kill me and the guy who sold my soul. Here, I'm going to make you the last speed dial."

I pulled up the contacts and immediately changed Michael's name to JACKASS.

"Contestant Heart, you can do that in a moment," Master Lenin paused until I pulled my eyes up from the screen. "I want to remind you, it is immensely important that you call everyone by their title. I know you weren't born in this world, but if you call someone by the incorrect title or if you don't use it at all, they won't be forgiving or even merciful. For your time in The Trial, your Guardian won't have his Master title to protect you and I can't interfere."

"What do you mean Michael doesn't have his title?" I asked.

"To make sure The Trial has our full focus, every Guardian with a title had to renounce it." Michael's abrasive tone suggested that was my fault, even though *he* signed up by himself.

Master Lenin nodded. "So, you will refer to him as Guardian Kale until your time in The Trial is over. Next, any talk of the war is forbidden. Your father is highly involved in this Trial. If you talk about the Achilles Heel or fighting with us, he has the means to take you off the board and get away with it."

"Why is he so involved?" I asked. "Isn't he too busy winning?"

Michael tensed.

"It helps his status with the war. The more his face is seen, the more traditions he follows, and the better he looks, the more he will sway people to his cause. Which is why you need to do the same. Don't give anyone a reason to look twice at you. Be the definition of a rule follower.

"This afternoon will be your benchmark exam. You get to show the judges and your Guardian where your skill level and stamina is."

Oh no. Did that mean cardio?

"Everyone will be interested to see why Master Kale picked you. I suggest you forget everything in your past and remember only that folder." Master Lenin pointed to the file in my lap.

I nodded.

Then a thought hit me.

Twisting in my seat, I looked at Michael. "What about you?"

"What about me?"

"I get to throw away my past. Why don't you?"

His eyebrows scrunched together with confusion. "You're going to have to explain that one to me."

How does he make everything I say sound ridiculous? "I have to forget everything that makes me hate you. You should do the same."

"Why on earth would I do that? Didn't you stab us in the back last night?"

"No. I just pulled a you on you. If someone sees us fighting, they'll know something's up. People don't hate each other like we do without a reason." I glanced at Master Lenin to find him nodding. "If you ignore that I'm Lawrence's kid and I ignore that you're going to kill me, there'll be less of a chance someone connects the dots."

Michael shook his head. "No way. I'm not going to ignore the fact you're related to the son of a bitch."

"It's not my fault I have Lawrence's eyes."

"You have a lot more than that."

I bit my tongue. "You're going to be working with me non-stop for months."

"And in front of Masters," Master Lenin added.

"Exactly!" I had forgotten about that. "You know how I get when I'm pissed off. I say things that should most definitely remain unspoken."

"She's got a point," Master Lenin noted.

"You can't be serious." Michael dropped his arms. "You want me to forget *decades* of good reasons and anger?"

"No, I'm rather fond of your anger. I'm just suggesting you forget your anger for this young woman." Master Lenin shot me a smile. "She's actually quite pleasant when she isn't doing something stupid."

"Thanks." I faced the Master Hunter. "I'm game if you are."

His jaw popped but said nothing.

"Just for this year. Then you can hate me until your blackened heart is content." *Or until I get a title and you can't do shit.*

He exhaled sharply. "Fine. But I have one condition."

I rolled my eyes. *Naturally.*

"If you don't follow every single thing I tell you to do, I'll go back to treating you like the spawn that you are. Consequences be damned. Understood?"

"Deal." I got to my feet and held out my hand. "Hi. I'm Charlie Heart."

His obsidian eyes bore down into mine with threats of dismemberment and bloodshed. But begrudgingly, he grasped my forearm. "Michael Kale. I look forward to working with you."

I bit my tongue to keep from smiling. It didn't work.

He released my arm. "Don't mess this up."

"I won't."

"Oh, God. Stop smiling at me."

23

Sooner or Later

I had no idea what to expect on my first day being a Trial Contestant.

I spent a good amount of time in front of the mirror, making sure all my scars were covered, and the potion Master Lenin gave me was soaked in. As I walked down the stairs, I noticed more looks than usual being cast my way, and heard my name whispered between students.

As I made it to the bottom of the stairwell, I saw the guards in black and gold were back in place around the perimeter of the room. *Was that going to be a normal thing now?*

Entering the dining room, I located Blake. My heart glowed at the sight of him. Just as I was about to make my way over, my attention was drawn to the far end of the room. On the long stage was a tall, white statue.

Instantly, I recognized the crest of a double-sided axe on the chest of the statue. He was from the University. He stood with his back straight and proud. In one hand, he held an axe.

It wasn't a part of the statue; it was real. Blood stained the handle but the blade gleamed without tarnish. On his head was a crystal crown with reflections of faces in the stones.

The base of the statue read, *Trial Winner, Victor Haltland. The University for Advanced Tactical Magic.*

So that's what a Trial Winner looks like. As I moved to get a better look, my way was blocked by Amelia Markus, an Aquarius Contestant. I had barely looked at her the night before. She was basically a surfer stereotype: long blonde hair, broad tan shoulders, and a lopsided grin.

"Good morning, Contestant Fifteen," she said with a crooked smile.

"Uh, hi." I tried to move around her.

She stepped in front of me. "Listen. You're a Contestant. I'm a

Contestant. I'm hot and you need as much help as you can get. Seeing as I'm in a charitable mood, I decided to let you be my girlfriend."

I stopped. "Excuse me?"

"It's a brilliant plan. We would look amazing together as we match in The Trial colors and go to Trial parties."

My head actually started to hurt as it tried to understand what she was saying. "I don't know what to say."

She grinned. "Don't worry. I have that effect on people." She draped her arm over my shoulders. "Now give me a kiss so we can—"

I ducked out from under her arm. "Not going to happen."

Now it was her turn to look confused. "Excuse me?"

"I don't want to be your girlfriend. Thanks for the offer . . . I think."

A smile as fake as plastic popped onto Amelia's lips. "Are you turning me down?"

I hesitated. Then I looked her over and decided I had dealt with bigger and scarier Users. "Yeah, I am."

"I don't think you understand—"

"I understand perfectly. If I date you, my status in this black stone coffin goes up and you look even better. The thing is, I don't care." *I just want a title.*

Her eyes narrowed. Her glare was laughable compared to Michael's. "You have no idea what you're passing up."

"I think I do."

"When you fail, see if I care." She shouldered her way past me.

As I watched her tall figure saunter away, I shook my head. *That has to be the weirdest conversation I've ever had.*

I didn't take more than two steps before my path was blocked again. This time it was by some kid I had never seen before. Paired with mousy brown hair and a flirtatious grin, he held out his hand. "Davis Smith. Your soulmate."

What the hell is going on?

"Listen, David—"

"Davis."

I gripped my bag. "You seem like a nice guy—"

"For you, I can be anything."

Wow. "I'm not interested."

His smile dropped. Tears entered his eyes. "But we're—"

I bolted. Ducking around him, I almost sprinted through the dining room. I glanced back to see his shoulders jerking with sobs.

As I turned back to my destination, I almost collided with a bouquet of roses.

"Contestant Heart, I—"

"NO! The answer is no!" I ducked under the small rose bush and ran to Blake's table.

I slipped into the seat next to him. Keeping my shoulders low, I said, "If anyone asks, you haven't seen me."

"Good morning to you, too." He sank his teeth into jam-coated toast. "What happened?"

I lifted my head just enough to look at him. "Do I have something on my face that says 'single and ready to mingle?'"

He lifted the hair from my forehead. "Nope. But you're a Contestant."

I then noticed the number of flowers and cards piled in front of him.

I scanned the room and found Daniel in the buffet line with a small crowd of girls around him. He looked so uncomfortable I thought he might dissolve into thin air at any moment. Clarence, on the other hand, was licking it up like a fine dessert.

"I didn't get a chance to congratulate you on the Kale grab last night." Blake finished off his toast. "I think."

I looked up at his tone. "You think? Not twelve hours ago, you practically said he was the only way to the Top Seven."

"Doesn't change the fact that he's dangerous. He eats dragon hearts once a month to give him strength. It's also the reason he's immune to fire."

Laughter burst out of me. "You're kidding."

"Nope." There wasn't a trace of humor on his face. He was completely serious. "I heard one time he was poisoned and the only cure was in the other guy. So, Master Kale killed him and drank his blood."

I opened my mouth to tell him that it was ridiculous. But was it? The more I thought about it, the easier it was to picture him cutting someone's throat and draining the blood in a goblet. I hardly knew anything about the Master Hunter Michael Kale.

"He even cut out his own kidney because it was failing. The man may be the best in his trade, but people call him Hades for a reason. Just be careful."

He dropped his voice and leaned closer. "People like him don't care much about those around them, unless you can help him achieve his goal. Plus, he's the king on the opposing side of the war. Not a lot of people are fans."

The air around us seemed to still, like we stepped onto thin ice. Michael and Master Lenin warned me not to talk about the war with anyone. But this was Blake.

"And which side is that?" I asked. Every cell in my body went still with anticipation for his answer.

"Right or wrong, I haven't decided and I hope I never have to. If Master Kale keeps his head down and Master Hart isn't opposed, the war won't get any more out of control."

"Lawrence is killing Deficients, Blake." My voice dropped to a whisper. I gestured to the number six on my uniform. "That would be me if I were a couple statuses lower."

His lips paled as he pressed them tightly together. "There's a reason why there are wiser people to worry about this, so I don't have to."

"You'll have to, sooner or later."

A sad smile crossed his lips. "I distinctly remember a girl who used to live by the phrase 'out of sight, out of mind.'"

That was before I got dropped right in the middle of it.

Shrugging, I looked down at my hands. Underneath Helen's potion were the scars from the binding curse. "I learned you can't run from everything."

As if he sensed the mood was getting too grave, he smiled. "My point is, be careful around him. I don't want you caught up in his idea of a good time."

Daniel dropped onto the bench beside me with a cinnamon roll. He had his hood pulled over his forehead. "If anyone asks, I skipped breakfast and you didn't see me."

"You're not basking in your new-found fame?" I asked, jumping at the chance to change the conversation.

"God, no." He looked at me with a smile. And then he saw Blake. "Hey, I'm Daniel."

Blake reached over me and grasped his forearm. "Blake."

"How do you know each other?" Daniel gestured between us with his fork.

"We used to be neighbors," Blake answered.

"No kidding?" Daniel took a bite of his cinnamon roll. "Small world."

The sounds in the dining room changed. The usual roar of conversation dipped to an awed whisper. Benches scraped across the floor as students clambered to their feet. Blake went completely still.

Those standing turned to look at the man who entered. The few who remained in their seats also turned, but with looks of malice. Following their gaze, I saw who walked in.

It was Michael. With a plate of food in one hand, he casually walked toward my table, oblivious or ignoring the attention around him.

"I hope you haven't eaten anything yet," he said coolly.

Blake's stories about the Master Hunter came back in a rush. I could all too easily picture blood running from his lips. Shaking that nasty picture from my head, I asked, "What?"

He placed the plate of food in front of me. "From now on, if I don't give it to you, you don't eat it. The last thing I need is for you to get poisoned. Understood?"

"I'm not a pet. You can't—"

"Ah, but I can." He tapped the tattoo on his wrist. "This gives me all the permission I need." He leaned down to whisper in my ear, "Are you regretting having me as your Guardian, yet?"

I shivered at the feeling of his warm breath. "Nope. Best decision I've ever made."

He straightened and pointed to my plate. "All of that needs to be gone. You need to gain weight so training doesn't kill you. Tonight, we'll see what we have to work with." His eyes traveled over me, picking out my thin wrists and the skin sagging under my arms. "It doesn't look like much, but after tonight, I'll know where to focus."

He glanced around at those trying to eavesdrop. He stopped when he saw Blake. "I don't think we've met."

Blake, completely star-struck, shook his head as he got to his feet. "No, sir. Blake Johnson."

The Master Hunter extended his hand. "Michael Kale."

Everything blurred to slow motion as I watched Blake clasp his forearm. My eyes snapped to Michael's face. *Don't you dare hurt him.*

With a nod, he dropped Blake's arm. "You're Atlas's Contestant."

"Yes, sir." Blake stuffed his nervous hands into his pockets.

"I've worked with him for over seventy years. He's a brilliant User. Very loyal. He'll do right by you."

Relief made Blake stand a bit taller. "Thank you, sir."

Then Michael turned to Daniel. "You're Daniel Phillips."

Daniel surged to his feet with his hand outstretched. "Yes, sir."

"Master Lenin speaks very highly of you." Michael grasped his forearm. "As does your father. I always expected you to have a title, but it looks like you'll be getting one sooner than expected."

Michael knows small talk? Astonished, I watched him act mildly normal.

"That's if I make it past you and your Contestant to the Top Seven," Daniel said with a nervous laugh.

Michael looked down at me. His eyes spoke of how unlikely that was going to be.

Jokes on you, jackass.

"I guess we'll see." Michael stepped back from the table. "Contestant Heart, I'll see you in the training room. Don't be late." With that, he turned and left.

"Damn." Blake sagged into his chair. "I thought he was going to knife you . . . and me."

Daniel lowered himself back to his cinnamon roll, but he didn't touch it.

"He has that effect on people," I muttered, trying to get my heart to settle down. Turning back to my plate, I realized I had a lot to eat.

The clock chimed, signaling the final warning before classes. Cursing, I dug in. When I was full, there was still half of a plate left. By the time I finished, I felt like I was going to puke. Blake just laughed.

Shoving the rest of my breakfast into my mouth, we ran out the door. I cursed when I saw I had dripped yellow egg yolk down my white t-shirt.

Taking the stairs two at a time to the fifth floor, Blake, Daniel, and I ran down the East Wing. The room numbers slid by in a blur. Moving too fast, we almost ran by the classroom.

Bursting into the room, I winced when I saw that not only was everyone already seated, but everyone was looking at us.

"Contestant Heart."

My back stiffened. I turned toward the woman standing at the front of the room. *No way.*

Gripped in a dark green turtleneck dress was Brandy.

24

Dellamora

"You're late. I'll be reporting that to Master Lenin." Brandy motioned toward Blake and Daniel. "The same goes for you two. Have a seat."

I stood there in shock, staring at the blonde. Blake took my arm and guided me up the stairs to a pair of empty seats. The classroom was built like an auditorium, the tables and chairs at the front were lower than the ones in the back. Royals sat up close, while Deficients sat in the back, leaving the middle for Commons.

"Now that everyone is here," Brandy shot me a pointed look, "we'll get started." Clarence laughed somewhere in the room. "My name is Brandy Charles. I've studied under four different Masters in creature behavior and tracking. I'm Mr. Harrison's replacement."

She's going to be here for the entire school year? What the hell?

"I don't care which school you come from. In this class, we do things my way. If you don't like it, I suggest you get over it, or fail." Her red lips curled. "Open your books to chapter eight."

"She sounds like fun." Blake pulled out his book and flipped to the right page.

I made a noncommittal sound in the back of my throat. I stopped when I saw a picture of our subject.

"Dellamora, or more traditionally, known as The Tainted. Can someone tell me why?" Brandy waved her wand, enchanting a piece of chalk to write across the blackboard.

I smiled when Daniel raised his hand beside me.

"It's said a Royal tried to make his Regular wife live longer," Daniel answered. "He injected her with a mix of wards and potions, tainting her.

Instead, it turned her into something neither dead nor alive. Their bites are infectious, but treatable. Regulars call them vampires or zombies."

Brandy nodded. "Correct. Where can they be found?"

Daniel cocked his head to the side. "Uh, nowhere. A Hunter Trio wiped them out a few decades back."

"Wrong." She smiled smugly. "They were contained." That's when she turned to a wooden crate on her desk. It was so large, it nearly took up the whole surface.

With a flick of her wand, the wood fell off, revealing a metal cage underneath. Inside was a creature that resembled a human, but barely. The only thing familiar about it was that it had a head, two arms, and two legs. That's where the similarities ended.

It hung from the top of the cage with curved, black claws that replaced its fingers and toes. They easily cut through the metal on top to keep it suspended. Its head was twisted around at a sickening angle. Eyes, completely black from lid-to-lid, tracked every movement of each student. Instead of skin colored by the warmth of blood, it was a sick white. Then it opened its mouth and screamed.

The sound was a shrill mix of nails on a chalkboard and a cat screech. Goosebumps rushed over my skin. In its mouth were bloodstained razors. Drool dripped to the bottom of the cage. Its nostrils flared.

"Ugly, isn't it?" Brandy turned her sapphire gaze toward the cage. "Can someone tell me what they were used for?"

Cornelia slowly raised her hand. Her face was so pale, it made her blonde hair look yellow. "Th—they were used as trackers."

"Explain."

"They have an amazing sense of smell. They can track a User days after they're in an area." Her eyes were glued to the thing in the cage.

"Thank you." Brandy stepped toward the cage. "In addition to their sense of smell, Dellamora can tell how much magic a User has. Some specialists think they prefer to eat Users with the most magic."

My stomach rolled. *Making me a five-star meal.*

"Does anyone know how to kill one?"

The class remained still and quiet.

"No one? Huh." Brandy straightened from her leaning position. Her bright pink nails flashed as she flipped the latch on the cage. "Whoever figures it out gets an A."

What?

She stepped back as the creature dropped to the floor.

My heart stopped beating. The room erupted with screams. Students pushed me into the table as they shoved their way toward the door. With an irritated scowl, Brandy waved her wand and the door slammed shut.

Blake grabbed my arm and yanked me to the floor. A shoe was planted in my back as someone bolted over me. Blake quickly pulled me under the desk. Daniel snatched a textbook from above us and frantically flipped through the pages.

The creature screamed.

I watched as it leapt out of the cage and crawled up the wall like a spider. The claws on its hands and feet cut through the stone as if it were wet sand.

Through the sea of students, Cornelia stumbled. Her hand sliced against the sharp edge of a broken chair. The Dellamora screamed again.

"Daniel!" I yelled over the noise. "How do you kill it?"

"I don't know." His hands shook as he looked over a couple pages. He turned a few more and then flipped the book around. He had it upside down. "I don't know!"

The creature dropped from the ceiling and landed on a tabletop a few levels below us. It ignored other students closest to it; it even climbed over a few as it made a straight line to Cornelia.

I was about to dive out from the table, but stopped. *What could I do?* I was worried if I used magic, I'd end up decapitating a student. I could levitate it away from everyone, but then what would I do with it? A thought came to me.

Brandy said they were attracted to high statuses. *Then let's give it a good whiff of a Royal Nine.*

Quickly, I broke the scab on my thumb I'd gotten from signing the scroll the night before. Blood beaded to the surface and the creature went quiet.

I looked out from under the table. The Dellamora stood still. Its eyes scanned the room. It lifted its nose and took a deep breath. Then its eyes locked onto mine. Something that resembled a smile crossed its pale lips. It launched off the table and landed above me. The table rocked and almost tipped over. Blake yelled. Daniel threw the textbook at it.

Its claws lashed under and caught the floor beside me.

I rolled down to the next landing. The Dellamora dropped onto the neighboring table and threw the one covering me across the room. Uncovered and screwed, I raised my wand.

Too quick for me to pull on my magic, the creature pounced. Squeezing my eyes shut, I waited for impact.

But it never came.

Cracking open an eye, I found the Dellamora levitating above me. Twisting and reaching, it squirmed in midair. It wasn't from my magic.

The monster screamed in frustration. My heart beat so fast, I was surprised nothing was on fire. The lights were sure dancing.

The creature lifted further into the air before being sharply tossed into the wall. As it recovered, a tall student from Lions of Magic jumped in front of me and pointed his wand at the monster. With a sharp slice of magic, the Dellamora's head rolled away from the body.

The volume from the students swarming the door quieted until the room was silent once again. Black, thick blood oozed from the severed tissue of the Dellamora, releasing a sharp, earthy stench.

Brandy clapped once, twice, and then a third time. Each slow, with mocking celebration. "You'd think with the number of Trial Contestants in here that that wouldn't have taken so long. What's your name, kid?"

"Emeka Selasi." He straightened his back and placed his wand in his pocket. Breathing heavily, he faced her.

"Congratulations, Contestant Selasi. You just got an A." Turning, she called over her shoulder, "Class dismissed."

The door burst open. The students rushed into the hall without waiting a second longer.

I dropped my head to the floor and stared at the ceiling. *Cheese and rice.*

A shadow fell over me. I startled, and found it was only Emeka. I had seen him the night before at The Trial orientation, but hadn't had time to really look him over. He was tall and fit with short cut hair. The dark color of his suit and his skin only made him look more impressive.

"Hey, thanks." With shaky hands, I pushed myself into the sitting position.

"Emeka." He held out his hand.

"Charlie." I grasped his forearm and to my surprise, he helped me to my feet. At the same time, we looked at each other's status pins. He was a Common Seven.

His nose crinkled at the sight of the six pinned to my shirt. Without another word to me, he walked over to the dismembered monster.

And then I remembered Cornelia. My legs shook as I bounded up the steps toward her. She was huddled under a table with her knees hugged tightly to her chest. Tears clung to her long lashes as she stared at the beheaded creature.

"Hey," I said softly, blocking her view of it. "Are you ok?"

Her eyes focused on me and, with jerky movements, she shook her head.

I held out my hand. "Come on, let's get out of here."

Her arms tightened around her knees. She stared through me as if she could still see the dead monster.

Blake squatted beside me. "Are you alright?" he whispered.

I nodded. "Yeah, I'm fine." Then I saw an opportunity to distract the frightened girl in front of me. "Cornelia, this is my best friend, Blake. We grew up in Kansas together."

Her large sapphire eyes looked up into his face.

"Ello," he said gently. "I saw that thing come after you. Are you alright?"

She shook her head.

"Cornelia, is it? Can you take my hand? I'm going to help you up, and then we're going to walk out of here. Charlie and I will be on either side of you, so you don't have to see the Dellamora. Does that sound alright?"

"I don't know if I can move," she whispered.

"Then let us help." Moving slowly, he rose and pushed the table so she was no longer under it. Signaling to me, we each grabbed her elbows and helped her to her feet. I wrapped my arm around her waist and he covered her shoulders. She shook like a cold puppy as we moved toward the door.

I looked back for the hero of the day, but Emeka had already left the classroom. *What the hell do they teach at his school?*

Keeping a tight grip on Cornelia, we slowly walked her into the hallway. All along the walls, people were bent over trying to catch their breath. Some were even crying.

"Did you see the way that thing climbed?" someone gasped.

"I could've taken it if I were closer." The speaker was a couple shades paler than he used to be.

"They should have let it eat the Low Common," a Royal laughed.

I whirled toward the voice, but they were lost in the crowd. *They were talking about—*

"Cornelia! Thank God." Nirean shouldered her way past a group of students. "We just heard what happened. Are you alright?"

Clarence was right behind her and, to my surprise, so was Ace Navarro.

"She's fine," I said. "That thing came straight—"

"I wasn't talking to you," Nirean snapped, her eyes keenly focused on Cornelia.

My mouth snapped shut. I looked to Ace behind her. She rolled the lollipop across her tongue but she too refused to look at me.

"Come here, sweetheart." Clarence pulled Cornelia toward him. "Let's take you to the infirmary."

"We were just about to take her," I said, but he continued to pull her from me. "Can someone tell me what's going on?"

"Simple." For the first time, Clarence met my gaze. "Did you find Blaine Willow's diary?"

The sudden swerve on to Memory Lane caught me so off guard, I blurted without thinking. "Yes."

"See." He tapped my nose, but it wasn't gentle or endearing. "We don't hang around liars; they can't be trusted." With his arm securely around Cornelia's waist, he started down the hall. Ace and Nirean followed without another word.

"What was that about?" Blake asked, watching them retreat toward the stairwell. "Are they friends of yours?"

"Not anymore." Those words were like an ice pick to my heart.

25

Benchmark Exam

The rest of the day was thankfully uneventful.

The school buzzed about Emeka and how brave he was, how strong, how fast. It provided the perfect distraction. Whenever he was near, students flocked to him, leaving me alone.

Brandy's class did enforce one of Michael's points. I hardly knew anything about magic. These kids had years on me.

What was the benchmark exam going to be like? All I could picture was myself finishing dead last.

Too nervous to really eat, I had only a few bites of dinner before I made my way down to the training room. When I reached the guarded doors, I stopped. On the floor was a magazine, the same one Master Lenin had that morning. I scooped it from the floor. Sure enough, I was on the cover.

Cheese and rice. The picture was of me mid-gasp when I saw Blake. My eyes had a far away, cross-eyed look.

The caption caught my attention. 'MASTER KALE'S FIRST MISTAKE?' Flipping through the other, more flattering, pictures of other Contestants, I found the cover article.

As I read through it, my uneasiness left. It was replaced by boiling rage. The lights flickered, as I stormed into the training room.

Ignoring all of the other Contestants, I burst into my training room where Michael was already waiting.

I showed him the cover. "What the hell is this?"

He looked amused. "Coverage of The Trial."

"*Coverage of The Trial?*" I felt my skin heat up as I flipped to my article and read, "This takes scraping the bottom of the barrel to a whole new level. Our world's finest, Master Michael Kale, has stooped quite low to accept the invitation to be Contestant Fifteen's Guardian. I cannot help but wonder, 'why?'. Does anyone else think it's a bad idea that a Heart, no matter how it's spelled, and a Kale are working together again? They mix like oil and water.

"This barely pretty, final-year student somehow managed to get Master Kale to accept being her Guardian. By the looks of it, she'll need it. There's nothing outstanding about this Magisterium of Magic's Contestant. Her grades hover around average and her magic status, a measly Common Six, leaves something to be desired. In fact, I couldn't find anything that would make her even remotely appealing to the Master Hunter. She's hardly his type, in looks or skill.

"Why Master Kale accepted to be Miss Average's Guardian, I'll never know. Maybe years of social purgatory have made him desperate to get back in the headlines. If anyone is going to get crushed in November, it will be this pair. I almost feel sorry for them.

"If this is the kind of Contestants The Trial is choosing, then it's going downhill. Master Kale must have seen something in Contestant Fifteen, but from where I'm sitting, I can't see it. My advice to Master Kale? Drop Contestant Fifteen. You have enough to worry about."

By the time I was done reading, my nails had pierced the pages and smoke slid between my fingers.

Michael calmly pried the smoldering magazine from my hands and dropped it into the trashcan. "This happens with every Trial. Don't get so worked up about it." He stripped his jacket from his shoulders.

"That's easy for you to say!" The lights brightened. "She called you 'our world's finest' while I got nicknamed 'Miss Average'!"

Sighing, he turned back to face me. The look on his face told me I was acting like a child. "This is a good thing. If everyone thinks you can't do anything, they'll leave you alone."

He's kidding. "When was the last time you were in high school? No one leaves you alone."

"You chose this, remember? So, stay away from magazines. This won't be the last one to call you out." He grabbed a bundle of clothes and tossed them to me. "You're wasting time."

Cursing under my breath, I went to the small bathroom in the back and quickly pulled the clothing on. Everything was in the colors of black and gold, from the t-shirt with my Contestant number, to the sports bra, shoes, and leggings.

Seeing the whole outfit together made reality settle coldly into my chest. When I emerged, all thoughts of the article were gone. Butterflies swarmed my stomach as I approached Michael.

He looked me over when I got closer. He didn't look too happy to be seeing me dressed as a Contestant.

"Does everything fit?"

Not trusting my voice, I nodded. *Think of the title.*

"Then let's go." Michael pushed open the door of our room and led me back into the main training area.

Unlike the night before, where everything was neatly lined up on the walls, today all the weapons were organized across a long table. On the other side of the room, directly across from the weapons, were twenty-one target posts, one for each Contestant.

Tala Abalos, from The Magical Academy of the Earth, had her target filled with small knives. She and her Guardian were already on to another weapon.

The Tactical University Contestants were throwing every weapon they could get their hands on. Each weapon they threw sank into the center of the target.

Even Blake had his target looking like a porcupine. With a quiver of arrows at his hip, he pulled back on his bow with perfect, practiced form. Atlas stood behind him with a smug look as each landed in the center of the bullseye.

"The objective of this evening is to see what you can do," Michael explained quietly. "For me, the judges, and everyone in this room. At the table," he motioned toward the weapons, "you'll pick whatever suits you and show off."

"The only weapon I've handled is my wand and a pair of scissors," I whispered back.

"The same goes for the majority of the Contestants." He nodded to Daniel who was looking over the table with a mix of curiosity, apprehension, and straight-up nerves. "Pick something. If you don't, I'll pick for you. Most Guardians have an instinct about what their Contestant will have the most success with after a few moments. I, however, have the advantage."

"What's that?"

He smirked. "I'm the best Hunter the Guard ever trained. I can tell you which weapon would suit the Pope just by looking at him."

Arrogant, jackass. But I'm glad he's on my side.

We walked to the table and split to opposite sides. My hands clenched tightly around each other as I looked over every sharp edge, blunt force object, and shiny surface.

Half of them I had never seen before and the other half I'd only seen because I had watched some whacked out horror films. I feared if I picked one up, I'd take off my own arm by accident.

"Would you like some assistance?" When Michael spoke, it was loud enough for those nearby to hear. His voice was cold and refrained.

I nodded. "Please."

"Come this way." He beckoned me further down the table.

The weapons we passed grew in size and the edges looked so sharp my eyes hurt.

Nearly half way down the table, he stopped. He looked over the collection of knives before picking one and handing it to me. "Try this."

The blade was about half a foot long with jagged teeth. With shaking hands, I reached for the knife. It fell through my clammy fingers and sank into the table with a dull *thunk.*

Snickers from those watching pushed blood to my cheeks. I grabbed the handle and yanked the blade from the wood. The reflection in the blade showcased a girl seconds away from having a panic attack.

"Just breathe." Michael Ported to my side of the table and turned me to face a target with my Contestant number above it. "Just do what you can." He placed me directly parallel to the target and stepped back.

My stomach was pulled so tight, I had to remind myself to breathe. I glanced at Michael, remembering how he drilled me over the summer to always breathe.

A couple targets down, Clarence laughed. "This will be good."

My eyes shot toward his target without my permission. Multiple machete-like knives jutted from the surface.

I glanced back at Michael, but he wasn't looking at the other Contestant. He was looking at me. He nodded for me to proceed.

I loosely held the knife between my fingers and lifted it above my shoulder. I breathed in and held it for a count of three. The shakes in my arm stilled. As I exhaled, I sent the blade flying.

I held my breath as it soared. With a hearty *thunk,* it sank into the target.

"No way," I muttered.

I blinked rapidly, wondering if my eyes were playing tricks. But no matter how many times I blinked, the knife stayed in place. It wasn't in the center. Not even close, but it had made it onto the face of the target.

Michael came up beside me, staring hard at the target. Like if he blinked, the knife would dissolve. Without turning away, he reached behind him and grabbed the nearest knife. "Try again."

It didn't take me as long to talk myself into throwing it. The knife zipped across the room and sank into the target closer to the center.

This time I turned and grabbed another knife from the table. When this one landed, it cut through the heart of the bull's-eye.

Clarence wasn't laughing anymore.

"That is something I can work with." Michael's lips were just barely turned up into a smile as he examined the target. "Not bad."

Holding back a smile of my own, I felt my back straighten. "What's next?"

We tested with more weapons, but I was best with the knives. Next, we were tested on strength: lifting, pressing, and throwing weights. Then we were evaluated on how hard we could punch and kick. There was more and all of it sucked. And I was last. On nearly every level. I could feel Michael's "not bad" dissolve into disappointment and embarrassment with each passing exam.

And then I was proven right. There was cardio.

Each Contestant was put on a treadmill. The Guardians were instructed to increase the speed after each minute. For this portion of the exam, Helen waited near a cart of potions.

"If you can't take it, I'll shut it down." Michael pointed to the red button that would kill the machine. Judging from his tone, he thought that was going to happen sooner than later.

But if there was anything I was good at, it was running. He should've known that after spending five months chasing my shadow.

Standing on my treadmill, I looked down the line. Daniel stared intently at the belt in front of him. Clarence caught me looking and gave me a once over. With a scoffing laughing, he looked away with a shake of his head.

"Just focus on you." Michael moved to the front near the button that increased the speed. He shot a glare at the Contestant Sixteen, Marina Rafael, on my right as she tried to eavesdrop. The poor kid almost tripped backward.

What I needed was for him not to be in my line of sight, judging me.

"Start the machines!" Master Lenin ordered.

Think of the title.

Michael pressed the button. From the corner of my eye, Marina, Daniel, and I stepped in unison. The speed was painfully slow. I struggled not to outpace the belt.

After one minute, Michael leaned forward and increased the speed, forcing me to lengthening my strides. Three minutes went by before I had to move into a jog.

My hair clung to my neck as Michael reached forward again. I cursed as I was thrown into a sprint. Each time my lungs expanded my ribs ached in response. I tried to ignore how, every so often, Michael glanced to his left or right.

I forced myself not to look as my legs started to shake.

I lost track of how many times Michael hit the button. No matter how deeply I breathed, no amount of air satisfied the hunger in my lungs. Sweat poured down my spine and pulled my shirt close, suffocating my skin.

Think of the title, I chanted. *Just think of the title.*

Michael hit the button again.

The belt zipped away from my feet. My knee hit the machine. Before my brain could process, I was rolling across the floor. I ended up on my back panting for air.

"Charlie?" Michael's shadow loomed over me. "Charlie, look at me."

I couldn't open my eyes. I couldn't do anything other than gasp.

Following a sharp prick on the side of my thigh, a cooling sensation worked up my body. After a few seconds, the fire in my chest eased and the weak, dead weight in my limbs lifted. Forcing my eyes open, I looked down to see an empty syringe sticking out of my leg.

"Are you alright, Contestant Heart?" Master Lenin peered down at me. Blake, Daniel, and Atlas stood around him.

"Yeah." I allowed Michael to help me sit up. The following headrush was insane. "I'm good."

"I had no idea you could run like that." Michael nodded his head toward the machine.

Over his shoulder, most of the treadmills were empty. The only Contestants still running were the three from the University, one from The Magical Academy of the Earth, and Emeka Selasi from Lions of Magic. Every other Contestant sagged against the wall across from the machines drenched in sweat and breathing hard.

"You should've seen her in Kansas." Blake grinned. "Sometimes I wondered if she was trying to fly."

"She should get looked at. And you two should move to your next station." Master Lenin gestured to Blake and Daniel before wandering back to those still running.

Next station? I groaned.

As Blake and Daniel left, Michael gripped my elbow and rose from his crouch, pulling me up. With Helen on one side and Michael on the other, they guided me to a bench along the far wall. My knee burned with every step. Once seated, I saw the skin . . . well . . . there was no skin.

"How did I do?" I asked as Helen started mixing something as green as toxic waste.

Michael's gaze wandered to those still running. "You outran over half of them."

"You sound surprised."

"Can you blame me?" His phone dinged, drawing his attention and smirk away from me. He turned to answer it, leaving me to be put back together by Helen.

Leaning against the wall, savoring the feeling of not being out of breath, I couldn't help but smile to myself. *I did good.* My victory turned into a wince as Helen applied the goo to my raw knee.

"No one cares, you know." A few feet down, Clarence was on the same bench as I was. "So what? You can run. That only means you're good at fleeing."

"I think out running you is something worth mentioning." I met his gaze with a smirk.

Helen coughed into her elbow, covering a smile.

"Good luck convincing the rest of the world that." He jerked his head to where the University students still ran without signs of slowing. "They'll eat you alive when they catch you. And so will everything else." He got to his feet and limped toward his training room.

"He's right."

I jumped when Michael stepped out of my peripheral vision. Pocketing his phone, he crossed his arms and glared at the retreating Contestant.

"Then it looks like we get to prove him wrong." I smirked up at him. "Right, *Guardian* Kale?"

He turned his glare to me. "Then you have a lot of work to do."

26
The Theme and Challenge
of the First Trial

I stepped into my apartment and fell against the door.

Through half-lidded eyes, I looked toward the bedroom. *Was the apartment always this big? I don't remember my bed being so far away.*

It had been thirty days since The Trial started. Thirty days of running exercise circuits, weapons and magic training. They were much like night lessons, but so much longer.

Michael was hell-bent on making me regret entering The Trial. We were one of the first to get into the training area and the last to leave. On top of that, I somehow had to fit in homework. I wanted nothing more than to lay down and sleep for a week straight.

From the corner of my eye, something rose up at the center of the living room. I whipped around, yanking my wand out from the pocket on the side of my jeans. Magic surged down my arm and flared through the carvings.

But it was just a levitating garment bag. The material gleamed as brightly as the gold doors of the castle. Stuck to the front was an envelope addressed to Contestant Fifteen.

Cursing, I clutched my wand to my chest. The lights mimicked the frantic beating of my heart.

I dropped my school bag on the couch and glanced toward my bedroom. I was tempted to ignore it and take a nap anyway. *Remember, you're doing all of this for a title.*

Sighing toward the ceiling, I rounded the couch and snatched the envelope from the floating bag.

Contestant Fifteen,

Tonight is The Magisterium of Magic's annual Halloween Masquerade. It is also the First Award Challenge, a precursor to your First Trial in a few weeks.

Your objective is to show how much you have connected with your Guardian in the last month. Tonight, you will dress without informing anyone, in a costume you think will best correspond with what your Guardian will be wearing.

Everyone will be in masks during the evening. Keep your identity a secret until I, Master Lenin, call the Contestants to the front. Only then may you reveal who you are. In the meantime, walk around and see if you can find your Guardian. For the Award Challenge, you will have three guesses to identify him.

The winner will be awarded a sneak peek into the First Trial.

The Award Challenge starts at 6:00 pm. Please arrive on time.

Master H. Lenin

There was another note in the envelope. It was short and consisted of five words.

PUT ON THE DAMN COSTUME.

He didn't have to sign it. The implied threat was as good as any signature Michael could give.

Tossing the notes aside, I unzipped the gold bag. The dress inside was simple, with no ribbons, no embellishments, and no color. In addition to not having sleeves, there was no form. Basically, it was a white pillowcase with holes for my head, arms, and legs. Pinned to the hanger was a mask that was just as simple.

What the hell is this supposed to be?

White was the last color I would *ever* associate with Michael. Master Lenin gave me this hideous sack for a reason. If winning the Award Challenge earned me more points in The Trial, then I couldn't half-ass it.

Turning away from the levitating garment, I exited my apartment and knocked on the door directly across the hall.

The door swung open revealing Snow White. The yellow and red dress reached halfway down her thighs. The full skirt flared out with ruffles and lace. The front of her red pumps looked like juicy apples.

"Hey, Charlie!" Cornelia smiled. Her usual blonde hair was a rich, curly black with a bright red bow. Behind her yellow-gold mask, her magically colored green eyes beamed at me.

"Cheese and rice, you look awesome!"

Her smile grew. "Thanks." She looked over my jeans and t-shirt. "Are you wearing that?"

"No, I haven't started yet. You did such a good job helping me get ready for the Valentine's Day party last year, I was wondering if you could help me again."

She stuck her head out the door and looked both ways down the empty hall. "I'm a bit low on magic," she whispered.

Much like me, Cornelia was lying about her status. She claimed to be a Common Four but was actually a Deficient Three. Both of us were lying so we could fly under the radar, but her lie was coupled with self-preservation.

"You tell me what to do and I'll do it." I clasped my hands in front of my chest. "Please, please help me."

"You don't have to beg," she laughed. Pulling her door closed, her heels clicked against the floor as she stepped into my apartment. "Where's your costume?"

"Over there." I gestured to the living room and pulled the door closed.

"Oh, my God." She stood in front of the bag with her hands hovering before the ugly garment. Her ruby lips hung open. "Do you know what this is?"

"The ugliest dress I've ever seen?" I came to stand beside her.

She shook her head. "It's a transformative garment, super rare. It will change into anything the wearer is thinking."

I reached in and touched the smooth fabric. Magic tickled my fingertips. At least Master Lenin wasn't expecting me to dress as a pillowcase.

"I've never seen one in person." Cornelia reached forward but stopped before she touched it. "Where on earth did you get one?"

"Master Lenin sent it."

"The perks of being a Trial Contestant, I guess. Who are you going as?"

That was an excellent question. I was supposed to dress in something that would match whatever Michael was going to wear. He was about as talkative as a rock when it came to his personal life. During our training sessions, when we weren't running through drills, we were silent.

All he ever wore was black. I knew he grew up on a ranch, but I doubted he would go as a cowboy. I almost laughed thinking about him in a cowboy hat.

Something tickled in the back of my mind. Michael nicknamed my father Lucifer. Michael had a nickname, too . . .

Hades.

"Persephone." I turned to Cornelia. "Can you help?"

"Of course! Do you have your wand?"

I pulled it from the pocket of my jeans.

"Remember how I curled your hair?" she asked as she walked toward my bathroom.

I nodded.

"You're going to do the same thing. Section your hair and then press your wand to the lock of hair. Your magic will do the rest."

Standing before the large mirror, I parted my hair and pressed my wand to my scalp. Golden magic bled into my hair, burning my head. The lock curved into a loose curl.

"Can you make the curl tighter? I'm going to need more texture."

Pulling on more magic, the curl gathered into a spiraling ringlet. Once all of my hair was in tight curls, Cornelia elegantly spun and twisted my hair into a pile at the base of my skull. She left a few locks loose to play around my shoulders. Then she directed me to turn it all blonde.

"Now, let's see what that dress can do." She slapped her handful of bobby pins to the counter and dashed out of the bathroom.

Biting back a smile, I followed her to the living room where she had carefully taken the plain garment from the bag. She practically shook with excitement as she handed it to me.

Closing my bedroom door, I quickly stripped out of my loose sweater and jeans and pulled the formless garment over my head.

"So, how does this thing work?" I asked, stepping back into the living room.

"It already is," Cornelia said breathlessly.

Following her downcast gaze, my eyes bulged.

The sleeves slid off my shoulders. The fabric lengthened and billowed around my arms in sheer loops before encircling my wrists. It was as soft as a lazy morning breeze.

The bodice pulled close to my chest and waist. The hem fell to the floor with an abundance of wispy layers. Flowers bloomed along the neckline, wrapping around my shoulders to the back. They sprouted down the tight bodice and the full skirt. Ribbon crisscrossed over the front to my waist, where they followed the skirt to the floor. All the while, the fabric darkened to a deep gold. With each breath, every rustle of the light fabric glinted with emerald streaks.

"Wow," Cornelia breathed.

Wow was right. I gently touched the skirt. The magic of the dress wasn't limited to the fabric. It leaked over my skin giving it a summer-kissed glow.

Magic is so cool.

Wordlessly, Cornelia handed me the mask. As soon as it touched my fingers, the white material darkened to match the color of the dress. Golden stalks of wheat and leaves twisted over the surface. Six ruby pomegranate seeds cascaded from the corner of one of the eyes.

As I pressed it to my face, magic kept the mask in place. The ruby seeds fell against my cheek like crimson tears.

"Can you recognize me?" I asked.

"If I didn't just see all of that happen, I wouldn't know it was you."

I sagged with relief. "Thank you."

With a few extra minutes to spare, we walked arm in arm to the dining room.

However, we never made it.

On either side of the gold doors were guards dressed in white and red armor. The open doors didn't show black stone or round tables, but a garden.

Tall trees with broad, white trunks loomed over us with a canopy of gold blossoms. Petals sprinkled gracefully to the ground. The air was rich with the smell of dark chocolate, only more earthy.

"Where are we?" I floated down the stairs into the small piece of paradise.

"This has to be The Magical Academy of the Earth." Cornelia sounded as in awe as I felt. "I heard we were going to visit the other schools . . . but I didn't think it would be right away."

This was a school? I wouldn't mind coming here if this is what it looked like.

"Well." Cornelia unthreaded her arm from mine. "You have work to do. The theme should be announced within the hour. I'll see you around." With a quick hug, she twirled out of sight.

I walked around the garden, unable to take my eyes off the magnificent trees. A floating tray drifted by, stacked with glasses of sparkling liquid. I reached to grab one, but remembered Michael's order. *"Don't eat or drink anything unless I give it to you."*

Reluctantly, I stepped back from the beverages.

Hades. I'm looking for Hades. My eyes sought out every costume relating to the Lord of the Dead. Whenever I spotted an all-black outfit, I carefully looked it over.

But I wasn't convinced Michael was behind any of them. One god of the dead had a suit made entirely of bones and strips of decaying skin. I thought that was too dramatic to be Michael.

Another costume was outfitted in black gems and gold stitches. The mask was made entirely of jewels, distorting the face beneath it. Everything about his shining costume was drawing attention to him, which was something Michael would never do.

Finally, I recognized someone in the crowded garden.

Robin Hood dragged his hands through the curls of black hair at the top of his head. The green leotard complemented his olive skin, making his candy apple green eyes more dazzling. The smile he gave to Captain America in front of him might as well have been a nametag.

Blake.

"Good evening, gentlemen," I said, stepping into their conversation. "Don't you two look dashing?"

"Thank you, my lady." Blake dipped into a bow. "Well, well, well. Look at you." He made a show of stepping back to look me over. "How did Guardian Kale get you into a dress?"

"He threatened to kill me."

He laughed, thinking it was a joke. I smiled so he would believe it.

"Where is he? I might have to thank him," Captain America asked. His warm brown eyes twinkled in the bright light of the party. *Daniel.*

"Your guess is as good as mine." I scanned the room once more. "Maybe he's not here."

"He's a Guardian. He's required to be here."

"Do you have any idea who your Guardian is dressed as?"

Daniel nodded to a centaur about twenty feet away. "Either him or the Minotaur over there. Sean mentioned something about mythical creatures but, for the life of me, I can't remember which one."

"Not to brag, but I have this in the bag." Blake leaned against his bow. "Don't cry too hard when I win, alright?"

I stuck my tongue out at him. "Any bets on what the theme will be?"

"I've got nothing." Blake's eyes lingered on a particularly cute Snow White a few trees over.

"Judging from the other Trials, I think they're going to make it more personal." Daniel swirled his drink around the bottom of his glass. "Something general so it can be judged the same, but different for each Contestant to showcase their experience."

"Why do I not like the sound of that?"

"Could be worse. We could be infected with a disease and have to diagnose it," he said.

"That happened in the last Trial, right?"

"Yep."

"Are you sure they won't reuse it?"

Blake laughed. "They don't recycle themes. Kinda defeats the purpose of 'being the best' if you already know what to expect."

"Thank God for that," I mumbled.

"Here we go." Blake pointed to the front of the room as Master Lenin, disguised as Julius Caesar, stepped up to the microphone. "Contestants! Please come to the stage. It's time!"

Butterflies attacked my stomach; a curse dropped from my mouth. I still hadn't seen anyone that could be Michael.

Once we were lined up in order of our Contestant numbers, Master Lenin took his place in front of us. "Good evening, ladies and gentlemen, Guardians and Contestants. Tonight is a big night. Tonight, we learn the theme of the First Trial. Master Lawrence Hart will do the honor of revealing it to you." He stepped back from the microphone and applauded politely.

Lucifer bounded up the steps. Sprouting from his back were four large white wings. His usual red suit was accented with char and rubies. In his left hand was a pitchfork with three barbed prongs. Lawrence Hart removed the mask covering his whole face and grinned at the crowd.

"Good evening! What a marvelous party! Thank you, Master Loran, for having us at your school. I'm excited to announce the theme of The Trial you will be facing next month.

"Over the last couple of years, the School Masters and I have been hard at work designing it. We wanted something interesting and dangerous, but we also wanted to know more about our Contestants. Do I dare ask for a drumroll?" His lips curled into a smile.

The crowd chuckled and obliged. A low rumble filled the room.

"The theme of the First Trial is," everyone fell silent, "what you fear the most."

27

Persephone's Guess

"Cheese and rice," I muttered.

What I feared most? That list was the only one in my life that was constantly growing. My mind dredged up one horror after another.

Past foster parents.

Mr. While.

Falling from the North Tower.

Ghosts.

My nails curled into my palms. I knew getting a title wasn't going to be easy, but this was something else. And this was only the theme of the First Trial. If they were this strong coming out of the gate, what were the other two going to be like?

I am so screwed.

"In this Trial, you will come to three doors," Lawrence said over the excited whispers. "Behind each door, you will face one of your nightmares. This is to test whether you can conquer and think through fear."

I glanced down the row of Contestants. Some had gone dangerously pale. Others looked at each other with confusion. A couple were shocked, neither moving nor breathing.

"With that in mind, whoever wins the Award Challenge tonight, gets to know one of their fears in advance."

I want that. I was already behind the curve when it came to magic. I needed that sneak peek if I was going to make it to the finish line.

Lawrence looked at the Contestants behind him. "Let us begin. Contestant One, Lin Cho-Hoy. Who have you dressed up as this evening?"

I blocked them out completely. From my vantage point on the stage,

I could see almost everyone at the party. I kept my posture relaxed as I searched the crowd feverishly.

Michael is required to be here. He has to be here somewhere.

I looked over every costume that vaguely resembled a Greek god. I paused on someone who was dressed up like the Grim Reaper, but I couldn't see Michael putting that much effort into it.

"Contestant Twelve, Blake Johnson. Who did you dress up as?"

"Robin Hood, sir." Blake bowed his head toward the Master.

"Have you found your Guardian?"

"Yes, sir." Blake removed the dark green mask from his face. He wore a blatant grin of victory as he pointed into the middle of the crowd, toward a man decked out in black leather with a sheriff's star on his vest. "The Sheriff of Nottingham."

Atlas removed the leather mask and pointed at his Contestant with pride.

"Well done, Contestant Johnson!" Lawrence Hart clapped, clearly impressed. "On the first try, and your costumes correspond. We have a competitor for the first fear."

Atlas bounded up the stage and slapped Blake on the back. "Bloody well done, mate."

My stomach contracted, making me nauseous. I barely calmed myself before the lights flickered. I still had a few more Contestants before I was called to guess. My gaze continued to rake through the crowd.

I looked over a mortician, a vampire, a deranged ghost, a shadow man, a devil, a fire creature—

"Contestant Fifteen, Charlie Heart." I startled when my name was called. "Who did you dress up as?"

"Persephone, sir." Following Blake's lead, I bowed to the Master dressed as the devil.

"Who is your Guardian?"

My labors were fruitless. Michael was the best Hunter in the world. Hiding was as easy as breathing to him. My shoulders sagged in defeat. I could almost hear the title of the next 'Trial coverage.'

Trial's Biggest Failure

The Magisterium's Dud.

Not Worth the Time.

Removing my mask, I prepared to tell him I didn't know when a shadow at the edge of the room caught my attention.

Leaning against a tree was a tall man dressed head to toe in black. A floor length black coat housed a silver pocket watch. A long, thick scarf draped around his shoulders. A skull-white mask covered his whole face, but the eyes beneath it were as black as a starless sky.

"Hades." I pointed to the daunting figure. My breath stalled in my throat. I crossed my fingers behind my back.

The man reached up and pulled the mask from his face. Michael Kale smirked back at me.

"Well done, Contestant Heart." Lawrence applauded with the whole room. Without sparing Michael a glance, he said, "Contestant Sixteen, Marina Rafael. You may guess."

Michael bounded up the stage and slipped into the space beside me. "I thought for sure you wouldn't get it," he mumbled.

"What breathtaking confidence you have in me." I sent him a sharp look from the corner of my eye. "One of these days, you're going to stop underestimating me."

Laughter snorted from his nose. "Sure."

"You're lucky I remembered some obscure conversation about that nasty nickname of yours or you would still be standing out there."

"When did we talk about that nickname?"

"We didn't. My friend Moose told me."

At the sound of her name, Michael turned his gaze to me. His eyes dropped to the golden gown, shimmering with an emerald hue.

"It wouldn't kill you to tell me I did a good job." I clapped as another Guardian made their way onto the stage. "Plus, the costume is rather fitting for this arrangement between us."

"Because I kidnapped you and dragged you to the Underworld?"

"You might as well have."

Michael shook his head. "Rumor has it, Persephone begged the Lord of the Dead to take her. She reveled in the idea of being the goddess of both life and death and wanted to stand beside the most feared god."

A shiver ran down my spine. Hades may have just been his nickname, but it wasn't hard to believe.

"Speaking of fear, what are yours?"

Now it was my turn to laugh. "Like I'm going to tell you."

"You're supposed to. I'm your Guardian."

"You're also the guy who's going to kill me. Forgive me for not willingly handing over my nightmares."

"First off, I thought we were forgetting that little tidbit for the duration of The Trial, per *your* request."

I rolled my eyes. *Of course that was coming back to bite me in the ass.*

"Secondly, I'm the only person helping you through The Trial. So, you can either give me your fears so I can help you fight them, or I can watch them kill you and laugh at your stupidity for entering yourself." He paused to let that sink in. "So, what are your fears?"

He was right . . . and I hated it. "I'm afraid of some of my foster parents. Denny, for sure. There were others." I cast a look to see his expression.

His eyebrows pulled together. "You're afraid you'll have to face them again?"

"I barely made it out the first time."

"You got out once, right?"

Slowly, I nodded.

"Then you'll do it again. Back then you were a different person. Now you know how to give it back."

"Michael—"

"If you don't stand up for yourself, you'll always be the punching bag. With your magic status, you're at the top of the food chain."

Top of the food chain. Ha. When I was a baby, I was dumped out with the Tuesday trash. If that wasn't the universe saying how low on the food chain I was, then I don't know what was.

"What about demons?"

My eyes bulged. I would have whipped around to look at him if he didn't wrap his hand around my arm, keeping me in place. "Please tell me I'm not going to see another one of those," I hissed.

"It's a possibility." He relaxed his hold when he was sure I wouldn't freak out. "Luckily, I have a whole month to teach you how to handle one without skydiving out of a tower."

"I'm glad you think that was funny," I quipped.

"I'm not poking fun. I'm serious." He clapped with the crowd. "Keep going. What else?"

The next thought made me go cold.

You.

I looked at him from the corner of my eye. From his long coat to the shiny shoes stitched together with animal bones, he was a vision straight out of nightmares. The harsh stage lighting hit his cheek bones and shadowed half of his face. It was entirely believable that he reigned over the Underworld in his spare time.

I knew the darkness in his eyes wasn't a costume. It was put there by broken bones and spilled blood. This was a man who was used to getting what he wanted by any brutal means necessary.

This was the man who wanted me dead from the moment he saw me. The only reason my heart was still beating was the order from Master Lenin to use me for the Heel's war. But if that order wasn't there . . .

How perfect would it be for him if I died in The Trial? If my fears caught up with me, would he even try to help? Or would he let them do what Master Lenin's order kept him from doing?

Cheese and rice.

He had no intention of getting me out alive. And like an idiot, I gave him the tools to paralyze and destroy me. And, here I was, thinking I was outsmarting him by earning a title.

The man in question turned to look at me, waiting for my answer.

Swallowing around my racing heart, I blurted the first thing that came to mind. "The dark."

He cocked his head as if he could smell the lie on my breath. He opened his mouth, but the final round of applause finished, and Lawrence stepped up to the microphone.

"Congratulations to everyone who found their Guardians. While the majority of you found your selected Guardian, in my mind, there is only one pair who truly fulfilled what was asked. Contestant Twelve, Blake Johnson and Guardian Atlas."

Blake launched into the air with a yell of triumph. Atlas wasn't too far behind him. Atlas gave him a hard slap on the back before shooting Michael a smug look.

"Congratulations," Lawrence called over the thundering applause. "Please follow me for the viewing of your first fear. For the rest of you, enjoy your evening and Happy Halloween." He walked off the stage, followed by the ecstatic duo. His armored guard followed after him.

Michael's hand was on my elbow again as he led me down the stairs. "What else do you fear?"

I turned away. I already gave him too much. "I'm going to wait for Blake. I'll see you tonight at ten." Before he could grab my arm, I slipped into the crowd, the golden skirts flaring around my retreating feet. I moved quickly in case he decided to track me down to finish our conversation.

On the other side of the party, I put on my mask and ducked behind one of the far trees. I wrapped my arms tightly around my middle, hoping it would stop my hands from shaking and my magic from moving.

I peeked around the tree at the rest of the party. Hades was nowhere to be seen.

From my hiding spot, I could see the small room that Blake and Atlas stepped into. A pair of red-armored guards stood on either side of the door; one arm crossed over their chest to grasp their holstered wand.

As good of friends as Blake and I were, I didn't know what he was afraid of. Nothing seemed to faze him. He barely jumped at scary movies.

A while later, the pair exited, shoulders tense, in deep conversation. I waited until Atlas patted Blake on the back and bid him a goodnight.

I quickly made my way to the spot Atlas left. Every question I had died on my tongue when I saw Blake's expression. Not really seeing, he stared blankly at the air in front of him.

"Are you ok?" I asked.

Blake shook his head. A trembling breath left his lips.

"What did you see?" Instead of curiosity, I felt my own fear rising.

Again, he shook his head. "Bloody hell, Charlie . . ." He grabbed my hand. "I don't have the words." He swallowed thickly. "I can't tell you. Master Hart told me not to. Prepare for anything . . . and everything."

My stomach flipped over. Squeezing his hand tightly, I tried to smile around the hurricane of emotions inside me. "Then it's a good thing we have a month to prepare."

"I need more time," he mumbled. Shaking himself out of his thoughts, he released my hand. "I'll see you tomorrow." Without waiting for a reply, he walked back toward the Magisterium.

I watched him leave. *What did he see?*
All the things I listed out loud to Michael swirled through my head.
What would I see?

28

You Want to Arm Wrestle?

Fear was a familiar emotion to me.

It was a warning system that kept me out of trouble. It kept my head down and shoved me into the shadows when I needed to hide. It was the humming verse before the chorus started in my blood, *run, run, run*.

After hearing the theme of the First Trial, I barely slept. I glided from one class to the next, barely retaining a word of the lectures. All I could think about were the nightmares I listed for Michael at the Award Challenge.

I liked it better when The Trial didn't have a theme, when it was a source of hope for a title. Now that we had a destination harboring every horror imaginable, it just felt like I was headed for a cliff.

Barely touching my dinner, I headed down to the training room. Michael was already waiting inside our designated training area. Dropping my bag by the door, I ducked into the back to change. My shaking hands added another layer of difficulty to pulling on the tight workout clothes.

"Nervous?" Michael asked as he dragged his leather jacket from his shoulders. The sight of his double holster, housing his wand on the left and four sharp, menacing blades on the right, reminded me how many ways he could kill me at any given moment.

I swallowed hard. "I'm fine."

"Really?" His black eyes darted to the fluttering light closest to the door.

"You make it sound like there's nothing to freak out about." I forced myself to take slow, deep breaths. Gradually, the lights returned to normal.

"There's nothing to freak out about."

"Of course, you would say that, you self-centered jackass," I quipped. "You're not the one headed for your own personal hell."

He looked down at me, bored with my tone. "Lenin gave you an out by pulling your scroll. You wanted this."

"No, not *this.*"

"If you had done any research on The Trial before you finagled your way in, you would know they're all like this."

The bastard was right. And I hated it.

"We have the next month to come up with a game plan." Michael moved on from gloating. "Lucky for you, I specialize in fear."

My heart dipped toward my toes. I didn't need a reminder of that.

"We're going to dissect your fears and then I'm going to teach you how to overcome them. Deal?"

He made it sound so simple.

"Let's start with your foster family."

My heart jumped. The lights flashed.

"Tell me what Denny did to you."

All across my back the scars tightened with memories of when they bled. My skin ached with long forgotten bruises and broken bones. "No."

"What do you fear about him?"

"I said *no.*" The light beside me shivered and sparked.

"You're not doing yourself any favors by keeping it to yourself."

My clenched hands ached with white-knuckle tension. "I'm just scared of him, ok? There isn't anything specific."

"There's always something specific. Fear is a side effect. No one is afraid of heights; they're afraid of falling. So, what does Denny do that makes you afraid of him?"

Five years' worth of memories threatened to overtake me. I looked up into his scarred face. "He . . . he knows how to get in my head. He knows exactly what words to say to back me into a corner. And then he—" I put my hands to my throat to illustrate what I couldn't say out loud.

Michael nodded thoughtfully. "Ok, we're going to try something." Moving slowly, he stepped forward. "But I need you to keep your magic in check." He placed his hands on my shoulders and backed me across the room.

I jumped when my shoulder blades touched the cement wall. My magic scalded the inside of my ribcage with a flash of heat.

Michael hissed through his teeth, jerking his hands back. "Rein it in."

"Sorry." I yanked my magic back into my core.

He flexed his fingers to work through the pins and needles. "I'm going to place my hands around your throat—"

My eyes leapt up to his. *He's out of his damn mind.*

"I'm not going to squeeze," he reassured me. "I'm not even going to touch you."

"Do you think I'm an idiot? You're just going to break my neck."

"I'm trying to help you." He poised his hands around my throat. True to his word, he didn't touch me, but that didn't mean I couldn't feel his scarred fingers close to my pulse. He stood close enough that I could just barely distinguish his pupils from his obsidian irises.

"If he gets you in a hold like this, raise the arm of your dominant hand." He waited for me to move.

My mouth was so dry, the Sahara Desert would've been an oasis in comparison. My hand shook as I raised my right arm, bringing my elbow over my head.

"Twist in the opposite direction of the arm you have raised." He jerked his chin toward the left.

I turned.

"Then drop your elbow onto my wrists."

I dropped my hand, the back side of my arm connected with his outstretched hands. What happened was exactly what I thought would happen. Nothing. His hands didn't even twitch away from my neck.

He gave me a dry look. "You'll need more force than that."

I pushed his hands away. "I don't see what the point is. He's stronger. Even if I did that perfectly, it'll just piss him off."

I got six new scars for fighting back. They were the deepest lashes he ever gave me. After that, I took my punishment with clenched teeth. It wasn't worth it to double the amount of split skin.

"Strength doesn't have anything to do with this," Michael said. "If you strike his joints, they'll buckle and his grip will break."

I shook my head. "When he's angry, there's nothing that'll release his grip."

"Your magic fuels your entire body. With your status, you have an unbelievable amount coursing through your veins. What do you think that does to the rest of you?"

I shrugged. "It shocks people when I touch them."

"That's just a reaction. I'm talking about what it does to you." He pointed at my chest. "It makes your bones harder to break. It makes you run faster and doubles your endurance—which is why you were able to outrun more than half the Contestants at the benchmark exam. But most of all, it makes you stronger."

"You're saying I can out-muscle him?" I asked incredulously.

"Yes." Michael glanced over his shoulder at the room behind him. "Come here." Turning on his heel, he walked toward the bench by the door. He dragged it away from the wall and knelt on the other side.

He shoved his sleeve up his arm and propped his elbow onto the smooth surface.

My eyebrow lifted. "You want to arm wrestle?"

"Will you just get down here?"

I dropped my voice. "But won't my magic hurt?"

"I'm used to it." When that didn't persuade me, he added, "I've felt worse. Now, come on."

Chewing on the inside of my cheek, I shot a glance at the rest of the training room. No doubt, what was about to happen was going to be humiliating. Thankfully everyone was preoccupied.

I lowered myself on the other side of the bench and grasped his hand.

"On the count of three. One . . . two . . . three."

Michael flexed and pushed into my hand. Just as I expected, my knuckles touched the bench.

He gave me the same bored look over our interlocking hands. "You're holding back. Put your shoulder into it." We reset. "One . . . two . . . three."

Taking a deep breath, I pressed forward. Digging my elbow into the bench, I put my back into it until a sweat broke out along my hairline. The muscles in Michael's forearm flexed as his fingers tightened around mine.

Slowly, his hand inched backward.

My eyes widened. "You're going easy on me."

Michael gripped the edge of the bench. "Does it look like I'm going easy on you?" His hand inched back up until it was centered with mine. Neither moved.

Pulling his hand back, he pushed himself to his feet.

All I could do was stare at my hands.

There's no way . . . but if I can do that . . . there's no way!

"Let's try again," Michael said, moving across the room. "Charlie. Back against the wall, let's go."

Snapping out of my shock, I jumped to my feet and aligned my spine against the wall.

Stepping forward, he wrapped his hands loosely around my throat. "Up, over, and drop."

I found myself a little eager to see what I could do. Quickly, I raised my arm, twisted to the side, and dropped my elbow to his wrists. This time I put some force into the down strike.

His hands jerked away from my neck. Due to our height difference, the motion caused him to stumble forward.

"Ok, I'm adding another step." He moved back and repositioned his hands. "After you drop your elbow, throw it back into Denny's face. That should knock him back so he doesn't fall into you."

I reset my hands by my side. When he was ready, I lifted my arm, twisted, and slammed it down. Just as Michael pitched forward, my elbow sailed toward his nose.

His forearm shot up and took the blow before it could clock him in the head.

"Good." He kneaded the flesh that took the blunt of the hit. "The key is to strike and move away from him."

We ran through a few more sets. With each reset, Michael moved his hands closer and closer until they were cupped around my neck and I didn't hesitate. By the tenth try, it was a fluid motion.

"Good." Michael stepped back. "How else has he restrained you?"

"He pinned me to the floor once." Maybe it was because I was warmed up, or maybe it was because I had just managed to maneuver away from someone like Michael Kale, but I was looking forward to what he would say.

"That's actually a good one for you to learn to get out of." He nodded to the mat. "Lay on your back."

"You haven't said that to me in a while." For my first three days in the magical world, he had me lay on the floor to connect with my magic.

"And look how far you've come." He smirked. "You're still a huge pain in the ass, but at least you can do magic."

I stuck my tongue out at him.

Kneeling beside me, he swung his leg over and straddled my midsection. Then he placed his hands loosely around my neck. A tendril of black hair fell across his forehead. As close as I was, it looked surprisingly soft.

"If you get in this position, you need to move fast," he instructed. "He'll have the high ground. He can use his bodyweight to crush your windpipe."

"Noted."

"But, if he's pressing on your windpipe, that means his balance is shifted forward. He'll be leaning into you, not on his knees."

Reaching behind him, he grabbed my right knee and pulled it up, planting my foot on the floor. "Since he's twice your size, you'll need a little help. Move your leg like this and press up through your heel, throwing your hips to the side. He will be thrown off." Michael illustrated by rolling to the side, taking me up with him. I planted my hands on his chest to keep from headbutting him.

"Then you'll have the high ground. Knee him in the groin or strike his face to give you some time to get to your feet." With a quick twist of the hips, he flipped me on my back.

"Ready?" He placed his hands around my throat. "Go."

I planted my foot on the floor and pushed. Twisting my hips, he fell on his back. My knee jerked forward.

"Wow!" Michael crossed his leg in front of him, catching the knee before it could connect between his legs.

"Sorry." I scrambled off him.

"You apologize too much." He pushed himself up onto his elbows. "I'm starting to think it's your catch phrase."

I opened my mouth, but immediately clapped it shut when I realized I was just going to say the exact same word.

He patted the mat beside him. "Let's go again."

29

The Trial Field

Time didn't fly.

It sprinted.

It slipped through my fingers, leaving me with sleepless nights and panicked mornings. Days of training and classes felt like hours. Weeks passed by like days. Before I was ready, the First Trial was a week away.

Seven days.

I had seven days before I stared my fears in the face.

Michael's boots stomped across the hardwood in the other room. After he brought me breakfast from the dining room, he left so I could eat and he could pack. My plate sat beside me on the bed untouched.

As soon as he was done, we were going to the Trial Field. Once there, it would be impossible to ignore what was coming.

The silence in the living room pulled my attention to the doorway where he stood waiting. Michael sighed when he saw my uneaten breakfast.

"Are you packed?"

I nodded, too nervous to speak.

He shook his wrist to reposition his watch. "Then let's go."

The lights flickered. With shaky hands, I grabbed my bag. He slung his duffle over his shoulder and dug into his jacket pocket.

When he pulled out a transporter, my heart skipped another beat. Without giving me time to pass out, Michael grabbed my arm. The stone glowed brightly and the castle vanished.

Sunlight blinded me. A rough wind blew around us. Blinking back tears, I saw we were in the middle of nowhere. Sprinkled with little white flowers, endless green hills stretched until they met a deep blue sky. A canyon of white stone cut sharply into the earth, dividing the sea of grass.

Beside the canyon was a single tree, blowing madly in the wind. The twisted trunk looked like it had been used for sword practice. The chalky white surface was scarred by random lines and curves.

"What are we doing here again?" I asked over the wind.

"One school hosts The Trial, while the other six either build a Field or host an event. The European Academy built the First Trial Field." He started walking toward the lonely tree.

Standing beneath its mighty branches, it looked like it stabbed right into the heart of the sky.

Michael took out his wand and tapped the white bark twice. Golden magic sparkled in the crevasses. With a groan, the tree started to straighten and untwist. The random lines in the bark lined up one by one until they formed a door.

Without hesitation, Michael pushed it open. To my surprise, the inside was hollow, revealing a downward spiraling staircase.

"After you." Michael gestured inside.

With my interest piqued, I started down the staircase. When the door softly closed behind Michael, the walls groaned and twisted as the tree went back to normal.

At the bottom, my jaw dropped.

The European Academy was housed in the walls of the white stone canyon. Eight stone bridges reached across to the other side where the school continued. Vines grew peacefully on the walls and moss spread across the floors. Birds darted in and out of classrooms with open windows. At the bottom of the canyon, a lazy river moseyed on by. Sunshine poured over everything.

I had school envy.

I followed Michael over a bridge. Despite my uneasiness about heights, I peeked over the edge. At first, I thought there were fish in the water. But then one jumped up. A child, with two fins and as translucent as the water, splashed back into the river.

"What are they?" I whispered, not wanting to frighten it away.

"Water nymphs," Michael called over his shoulder as he continued across.

On the other side of the canyon, he held open one of the white doors.

Even though we were eight stories underground, sunlight continued to pour through the ceiling.

"How does the light get in here?" I asked, loving how bright it made everything.

"Daylight buds." He pointed to the white roots growing out of the ceiling. At the end of each sprout was a warm, bright orb. "The flowers soak up the sunlight above while their roots project it down here."

"That is so cool." All the way down the hall, I couldn't stop staring at the sparkling ceiling.

On either side of us were classrooms, much like the ones at the Magisterium. Except here, they felt alive. Moss grew up the legs of the desks. In one classroom, flowers sprouted from the chalkboard.

At the end of the hall was a gold door guarded by two soldiers in sage green armor. As we approached, they opened it. Down a long staircase was the Trial Field.

Oh right. I had forgotten why we were there.

Encased in grey stone, was a lawn no bigger than a high school football stadium. Sitting on the manicured grass were twenty-one doors, each in the color of the schools. Their frames anchored them to the ground, allowing them to stand freely. I quickly spotted the Magisterium's doors, black with gold frames. Opposite the line of doors was a building made mostly of glass.

On the grass, we joined the other waiting pairs of Contestants and Guardians. Master Lenin stood off to the side talking on his phone.

As Contestant-Guardian pairs slowly arrived, I looked closer at the wall of glass. The lowest level, right off the lawn, was the apartments. The two levels above that were dark, giving me more questions. At the very top was a terrace.

"Welcome, Contestants," Master Lenin said when everyone arrived. "In a week, this is where you'll participate in the First Trial. Those are your quarters for your time here." He gestured to the wall of glass.

When they said we were going to stay at the Trial Field, I didn't think they meant it literally.

"On Trial day, you'll get ready in your rooms and then step out here when your name is called. You'll take your place before one of the doors." He gestured to the line behind him.

"The floor above that is where your Guardians will observe and guide you. The third floor is for the judges. All of the Masters will be at the top with the best view. Let's head inside." Master Lenin turned and walked *through* the glass.

Everyone followed after him without a second thought.

We can walk through glass? Tentatively, I stepped forward. The glass was cold and almost slimy, not a feeling I enjoyed.

Once through, I stood on my tiptoes to look over everyone's heads. There was a kitchen, plenty of couches, a TV, and a long table for meals. *Were we expected to hang out together?* Beyond that, there was another glass wall that led to a training room.

"Contestants, you may find your quarters and get settled. The rest of the day is yours. Guardians, I'll meet you back here in five minutes."

Taking me by the arm, Michael steered me down the row of doors. At the one marked fifteen, he shoved his way inside.

The room was as beautiful as the school, with walls of grey stone and white tile floors. Dark wood furniture housed olive green cushions. The two bedrooms were on opposite ends of the living room. As Michael headed for the one closest to the door, I headed to the one deeper in.

Inside, tall posts carved to look like trees stood at each corner of the bed. Thick white curtains draped between the branches to block out the light.

Trying to keep my mind busy, I unpacked what little I brought and put it in the dresser. When I was done, I found a stack of neatly folded clothes on the bed.

I immediately put them on. The outfit consisted of a tank top, a hoodie, and tight pants. The back had my Contestant number in large, gold numbers. There were even shoes.

With nothing else to do, I stepped back into the living room. Michael stood with his back to me, looking over the Field. His shoulders looked tense.

He must have heard me, because he turned. He froze when he saw the outfit.

My hands jumped to fiddle with the hem of my shirt. I felt like a fool. "I found them on the bed."

He nodded. "I have some as well . . . are they comfortable?"

My eyebrow popped upward. "Small talk? Really?"

"Would you rather I ignored you?"

"No!" I dropped my gaze to the hem. "Sorry. Yes, they feel fine."

"Good. You'll be training in them until The Trial starts." He slid his hands into his pockets. "Alright, let's set some ground rules."

I gave him a questioning look.

"Don't go near any Contestant without me. Just because Lenin said no foul play doesn't mean there won't be any. If you give a Contestant an opening to take you out, they will."

My throat went dry. "Why?"

"Because you're competition. They don't know what you're capable of, so they see you as a threat. Me choosing to be your Guardian doesn't help. They think I saw something in you and they don't know what it is, which frightens them. They'll want me out of The Trial as soon as possible."

"Why don't they want you in The Trial?"

"I'm a Master Hunter. I could kill each of them six different ways before they could think of one. They think I will pass that on to you, which I will. That makes you a threat."

Cheese and rice. I never thought having Michael's help would be a bad thing.

"To them—especially for the Tactical University Contestants—if they eliminate you, you're one less person standing between them and a title. Their school is brutal, blood thirsty, and full of sore losers."

I lowered myself to the couch before my knees gave out.

"Use your head. Even the Guardians have training events and that will leave you alone with the other Contestants."

"Should I stay in my room when you're gone? The less I'm exposed, the less time there is for someone to do something."

He smirked. "You've never asked permission before. About damn time. Yes, that would be helpful." His dark eyes moved over my face. "You look like you're about to be sick."

"I might be."

"You'll be fine. Just stay in here." He twisted his wrist to look at the watch. "I'll see you later tonight. Lock the door behind me." Without another word, he left the room.

My legs shook as I walked toward the door. The deadbolt slid into place with a low click. That sound used to give me comfort. But now, I wondered, if someone really wanted to, they could just use a ward to blast their way in.

I pressed my forehead to the cold metal and breathed. The light beside me pulsed with my heartbeat.

A fist pounded against the door.

Jumping back, I had my wand out and aimed in a second. Magic smoldered in the fire designs engraved in the black wood.

A knock came again.

"Charlie, it's me," Blake whispered.

At the sound of his familiar voice, I pocketed my wand. My hands shook as I turned the deadbolt and cracked the door.

Blake was dressed in something similar to me. His fitted t-shirt and jogger sweats were the same color of olive as the couch cushions. His Contestant number with his last name was painted in white across his back. The crest of his school, a circle with a twisting tree, was embroidered on the front pocket. Despite the Contestant getup, his grey beanie was pulled low over his ears.

"You scared the shit out of me," I said, holding the door open.

"I just knocked," he laughed, stepping inside.

"I wasn't expecting anyone."

"Atlas ditched me to learn about the observation box where they'll watch us during The Trial. So instead of staring at the walls by myself, I thought I'd stare at the walls with you." He spun around with a smile.

"I'm not the best company at the moment." I re-bolted the door and started pacing the length of the room.

Blake, on the other hand, plopped onto the couch and draped his arm over his tired eyes. His long frame took up all the space between the armrests.

"You're better than an empty room," he sighed. "Hey, what are you doing for Thanksgiving?"

"Knowing my Guardian?" I headed for the other side of the room. "Training."

"Hades has you on a tight schedule, huh?"

"I really wish you would stop calling him that. It's not like he doesn't terrify me enough as it is."

"You chose him as your Guardian."

"You wanted him, too."

"Touché." He moved his arm over his head to look at me. "Back to my original question. Did you want to come over for Thanksgiving tomorrow? I'm sure my parents would be delighted to see you . . . you know, since they thought you were dead and all."

I stopped behind one of the armchairs. My heart warmed at the thought of his parents. When I lived in Kansas, Blake's house was the only haven-like place on Haven Avenue. Despite being a foster kid from a house the police frequently stopped at, his parents welcomed me every summer and holiday.

It sounded like just the perfect thing to get my mind off what would be happening at the end of the week.

But then my mood took a sour turn. There was no way Michael or Master Lenin would let me out of their sight. But maybe . . . If I was on my best behavior, maybe I could convince them.

Blake mistook my hesitation. "We'd Port into my backyard, and after we stuff our faces, we can leave the same way. You'd never have to see the house across the street."

I didn't want to get his hopes up, or mine for that matter. "I don't know." I fiddled with the ends of my hair. "Going back to Haven Avenue . . . Can I think about it?"

"Of course."

As we lapsed into silence, I continued my pacing across the living room.

How am I going to convince Michael to let me go? My mind spun with ideas. At least I wasn't thinking of The Trial anymore.

30
Thanksgiving

The next day, I had a plan.

I was going to placate Michael with good behavior.

I woke up early so when he meandered out of his room for coffee, I was ready to jump into training. I kept quiet, just in case the sound of my voice irritated him more than usual. I ate all the food he set before me. During lessons, I didn't hesitate or complain about the sets he gave me.

My hopes gradually lifted with each passing hour. His short comments and insults were at an all-time low.

As the afternoon drew closer, I gathered my courage to ask. He was in as good of a mood as he could get without me spiking his water bottle.

I planned to ask once we completed a set of drills, but his phone rang in the middle of it.

Holding up his hand, he stopped me from throwing another punch. He retreated to his jacket draped by the door and dug out his buzzing phone.

"This is Kale." Leaning all his weight on one leg, he looked at me over his shoulder. "I'm training Charlie. So, it could be better."

I fought the urge to stick my tongue out at him. *You've spent the entire morning kissing his ass. Don't blow it now.*

I wiped the sweat from my forehead and went over how I was going to ask, and all the things I was going to do to put his mind at ease. This was going to work.

By the time he hung up, my breathing had evened out.

When he faced me, he didn't meet my gaze. "We're, uh, going to the ranch for dinner. For Thanksgiving."

"Oh. I actually wanted to talk to you about that." I crossed my fingers behind my back. "Blake invited me to eat with him and his parents. I was wondering if I could go."

His eyes instantly narrowed.

"I'll check in every thirty minutes," I rushed on. "I mean, I do have this." I raised the wrist encircled by the silver tracking bracelet. "So, it's not like you won't know where I'll be."

"You think I'm going to let you go to another state with a boy who's already helped you run away? Not a chance."

My heart sank. "I promise I won't leave his house."

"Your promises are worthless. I've honestly lost track of how many times you've lied to me."

"But—"

"No, Charlie."

I clamped my teeth around the rest of my argument and stamped them back down my throat. Through my disappointment came the sour note of reality. I don't know why I expected anything different. Rule number one: don't let anyone know that you care. Because then they can take it from you.

"Let's go." He grabbed his jacket and headed for the door.

I looked for Blake in the training room, but he had already left. Helpless to do anything else, I followed Michael out of the training room. Once we were out of sight, Michael dropped a hand on my shoulder and Ported us to the ranch.

The crisp autumn air was sharp on my heated skin. It clung to the damp material of my shirt and the sweat on my back. No breeze moved through the naked branches. As we walked up the leaf-covered drive, our breath crystalized in curling white clouds before us.

My mood turned bitter upon stepping into the house. The scent of roasted, buttery turkey floated down the hall. The afternotes of sugar and cinnamon warmed the autumn chill. I heard Mrs. Kale and Meg talking in the kitchen.

Shoving passed Michael, I went straight to our room and into the connected bathroom. I slammed the door, shaking the walls.

Pressing my back to the door, I closed my eyes. Disappointment crawled up my throat with sharp little fingers, pushing tears into my eyes.

I shouldn't have expected anything different. Michael is my jailer, nothing more.

After a ridiculously long shower, I dressed in a thick sweater and leggings. When I stepped out of the bathroom, a plate of the Thanksgiving feast sat on the bedside table.

It was so full I couldn't see the plate beneath it: two slices of glistening turkey, creamy green bean casserole, sweet potatoes dripping in syrup, mashed potatoes topped with cheese and bacon, two bread rolls with their own crown of butter, and a small mountain of steaming golden-brown stuffing.

I should've just eaten it. But looking at that plate and hearing the warm conversation mumbled through the closed door made me think of where I *could be* if Michael wasn't a jackass.

Well, screw him.

I crammed my feet into my shoes and headed for the window. I paused before I touched the latch, remembering that the front gate was warded to only open for the Kales.

Then I got an idea. *Can I trick the magic into thinking I was a Kale?*

On quiet feet, I threw open the closet door. The rich scent of ground sage rolled from the hung garments. I grabbed one of Michael's shirts and went back to the window.

Quietly, I pushed it open. The still autumn air wasn't as abrasive as it was before. It smelled like freedom and friendly smiles. Stepping onto the porch, I eased the window closed behind me. Leaves and pine needles crunched under foot as I approached the gate. My heart thumped excitedly against my chest.

I wrapped the shirt around my fist and grabbed the gate. *Please let this work.* With a deep breath, I leaned back . . . and the gate cracked open.

Yes!

The brilliant blue sky flared with a spiderweb of magic.

My heart sank. There was no way someone didn't see that.

I looked up the road just as Michael Ported to the top of the hill.

Dropping the shirt, I dove through the gate. I yanked sharply on my magic to Port. Before I took two steps, Michael was in front of me.

He knocked my feet out from under me. I landed on my back with the crunch of rocks and dried leaves. My magic snapped back into my core.

Michael lifted his boot with a look of pure rage. As he aimed it at my chest, I pitched my weight forward and swept my legs into his. He stumbled back, fighting for his balance.

"What the fuck are you doing?" he snapped, as I got to my feet.

"Since you were preoccupied with your feast, I thought you wouldn't miss me." My tone matched his.

"I told you no."

"You don't even want me here!" My voice bounced from one side of the pine trees that lined the road to the other. "So why does it matter? I'd be doing us both a favor if I left for the night."

"Remember the last time I let you out of my sight?" he hissed. "You disappeared for *five months*. So, forgive me if I'm a little hesitant."

"What if I promised I'd stay—"

His bitter laugh silenced my argument. "You can't make promises *while you're sneaking off the property*." He struck my shoulder, spinning me toward the gate. Planting both hands against my shoulder blades, he shoved me through the gate and slammed it closed behind us.

With a flare of gold, the magic resealed the property. He scooped his shirt from the gravel and stormed back up the drive.

That son of a bitch.

My anger erupted like a volcano. My hands clenched at my sides and for a blink I saw red.

"You're not planning on getting me out of The Trial, are you?" I stormed past him. Spinning around, I walked backwards to nail him with a gaze so intense only molten lava could replicate it.

"You almost convinced me, with everything you've been saying in training, and the cute little defense moves you've been teaching me. Seriously, *Oscar*-worthy performance." I gave him a double thumbs-up.

"But then I started thinking . . ." A stiff breeze whipped my hair from one shoulder to the other. "If Lawrence can use this Trial as his own personal playground, why couldn't you? How did Master Lenin phrase it?"

I paused, but the silence was anything but thoughtful.

"If Lawrence plays his cards right, he gets more ammo for this bullshit war. So, that means you," continuing my stride backward, I pointed at his chest, "are making the same play. Except you have another goal aside from Master Lenin's."

At the top of the hill, I pivoted on my heel and faced the yard. It took a great deal of effort to keep the tears out of my voice.

"It would be perfect if I died in The Trial. No one would blame you. How could they if my greatest fears just ripped out my throat? The Masters might even feel sorry for you and then you'd get twice the points." Now I was yelling. "That's why you ran into the room to be my Guardian. This was your plan all along!" Pulling up short, I spun toward the silent man in black. "Are you going to say anything?"

"I would if you stopped to take a damn breath," he snapped. "You're my assignment."

I flinched.

"I signed a contract vowing I would do everything in my power to help you through The Trial. Unlike you, my word actually means something."

"I don't trust you."

"Fine by me." Shoving past me, he yanked open the door. "This Trial is a means to an end. You are a means to an end. The sooner you get that into your head, the better."

"Screw you, Michael."

Ducking my head, I didn't let him see the tears falling down my cheeks as I brushed past him. Flying down the hall, for the second time that day, I slammed the door.

My face was cold from the autumn air, making my tears feel as if they were on fire. I kept quiet, not wanting to give him the satisfaction of knowing he hurt me.

I brushed away the tears with the sleeve of my sweater and texted Blake. I told him Michael kicked my ass during training and I was planning to sleep the rest of the day. He responded with disappointment and tried to convince me otherwise. I didn't answer, hoping he thought I had fallen asleep.

I sat on the bed and pulled the full plate into my lap. The stuffing no longer steamed. The sweet potatoes lost their shine, and the turkey gravy had a film over the top.

I ate the cold feast only out of principle; I wasn't about to waste food. I had gone hungry too often to ignore a full plate.

31

The First Trial

The day of the First Trial, my stomach was in knots.

I could barely swallow my own spit without wanting to throw up. As Michael and I sat in our shared living room, a breakfast of orange slices and toast between us, he watched every flinch and nervous bounce of my knee.

"Charlie," he said, pulling my attention from the door. "Eat something."

My stomach rolled. I shook my head.

"You'll pass out if you go into The Trial on an empty stomach." He picked up an orange slice and peeled off the rind. "Come on."

He seemed to be as cool as a cucumber. Despite what he said, his dream was about to come true. There was about to be one less Hart in the world.

Classic Charlie move, I thought dryly. *Jumping into something before testing the waters. Why did I put my scroll in that chest?* I was too scared to remember how much I wanted a title.

I picked up a piece of toast and tore it in half, and then in half again and again. Crumbs bounced off the plate and sprinkled the table top.

Michael tossed the orange into his mouth. "Charlie. Eat."

Knowing that he would start threatening next, I lifted the toast to my mouth and nibbled on the crust. It sucked all the moisture from my mouth.

Knock, knock.

I jumped to my feet, dropping the toast. An explosion of crumbs fell to the floor.

Licking the juice from his fingers, Michael coolly rose and opened the door.

"Good morning, Master Harlan." He bowed his head.

"Morning, Guardian Kale." The European Academy School Master looked past him. "Morning, Contestant Heart."

I managed a small wave, but my arm trembled.

Master Harlan lowered his voice, probably hoping to spare me another rush of nerves. It didn't work. "The Masters have arrived. Here is a change of clothes for Contestant Heart." He handed Michael a black briefcase with my Contestant number painted in gold. "Your earpieces are in there as well. We'll be starting in fifteen minutes."

"Thank you, sir." Michael took the briefcase.

"Good luck, Contestant Heart," Master Harlan called to me.

Michael closed the door and relocked it before I could thank him. He placed the briefcase on the coffee table and grabbed the latch. Magic shocked his thumb with a sharp pop. Mumbling a curse, Michael jerked his hand back.

The lid opened with a click. In the largest compartment was a stack of clothes. Michael tossed them to me.

"Go change. I want you to stretch in them so they don't pinch you."

The stack shook in my arms as I closed myself in my room. The outfit consisted of a brown tank top covered by a leather jacket and a pair of brown fitted pants. The shoes were light with good traction. It almost felt like I was barefoot.

When I stepped back into the living room, Michael looked up from his phone. Rising from the armchair, he handed me a black bead no bigger than an M&M.

"Put this in your ear. It'll enable us to talk while you're in The Trial."

If I had a dime for all of the times I was handed a random magic object, I would have enough money to live on the moon.

I slipped the bead into my ear. With a tingle of magic, it expanded, shaping perfectly to my ear.

Michael's eyes locked on to my shaking hands. Taking a knife from the right side of his holster, he stepped close to secure it to my belt.

"Have you picked out my headstone?" Walking away from him, I stopped before the wall of glass overlooking the Field. "Who am I kidding? You'll probably just leave my body in The Trial, right? Why waste the time burying me?"

"During Guardian orientation, Lenin told us we had one job," he said evenly. "And that was to get our Contestants across the finish line. I'm going to get you out of this alive."

I believed him just as much as he believed me. My fingers curled painfully into my palms.

"Start your stretches," he said, as he headed back to the door. "And lock the door behind me." The door closed firmly behind him.

As I slid the deadbolt in place, I wondered if that would be the last time I saw the smirking bastard in black. Before I could take joy in that thought, my stomach rolled.

I barely made it to the bathroom before I rejected the few nibbles of toast. Spitting into the toilet, I rolled onto my back. The cold tile felt good against my feverish skin.

"Contestants," Master Lenin's voice blared through the room. "When your name is called, step through the glass and up to the door with your number. Good luck."

If there was anything else in my stomach, I would've puked again. Rising on unsteady legs, I returned to the wall of glass.

One by one, Master Lenin called out each Contestant.

Emeka stood tall.

Anna was gorgeous with her flaming hair.

Blake looked strong.

Clarence's ruffled hair looked as if he had just woken up from a nap and this was a mild inconvenience.

Daniel showed his nerves by clenching and unclenching his hands.

"Contestant Fifteen, Charlie Heart."

My stomach clenched so hard I thought it was trying to strangle itself.

I stepped through the glass and shivered at the cold, slick feeling. As I crossed the grass, a piano played from somewhere on the terrace. I stopped a few feet from my door. A gold fifteen was pressed into the middle of it.

I looked over my shoulder as Contestants continued to file out onto the grass. The Masters stood near the railing, looking down at us with mild interest. Soft conversations played from cluster to cluster.

The women were dressed elegantly in gold gowns. A few men wore gold suits. Even the tall tables they stood around were draped in golden cloths.

Upon seeing me, some Masters leaned closer together. The whispers grew louder. One of them caught my eye, a red-haired woman by herself. She was too far away to confirm, but it looked like she was staring right at me.

I looked at the third floor where the judges were hidden behind black glass. I wondered how many were up there. *How many did I have to impress to earn a title?*

"Here's how this is going to work."

I jumped, hearing Michael from the earpiece.

"When Master Lenin tells you, you'll step forward and open the door. The Masters have a tablet where they can pick which Contestant to watch. They can hear everything we say, so don't say anything you wouldn't say to the world."

"Noted." I clenched my shaking hands into fists.

"Remember to say what's wrong or I can't help you. I can see everything you see, but I can't read your mind."

Yeah, help kill me. My knees started to feel weak. "I hope this is worth it."

"Here are your twenty-one Contestants." Master Lenin's voice boomed over the stadium. "Are we ready?"

The Masters went completely silent.

I closed my eyes. If my heart pumped any faster, I was going to pass out.

How can a door be so threatening? It looked so ordinary; black wood, a gold frame, and an unassuming door handle.

"Get ready," Michael said.

My heart doubled its gait.

"Contestants!" Master Lenin's voice echoed from one side of the Field to the other. "You may begin."

Contestants launched forward. The Masters cheered and clinked their glasses as Contestants flung open their doors.

"Charlie, move!"

My feet were still firmly planted in place. I forced myself forward, to close the space between me and the door.

So, this was it. My first fear.

"Did Master Lenin or Master Hart say which order the fears came in? Like mild to strong?" I asked, clutching my hands like a desperate prayer.

"No."

Oh, God. I forced myself to take my wand from the sheath on my hip; it shook in my grasp. Then, against everything logical, I gripped the cold door handle.

Come on, Charlie. You faced a demon and jumped seven hundred feet out of a tower. You can walk through a door. You can prove him wrong.

As I turned the handle, the door pulled out of my hand and swung open without a sound. I raised my wand, expecting something to jump out.

But nothing did. Silent darkness stared back at me.

Before I could talk myself out of it, I stepped forward.

As soon as my foot hit the floor, color flared. Carpet grew out of it like grass. Paint rippled over the walls. Pictures, bookcases, and a bed blossomed from the drywall. At the foot of the unmade bed, a body manifested out of the dull carpet.

He was sprawled across the floor on his belly, shirtless. Both of his arms were thrown protectively over his head. Deep slashes split his dark skin, pulling away from the spine and ribcage.

"No!" I would know that head of curls anywhere. Blake.

Jumping through the door, I fell to my knees beside him. The metallic stench of blood almost made me gag. My hands trembled as I grabbed his shoulders. They were cold.

"What am I looking at?" Michael asked, but I could hardly hear him over my racing heartbeat.

I blinked rapidly, trying to disprove the reality in front of me. I had just seen Blake on the Field. I knew that. Yet, when I turned over the body and saw his colorless face and dull eyes, I couldn't stop the sob that shook my shoulders.

"Behind you!"

I was grabbed by the hair and yanked to my feet. My back slammed into his flabby chest.

"So, you finally decided to come back?" Denny hissed in my ear. The sound of his voice took me back to the small house on Haven Avenue in Salina, Kansas. As easily as he had spoken, my resolve was stripped. In a flash, I was the scared girl with no last name and no way out.

Denny shoved me forward. I slammed into the bookcase. It rocked back into the wall with a heavy thud. Books tumbled to the carpet as I spun to face him.

"You know what the punishment is for leaving. Who's going to stop me now?" He motioned to the body on the floor. His belt clinked as he loosened the clasp and pulled it free from the loop of his jeans. "Your charming Brit got what was coming to him. It's just you and me now."

Wrapping the belt around his knuckles, he slammed his fist into my face.

I landed hard on my shoulder. Flipping onto my back, I scrambled away from him. My heart nearly stopped when my back hit the wall. I had nowhere to go.

My wand. Where's my wand?

My eyes flew around the carpet. It was still beside Blake's broken body. I dove forward. Denny grabbed my ankle and dragged me farther into the room, away from my only defense.

Reaching down, he grabbed me by the throat and hauled me to my feet. Slamming me back into the wall, he squeezed.

His fingers dug into my skin, barring the air from my lungs. Black dots began to fill my vision. Instinctively, I moved my arm up and over. Slamming my arm on his wrists, I broke his hold and whipped my elbow into his nose.

With a crack and a scream, he let go. I slid to the ground. I would have loved nothing more than to sit and get drunk on oxygen, but I couldn't let him get the upper hand.

Pushing myself to my feet, I balled my hands into fists. The scars on my back prickled with memories.

All fear dissolved when I looked at him. My blood went hot as the magic in my chest ignited and rolled through my veins.

I planted my shoe into his stomach. The sneaky bastard grabbed my ankle and pulled me to the ground. He jumped up, ready to kick, but I slammed my foot into his knee. He tipped backward. The base of his skull caught the edge of his bookcase.

I dove for my wand and jumped to my feet. Panting, I stood over him with it aimed at his chest.

But he wasn't moving. His eyes gaped at the ceiling. A puddle of blood grew out from under his head.

I staggered back and dropped onto the bed, unable to look away.

" . . . you listen to me!?" Michael yelled from the earpiece.

"What have you done to me?" My hands shook.

"I taught you how to protect yourself. It's nice to know you were paying attention. Remind me when this is over to take you to an ear specialist. Your hearing is shit," he growled.

"I'm sorry I couldn't hear you while I was being choked." I meant to snap but it just sounded tired.

That got his attention. "Are you ok?"

"Nothing's broken."

"That's not what I asked."

I tried to wipe the feeling of Denny's skin off me. "I killed him."

"Unfortunately, he's just a projection from your mind. The real son of a bitch is very much alive. Despite not hearing a word I said, you did good."

"Don't." My hand twitched toward my ear with the intention to remove the earpiece. "Don't congratulate me on this."

"Looks like the bastard deserved it. Do you want to cut out his heart? It brings another level of satisfaction."

"You're disgusting." My stomach contents started to climb up my throat.

"Don't knock it till you try it."

I refused to respond or even look at either of the bodies behind me as I struggled to my feet. I turned toward the bedroom door, but there wasn't any. The wall where the door used to be was smooth and whole.

Where am I supposed to go? I looked back over Denny's room but everything was the same. My eyes landed on the closet. *That couldn't be it.*

Then again, if I could walk through glass and doors can open to different countries, maybe this one could lead to the next fear.

I walked over to the closet and pulled it open. Just like the first door, I was met by the darkness of The Trial.

I took a deep breath and looked behind at my past. "Wanna bet on what comes next?"

"I don't have a clue," he said. "You?"

"Not one." I stepped into the darkness.

32

The Second Fear Escape

My foot didn't hit the floor.

Before I could grab the doorframe, I fell over the edge. I didn't have time to scream as I tumbled through the air.

Flashbacks of when I fell from the North Tower blurred the lines of reality and memory. I couldn't tell if I was thinking about it or reliving it as I—

I hit the ground, *hard*. All the air ejected out of my lungs, making them feel like they were going to burst. Vaguely, I heard Michael talking but I didn't catch a word over the pounding in my skull.

Finally, I was able to gasp for a breath. I choked and coughed.

"Are you good?" Michael asked.

I nodded, still coughing.

"Good, then you need to get up. You're wasting time."

"Give me a break," I wheezed. "I can hardly breathe—"

"I need you to see this because I don't know where you are." The urgency in his voice forced me to open my eyes.

Above me, the sky was a dismal grey. That's when I noticed the lack of sound. I strained my ears for even the faintest noise. Dread seeped into my bones. Nothing good came from silence.

I sat up. In front of me was a city of tall skyscrapers unlike any I had ever seen. It was dark and the air was humid. It was clean of dust and trash. The street in front of me stretched beyond the range of my vision. Cars sat in the road like they were frozen in traffic. They weren't running and no one was inside.

"What is it?" he asked.

I shook my head. "I don't recognize it. Do you see anything?" My eyes darted from one shadow to the next. I gripped my wand so hard, it only caused the shakiness in my hands to be more prominent.

Michael didn't answer right away. "I'll tell you, but you need to keep it together."

I really don't like the sound of that.

"The city is infested with Dellamora."

I slapped a hand over my mouth to keep any panic from escaping. My eyes scanned everything, waiting for something to move. Everything in me was running: my heart, my blood, my magic, and, worst of all, my imagination.

Run.

Run where? There was darkness to my back and the city in front. There was nowhere else to go.

"Right now," he continued calmly, "they have no idea you're there. If you keep quiet, I can lead you to your next door without you having to encounter any."

I clenched my teeth to keep my mouth shut. I breathed through my nose to slow my panic, but it did nothing to loosen fear's strangling grip.

"Do you know how to kill one?" His smooth tone helped a bit.

I nodded, recalling Brandy's lesson at the beginning of the year. "Take off the head."

"Correct. That means you need to be ready to do that. Take out the knife."

It felt like my whole arm shook as I traded out my wand.

"When you go to take off the head, stab deep. Start on the far side of the neck and pull it to the other side. Use both hands. You might have to do it twice to fully sever the head. You'll need to be quick. It won't sit still while you do this."

A gag worked up my throat. Hopefully, I wouldn't have to do any of that.

"Start moving."

I gripped the knife with both hands and a prayer. When I stepped forward, the large city swallowed the sound of my footsteps.

"Stick to the buildings. You don't want to be in the open."

Keeping close to the sidewalk, I ventured a block and then another and another. My head was on a swivel. I left no shadow unchecked and then I checked again.

"Stop."

My feet instantly obeyed.

Clicking, like the sound of a tongue, drifted around the corner. I flattened myself against the skyscraper. That sound matched what I heard during Brandy's lesson.

"There are three around the corner." Michael kept his voice low and even. "They haven't smelled you yet."

My heart jumped at the word 'yet.'

"So, I need you to do something."

I squeezed my eyes shut.

"Look around the corner. Tell me what you see."

I rested my head against the cold wall of the building. "Isn't that your job?"

"If you don't look for yourself, you could miss something and ruin what I'm trying to teach you. Take a look."

"I can't." Even whispering felt dangerously loud.

"You have to if you want to get out of there."

I captured my bottom lip between my teeth. I counted to five and opened my eyes. My legs shook as I moved toward the edge. When my shoulder was aligned with the corner, I leaned around. Even though I was expecting it, that didn't stop my heart from freaking out when I saw them.

The horrible creatures were on the side of the building. Their clawed appendages sank into the wooden scaffolding of the building construction. Suspended over the sidewalk, their pale bodies seemed to glow in the dim lighting.

I flipped back around the corner.

Run.

"What did you see?" Michael asked.

"Th—they're on the walls." Hardly any sound passed my lips.

"What else did you see?"

"Nothing."

"Then look again."

Run.

Never before had I been so paralyzed by fear that I couldn't follow my core instinct.

I clenched my hands tightly on the knife; my skin stretched painfully over my knuckles. I forced myself to lean around the corner again. I locked my knees to keep myself from moving prematurely.

The Dellamora were completely still. As my eyes ran over their bony bodies, I saw what Michael wanted me to notice.

"Their eyes are closed."

"Good. What does that mean?"

Turning back around, I shook my head. "I don't know."

"Didn't you have a lesson on Dellamora?"

"Yeah, but that implies the teacher actually taught us something."

"Who was your teacher?"

"Brandy Charles."

"Huh." There was too much disdain and loathing for that one word to carry. "It seems the teaching quality at the Magisterium has gone down since I left."

If this were a normal situation, I would've laughed.

"The Dellamora are resting," he explained. "They don't sleep. This state is as close as they get. Basically, their senses aren't as sharp. That doesn't mean you can start singing, but you can run across the street without being noticed if you remain quiet."

Finally. Somebody, somewhere was smiling on me. I peeked around the corner once more. They hadn't moved.

You can do this, Charlie. You're good at running.

I took a deep breath and stepped into the open. Rising onto my tiptoes, I bounded across the street and flattened my back against the adjacent building. Looking back, the monsters hadn't moved.

Cheese and rice, it worked. I leaned against the skyscraper and let relief drown me.

"Well done." From the sound of his voice, he might have been smiling.

Not wanting to hang around any longer, I started down the deserted street. Moving more quickly, I crossed two more city blocks.

"Stop."

I froze, not because of his command. My muscles were pulled tight with fear as a Dellamora stepped into the street.

Hunched over at the waist, its glassy black eyes scanned its dismal surroundings. It almost looked bored.

Like a serpent, its tongue lashed out of its mouth. It raised its nose into the air. Its curled spine kept it from rising too high. A growl purred out of its throat.

It smelled me.

Run.

My foot slid back. There was a doorway to my left. Maybe I could duck in before—

"Stay where you are. It hasn't seen you."

The creature turned its head to look further up the street. I didn't hesitate. I leapt into the alcove and pressed my back firmly against the cool stone.

"Congratulations. It heard you." Irritation rimmed his voice.

My lungs refused to hold a good breath of air. My whole body shook against the wall.

Run.

"It's coming around the corner."

Every joint and muscle locked as if they were trying to imitate the wall behind me.

"Charlie, you need to pin it face down. Then you have to sever its vocal cords before it can scream. If you don't, the three around the corner, and the four down the street are going to join the hunt."

There were more? Cheese and rice.

The knife was slick with sweat in my hand.

"NOW!"

My stomach lurched. I sprang around the corner and knocked into the creature. We tumbled over until I pinned it on its back. Without thinking, I sliced the knife across its throat.

Hot black blood sprayed across my chest. The Dellamora opened its mouth, but no sound came out.

I drove the knife into the left side of the neck. Readjusting my grip, I yanked it to the other. I miscalculated how much force to use. The head was still attached.

The creature struggled under me. Its clawed fingers punctured my jacket and ripped into my shoulders. I cried out as the monster rolled me onto the sidewalk.

I managed to bring my knees between us, giving me enough leverage to put my forearm on its chest.

The nearly decapitated head dangled from the last few surviving ligaments. It continued to snap at me. Its horribly long teeth grazed my cheek. Blood, black and thick as syrup, sprayed from its wound, clotting in my hair and my skin.

At the near taste of human flesh, the Dellamora doubled its efforts to bite me. The clawed feet cut into my shins.

"Grab the knife!" Michael yelled.

Somehow the blade was still embedded in its flesh. Bracing the weight of the monster on one forearm, I grabbed the hilt. The Dellamora pulled one clawed hand from my shoulder and grabbed my arm. As its claws broke my skin, I reinserted the knife and sliced.

The snapping head dropped to the cement and rolled into the gutter. The body went limp above me.

Gagging, I shoved it off of me and scrambled back.

"Time to go. You've got the attention of the others."

Cheese and rice. Staggering to my feet, I collected the blood-slick knife and bolted down the street. I followed Michael's voice without hesitation. He directed me down alleys and across streets. All the while, the scampering of clawed feet pursued me.

Turning the corner, right in the middle of the intersection, was the door. I had never been so excited to see an inanimate object in my entire life.

Without slowing down, my shoulder slammed into the wood at the same time my black bloody fingers grabbed the handle. The wood darkened as the frame glimmered with gold.

I twisted the handle and threw open the door, ready to get out of this particular hell.

A scream ripped through the air.

I spun around expecting to see a horde of Dellamora charging me, but the streets were empty. The scream was different. This one sounded . . . human.

"What was that?" I asked, searching the shadows.

"Don't worry about it."

Another yell followed.

"That sounds—that doesn't sound like a Dellamora."

"Charlie," Michael said sternly. "Go through the door. You're about to have company."

That didn't answer my question. "They wouldn't put two Contestants in the same Trial, right?"

Silence.

"Michael." I released the door knob. "Tell me there isn't someone else in here."

He sighed. "It's Contestant Eight."

33

Contestant Eight

Emeka Selasi?

"He's handling his own Dellamora problem, which means they're distracted," Michael said. "*Go.*"

That scream sounded like he wasn't handling anything. Since I was no longer touching the door, it started to fade back to its blank state. I thought of how he helped me in Creature Studies. With a curse, I bolted toward the sound.

"Wow!" Michael exclaimed. "What are you doing?"

"He needs help."

"Who cares?"

Another scream from Emeka echoed down the street. I pushed myself faster.

"Charlie, this Trial is meant to test its Contestants. If he can't handle it, he's not worthy of a Master's title."

"And if he fails and dies? That's all just a part of The Trial?"

"Yes."

"Screw that."

"Head back to the door," Michael snapped. "You can't save him."

"Watch me!"

The sound he made was a mix of curses and exasperation. "Will you at least stop before you go barreling in like an idiot? You're bleeding and he has company that would love to eat you too."

That got my attention. I ducked into a tight alley. "You have sixty seconds."

He muttered something under his breath before saying louder, "There are three Dellamora with him and more on the way. Four more are tracking you a block over." Just as he said this, one of the beasts charged right by where I was hiding.

"How many are coming?"

"Ten—it's getting close to fifteen."

Maybe this wasn't such a good idea. Shaking that thought from my head, I peered into the street. It was empty at the moment. "I have to help him."

"Actually, you don't. I'm not letting you rui—"

"I'm not asking for permission. When Miss Charles," her name even tasted bad, "taught our class about Dellamora, she brought one into the room and let it out of its cage. It came toward me and Emeka cut off the head. I owe him."

A growl of exasperation rumbled from the earpiece. "Down the alley to the right. Take out your wand."

Trading the knife for my wand, the carvings lit up the moment I touched it.

I sprinted down the alley and took the first right. A block down, I burst into the street and saw him.

Emeka was on his back. There was a Dellamora a couple feet from him without a head. He was barely keeping the remaining two from latching onto his neck. Excited screams from the other creatures echoed in the distance.

I charged out of the alley and fired. My ward struck the Dellamora, sweeping them off him. The creatures flipped back to their feet. Their lips pulled away from their hideous teeth as they smiled at their new dinner guest.

"Slash your wand in a horizontal movement," Michael barked. "Picture your magic being sharp like a sword."

The Dellamora leapt forward. Whipping my wand over my head, a thin trail of magic cut through the air and severed one head. As the body fell, it tripped the other one. The second didn't care much about me, it dove back to Emeka.

My magic arched across the street and sliced it through. Its body crashed to the asphalt in a tumble of limbs as its head bounced onto the sidewalk.

I picked up Emeka's fallen wand and knelt by him. "Are you ok?"

He stared at me, breathing hard.

I slapped his cheek. "Hey. Are you hurt?" I looked around to make sure we were still the only two things moving.

Slowly, he nodded. "My ankle, but that is all."

His ankle was a bloody mess of claw marks. "Shit."

"Time to go," Michael urged me.

Ignoring him, I tore off my jacket. Taking the knife to the leather, I sliced it in strips. I had no idea what I was doing. I just covered the wounds the best I could.

"What are you doing here?" Emeka asked, watching me closely. "I thought we could not enter each other's fears."

"Based on this shit," I wiped his blood off my hands, "I think my fear is being hunted. What about you?"

"Being helpless."

"Looks like you're in the right place for that." I got to my feet and held out my hand.

He didn't grab it. "Why help me? It was stupid. Even my Guardian saw I was past helping and stopped instructing me."

"He has a point," Michael muttered.

I ignored both of them. "Unless you want to meet their friends," I nodded toward the bodies oozing black goo, "I suggest we have this conversation while we're moving."

A bit impatient, I grabbed his arm and hauled him to his feet. I shoved his wand into his hand and turned back to the alley.

"Don't you fu—" Michael groaned. "Charlie. Turn around."

I turned to find a wand in my face. My eyes narrowed. "You're kidding me."

"This is where I say I told you so," Michael said flatly.

"Shut up," I growled.

"Quiet!" Emeka tightened the grip on his wand. Magic flared in the designs. "I'm not stupid."

"I never said you were. But I'm starting to think otherwise."

"For the love of God, now is not the time to be a smartass!" Michael hissed.

"Stop talking to your Guardian." Emeka limped forward. "You think I'm an idiot? You're just going to help me? No. You're going to use me to earn more points with the Masters. Give me your earpiece. Now!"

Irritation ignited in my chest. *Really? I just saved his life and this was how he was going to thank me?*

I slammed my foot into his ankle. He screamed as blood seeped from my poorly wrapped bandage. He fell back to the ground.

I stomped my foot over his hand, crushing his wand to the asphalt. "Listen carefully because I'm only going to say this once." I paused to make sure I had his attention. When he didn't interrupt, I went on. "I'm here to help you—"

"You did. Now—" Michael started.

"I'm not talking to you," I snapped. I turned back to Emeka. "If I wanted to kill you, I would've let you be the distraction while I ran to my door. That's what my Guardian was telling me to do."

A shriek echoed down the street.

"Your loyal followers are right around the corner," Michael growled in my ear.

"We can go to the door together," I told the other Contestant, "or I can leave you here to be chewed on like a stick of gum. Your choice."

"Why?" he asked. "You could be out of here and place."

"You helped me in class. I owed you."

Emeka looked at me for a couple seconds. Then he nodded. "Alright."

I helped him back to his feet and stooped down to grab his wand.

"If you hand that to him, I swear—"

"Swear all you want, Guardian Kale," I said as I handed the wand to Emeka. But I tightened my grip before he could pull it away. "If you use this on me, I will leave you here. I'll hate it, but I'll do it."

"You have my word." Emeka took a step back, taking his wand with him. We stood there for a couple seconds, testing to see how much his word was worth. When nothing happened, I nodded.

"Guardian Kale, can I have directions back to the door please?"

He took a slow, calming, deep breath. "Take the alley to your left."

"How fast can you run on that ankle?" I asked Emeka.

He looked down at the poorly wrapped mess. "Fast enough."

"Good. Let's get out of here." I started off toward the alley.

We made it out and across the street before he started to fall behind. Keeping my curses to myself, I slowed down. After a few more blocks, he fell against the wall.

"He's slowing you down. And you've got incoming," Michael announced.

I looked down the street and then back to Emeka. If I stuck with him, both of us could get killed. Ignoring Michael, I pulled his arm over my shoulders. "Come on. We're close."

We moved slower than either of us liked. With every step Emeka took, blood seeped from the bandage. We were leaving a nice, bloody bread-crumb trail for the Dellamora to follow.

Finally, we turned the corner and there was the door; our ticket out of hell.

I dragged him faster across the intersection. My shoulder burned under his weight, but I didn't want to stay longer than I had to.

A growling screech came from down the block.

At the door, I grabbed the handle and pushed it open. Darkness never looked so appealing. I moved to step through, but I slammed into a wall of glass, or what felt like glass.

"What the hell?" I tried to push through again and was met by the same force.

Emeka mumbled something that sounded like a curse. "It won't let both of us through."

"He's right," Michael confirmed. "The portal is only made for one. That's how they keep the Dellamora in here."

The Dellamora cries grew louder. One rounded the corner, its nose close to the ground, sniffing the bloody trail. When it saw us, it screeched with delight. Two more bolted around the corner. And then three more, then five. A large group bolted into the street and I lost count.

Emeka tugged out of my grip and shoved me. I landed on my tailbone just as he grabbed the door handle. The wood changed to colors of sand and yellow.

Without a word, or even looking back, he opened the door and jumped through. The door slammed closed behind him and disappeared with a flash of gold.

34

Get Out of the Water

I gaped at where the door used to be. *That son of a bitch.*

"This is where I say 'I told you so'," Michael snapped. "You need to get up. Now!"

I jumped to my feet and slashed my wand at the newcomers. My aim went wild with panic. The ward sliced one Dellamora in half while it only hacked off limbs from a couple others.

Leaving the Dellamora to crawl after me, I bolted down the street. "Please tell me there's another door." I crossed my fingers as I took alleys and shortcuts to lose the pack of Dellamora.

A blast of wind tore around the corner and blew around me. Magic scraped and stung my skin.

The buildings groaned with a metallic whine as their windows rattled in their frames. It sounded like a thousand rattlesnakes rose into defensive positions. The cars along the side of the street vibrated into each other, setting off their blaring alarms.

All of it stopped as suddenly as it started. All was quiet. Even the Dellamora.

I pushed the hair out of my face. "What was that?"

"Your Trial is changing." The anger in Michael's voice was gone. If anything, he sounded curious.

"Changing?" I looked up and down the street. As far as I could see, nothing had moved an inch. "What do you mean 'changing'?"

"It's making room for something."

Before I could ask what, a groan slithered down the street. One of the tallest buildings of the skyline tilted toward the ground.

The windows shattered as it split in half. The skyscraper crashed into

222

the surrounding buildings and then toppled into another. The deafening crash of glass and metal rolled down the street, creating a cloud of dust. The growing storm consumed everything as it rolled toward me.

"Get into one of the cars and shut the door," Michael barked.

Doing as he ordered, I threw myself into a minivan and slammed the door. I curled up on the floor, wrapped my arms around my head, and waited.

Slowly, the sharp taps of glass shards pelted the car. Gradually it built until it was pounding. The car jerked. The sun was blocked out.

The wind flipped the car, causing the windows to shatter. Digging my knees into the seat, I tried to stay where I was. The vehicle skidded. Sparks shot across my skin and glass tangled in my hair.

The car slammed into a light pole, jarring me from my hiding place. I fell onto the glass-coated ceiling. The dust cleared and the wind calmed. Rolling on my side, I winced as glass cut into my hands.

"Hey, Guardian." I gritted my teeth as I crawled out of the car. "Do you mind telling me the next time a building is going to spontaneously snap in half?"

"None of this would've happened if you had just left him." The bastard sounded way too calm for the situation.

"You know," I pulled myself out onto the asphalt, "Blake was bragging about you. He said you knew things were going to happen before they did. Remind me to tell him he's full of shit."

"Contestant Heart, I'd appreciate some respect, seeing as I'm giving my time to help you."

Getting to my feet, I leaned against the car and picked a few shards of glass from my palms. "Of course, Guardian Kale. Please accept my sincerest apology."

"You're wasting time."

Now, I did roll my eyes. If I had a dollar for every time he said that, I could buy myself a title.

I wiped my hands on my pants to get the blood off. After a couple swipes, I gave up. I was about to leave when I saw my wand wasn't in the pocket of my jeans. Peering back into the car, I found it surrounded by glass.

"Is there another door?"

"Yes. It's ten blocks to the—Don't move."

I scooted further into the car. "What?" I cursed as glass poked into my knees. "Do you even know the word . . ." Not a foot from the car was a Dellamora. The monster looked like a porcupine with glass for quills. Black blood painted most of its skin.

"I told you not to move."

"Are you really scolding me right now?" I hissed. I looked at my wand. It was two inches from my hand. Then I looked back at the Dellamora.

Its nostrils flared as it lowered its head to the ground. Its tongue scraped across the asphalt right where a bloody shard of glass rested.

Brandy's words echoed back to me as its eyes locked on my bloody hands. *"Some specialists think they prefer to eat the ones with a lot of magic."*

It lunged forward.

I grabbed my wand and threw myself backward. Crazed with hunger, it wormed its way into the car. Its clawed hands groped for me. I scrambled back, through the broken window, and onto my feet.

It screamed in frustration. Another creature answered its call as it turned the corner. It brought friends. Lots of them.

"Run! Take the first left."

Following the angry GPS in my ear, I squeezed into a tight alley. Shadows played along the ground. I looked up. They were running across the roof.

I burst back into the open. More spilled into the street from other blocks and buildings. I grabbed a light post and swung myself around the corner.

"No! You needed to go left."

"I can't!" I yelled over their shrieks. Between two buildings I saw what looked like a lake behind them. When the building had crashed, it must have been from a change in the landscape. I ran toward it, hoping the Dellamora didn't like water.

Running into the cold waves, I clenched my wand between my teeth and dove under the surface. Exhausted, I couldn't stay under very long. I pulled up, gasping for air, as my feet found the bottom. The waves lapped against my chest.

Spinning around, I watched the Dellamora crowd the shore. They had stopped right before the water's edge.

My heart jumped when something brushed across my ankle. The murky water hid whatever it was.

"This lake is empty, right?" I looked at the rippling water. *Please be a goldfish.*

Michael cursed, causing me to jump. "Get out of the water."

"And go where? Michael—"

A shriek stopped me.

One Dellamora had entered the water. It stumbled through the waves toward me.

I lifted my wand to cast it ashore but the Dellamora stopped. It tilted its head at the water. With a jolt, it spun back to shore just as it was pulled under the surface.

"Charlie, get out of the wa—"

Something wrapped around my leg seconds before I was jerked beneath the surface. Blindly, I fired. What the burst of magic illuminated made me scream.

Wrapped around my leg was a tentacle, and it was connected to a giant squid.

Another tentacle bound my legs together. Another cold and slimy appendage wrapped around my neck. With one powerful tug, it dragged me through the water toward a mouth lined with teeth.

My wand was trapped at my side. My lungs burned for oxygen and my panicked heart raced frantically in my chest.

From my earpiece, there was only silence.

Michael was finally getting what he wanted.

Desperate for air, my lungs forced me to take a deep breath. But no air came. Just cold, brown water.

35

So That's What Drowning Feels Like

It was like someone punched me in the chest with a sledgehammer. My lungs contracted. Cold water surged up my throat and spilled over my cheeks. Air rushed into my lungs. I gasped, sputtered, and coughed like I was trying to expel all of my organs.

Strong hands rolled me to my side as I sucked in air like a vacuum. A sharp ringing filled my ears.

"Charlie, honey, can you look at me?"

Breathing hard, I flopped back onto the grass. I squinted against the bright stadium lights. Someone leaned over me. My eyes focused on Helen and . . . Michael?

"What are you doing here?" I croaked.

"I told you I'd get you out." A drop of water slid from his hair and landed on my cheek.

I looked around and saw we were in the middle of the Trial Field. Helen was on the other side of me, getting ready to stick my arm with a needle. At my feet was a Trial door.

I was out.

And I was alive.

I looked back at Michael. Breathing hard, he sat back on his knees and closed his eyes. If I didn't know better, I'd say he looked relieved. Soaking wet, his shirt clung to his chest like a second skin. On his belly was a divot. *So he does have a belly button.*

"You're welcome for saving your ass." He raked his hands through his wet hair. "By the way, I used the Save."

A laugh tickled up my sore throat. "There's literally nothing I care less about than that Save." I closed my eyes and just breathed. I would never take air for granted again. "Thank you. Drowning really sucked."

"Charlie, can you look at me?" Helen asked again.

Forcing my eyes open, I rolled my head toward her.

"How many fingers am I holding up?" She held up one hand.

"Four."

"What's your middle name?"

"I don't have one."

"Can you feel this?" She ran her finger along the underside of my foot. Lifting my head, I saw I was missing a shoe.

Nodding, I dropped my head back to the grass.

"You were out for almost three minutes," Michael said. "How do you feel?"

"Been better. You?"

"Been worse." Another smile softened his face. "You had me worried for a moment."

"I thought you couldn't feel anything besides anger and disgust."

"What can I say? You bring out the worst in me."

"Guardian Kale." Helen shot an uneasy glance over her shoulder. "Maybe we should move this conversation elsewhere."

His dark eyes followed her gaze to the terrace of Masters. With a sharp nod, he knelt beside me and helped me sit up.

With my head swimming, I gripped his arm until I could see again. Then Michael pulled me to my feet.

My eyes jumped to the balcony. None of the Masters were interested in our trio. They were in tight clusters watching Contestants who were still in The Trial. But there was one Master who wasn't around any of the others.

A woman with bright red hair stood by herself before the railing. It was the same woman I had noticed before The Trial started. Motionless, she watched us cross the lawn.

Keeping close beside me, Michael guided me toward a first-aid tent secured by two guards in black and gold armor. Inside, away from the bright lights, he helped me onto a stretcher. I hadn't been sitting for more than a few seconds before Helen stuck a needle into my arm.

"Ow." The potion spread through my body, warming as it went.

The Masters' whispered conversations rose with excitement as another Contestant crossed the finishing line. The fact I could hear them surprised me. I thought I would be getting yelled at by now.

Michael stood on the far side watching me. Of course, there was no readable emotion on his face, but there was also no glare.

Helen stuck me with another needle. As soon as the potion entered my blood, my skin itched.

"Well," I took a deep breath. "Let me have it."

His eyebrow twitched with a question. "Have what?"

"You're supposed to be yelling at me because you think what I did was stupid—"

"It was stupid. He left you."

"It was still good." He didn't respond. "So, go on and get it out. How badly did I mess up?"

"I'm not going to yell."

I balked. "Really?"

Helen even stopped to look at him over her shoulder. When he caught her looking, she quickly went back to mixing potions.

"I don't know whether I should strangle you or shake your hand. No one saves another Contestant in The Trial. Especially a Hart." His eyes dipped over me like he was trying to find something he had overlooked. "You surprised me."

That was something I thought I would never hear him say.

He turned to Helen, who was coming at me with another needle. "Is she ok?"

"She's more than ok," Helen said cheerfully. "She's resilient. Once her wounds are disinfected, she'll be right as rain. Although she may slur for a bit."

A giggle filled the tent. It took me a few seconds to realize it came from me. I slapped my hand over my mouth to silence it but the giggle continued to bubble through my fingers.

Michael shot a concerned look at Helen. In reply, she held up an empty syringe.

The tent flap moved aside for Master Lenin to step inside. Today he chose a navy suit with gold lining the lapel and the buttons of his coat. On the right sleeve of his jacket were the numbers thirteen, fourteen, and fifteen in gold.

"Hiya." I waved. My fingers blurred before my eyes, looking like hummingbird wings in flight. *Wow.*

"Guardian Kale," Master Lenin said tightly, "can I speak to you for a moment?"

"Wasgoinon?" My tongue felt like the size of a basketball. I stuck it out, going cross-eyed to look at it. It looked normal. Blinking slowly, I turned to Helen. "What'd ya gimme?"

Helen pressed her lips together to keep from laughing. "Is everything alright, Master Lenin?"

"I'm afraid not." His galvanized gaze didn't leave Michael's. "In order for The Trial to finish, all living Contestants must cross the finish line. You took her out of The Trial. *Not* to the finish line. Therefore, The Trial isn't over."

"Why does that man?" I shook my head. "I mean . . . what does that mean?" *Did I say that whole sentence backwards?*

"Trouble," Michael muttered.

Master Lenin nodded tightly. "Come with me, please. Helen, when Contestant Heart is cleared, send her to Harlan's office."

"Yes, sir."

Michael followed the School Master from the tent. I wasn't sure if they floated or walked.

"Alright." Helen exposed the inside of my elbow again. "This is your last shot. It should calm the reactions from the disinfectant." She pressed the needle into my skin and squeezed the green liquid inside.

I gritted my teeth as a cold sweat broke out over my body. It stung wherever there was a wound. After a few minutes, my temperature mellowed and my brain cleared.

Helen pulled a stool from under the bed and sat beside me. She handed me a small bottle that smelled like rotting meat.

I took the bottle of healing potion and tipped it back. As soon as it hit my tongue, it melted into the taste of fresh peaches. My toes curled and my stomach warmed. The throbbing in my throat and arms faded. When I was done, my nose burned, but I wasn't bleeding or sore.

"I don't care what anyone says," Helen said, breaking the silence. "I appreciate what you did for that Contestant. It's refreshing, especially in The Trial. But be prepared. You're going to get a lot of backlash for it." She squeezed my arm.

When didn't I get backlash for something I did?

"You're free to go to Master Harlan's office. But take it slow." Her nose crinkled. "I would suggest you shower first. You smell."

I lifted a lock of hair to my nose and winced. It reeked of lake water and mud. "Noted."

I slipped through the tent flap and back to the Trial Field. Keeping my head down, I made a beeline for my room. I was picturing fuzzy socks and a thick sweater.

Just as I was about to step through the glass, something silver flashed in the corner of my eye. A knife slammed into the glass, centimeters from my head. A severed lock of hair slipped from my shoulder and drifted to the ground.

I spun around, breathing hard. Contestant Nineteen, Dmitri Theodore, stood a few paces away.

I glanced back at the knife. The handle was made of ivory. Carved into the bone was the letter 'T.'

"Nice throw." My hands shook at my sides.

"Why? I missed." His large hands played with a matching knife. Something glowed between his fingers. The knife beside me ripped out of the wall and spun back to him. He caught it easily.

Now he had two knives and I had nothing.

"You flinch," he chuckled. "Like a little bird."

He jolted forward.

My breath hitched as I jumped back through the glass. What was I going to do if he followed me?

But he didn't. He had faked coming closer to get a reaction. Twirling the knives through his fingers, he shook his head. Laughing, he turned and walked away.

36

Consequences

Breathing heavily, I stood there until he was out of sight. Still shaking, I turned my back to the Trial Field. The afternoon sun cast elongated shadows across the apartment.

Darkness was my friend in Kansas. But after everything I had gone through in The Trial, it wasn't friendly at all.

You're safe, I chanted to myself, but it did no good. I pulled out my wand and crept into Michael's room. I checked his bathroom and closet before doing the same to mine.

I closed my bedroom door and levitated my dresser in front of it. Exhausted, I fell onto the bed. Staring at the ceiling, I felt hollow.

For two months, my life had revolved around the First Trial. Now it was over.

I made it.

I faced two out of three of my fears and lived. I finished the First Trial, which meant I could survive another.

I wasn't delusional to think that the first one didn't kick my ass. But now I knew what to expect. Michael and I could double down, and I would do better in the second one.

If I made it to the Second Trial.

I have to keep going. All of this couldn't have been for nothing.

I jumped into the shower and washed The Trial from my skin. Twisting my wet hair into a knot on top of my head, I pulled on my light blue hoodie, sweatpants, and the thickest socks I could find.

Leaving the apartment, I went into the European Academy and followed the signs to Master Harlan's office. Outside the door were two guards in sage green and white.

They must have been expecting me, because I didn't have to say anything or even knock. They opened the doors and released a torrent of sounds.

All seven School Masters crowded in front of Master Harlan's desk, and all of them were talking at once.

Passionate hand gestures, crossed arms, kneading foreheads, shaking heads . . . it was a mess. Tension was so high, the lights were pulsing. And it wasn't because of me.

At their center, with his hands in his pockets, Lawrence Hart looked from one Master to the next. The guard with the grey streaked hair and dark red armor stood in the corner.

I spotted Michael on the other side of the room.

While every School Master was too busy arguing to see me enter, the guard with the cobalt eyes latched onto me. Without turning his head, he watched me move toward my Guardian.

Master Harlan's office was much like the rest of the school: grey stone and white tile. Bright green moss grew out of the corners of the room and along the sides of the desk. The same white flowers covered the ceiling to bathe the room in light.

The walls were completely covered in pictures of students. The wall directly behind the desk housed Trial Winners. Master Lenin kept his pictures in neat rows, while Master Harlan had his spaced randomly in different sized frames. Some were even on top of each other to make room for other photos.

"What's going on?" I asked Michael over the noise.

"You didn't cross the finish line, which means the First Trial isn't over."

"Ok . . ." I wasn't really sure what that meant. "Can I just go to the finish line and skip over?" *No way it's going to be that easy.*

Michael shook his head. "Once out of The Trial, you can't go back in unless you go from the start."

My heart dropped. "Why?"

"To keep Contestants from cheating, the creators put up wards that only allow you to get there by the doors inside The Trial. You would have to go through each fear again."

My heart squeezed in panic. "I barely survived the first time."

"My thoughts exactly."

"So, if I can't go back in, does that mean I'm disqualified?" My heart sank. *So much for earning a title.*

He pointed to the tattoo around my wrist. "Your Contestant tattoo is still active. The wards in it were created to protect you. If anyone outside The Trial staff tried to hurt you, the same thing would happen to them instead." Seeing my confusion, he elaborated. "If someone hit you, their cheek would sting instead of yours. Since I'm your Guardian, a member of The Trial staff, if I struck you, you would still feel it.

"A couple Trials ago, a Contestant tried to keep that protection and ran. The Trial went unfinished for two years before they found him and forced him to finish the remaining Trials. After that, the Masters created a failsafe. If a Contestant doesn't cross the finish line within a year of the start of The Trial, the tattoo will release a poison. Once the Contestant is dead, The Trial would be over and the winners could be named. The magic at the finish line disarms the ward in the tattoo."

"So, it's either go back in or get poisoned?" With each word, my stomach dropped lower.

He nodded his head toward the arguing Masters. "They'll think of something."

Lawrence raised his hand. Instantly, the Masters stopped talking. "I hear your frustrations and I share them. But we aren't going to accomplish anything if we cannot hear each other." He replaced his hands in his pockets. "A Contestant not crossing a finish line with the failsafe tattoo has never happened. So, we need to work together to decide the best course of action."

Master Lenin didn't waste any time. "We should send her back in immediately."

"Of course you would say that," Markus Han, the Serpentine Master, said. "She already knows her first two fears. If we send her back, she'll do better than her first performance. She could get higher marks from the judges."

"I don't think we should be worrying about the competition aspect right now," Master Lenin said icily.

"Han is right." Master Finch nodded. "That's giving the Magisterium an unfair advantage."

"We could create another Trial for her to go through," Master Harlan suggested from behind his desk.

Lawrence shook his head. "It would take at least two months to come up with another Trial. That would put everything behind schedule. The

Contestants signed contracts binding them until the end of the school year. We would have to write up new contracts extending into the summer."

"Her Trial would not be judged the same as the others," Master Theodore added. "I prefer to win fairly."

"Would you please shut up?" Master Aluna snarled. "No school has won twice in a row. Your school won't change that."

"Let's stay on topic." Lawrence looked between the two. "Guardian Kale, you've been quiet. I'm sure you have something to add."

All the Masters turned in our direction. Many of them blinked in surprise, as if they hadn't expected me to be there.

Michael straightened. "We could send her back into The Trial, but don't have the judges watch until she's facing her third fear."

My heart skipped and my magic bubbled through my chest. Denny and belts, Dellamora and underwater creatures flashed through my mind.

"Unfortunately, The Trial has already started to deteriorate," Lawrence said. "If we send her back in this state, she could get trapped. If we want to revive it, we would need a substantial amount of magic and time."

"What about a dream walking potion?" Master Loran asked in a gentle voice. "It has the same effects of drawing out fears. The judges can use a projection stone to watch how she does."

"Dream walking potions are detrimental to the mind, even if you dilute it," Michael scoffed. "*If* she woke up, she'd be insane."

"That would make it easier for the judges," Master Theodore chuckled.

"We could tap into her mind and create an illusion," Master Finch offered.

"It wouldn't be dangerous enough." Master Lenin aggressively kneaded his forehead. "The illusions wouldn't be able to harm her, so there wouldn't be any incentive to try. Plus, that still doesn't solve her crossing the finish line." Master Lenin shook his head. "I'm not seeing how we can send her back."

I was almost dizzy with all of the options being thrown around. None of them were particularly kind to me. I needed a Master's title, but I also couldn't go back into The Trial of my fears.

And with that, the answer was simple.

"Maybe you don't have to," I blurted.

All eyes turned to me.

I swallowed around my racing heartbeat. "The contract doesn't say which finish line I have to cross. You could send me to the Second Trial. And I'll cross that finish line."

Guardian Theodore laughed. "You did not finish the First Trial. What makes you think you could do any better in the second?"

"I agree," Michael said, glaring down at me. "You can't handle another Trial." He looked to the Masters. "Is there some sort of ward or enchantment that can keep the tattoo from poisoning her?"

Master Lenin shook his head. "The tattoo cannot be tampered with. If someone tries, the poison would be activated immediately."

"You could just cut off her arm," Master Han said in a bored tone. "Then the poison wouldn't have a body to destroy."

I grabbed my wrist, squeezing until my hand went numb.

Master Lenin gaped at the other School Master. "You want to cripple one of my students?"

"You can give her an enchanted hand as a replacement." Master Han shrugged.

"There's no reason to maim the child," Lawrence said evenly, putting a halt to Master Han's next remark. "I think the solution is clear. Contestant Heart should Ascend to the Second Trial where she can cross the finish line. If," his blue-grey eyes cut to Michael, "her Guardian doesn't make the same mistake."

"She can't handle another Trial," Michael said sternly.

"You should've thought of that before you pulled her out," Lawrence said.

"She wasn't breathing."

"With your reputation, that shouldn't have been an issue. You could've revived her in The Trial and then taken her to the finish line. Unless you think you're incapable of saving people."

Michael flinched ever so slightly.

"So, we're going to rig our own game now?" Master Finch asked. He tapped his cane against the stone floor. "If we do this, we ruin the integrity of the whole Trial."

"If we don't, we condemn my student to death." Master Lenin bristled.

No one argued that.

Lawrence nodded. "Then she continues."

I bit the inside of my cheek to keep my expression blank. I was a mess of conflicting emotions. I was still on the road to a title, away from Achilles Heel. But I was also continuing in The Trial. I almost didn't survive the first one. Would I survive another?

Lawrence glanced at his watch. "I'm going to inform the judges of our decision. At the Ascending Ceremony, it will appear as if she was chosen for the Second Trial. No one outside this room will know the real reason she is there." He looked at each Master until they nodded.

Then his gaze locked onto mine. "Contestant Heart, you have two more months in my Trial. That means you have two months to do a better job than what you did today." His eyes flickered to the man beside me. "I suggest you find yourself a better Guardian; one who thinks before he acts."

With that, he strolled from the room with his armored guard in tow.

The School Masters quickly followed after him. None of them were stupid enough to glance Michael's way. The only one who made any noise as he left was Master Theodore, who chuckled all the way down the hall.

Master Harlan followed the last School Master and closed the door behind them. He stood by the door, tapping his shoe against the stone floor.

"If I didn't know any better," he said, looking at Master Lenin, "I'd think Master Hart planned that. You both look like idiots and he's the reluctant savior."

"Which proves my theory that he's trying to earn points with all the Masters, School Masters included." Master Lenin's eyes shifted to Michael. "You're down one."

"I don't play games, especially ones involving Lawrence," Michael said dryly.

Master Harlan chuckled. "Too bad. Masters love games. Present company included. From what I've been hearing, they've been looking forward to this for years. Bets have been cast and now the race has started."

"Are you insinuating that I'm a racehorse?" Michael asked.

The European Master nodded. "If it makes you feel better, you're the best horse we've got."

Michael shook his head.

"After today, that's debatable." Master Lenin crossed his arms. "You do realize he's going to use this to his advantage."

"She's breathing, Lenin." Michael gestured toward me. "I'm not going to apologize for that. If you're so worried about him using it with the other Masters, then get ahead of it." Michael put a hand on my shoulder and guided me to the door.

Without saying a word, Michael opened the door and marched down the hall. Between a jog and a brisk walk, he threw open the door to our apartment and he stalked toward his bedroom.

"Why'd you do it?" I called after him.

He stopped in the doorway.

"Pull me out of the water. Why did you do it?" I stuffed my hands in the pocket of my hoodie. "You want me dead. You could have let me drown and been done with it."

He nodded slowly. "I could have . . . when I saw you drowning, I didn't think. I just used the Save."

That surprised me. I felt like all he ever did was think. "Thank you." I cleared my throat. "I'm sorry for everything I said before. About you using The Trial to kill me."

"It was a good plan, if I wasn't a man of my word. I signed a contract saying I would get you out, and I told you I would. And then you threw that away by suggesting that you Ascend to the next Trial." He slammed his fist into the doorframe. "Dammit! None of this would've happened if you had just left that Contestant. Better yet, if you had stayed out of The Trial."

This was the reaction I had expected in the medical tent.

"I helped Emeka because it was the right thing to do," I said evenly.

"It was stupid and reckless and it almost cost you your life."

"I thought you brought me into this war to save people."

"Is that what you're doing in this Trial? Trying to save people or yourself?" he snapped.

"Both. I am doing this for me *and* to keep Blake from your butcher knife."

"That wasn't me," he said, referring to Blake's severed finger.

"I don't care."

He shook his head. "You can't always be the hero. It'll get you killed."

"You seem to be doing just fine."

"Yeah, well, I ruin everything, one way or another." Leaning against the doorframe, he pinched his eyes closed. "In this world, everything comes with a price. You need to think before you rush into things."

I dropped my gaze to my fiddling hands. *What would saving someone cost?*

"Three Contestants died today. That number could double for the next Trial and you just threw yourself in without looking."

"Three?" I had to have heard him wrong.

"It's what happens when Contestants clash and they want to come out on top." He scrubbed a hand over his tired face.

"How can you say that so calmly?" My stomach pinched. "Who were they?"

"Marissa Larson from Aquarius, Leon Smith from the European Academy, and Josephine Gloriana Paulo from Serpentine."

My relief was short-lived when I asked the next question. "How?"

"Larson and Smith were killed by their fears. Gloriana Paulo got between another Contestant and the finish line."

"Which Contestant?"

"Contestant Nineteen."

I had already come to the conclusion I didn't like Dmitri Theodore. This added to my case.

"You still want to participate in the next one?" Michael asked.

My confidence wavered. But I lifted my chin. "Yes. Are you still going to help me?"

He nodded. "Against my better judgment, I've got your back."

I paused, taken aback. "Really?"

"Really." He nodded to my bedroom. "Head back to the Magisterium. Don't talk to anyone about Ascending to the next Trial." Turning on his heel, he shut the door behind him.

I stood there. Stunned.

37

Seafood and Fries

The transporter took me to the heart of the Magisterium by the clock tower.

My stomach grumbled at the tangy scent of barbeque. But it dropped at the sight of the full dining room. Luckily, none of them were able to watch The Trial. But once they saw me, I assumed they would pepper me with questions.

I remembered there was a bag of chips in my room. That paired with peace and quiet sounded like a great dinner. As I made my way to the stairs, I spotted a familiar face in the infirmary.

With closed eyes, Emeka leaned back against the headboard. His ankle was wrapped in blue gauze. There was an IV bag hanging beside his bed filled with a pink potion. Other than that, he looked unscathed.

Just as I was about to head up to my room, he opened his eyes and saw me.

"Hi." I gave him a little wave, feeling awkward. "Glad to see you got to the finish line."

He said nothing.

Clearing my throat, I stepped closer. "How are you?"

"Alive." He shifted away from me. "What are you doing here?"

"I was on my way to dinner." There was a pause. "I'm glad you're ok."

"I said I'm alive," he repeated tightly. "What happened in that Trial . . . don't act like we're friends. You didn't do me any favors by helping me."

Confusion clouded my head. "If I didn't, you never would've gotten to the door. *My* door, by the way."

"My School Master thinks I can't complete a Trial by myself. She doesn't think I should Ascend. My Guardian is thinking of dropping me," he said bitterly.

My head reeled. *But I—I helped him. It was the right thing to do. Right?* "I didn't mean for that to happen."

"Obviously." He stared across the room, refusing to even glance my way. "Just . . . leave me alone. You've done enough."

Flinching, I dropped my gaze to the floor. I wanted to defend myself, but talking back never got me anywhere good. Keeping my eyes on the floor, I left the infirmary. *So much for doing something good.*

"Hey, you."

Daniel stood in the doorway of the dining room with a soft smile. "Glad to see you made it out." He studied my expression. "You don't look too happy."

"Well," I leaned against the stair banister, "I spent most of the afternoon making a fool of myself in front of the most powerful people on the planet. My Guardian is getting lip for my performance. And I could've just single-handedly ruined Emeka's chances in The Trial. But other than that, I've had a great day."

"What about Emeka?"

I shook my head. "Nothing. I'm just really ready for today to be over."

Daniel crossed the space between us and leaned against the railing next to me. The silence of the stairwell made the roar of the dining room sound even more daunting.

"I got permission from Master Lenin to go home for dinner," Daniel said after a minute. "You can come, if you like."

I looked at him in surprise. "What?"

His dimple deepened. "You're going to make me say it, aren't you?" Color settled into his cheeks as he awkwardly rubbed the back of his neck. "Would you . . . like to have dinner with me?"

Maybe it was because I faced some of my nightmares and survived, but I was feeling a little brave. When I met his hopeful gaze, I didn't shrink away.

My heart felt like it was glowing. "I'd love to."

He smiled wide enough to make his eyes squint. "Your Guardian won't mind?"

I haven't given a damn what he minds since I met him. "Not at all."

Grinning from ear to ear, he threaded my arm through his. Pushing his sleeve up his forearm, he pressed the face of his watch. It glowed a familiar gold and Ported us out of the Magisterium.

When my eyes refocused, we stood on the beach.

I breathed in the familiar smell of salt and tide. As sand shifted under my feet, my muscles started to relax. The rolling waves of mixing blues brought me the first sense of peace since I had gone back to the Magisterium.

"That's a cool watch." I gestured to his wrist. "I didn't realize transporters could be anything but marbles."

"Master Lenin gave it to me when I made Records Keeper. It can be enchanted to Port to a couple different locations. It's how I get into the Magisterium." Daniel unthreaded my arm from his and started down the boardwalk.

A little way down the beach, he stepped into a small seafood restaurant. As soon as he crossed the threshold, shouts filled the air. People stood on their chairs and clapped. Others waved from their tables and called out his name. Some even came up and slapped him on the back.

He smiled wide, his dimples in full view. As he moved through the crowd, he waved to the hostess. A pretty black-haired girl gave him a hug before leading us to a table in the back.

The restaurant, still electric with energy, went back to their meals. The waitress came over with two glasses filled with a clear liquid. As soon as Daniel grabbed his glass, the liquid fizzed and darkened into a root beer.

"Does this place have," I dropped my voice, "magic?"

Daniel nodded. "But only if you look for it. Just in case Regs come in."

I settled against the red leather booth and grabbed my glass. The liquid inside immediately brightened to a cheerful yellow. I took a sip of the lemonade and looked at the pictures covering the wall of our booth. Instantly, I recognized Daniel in a few, varying in age.

As silverware scraped against plates and mindless chatter filled my ears, my mind wandered. Everything I had been through flashed before my eyes. Then it faded into questions.

What would've been behind the third door? What would've happened if Michael hadn't pulled me out?

A warm hand brushed across mine. "Where are you?"

Words came without me realizing it, "The Trial."

His hand stilled. "What about it?"

I was about to blurt out that I didn't face my third fear. But his Contestant tattoo caught my attention.

Pulling his arm toward me, I ran my fingers over the ink. Magic tickled my fingertips. Inside the black band were pictures. The one closest to his Contestant number was a throne. Next to it was a castle that melted into a crashing wave.

I looked down at mine, but it was still empty and black.

"When did this happen?" I couldn't stop looking at it.

"Right after I crossed the finish line."

Ah, that's why mine hadn't changed, because I didn't cross the finish line.

"Each picture is for a fear I conquered." He pointed to the first one. "A School Master."

I bit my tongue. *Don't ask, don't—*

"If you bite your tongue like that, you'll chomp right through it," he chuckled.

My cheeks heated. "Why are you afraid of a School Master?"

"I'm not. My father, my biological father is Thomas Harlan, the School Master of the European Academy."

I fought for control over my face. Judging by the amusement on his, I was losing that battle. "I never would've guessed—just because I didn't know they had time for families."

"They don't. That's why my mom left."

Curiosity took over me. "Why are you afraid of him?" *Stupid Charlie!* "Sorry. You don't have to answer that."

"You don't have to apologize. It sounds pitiful, I know . . . But I think everyone's afraid of their father in some way."

I swallowed my laugh. *He's preaching to the choir.*

"What about the others?"

He pointed to the castle. "My failure in the form of the Magisterium. Each floor contained something to conquer from my classes through the years."

I smiled. "I have no doubt you passed that with flying colors."

His smile returned. "It was easier than I thought it was going to be." He looked at the last image. By the look on his face, I knew this was the hardest part of The Trial. "A tsunami hit my house. It was weird . . . When I stepped through the door, I thought I was Ported home. We sat down and had dinner. A part of me kept trying to remind myself it wasn't real; it was just The Trial. But it felt so real . . .

"The ground started to shake. A wave flew over the house and we were covered in seconds." He was staring so hard at the tabletop I thought he was going to burn a hole through it. "There was a lot of debris in the water. I almost didn't make it to the surface. Even when I did, I kept ramming into stuff."

My eyes jumped up from his tattoo. The bright afternoon sunshine hit his skin. Against the black stone of the school, I had missed the faint bruises marring his face.

"How did you find the door?"

"I didn't." He looked at the picture on the wall. "My sister did. It was in a flooded building."

A memory flashed to when I was under water. The ceiling and walls suddenly felt like they were pressing in. I tugged at the collar of my shirt.

"What about your Trial?" he asked.

I ran my fingers through the condensation on the outside of my glass. "My Trial started with my foster dad. My second door led me to a city full of Dellamora."

"Damn." His eyes dropped to my wrist.

I quickly pulled my sleeve over my tattoo that hadn't changed.

"Here you go!" An older woman approached our table and set down two plates of snow crab legs, even though we hadn't ordered anything yet. There was a small cup of butter and a large basket of french fries. But she didn't move away.

Daniel cleared his throat. "Thanks, Mom."

Right away, I could see they shared the same warm brown eyes and caramel hair.

She nudged her son. "Do I have to ask to be introduced?"

His cheeks pinkened when he glanced at me. "Charlie, this is my mom, Kathy."

A broad smile revealed her own dimples. "Stand up and give me a hug."

I jerked to my feet at the order and was immediately enveloped in her warm arms. She smelled like butter. When she pulled back, she kept her arms on my shoulders.

"You're even prettier in person."

Wow. I was so taken aback I had to remember how to string words together. "Th—thank you."

She shot a glance at her son. "We've heard so much about you."

"Mom," Daniel dropped his head into his hands. "I just got her here. Please don't send her running."

"Sorry, sorry." Not two seconds had gone by before she blurted, "Your father will want to meet her. Tim!"

"I knew there was a reason why I wasn't going to bring you here," he muttered. "This is why."

A short man with glasses came through the kitchen doors. He was splattered with various cooking ingredients and sprinkled with flour.

Daniel got to his feet with a sigh. "This is my stepfather, Tim." He glanced toward the back. "Since you've met my parents, you might as well meet the rest of the family. Where's the monster?"

"Erin's learning to fry shrimp with Sam." Tim looked over his shoulder.

Following his gaze, I saw a girl with a bright auburn ponytail. Beside her was a lanky man, much taller than Daniel. Both of them jumped back as flames flashed from the fryer.

"Oh, dear! It was nice to meet you, Charlie!" Kathy briskly walked back to the kitchen.

"It's weird having a son for a Contestant, but to have two in the same room!" Tim slapped Daniel on the back. "Are you going to help my boy win?"

"Dad." Daniel's eyes nearly popped out of his head.

"I'm just asking. If any of the Magisterium Contestants are going to Ascend, it's going to be you. I doubt their performances even compare—"

"*Dad.*" There was a hint of embarrassment on Daniel's face.

"I thought no one could see the performances but Masters," I said.

"Families are the exception," Daniel explained.

I smiled at Tim. "From what I know of Daniel, he doesn't need much help."

Tim Phillips beamed. "Me neither. Master Lenin called right after he crossed the line. He said that his performance was one of the better ones. Erin was excited that she was on TV."

Daniel's eyes widened. "You let her watch?"

"Of course not. She used an invisibility charm and stood behind us. Didn't know she was even there until she cheered when she saw herself on the screen." Another blast of fire came from the kitchen. "Excuse me." He ran into the kitchen waving his wand. Erin laughed at Sam's missing eyebrow.

Daniel slid back into his booth and grabbed a crab leg. "Teaching Erin to fry is a bad idea. She can bake anything, but if it isn't a dessert, she burns it." He snapped the leg in half and dunked the pink meat in the butter.

"At least she can cook. I nearly burned my house down trying to make boxed mac and cheese in the microwave." Copying him, I grabbed a leg and broke its shell. The fleshy center flew across the table.

He jerked out of the way just in time for it to miss his eye. Fighting a smile, he handed me a shell cracker. "How'd you manage to do that with mac and cheese? From a box, no less."

Blushing, I grabbed the utensil and placed a new crab leg inside. "I put the mac and cheese in a pot and then put the pot in the microwave."

A laugh snorted out of his nose. "You did not."

"Oh, I did." My hands stilled. *I learned true, desperate hunger in that house.*

I squeezed the two metal arms of the cracker. The shell broke apart violently. Shards exploded across the table.

Daniel flinched back as one went for his forehead. "How old were you?"

"Ten, I think." Carefully, I put the utensil on the plate. I ate what crab meat I had collected, but decided to turn to something safer, like french fries. I grabbed the bottle of ketchup and put a small puddle on the corner of the plate.

"And no one taught you that metal in the microwave was a bad idea?" he chuckled. He cracked the crab shell and broke it the rest of the way with his fingers.

"No one taught me how to cook. After that whole incident, no one even let me near a stove." I took a french fry and dunked it into the ketchup puddle.

Daniel shook his head and tossed his bite of meat into his mouth. "Erin would probably love to teach you a few things, if you want."

"Somehow, I'd manage to cut off her hand, or mine—with a spoon."

His eyebrows rose. "Now that's talent."

"I'm talented at creating disasters." I dipped another french fry.

"I doubt that." He gave me a skeptical look as he picked up another crab leg.

"Just give me time, and I'll prove it."

He paused long enough to swallow. "I have a disaster story for you. One time I decided to bake cookies for the family. I thought the recipe called for too much butter and sugar, so I just didn't add it."

I saw where this was going. "Oh, no."

"They were like rocks. You think I'm kidding? They were so bad, my mom put them outside for the birds. After a whole week, we threw them away because not even wild animals would touch them."

I threw back my head laughing. "Ok. My mac and cheese, while a little bit charred, was still edible."

His eyes widened. "You ate it?"

"Of course. I was starving." I struggled to keep my smile in place.

"Good God, how are you alive?"

"Pure dumb luck."

A sharp ringing cut through our laughter. Daniel licked his fingers clean and dug his phone from his pocket.

"It's not me." He looked up from his cell. "I think that's your phone."

"Oh." I pulled it from my back pocket. My mood cooled when I saw the name on the screen; JACKASS. Reality dropped into my stomach.

Somehow, I had forgotten everything outside the restaurant. I hadn't felt that normal in—well—I had never felt that normal. I forgot the effect Daniel had. With him, I wasn't a foster kid or the daughter of a dangerous Royal. I was just Charlie.

"I'll be right back." I slipped out of the booth and stepped outside. Taking a deep breath, I answered. "Hello?"

"I don't recall the Magisterium being in Camden, Maine," came Michael's greeting.

I glared at the tracking bracelet around my wrist. "Really? I had no idea."

"Don't be a smartass with me."

"I was just getting something to eat."

"I don't recall you asking for permission."

"Because I already knew your answer. Calm down, I'm coming back."

"Calm down?" he scoffed, barely handling his rage. "Get back to the castle before someone, maybe me, kills you." The connection died.

Without a choice, I replaced the phone in my pocket and returned to our booth.

Daniel smiled when he saw me coming. My heart ached when that smile dimmed at my expression. "Time to go back?"

I nodded. "I'm afraid so."

Snatching his napkin from his lap, he quickly wiped his mouth and hands. Sliding out of the booth, he waved to his family and led me toward the door.

Outside he grabbed my hand and pressed the face of his watch. When we Ported back to the Magisterium, we stood on the apartment level.

"I'm glad you came." Daniel gestured down the hall for me to go first.

"Thanks for rescuing me." I tucked a rebellious lock of hair behind my ear. "I've never had seafood before."

"That was obvious," he chuckled. "Next time, I'll ask my mom for popcorn shrimp. That way I won't have to dodge anything. But I'll make sure Erin isn't the one frying."

My cheeks ached from how wide my smile was. "Next time?"

He rubbed the back of his neck. "Would it be a bad idea if it happened again?"

"Not at all." I stopped in front of my apartment. Butterflies fluttered through my stomach when I faced him. "I'd like that."

His eyes dropped to my lips. With a sheepish grin, his gaze fell to his shoes. "Have a good night, Charlie."

"You too."

With one last smile, he slipped his hands into his pockets and turned down the hall.

I watched him go as an unfamiliar warmth spread through my chest. When he reached the stairwell, he glanced over his shoulder.

I gave a little wave, unlocked the door, and threw myself inside.

He said there would be a next time.

I felt another smile stretch over my lips. Pulling off my hoodie, I tossed it across the back of the couch. Humming, I pushed open my bedroom door. The perfect way to end today was with a tub of chocolate covered raisins.

The lights flickered on as soon as I stepped inside. I paused. A weird smell met my nose. Looking around, I found a dead mouse lying at my feet.

The Magisterium gets mice? You'd think with magic that wouldn't be an issue . . . and the fact that I'm seven stories up.

Bending down, I reached out to pick up the carcass and throw it away. I stopped when I saw it wasn't just dead. Its tiny throat was slit. A small puddle of blood surrounded the body.

From the corner of my eye, the closet door swung open.

From the darkness, something crept into the room. Clicking, like that of a tongue against the roof of a mouth, came from the creature.

I turned my head. With every inch, I prayed I wouldn't see what I thought was there.

The Dellamora's black eyes locked onto mine. Thick drool dripped from the row of narrow teeth.

It opened its horrible mouth and shrieked.

Then it jumped at me.

38

Surprise!

I Ported into the living room.

The Dellamora screamed, an earsplitting combination of a cat screech and distressed metal.

My feet slid across the hardwood as I spun toward my hoodie. My hands fumbled through the pockets. The creature crashed into the bedroom door with a hungry snarl. Sitting back on its hind legs, it pounced.

I yanked the knife from the pocket just as we collided. We tumbled onto the hardwood.

Wrapping my legs around the monster, I rolled upright and slammed the knife into the side of its neck. The tip stabbed into the floorboards. Twisting my grip, I yanked the blade over, severing the head in one clean swoop. Hot black blood sprayed up my chest and neck.

Jumping to my feet, I flipped the knife around. My eyes flew around the room. *If there was one—there had to be another—*

Something moved by the front door.

Magic sparked through my fingers as I hurled the knife.

Michael grabbed it before it could sink into his neck. His wide-eyed gaze dropped to the motionless Dellamora.

"There—" I gasped. "There was a Dellamora in my closet."

His head snapped toward the bedroom.

"I—it just came out." I pushed my hair out of my face, smearing a thick layer of black gore across my forehead.

Cheese and rice, would today never end?

Wait.

What if it never ended?

My heart skipped. My magic flared.

All around the room the lights buzzed and brightened. Michael flinched back from the sudden change.

"I never made it out," I realized, backing away from Michael. "I never made it out of The Trial."

How could I be so stupid! When I was under the water, The Trial must have changed again. It must have spat me out at the starting line with Michael.

He was my final fear.

My eyes snapped from one doorway to the next. If I opened one, would I see the waiting blackness of The Trial behind it? I had to get out. I had to get away from him.

The lights in the kitchen popped, spraying sparks and glass across the counter.

Michael dropped the knife and stepped toward me. "Charlie—"

My back hit the wall. I startled with a scream. The living room exploded with light. Fire whooshed out of the fireplace, blasting the room with heat and blackening the coffee table.

"Hey!" Michael jumped over the decapitated Dellamora and grabbed my shoulders.

My heart jumped as my magic flared brighter.

This is it.

Michael is going to kill me.

"You're out!" Michael pressed me back into the wall. He flinched as another light popped and glass rained over his head. "You're not in The Trial! I got you out!"

I grabbed his wrists. My magic flared down my arms. Just as I was about to wrench them off my shoulders, I stilled.

He wasn't reaching for my neck.

There were no weapons in his hands.

He was just holding me.

I looked up into his face, tears slipping down my cheeks.

"You're safe." His gaze held mine steadily and without malice. He wasn't glaring or smirking. His expression was earnest. "You're safe."

A sob broke through my chest. Doubling over, my forehead dropped to his chest. I cried with relief. My magic eased back into my core. The surviving bulbs returned to normal, but they barely offered any light.

Cheese and rice. My hands shook with the aftermath. I focused on my breathing, trying desperately to calm my pounding heart. All the while, I gripped his wrists, anchoring myself to reality.

I made it out.

I'm safe.

Pulling in a shaky breath, I leaned back and aligned my spine to the wall.

"I'm sorry." I raised a trembling hand to brush the tears from my cheeks.

He grabbed my wrist before I could touch my face. "You should clean up," he said softly.

My hands were completely covered in black gore. My stomach twisted at the sight.

"Come on." Releasing my wrist, his hand slid up my forearm to my elbow. "Let's get out of here."

I sniffed, shaking my head. "I should clean this up—"

"I can do that. I know how."

"You shouldn't have to—"

Pulling on his magic, he Ported us from the Magisterium. I jumped at the sharp sound of gravel beneath our feet. Seeing the darkening shadows of the ranch, my heart rate doubled.

Keeping me close, Michael guided me through the gate and into the house. The once-comforting sounds of the kitchen now sounded too loud, too sharp. I flinched at each one.

Moving quickly, Michael took me into our shared room.

"Sit." He led me over to the bed.

Dropping onto the mattress, I shoved my hands into my hair. I didn't care if they were disgusting and covered in dark goo. Closing my eyes, I breathed deeply and slowly.

I made it out.

I'm safe.

Michael left the room, and, a moment later, returned with Mrs. Kale. Wordlessly, she knelt in front of me and unzipped her white medical case.

Taking one of the syringes, she filled it half with an orange potion and then the rest of the way with one that was bright pink. I didn't feel the needle enter my skin.

"That should help her relax." Mrs. Kale closed her medical kit and stood. "I don't see any injuries."

"She doesn't have any." Michael sounded impressed.

Mrs. Kale grabbed my hands and got me to stand. Slowly, she led me to the bathroom.

"What happened?" Meg asked, hovering in the doorway.

Mrs. Kale closed the bathroom door just as Michael started his tale. Meg's curses made their way through the wood without any problem. Mrs. Kale turned on the hot water and helped me out of my ruined clothes.

When the hot spray hit my head, I sucked in a deep breath. The numb shock shrouding my body faded as the black gore ran down the drain. Retaking control of my limbs, I scrubbed until I was raw and clean.

Once I got out of the shower, I pulled on clean pajamas and slipped into bed. The room was empty and the door was firmly closed. In the stillness, a thought raced around and around my skull.

Why was there a Dellamora in my room?

That question kept my eyes from closing. I'm not sure how much time passed before Michael slipped into the room, smelling faintly of bleach.

"How did a Dellamora get into my room?" I asked when he tried to sneak by.

"You know as much as I do." He leaned against the wall and rubbed the back of his neck. "There wasn't any magic on your door and there were no signs of forced entry."

My stomach dropped. "Someone has a key to my room?"

"Not anymore. I enchanted the locks."

I nodded. "Any idea who it was?"

"There's a short list of people who know what you faced in The Trial. My money's on someone who's upset Lawrence passed you on to the Second Trial." He leaned his head against the wall.

I clutched the covers closer to my chest. For the first time, I truly wondered if I should have left Emeka and gone through the third door.

"From now on, before you go into your room, text me and I'll go in before you."

I really liked the sound of that.

He pulled his jacket from his shoulders. "Get some rest." He closed himself in the bathroom. A few minutes later, the shower facet squeaked and water sprayed against the tile wall.

I snuggled into the blankets, but I laid awake.

39

How'd You Do?

Michael stuck his head into the room before the sun was fully awake. He looked like he had slept about as well as I did. His black hair was ruffled from tossing and turning all night. His eyes were hollow and sunken.

"What time is it?" I asked. My back was to the headboard with my knees pressed against my chest.

"Six-thirty. Did you get any sleep?"

I shook my head.

"Breakfast starts at seven."

My bottom lip slipped between my teeth. Placing my wand between my hands, I twisted it back and forth.

"I have to go back?"

He nodded, sending a thick lock of hair over his forehead. "Whoever put that Dellamora in your room is going to be watching. If you don't show up, they'll think they got to you."

They kind of did. I continued to twist my wand back and forth, back and forth.

"I'm going to get some coffee." He stepped back into the hall. "Did you want some?"

My hands stilled. Bringing my gaze to his, sure enough, he was waiting for an answer. Michael had never asked to get me anything. I was almost certain he wasn't capable of it.

I shook my head.

He massaged the back of his neck. "How about some hot chocolate?"

"Pity isn't really your thing."

His eyes narrowed at my tone. "Do you want hot chocolate or not?"

There was the Michael I knew.

But still . . . why was he offering? Would he poison it? After everything he did yesterday, I doubted it.

"Will you put marshmallows in it?"

"It's too early for that much sugar."

"You can't have hot chocolate without marshmallows. It's like having a peanut butter and jelly sandwich without jelly."

Michael rolled his eyes. "Fine. It'll have marshmallows. Get dressed. We're leaving as soon as you're finished with it." He turned to the kitchen.

I sat there for a second longer, running the last few minutes through my head. That was the most normal conversation I had ever had with him.

Am I even awake?

Releasing my wand, I pinched the inside of my wrist. *Definitely awake.* I pulled on a deep blue sweater with sleeves that fell past my thumbs. I slid my wand into the side pocket of a pair of holey jeans, then laced up my white converse.

The conversation stopped when I stepped into the kitchen.

"Morning," Mrs. Kale said brightly, keeping her voice low. She picked up the orange mug beside Michael and stepped into the pantry. When she came out, there was a small mound of marshmallows floating on top.

My soul instantly warmed as I cradled the mug between my hands. Michael took a sip of his coffee and left the room.

"How are you feeling?" she asked, giving my shoulders a comforting squeeze.

"Tired. I'm really glad yesterday is over." I took a sip. The hot drink made quick work of dissolving the marshmallows into a thick, sweet foam.

"I can imagine." Dropping her hands to her sides, she stepped back into the pantry. "I think you need more marshmallows."

Before I could object, not that I wanted to, she dumped another handful into the mug.

"Would you like something to eat?" She pinched a stray curl between her fingers and tucked it behind my ear. "That's a lot of sugar to have on an empty stomach."

"We're going back to the Magisterium for breakfast."

Her lips twisted with disapproval, but she didn't voice anything she was obviously thinking. "I still think you should eat something. I made some banana muffins yesterday. Did you want one?" She was already on her way to the other side of the kitchen.

"Yes, please." I took another sip of hot chocolate.

"I'm going to take a shower. But in the meantime," she placed the muffin tin beside me, "help yourself to as many as you would like." She brushed my hair back with a smile and then, with a flurry of honeysuckle perfume, she disappeared down the hall.

Leaning my elbows against the counter, I peeled the floral wrapping from the warm muffin. The combination of banana and marshmallow-flavored hot chocolate was the best way to start the morning.

Michael's heavy boots sounded down the hallway as I was licking the crumbs off my fingers. I cradled my hot chocolate close to my chest in case he was stupid enough to try and take it away from me. If he tried, he was going to lose a hand.

I turned just as he passed the kitchen island.

"Here." He extended his hand palm up. Sitting in the center was a plain silver ring. "It's a sync ring. They're made for long distance relationships—Lauren and I used them when I went to summer camp and she was grounded."

Oh, my God. Did that mean Lauren was the rebellious one of the twins? A hundred questions rushed to my tongue.

"The ring," he said quickly, "is enchanted to connect to its twin." He held up his hand, showcasing the other ring on his thumb. "If you tap yours, I'll feel it and vice versa. Next time, if something happens and you can't call me, tap it and I'll come to you."

Careful not to touch his skin, I plucked the silver band from his palm. A slight bit of magic made the cool metal tingle against my fingertips. The ring was large, so I slid it onto my thumb. Tentatively, I tapped my finger against it.

He nodded and did the same. My ring buzzed in response.

"I'll tap twice to ask if you're ok. You'll tap twice for yes and once for no. Got it?" Gulping the rest of his coffee, he set the empty mug into the sink.

Twisting the ring around my thumb, I nodded. I didn't know why he gave it to me. I didn't think he cared that much, but I wasn't about to question it and have him take it back. Just the knowledge of having it made me feel a hundred times better.

"Are you done?" He nodded to the nearly empty mug in my hands.

I scooped out what was left of the marshmallows and licked them off my fingers. Setting the mug in the sink, I followed him down the hall and to the front gate.

On the gravel drive, he took a card from his wallet and placed it in the dirt. After he tapped it with his wand, the card glowed bright gold. It expanded and rose into a full-sized door, just as I had seen it do before.

He held it open for me to go first.

I held my breath as I stepped back into my living room at the Magisterium. I expected to see signs of the Dellamora attack, but Michael was thorough in his clean up.

A knock came at the front door.

I froze.

Michael closed the enchanted door, letting it dissolve back into the small card. Stepping in front of me, he pulled out his wand and soundlessly approached the front door.

Drawing on his magic, he slid back the deadbolt and pulled it open just enough for him to peer outside.

"Mornin'," Blake said with a tone of surprise. "Is, uh . . . is Charlie here?"

Magic slipped from Michael's wand, curling like golden smoke, to the other side of the room. The concealing charm draped over the couch, dissolving Michael's pillow and blankets from view.

The Master Hunter jerked open the door and stepped aside.

Blake's shoulders sagged when he saw me. "Hey."

My breath left me in a rush. Moving around my Guardian, I pulled Blake into my arms and held him as tightly as I could.

"What are you doing here?" I asked.

"I was in the neighborhood and thought I'd walk you to breakfast."

I knew for a fact that his room was at the very end of the South East Wing, but I wasn't going to mention it. Smiling, I stepped into the hall and together we headed for the staircase.

"What's he doing here?" Blake asked, sneaking a glance over his shoulder. Michael quietly followed a few paces behind.

"He never really left last night. We were debriefing my Trial."

Interest lit his eyes. "How'd you do?"

"I was a complete disaster. You?"

"'Bout the same, I guess. I don't know how you can face your fears and not be a sodding mess."

"Did your sneak peek help at all? The one you got for winning the Award Challenge."

He shrugged. "Knowing the fear and actually facing it are two different things. I survived, so I guess."

A moment of silence fell between us. My growing interest itched to ask what Blake had seen behind his three doors. But if I did, I would have to answer the same question, and there was no way I was going to relive that again.

I kept my eyes locked in front of me to keep myself from looking at his tattoo. When we reached the intertwining staircases, the thundering clatter of breakfast rose from the dining room to meet us. Along with the noise was the greasy scent of bacon and sausage.

Blake's stomach gurgled. "I honestly don't think I've ever been this hungry in my entire life. I hardly eat yesterday."

"I tried before The Trial. I threw up."

"Who knew you had such a nervous stomach?"

I bumped my shoulder into his. "Like you were any less nervous!"

"Oh, I was completely beside myself. Atlas hovered around me like he thought I was going to have a heart attack."

"At least you didn't hesitate before your door."

His head whipped around. "You didn't."

"Oh, but I did."

He winced.

"Charlie!"

Coming to a stop, Blake and I broke apart and looked up. Daniel rushed down to meet us, his hair wet from a shower. In his hurried descent, he brushed by Michael.

"Sorry—" Daniel stopped short when he recognized the man in black. "Oh, my God. Master—I mean, Guardian Kale—Or Master Kale. I'm so sorry. I didn't know it was you." Daniel stumbled down a few steps, giving himself more room between them.

"No harm done," Michael said coolly.

Swallowing nervously, Daniel turned around and walked at a much more controlled pace toward me and Blake.

"Mornin'!" he said cheerfully. "Did either of you get any sleep?"

"Not a damn wink." Blake continued down the stairs.

I shook my head. "I might as well have pulled an all-nighter."

"Honestly, it'll be a miracle if I ever sleep again," Blake said as he adjusted his beanie.

Sensing the conversation was spinning back to our fears, I clapped my hands in front of me and smiled. "The great news is, now that we've faced our greatest fears and survived, I have a feeling the rest of The Trial will be a breeze."

"Don't say that too loud," Daniel muttered. Placing his warm hand on the small of my back, he glanced over his shoulder at my silent Guardian. "You don't want to give them ideas."

"After yesterday," Blake shook his head, "I doubt I'll scare at anything."

Passing through the guarded dining room doors, we made our way to our usual table near the windows. Cornelia was already waiting for us with a plate of pancakes. Michael spun on his heel and headed for the kitchen doors, leaving a trail of whispered conversations in his wake.

"You did it!" Cornelia exclaimed, throwing both hands into the air. A pop and a flash burst from the center of the table. In unison, the three of us grabbed our wands.

Brightly colored confetti fluttered around our heads and landed on our shoulders. Quickly, I released my wand and smiled at her. My heart was still racing, so it felt like I was just baring my teeth at her.

"How does it feel?" Cornelia asked brightly.

"Best damn feeling in the world." Blake walked around to the other side of her and took a seat on the bench.

"You better clean this up, Common," a Royal from our Wand History class said as she stepped over the confetti.

Cornelia slouched her shoulders.

"We've got it, thank you," Daniel said coldly.

The Royal paused. "Good. We already have enough trash floating around the school." Her eyes dipped to the four pinned on Cornelia's shirt.

"What did you just say?" Blake rose to his feet.

The Royal walked on, as if he hadn't spoken. Blake moved to step over the bench, but Cornelia grabbed his hand to stop him.

"It's so unfair that we have to wait until the Viewing to see The Trial." She sat before her breakfast and cut into her pancakes. But she didn't eat.

"What's the Viewing?" I asked, trying to steer the conversation.

Blake slowly sat down.

"After the Top Seven are chosen for the Final Trial, their first two Trials are released to the public." Daniel grabbed the pitcher from the center of the table and poured himself a glass of orange juice. A slight tremor shook it as he poured.

I winced. "Cheese and rice, no one needs to see that."

"Clarence seems to think otherwise." Cornelia looked over my shoulder.

Following her gaze to Contestant Fourteen, I found him sitting at a table surrounded by other students. Leaning back onto his palms, he retold his Trial with a smirk and arrogance.

"He's been telling the same story on a loop for the last twenty minutes."

My nose wrinkled at the sight. "What an ass."

"What did he face?" Daniel asked.

"That's the thing," Cornelia turned her back to him, "he never actually says what. He only says how *masterfully he performed* and what casts he used."

"I bet he pissed himself," Blake said. "There's no way he didn't."

"He would if he had a soul." I turned my back to him, too. On the other side of the dining room, Emeka sat with a close group of his friends. They leaned forward, listening intently to every hushed word.

A wave of whispers rushed over the dining room. I didn't have to turn to know my Guardian was making his way back.

"Speaking of nightmares." Blake watched the Master Hunter cross the room. "Here comes your Guardian."

"Be nice," I laughed.

"I honestly don't know how he doesn't make your skin crawl," Cornelia said softly, as if the Master Hunter could hear her from that far.

"He's not that bad." *Cheese and rice, did I really just say that?* "I sort of . . . drowned yesterday. And he saved me." My nails bit into my palm as my lungs contracted with the memory of cold water.

"Sort of drowned?" Cornelia blurted.

"Bloody hell, Charlie." Blake's eyes flickered to my wrist. Thankfully, the blank artwork was covered by the sleeve of my deep blue sweater. "All I got was a broken arm and a couple dislocated fingers."

Daniel set his cup down with wide eyes. "You let me go on and on about how terrible my Trial was last night. You should've shut me up."

Blake's eyebrows rose at the mention of last night.

"I'm fine," I assured them. "I just might not go swimming for a while."

Michael reached our table and placed an omelet in front of me. A small chunk was cut out of the center from him testing for poisons. I picked up my fork and dove right in.

Bending toward my ear, Michael muttered, "After your last class, head back to your room. We'll have dinner at the ranch and then we can get ready for the Ascending Ceremony there."

I quickly swallowed the warm eggs. "Ok. See you later."

Straightening to his full height, Michael walked leisurely out of the room.

"I still think he's made out of nightmares," Blake said as he pulled the plate of pancakes toward himself.

Daniel and Cornelia nodded in agreement.

40

Like a Royal

Compared to the day before, the rest of the day was a breeze.

I was left alone for the most part. The arrogant Contestants like Clarence, those from the Tactical University, and the remaining Aquarius students, were plenty vocal about their Trials. Anyone curious enough to listen went to them first and left me alone.

When my last class was over, I headed to my room where Michael was waiting. Then we Ported back to the ranch. Mrs. Kale met us as soon as we came through the front door.

"Dinner is about ready. And this came for you." She handed me a silver tin with the Magisterium's crest pressed into the lid. "It's from Master Lenin."

"What is it?" Tentatively, I took it from her. I never got mail.

She shrugged and turned back to the kitchen.

"I'm going to shower." Michael moved around me to his room.

I tried to open the tin, but it wouldn't budge. I found a latch, and inscribed on it was: "open in a large area."

I headed for our shared room, but Michael was showering. I pivoted to the room across the hall. It was still empty since my bed was in Michael's room.

Standing in the doorway, I lifted the latch.

A cloud of grey and silver exploded from it. With a cry, I jumped out of the room and dropped the tin.

The mass separated and solidified into a line of dresses. Each gown floated to the far side of the room and hovered, as if they were on an invisible clothesline. They continued to fly out of the tin until the whole wall was covered.

"What the hell?" I stepped slowly toward the line of gowns. I reached out and, sure enough, they weren't an illusion. Materials of silk, sequins, satin, and chiffon met my fingers. All of it was silver or grey. Gold was the color of the first Trial, silver must be the color for the second.

"No way."

Meg stood in the doorway with her mouth open.

"What am I supposed to do with all of these?" I gestured helplessly at the line.

"You pick one to wear, obviously." She waddled out of the doorway to stand beside me. "I heard about this for Trial Contestants. Famous designers donate clothes from all around the world. If a Contestant is seen in their design, they're basically set for life."

She turned toward me with her hands clasped under her chin. "You have to let me help you pick one."

"Uh—"

"Please. God, I need something to do that doesn't involve manure or birthing facts. Please, please, please—"

"Ok, fine," I laughed. "Have at it." I stepped back from the display of silver.

Grinning like a fool, she started flipping through the collection. Her smile faded into a look of determined concentration with each dress she passed.

"I've never seen so many bows in my entire life," she said halfway down the silver line. "It's like they want you to look like the girl next door."

For the last half of the dresses, the bows were replaced by sparkles and puffy, billowing skirts.

"Am I supposed to like any of these?" I asked. "I think I hate all of them."

"Hold the phone." Meg waved her wand. All of the dresses crowded to the other side of the room, except for one. It had tight sleeves and a simple skirt that fell to the floor. Every inch of it was overflowing with silver sparkles.

"I'm not wearing that." I crossed my arms. "It looks like a fairy murder scene."

"You gave me selection privileges. No take backs."

"Did I though? I said you could *help*."

"You just said you hated them all. You're welcome to look through them to find something else."

Ugh. I had no desire to do that. The dress she picked was pretty, in a disco ball sort of way. I just wasn't used to wearing something that was supposed to draw attention. It went against my super power of blending in.

"Fine," I conceded. "I'll go with that one."

She grinned. "Wise choice. But I have just one adjustment." She aimed the glowing tip of her wand at the skirt.

I jumped forward, grabbing her sleeve. "Wow! What are you doing?"

"I think it would be cuter if it was shorter."

"You're going to make it look like I forgot pants!"

With a huff, she gave me a bone dry look. "Why are you in The Trial?"

"So this stupid tattoo doesn't poison and kill me." I held up my inked wrist.

She leaned her weight on one leg and crossed her arms over her belly. "Why are you really?"

I paused. "I want a title."

She nodded. "Exactly. If you're going to be someone the judges should award a title to, you need to look like someone who deserves one. You need to stand out and make them pay attention."

That went against everything in my nature. "But that's so short."

"Think about it like this." She put her hands on my shoulders. "Everyone is expecting a scared little girl dressed like a doll to show up and then not Ascend. If I didn't know you, I would've put money on you fainting when anyone just looked at you. You need to look like a woman who can stand by my brother and own the spot next to him. Shock and awe, babe." She flashed me a smile.

She made some good points, but there was no way I was going to show that much leg. "I'll just pick another dress."

"If you pick anything else, I'll set it on fire." When that didn't move me, her eyes narrowed. "How about this, you can cut it, or I will."

What was up with Kales and ultimatums? I took her wand and turned to the dress. Pinching the thick fabric, I moved the glowing tip toward it.

"Higher."

I moved it up an inch.

"Higher."

It had to be at my knee now. I was about to cut it when Meg rolled her eyes. "Oh, for crying out loud." She took the wand and moved it up another foot. A thread of gold sliced through the fabric before I could react.

Both of us stared at the excess fabric on the floor.

My mouth hung open.

Meg stifled a giggle. The hem was nowhere near the knee.

I stepped back, staring at the mess we had created. "Can you put it back on?"

"Yes, but I'm not going to." The look on her face scared me. She was wearing her brother's smirk. "Wait here." She came back with a pair of tall black boots.

"Oh, come on." I crossed my arms, refusing to take them from her. "You've got to be kidding."

"I'm afraid not." She offered them to me again. "I'm not letting you leave this house in anything else. You can go—"

The door squeaked open.

Meg lunged forward, yanking the dress out of the air. She hid it behind her back just as Michael stepped into the room.

It felt as if my brain had shut off and was rebooting. I could barely process what I was seeing.

He wore a tux made of velvet. Matte leather made up the collar and lapel. The shirt beneath and the tie were midnight black. The soft material was a stark contrast to the angular folds of leather that I was used to seeing.

Tonight, his hair was combed and styled. Clothed in expensive fabric, he seemed to stand straighter. Cologne drifted off his skin. The scruff shadowing his face was more sculpted.

Holy shit. He looked deadly with his leather jacket and double holster. But in that suit, he was lethal for a completely different reason.

He blinked in surprise upon seeing Meg beside me. "Why are you in here?"

"I'm bored."

Michael's eyes narrowed at my light blue hoodie. "I thought the dresses made it obvious that this was a formal event."

"I did gather that, yes," I said with a nod.

"Yet," he glanced at his watch, "we're ten minutes from leaving and you're not dressed."

"We're almost done," Meg assured him. She struggled to keep the lines of her mouth flat and unamused.

"Ten minutes." He grabbed the doorknob. "Then we're leaving in whatever condition you're in."

"I wouldn't expect anything else," I called as he closed the door.

Meg faced me with a smirk. "Case in point. Do you really want to find something else when my brother looks like that? Your best chance is in this dress." She held out the sparkling garment.

With my teeth clenched, I snatched the dress from her and stormed into the bathroom. The dress was tighter and even shorter than I expected. Saying it went to the middle of my thigh was pushing it. Between the tall black boots and the dress was a three-inch gap of skin.

"Meg, we have to pick something else." I stepped out of the bathroom. "I look—"

"Like a Royal," she finished for me. "You're enrolled as a Common, right?"

I nodded. "A Common Six."

"Well, now you look powerful. Like your real status."

"I think that defeats the purpose of enrolling me as a lower status."

"Low Commons don't get titles through The Trial." She stepped forward and thrust her hands into my hair.

"Ow, what—" I stepped out of her ruffling hands. "What was that for?"

"Just topping off the effortlessly powerful look you've got going on." She looked around. "Where's your wand?"

"In my hoodie." I threw my tousled hair over my shoulder. "Meg, I'm serious. This is too much."

She flicked her wand toward the bathroom. A second later, my wand shot out and into her hand. She then stuck it into the side of the right boot, leaving the handle in full view.

"Too late." She grinned. "You've got to go."

"No, we have time—"

The door opened and Michael's tall frame filled the doorway again. Even with the tall heeled boots, he could still look over my head. Although that's not what he was doing.

"Meg, what did you do?" His eyes jerked over me like he didn't know what to look at first or even if he believed what he was seeing.

"I just came in here to see the dresses. I didn't do a damn thing." She brushed by him. In the hallway, she shot me a wink before disappearing.

"This was your idea?" he gestured vaguely toward me.

I didn't like his tone. I squared my shoulder. "I'm wearing it, aren't I?"

His mouth opened and then immediately snapped shut. "We're going to be late."

He turned sharply on his heel and headed for the front door. *Michael was flustered.* Smiling to myself, I followed after him, with the heels clicking loudly against the floor.

On the other side of the gate, Michael Ported us from the property and onto a dark street. In front of us was a long line of limos. Each one was painted with a different Contestant number.

Playing the part of a gentleman, Michael stepped up to the limo painted with the number fifteen. He popped open the door and waited for me to get in.

Wordlessly, he slid in after me. The driver came around and closed the door after him seconds later. When the car rounded the corner, cameras flashed through the window.

Bzz.

The sync ring tapped around my thumb.

Bzz. Bzz.

Turning away from the window, I glanced across the cab. Michael looked rather calm. His watchful dark eyes peered out the window. In his lap, his fingers twisted the sync ring around and round his finger.

Bzz.

"Michael," I said softly as the ring buzzed against my thumb again. "You're tapping your ring."

He turned from the window. "What?"

I pointed to his hands in his lap. "The sync ring. You're tapping it."

His hands stilled.

"Are you ok?"

He nodded. "I don't like crowds."

The limo rounded a hedge of thick foliage and our destination came into view. The structure was old and broken down by time. There was a line of pillars, some crumbled, others cracked. At the center was a tall, arched doorway.

"Where are we?" I asked, scooting closer to him to get a better look.

"Greece." Michael smoothed his hands over his jacket. "The Trial originated here. It's tradition for Contestants to Ascend here." Michael cleared his throat when I tried to lean over him to get a better look.

I settled back in my seat.

As we drew closer, the limo passed through a wall of magic. On the other side, the building wasn't crumbled. It was as if time had never touched it.

Hundreds of torches lit up the ancient stone theater. The columns were whole and strong. The steps leading up to the arched doorway were draped with red carpet.

When each limo stopped at the bottom of the stairs, Contestant-Guardian pairs stepped out and walked to the tall door at the top. Hundreds of people and photographers lined the stairs all the way up. Keeping the crowd and photographers at bay was a line of guards in bright red armor.

Who did they belong to? The red armor of Master Theodore's military was dark and rimmed with black. These guards were in all red.

My heart hammered against my ribs when our limo stopped at the bottom. Michael popped open the door and slid out. The crowd roared and cheered. People screamed and cameras flashed from every direction.

He nodded to the crowd and offered me his hand.

Taking a deep breath for courage, I took his hand and pulled myself out of the car. The flashes of the cameras reflected off the sparkling fabric, adding another blinding element.

My nervous gaze shifted to the cameras. Every single one was looking at me. They weren't even looking at Anna Clarkson, who was dressed in a tight silver gown.

Think of the title. Act like you deserve it.

I straightened my spine. When Michael tried to place my hand on the crook of his arm, I pulled out of his grip. I planted each foot firmly on the ground and propelled myself confidently forward.

With a tight jaw, Michael fell in step with me. With matching strides, we walked side by side up the stone steps. When we reached the top, the theater was displayed before us.

The room was carved into the earth. Rows and rows of stone benches curved around the stage. A rumbling crowd eagerly sought out their seats. Just in front of the stage, the first row was made of padded silver chairs. Tall pillars outlined the whole theater. Stationed in front of each was an armored guard in bright red.

Stepping ahead of Michael, I kept walking. I didn't look at my feet. I didn't hold the railing. I kept my eyes focused on my destination.

As I approached, I saw Daniel talking with his Guardian. He wore a three piece suit and a bowtie. Each piece was a different shade of silver, ranging from dark to metallic. When he saw me, his lips parted. That look sent a smile across my lips. Feeling braver than I had ever felt, I winked.

The lights dimmed as Master Lenin walked toward the podium. Michael tapped my elbow, and led me down the row to our marked seats. All the other seated Contestants wore varying shades of silver. Seeing them all dressed to the nines with confidence in their postures, it made me glad I had worn the dress Meg picked.

Master Lenin stopped before the microphone. "Welcome, ladies and gentlemen, to the Ascending Ceremony. I know you're very eager to see who will participate in the next Trial, so I won't keep you waiting any longer.

"Please welcome Master of Combat Power, Master Hunter Lawrence Hart, who will tell us the names of those Ascending." He pulled two silver envelopes from his jacket.

Lawrence gracefully strolled up the stairs and took Master Lenin's place. The color of his suit matched the armor of the guards at the entrance and throughout the theater. *Are they his?*

"Good evening, Contestants." He carefully inspected the front row. "I was trying to think of something clever to say but I don't think we should draw this evening out any longer." The crowd cheered and he smiled in response.

"We'll start with the first string of Contestants Ascending to the Second Trial." He took the first envelope from Master Lenin. "These Contestants outshined the others from their school. Their performances demonstrated true survival skills and magical technique. The first Contestant to Ascend, from The Magical Academy of the Earth is . . . Contestant Three, Tala Abalos."

The crowd erupted when the Guardian-Contestant pair rose. They grasped forearms and moved up the stairs.

"From Aquarius: The Undersea School of Enchantments, Contestant Six, Bailey Jones."

Michael nodded, not surprised.

"From Lions of Magic, Contestant Seven, Aboiy Dlamini."

"From The European Academy for Practical Magic, First Challenge Winner, Contestant Twelve, Blake Johnson."

As he walked past, I couldn't tell if he was happy or anxious. To be honest, I couldn't tell what I felt either. Another step closer to a title, but the three Contestants who died put that in a brutal light.

"From The Magisterium of Magic, Contestant Thirteen, Daniel Phillips."

I wasn't surprised. On the other side of him, Clarence glared as Daniel rose and moved onto the stage. His hands gripped his armrests. His eyes never left the spot next to Daniel, the spot for the next Magisterium Contestant.

"From The Serpentine School of Magic, Contestant Sixteen, Marina Rafael." Lawrence waited for the round of applause to quiet down.

"From The University for Advanced Tactical Magic, Contestant Nineteen, Dmitri Theodore."

Dmitri jumped up from his seat with a holler. His Guardian ruffled his blue hair. Throwing their arms around each other they walked up the stage.

Once they were in place, Lawrence took the second envelope from Master Lenin and stepped back up to the podium. "Now we move to the second string. These Contestants showed potential and the judges hope to see them improve. The next string of Contestants, moving to the Second Trial, are . . . from The Magical Academy of the Earth, Contestant Two, Malan Thompson."

I snuck a glance at Lin, the third Contestant. A look of relief passed her face when her name wasn't called.

"From Aquarius: The Undersea School of Enchantments, Contestant Four, Amelia Markus."

"From Lions of Magic, Contestant Eight, Emeka Selasi."
Held him back, my ass.

"From The European Academy for Practical Magic, Contestant Ten, Anna Clarkson."

I rolled my eyes as Anna and Brandy sauntered up the stairs and stood beside Blake.

"From The Magisterium of Magic, Contestant Fifteen, Charlie Heart."

41

The Next Fourteen

"What?" Clarence gaped up at Lawrence. Shaking his head, he threw himself back into his seat. The scar cutting through his eyebrow looked even more sever with his anger.

His Guardian had no problem openly glaring at me. Michael smirked at him as he helped me to my feet.

A rush of relief flooded through my body. Even though I knew it was coming, in the back of my mind, I wondered if the School Masters would take it back. But Michael and I walked together onto the stage.

Daniel gave me a smile brighter than the theater lighting as I took the spot beside him.

"From The Serpentine School of Magic, Contestant Seventeen, Thiago Luis. Last, but not least, from The University for Advanced Tactical Magic, Contestant Twenty-One, Igorek Len."

Igorek raced up the steps and tackled Dmitri in a hug.

The crowd roared even louder with the announcement of the final Contestant. Cameras flashed from the audience like stars in a sea of silhouettes.

"Ladies and gentlemen, I present the Next Fourteen!" Lawrence spread his arms wide.

The crowd rose to their feet, clapping wildly.

I have another chance to win a title. I grinned.

"The Second Trial will take place February twenty-first. Contestants," Lawrence turned to look down the line, "I'll see you then. Have a good night."

As the cheers of the crowd died down, I turned to Daniel and crushed him into a hug. "Congrats!"

"And to you!" he chuckled. "First string! He named me first string!"

"I'm not surprised."

I was pulled around into another hug. Smiling, I squeezed Blake back.

His eyes locked on someone over my shoulder. "I guess I should thank you for keeping her alive." He held out his hand to my Guardian.

"It's not an easy job," Michael said dryly, grabbing Blake's forearm.

Atlas clapped Michael on the back with so much force that the Master Hunter stumbled forward a bit. "It seems we're in an awkward situation. We're going up against each other."

Michael shook him off. "We already did in the First Trial."

"The Second Trial is different and you know it." Atlas grinned. "Your Contestant could lose to mine."

Michael smirked. "That's unlikely."

"Oh, this is going to be fun," Atlas chuckled.

"I don't know if I've ever heard someone describe The Trial as 'fun' before," Daniel's Guardian, Sean Fields, said, looking at Atlas nervously.

"That's because no one's ever seen a Trial with me behind a Contestant." Atlas's grin grew.

I leaned toward Blake and whispered, "Why does that scare me?"

"Because you're smart." Atlas's sharp grin turned to me. He took his time letting his whiskey-colored eyes look over the sparkly dress and tall shoes. "Always good to see you, love." He took my hand in his. Tattooed on the back was a black heart. Stooping over my hand, he placed a kiss on my knuckles.

"Get your hands off my Contestant." Michael swatted him away.

Atlas did what he was told, but that didn't diminish the innuendo in the curve of his lips in the least.

"I heard Blake did really well," I said to the Irishman. "Thanks for getting him out in one piece."

"I only did part of it. Your friend did most of the work."

"Most of it?" Blake blurted, shaking his head. "More like all of it. The man speaks in fragmented sentences. It's like learning a whole new language."

"At least yours knows how to speak with a pleasant tone," I countered. "Mine sounds like he's reprimanding me all the time."

"That's because I am," Michael said flatly.

Blake and I turned to the third Contestant in our circle.

Daniel looked at his Guardian. They shrugged.

"No complaints here," Daniel admitted.

"Yes, I think we work rather well together," Sean agreed. He pulled out a pocket watch and checked the time. "Are you all going to the Glasshouse? Master Lenin mentioned there would be a party to celebrate the Next Fourteen."

"Is it mandatory?" I asked, looking to Michael. He hated crowds and my feet were starting to hurt.

Michael nodded. "It would be good for you to go. You could stand to learn a couple social cues."

Blake choked back a laugh.

Reading my glare, Michael added, "I'll give you some chocolate covered raisins if you go."

Damn. He knows me too well.

"Do you actually like chocolate covered raisins?" Atlas asked with his disgust thinly veiled.

Sean nodded in agreement. "There are snacks that are so much better."

"That's what I've been telling her for years." Blake grinned cheekily at me.

"You can accept the bribe, or I can make you spend the whole day in the gym tomorrow," Michael continued. "Your choice."

He not only knew how much I liked chocolate covered raisins, but he also knew how much I hated working out.

"Fine."

With a smirk of victory, he took a transporter from his pocket. Atlas did the same and Daniel twisted the face of his watch. The magical objects glowed gold before we were Ported off the stage and into the middle of the Magisterium.

Following the stream of students, we walked to the far end of the South Wing and into the tower. The three other towers in the school only went up, but this one was the exception; it also went down. Situated at the bottom of the staircase was the Glasshouse.

Warm wood covered the walls. A fireplace stood in the center of the room, surrounded by tables covered in dark brown leather. There was a bar and, by the smell of it, they made coffee. I guess what gave it its name was that the floor was made of glass. Under our feet, the river surged in hues of blue.

Atlas draped his arm over Daniel's Guardian's shoulders and led him to a table in the darkest corner of the room. Alone with the Hunter, Sean looked like he might pass out.

As Daniel and Blake moved toward the bar, I grabbed Michael's coat sleeve. "How long do we have to stay?"

"You know, normal kids stay out past curfew and spike their drinks at these things."

"Normal kids also enjoy these things. I, however, have an ongoing relationship with my bed, and I'm missing it. I'm exhausted and my feet are starting to hurt. So, when are we leaving?"

He looked at his watch. "How about an hour?"

"Perfect. I'll meet you back here."

Before he stepped away, he said, "In the meantime, try to be normal. I'd love an hour where I can simply enjoy a cup of coffee and not pull you from a stupid situation."

"This place is crawling with Guardians and teachers. I don't think I can even find a stupid situation here."

"I wish that reassured me."

I rolled my eyes. "Go to hell."

"I'm already there." With his hands in his pockets, he walked toward Atlas and Sean.

42

The Glasshouse

At the bar, I slipped into the seat between Daniel and Blake to find a hot chocolate waiting for me. Decorated into the whipped cream was my Contestant number, fifteen.

"A toast to our success in The Trial." Blake lifted his cappuccino. "It's nice to know at least two people won't stab me in the back."

"I'll toast to that." Daniel clinked his mug of tea against ours.

I took a sip of the hot chocolate. Warmth spilled into my stomach and wove through my chest as I licked the whipped cream from my upper lip.

"I did not think you would Ascend."

Spinning on our stools, Blake, Daniel, and I turned toward the Russian voice. Dmitri Theodore's dark blue eyes focused on me over the rim of his steaming mug. With the ceremony over, he had loosened the silver tie from around his neck.

"It was very surprising," his friend Igorek added.

I glanced around the room. *Out of everyone, why were they wasting their time with us?*

"Not finishing The Trial was a smart move," Dmitri said.

Igorek shrugged.

Shock bolted up my spine. Blake jerked his eyes to me. Daniel went completely still.

"I don't know what you mean," I said slowly. "We aren't supposed to see each other's performances."

The sync ring around my thumb buzzed twice; *You ok?*

"My father is a School Master. I can see what I want." He gestured toward me with his coffee. "Your Guardian is smart. Now, everyone will underestimate you. That was the reason Guardian Kale pulled you from The Trial, was it not?"

"Had to be," Igorek muttered.

I tapped the ring twice; *Yes.* "Master Kale pulled me out so he could get my heart beating. Nothing more."

"He's not a Master now," Dmitri reminded me with a smile.

"Neither is yours. *All* Guardians dropped their titles, right? So, does that make daddy dearest a cheat?"

"Watch your mouth," Igorek snapped.

"Sounds like it to me," Blake chimed in.

"Did your fears kick your ass?" I asked, tilting my head. "Is that why he wanted to give you a leg up?"

Dmitri's nostrils flared. "I was a first-round pick."

"That's not saying a lot about your school then." I shrugged. "Your aim is shit."

Igorek stepped forward with a snarl.

Dmitri put his arm out, halting Igorek's advance. With white knuckles, he gripped his mug. "My father told me you were sent to the Second Trial to cross the finish line." He took a sip of coffee. "I will personally make sure you never cross it."

My eyebrow lifted. "Was that a threat?"

"Of course." His lips curled. Igorek wore a matching smile.

There was something brutal in his eyes, something I had seen shadows of in Denny's. I expected the familiar hum to warm my blood. But I didn't hear the call to *run.* In fact, I wasn't afraid, just uneasy.

He wasn't Denny. He wasn't a Dellamora. He wasn't even a Hunter. He was just a boy steeped in arrogance with blue hair.

"Thanks for the heads up." Daniel set his tea aside and fully faced the taller Contestant. "Now you'll be the one that won't finish the Second Trial."

"And since you just threatened our friend," Blake crossed his arms over his chest, "that's three against one, mate."

"Three against *two,*" Igorek corrected.

Dmitri's eyes brightened at the challenge. "I welcome the chance for you to prove that. But I doubt you will do much."

"Do I smell threats?" A fourth member joined our group. Thiago Luis,

Contestant Seventeen from Serpentine. "Was this threat an exclusive offer or something I can look forward to as well?"

Dmitri and Igorek looked over the new arrival from head to toe. Their eyes were slow and careful. It reminded me of the look Michael gave me when I first came to the Magisterium. They were looking for weaknesses.

"The threat extends to the entirety of the Next Fourteen," Dmitri said finally. "The Second Trial will do as it always does. Weed out the weak." He held my gaze to ensure I knew he was talking about me. "But, I think I can change that. Swap it if you will."

"Well, now I'm intrigued." Thiago smiled, but without teeth. Somehow, that was even more menacing than Dmitri's wide grin.

Dmitri pointed to Blake and Thiago. "You are good with magic. I would prefer to face your fellow Contestants." He nodded to Daniel. "You are weak, all brain, no strength. Going against you would be like taking candy from children." He looked at me. "After watching your performance, I found you disappointing. Too emotional."

"Judging by that description, I don't sound like much of a threat," I said dryly.

"You aren't, but your Guardian is. He proved how smart he was by how he got you into the Second Trial."

"I already told you, it had nothing to do with me Ascending."

"You're inclined to lie," Igorek drawled.

"This does not matter." A shark-like smile stretched Dmitri's lips. "If I kill the strong, then only the weak will be in the Top Seven. It'll be like pie."

"Pie?" Blake raised his eyebrows.

"I think he means cake," Daniel grumbled. "It'll be a piece of cake."

"Sure. Do you know what the best part is?" Dmitri asked. "By killing you," he gestured to me, "Guardian Kale loses. No one will trust a Guardian who could not keep his Contestant alive. Master Hart will offer me anything I want."

"If that's going to happen, you better start working on your aim," I growled.

"I will. The next time I throw my blade, you will die and I will cut the head off the Achilles Heel."

"What do you say here?" Igorek pondered sardonically. "Two birds, one stone?"

Laughing, the pair moved deeper into the room.

"They're the reason this Trial has such a bad rap." Blake glared after the pair.

"Can you blame them?" Thiago asked, reaching into his pocket for a pack of cigarettes. "This is the fastest, laziest way to become a Master. They'd be idiots to half-ass it." He put one between his lips, but didn't light it. "We haven't officially met. Thiago Luis." He clasped each of our forearms.

"Why did you get in the middle of that?" Daniel sat back on his stool and grabbed his tea.

"Would it be so hard to believe that I'm a good guy?"

"You go to Serpentine," Daniel said slowly. "Your school doesn't have the greatest reputation for teaching good guys."

Thiago tilted his head from side to side, pondering. With a shrug, he accepted that to be true. "Contestant Eighteen, Josephine Gloriana Paulo, was my ex-girlfriend."

My eyes widened. *That was the girl Dmitri killed in the First Trial.*

Thiago shrugged at our shocked and then pitiful expressions. "We dated in basic school, but still, she was a friend. If you decide to go after him, loop me in. I would do it myself, but Contestants from my school are more closely watched than others."

There was a crash of broken glass, and a yell from the other side of the bar. Igorek had dropped his mug. Bright yellow foam erupted out of his mouth.

Marina Rafael, Contestant Sixteen from Serpentine, rushed up to Thiago. "Time to go," she said, a little out of breath.

"How much did you give him?" A feverish glow lit his eyes as he watched Igorek continue to retch.

"Enough to ruin his week. Let's *go.*" Marina tugged on his sleeve.

"Like I said," Thiago turned to me, "if you're going in on him, give me a heads up." With a mock salute, he and Marina left the Glasshouse.

Daniel, Blake, and I immediately put our drinks down and pushed them away.

"I can't decide which was weirder," Daniel said as he watched Thiago leave. "The Russian blatantly threatening us, or him."

"Him. Definitely him," Blake said. "Did you really not cross the finish line?"

Daniel's eyes dropped to my tattoo, still covered by my sleeve.

I glanced across the room to where Michael sat. At the moment, his attention was diverted to a snake dressed in the skin of a stunning blonde. Brandy leaned her body into Michael's. He pried her hands off him like they were leeches.

Dropping my voice, I told them, "When I was drowning, Michael pulled me out of The Trial to get help instead of to the finish line. It really had nothing to do with Ascending."

"I believe you," Daniel said in a rush.

Blake hummed in agreement.

With a breeze of vanilla, our trio was joined by another. But this time, the additional company was most welcome.

"Congratulations!" Cornelia stepped up to the bar with a wide smile. She quickly pulled me into a hug and then Daniel. When she turned to Blake, a blush of color rushed into her cheeks. "How does it feel to be in the Next Fourteen?" she asked as she wrapped her arms around his neck.

"Can't complain." He coiled his arms around her waist and held her a second too long.

Daniel wore a knowing smile, but quickly hid it with a fake wipe of his nose.

Cornelia pulled back and ducked her head. Her long blonde curls fell before her face, hiding her blush from Blake's fascinated eyes.

"No confetti?" Daniel grinned.

"I decided against that when all three of you jumped for your wands last time," she laughed.

I winced at the memory. "Sorry."

"That was totally on me," she assured us.

"It was very sweet of—"

The hot liquid and foam sloshed forward, dowsing the front of Cornelia's gown. My empty mug rolled across the bar top.

Cornelia gasped. I stared, opened-mouthed. *What just happened? I wasn't touching it.*

"Bloody hell, Charlie." Blake reached around Daniel to grab napkins off the bar.

"That wasn't—I didn't—" My eyes flew around the crowd.

On the other end of the bar, my eyes landed on Clarence. Without breaking eye contact, he pocketed his wand. My magic churned as I dropped off the stool and pushed my way through the crowd.

"What the hell, Clarence?" I snapped. "That wasn't funny."

He smirked. "Maybe not to you."

"Apologize to her," I said through my teeth. "Now."

"That's not going to happen." He finished the rest of his drink and slid the empty mug toward the barista. "She's barely a Common."

My anger rose a couple notches, and with it, my magic started to boil.

"If you're pissed at me Ascending instead of you, take it out on me. Not my friends."

Clarence gripped his glass so tight, I wondered if it would shatter in his hand. "Are you sure you can handle another Trial? You didn't even finish the last one."

How did he know that? "You haven't talked to me in months, and that's what you're going to say to me?"

"Are you saying you don't deserve it? Remember last semester when you found Blaine Willow's diary and then bailed without telling anyone?"

"It's not like you wanted any part of it," I whispered harshly. "If I remember correctly, after Moose was killed, you jumped ship."

"You still should've said somethin'! You found the diary." Clarence's eyes lit with intensity. "At least tell me what it said."

That's when it clicked. Cruel laughter shook my shoulders. "You're not mad that I found it without you. You're pissed that I read it and you didn't."

"I had every right to that information, same as you."

"You gave that up when you threw in the towel."

He stepped so close that when he spoke, his spit hit me in the face. "Tell me or I'll make you."

The sync ring buzzed twice; *You ok?*

I smiled right in his face. "Do you think you scare me? I've seen scary and you don't have his smirk."

"You're fooling yourself if you think you're going to get through this next Trial. You should forfeit and let me Ascend."

"Not a chance."

"Listen, darlin', you ain't good enough for what's coming. If you continue, you'll fail even worse than you already have."

Anger filled my chest. "Now I get it. You can't stand that I found the diary and you didn't. I Ascended and you didn't. How does it feel to always be in second place?"

His scarred eyebrow twitched.

I should've seen it coming.

The fury in his eyes screamed to the whole room.

His hand whipped across my face.

My magic flared. A light bulb exploded over the bar as I stumbled back. I felt the sting of his slap all the way to my bones. My cheek flushed bright red.

The magic in my chest coiled around my shoulder, then down to my hands. I took a step forward with every intention to hurt him back when Michael Ported between us.

The Master Hunter's hand latched around Clarence's throat. His fingers pressed tightly into the boy's skin as he lifted him off the floor. Clarence's silver shoes dangled a couple inches over the glass.

The room went so still, I could hear the water rippling under the floor.

"Apologize." Michael inched out of the way so I could see Clarence's face.

Any sane man would have eyes wide with fear. The rage on Clarence's face flushed his cheeks and clenched his teeth. He wasn't afraid.

"I said," Michael dragged him closer, "*apologize.*"

Clarence gathered the saliva in his mouth and spat. The glob landed on Michael's shoulder. "Over my dead body," he rasped.

Michael's fingers tightened around his throat. Clarence's skin darkened under Michael's fingertips.

Cheese and rice, he's going to kill him.

"Michael." Stepping forward, I placed my hand on his arm. "He's an idiot. He's not worth it."

Clarence sputtered and gasped. As he struggled for air, his dark blue eyes didn't leave Michael's. He met his gaze with a reckless challenge.

"Let him go," I said gently.

Michael took a slow, deep breath. "You're lucky I'm in a good mood. Tonight, I'm celebrating my Contestant Ascending, so I find myself feeling merciful. But if you *ever* touch my Contestant again, I'll slit your throat. Do I make myself clear?"

"I'd like . . . to see you try . . . pretend king," Clarence hissed through his teeth.

The muscles in Michael's arms tightened. I knew he was getting ready to throw him head first across the room.

"Hey." I drew the Master Hunter's dark gaze to me. "Let's just go."

Michael held on for a second longer. Clarence was almost cross-eyed when he relaxed his fingers.

He slumped to the floor, holding his raw throat. Wheezing, he looked up at Michael with a look so bloodthirsty it chilled my blood.

Smoothing his hands down his suit, Michael's eyes never left the rasping boy in front of him. He offered me his arm. As soon as I took it, Michael Ported us from the Glasshouse. We appeared in the middle of my room on the top floor.

Instantly Michael turned toward me. With more gentleness than I thought he was capable of, he turned my face to the side, exposing the cheek Clarence struck

"Are you alright?" He dropped his hand and stepped back.

I nodded, touching my cheek. The skin was hot beneath my fingertips. My eyes dropped to the tattoo on my wrist. "I thought this was supposed to keep people from hurting me."

"The magic only protects you from people outside of The Trial," Michael said stiffly. "Technically, Clarence has been benched. He may not be participating, but he's still a part of it until it's over."

Bummer. I would have liked to have seen Clarence's cheek red from his own slap.

"Are you ok?" I asked.

His jaw clenched. His eyes hardened and I readied myself for what was about to come out of his mouth. "What happened?"

"He was pissed that I found Blaine Willow's diary without him. That, and I Ascended and he didn't." Again, I touched my cheek. "I'm sorry for ruining your coffee break."

Under his breath he muttered, "Of course you would apologize for someone hitting you." With a sigh, he said, "Don't be. It was a lousy cup of coffee."

Something tickled my wrists. Looking down, I watched as silver sequins sprinkled to the floor. The tight sleeves of the dress had melted around my wrist as if my magic had scorched them during the conversation with Clarence. My hands, however, were fine.

If I struck Clarence, what would've happened to his face?

"If that kid comes near you again, call me." Michael jerked his jacket from his shoulders.

Chills danced down my spine as I remembered him vowing to slit his throat. "I don't think that'll happen. He's an idiot, but he's not stupid."

He huffed. "You'd be surprised what people do when they're angry."

Something slammed into the front door.

It wasn't a knock. It was a single thud. Michael and I both froze, waiting for another. When none came, Michael pulled his wand from the left side of his holster. Without realizing it, I had drawn mine too.

Silently, he crept to the door and tapped his wand against the wood. For a split second, the door faded, allowing us to see into the hall. It was empty.

Michael swiftly pulled the door open. He looked up and down the hall. But he found the same thing: nothing. Just as he was about to close it, his eyes settled on the outside of the door. His eyes narrowed.

"What?" I slipped my wand back into my boot.

He pushed open the door further, letting it bump into the wall.

Stabbed in place by a thin rod of silver, was a mouse. Its tiny throat was slit, letting its blood spill down the wood. A crudely finger-painted crown sat above its limp head. Below the dead creature, written in blood, was the single word, "PRINCESS".

"Dead princess . . . Any idea what it means?" Michael asked, regarding my expression closely.

I shook my head. My eyes jumped from the bloody letters to the dead animal. With a start, I remembered the night after the First Trial.

"When the Dellamora was in my room, there was a mouse on the floor with its throat cut." I wrapped my arms around myself.

Michael sighed. "Shit."

"What?"

"Someone doesn't want you in The Trial. First, they tried to take you out by force, now they're trying to scare you out." With the tip of his wand, he lifted the mouse's head. A small trickle of blood ran down its body.

"If anything like this happens again, call me immediately." Grabbing the spike skewering the mouse, he yanked it from the wood. The dead animal fell to the floor with a soft squish.

43

Got Anything Better to Do?

Screams filled my ears.

My feet pounded down an empty street.

No matter how fast I ran, I didn't move. Red eyes stared out of the shadows. The wide mouth of a Dellamora flashed, highlighting every tooth.

Rank, hot breath blew across the back of my neck. Saliva dropped on to my shoulder as—

"Charlie, wake up."

I flinched deeper into the mattress. All around the darkened room, the lights flickered like sleepy fireflies with the leftover panic from my night-mare.

"Wh—" Shoving the hair out of my face, I looked around. Michael stood beside the bed with pillow-mused hair. "What time is it?"

He glanced at his watch. "Just after three."

With a shaky breath, I dropped back to my pillow and pressed my palms to my eyes. "Did I do anything?"

The mattress bowed as he sat beside me. "You'll have to shower in the dark until the bathroom light gets fixed."

Of course, I broke something. When wasn't I breaking something? With a sigh, I dropped my arms; one landed above my head and the other on my belly. Mindlessly, I twisted a lock of hair around my finger.

You'd think after the excitement from the Ascending Ceremony and the daunting two months ahead would have been a great incentive to go back to sleep. It did nothing of the sort. In fact, the more I thought about it, the more awake I became.

Rolling my head across the pillow, I looked down the length of the bed. The bright blue glow from my clock hit Michael's sharp profile and the unkempt curls of his midnight hair. The rest of him was lost to shadow.

"Are you tired?"

"Not even a little," he said, not looking up from his hands.

"Same." I paused. "You're going to make me train, aren't you?"

"That hadn't crossed my mind, but now that you mentioned it—"

"Oh, come on!" I sat up.

"Got anything better to do?"

"I can find something."

"I bet you could," he chuckled. "We'll have the whole training area to ourselves. It'll be quiet for once."

While that might have been something Michael was excited about, it brought me no such joy.

He stood and pulled his arms over his head to stretch the sleepy muscles. "Come on, I can see you're amped up. It'll be good to work off the energy."

"It's dark, you can't see anything."

"I'm a Hunter. Do you really think something as simple as the lack of light is going to slow me down?" Leaning closer, he flicked the loose lock hanging before my face. "Come on. I'll make you some hot chocolate."

"You've been bribing me a lot lately." Shoving the covers from my legs, I groped around the nightstand for the lamp.

"When it stops working, I'll find something else." He turned to the living room and called over his shoulder, "You have ten minutes to get dressed or we're starting with pushups right here."

I grabbed my pillow and hurled it after him. The door shut just in the nick of time to save the back of his head.

Wandering around the room, I pulled on my light blue hoodie and a pair of baggy sweatpants. I brushed my teeth and splashed some cold water on my face before stepping into the living room.

"I think I should get bonus points for being ready in seven minutes." Gathering all my hair, I knotted it at the top of my head.

"I should get bonus points for dealing with you before coffee."

I stuck my tongue out at him.

Smirking, he grabbed his holster from the recliner and threaded his arms through the loops. After he had a cup of coffee and I had hot chocolate, we set out for the training room.

Despite the hour, the stairwell was still guarded by Users in black and gold.

"Are they always here?" I whispered.

Michael nodded.

We followed the staircase to the bottom. For the first time, when we stepped into the training room, we had to turn on the lights.

The room was usually filled with grunts and the clanging of exercise equipment. The air was humid with sweat and swear words. But, at three in the morning, it was spotless. The air had a bit of a chill and the strong scent of lemon.

There was a visual difference as well. Beside the door in every training room was a small mailbox. Each one was stuffed with letters marked with important wax seals. Some Contestant's mailboxes were so full, letters were piled on the floor beneath.

When we stepped closer to our training room, my eyes went to the mailbox by the door. It appeared empty. *Figures.*

Setting my hot chocolate on the bench by the door, I dropped to the floor and started stretching. I looked over my shoulder when Michael didn't join me.

He stood in front of the mailbox holding an envelope with a pale pink seal. The wax had an eyeball stamped into it, round, without lid or lashes.

"What's that?" I asked.

"Guardian feedback," he mumbled. Breaking the seal with his thumb, he pulled out a small square of pink paper.

"Does it suggest you find another Contestant to Guardian?" I asked. Tucking my right leg beneath me, I leaned toward my extended leg and grabbed my toes.

"Surprisingly, no." Smirking down at me, he tucked it into his pocket.

"Who's it from?"

"It doesn't matter." Coming to stand behind me, he pushed my shoulders forward into the stretch. The back of my leg lit up with fire.

After stretching, we jumped into our usual sets, first warming up with magic, focusing on enchantments and intermediate wards. Then, we took a break to work on hand-to-hand combat and weapons. After a hot chocolate and coffee break, we returned to magic.

Without prying, judging eyes, I didn't hesitate or get distracted by looking at the other Contestants. Judging from Michael's lack of brisk comments, he was pleased.

Around six, our private training ended. Dmitri and Igorek and their Guardians threw open the doors with an air of confidence that only belonged to assholes.

My mood instantly soured.

Their conversation halted when they saw us.

"What are you doing here?" Dmitri called through the glass. "You're never here this—"

"What?" I squinted, cupping a hand around my ear.

He raised his voice. "What are you—"

"I can't hear you!" I shook my head. "The glass." I shrugged, barely keeping the smile off my face.

His Guardian grabbed his shoulder and steered him to his own space at the end of the room. Igorek glared as he followed after.

"You're poking a very dangerous and easily irritated bear," Michael noted. He didn't sound disapproving. Maybe a little amused.

I shrugged.

We took a much-needed break for breakfast. I passed out for a couple hours before we went back to the training room. Having been at it for a few hours already, both of us moved slower. My casts and strikes lacked their usual potency.

It was around lunch when we were interrupted for a second time.

A knock on the glass came just as Michael flipped me onto my back. My skull struck the mat. I felt the blow all the way to my forehead.

"Ow."

"Baby." Michael reached down and grabbed my forearm. "I went easy on you."

"Didn't feel like it." I let him pull me upright. At the sound of the door opening, I turned and instantly dropped Michael's arm. "Hey!"

"Sorry to interrupt." Daniel tentatively stepped into the room. His warm brown eyes flickered to the man in black beside me. "Good afternoon, Guardian Kale."

Michael nodded.

"Sean and I were thinking of calling it a day to celebrate Ascending. Guardian Atlas and Blake are in. I was wondering if you'd like to join us."

Instantly, I checked my face. Trying to remain nonchalant, I looked over at Michael. If he knew how badly I wanted to go, would he refuse out of spite?

"Atlas agreed?" Grabbing the hem of his shirt, Michael pulled it up to wipe the sweat from his forehead. Just as quickly as he lifted it, he let it drop, hiding the collage and scars scattered over the hard muscles of his abdomen. "It's not exactly safe for Contestants to be out."

"If we go," I jumped in, "that would be three Guardians in one place, two of which are Hunters. We'd be the safest people outside of witness protection."

Daniel's grin said I wasn't doing a good job of hiding my excitement.

Michael shook his head. "Not a good idea."

I turned my back to Daniel, dropping my voice. "Please. I've been really good today."

"I'm not doing this to punish you," he said gently. "If Clarence Hardy is still pissed, which I guarantee he is, I don't want to give him an opening."

That was actually a good argument. With a sigh, I turned to Daniel and smiled. "Maybe next time."

"Ok, yeah." Daniel stepped back toward the door. "I'll save you a seat at dinner."

I waved as the glass door closed behind him. I wondered if I would ever be able to have his attention again like when he asked me to dinner.

Don't kid yourself, Charlie. Attachment is an anchor, remember? I hadn't thought that in a long time.

Focus on training for your title.

When I turned back to Michael, I kept my face clear of disappointment.

"Fists up," he ordered.

My hands snapped up from my sides, clenched tight. I slid my dominant foot back and angled my shoulder toward him.

Him and his stupid rules. A familiar pinch of anger rose up through my chest. It was the same temper that got me the majority of the scars on my back, and yet that realization couldn't stop me from getting in trouble. If

Michael was going to keep me here, I was at least going to leave a bruise on his jaw.

I swung toward his head. Michael parried. I ducked as he aimed for my shoulder. I straightened and drilled my fist into his gut.

Booya!

Now, time for the aching jaw. Pulling back, I put my entire weight behind my fist. Unfortunately, he caught my hand and twisted it behind my back. He hooked his foot around my ankle and pulled my legs out from under me. I hit the ground flat on my back.

"Oi!" Atlas threw open the glass door. "We're leaving right now and you're coming. Don't make me kidnap your Contestant, mate. Let's go."

"We're in the middle of something," Michael said.

"Really?" Atlas pointedly looked at me breathing heavily on the floor mat. "Looks like you just finished."

Michael took a deep breath, probably to order the tattooed Hunter from the room.

"Come on, love," Atlas said to me. "I know you don't want to be stuck in this sweaty room with this wanker any longer."

I looked at Michael. His eyes were narrowed.

"If you want to save face, I can throw you over my shoulder and you can pretend I'm taking you against your will."

I laughed at the image of it. Especially the part of Michael running after us cursing through his teeth.

Atlas turned his whiskey-colored eyes to the silent man beside me. "I'll keep an eye on her, too. All of this black stone is suffocating me. *Let's go.*"

I jumped to my feet and took one step toward Atlas. I looked at my Guardian with the best puppy-dog look I could muster.

He rolled his eyes. "Fine."

44

Candied Dandelions

I grinned.

"*But*," Michael stressed, "you don't leave my side for a second. Understood?"

"Consider me your new shadow." Before he could change his mind, I grabbed his arm and tugged him out of the training room. When the door closed behind us, I jogged past the other rooms filled with sparing Contestant-Guardian pairs to the group waiting beside the door.

"Did you decide to join us after all?" Daniel asked, turning away from Blake. His dimpled smile was tentative.

"Atlas threatened to kidnap me if we didn't."

Blake looked over my shoulder. "Not the way I would've done it, but I'm not complaining."

The two Hunters walked easily toward us, oblivious to the effect they had on the room. In each training space they passed, the Contestant-Guardian pair inside paused, as if their movement would attract the attention of death and his henchmen.

"With Michael, you have to be dramatic. He's more stubborn than a meteor." Turning my back to him, I smiled at my fellow Contestants. "So, where are we going?"

"Have you ever been axe throwing?" Daniel asked, lifting an eyebrow.

"Uh, no."

"Sean knows of a fun bar in San Francisco that just installed it."

"Axe throwing with booze?" Blake waited for Daniel to contradict him. When he didn't, he shook his head. "Why not? What could go wrong?"

"Oh, come on!" I laughed. "It sounds fun."

"I'll remind you that you said that when you're getting your foot sewn back on."

"Daniel." Sean gestured for him to come closer. Immediately, Daniel pulled himself from our conversation and joined his Guardian. Blake and I followed suit.

As Michael took my wrist, he asked, "Where are we going?"

"The Garage," Sean said.

Michael tensed.

Daniel pressed the face of his watch. With a flash of gold, he and Sean Ported from the training room. Atlas dropped a hand on Blake's shoulder and followed a split second later.

"Charlie." Michael turned to me with a little less color in his face. "The Garage . . . Zak owns it."

"Oh." Surprise zipped up my spine.

"No one knows that—at least, they don't know he's my brother. We'd like to keep it that way."

A hundred questions thundered through my mind. *Why didn't they want anyone to know they were related? I would've thought that would be a big advantage.* But the tight clench of Michael's jaw halted every question. So I nodded.

Pulling on his magic, he Ported us from the training room to the humid coastal air of California. The scent of sea mist and rain paired perfectly with the smoggy, grey sky. A large neon sign battled against the afternoon gloom. Over a metal door, it read: *The Garage.*

The entrance to the bar was a raised garage door with glass window panes. At the center of the large space, surrounded by tall cocktail tables and leather chairs, was an oval bar with an impressive display of bottles and bare light bulbs.

The others were already inside winding their way through the tables to the back of the room. Michael, however, was frozen on the sidewalk. His black eyes stared unblinkingly at the bar in front of him.

I tapped the sync ring around my thumb. *You ok?*

His gaze snapped away from the building. With a tight nod, he stepped inside.

The walls were whitewashed, except for the dark support beams overhead.

Most of the tables were stainless steel, accompanied by black leather seats. Cool jazz streamed from the speakers in the bar display.

The far side of the room housed five stalls. Each had a red and white target hung between the separating panels. An axe was planted firmly in each.

Daniel's Guardian led our group toward the throwing stations. People turned as three Trial Contestants and three Guardians cut through the room. The robust sound of laughter and loud conversations dropped to a simmer as we claimed a high table for our party of six.

At the center bar was a familiar face. Zak tossed a rag over his shoulder and ducked under the counter. Most of his long hair was tied back, except for a few strands that fell over his forehead. His sauntering gait was accentuated by the loose straps of his suspenders dangling from his belt.

"Welcome to The Garage," he said coolly as he stepped up to the table. "It's not every day I have almost a fourth of The Master's Trial at my bar. I'm Zak. I own the place."

"Hi!" Reaching across the table, I offered him my hand. "I'm Charlie."

A smile flickered across his face. Rolling his toothpick to the other side of his mouth, he clasped my forearm. "Pleasure."

Atlas joined in and introduced himself. The rest of the table followed.

Zak's dark brown eyes shifted to his younger brother. "It's been a while since we've had Hunters here."

Atlas shot a glance around the room. Those sitting close to us didn't bother to hide the fact they were eavesdropping.

"Hunters are welcome," Zak went on. "Always have been. Anything you want, it's on the house." He nodded to Atlas as well.

"Thank you, mate." Atlas's usual smirking amusement was replaced with genuine gratitude. "We appreciate it."

The table directly to our left slipped off their stools and promptly left the bar. The table on the other side hunched together in a cluster of whispers.

"What can I get for you?" Zak didn't pull out a pad of paper. Instead, he casually leaned his elbow against Sean's chair.

"I'll have a Wolfbane Shandy." Blake crossed his arms on top of the table.

My eyebrows shot up. *Does he think Zak's not going to card him?*

Michael leaned over and whispered in my ear, "The drinking age in the magical world is sixteen."

"Oh." *Of course. Why wouldn't that be different too?*

Daniel ordered a Cornwall Bourbon, and Atlas a tonic water with lime. Sean asked for Willow Tree Rum.

"What about for the lady of the table?" Zak nodded his head toward me.

"I'm fine with just a water." I smiled politely.

"We'll both have a Dandelion Porter," Michael said. "With a drop shot of Hell's Whiskey with mine."

"Thank God." Atlas shook his head. "I thought you were body snatched. Since when do you drink porter?"

"Since she became my Contestant." He smirked in my direction. "If I get too drunk, she'll set something on fire."

I was about to blurt that I wanted to set him on fire, but those around us were still eavesdropping. So, I settled for scrunching my nose at him.

"You got it." Zak returned to the bar and drew his wand.

With small bursts of magic, bottles from the center display levitated to the bar top as he prepared the glasses. When everything was mixed and garnished, the drinks rose into the air. Winding around the light fixtures, they made their way across the room and settled around our table.

Michael took the sugared dandelion from the mouth of his bottle and tossed it to the center of the table. He dumped the dark liquid into the accompanying empty glass. As soon as the bottle was empty, he dropped in the shot of Hell's Whiskey, glass and all.

Atlas grabbed his fizzing water and raised it. "Cheers to surviving two months of this shit show and looking forward to two more."

Arms crisscrossed, reaching over and under, to clink glasses with each other. A moment of silence passed as everyone took their first drink.

I tucked the sugar-crusted dandelion behind my ear and took a sip. The liquid fizzed across my tongue and down my throat. A dry, sweetish flavor of citrus and wild herbs rushed up my nose.

Michael took a large mouthful of his dark mixture. As the gulp slid down his throat, he slowly exhaled. The Hell's Whiskey colored his breath like dragon flame as it left his lips.

"Alright." Blake set his rectangular bottle on the table with a clang. "Who's going to throw axes with me?"

Daniel shook his head. "I'll probably take off my foot if I try. Or somehow, I'll end up throwing it behind me."

"It's all about form, mate." Atlas shook his head. His earrings rocked and twinkled in the light.

"That's my fault," Sean said. "I haven't been able to teach him much in that department. I was raised by scholars. We had a drawer full of pens, which my father insisted was the best weapon a man could have."

"You outrank Atlas there." Michael savored another swallow. "He was raised by wolves. Some days I'm surprised he can read."

"I've heard you don't have a belly button," Atlas countered, "because you were born out of the darkest shadows in hell."

Meeting Atlas's eyes with a dry look, Michael grabbed the bottom of his shirt and raised it. He exposed not only his belly button, proof that he was actually born, but also a plethora of scars.

The tough tissue covering my back burned in sympathy. While mine were all inflicted with a belt, minus the one under my heart, his looked to be made from all kinds of weapons. There were slashes and jagged cuts, round patches and starbursts. The two most devastating were the thin scars of a knife. Close together, one was small while the other trailed up his chest toward his heart.

Oh, God.

Daniel and Sean had gone pale with matching looks of horror. Blake reached for his drink as if to stop himself from staring. Atlas was the only one who looked unaffected.

"You could've used an illusion," Atlas chided.

Rolling his eyes, Michael dropped his shirt and grabbed his drink.

"No one answered my question," Blake blurted again, pulling everyone from their shock of seeing so many scars. "Who's going to throw with me?"

"You should, Charlie." Leaning protectively over his beer, Michael nodded toward the axe wall. "You could probably teach him a thing or two."

"Oi!" Blake held his hands palm up in a 'what the hell' gesture.

"I don't know how to say this nicely," Atlas said, leaning into the table. "So, I'm just gonna say three words. First. String. Contestant. Sounds like your Contestant can learn a thing or two from *mine*." He sent an apologetic glance my way. "No offense, love."

How was I not supposed to take offense at that?

I took another drink from the dark beer and dropped from the stool.

Pulling my light blue hoodie over my head, I straightened the white under-shirt. I walked up to the target and yanked the axe out of the wall.

My shoulders tensed and shifted, growing accustomed to the weight of the new weapon. Walking back to the starting line on the floor, I swung the axe a couple times, testing the weight and balance.

I raised the axe over my head, took a deep breath, and threw it. The axe cartwheeled through the air and planted dead center in the target with a satisfying *thunk*.

Michael whistled from the table.

I spun toward him. A flash of silver streaked through the air. I snatched the knife coming for my chest and, in the same fluid motion, flung it at the target. The knife landed right beside the axe.

I raised my arms in victory. Turning back to the table, I bowed at the applause from Sean and Daniel.

Michael looked at his coworker with a look so smug, Mother Teresa would've wanted to slap it off.

"How'd you get her to do all that in a couple of months?" Sean blurted. He couldn't take his eyes off the target.

"What can I say?" Michael shrugged. "I'm a brilliant teacher."

Atlas nodded toward the target. To Blake he said, "Beat that."

"Done." Blake quickly retrieved the weapons. After returning the knife to Michael, he stepped up to the starting line. The axe embedded in the center of the target.

"Your turn, mate." Atlas nodded for Daniel to step up.

"No thanks," he said with an uneasy laugh. "I can handle written exams and casts. But axes?" He shook his head.

"It's all about form." I hoped to reassure him. "You place your dominant foot back. Then you use the weight of the blade to propel the throw."

"The nondominate foot should be back," Blake interjected.

I shook my head. "The dominant foot is stronger, so it'll give you more support." I peeked at Michael to see if I said it correctly. He nodded.

Blake scoffed. "Yeah, so when you swing and miss, you take out your best leg. Blood goes spraying everywhere. Then you drop the axe on your other foot, and you're bloody incapacitated because you're an idiot."

I turned to Daniel with additional instructions on my lips, but they vanished in a butterfly flutter when I met his laughing gaze. His warm brown eyes flickered over my face, absorbing every detail.

Another rush of heat flooded my cheeks. I turned back to Blake. "No offense, but I think, since my Guardian is a *Master* Hunter, that he has the leading authority on form."

Atlas choked on his soda.

"Bullshit." Blake stood up straighter. "Everyone knows Master Kale is good with his hands, but my Guardian has every knife known to man."

"But does he know how to use them?"

Atlas balked. "Did she really just say that?"

Michael grinned, dimple flashing. "It's a valid question."

"I bet Atlas can outthrow Master Kale," Blake declared.

Michael's eyes narrowed. "Come again?"

Atlas cocked his head at Michael's tone. "Maybe I do have a better throwing arm than you."

Michael shook his head. "Not a chance."

"Prove it." Blake nodded to the line of targets.

Michael smirked at him. "Throwing an axe is elementary."

Blake smirked at me. "See? He's chickening out because he knows my Guardian can outthrow him."

"I didn't say I wouldn't," Michael corrected him. He slid from the stool, placing his boots firmly on the cement floor, towering over us. "I just meant that throwing a single axe at an unmoving target is child's play."

Michael reached beneath his right arm and grabbed the knives secured there. One by one, he set the blades on the table.

The first was small with a rounded end. The second had a curve in the blade so sharp, it was almost painful to look at. The third was a replica of the one he gave me for the First Trial; one side was serrated while the end was smooth. The fourth blade looked like a butcher knife found in meat shops. The large knife clinked against the table.

Blake, Daniel, and Sean stared at the knives with mild alarm. The drinks and casual atmosphere made them forget they were in the company of one of the most dangerous men alive. Atlas and I barely kept our grins to ourselves.

"I can sink each of these into the center of every target, moving from there," Michael pointed to one side of the room, "to there." He pointed to the opposite side.

"So can I!" Atlas exclaimed. "That's nothing special."

"Then let's see you put your knives right next to mine."

"You're on!" Atlas quickly cleared the others in the bar away from their targets, saying it was 'official Trial business.' Once the way was clear, Atlas inclined his head toward his boss as if to say, "go for it."

Michael collected all of his blades, placing the handles between his fingers so he grasped all of the knives in one hand. Crossing the room, he lined himself up with the first target.

I stared, gripping the neck of my beer bottle with excitement. In training, Michael broke everything down to teach me the flow of each move. I knew he held himself back when we were sparring. It was a rare occasion to see what he could do. I wanted to see him take off the training wheels and show off.

Michael let the first knife fly. He was on the move before it even landed. He threw the following knives in quick succession. When he came to a stop, at the center of each was a gleaming silver blade.

Picking my jaw off the floor, I clapped with Daniel and Sean. Blake was trying not to look impressed.

As Michael made his way back to the table, I extended my fist toward him. Smirking at Atlas, Michael bumped his fist against mine.

The Irishman reached into the lining of his trench coat and pulled out three identical knives with serrated edges. He positioned them between his fingers the same way Michael had done.

As he moved toward the starting line, I leaned closer to Michael. "You're going to teach me that, right? Because that was so cool."

He smirked down at me. "I've already started laying the groundwork."

Awesome. "Who knew you were good at something other than scowls and insults?"

"This might come as a shock to you, but I am extremely good at my job. In fact, when the Hunter Guard was still running, I was called the best Hunter the Guard ever created."

"So you've said multiple times. It's nice to see that that hasn't gone to your head." I took another sip of my beer to hide my mocking smile. I collected Michael's candied dandelion and tucked it into the knot at the top of my head.

"Oi, pay attention." Blake nodded his head toward the targets.

In a whirl of his trench coat, Atlas started. While Michael threw with elegance, Atlas's throws were brutal. Each blade struck the target with a bang. At the last target, when Atlas was out of knives, he pulled his wand from the holster riding low on his hip. He tossed the black weapon into the air.

For the split second it moved toward the ceiling, a golden sheen glazed over the dark surface. The magic lengthened it and twisted it into the shape of a black sword with no decoration. The plain look drew attention to the long, gleaming blade.

Atlas caught it by the hilt and threw it like a javelin. It split the air and slammed into the target with a crack that echoed around the bar. If people weren't paying attention before, they were now.

"My God," Daniel muttered.

"I'm starting to think you need a new Guardian," Sean said slowly.

Atlas spread his arms wide, daring our party to judge him. Blake and I were the first ones at the targets. With narrow, focused eyes, we looked at each knife.

Michael's knives were deeply embedded in the center of each target. The serrated knives and sword Atlas threw were right next to them. They were so close that the two blades were almost pressed up against each other.

At the final target, the corner of my lips lifted. "The sword is off-center."

"No!" Blake rushed over and leaned close to the two blades. "It's the lighting."

"No." I pointed to Atlas's blade. "It's definitely not as close to Michael's as the others."

"Like hell it is." Atlas practically shoved Blake out of the way. "Not even a damn sprite could fit between them."

I took a candied dandelion from my hair and placed it between the two weapons. The gap between the two was large enough to let the small flower slip between the sleek steel to the floor.

I turned to Blake. "My Guardian is better than yours."

Michael quickly smothered his amusement. "He's an arrogant son of a bitch, but it looks like the lighting is playing with your eyes."

Smirking with satisfaction, Atlas yanked his sword from the target. The blade dissolved, the wand shrinking back to its original size. Slipping it into the sheath running parallel with his thigh, he returned to his drink.

I stepped close to Michael and lowered my voice. "You totally won that."

"Of course, but Atlas's feelings are sensitive."

I nodded, keeping my expression earnest as laughter threatened to escape me. "We have to protect him from the truth."

"At all costs."

We locked eyes and, unable to continue the joke any longer, we broke into grins. Maybe it was the liquor, but when he chuckled, some of the darkness faded from his eyes.

After Michael collected his blades, we returned to the table and finished our drinks. Another round was ordered, taking us from the afternoon crowd to the early-evening drinkers. By the third round, Daniel was starting to slur and everything was impossibly funny.

"Gentlemen," Michael slid off his stool. "I think this is where we call it a night."

"Oh, come on," I unabashedly whined. "Can we stay a little longer?"

"You've been awake since three."

"So have you!"

"I can handle little sleep and alcohol. I'm not sure I want to see you try. Let's go. You need food."

I shook my head and, I swear, the entire room shook with it. Bidding my fellow Contestants goodbye, I headed for the front of the bar.

The music was a lot more intoxicating than when we first arrived. On the sidewalk, it spun me in circles. Catching my hand, Michael pulled on his magic and Ported us from the sticky air of San Francisco.

Michael pushed open the gates to the ranch and together, me humming and him trying to keep my feet from betraying me, we headed up the drive.

45

At the Table

"Congratulations on Ascending!" Mrs. Kale exclaimed as we entered the kitchen. The bright burst of energy brought a smile to my face.

"Sorry, I should've called." Michael shrugged off his jacket and draped it across the chair beside Meg.

"Don't even start." Mrs. Kale waved off his apology. "There's always plenty of food for whenever you two want to stop by."

Leaning against the wall, I crossed my arms behind my back and watched Michael wrap his arms around Meg.

"How are you?" he asked. He almost sounded affectionate. *Was that even possible?*

"I would be fine if this baby stopped kicking my internal organs." She winced, placing both hands on her stomach. "Would you stop that?" she hissed.

"I remember when I was pregnant with Michael and Lauren," Mrs. Kale said from the stove. "It was like they were fighting for the right to be born first. Michael actually broke one of my ribs."

"Damn." Meg looked down at her bulging stomach. "Please be nice to Mommy. You can use my kidneys as punching bags for as long as you want. Just leave my bones alone."

Michael smiled down at her with a look so soft his scar seemed out of place. When he was around his family, he seemed more human than I had ever seen him. *That has to be the beers talking.*

"No weapons at the table," Mrs. Kale called from across the kitchen.

Michael paused, mid squat. Rolling his eyes, he straightened and un-clipped his holster. The gentle expression on his face made him look closer to who he was in the picture where he was kissing Lauren's cheek. He caught me looking just as he pulled his arms free from the straps.

"What?"

"Nothing," I said in a rush.

"When you've finished hanging that up, can you poke your head into your father's office and let him know dinner is about ready?" Mrs. Kale asked.

"Sure, Ma." He headed for the hallway.

I watched him as he grew closer. I guess no matter what title sat before your name or what the world called you, or what war you were involved in, you were never too important to get ordered around by your mom.

I was definitely buzzed from the drinks, but I wasn't buzzed enough to make fun of him about it in front of his family.

As he brushed by, I pushed away from the wall and headed for our shared room.

"Charlie, honey, can you grab the butter from the pantry?" Mrs. Kale called over her shoulder.

I paused in the mouth of the hallway. Michael even turned to look back at me.

"Uh." I waited for him to give me the nod toward my room, but he continued toward the study.

"Sure." Stepping back into the kitchen, I found the butter dish beside the pancake syrup. My vision blurred as I spun toward the table too fast. Blinking rapidly, I walked, or maybe I floated across the kitchen and placed the dish on the table.

Michael stepped into the kitchen just as I was making my retreat down the hall.

"I'll be in my room," I announced to no one in particular.

"How about you eat at the table tonight?" Mrs. Kale turned off the oven and pulled open the door. "Zak called and said the bar is swamped. He's short-staffed thanks to the flu that's been going around."

My eyes cut to Michael.

He was just as surprised as I was.

"I don't think that's a good idea . . ." I trailed off, waiting for Michael to jump in.

"Why not?" Mrs. Kale set a platter of pork chops in front of Meg. She was still trying to convince her baby to stop beating her from the inside. "We have an open spot at the table."

"Well, you know, because I'm a—I—I've always eaten in my room," I finished in a hurry.

"Mom—" Michael finally jumped in to save me.

"I think we can stop that now since we've gotten to know each other." Mrs. Kale looked right into Michael's eyes, daring him to contradict her.

One of the first things he said when he brought me here was to keep interactions with his family to a minimum. There's no way he was going to—

He looked at me. "Up to you."

Cheese and rice, what is going on? If I had a direct line to hell, I would've called to see if they were having a freak blizzard.

Maybe it was the beer, or maybe it was that he had pulled me from The Trial, but I actually believed he really meant it was up to me. I wasn't ready to be alone just yet. Humming with courage that didn't belong to me, I pulled my sleeve over my Contestant tattoo and made my way around the table.

I slowly pulled out the chair beside Michael's leather jacket, giving anyone a chance to object. When I sat down and no one flinched, I looked at Michael.

He stared at me for a second and then two. Then he nodded. It was ok.

Mr. Kale came in just as a bowl of fruit was placed on the table. "Hey." He grinned at his son and then me. "Congratulations on Ascending."

"I told you she would after she didn't cross the finish line," Michael corrected.

Mr. Kale went over to the sink and dropped his hat on the counter. "It still deserves a 'congratulations,' especially after what you went through."

I shrank down in my seat. "I thought no one was supposed to see the first two Trials but the Masters."

"Michael rewatched it here and we may have been in the same room when he did." Meg picked an imaginary piece of lint off her shirt.

I sighed. "Great."

"It was very courageous what you did for that other Contestant." Mrs. Kale set a bowl of crescent rolls in front of me.

"Even if he was a total dick and stole your door," Meg added.

"Most people are calling it stupid," I said.

"Well, I don't think it was stupid at all." Mrs. Kale pulled out her chair and sat down.

"Neither do I." Mr. Kale joined us at the table and took the first pork chop.

I wasn't convinced.

"Anyway, I'm sure you're sick and tired of talking about all of that. How's school going? Is Mrs. Hoehn still the substitute for Potion Chemistry?" Mrs. Kale asked, taking my plate.

She didn't skimp on the serving sizes. Any time Michael started to object on the amount of carbs, she silenced him with one look.

I expected the meal to be awkward, or at least filled with glares, but conversation flowed easily. Every time I thought the conversation had found its end, Mrs. Kale would jump in with another question.

This was something I wasn't used to. I wasn't invisible. She wanted to know about school and training. Mr. Kale and Meg joined in with the perfect quip. With each burst of laughter, breathing got a little easier.

I kept waiting for the other shoe to drop and crush me. I figured me being there would set one of them off. If the air filled with apprehension, I figured I could push away from the table and be in my room before something went flying.

But nothing happened. It was just dinner. A really fun dinner. The only way I could describe it was that I fit in. But that couldn't be it. I was a Hart and they were Kales.

As the plates were cleared, Meg recounted her adventure of putting the crib together. The charm they had suggested to assemble it kept leaving out screws. It took her nearly two hours to give up and call in the reinforcements. Mr. Kale was even unable to get all the pieces together.

"I'm convinced there's an extra screw," Mr. Kale said from the sink. "No matter what enchantment we used, there was always one left out. I even went as far as building the damn thing by hand."

"And there was still a screw missing?" Mrs. Kale asked, surprised.

"Yep." Meg readjusted in her seat for the fourth time.

"Well, we can always use a strengthening charm on the joints just in case." Mrs. Kale levitated another container of leftovers into the fridge.

"We could just order another one," Mr. Kale said.

"Why waste the time?" She shook her head. "The charm will—"

"Mom."

All heads turned at the sound of Meg's breathy and strained voice. She gripped the edges of the table with white knuckles.

"My water just broke."

Mr. Kale dropped the pan he was washing. Water and suds splashed over the sink and sloshed to the floor. Michael slowly rose from his seat.

"Atticus, take her upstairs." Mrs. Kale opened drawer after drawer, and grabbed every towel in the kitchen. "Michael, get the lights." She dashed down the hall. Her feet pounded up the stairs.

Mr. Kale rounded the table and slid his arms under Meg. Swiftly, but carefully, he took her from the room.

Michael ran down the hall and came back with his wand. Magic burst from the tip, darting toward the ceiling. His magic twisted the light bulbs from their fixtures and gently floated them to the floor. One by one, each room darkened, first the living room and then the kitchen.

"What can I do?" I asked.

"Unplug anything electric." He ran to the other side of the kitchen island.

"You're not taking her to the hospital?" I unplugged the coffee pot and then the toaster.

Michael shook his head. Grabbing the underside of the refrigerator, he dragged it away from the wall.

"It's not safe. No one will help a Kale." Bending over the counter, he reached between the wall and the fridge and yanked out the plug.

The walls shook as Meg's groans traveled down the stairs. The windows rattled. The lights that were still on flared brightly.

Michael ran down the hall without another word. Each room he passed darkened until the house was void of light. His boots pounded from room to room.

I stood helpless in the dark kitchen with my hair full of candied dandelions. Just like that, my perfect evening at the table was gone. Once that baby was born, would they want to see a Hart?

Retreating to my room, I collected my coat and threaded my arms through the sleeves. Snow flurried across the ground; it wasn't from any breeze.

Meg screamed. The house shook violently. The alarm clock by my bed had been forgotten when he took out the lightbulbs. It sparked and exploded.

I caught myself against the wall. When the shaking stopped, I darted to the front door and stepped outside.

Stuffing my hands into my pockets, I crossed the cold yard into the barn. With a full belly, I was finally starting to feel the fact that I had been up since three in the morning.

I took the familiar route up the ladder and into the hay loft. The last time I was up here, I set the entire barn on fire. It looked like that horrible night never happened. Stacks of hay reached toward the ceiling and there wasn't even a whiff of smoke.

Scooting between the hay bales, I retreated to the corner in the back. It was a little warmer up here, but not by much. Stuffing my hands into the front pocket of my hoodie, I scrunched down and leaned my head back. A chill bit at my nose, but the exhaustion from the long day lulled me to sleep in no time.

A hand dropped to my shoulder.

I startled awake. Magic flared down my arms.

Michael winced, pulling his hand back.

"Sorry." I yanked my magic back into my core, restoring the coldness of the hay loft. As my racing heart settled, I leaned back into the wood. "Is Meg ok?"

He nodded. "She and the baby are fine. What are you doing up here?" Shifting forward, he turned his shoulder and leaned against the wall beside me. With a sigh, he closed his eyes.

"I'm hiding. I figured I'd be the last person anyone wanted to see."

He turned his head with questions in his eyes. But the moment his gaze met mine, he caught my meaning.

"Lauren would've loved this," he murmured. "She couldn't wait for Meg or Zak to give her son cousins."

"But not you?"

Michael shook his head. "That life was never meant for me."

That was a can of worms to open at another time. "Why didn't you take Meg to a hospital?"

"For the same reason Zak doesn't tell anyone we're brothers. Being a Kale is dangerous. Thanks to me."

At that moment, I felt something I never thought I would ever feel for that man. I felt sorry for him. Was that why he stayed away from his family for so long? He wanted to keep them out of the spotlight and away from the war. I had spent one night eating at their table, surrounded by their family, and I had fallen head over heels. I couldn't imagine giving that up.

Hoping to turn the conversation to brighter things, I asked, "Did Meg have a boy or a girl?"

"A boy," he yawned. "She named him Quinton James."

I smiled at the sound of it. "That's a good name."

"It's a miracle that's the one she chose. She was throwing around names like Pixie and Oz at the beginning."

"Oz is cute. You could call him Ozzie for short."

"Oz doesn't need a nickname," he chuckled. "It's already short."

"Everyone needs a nickname." Fabric rustled and hay shifted as I turned toward him. "Does anyone ever call you Mike?"

"God, no. I think I'd break their neck just for trying."

"Someone somewhere during your three hundred years—"

"Two hundred and eighteen," he corrected.

"Whatever. Someone has to have given you a nickname." I nudged him. "You're avoiding the question. Are you scared I'll use it against you?"

"The day you scare me, Charlie Heart, is the day I'll hang up my leather jacket." Yawning, he scrubbed a hand across his face. "People have called me Master Kale for most of my life . . . I guess you calling me Michael is some form of a nickname."

"That's really sad."

"You're really sad." Groaning, he pushed himself to his feet, pausing to brush the hay off his pants. "Come on, Sunshine, let's go inside."

"Sunshine?" I took his hand and let him pull me to my feet.

"Yeah." He shrugged in the darkness. "Every time I look at you, I have the same feelings as if I'm looking at the sun. My eyes hurt and I'm annoyed."

I playfully swatted his arm. "Rude."

I was thankful for the shadows that hid my smile. I didn't want him to get any crazy ideas that I had enjoyed the conversation. Brushing past him, I squeezed through the stacks of hay and climbed back down into the barn.

In silence, we trudged through the freshly fallen snow and into the house. All the lightbulbs were still on the floor, locking in the shadows at every corner. Yawning, we stepped back into our room and we both went straight for our beds. Without another word, we went to sleep.

46

Three Steps Back

When I woke up, his bed was empty.

Early morning murmurs came from the kitchen, matching the soft morning light filtering through the blinds. Stretching my arms over my head, I yawned. After being awake for so long the day before, I slept like a rock. It might have been the best night of sleep I'd had in a long time.

I sat up and brushed the hair from my face. A stalk of hay poked out of the tangled mess. Rubbing the sleep from my eyes, I made my way into the bathroom for a shower. Once I smelled of citrus and was dressed in comfy layers, I advanced toward the door.

Just as I was about to open it, the handle turned. I jumped back as Michael entered.

In his hand was a plate of food.

My heart slowly slid down to my toes.

He set the full plate on the end of my bed. He didn't say anything and he didn't have to. We both knew what it meant. No one wanted Hart's kid around the baby. The step forward that took me to the table, was traded for three steps back.

My wet hair covered my face as I looked down at the plate. I used all of my energy to keep my voice light. "Wow, three whole pancakes. With syrup? Are you sure you didn't grab the wrong plate?" Taking the breakfast, I turned my back to him.

"Charlie . . ."

Keeping up the charade, I smelled the steaming food. "Your mom is a cooking genius." I picked up a piece of bacon and bit into it without tasting it.

If he was fooled by my act, he didn't say. He backed into the hall, pulling the door with him. "When that's gone, knock, and I'll take your plate to the sink."

"I know the drill." I sat on the bed and set the plate on my lap.

"Get as much homework done as you can. We might train later this afternoon if you don't mind the cold."

"Of course I mind the cold. I'm human."

"That's debatable." After a pause, he closed the door, leaving me alone.

A small squawk came from the kitchen. Another followed and Mrs. Kale crooned to the newborn.

I stared at the food in my lap. *And there was the other shoe.* I was a fool for thinking I belonged here. I learned a long time ago that fireplaces weren't meant for stray dogs. Definitely not ones found in trashcans.

When I was ten, I used to love Christmas: the lights, the decorations, the music. Best of all, I was placed in the best foster home I had ever been in.

The parents were in love. Loraine made cookies and smelled like pumpkin pie. Evan read the newspaper at the breakfast table and played cards with me when he got home from work.

They wanted to adopt me. The paperwork was filed. And then they got pregnant with twins. Since I was going to be a part of the family, they said I could help name them. I even got to paint their room.

But then Evan lost his job. They soon realized four mouths were easier to feed than five. On Christmas Eve, the social worker picked me up and I spent the remainder of the holiday sleeping on an office floor.

For the second time in my life, I was pushed aside. But this one with the Kales hurt more than the first. No one wanted Lucifer's daughter around a newborn. After everything they had been through, I didn't blame them.

47

The Dragon Farm

A few weeks had passed since Meg had her baby. We hadn't been back to the ranch since that night.

But on the day Christmas break started, as soon as I stepped into my room at the Magisterium, Michael Ported us to the ranch. I didn't even get a chance to say goodbye to Blake, Daniel, or Cornelia. That was probably for the best, since my mood was always sour during the Christmas season.

As soon as I stepped into the house, I went right to our room. Sitting cross-legged on the bed, I did my best to lose myself in homework.

Around noon, I expected the knock that announced lunch. I didn't bother looking up as Michael came over. He stopped beside me and dropped a letter on top of the open textbook in front of me.

Contestant Fifteen,

Please make your way to the Dragon Farm this afternoon at 3:00 pm for the second Award Challenge. Further instructions will be given when everyone arrives.

Master H. Lenin

"That's cryptic." I glared down at the letter. "What's the Dragon Farm?"
"A zoo."
My eyebrows shot up. "Like . . . a magical zoo?"
He nodded.
"Are there . . . dragons there?"
Michael shrugged. "That and other things."
I wanted to follow that line of thought. *What did he mean by other*

things, but there was an award up for grabs. "Do you know what the Award Challenge is?"

Michael walked back to the door. "I'm not allowed to say anything."

"Not even a hint?"

"Nope."

Sighing, I closed the textbook and dropped my feet to the cold floor. Thankfully, my over-the-knee socks kept most of the cold from berating my toes.

"When do we have to leave?" Stretching my arms over my head, I moved toward the bathroom.

"Two-thirty at the latest."

I glanced back at the Master Hunter. He was in his usual fitted black jeans and Henley shirt with two of the three buttons undone. His shoulders usually supported his double holster and his boots were laced. Sometimes I wondered if he actually slept with them on.

This morning however, his shoulders and feet were bare.

"Seeing as your boots aren't on, are we skipping training today?" I leaned my head and shoulder against the bathroom door frame.

"Nope. You're going to run a lap around the lake." He smirked.

"Didn't it snow last night?"

"It sure did. So, you better not slip and fall in." He dug a transporter marble from his pocket and tossed it to the bed. Lastly, he threw a blue mitten on top. "The glove will let you open the gate. The transporter will get you to the Award Challenge."

"You're not coming?"

"I'm leaving in twenty minutes. Guardians have their own *fun* day planned." He did not look like he was looking forward to it.

"You're really not going to tell me anything?"

"Nope." He nodded toward the door. "You should get going if you don't want to be late."

Rolling my eyes, I dressed in thick layers and pulled a beanie over my ears. When I stepped into the kitchen, Michael leaned against the counter beside a steaming bowl of oatmeal and a cup of hot chocolate, with no marshmallows.

As much as I wanted to forget what time of year it was, the moment I stepped into the heart of the house, there was no ignoring it.

A Christmas tree, just an inch shy of the ceiling, was tucked in the corner of the living room. The evergreen was wrapped in strands of gold ribbon and tinsel. All the ornaments were mismatched. Some were definitely handmade by the Kale children: popsicle stick sleds, roughly drawn reindeer, and something that vaguely looked like a star.

Cast on top of the tree was a golden orb that expelled refracted light on the walls. Flying around it, in unhurried laps, were three angels.

The fireplace had red stockings with fluffy white trim for each family member. There was a new one next to Meg's for Quinton. From there, every surface of the living room had at least three candles and one jar of candy.

The kitchen had frosted garland along the top of the cupboards. Gold pinecones, glittering frost, and ivory antlers poked out of the thick greenery.

The table was draped with a red and green checkered tablecloth. At the center was a tri-layer display of cookies: frosted sugar cookies, chocolate crinkles, and folded prune tarts.

The air smelled like cinnamon and nutmeg. I wondered if it was a charm placed over the house to make it smell like that, or if it was just the Christmas spirit.

Not wanting to give Michael a reason to make it two laps around the lake, I quickly devoured my breakfast and stepped out the back door. The air was brutally cold against my cheeks. The fresh blanket of dazzling snow was blinding.

Breathing in the sharp air, I slipped in my earbuds and stepped off the back porch. My feet broke through the fresh layer of snow. Reaching the shoreline, I picked up the pace.

It was hard to think that a year ago I was in Kansas working two jobs with no end in sight. And here I was jogging around a lake while on a holiday from a school that taught magic. I didn't know if it was fate's best joke, or the biggest glow-up in history.

Lost in thought, the new snow took my foot out from under me. I landed on my hip. The fresh powder sifted down the neck of my shirt and into the tops of my shoes. Biting back curses, I pushed myself back up and continued my run.

I fell twice more. When I made it back to the warmth of the ranch house, I might as well have gone running without a coat. I was damp and chilled to the bone.

I thought about going to the Award Challenge in sweats and my hoodie, but Daniel was going to be there. That thought sent me into the shower.

At two, a tap came from the cracked bathroom door. It swung open as Meg leaned her shoulder against the doorframe. Quinton was wrapped against her chest.

I hadn't seen her since that night at the table. She practically glowed with happiness. My eyes were drawn to the tiny bundle with bright red curls on her chest. I took a step away from the pair.

"Michael told me to give you a thirty-minute warning." Her eyes darted from my iPod playing on the counter to my wand pressed to my scalp.

Magic singed my head as it wrapped around a lock of dark brown hair and pulled it into a spiral. I selected another section. "Did he tell you about the Award Challenge?"

"Nope."

I didn't buy it.

"Why are you dressing up?" she countered.

"I'm not." Avoiding her eyes, I set my wand on the counter and combed my fingers through my hair, breaking up the curls.

"Yeah," she said dryly. "That was really convincing. Want to try again?"

I tucked my wand into the lining of the jean jacket and brushed past her into the bedroom to grab my status pin.

"Is it for a boy?" she asked from the doorway.

"Of course not," I said, maybe a little too quickly.

"Mhmm," she said knowingly. "What's his name?"

Tossing the transporter from one hand to the other, I stepped into the hall. "I need to get going. Don't want to be late!"

"Hey, are you ok?" she called after me. "You seem mad at me or something."

"No, I'm not—I'm not mad." I shook my head and faced her. "I'm a Hart. I shouldn't be around—" I gestured to the baby. "Him."

"Who said that?"

"It didn't need to be said."

Her expression softened. "You know, growing up, I had three older brothers: Zak, Michael, and Lawrence. We all grew up together. So, I think I have the authority to say you're not Lawrence. Your First Trial proved that." She patted Quinton's back. "If you want, you can hold him."

"I've never held a baby before."

"It's surprisingly easy." She tugged at the corner of the wrap. It slithered away from the baby and draped around her neck like a scarf. One of the girls in my foster home had a water baby doll. The baby Meg held to her chest was just as small.

"Oh, wow," I breathed.

"Hold out your arms," Meg directed. Moving carefully, she repositioned the baby and held him toward me.

"Wait, what about my magic? Will my status hurt him?"

"You're wearing sleeves and he's in a blanket. He'll be fine." She set him in my arms.

He was smaller than a popcorn bag. I wanted to hold him tighter, but I didn't want to crush him. I took in his rosy cheeks, his long eyelashes, and the coils of red hair. "He has so much hair," I whispered.

"It looks like a little wig," Meg laughed.

"He's really cute."

"I think he looks like a baked potato." Meg brushed a curl off his forehead. "But he's the cutest baked potato," she crooned.

Quinton started to squirm and whine. If it was possible, more wrinkles appeared on his face and it made him even cuter.

"That's his hungry cry." Meg pulled him from my arms. "And I've almost made you late."

"Shit." I bolted for the front door.

"Good luck!" she called after me.

Running down the drive, I skidded to a stop at the gate. Using the mitten, I grabbed the iron and pulled. The wards broke apart with a flash of gold. As the gate closed behind me, I took the transporter from my pocket. With a deep breath, I pulled on my magic and the transporter ripped my feet from the gravel road.

I appeared on a long sidewalk. On either side were statues of monsters: a griffin, a hippogriff, a snake with wings, a sphynx, a three-headed dog, and a giant spider. On and on went the line of mythical creatures. They were so life-like they could have been real monsters painted white. As I passed underneath, their eyes seemed to follow me.

The sidewalk led to a large archway of thick green vines. Large orange flowers clustered together to spell "The Dragon Farm." Beneath it was a sign: "where the past and the present breathe the same air."

As I passed under the arch, magic glided over my skin. I turned back and saw snow covering the ground, but on the side where I stood, it was sunny and the grass was as green as if it were the middle of summer.

Murals were carved into the sides of the welcome center and the gift shop sparkled with jewels. Joyful music played from hidden speakers that lined gleaming white sidewalks.

"Contestant Heart."

I startled, but found no one. There were only leaves, florals, and a little golden bird—a little bird that glowed as bright as magic. With a cheerful chirp, it soared closer and landed on my shoulder.

"You're a little early," the bird said in Master Lenin's voice. "The Award Challenge is this way." It jumped off and glided down the center path.

For the first time in my life, I found myself following a bird.

The sidewalk was hedged with thick bushes; tiny flowers that looked like orchids sprinkled through the dark leaves. As I passed, the blooms moved out from the shadow and back to the light. Some of the trees moved without wind and, I swear, I heard a couple flowers giggle as I walked by.

"Contestant Heart," the bird prompted as I took too long watching the flowers.

"Sorry!" I jogged farther down the sidewalk.

I hadn't taken more than a dozen steps before I slowed again. The sidewalk split, going to the left or the right. The pen in front of me was filled with wild flowers, a running brook, and a unicorn.

I laughed. "You're kidding."

The beautiful creature lifted its head at the sound. His black coat glinted with rainbows in the afternoon sunlight. I walked up to the fence and was surprised when he took a few steps closer.

"Hi." Leaning over the railing, I held out my hand.

The unicorn extended its neck. Just when his fuzzy muzzle was about to touch my fingertips, he jerked his head back.

"You're not supposed to do that."

I spun around, clasping my hands behind my back. Daniel walked toward me, pointing. Right beside me was a sign. *Stay behind the fence.*

"Oh." My cheeks flushed. "But come on. It's a *unicorn*."

He grinned. "Never seen one before?"

"No!" I turned back to the enclosure. The unicorn watched curiously from where he stood. "I'm guessing by your lack of enthusiasm, you have."

Daniel joined me at the railing. "When my mom and Master Harlan were still married, he was putting the final enclosures together. He wanted this place to be the Eighth Wonder of the World. I spent a lot of time here."

"Do you think we have time to look around? I've always loved zoos." Blake had taken me to my first one a couple years back. It was where I got my light blue hoodie.

Daniel looked like I had just called his mom a pole dancer. "It's not a zoo."

I bit back a smile. "A place where animals are in enclosures and people pay to see them is, by definition, a zoo."

"A zoo implies a smelly, tourist trap," he countered. "The Farm has far more class than that. It holds our world's most exotic, beautiful, and dangerous creatures."

"Then it's a magical zoo."

He rolled his eyes. "If we had time to look around, we wouldn't have that," he pointed to the gold bird, "leading us. Which is too bad. Last time I was here, they hired an arctic mermaid."

Did I hear him right? "Hired?"

"Most of the sentient creatures get paid to be here. The dangerous ones are here as a sort of prison sentence. There are some that basically rent their enclosure."

That is so cool. I pushed off the railing and walked to where the little bird was waiting a few yards off.

As we made our way down the winding sidewalk, Daniel pointed out different buildings and enclosures. The aquarium was one of the biggest with blue and green glass walls. Not only were there mermaids, but he told me about sea serpents, megalodons, and even a Loch Ness monster.

There was a petting zoo with a mini-Pegasus, a three-headed puppy, a miniature light blue unicorn, a sphynx cub, and something that looked like a baby long-neck dinosaur.

Farther in, we walked by an enclosure with a spider the size of a medium dog, known as a Talker. It had a yellow ring around each leg. Daniel called it the zombie spider because the venom made the dead move and talk like it was in pain to draw in more prey.

If I thought that was bad, the next creature topped it.

The Dresser sparked the story of Frankenstein. It looked human—sort of—with body parts from both men and women. It killed people and used their body parts to replace the ones that had started to rot. It ate what it didn't use.

We walked by a fairy pavilion. Tinkling music could be heard through the glass doors. Right next to it was the pixie pavilion. It sounded like a boulder was rolling through a china cupboard.

All the while, there were signs along the path: playgrounds, restaurants, a carousel, a Ferris wheel, parks, ponds with paddle boats, and even a Pegasus-riding enclosure.

Master Harlan wanted it to be the Eighth Wonder of the World, and I was starting to think he had succeeded. Surrounded by foreign vegetation and strange creatures, the Award Challenge slipped from my mind. For a moment, Daniel and I were just taking a weird walk. I wondered what it would be like to hold his hand.

The golden bird took us around the corner and landed on a lamppost. "Please wait here." And then it disappeared in a flurry of sparkles.

A few Contestants were milling around before a chain-link fence. Thiago was sprawled across a bench with his arm over his eyes. Blake stood looking over a rolling landscape of green hills. Dmitri and Igorek leaned against a tree smoking. No one else hung out together.

As Daniel and I came closer, each looked at us with wary expressions. Not that I could blame them. I looked at them the same. The last Award Challenge gave the winner a look at their first fear. The award today had to be just as good.

Moving away from the majority of the Contestants, Daniel and I made our way over to Blake.

As we drew closer, I saw that the fence gleamed with magic. It was so tall, it seemed to disappear into the sky.

I skipped over and bumped my shoulder against his. "Hey. What are you looking at?"

"That," he breathed, nodding to the enclosure.

I followed his gaze in time to see a hill move. But it wasn't a hill. Now that I was paying attention, I saw it was covered in scales the size of dinner plates. The beast rose until it was as high as a three-story house.

"Cheese and rice," I stumbled back from the fence. My neck hurt as I looked up at the massive beast.

It planted its front feet into the ground and arched its back. As it stretched, its claws sank easily into the ground. From its sides, two wings fanned over its head. They were so thin I could almost see through them.

Finally, it opened its mouth and let out a yawn. Large teeth gleamed in the sun. Then its yellow eyes opened. They were so big my reflection, from head to toe, stared back at me. Its head and neck reminded me of a snake. The body was lean and agile with a lazy, swishing tail that looked like the head of a spear.

It was a dragon. A living, breathing dragon.

"Beautiful, isn't she?" Blake craned his neck to look up at it.

"That has to be one of the ten still awake," Daniel said in awe.

"I've always wanted one," Blake said longingly. "I've heard of a couple Royals who have them as pets."

"Not any of the cool ones, though," Daniel countered.

"What do you mean still awake?" As hard as I tried, I couldn't look away from the glittering creature. It was equally frightening and stunning. I was torn between being dazzled and horrified.

"Dragons used to roam all over," Blake answered first. "They were the number one predator, eating Royals and Regs. Everyone. It takes a lot of magic to kill something that big, not to mention, they are ridiculously hard to kill." He gestured to the towering beast. "Instead of wasting the magic and the lives to get rid of them, the School Masters ordered all the dragons to be enchanted to sleep and covered in dirt. As time passed, trees and plants grew over them."

I snuck a peek at him. *He's totally geeking out.*

He rolled his eyes. "Laugh all you want."

"I didn't say anything." I tried to keep my smile in check. "So, dragons are sleeping underground?"

He shook his head. "They're in the majority of the mountains and hills around the globe."

I turned my gaze back to the dragon. *There was one of those under every peak and slope?* I was suddenly very happy I grew up in the flatlands of Kansas.

"If I win The Trial, I'm going to buy one." Blake stared longingly at the dragon as it lumbered away from the fence.

"What on earth are you going to do with a dragon?" Daniel laughed.

"Have the coolest pet ever." He grinned.

A little golden bird dropped on his head.

"What the—" Blake swung at it like it was a fly.

The bird easily dodged and flew around my shoulders, catching Daniel's attention. It darted between each of the Contestants, tweeting happily, until everyone was awake and watching.

It landed on the handle of the door to the dragon enclosure.

"Contestants, come this way." It hopped into the air just as the door swung open. Then it darted into the enclosure.

"We're going in there?" I hissed. "With that thing?"

Daniel took my hand.

My heart somersaulted around my chest. It wasn't because of where we were going. He was holding my hand.

My magic. Just as I was about to pull my hand free, I realized that he hadn't flinched. Master Lenin mentioned that only certain statuses could feel mine. Maybe he couldn't feel it. I dared to tighten my hold on his hand.

"The fence is for people coming in, not her getting out," Daniel said gently. "She's well-fed and happy. She has no reason to come near us." He pulled me toward the door.

"What if fighting a dragon *is* the Award Challenge?"

Daniel's hand tightened.

"No way." Blake shook his head. "They would put us in one at a time. Not all together." With much more confidence than I had, he headed for the door.

That did very little to reassure me, but everyone else was walking in like it was completely normal. So, I let Daniel pull me in.

We walked in silence, up and down the hills of the dragon's enclosure for a few minutes. Just as Daniel said, she stayed on the far side. She didn't even look our way, as if we were only ants walking through her yard.

The golden bird led us up the crest of a hill and glided down on the other side. At the bottom was a circular, one-story building. The School Masters stood by a single door talking excitedly. Well, some of them were. Dmitri's Guardian leaned against the wall with a strong look of boredom.

All the observing Masters were there, chatting in tight groups. Most of them held glasses with tall stems and small colorful umbrellas.

In a group next to them were all the Guardians. Unlike the Masters, none of them were talking. When they saw us walk up, they made a beeline for their Contestants.

I spotted my Guardian on the outskirts of the group and immediately dropped Daniel's hand. I stuffed my hands into the pocket of my jacket and made my way over, hoping he didn't see me with Daniel.

"You made it on time," Michael noted.

"Always with the tone of surprise." My eyes drifted toward Daniel. He met my wandering gaze with a smile. I turned back to Michael and found him watching.

"Contestants!" Master Lenin called. He stood in front of the door to the round room. "Thank you for being prompt. We are excited to have you participate in the second Award Challenge."

Hushed excitement rolled through the Contestants. Butterflies fluttered through my stomach.

"Masters and Guardians, please follow Master Harlan to your viewing room."

My stomach twisted as Michael walked toward the other School Master. Whatever was about to happen, I was going to do alone.

Once the crowd threaded through the door, leaving us alone with Master Lenin, he turned to our group of fourteen.

"Contestants, please follow me." The School Master moved through the same door.

We walked into a room barely big enough to fit all of us with a low ceiling. Inside, there were fourteen chairs and nothing more. Once the door was closed, the only way out was on the other side of the room.

Master Lenin stood in that doorway and waited for us to take a seat. Shoulder to shoulder with Daniel and Blake, I felt uneasy about whoever was sitting directly behind me.

"Behind this door," Master Lenin pointed his thumb over his shoulder, "is a suit of armor. Your objective is to injure the mannequin underneath it.

"You'll have access to all of the weapons in your training room. You'll be timed and your wards, whether they hit or miss, will be counted. The Contestant who takes the least amount of time and casts the least amount of magic will gain a five-minute head start in the Second Trial."

"Bloody hell," Blake breathed.

Thiago let out a low whistle across the room.

Five minutes without any other Contestants breathing down your neck? Sign me up. I needed all the help I could get to make it to the Third Trial.

"We'll go in order of Contestant number. Contestant Three, Tala Abalos, you are first. As soon as you're ready, step through and we shall begin. Good luck." Master Lenin disappeared through the doorway.

The room fell silent in his wake.

Tala stood from her seat. She sent a nervous glance around the room and headed toward the door. Rolling her shoulders, she pushed through it.

"Five minutes," Blake muttered. He might as well have said it at full volume. No one else was talking.

I snuck a glance at the rest of the Contestants. Anna pulled out her phone and started watching a movie. Thiago took out a book and started reading, although he didn't turn a page. Malan jiggled his leg. Amelia chewed on her nails.

Dmitri chuckled. "Everyone's so nervous." He clicked his tongue in a condescending manner. "Are you nervous, Iggy?"

"Nope." Igorek was slouched so low in his seat that his head rested against the back. He even had his eyes closed.

"Do you have to be talking right now?" Emeka grumbled from the front.

"Of course he does." I glared at Dmitri from the corner of my eye. "He loves the sound of his voice too much."

"I wasn't talking to you," Emeka snapped.

I slid a little lower in my seat.

"Alright kids, let's settle down." Blake put a comforting hand on my knee. "They obviously put us in a small room, hoping we'd tear out each other's throats. I, for one, like my throat. So, let's play nice and get out of here."

I shot Dmitri one last glare and turned my back to him. His chuckle made the hairs on the back of my neck stand straight up.

After that, no one broke the silence. One by one, Master Lenin called each Contestant. Once they passed through the door, we didn't see them again. There was no clock in the room to track each Contestant's progress. Some definitely took longer than others.

As the room emptied, the tension level rose close to suffocating.

The sync ring around my thumb buzzed twice. *You ok?*

My nervous fingers tapped back. *Yes.*

When Blake was called, I gave him a high-five before he left the room. Then it hit me. He was Contestant Twelve. After Daniel, it was my turn.

Think, Charlie, think! Michael had to have mentioned something about this. *What's the first thing you do when you face a new opponent? You look them over for weakness.* Quickly, I drew up a game plan.

I was so lost in thought, I almost didn't notice Daniel stand up for his turn.

My stomach churned with butterflies. *I can do this.* No matter how many times I ran through the steps, when my name was called, everything that could go wrong filled my mind.

With shaky hands, I started toward the door.

"Say hello to my head start for me," Dmitri called. Igorek chuckled from his seat.

Clenching my teeth, I ripped the door open and slammed it behind me.

48

The Second Challenge Winner

If I thought the last room was cramped, the hallway on the other side of the door felt like a shoe box. The low ceiling held only two lights that barely did anything to illuminate the room.

Lining the walls were all the weapons Michael and I had worked with over the last three months: knives, a few short swords, and darts.

Did they want me to select a weapon?

"Never take a weapon you've never used into a fight," Michael told me once. *"You don't know how it works or how it doesn't."*

Leaving the wall of weapons, I stepped out of the narrow hallway and into a room in the shape of a perfect circle. Encasing the entire space was the familiar black glass I had seen everywhere in The Trial. Now I knew where all the Masters and Guardians had disappeared to. They were watching.

At the very center stood a mannequin dressed in armor as red as a maraschino cherry. Around the perimeter of the room was a red circle ten feet from the mannequin.

I looked carefully around the room and noticed there was no clock. They set it up so we had no way to tell how much time was passing.

Shit.

I shoved my hands into the pockets of my jean jacket and found a surprise. Before leaving the ranch, I had taken my iPod. With each song that passed, I would roughly know how long I was working.

I took out the iPod, not bothering to hide it. When no one called me out, I untangled the cord. Hooking the buds in my ears, I stepped over the red line and hit play.

Bobbing my head to the music, I circled the armor. It was unlike any

325

I had seen. I was expecting the kind that knights wore or what I had seen on all of the Masters' personal guards. Instead, it was smooth and athletic. There were no sharp edges. It curved around the shoulders and down the arms. Between the pieces of armor was a thick black material. It reminded me of the armor I saw Lawrence's shadow wear.

I looked over its red surface and came up empty. I had no idea how to make it break.

Each second that ticked by made my nerves ramp up.

"*Slow down,*" Michael's voice told me. "*Rushing won't do you any favors.*"

I looked at every crease and dent on the armor. I walked around it twice to make sure I saw everything.

Coming back to the front, I gently traced my fingers over the cold metal. Magic tickled my fingers. It was infused with magic. *Does that mean it repels wards? What about knives?*

I dashed back to the cramped hallway and grabbed one of the knives from the wall. Stopping before the broad chestplate, I dragged it across the bright red surface. The blade slid across with a high-pitched shriek, but it didn't leave a scratch.

Any direct attack would bounce off, like light on a mirror.

There had to be a way to get into the armor; therefore there was a way out. If there was a way out, then there was a weak link somewhere.

When I looked over the armor, I didn't find any vulnerabilities. Then I realized I hadn't looked everywhere. Rolling onto my back, I looked up. That's when I saw it. There was a small clip on the left side, beneath the arm. *If I broke it, would it open?* I quickly searched for any other visible clips and found none. It was my best bet.

I got to my feet as the third song started. Taking my wand from my jacket, I flexed my nervous fingers around the shaft. Then I pulled on my magic.

I snapped my wand at the armor. The ward curved under the arm and struck the clip. The chestplate burst open like a water balloon, revealing a target painted on the mannequin beneath.

Not wasting another second, I fired the kill shot. The dummy fell to the floor, smoking and broken. The door on the other side of the room opened with a click.

I jerked the headphones out of my ears. I did it.

"Yes!" I did a little happy dance before I remembered people were most likely watching.

Too excited to care, I quickly curtsied to the glass walls. Stepping over the smoking metal, I left the round room and stepped back into the dragon enclosure.

Coiling my earbuds back around my iPod, I walked over to Blake and Daniel. Both boys lounged against the wall looking thoroughly stressed.

"How'd you do?" Daniel asked.

I took the space next to them and leaned my back against the cold siding. "I'm not going to lie. I think I kicked ass." I couldn't help the smile that followed.

"Are you sure?" Blake leaned around Daniel to shoot me a smile. "If you listen closely, you can hear those five minutes calling my name."

"I don't know . . . 'Daniel Phillips, Second Challenge Winner,' has a nice ring to it," Daniel said.

Blake rolled his eyes and muttered something about arrogant Americans.

I smothered my laugh and kept any additional comments to myself. I crossed my fingers and hid them behind my back. *Please, let me have those five minutes.*

"Ok, I can't just keep standing here." Blake pushed off from the wall. He paused. "Do you think if I tried to pet the dragon that she would eat me?"

Daniel shook his head. "She likes chin scratches."

Blake nearly bolted across the enclosure.

"Are you sure?" I asked as he got closer to the large creature.

Daniel nodded. "She grew up here. She's as tame as a kitten."

I snuck a glance at him. While Blake had been about to combust with nerves, he looked rather calm.

"You seem to be handling this well," I noted.

He gave me a small smile. "This is one of my favorite places. I spent a lot of summers here. This was the last enclosure to be built, so while there were construction crews on the other side of the island, there was nothing here but open land. I came back here and studied a lot."

With the bright sunset colors and a lazy breeze, it was paradise. Or, close to paradise, since there were monsters everywhere.

He uncrossed his arms. "Did you have a place like this?"

I thought for a moment. "My roof. After work, I used to pop the screen out of my window and sit outside. I didn't study out there."

He chuckled.

"But it was kind of like this. Peaceful and away from everything."

His hand shifted closer to mine. The side of my hand tingled with anticipation. His hand was so close, just a breath away.

"Are you scared?" he asked quietly. "For the Second Trial?"

"Oh, yeah. I have no experience, no Save, and an angry Russian who wants to use my back for target practice." I looked down at our close hands. "Are you?"

"I haven't been thinking about it, to be honest. That's the only thing keeping me sane. But now that I know how they work, it makes it so much scarier."

"You said so yourself that they don't reuse themes. So, we know the Second Trial won't be based on fear."

His smile came back. "There's that."

"Nothing's as bad as fear, right?"

"I guess we'll find out." His hand brushed mine. "I'm glad you're going in there with me. I know we're competing against each other, but I'm glad you'll be there."

"I'm glad you'll be there, too."

The afternoon breeze brushed a lock of hair in front of my face. With nervous fingers, he tucked it behind my ear. His fingers lingered at the corner of my jaw. His gaze dropped to my lips.

A cry of excitement pulled our attention to the door. Marina, from Serpentine, pounded her fist against her chest. "Now that's what I'm talking about."

Laughing, I watched her wander away from the group. She continued to nod to herself. Too nervous to look back at Daniel, I pretended to look for Blake.

When Igorek, the last Contestant, shut the door behind him, it wasn't long before the Guardians came out. As soon as I saw Michael and Atlas, I moved away from Daniel.

Everyone refused to walk within five feet of the Hunters. Seeing Blake by the dragon, Atlas peeled off to get him. Michael strolled over with a rare crooked smile.

"Can I borrow you for a moment?" he asked.

With a nod, I followed him away from the group of Contestants. When we were out of eavesdropping distance, he bent down to my ear. "How do you think you did?"

My hopes dropped. Looking down, I fiddled with one of the silver buttons of the jean jacket. "Since you're asking, poorly."

"On the contrary, you beat every single Contestant."

My eyes snapped up to his. In the fading afternoon light, they were so dark I could hardly tell where his pupils started. "Are you serious?"

He broke into a full-out smile. "I've never been more serious in my life."

I stared at him. "We got the head start?"

He dragged a hand over his face and nodded. "There's no way the judges would give it to anyone else. You finished in nearly nine minutes. The shortest time was Contestant Seventeen, and even then, it took him four strikes to break the armor."

"Oh, my God." I suddenly wanted to sit down, or hug him, or do a happy dance. Or a combination of all three. "Oh, my God!" I threw my arms around him.

He went rigid.

Oh, right. No touching. I quickly pulled back. For the first time, I was starting to feel real hope. *I could get a title. My life.*

He cleared his throat. "It looks like you're paying attention after all, Contestant Heart."

I grinned up at him.

Master Lenin Ported in front of the group. "Thank you for your patience and for your time today. Before I dismiss you for your holiday break, I think you all would like to know who won the Second Award Challenge."

I bit the inside of my lip to keep the smile off my face. Stepping around Michael, I moved so I could see Dmitri's face.

"It was a close call, but only one stood out." Master Lenin drew his wand from his pocket. "Here are our top three finalists. For the rest of you, your ranking is beside the door."

With a jerk of the wrist, a gold spark shot out and outlined a chart with three sections. Name, time, and strikes against the armor.

Starting from the bottom, it filled in three names.

I looked at the empty spot at the top. Instantly I knew something was wrong. Michael said I had the least amount of time. Whoever got first took fifteen minutes and had three strikes.

When a name filled the top spot, my heart dropped. Curses growled out of Michael.

"Contestant Eight, Emeka Selasi!" The group applauded, although the Contestants only did it out of obligation.

My eyes scanned the list until I found my name. I placed second. Beside my time, the quickest out of the three, it said I had four strikes.

"I don't understand." I turned to Michael. "I only used two wards against the armor."

His jaw popped in irritation. "They must have counted when you touched it with your hand and with the knife."

"But I got the shortest time."

He paused, and then shook his head. "Lawrence won't let me win."

"What?"

The muscle in his jaw flexed. "This is his Trial. He's using it to build credit among the traditionalists. I didn't play when I was chosen, but if I help someone win now, I get the credit he's been counting on."

"Are you kidding—"

"Keep your voice down." He shot a glare to a Contestant who dared to look over at my outburst.

"Well, it's stupid."

He gave me a scolding look, telling me to be cautious. But he didn't object.

"Why aren't you more pissed off about this?" I asked. "Those five minutes should be ours."

"Because I've been expecting him to do something like this sooner or later."

Screw that. But I bit my tongue. I turned back to glare at the chart. My anger dissolved when I saw the name underneath mine.

Contestant Nineteen, Dmitri Theodore. Fourteen minutes. Six strikes.

I beat him. Noticeably.

My gaze sought out Dmitri. He combed his hands wildly through his blue hair as he spoke furiously with his Guardian. His eyes flicked over to where I stood.

I met his heated gaze with a grin of victory.

Michael placed his hand on my elbow. With a sharp sting of magic, he Ported us out of the enclosure before the other Contestant could react.

49

Christmas Morning

I snuggled deeper into the covers.

With a yawn, my eyes popped open. I knew it was late morning by the amount of sunlight streaming through the window.

Past the curtains, the sun was high without a single cloud as a companion. A thick layer of snow cloaked the yard and piled on the naked tree branches. The wind must have taken a holiday too, because nothing moved. It was a beautiful morning. It was also Christmas.

The bedroom door creaked open. Pushing the hair out of my face, I squinted across the room. Mrs. Kale wore pajamas covered in penguins with Santa hats. She had on a red robe to match.

She winced when she caught me looking. "Did I wake you?"

I shook my head. "I was awake." I scrubbed a hand over my face. I expected the Kales to leave me alone today. Seeing Mrs. Kale started the day with a surprise.

"I've been keeping breakfast warm for you." Crossing the room, she sat next to me. With a soft smile, she tucked a tangled lock behind my ear. "But I was worried it wouldn't be any good if I waited much longer. It's almost ten o'clock."

I shot a glance at the clock to confirm the time. That's when I noticed she didn't bring the food with her.

"I'm surprised you slept so long. With as much noise as Meg and Zak have been making, you would've thought they were six." To illustrate her words, a wave of laughter rolled down the hall.

Along with the sounds of merriment, there were delicious smells. I couldn't name what I was smelling. But it made my stomach growl.

She looked at the hallway with a smile that crinkled her eyes. "I've always loved that sound." She turned back to me. "You missed the initial present opening, so I thought I would just give this to you myself." She pulled a small red box, topped with a green bow, from her robe and set it beside me.

"What is it?"

"Your Christmas present."

My gaze jumped back to her. I looked at the open door behind her. *Did Michael know about this?*

"Anyone who stays in my house over Christmas gets a present."

"Even me?"

She smiled. "Even you."

"But I didn't get you anything. Or anyone else."

"You did." Her smile grew when another wave of laughter moved down the hall. "This is the first time my family has been together for Christmas in seventy years. You brought Michael home. You gave my family a chance to fit back together."

"I wouldn't say that—"

"Yet here we are. All of us." She nodded to the wrapped box. "Open it."

The first and last present I had gotten was a bus ticket from Blake. I plucked the small box from the rumpled comforter and peeled the wrapping paper back to find a plain white box underneath. Inside was an old bronze key.

"It's a key to the front gate," Mrs. Kale explained.

I froze. When I first came here, Michael mentioned the protection wards around the ranch. No one could get in or out unless it was through the gate. It only opened for the Kales.

She just gave the daughter of Lawrence Hart a key to her home.

"I can't have this." I dropped the lid back on and shoved it back at her. "If Michael knew—"

"This is my ranch. I can invite who I want."

"But . . . Lawrence is my—"

"You're nothing like that man, honey. Trust me. I watched him grow up under this very roof." She picked up the box and grabbed my hand. "Michael told me a little of what you went through growing up. About how many places you lived. With this," she placed the key in my palm, "you'll have a home here. If you want it. Everyone needs a safe place they can go where a hot meal will be waiting. And I want that for you. Here."

I stared at the key, unable to take my eyes off of it. Something bloomed in my chest, making it hard to breathe.

She patted my knee and rose to her feet. "I've left breakfast on the table. And I talked Michael into letting you eat whatever you want."

Still reeling, I asked, "How'd you manage to do that?"

"He really didn't get a say in the matter. Come out when you're ready. I think from now on, you can eat at the table with us." She went into the kitchen. A few seconds later, the microwave hummed.

I looked back at the key in the center of my palm. The cool metal tingled with magic.

A home.

The pressure in my chest built and my lip trembled. A tear rolled down my cheek. At a very young age, I had given up hope that I would have a place like this. When you're thrown out with the trash, no one wants you. Yet, here I was.

It didn't matter if I got a title, left the Heel, and Michael hated me for it. It didn't matter if I was forced to fight. It didn't even matter that Michael was going to kill me at the end of all of this. Wrapping my fingers around the key, I hugged my fist to my chest. Another tear threatened to run down my face.

A home.

Sliding out from the sheets, I pulled on my light blue hoodie and tucked the key into the main pocket. I wanted it with me always.

Wiping my face dry, I followed the delicious smells to the kitchen. Mrs. Kale was in front of the microwave, heating up a hot chocolate. A can of whipped cream sat beside the Christmas tree mug.

I grabbed the last empty plate on the table. Laid out on a red tablecloth was a plate of pancakes splattered with green and red sprinkles. There was a pan of bacon and sausage links.

I snuck a glance at the living room where the rest of the Kales sat. This wouldn't be the first time one member of a family wanted me and the others wanted me in the backyard.

But none of them turned to glare.

The whole family was still in their pajamas watching *It's a Wonderful Life*. Scattered across the carpet were bits of crumpled wrapping paper and discarded bows. Various boxes and clothes with tags still attached were inter-mixed in the mess. The tree was empty underneath and the stockings above the fireplace were limp.

The black and white film held everyone's attention. Mr. Kale was in his recliner, closest to the fireplace, directly across from the TV. Meg was snug-gled against one armrest of the couch. A fluffy blanket was sprawled across her lap, and on top of it, was Quinton, sleeping. Zak sat beside her with his arm around her and a cup of steaming coffee in his other hand.

Michael was on the other end of the couch, sporting a new dark blue sweater. He took a savoring sip of his coffee.

I grabbed a sprinkled pancake and a couple sausage links.

Mrs. Kale came over and handed me the mug of steaming hot choco-late. When she saw what I picked, she grabbed a couple more pancakes and plopped them onto my plate.

"You should try the strawberry syrup on those," she said in a hushed tone. Rubbing her hand across my back, she joined her family in the living room.

I picked up the small pitcher of red syrup and poured it over the pan-cakes. I debated going back to my room, but the thought of eating alone was too heartbreaking.

My feet took me to the edge of the dark green carpet in the living room. Nervously, I looked around for a spot to sit.

I wouldn't dream of sitting on the couch. That would put me in a Kale-brother sandwich. I wasn't ready for that, and I didn't think they would be either.

However, on the floor, closest to the door and Mrs. Kale, was a fine spot.

Gripping my plate even tighter, I stepped onto the carpet and quickly dropped into the place I scouted. Curling my legs under me, I placed my back against the armrest of the couch.

When no one immediately threw me out, I released the breath I was holding. I dared a peek at the family.

No one paid me any hateful attention. No one was tense or holding a wand. Even Zak remained casual as he lounged against his sister.

Still clutching my plate, I peeked at the only person who mattered.

Michael looked down at me over the rim of his Santa mug. His eyes flickered to my plate with a ghost of a smile. When his dark gaze met mine, his eyes didn't narrow or glare. Instead, he scooted over to give me more room.

I tapped the sync ring around my thumb. *Ok?*

He nodded and tapped back. *Yes.*

Relaxing against the couch, I picked up my fork and started in on my pancakes.

"Have you seen this movie, Charlie?" Mrs. Kale asked.

"Best Christmas movie ever, and no one can say otherwise," Zak said firmly.

With my mouth full, I shook my head.

"I remember when it came out," Meg mumbled sleepily.

I nearly choked. "Didn't it come out in the sixties?"

Michael shook his head. "Forty-six."

"Magic-User aging freaks me out." I took another bite of my pancakes.

"Why?" Meg laughed.

"You're all so old, and you don't look it."

"For Royals, we're fairly young," Meg argued. "Mom and Dad didn't have us until they were in their three hundreds."

"Cheese and rice," I muttered.

"Since when did we talk during movies?" Zak asked, looking pointedly at his family.

Mrs. Kale pretended to zip her lips closed. With a wink, she turned back to the TV.

Pulling my plate closer, I ate slowly, enjoying each bite. Sipping my hot chocolate, I watched my first black and white movie surrounded by the last people I thought I would ever be comfortable with. For reasons beyond me, despite everything, I didn't want it any other way.

50

Don't Be Late

"Eyes on me," Michael barked.

A week before the Second Trial, I was where I always was when I wasn't in class. Training. Two months passed rather quickly, and before I knew it, I was staring down the barrel of The Trial's loaded gun.

Unlike the First Trial, getting closer to the second, I found my confidence growing. I could throw a knife at moving targets and get a fair number of bullseyes. My wards were precise and sharp. I was leaning into the strength of my Royal status with hand-to-hand training. More than once, Michael pulled back with a hiss of pain. I may have lacked textbook knowledge, but I was catching up in my physical abilities. At least, that's how it felt.

I held up my knife and glanced over Michael's body, looking for the telltale signs of his next move. When I found none, I realized he was waiting for me.

I faked left.

Flipping my knife around, I moved to sink it into the right side of his neck. Like always, his forearm was there to stop me. "Good. Remember to keep your body angled away from your attacker." He moved my arm away and took a step back.

Brushing the hair from my eyes, I repositioned with my fists in front of me.

"Are you going with Phillips to the theme party tonight?"

I blinked. "Wha—"

He lunged.

I barely blocked the knife speeding toward my liver. His fist found its way into my kidneys as his leg hooked around my ankle.

When I was staring at the ceiling, he said, "You get distracted too easily."

I groaned. "You say that a lot."

"Maybe because it's true." He held the knife over my head and dropped it. I jerked to the side, just as the blade embedded into the mat beside my ear. "That's only one of the ways I could have killed you in this position."

He smirked, looking too good in his own sweat, and helped me to my feet. "You need to pay more attention. If you don't, you might get an axe in your back." He glanced across the room at Contestant Nineteen. "He seems determined to see you bleed. What did you do?"

"Why do you assume it was me?"

He raised a single eyebrow. "Because you're you."

I stuck my tongue out at him.

A soft knock came from the glass door. Master Lenin didn't wait to be admitted. He didn't seem to mind that he was interrupting either.

"I came to give you these," he said without a hello. Stopping before Michael, he held out a silver box. "Transporters to the party tonight."

When Michael lifted the lid, his eyebrows pulled together. "There are two."

"Do you have to hit me so hard?" I asked, rubbing my side.

"I'm building up your pain tolerance," he said without removing his gaze from Master Lenin.

"I need you to come see me before the party, and I can't have Contestant Heart being late. I got news that Master Harper Landin has agreed to speak with us and . . ." he trailed off with a pointed look at Michael.

Michael went still. "That's ten thousand wands," he said in a near whisper.

Master Lenin nodded. "They are ours, under the condition that Master Shelly Moondra joins as well. She said she is coming tonight. I need you to sweet talk her."

"You know I'm not good at that."

"Then I suggest you make it something you're good at." Master Lenin turned. In a matter of seconds, the door was closed, and he was out of the training room.

"Good to see you too, Master Lenin," I said to the space where he used to be. "I'm fine, thanks for asking. Michael and I were just—"

"Are you packed for the Trial Field?" Michael interrupted.

"Yeah."

He glanced at his watch and headed toward his jacket. "If I pick you up in ten minutes, does that give you enough time to shower?"

"Technically, yes. But—"

"Be ready or I'm taking you with suds in your hair."

"What's going on?" I asked, wiping sweat from my forehead.

"Tonight is about more than The Trial." He swung his jacket over his shoulders and headed for the door. "So don't be late."

"I won't."

He stopped at the door. "Have I entered an alternate universe where Charlie actually follows orders?" With a smirk, he left the room.

I stuck my tongue out at the door. Gathering my things, I went back to my room and jumped into the shower. Michael arrived exactly ten minutes later. With my hair still wet, I grabbed his arm and we Ported out of the Magisterium.

We reappeared on a beach.

I hadn't given much thought to what Aquarius would look like. Maybe a sand castle or some really nice beach tents. Based on the students' tan skin, I figured it was outside.

But as I looked around, there was nothing that remotely resembled a school. There were some shrubs, seashells, and a lot of sand, but no structure. The only thing in front of us was a beat up, wooden sign that read: no swimming.

"Are we lost?" I asked, pushing my windblown hair from my face. "I thought we were going to Aquarius."

Michael took out his wand. "We are." He gave me a mischievous little grin.

Just like the tree guarding the entrance of the European Academy, Michael tapped his wand twice against the weathered sign.

The ground trembled, shaking the dunes flat and sending seagulls fleeing into the sky. Directly behind the sign, the earth sank, creating divots that looked like a staircase leading into the ocean.

Michael started toward the staircase like it was the most normal thing in the world. When his foot landed on the first wet step, the water rushed away from his boot, leaving the sand dry. The waves rushed toward the shore, but when they drew near the staircase, they swirled over the steps as if a tunnel protected them.

Aquarius: The Undersea School of Enchantments. Duh, the title said it was underwater.

Grinning, I raced after him.

A wave broke over our heads, covering the tunnel completely. The water was so clear it could have been glass. Vibrant coral formed an underwater forest. Fish of every color, shape, and size swam over us. A couple dolphins swam alongside for a few feet before getting bored. All the while, the sun streamed through the water in refracted ribbons.

A large shadow approached the wall.

At first, I thought it was a student swimming toward us . . . until I saw he had a nine-foot-long green tail. It was a merman. *Aquarius had merpeople!*

He darted by and was quickly followed by another. Their tails caught the sunlight and reflected it back in a rainbow of colors.

He swam down into the coral and scooped something off the ocean floor. Reaching through the wall of water, he handed me a sand dollar.

"Show off," Michael muttered.

The merman smiled at Michael, showing off a mouth full of shark-like teeth. With a departing wink to me, he flipped backward and swam off into the blue.

The tunnel grew colder the deeper we walked. Once the water was as deep blue as an evening sky, we came to a pair of doors made of pink coral. The handles were molded mermaids holding a trident. On either side stood a pair of guards in bright blue and gold armor.

"Identification," one guard requested.

Michael pulled up his sleeve to expose his Trial tattoo. Following his lead, I did the same.

The guard removed his wand and tapped each of our tattooed wrists. There was a flash of gold. With no other reaction, the guard stepped back and opened the doors.

Inside, my mouth dropped. Before us was a staircase mimicking a branch of coral, starting as a single staircase and then splitting off into different directions to different floors.

The outside walls were made of glass, offering a view of the sea in every direction. The inner walls were made of different colors of corals, changing to differentiate each floor. The lowest level matched the doors, a bright orange-tinted pink. Above that was dark blue, then a feather grey, plum purple, banana yellow, avocado green, and white for the top floor.

Michael led me up the sand-packed stairs to the white level. On the highest floor, the ceiling was made of glass. The afternoon sun rippled across the floor.

At the end of the hallway was a set of silver doors guarded by more soldiers dressed in blue and gold. When Michael grabbed the mermaid door handle, her tiny metallic arm moved the trident over his Guardian tattoo. The black ink glittered with gold under the three prongs.

She rolled her shoulders back, bringing the trident back to her chest, and the doors unlocked.

The room was similar to the First Trial. Directly in front of us, before a wall of water, was a long table for meals. The rest of the room was filled with training equipment and designated workout areas.

Encircling the room were seven doors on each side. Hammered into the silver doors were the numbers for the Next Fourteen.

With his hand on the small of my back, Michael steered me to the door marked with the number fifteen.

The room was made of white coral. All the furniture in the living room was midnight blue, a startling contrast to the white walls and floors. The pillows were silver, a reminder that this wasn't a resort but a Trial room.

Michael took the room closest to the door. Soaking in the sunshine pouring from the ceiling, I practically skipped to the room on the far side of the apartment.

In the bedroom, the walls were also made of glass. Blue water striped with shadows and greens was the best view I had had for The Trial. It almost made me forget what was going to happen next week.

"Charlie, let's go!" Michael called from the front door.

I tossed my bag to the bed. The mattress undulated and rolled. I clapped a hand over my mouth before I made my excitement audible.

It didn't last long. As soon as I stepped into the living room, I blurted, "Does your room have a water bed too?"

"Yes." Stepping into the hallway, he pulled the door closed behind us. "I can enchant it to act like a normal mattress."

"What? No. That would take all the fun out of it."

"When it puts a kink in your back, I'll remind you of this conversation."

He walked through the workout equipment toward the spiraling staircase by the dinner table.

"That might be the most 'old man' thing you've ever said," I laughed.

He ignored me.

The staircase led back up to the surface and onto the Trial Field. I should've known what the Field would be like before we got there. The school was a big hint.

At the top of the stairs was a dock with fourteen diving boards hanging over the ocean. Right above the diving boards were the Guardian observation boxes. Above them was the black glass that hid the judges. The highest level, directly in the sunlight, was a balcony to entertain the Masters.

Below us, a few yards away, was a floating platform with fourteen doors. Each one was decorated with our Contestant number and school colors.

"How do they keep all of this hidden?" I asked.

"Concealing charms." Michael looked down at the water twenty feet below. "You know how to swim, right? Or should I get you floaties?"

I gave him a dry look. "I lived in Kansas. Not under a rock."

"Thank God."

I knocked my elbow into his ribs. "Why are the doors so far off?"

"Because the Masters want to see how badly you want a title."

"Welcome, Contestants!" Master Lenin called over the chatter. "I can't believe your Second Trial is only a week away. As you can see, it's a little different from the first."

He walked through the group and stood before the diving boards. "When your name is called, you'll proceed up those stairs to your starting board. When I tell you to go, you'll dive in and swim to the door with your number on it. Our second Challenge Winner, Emeka Selasi, will start five minutes before everyone else."

I bit the inside of my cheek. I was still sore about losing that head start.

"Once you're through the door, you must remember two riddles that you will need to solve in order to cross the finish line."

"You better remember, little bird," Dmitri Theodore said with a husky laugh behind me. "Not crossing twice would be humiliating."

"Not as humiliating as you placing after me." I grinned at him.

"Unlikely," Igorek laughed.

"Contestants," Master Lenin called from the front. He shot me a strong look because, obviously, it was my fault for the interruption.

Atlas poorly smothered a laugh.

"You'll get the riddles tonight at the party," Master Lenin continued. "But that's not the main focus of tonight's gathering. The Masters who watched your First Trial are interested in meeting you. You get the rare opportunity to talk to every Master of every trade."

My stomach dropped. *Cheese and rice. I have to talk to them?*

"This upcoming Trial is crucial. You've separated yourselves from the mediocre in the First Trial. What you do one week from today will either put you in the class of the elite or it will end your time in The Trial."

No pressure.

Master Lenin took a moment to look every Contestant in the eye. "You have access to every Master, the roots of our kind, for one evening. Use it wisely." He stuffed his hands into his pockets. "The party is at The Serpentine School of Magic at seven. I'll see you all there."

Dmitri rammed his shoulder into mine as he headed to the stairs. Igorek snickered close behind him.

Michael openly glared at the boys. "In a week, you won't have to see him ever again."

Not when I make it to the Third Trial.

"In the meantime, I'll just picture myself ripping off one of his arms."

Back under water, I looped my arm through his and steered him away from the Russians. "Don't hog all of the fun."

"I wasn't. He has two arms." When we reached our shared room, his phone chimed. He quickly scanned the message with a frown. "Lenin wants to see me now. I'm trusting you to get to the party on time."

"Is leaving me alone the best idea?"

"Definitely not." He smirked. "You'll be fine. The door will only open for you or me. Meg sent over a dress for you this morning, and there is a transporter in your bag so you should have no excuse but to arrive on time."

Rolling my eyes at the same speech, I pushed open the door and stepped into our apartment.

"Don't be late!"

I promptly closed the door in his face.

A garment bag hung from the bathroom door. Inside was a silver floor-length gown with silver flowers making up the straps, the wide neckline, and a belt around the middle. Once my sparkly shoes were on, I had five minutes before it was time to leave.

After making sure my scars were hidden, and all my exposed skin was covered with the potion that hid my status, I walked into the hall with the transporter in hand.

I leaned against the cool wall. Colors mingled as the sun set over the ocean. I would have given anything to stay, staring at the wall, rather than leaving to a party to talk to hundreds of Masters.

I jumped when a Contestant door opened to my right. My hand moved toward my wand, expecting Dmitri.

But it was Daniel, looking too good to be fair. His suit looked like it was made of tarnished silver. The matte finish made his skin more golden and the hues of his eyes warmer.

"Hey." He grinned, closing the door behind him. "You look amazing."

"Thanks." My cheeks were bright red as I tucked a rebellious lock of hair behind my ear. "You look pretty good yourself."

"What are you doing out here?"

"Waiting to leave." I held up the transporter. "I'm trying to put it off for as long as possible."

"You and me both." He showed me his own transporter. "Is Master Kale not escorting you?"

I shook my head. "I'm meeting him there."

He came to lean against the wall next to me. "In a few days, this whole thing will be over."

"You think you won't Ascend?"

"Someone needs to participate in the Third Trial and it's not going to be me."

I arched my eyebrow at him. "I didn't finish the First Trial. You, on the other hand, were picked first to Ascend. With those odds, you're Ascending." My heart sank a little, knowing it was true. *If I lost a title to anyone, I'd rather it be him.*

He just shook his head. "Are we still going to go for dinner after The Trial?"

Butterflies fluttered around my stomach. "Yeah. Unless you've changed your mind."

"Not at all. Have you?"

I shook my head. "I'd still like to."

"Good." He took his transporter from his pocket. "We should get going. Our Guardians might reject us if we show up late."

"Right. That would suck." I took the transporter from my clutch.

Neither of us moved.

With a sigh I slouched against the wall. "I really don't want to go."

"You and me both." He stuffed his hands into his pockets.

"What was that whole speech from Master Lenin about the Masters wanting to talk to us? Was that supposed to inspire or scare the hell out of us?"

"Both?"

I groaned. "I make a fool out of myself when I'm by myself. I can only imagine what I'll say in front of our world's most important people."

"Oh, come on. You'll do fine." His smile dropped as he took out his transporter again. "I'll see you there." The transporter glowed seconds before he blinked out of the hallway.

I rested my head against the wall just for a second longer. I took one last deep breath of silence and then I pulled on my magic.

A slight glow moved down my arm and into the black marble. The transporter shocked my hand and took me to the middle of a rain forest.

Cameras flashed, shocking my eyes.

"Contestant Heart!"

"What has it been like working with Master Kale?"

"How do you think you'll handle the Second Trial?"

The mess of voices put my teeth on edge. I couldn't pinpoint who asked what. Blinking against the glare, I tried to locate the school in all of the foliage. The light wasn't coming from the ground, but from the trees.

The red carpet led across the forest floor to a tree the width of a minivan. A wrought iron staircase wound around the trunk with railings that looked to be made of iron snakes twisted and coiled together.

In the trees was The Serpentine School of Magic. Rope bridges connected different classrooms in the branches of neighboring trees. Their walls were thin rice paper painted with victory stories and myths. Paper lanterns of all different colors floated through the air. The night sparkled with fireflies.

Daniel fell in step with me. Waving politely to the cameras, he guided me to the trees. More than ready to be away from the crowd, we moved toward the staircase with guards on either side in green and yellow.

Before we could move up one step, our way was blocked by a woman. It was the same Master I had seen from afar. She always wore a light shade of pink, but her flaming-red hair was her most distinguishing feature. Or so I thought. Up close I noticed one eye was blue and the other was green.

"You're just in time," she said coolly. "The crowd is primed and ready for your compliments and speeches of why you're worth their attention. With your First Trial performance," she nodded to Daniel, "and your Guardian," she looked at me, "I think you'll find your time hard-fought for." She looked down at Daniel's hand on the small of my back. "Be careful who sees your affections. Some will exploit it." Without another glance, she moved around us and Ported with a twirl of fabric.

"What on earth was that?" I asked, looking at her Porting circle.

"I have no clue. I've heard about Master LeOnie's cryptic speeches."

Why have I heard that name before?

"Well, she really made this evening sound fun," I said dryly.

"No kidding." Daniel looked up the stairs and then back at me. The look on his face was one I knew too well; my interest piqued. Trouble sparkled in his rich, brown eyes. "You know . . . the contract doesn't say we *have* to be here."

My rebellious side cheered.

"And . . . we have two Guardians who are more than capable of writing down the riddles we need."

"What are you suggesting?" I asked slowly.

"That you run away with me. Just for the night."

My heart skipped. "What about the Masters?"

"Tonight is just another way for them to know which Contestant to bet on. If we're really worth their time, they'll see that in The Trial."

I looked back toward the stairs. Michael would have my head if I didn't go up. I had only seen him really angry a couple times. If I went through with this, it would not only earn his rage but also Master Lenin's.

Would it impact my chances of getting a title?

I looked back at Daniel. Even though the reporters called out our names, his gaze didn't stray. Under that look, everything faded away. I didn't want to be in a room full of strangers when all I wanted was that look all to myself.

I nodded. "Let's go."

51

Weightless

Daniel didn't hesitate.

He grabbed my hand and pressed the face of his watch. We reappeared back in the sunset glow of Aquarius.

"What time do you think everyone will be back?" I asked, moving toward the wall of water.

"I would guess around one. That's when we came back the last time." He came to stand next to me. "Master Kale won't hurt you, will he?"

To be honest, I wasn't sure. "No. I'm a Contestant. Even he can't do much." What surprised me was the guilt lining my stomach.

"Well . . . then I guess we have to do something worthwhile." He glanced toward the ceiling. "How adventurous are you feeling?"

"That depends. What do you have in mind?"

Wordlessly, he raised his eyebrows and sauntered down the hallway. I followed after him as if pulled by a magnet toward the exit for The Trial. When we stepped above the surface of the water, warm air rolled over my skin.

He walked right onto his assigned diving board. When he reached the end, he started pulling off his jacket. He turned to me with a smile. "Are you up for a swim?" He kicked off his shoes.

My eyes dropped to the water below. "Is there anything in there?" I thought back to the giant squid in the First Trial that drowned me.

He shrugged. "I guess we'll find out." He laughed at my expression. "We're at the top of the food chain. Plus, if anything is down there, it won't attack us until The Trial starts."

"How sure are you?"

"Almost positive."

My hand hesitated over the zipper of my gown. I thought of the scars on my back and the questions they would prompt. Quickly, I yanked at the zipper and pushed the sleeves off my shoulders. The dress pooled at my feet in a puddle of silver fabric. The slip beneath caressed my skin as it moved with the evening breeze.

With a running start, I leapt off the diving board. I hit the warm water and looked through the stinging salt water. I didn't see anything reaching or swimming toward me.

Kicking back up to the surface, I wiped water from my eyes and smiled up at Daniel. "What are you waiting for, slow-poke?"

He laughed. "I was going to show you how to dive."

"And why do I need to know that?"

He pointed at the platform of floating doors. "The way I see it, it's a race from here to there and we need to get there first."

"You're being a kill-joy."

He raised his finger. "Actually, I'm being educational."

"Alright then, Professor Phillips of the Diving School, teach me how to dive."

He shimmied out of his dress pants and ducked out of his shirt. Even his boxers were silver. The low evening light highlighted the muscles of his athletic build.

He backed up to the dock. Planting one bare foot behind the other, he rushed to the end of the diving board. Bouncing off the end, he threw his hands in front of him in a V. He sliced through the water like a bullet and came up a couple yards from the doors.

"If I wasn't treading water, I would clap."

"The thought is appreciated," he said with a smile. "The goal is to go far, not deep. If you go deep, you have to swim up. If you go far, you cut in front."

"Noted."

"And that ends class for today." He pushed a wave of water toward my face. "Race you to the dock." He plunged under the water.

I swam after him but wasn't anywhere near as fast as he was. When I reached the dock, he helped me up. We jumped off a couple of times, each practicing our dive. Then it was a contest of who could make the biggest splash. Every muscle burned by the time I climbed onto the dock and fell flat on my back. Breathing hard, I stared at the darkened sky. Thousands of stars broke through the darkness.

"Charlie," he said after a few moments of silence.

"Yeah?" I turned my head and found he was already facing me. Shoulder to shoulder, his breath caressed my cheek.

He hoisted himself onto his elbow and looked down at me. "Whatever happens next week, I need you to know . . ." He cleared his throat. "I really like you. I have since the first time I saw you at the Magisterium."

My heartbeat hitched and slowed so much I wasn't sure it was moving at all.

"I tried playing it cool. Or maybe I didn't." He laughed. "Oh, I'm botching this. What I'm trying to say is . . . I want to take you on a proper date when this is over."

I smiled up at him. "Really?"

He nodded. "No matter which of us Ascends. I just . . . I really like you." He bent his head forward. A wet lock of hair fell over his forehead.

All the air seemed to rush into my lungs all at once as he leaned in. And when his lips touched mine, I was weightless, as if I had slipped onto an ocean breeze. Stars danced under his fingertips as he touched the corner of my jaw.

"Contestants."

We jerked apart.

By the diving boards, Master Lenin, Master Harlan, and both of our Guardians were accompanied by Lawrence Hart himself.

"Please, join us." Judging by Lawrence's tone, it wasn't a request.

52

Hart Consequences

"If they kill me, please visit my grave."

"I'll probably be in the hole next to you," Daniel muttered as he slipped back into the water.

I found that I didn't care about any of the others standing by the diving boards. I only looked at Michael. I couldn't read his expression. He stood impossibly still.

Pushing off the dock, I dropped back into the water. In silence, the group of Masters and Guardians watched us swim closer. Something whispered from the back of my mind that this was going to end horribly.

When I reached the ladder, I looked twenty feet above me to where Michael waited. Another wave of guilt slammed into my stomach as I made my way up.

When I got near the top, Michael reached down and forcefully helped me up the rest of the way. A cool breeze sent chills over my skin. I was very aware that I was in a soaking-wet slip. I crossed my arms over my chest.

Seeing the goosebumps on my arms, Michael tugged off his suit jacket and draped it over my shoulders. The shirt he wore for the evening was thin as chiffon. In the fading light, I could make out the larger scars on his chest. A dark shadow coiled around his arm and over his shoulder.

But I didn't look long enough to study the tattoo. I looked up to meet his gaze. I wanted to say something to him, but the words died on my tongue. He refused to look me in the eye as he stepped back.

I slouched, letting the large jacket swallow me. It smelled like him, ground sage. For some reason, that made me feel even worse.

"I'm glad to see both of you are alright." Lawrence broke the silence with a cold tone. "I wondered if another Contestant had tried to subtract you from the competition, but it seems that poor judgment was to blame. Which of you would like to explain why you weren't where you were supposed to be?"

Neither Daniel nor I were eager to explain to the Master in red our reasoning. I'm not sure what was going through Daniel's head. It was straight up fear on my part.

"One of you needs to answer," Master Lenin said through clenched teeth.

Daniel pushed his wet hair from his face with a nervous hand. "We signed a contract saying we'd be at the Trial Field at our appointed time—which we will. It said nothing about attending parties."

Master Harlan's shoulders tensed. "Daniel, shut up."

Fire lit inside Daniel's eyes. "I'm sorry. You're neither my School Master, nor my Guardian. Why are you here?"

"I am your father."

"Not one I recognize."

"Enough," Lawrence said, silencing them both. "Contestant Phillips, while you are correct about the contract, you're still wrong. There are expectations that, as a Contestant, you are required to meet. You represent an entire school: the Master, the teachers, the student body, and the entire exposition of the curriculum. By not fulfilling that role, you cast a rather hideous shadow on those who have spent years educating you."

Daniel's cheeks darkened. He dropped his gaze to his bare feet.

"Not to mention, this could be seen as testing the Trial Field for an advantage. I'm tempted to penalize you both by holding you back at the starting line next week."

My stomach bottomed out. *No.*

Lawrence turned to our Guardians. "You're supposed to be in charge of your Contestants. Yet, you couldn't even get them to where they were supposed to be. Not to mention, you had no idea where they were."

Daniel's Guardian, Sean Fields, stared at the dock with shoulders sagging with defeat. Michael's jaw was clenched so tight, his teeth were probably cracking.

"I'm starting to think the real problem is your incompetence and lack of anything useful to contribute to this Trial."

Sean flinched.

"Hold on a second." The words burst out of my mouth before I recognized anger growing in my gut.

Master Lenin shook his head, warning me to shut my mouth.

I locked eyes with Master Hart. "Our Guardians had nothing to do with this. We knew where to be. They gave us specific instructions, which we ignored. In fact, one of the reasons we could so easily ditch your party is because we knew they were fully capable of getting any information we needed for next week."

Lawrence tilted his head like he didn't understand the words coming out of my mouth. "Say what you will but, bottom line, they are in charge of you. And that means, your actions reflect on them."

"Contestants, go to your rooms. I will join you momentarily." When we didn't move, Master Lenin barked, "Now."

Grabbing our clothes, Daniel and I quickly descended the twisting staircase.

Below deck, away from our Guardians and the School Masters, Daniel stopped at his door. "Whatever happens, tonight was totally worth it."

"Don't say that too loud." I shot a look toward the stairs. "I'd hate for them to get even more pissed than they already are."

"But I mean it."

Guilt was still doing a number on my stomach, but looking into his bright eyes, our conversation on the water came back to mind. What he said made the warmth in my chest spread to my cheeks. "About what you said on the dock . . ."

"Yeah?" he prompted, with a hopeful step forward. His fingertips kissed the corner of my jaw.

"I like y—"

Heavy boots started down the stairs.

Jumping away from each other, both of us ran to our doors.

"Charlie!" Daniel whispered before I shut the door.

I stuck my head out into the hall. Standing in front of his door, he smiled broadly. "Tell me in the morning." He ducked into his room.

I looked toward the stairs just as Master Harlan and Sean came off the last step. The School Master met my gaze coldly. Shaking his head, he headed out of the room. Sean offered me an apologetic smile before heading into Daniel's room.

When Michael didn't immediately follow after, my stomach churned. I could only imagine what Master Lenin was saying to him.

A puddle had accumulated around my feet. Threading my arms through the sleeves of Michael's jacket, I stepped into the warmth of the apartment in search of a towel. Just as I was running it through my hair, the main door opened.

"Contestant Heart, can you join us in the living room, please?" Master Lenin called.

My stomach dropped. Setting the towel on the bed, I stepped out to meet them.

Master Lenin stood in the center of the room with his hands tucked into the pockets of his fine, grey suit. In the light of the apartment, it reflected light like it was made of metal.

I turned my gaze to the silent man in black by the door. Just before I could meet his gaze, he turned his head from me and leaned back into the wall.

"Do you have any idea what you've done?" Master Lenin asked, redirecting my attention. "I can overlook the fact you left Guardian Kale like a rejected blind date. I might even be able to forgive the stress you put us through, but I cannot get over the fact that you deliberately spat in the face of Master Han."

I looked back at Michael, but he was still looking at the floor. "Who?"

Master Lenin sucked in a sharp breath. "The Master of Serpentine. The school you didn't even step foot in tonight."

"How exactly did I offend him?"

A disbelieving laugh huffed from between his lips. "Of course you don't see it. By choosing not to come, you basically told him you didn't view his school as anything important. In this Trial, that means war."

I leaned against the back of the couch, crossing one ankle over the other. "So? It's not like they can do much. They haven't won a Trial in, like, a thousand years. Right?"

"Do you know why they haven't won? It's not because they lack knowledge or skill. Tell her, Guardian Kale."

Finally, my Guardian looked at me. His eyes were hard as obsidian covered in frost. "They play dirty. They've been known to poison Contestants before Trials and even kill some in their sleep. One Contestant used Seers Drops on a Contestant from his own school so he would Ascend."

I thought of the yellow foam that came out of Igorek's mouth at the party in the Glasshouse. "What's that?"

"It's a potion that allows complete control over another person. The Contestant made his fellow classmate die, so he would have a chance at the Top Seven."

Thiago's comment at the Glasshouse party finally made sense. The reason the Contestants from his school were under supervision is because they had a history of foul play.

"And now," Master Lenin continued bitterly, "you have the whole school's rage pointed at you and Contestant Phillips. And don't even get me started on the Masters. You could've made connections with important people, earning some real points for the Heel. Instead, they think you're a disrespectful brat."

I've been called worse.

"Remember how I said Master Hart is using The Trial to gather Masters to his side and that we could do the same?"

I nodded.

"That's what we were trying to do tonight. We could have added to our ranks if Guardian Kale had been speaking to Master Harper and Master Moondra. But instead, he was looking for you."

My eyebrows shot up. "So, when you said 'ten thousand wands,' you meant—"

"Ten thousand Users, yes. Which *you* cost us."

My heart sank a little more.

"I'm honestly considering not giving you the riddles for The Trial, and watching you fail. Or maybe I should just go to the judges and ask to have you expelled."

Michael dropped his head back against the wall and closed his eyes.

"What were you thinking?" Master Lenin demanded.

"I like him."

Michael's eyes snapped open. Master Lenin blinked once and then twice. The shock on their faces caused a twinge of anger to spark in my chest.

"Yeah, surprise! Lucifer's kid has feelings." The lights flared. I took a deep breath, pulling my magic back.

"Nothing good will come out of this," Master Lenin said, with a shake of his head. "This war is too important to risk on a boy you cannot have."

I straightened from the couch. "Oh, come on—"

"Lenin—" Michael's voice descended to a warning tone.

The School Master talked right over him. "Let's say you indulge this fantasy. What do you think will happen when your father figures out who you are?"

"He won't!" A chill sank into my bones.

"It's only a matter of time before he finds out or we tell him to throw him off his game. Either way, when he learns how dangerous you are to his reign—tell her what will happen, Guardian Kale. Tell her how her father breaks his enemies."

Again, Michael turned his guarded gaze my way. The muscle in his jaw clenched. "He'll go for the crack in your armor. He's done it to me, and Lenin, and he'll do it to you. You'll get Phillips killed."

Those last four words punched a hole in my chest. Flinching back, I wrapped my arms around my stomach.

"Trust me." Michael dropped his gaze to the sandy floor. "You don't want to be the reason someone you love is dead."

I looked at the scar cut into the side of his face.

"Magee is dealing with Contestant Phillips right now," Master Lenin continued. "As for you, I want—"

The lights flared as my heart clenched with fear. "What do you mean?"

The last time I had heard mention of Magee was when Master Lenin told me he had cut off Blake's finger.

"He's twisting Contestant Phillips' memories," Master Lenin answered. "The emotional response to you won't be there. Hopefully, that will keep him away."

I suddenly found it hard to breathe. My lungs wouldn't release air. "You . . . you can't just mess with people like that. I'll leave him alone, I promise."

"But we can't guarantee that he'll leave you alone. The closer he gets to you, the more at risk he becomes. I wish it didn't have to be this way. But there aren't any other options if you want him to live."

I wanted to hold on to the glow in my chest, the look in his eyes. But with every word, Master Lenin's argument loosened my grip on those memories. I couldn't stand by while what happened to Lauren happened to Daniel. I wasn't strong enough to hold that kind of grief. I wasn't as strong as Michael.

"Will he . . . will he remember me?" I whispered.

Master Lenin nodded. "Yes. But anything romantic won't be there."

A tear slipped from the corner of my eye. I swiped it away, but he already saw it.

"You won't be the first, or the last person, to give up what they want because of this war. But with your help, it won't have to be everyone." Master Lenin spun on his heel and jerked open the door. "You better get some sleep. I want you in the training room at six tomorrow morning. If your Guardian reports any complaints, I'll be forced to dish out a harsher punishment." Without another word, he pulled the door closed behind him.

I dipped my head, letting my wet hair conceal my face as tears rolled down my cheeks. Biting my lip, I pushed off from the couch and closed myself in my room.

Oh, God. I shoved my hands into my hair. *What have I done?*

I pressed my fingers to the corner of my jaw. I could still feel Daniel's fingertips on my skin.

I was a goddamn idiot. I ruined everything I touched. I knew that. I had years to prove that. Just because I had a new identity, that didn't mean I had changed. My touch was still poisonous.

A gag worked up my throat at the thought of what Magee was doing in the room next door.

Maybe I could get there before Magee started and convince him not to go through with it.

I pulled on my magic and Ported into the hall. The common room was silent and dark since everyone was still at the party. My bare feet took me across the sandy floor to the room marked with the number thirteen.

Just as I was about to grab the handle, the door swung open.

"Oh!" Robert Magee smiled as he shut the door behind him. "Hello, darling."

I stepped away from him. The last time I saw this man, he had taken over my war lesson for the night. That was when I learned that they weren't just teaching me how to use magic to protect myself, but for their war.

Dressed in a loose button up and slacks, he hadn't changed much. His slicked-back black hair matched his sleazy charm. His cool dark brown gaze made goosebumps rise over my skin, and not the good kind.

After what he did to Blake, and what he was prepared to do to Daniel, I knew that this man's attention was not a good thing to have.

"It's a pleasure to see you again," he said with a broad smile. His eyes jumped over me, taking in every detail of my appearance. I was thankful for Michael's oversized jacket. "How have you been?"

"I've been better." My eyes flickered to the door behind him. *Am I too late?*

Magee chuckled. "I'm guessing Kale has something to do with that." He was one of the few people who openly hated Michael to his face.

"It's The Trial, actually."

"Ah, yes." His eyes dropped to my wrist, looking for my Contestant tattoo. "I bet Kale was beside himself with how it played out." He chuckled. "I do feel sorry for you that you have to work with him. That man disturbs me. There's a controlled wildness about him." His eyes flashed over my shoulder toward my room. "Speaking of Kale, I don't think he'd let you wander about unsupervised this close to the Second Trial."

"I wanted to see Daniel."

His smile sobered into a thin line. "Contestant Phillips is asleep. Manipulating memories is taxing on the mind."

I'm too late. I fought to keep my breathing even as an ache exploded through my chest. "Did it hurt?"

"If you can't remember the pain, did it really happen?" With a comforting hand on my shoulder, he steered me away from Daniel's door.

I jerked away from his touch.

He gave me a look of pity. "He won't remember any of it. Altering memories is a specialty of mine."

My fingernails dug into my palms, biting painfully into my skin. *Would he tell me the truth?*

Stopping outside my door, Magee turned me to face him. He rubbed his hands in what he thought were comforting circles over my shoulders. It made my skin crawl. "This is for the best. It might not seem like it at the moment, but you will see it eventually."

His hands slid down my arms and took my hands in his. Bowing deep, he pressed a kiss to my knuckles. "Goodnight, darling. Good luck next week."

As soon as he turned, my worked-up magic easily filled me and Ported me back to my bedroom.

So that was it . . . It took minutes to uproot me from his mind and heart. *I never even got to tell him that I . . .*

I should have just gone to the party. I should have focused on getting a title.

I brushed the runaway tears from my cheeks. The long sleeves of Michael's jacket caressed my face. I looked toward the door. *Is he here?*

The rest of the apartment was dark as I crossed the flat toward Michael's room. My feet barely made a whisper on the sandy floor.

I stopped outside his room. Michael had been quiet while Master Lenin tore me a new one. By opening this door, I was giving him an opportunity to unleash everything simmering in his head.

That should have frightened me. But I still had one question.

Quietly, I twisted the knob and soundlessly pushed open the door. Keeping it cracked, I peeked my head inside.

His room was dark, like the rest of the apartment. I found him laid out on his bed, fully dressed, with his feet still on the floor. Even though he didn't turn his head when I entered, that didn't mean he wasn't awake.

Leaning against the doorframe, I willed the tears out of my voice. Twice, I tried to ask my question, but the thickness in my throat kept me back.

"Will it hurt him?" I whispered.

Michael pushed himself upright and braced his elbows against his knees. "It's completely painless. Magee is the best at what he does. He'll make sure of it."

Even though he echoed Magee's answer, it didn't console my weeping heart. "You were quiet through all of that. I know you're pissed . . ."

He remained silent.

With a shaky breath, I slipped his jacket off my shoulders. I stepped closer to the bed, but Michael refused to look at me. Folding the jacket in half, I set it beside him. "If there was anyone who could make you forget how hard life is, wouldn't you drop everything to spend just a moment with them? Even if it meant dropping something important?"

He didn't answer. Breathing deeply in the darkness, he stared at the sandy floor between his dress shoes.

I brushed the fresh tears from my face and retreated to the door. "I guess what I'm trying to say is that I'm sorry."

"No, you're not. You thoroughly enjoyed your night," Michael chuckled lightly. A sober moment of silence followed. "I thought one of the other Contestants got to you."

Another wave of guilt slammed into my stomach. "Would it have mattered if one of them had?"

"Yes."

My eyes snapped to him. The evening darkness kept me from seeing his expression, but I could hear it in his voice. He had been worried, truly worried that something had happened to me.

"We're in this together, you and I." Rising to his feet, he collected his holster and took out a flat, clear stone the size of an egg. Unsheathing his wand, he pressed the tip to his temple. The tip glowed bright and golden, like a firefly, before he moved his wand to the clear stone. It eagerly absorbed the magic.

When the glow dimmed, Michael walked over and pressed the stone into my hand. "This will tell you the theme of The Trial. We'll work on memorizing the riddles tomorrow." He headed for the bathroom.

"I'm sorry," I blurted. "About Master Harper and Master Moondra. I didn't realize . . ."

He closed the door behind him as if I hadn't spoken.

Silence screamed around me. Shivering against the ocean chill, I retreated to my room. I sat on the bed and ran my hands over the smooth stone. Finding no button or on switch, I tapped my wand against it. A bright light shot straight into my eyes.

Cursing, I dropped it onto the bed. Praying I wasn't blind, I rapidly tried to blink the dots from my vision.

When I could see again, I slowly lifted it off the mattress. The beam of light that nearly took out my eyes projected something onto the bed.

I moved the projection to the wall opposite me. It was a still frame of

Master Lenin standing on a stage. Before him was a sea of Masters dressed in silver and grey.

I tapped my wand against the stone again.

"Good evening, Contestants and Guardians! I apologize for interrupting your conversations. You can resume in a moment. Please give your attention to Master Hart for a few announcements."

A polite applause rumbled through the room as a tall man dressed in red stepped up to the microphone.

"Good evening, ladies and gentlemen. I am excited to share the new theme with you. The First Trial focused on your fears. You were faced with three of your own personal nightmares. They were meant to break you and challenge you. Based on the fact that you are standing here right now," his cool gaze swept the room, *"means you conquered the darkest parts of your mind while exemplifying The Trial's standards of showing your skills in magic, agility, and making the knowledge of your school into a weapon.*

"Keeping with the intention of getting to know our Contestants, we have selected the theme for the Second Trial to be based on the memories of the Next Fourteen."

My stomach dropped. I knew how powerful memories could be. They were what kept me up at night, and what made my magic dangerous when I slept.

"Contestants, I urge you to dig deep and find out what matters to you. What memories in your history brought you here? What makes you tick? Before you need those answers, you will need to solve two riddles."

Lawrence reached into his jacket and took out a silver envelope. *"Is everyone ready?"* With his thumb, he broke the seal. *"In no particular order, the first riddle is 'Hurry and choose the exit that means the most to you. Time is running short and you better not lose. For at the end of time's race you will be stuck, and for the next Trial, you will not place.'"*

A low murmur ran through the crowd.

"Your final riddle is 'Fire set. Fire burn. What is left will be yours for this turn.' Remember these riddles, solve them, and you may earn yourself a spot in the Top Seven. I look forward to seeing each of you perform next week."

The projection stone shut off, leaving me in silence. I had a feeling the Second Trial wasn't going to be any easier than the first.

I crawled further onto the bed and hugged the sheets to my chest. My eyes burned with tears.

Just for a moment I let my mind slip back into memories of Daniel—eating seafood with his family, touching his hand at the Dragon Farm, swimming, and then his statement on the dock. The weightlessness of my soul when his lips touched mine.

"I really like you."

I replayed that moment once more, letting it glow around my chest. I imagined what would've happened if I had said it back. If I had kissed him back.

Then I did my best to trick myself into thinking that that night didn't mean anything.

53

I Got an Idea

I opened the front door and peeked out into the common room.

Michael was at the main table seated beside Atlas. A plate of food was already waiting for me in front of the empty chair beside him.

For how quiet the room was, it could have been confused with being empty. But the table was almost full with people who were forced to sit next to each other. No one talked outside of their Contestant-Guardian pairs, and even then, it was in hushed tones.

The University Contestants were absent, having already left for the training room. The Lions of Magic Contestants were just about ready to join them. But best of all, Daniel wasn't there yet.

I darted out of the room and took the seat beside my Guardian. I picked up my fork and blindly started eating. I made it through half the plate before the seat beside me pulled away from the table. My heart dropped. I kept my attention locked on my toast, already knowing who it was.

"Hey," Daniel said cheerfully. "I was hoping I'd catch you before the day started. I'm sorry."

"For what?" Avoiding eye contact, I reached for an empty glass in front of Michael.

"Well . . . it was my idea to ditch the party, so I'm basically the reason we're in trouble. I hope you weren't reprimanded too harshly."

Grabbing a pitcher of water, I aimed it over my glass. "I agreed to go with you. We're both at fault."

"But I never should've suggested it." He moved closer, which only sent an ache through my bruised heart. "We have so much going on with school, The Trial, and training that I don't think we . . . will you look at me please?"

My heart tore a little more. I set down the pitcher and faced him.

His expression was pleasant, but not warm. His eyes were bright, but they didn't dazzle with the accumulation of stolen glances and secret wishes. When he smiled, it was one of politeness. He looked at me like he would look at anybody else.

"I don't know what got into me last night. I've never done anything like that before. I think it's a combination of stress, little sleep, and mortal peril." He laughed, but it sounded off. "I shouldn't have suggested what I did. I shouldn't have kiss—"

"It's fine," I blurted. I couldn't stand to hear him apologize for that moment. "I totally understand. We were both practically high on freedom and denial."

Relief sagged his shoulders, bringing another Playtex smile to his face. "Thank God, we're on the same page. I don't want it to be weird between us, not since we're in The Trial together. I don't want to go through this without you. Your friendship means a lot to me."

My face ached as it struggled to keep my smile in place. "Me too."

With another smile, he pushed away from the table to get his breakfast. I looked back at my plate, no longer hungry.

His eyes were so empty.

It doesn't matter. I had always been at the Magisterium for something other than the people in it. Last year was to control my magic, and now it was to earn a title. Each time I had let my attention stray to something else, it was taken away. First, Moose. And now, Daniel.

I shoved my half-eaten plate away and rose to my feet. "Guardian Kale, are you ready to get started?"

Michael stopped mid-conversation. He looked at me and then the food still on my plate. "You haven't finished."

"I'm done."

"You need—"

"I'd like to get started."

His dark eyes ran over my face, reading me like a book. I thought he would order me to finish my breakfast but he just rose to his feet.

After a final word to Atlas, he led me to our assigned training room. While he set up our equipment, my eyes wandered to Daniel at the breakfast table. Usually, I could catch his eye and get a smile from him. This morning, he was completely focused on his food.

"Good morning, little bird." Dmitri filled the doorway with his usual cocky grin. Surprisingly, Igorek wasn't with him. "You do not look so good. Too little sleep?"

"Not today, Dmitri." I grabbed the door and started pushing it closed.

"I thought for sure Master Hart would have thrown one of you from The Trial for your misconduct. I was hoping it would be you."

"Leave me alone."

"Forfeit The Trial. Then I will."

"Bite me." Slamming the door in his face, I turned to Michael with my wand drawn, ready to begin. He didn't give me any breaks or pauses. Which was just what I needed to keep me from thinking about last night.

The week continued like that.

I avoided Daniel. Michael and I trained until I couldn't think of anything other than food or sleep. It was for the best. Daniel was an anchor, and that was the last thing I needed in a Trial by the ocean.

The morning of the Second Trial, I was already awake as the sun started to ripple through the ocean walls. With a sigh, I got up and made myself a cup of hot chocolate. As I sipped the sweet drink, I started to stretch for the day.

When Michael stepped out of his room, he paused. Surprise flashed across his face. Recovering quickly, he poured himself some coffee and then helped me deepen my stretches.

Thirty minutes before noon, there was a knock at the door.

Just like the First Trial, the Master of the school came by to deliver the equipment for the day. Today, it was Master Harley Finch, the School Master of Aquarius.

Murmuring his soft greeting, he shifted his grip on his cane and handed Michael a silver briefcase with my Contestant number engraved on the side. Master Finch also handed him a box wrapped in brown paper.

Accepting the items, Michael bowed and closed the door.

"Charlie," he called over his shoulder without looking. "Here are your clothes."

My hands shook so hard, I felt it in my shoulders. Scooping the clothes from the case, I ducked into my room and quickly changed out of my pajamas.

The Trial attire wasn't any different than what I wore for the First Trial. There was a brown tank top with a tight jacket, fitted pants, and light shoes. I expected it to be a swimsuit. Pulling my hair into a loose ponytail, I stepped back into the living room.

Michael was still at the kitchen counter. Before him was the wrapped package. This time, it was open.

"What's that?" I asked, stepping up beside him to peer inside.

"A gift." Reaching into the box, he took out one of three pieces.

It was a belt, simple and undecorated, except for the silver buckle. The only thing breaking the smooth black finish was an image; pressed into the back was a crest of a wand, crisscrossed with a smelting hammer.

To my surprise, Michael crouched before me.

"It's for me?" I stood, shocked, as he moved my shirt away from the top of my jeans. My skin buzzed with magic as he threaded the belt through the loops of the pants.

He nodded.

"Who's it from?" I asked as he cinched the belt together.

"Anyone I name will be lost on you since you weren't at the party last week."

My heart dropped like it did every time I thought of the Second Trial's theme party.

Michael continued, but with a less confronting tone. "Walter J. West. He's a Master of Magical Technology."

"What does the J stand for?"

"I . . . actually don't know. I've never had the chance to ask."

"Why'd he send this to me?"

"Because I asked him to." He clipped the second piece onto the belt and then secured it with the strap around my thigh. He did the same thing with the final piece to my other leg.

He sat back on his heels, admiring the piece fully assembled.

On the outside of my right leg was a sheath for my wand. There was a strap just above my knee to keep it from flopping about when I ran.

The piece on my left thigh had a similar structure, but instead of one notch on the belt, it had three: one in the front, one on the side, and the last on the back. Two straps circled my thigh but the space between them was solid, dark leather.

Michael took the knife he had used to open the box and slid it into the first notch. The point of the blade settled into the bottom strap, securing it in place and protecting my skin from the sharp edge.

"Where's your wand?" Michael asked as he took two knives from the sleeves of his jacket.

"In my room." I held still as Michael put the knives in the remaining slots. When they were in place, he took another step back.

That looks so cool.

"How does it feel?" His gaze jumped up to my face.

"I can barely feel it, actually." I squatted low and bounced up and down. Jumping back to my feet, I paced the length of the room. None of the weapons jingled or shifted. They might as well have been a part of me.

"Go get your wand." He nodded toward my room.

With eager steps, I found it and returned to him.

"The leather is enchanted," he said as he slid my wand into the holster running along the outside of my right thigh. "No one can take your wand out but you." To prove it, he tried to yank it out. I stumbled forward, but my wand remained in the holster.

"That's helpful."

He smirked down at me. "Come on, we should get going."

Leaving the safety of our apartment, we joined the remainder of the Next Fourteen in the common area.

All the Guardians stood by the twisting staircase leading to the surface. Half of the Contestants were sitting on the couches, while the other half paced around the room or tried to work off some energy at weightlifting machines. Igorek was in the corner taking a nap. How he managed to do that was beyond me.

Michael turned on his heel and headed toward the group of Guardians near the stairs. Blake beckoned me over to the corner farthest from everyone else. I darted over and sat beside him.

"Ready to go swimming?" he asked in a hushed tone.

A fresh wave of nerves flooded my stomach. "I'm more ready for it to be over." I tucked a loose strand behind my ear.

"That makes two of us. After this is over, do you want to hang out? We can make popcorn and watch something mind-numbingly stupid."

Without my permission, my gaze was drawn across the room to Daniel. He sat low on the couch, trying to read a thick book on wand history, but his eyes kept darting to the clock on the wall.

After The Trial, we were supposed to go to dinner, like before. But that was before Magee twisted his memories.

I pinched the side of my leg as hard as I could. *Stop it. It's not going to happen so stop hurting yourself by imagining it.*

I turned back to Blake. "I'd like that."

Dmitri rose from his seat with a loud yawn. He stretched his arms over his head, letting the bones in his back crack. His eyes landed on the only Contestant who sat by himself.

Rounding the couch, he braced his forearms against the back and peered over Daniel's shoulder. With a smirk, he tore the book from Daniel's hands.

"Wand history? How will this help you?" he laughed.

Daniel spun around and reached for the book. "None of your business."

Dmitri stepped out of reach and thumbed through the pages. All the notecards Daniel had carefully stuffed in the pages fell to the floor. "Igorek," he bellowed across the room, startling his classmate awake. "This boy thinks his brain can overpower muscle."

Igorek managed a weak grin as he rubbed the sleep from his eyes.

"What can your brain do?" Dmitri's hand snapped away from his side toward Daniel's face.

I jumped to my feet.

Daniel flinched back and stumbled off the couch.

Laughing, Dmitri dropped his hand. "See? You flinch. Real men make a move."

I walked over and yanked the book from the Russian's hand. "Has anyone ever told you that you're a huge pain in the ass?"

Dmitri cocked his head to one side. "No one would dare."

"Then let me be the first. You're a huge pain in the ass."

"Why are you so angry? He was giving him tips for The Trial." Igorek smirked in Daniel's direction. "Not that it'll do any good."

"Do us all a favor and shut up." I pulled Daniel away to where Blake was standing with his hand on his wand.

Dmitri had other plans, of course. He grabbed my shoulder and spun me around. Before he could utter a single sound, I planted my hands on his chest and shoved.

Catching him by surprise, he stumbled back onto the couch.

"Contestants!" Master Lenin's voice swept across the room as all the Guardians turned our way. "May I remind you of the contracts you both signed? Particularly the part about assaulting another Contestant."

"Assaulting another Contestant is discouraged, and will result in revoking their Save," Dmitri rattled off flawlessly. His smug look was short-lived however.

"I already used my Save," I said with a grin.

"Contestant Heart, go stand on the other side of the room," Master Lenin said tensely. The steel in his gaze told me that force would follow if I didn't move myself.

I promptly walked back to my seat beside Blake. Daniel followed close behind.

"Thanks," Daniel mumbled.

I didn't look at him. His hollow expression would destroy my small victory over Dmitri.

"Since I have your attention," Master Lenin gave me a pointed look, "we're officially ten minutes from the start of the Second Trial. When your name is called, please walk up the stairs to your assigned diving board.

"After Trial Two Challenge Winner, Contestant Eight, gets his head start, the rest of you will proceed at my order. Remember the riddles. And make your school proud," he said with another sharp glare my way. "Good luck."

As soon as the period was at the end of his sentence, Guardians made a beeline toward their Contestants.

Michael took exactly one step in my direction before Master Lenin waved him over. I rolled my eyes. *Of course, he was ratting me out.*

They shared a brief conversation. Michael's eyes flicked briefly my way. It was too quick of a glance to read. Master Lenin's lips were pressed tightly together as he beckoned Dmitri over. Master Lenin made quick work of scolding the Contestant before moving upstairs.

Before Dmitri could step away, Michael grabbed his arm.

I almost laughed at Michael's expression. *Was he seriously threatening him?*

Michael waited for Dmitri to nod, then he headed toward me. Dmitri whistled for Igorek's attention. The pair huddled together in a tight conversation. Igorek grinned.

"Making new friends?" I asked when Michael got close enough.

"The opposite, actually." He handed me an earpiece. "How are you feeling?"

"I'm ready to get started." I stuck it in my ear and tried not to shiver as it expanded to fit my ear.

"Do you have the riddles memorized?"

I nodded, shaking the nerves out of my hands.

"How do your shoes feel?"

"A little tight." I bounced on my toes. "Do you know how they'll work in water?"

He put his hands on my shoulders, stopping me from bouncing again. "They shouldn't hinder you."

Good. One less thing to worry about.

He glanced at his watch as Guardians started making their way up the stairs. "In a couple of hours, this will be over. Remember to—"

"Let you know what I'm thinking and listen to you." Another wave of butterflies hit.

A shot of annoyance crossed his face at my interruption, but it was mixed with pleasure that I knew what he wanted.

"Your door is marked with your Contestant number. Once you get into the water, swim as hard as you can to your door. No one should fire at you while you're under, but once you're on the platform, you're fair game. Don't trust anything but my voice. Do you understand?"

I nodded.

He offered me his hand. "We're in this together. I've got your back."

I stared up at him. He looked like he truly believed that, that he truly believed in me. Despite everything, his war and my need for a title, we were on the same side. We were in this together, and together we would make it.

I grasped his forearm. "Damn right."

"Guardians, please report to your observation rooms. Contestants, roll call will start in one minute," Master Lenin's voice warned through the speakers.

Michael touched my arm, drawing my attention back to him. "You can do this."

He turned on his heel and Ported out of the waiting room.

My stomach clenched painfully. I sucked in a deep breath and held it, hoping my racing heart would calm.

Not soon after the last Guardian was out of sight, a line of Aquarius guards came down and stationed themselves along one wall. Master Lenin wasn't taking any more chances.

Then, through the speakers, he called for Contestant Three to make her way up. One by one, Contestants made their way toward the stairs.

"Contestant Thirteen, Daniel Phillips."

Daniel stood up from the chair where he had been nervously bouncing his leg. He straightened his jacket and smoothed back his hair. Taking one last deep breath, he climbed to the surface.

A huge body entered my peripheral vision. "You do not look scared, little bird," Dmitri said.

I didn't look at him. "After facing my fears in the last Trial, I found there's not a lot that makes my heart race."

"Not of The Trial. You should be afraid of me."

"Funny. You're not very frightening."

Igorek chuckled from the couches. "We'll see."

"Contestant Fifteen, Charlie Heart."

I sent them a smirk Michael would've been proud of. "I guess we will."

With my hands singing with nerves, I walked up the stairs. The sun blared down with all of its power, reflecting off the crystal-clear water.

Just like the First Trial, classical music drifted over the balcony of the Masters. Unlike the formalness of the First Trial, the Masters wore beach attire. The ladies' swimsuits and the men's flowery Hawaiian polos were all silver. Some crowded the railing with brightly colored drinks; their whispers fell to us below. Some lounged in beach chairs while others stood under umbrellas.

From the clusters, Masters pointed to different Contestants. Light laughter came from the ones scrutinizing me.

As I made my way to my diving board, I caught sight of the red-headed

Master. She was alone again, leaning against the railing. I looked away as her eyes drew closer.

Below the terrace of Masters was the black glass that hid the judges. I wasn't going to disappoint them again. I wanted a title. And I was going to show them just how badly I wanted it. No more cowering. No more running.

I turned to the water below and found my door. It was between Daniel's and Marina Rafael's, from The Serpentine School of Magic.

Once everyone was in place, Master Lenin gave Emeka his head start. He didn't waste any time jumping into the water and swimming toward his door.

Those five minutes crawled by.

My mind went wild with all the possibilities of what he could be doing, and most importantly, how close to the finish line he was getting.

"Time's up! Remaining members of the Next Fourteen, are you ready?"

My stomach dropped like I was on a roller coaster. I glanced over at Dmitri and startled when we made eye contact. Igorek was looking over too.

The look on their faces told me if they caught me in the water, they were going to drown me.

That should have scared me, but instead, I got an idea. It was incredibly stupid, but that was only if it didn't work. Dmitri talked about crippling the competition. I was going to take his advice.

I shrugged out of the jacket and tossed it behind me. I pulled my wand into my hand.

"What are you planning, Charlie?" Michael asked.

I glanced over at Dmitri and Igorek and pulled on my magic. "You'll see."

"Contestants," Master Lenin called, "you may begin."

54

The Second Trial

Running to the end of my board, I shot a blast of magic to my right.

Just as I hit the water, I heard Dmitri and Igorek's enraged cries as they fell from their shattered diving boards.

I dove into the waves like Daniel showed me and came up ten feet short of the dock with a smile on my face. Michael's laugh in my ear only made that smile bigger.

Cutting through the water, I wasted no time pulling myself onto the dock and bolting toward my door.

"Behind you!"

Without hesitation, I turned and fired. My ward collided with a shot from Amelia Markus.

I pointed my wand at the water and jerked it back to her. The ocean followed the motion of my wand and engulfed her. That's when I noticed Dmitri nearing the dock. Igorek wasn't too far behind.

Time to go.

Turning, I flung open the door and lunged through. Pulling it closed, I fell against the wood, breathing hard.

"Nicely done, Contestant Heart." I could hear a smirk of pleasure in Michael's voice.

"Thank you, Guardian Kale." *That should get the Masters' attention.*

Before me was a silent forest made of unusual trees. Their leaves were the color of bronze and their trunks a dull gold. They shone in the midday sun as if they were made of metal.

I stepped up to the nearest trunk and placed my hand on the sunlit metal. I found it to be warmer than it should've been. The surface swelled with the intake of a breath; the leaves rustled overhead.

I jumped back. "Are the trees anything I need to worry about?" I started moving through the quiet wood.

"No. Dryad trees won't bother you unless you bother them first. I would be more concerned with the Contestants that are looking for you. Nineteen is pissed."

A smile flitted across my face. "About which part? Me hitting the water before him, or him belly-flopping in front of the Masters?" I looked between the trees. So far, I couldn't see anyone.

"Both."

I chuckled. I couldn't wait to rewatch this Trial, just so I could see the look on his face when his diving board broke.

"So, what am I looking at?" I asked.

"You're on a circular island levitating three hundred feet above the ocean. There are fourteen groups of fourteen doors evenly spaced along the perimeter."

"Let me guess, one of those groups has my name on it."

"Pretty much."

I brushed back my wet hair. "Which way am I going?"

I followed Michael's directions across the island. The hot, still air seemed to weigh on my skin. Sweating wasn't even helping. My shirt stuck to me like it was coated in glue. Other than my footsteps, there was no other sound. No birds. No animals. Not even a breeze.

A slight rustle of leaves was my only warning.

Bony knees slammed into my back, throwing me to the ground. My cheek crashed into the earth. I felt a wand stick into the side of my neck as my own was ripped from my hand.

"Hey, Charlie."

I cursed. "Hey, Anna. What do I owe this pleasure?"

"Just looking to cut someone out of the Next Fourteen. Don't take it personally. You were just the first one I came across."

I rolled my eyes. "Brandy really doesn't like me, huh?"

"Nope. To be honest, neither do I."

"Does every Contestant in this Trial hate you?" Michael asked.

I shrugged my shoulders as much as I could under Anna's weight. "Probably."

"Oh!" Anna pressed my face into the dirt as she leaned down toward my earpiece. "Hi, Master Kale!" she yelled. "Sorry—Guardian Kale. That demotion must *suck*. Brandy has told me *so* much about you. I know how much you hate wasting time, so I expect a basket of flowers after I cut this pathetic excuse of a User out of The Trial."

Michael sighed in annoyance. "Are you going to shut her up, or just let her yell in your ear? You know what to do."

I did?

"Say goodbye, Charlie." I saw her wand glow from the corner of my eye.

I yanked a knife from the new holster and slammed it into her hip. With a shriek of pain, she slipped off me.

Quickly I rolled the opposite direction and whipped my foot into her face. The whimpering red head went motionless. Her head dropped to the dirt with a snort and a groan.

Rolling to my feet, I picked up my wand and replaced it in the holster. "You know what would've been nice?" I told Michael. "A heads up *before* I was jumped. Aren't you supposed to be the all-seeing eye?"

"I knew you could take her."

I couldn't tell if I should chew him out or thank him for the compliment.

My gaze was drawn to the knife sticking out of her leg. The dark material of her pants was wet with blood.

I stared down at her, torn as to what to do. If I helped her, would that hurt my chances of getting a title? Helping Emeka had brought me nothing but trouble. But she was bleeding a lot.

I looked at my hands and found a smudge of crimson.

Biting back a curse, I crouched beside her. "How do I stop the bleeding?"

"She just attacked you," Michael said slowly. "Let her figure it out."

I plucked the earpiece from my ear and stuck my tongue out at it, knowing full well he could see it. I dropped it into the dirt and took out another knife and cut the sleeve off her jacket. Using the fabric, I tied it around the wound.

I peeked at the earpiece, knowing Michael must be stewing with rage. I fought to keep myself from smiling.

When it was bandaged tight, I pulled the knife from her leg and cleaned the blade on her shirt. Then I picked up my earpiece and popped it back in.

"You idiot," Michael barked.

"Every time you say something that's not helpful, I'm taking you out of my head," I said as I got back to my feet.

"You can't honestly be that stupid," he laughed. "You could—"

I reached for the earpiece again.

"Ok! Ok!" He started cursing. "Charlie Heart, you're going to be the death of my sanity *and* my nerves."

"Personally, I take that as a compliment. So, where am I headed?"

"Go right," he said tightly.

I darted into the trees. Faintly, something started to break through the silence. It sounded like crashing waves. As the sound of the ocean grew closer, another noise came through: the sharp, guttural rumbling of tumbling rocks.

I broke through the treeline. A few yards in front of me, the ground dropped off to a sheer cliff. This must be the edge of the island Michael mentioned earlier.

The cliff was crumbling and falling into the water below. To my left was a clump of black doors with gold frames. As I stood there, a shard of the cliff slid back, taking a door with it over the edge.

"We're on a time limit," I realized out loud. Michael's silence confirmed it.

I stepped forward, but Michael stopped me. "Your doors are farther down."

I was just about to leave when movement near the crumbling edge caught my attention. Someone gripped the edge, struggling to grab something to pull himself up. Terror made his face nearly white.

Daniel.

Horror sliced through the center of my chest. "Michael—"

"I see him. Take out your knife."

The blade flashed in the sunlight as I pulled it into my hand.

"Cut the tree next to you," he directed. "Run and grab his forearm—don't grab his hand. You'll lose him if you do. Go!"

In one quick motion, I sliced the blade across the golden trunk. Then I ran as fast as I could toward Daniel. Tossing the knife, I dove across the ground as he lost his grip.

I grabbed his forearm before he went into free fall. With all the momentum I had, I went over with him. Something wrapped around my ankle and we came to a halt in midair.

"Charlie?" Daniel gasped. He pulled his wide eyes from the view below him.

"Hey," I said with a shaky smile as I tried not to look at the drop behind him. "Fancy meeting you here."

"Take his other arm," Michael barked in my ear.

I reached out my other hand as my opposite shoulder screamed in its socket. "Grab my forearm."

Daniel's hand shook as he reached for me. Once I had a firm grip on his other arm, I turned to look at the thing around my ankle. It looked like a black tree root.

Michael's words came back to me. *"Dryad trees won't bother you unless you bother them."*

The root tightened around my ankle, digging into my skin. *Oh no.*

Looking back at Daniel, I said with a shaky laugh, "This is probably going to hurt."

With surprising power, the root jerked us into the sky. We sailed past the ledge of the cliff and above the tops of the trees. Shock made my grip loosen, but Daniel didn't let go.

With another sharp tug, the root pulled us toward the earth. We were going to be smashed to pieces.

Why did Michael suggest this? I squeezed my eyes shut, preparing for impact.

We halted in midair.

I opened my eyes. I don't know what was the bigger surprise, that we were still alive, or that we were hovering a foot over the rocky ground.

With a pop, we dropped to the earth in a heap. Quickly, I jumped off Daniel. "Are you ok?"

He groaned. "Give me a second." He sat up and swayed. "My back is going to hurt tomorrow."

I looked up at the sky. "How—we were falling."

"A cushioning charm." He rolled his shoulders with a grimace. "Thank you . . . for grabbing me. I thought I was done for."

"For a moment, I thought we both were."

"Ye of little faith," Michael taunted.

I smiled, knowing he could see it.

Rolling to my feet, I limped across the rocky ledge and picked up the discarded knife.

Daniel pushed himself to his feet with a groan. "Will the tree come back for you?" He looked over his shoulder to the silent treeline.

"Excellent question. Guardian Kale?"

"No," Michael said. "It only does paybacks. If you tried to kill it, it would. You should be fine." I repeated his answer back to Daniel. He looked as relieved as I felt.

Keeping the weight off my ankle, I looked at Daniel's remaining doors. He had twelve left and they all looked the same; from their trim to the handle, they were perfect copies of each other.

"Which riddle do you think goes with this one?" I hobbled over and picked up my discarded wand.

"I was in the middle of figuring that out before the ground gave way." He stepped up beside me. "I was thinking the one about the exit, but it doesn't make sense in this context. As for the riddle about fire . . . I'm not sure."

"Aren't you the smartest student in the Magisterium?" I shot him an incredulous look.

"That doesn't mean I can hear a riddle and instantly know the answer," he chided. "I just need a minute to think."

"Remember you're on a time limit," Michael said as another crack splintered from the cliff face. "Which means you need to get to your own doors, Charlie."

I ignored him. "Fire set, fire burn. What is left will be yours for this turn," I muttered, as I replaced my wand in its holster. "You don't think we're supposed to—"

From the corner of my eye, there was a flash of silver.

A sharp sting sliced across my cheek. My hand jumped to my face and came away bloody.

"Behind you!" Michael yelled.

I spun toward the trees. I saw Dmitri and Igorek for only a moment. Dmitri was dripping wet; his blue hair was plastered to his forehead, and his face was flushed with fury.

His fist smashed into the side of my face. My skull cracked against the ground seconds before his foot slammed into my stomach.

Gasping for air, the metallic taste of blood filled my mouth. In the back of my mind, I realized I couldn't hear Michael. Struggling to breathe, I touched my ear and found it empty. Dmitri hit me so hard he knocked the earpiece right out of my head.

Igorek's boot slammed into my back. The air stilled in my lungs. Tears filled my eyes. Paralyzed with pain, I was unable to do anything as another kick landed between my shoulder blades.

My hand fumbled for my wand strapped to my hip. Pulling on my magic, I fired blindly. My ward hit Igorek in the chest, sending him flying back into one of the trees. He struck it with so much force the tree rocked out of the dirt.

The dryad shrieked with the sharpness of a mountain lion and the intensity of a jet engine. Roots unfurled from the dirt and coiled around one of Igorek's legs. The bottom of the tree opened up, revealing a mouth lined with row after row of teeth as thin as toothpicks.

The black roots dragged the struggling Contestant right toward the hideous mouth. Igorek's fingers scraped across the rock face, breaking his fingernails down to the nailbed. The tree clamped its mouth around his leg. With a wet snap, blood sprayed into the air. Igorek screamed.

Dmitri didn't even waste a glance on his classmate. He pulled out his wand and fired at my chest.

I rolled out of the way. The blast of magic slammed into the rock, searing my skin. Twisting onto my back, I barely had enough time to block his next ward. Struggling to back away from him, I continued to deflect his casts.

One after another, Dmitri kept firing. The hunger in his eyes intensified as he stepped closer and closer. Sending two wards back to back, he caught me off guard. I blocked one, but the second shocked my hand. Before I realized what was happening, I was unarmed and his ward slammed into my shoulder.

My throbbing head hit the ground and everything went black.

55

Fire Set, Fire Burn

With a groan, I cradled my head.

Blood dripped from the loose tendrils of my hair onto my knuckles. Breathing deeply, something nagged from the back of my mind. I needed to get up. I shouldn't be lying down, exposed. When I tried to open my eyes, the unforgiving sun acted like spears, shooting straight into my pulsing skull.

The nagging survival instinct grew louder. Forcing my eyes open, I turned my head.

I was alone. Daniel was on his back a few feet away.

A pool of blood was the only evidence that Igorek had been beside the tree. Drops of blood led into the forest. Somehow, he must have managed to get away. I was relieved Dmitri was gone as well. He probably thought he killed me.

"Daniel?" I struggled to sit up.

He didn't answer.

"Hey, are you ok?" I asked, staggering to my feet. My left arm swung limply at my side.

Daniel hadn't moved. Tentatively, I stepped closer.

At the center of his chest was Dmitri's dagger. His front was soaked. A puddle of crimson flowed steadily toward the edge of the cliff.

My heart stopped beating. I dropped to my knees beside him. My fingers sought out a pulse. His skin was cold. His blood was cold.

"No, no, no!" I pushed away from his body and clawed through the dirt. Gravel cut at my fingers until I found my earpiece. I shoved it into my ear, grabbed my wand, and dove back to Daniel.

I tried to clasp my hands around the blade to apply pressure, but my left arm was completely useless from magic-shock. I arranged my numb hand around the blade and pressed on the gaping wound with the other. "What do I do?"

"Charlie," Michael said somberly. "There's nothing—"

"Just tell me what to do!" Nausea rolled through my stomach as the smell of drying blood intensified. The edges of the knife cut into my hands.

"Charlie. He's dead."

My eyes finally focused on his face. His warm brown eyes stared at the sky without blinking. A dull line of blood left his mouth. His skin was bleached of all color. He was perfectly still, just staring at the sky.

I pulled my hands away. A cool breeze swept over the blood on my palms, making it impossible for me to forget it was there.

Dead.

No matter how badly I wanted to, I couldn't look away from his matte gaze. I wanted to wake up. I wanted this to be a nightmare, but the throbbing in my skull, the ache in my ribs and ankle, blatantly told me this was reality.

Dead.

My cheek tickled with the memory of his fingertips. Or maybe it was the blood dripping from the head wound. He couldn't be—we were right in the middle of a conversation. And then the glint of silver, the knife . . .

It was meant for me. The scratch on my cheek, from the blade that zipped by my face, burned. *Dmitri was aiming at me. And he missed.*

"*You'll get him killed.*" Michael's words stabbed through my chest. "*Trust me. You don't want to be the reason someone you love is dead.*"

The ground beneath me shook and cracked. I watched in slow motion as the ground gave way. One by one, Daniel's doors tumbled over the cliff and out of sight. The cracks in the rock face raced toward me.

Daniel slipped from my hands and tumbled over the edge. In vain, I reached for him. My blood-slick fingers only managed to glide over his skin before the air embraced him. Clinging to the edge, I watched his body fall out of sight.

I sat back. *That should've been me. Dmitri was aiming for me.*

Instead of bile rising up my throat, it was anger. It plumed up into my chest, tinting my vision red. My magic flared and burned against my ribs, begging for justice, demanding blood.

I jumped to my feet. "Where is he?"

"You need to keep moving. Your doors are almost gone."

"*Where is he?*" I yelled. My magic burned brighter, hotter.

"He's already left this part of The Trial."

"I have to follow him." Wheezing, I limped through the forest. "Tell me where he went."

"Now isn't the time." His voice grated against my anger, only making it burn hotter. I reached toward my earpiece. If he wasn't going to help me, then I would find Dmitri myself.

"WAIT! Just listen," he pleaded. "We don't know if there's a ward on the door he passed through that kills other Contestants who try to follow."

I stopped. He was right. In the last Trial, there was a ward on the door to keep out the Dellamora. Why wouldn't they use the same ward now?

"I know this is hard," he said evenly, "but you need to focus. Take everything you're feeling and lock it away. Your grief is only going to distract you. You need to focus on getting out of there."

He was right. I hated to admit it, but he was right. Dmitri and Igorek were out of reach . . . but once I got out of The Trial, we would be on the same playing field again.

I used that train of thought to lasso my emotions and pull them back. My magic cooled to a low simmer as I locked it all tightly in my chest. After a couple seconds, I was numb and as cold as the blood on my hands.

"Where are my doors?" I didn't even recognize my voice. It was as empty as I felt.

"Back the way you came, to the left." He sounded relieved.

I limped to where he directed. My doors looked just like Daniel's, black with a gold frame. Each one was no different than the next. Four of them were already missing, leaving me with ten.

"Fire set. Fire burn. What is left will be yours for this turn." I took out my wand. My eager magic slid into the shaft, ready for my command. "I'm going to burn them."

"Are you sure?" Michael asked. "We don't have a Save. I can't help you if this doesn't work."

What stands alone will be yours for this turn . . . whatever the fire left behind was my out. If not, then I was going to tear this place apart until I found a way to Dmitri.

"I'm sure." I circled my wand over my head. A wave of fire flew from the tip and engulfed the remaining doors.

Out of the corner of my eye, flames caught the closest dryad branches. The golden leaves started to melt. The dryads screamed as they curled their branches away from the flames.

Michael cursed.

The earth broke open. Black roots squirmed from the soil and tangled around my already injured ankle and yanked me to the ground. My chin struck the stone, clicking my mouth shut. With a mighty pull, the dryad tree dragged me back to the forest.

Twisting onto my back, I aimed my wand at the tangled knot of roots around my ankle. Fire pulled away from the doors and swarmed the mass pulling me across the ground.

With an even louder shriek, the roots loosened enough for me to kick myself free. The smoldering roots dove underground. The trunk shivered and the branches shook. Then the roots pulled the entire tree *forward*.

Jumping to my feet, I ran in the only direction I could: into the fire.

On the edge of the cliff stood a single door wrapped in fiery red flames; the black paint was untouched and the gold trim reflected the bright colors of the fire.

What stands alone will be yours for this turn.

I ran for it. Fire heated my skin as it swirled harmlessly around me. Reaching through the blaze, I grabbed the handle and threw myself into the waiting darkness.

I slammed the door shut, blocking out the heat and hair-splitting cries of the dryad trees. What was on the other side was a stark difference to what I left behind.

A clouded sky hung over me, casting everything in colors of grey and muted blue. Knee high grass moved like an ocean with a cool, dry breeze. Goosebumps rose over my skin.

In front of me was a two-story house that looked vaguely like the Kale's house, but something was off. Maybe it was the grey light of the sky or the dark windows or the quietness of the field, but it wasn't quite right. There were no obvious signs of life or that this place had ever been used as a residence.

"What's inside the house?" Without anywhere else to go, I started forward.

"I don't know."

That wasn't something I heard him say very often. After a heartbeat or two, I asked, "Care to elaborate?"

"I can't see inside. It must be touch-activated."

Grabbing the railing with my bloody hand, I pulled myself onto the porch. Favoring my right leg, I limped toward the door and peered through the window beside it. The shadows weren't playing nice. I couldn't see anything.

I grabbed the doorknob.

"Stop for a second," Michael said before I could twist it. "You just got the shit beaten out of you—"

"I'm fine."

"What hurts?"

Stepping back from the door, I leaned heavily against the porch railing. Tears stung my eyes. "My head and my ribs. I can't move my arm."

"Your arm's in shock from the ward. If Contestant Nineteen had a better aim, he would've stopped your heart."

I almost wish he had. I swiped at the tears running down my cheeks.

"Your head has stopped bleeding. You have a couple ribs broken." He paused. "Are you ok?"

Everything I had locked away in my chest threatened to consume me again. Clenching my teeth, I shook my head. Another tear dropped off my chin.

I had no words to describe how I felt. Broken was too simple. Grieving was too plain; devastated was an understatement.

"This is the final part of The Trial. Hold on just a little longer."

Pulling in a shaky breath, I dried my eyes with the bottom of my shirt. I winced as the rough fabric pressed against the scratch on my cheekbone . . . the one from Dmitri's knife, when it flew past me and—

I pushed off the railing, needing to move. Limping across the porch, I grabbed the handle and pushed open the front door.

"Any ideas?" I stared into the house. The light from outside illuminated only a few feet of the hardwood floors, but nothing else of the hallway. All I could make out was a small entry table. I stepped over the threshold.

"The theme has to do with memories. I'm going to guess—"

As soon as both feet crossed the threshold, light flared down the hall, bringing each room to life.

A loud, high-pitched shriek split through the house.

With only one good arm, I slapped my hand over one ear and pressed the other to my shoulder. The sound was so sharp, I felt the earpiece in my ear vibrate and pop. Pain, fiery and sharp, engulfed the right side of my head.

The front door slammed shut as my knees gave out. Squeezing my eyes closed, I curled into a tight ball. Dizziness overtook my head as something wet and hot ran between my fingers.

Then it stopped. But my ears continued to ring.

Opening my eyes, I looked around to make sure no one was standing over me with a weapon.

I was alone.

Pushing myself into the sitting position, a gush of hot liquid ran down my neck. My right hand smudged blood across the floorboards.

Reaching up, I touched my ear and pain flared. Pulling my hand back, it was wet with fresh blood. That meant—*oh no*.

"Michael?"

Nothing.

"Michael!"

I couldn't hear anything. Pushing through the pain, I reached up and felt around for the earpiece in my torn skin.

"Please say something."

I felt nothing but loose cartilage and blood.

My ear was in shreds, and my earpiece was gone.

56

Three Tries

My bloody hand fell to the hardwood floor. I sat there, shocked, as my ears continued to ring.

How the hell am I going to get out of here without Michael?

"Congra . . . tions, Contest—" Master Lenin's voice cut in and out from every corner of the house. "You've made . . . final stage of . . . before the finish line."

What is happening? I couldn't hear anything from my right ear. All I could get from my left was a ringing so sharp it made my head ache even worse than before.

I pushed myself to my feet, smearing the walls with bloody fingerprints. I couldn't tell if the blood was mine or Daniel's.

"As you walk—walk through the house . . . recognize the rooms. That's because you made this—or . . . subconscious did. Each room represents one of . . . final riddle comes into play."

I placed the back of my wrist against my mouth to fight back the nausea. But that brought my bloody hand right up next to my nose. Bending over, I retched all over the floor.

"You have exactly . . . to solve . . . exit, and cross the finish line. You have three tries . . . get out. When you cross the threshold of a . . . used. I suggest you . . . wisely. Your time starts . . ."

Outside, the landscape was bathed in a neon, red light. Peering out the window, I looked into the sky. A giant countdown started in the grey wash of clouds for sixty minutes.

"You've got to be kidding me," I muttered. *How the hell was I supposed to know what to do based on those broken instructions? I barely understood them!*

I tried the handle of the front door, but it was locked. I grabbed the small entry table and bashed it against the floor. Ripping off one of the legs, I thrust it through a window. I moved to reach my hand through the broken window to find the lock, but as soon as it crossed outside, my skin burned like it was put to an open flame.

Cursing, I jerked my hand back inside. Underneath the smears of blood and dirt, my skin, from fingertips to elbow, was now flamingo pink.

Alright, so I can't cheat my way out of the house. Looks like I have another riddle to solve.

Hurry and choose the exit that means the most to you. Time is running short and you better not lose. For at the end of time's race, you will be stuck, and for the next Trial you will not place.

I have to find 'the exit that means the most' to me. Or whatever the hell that means.

Since onward was the only way to go, I cautiously started down the hallway. It was bitterly cold. At any moment, I thought I would see my breath.

The house was set up like the Kale's house. Directly in front of the main door was the staircase to the second floor. The hall to the left led to the kitchen, living room, and back porch. The floorboards even creaked the same as I limped down the hall.

Coming to the first door, I leaned heavily against the frame and pushed it open. I jumped back. My eyes flew around the room, looking for the man it belonged to, but it was empty.

The office was simply furnished. A scratched and faded desk was shoved beneath the window. A mess of papers cluttered the top with a collection of highlighters and pencils sprinkled throughout. The chair in front of it was missing an armrest. The stout window showed the worn-down street of Haven Avenue.

That study was where Denny took a belt to my back for the first time after I ran my mouth.

I slammed the door closed. The sound barely cut through the ringing in my aching ear.

Master Lenin said my subconscious built this house, I think. Michael mentioned something about memories.

Sick to my stomach, I continued down the hall and stopped in front of the door that would've been the room Michael and I shared for the summer.

Instead of our two beds, the room led outside. A flurry of snow rushed from the room and dusted the hardwood around my feet, quickly dissolving into puddles. Inside was the 24/7 travel-store gas station in Salina, Kansas, the very same one where Blake brought me to get me away from Denny.

So each room housed a memory, and one of them, the one that meant the most, was my way out. And I had an hour to figure it out. My stomach filled with uneasiness over what I was going to see.

I turned to the room across the hall. Instead of the blue guestroom, the walls were made of grey cement. Bright fluorescent lights hung over a cherry red Honda with a sunflower sticker on the bumper.

It was the car I stole in New Mexico to drive to California. That little car, while it had no AC, was equipped with a killer sound system. Those wheels gave me the most freedom I had ever known. It took me to see the ocean for the first time.

Thinking of the ocean reminded me of the time Daniel took me to get seafood.

Before my mind could spiral, I pulled the door closed and stepped into the kitchen.

The table was set with Christmas breakfast. Red and green sprinkled pancakes steamed next to a plate of glistening bacon. A can of whipped cream sat in front of Michael's chair. A large mug of hot chocolate with a pile of marshmallows on top sat on the counter. The screen door was cracked open, inviting winter sunlight and snowflakes into the room.

For a brief moment, I was glad my earpiece was no longer functioning. I knew Michael would have questions as to why this room was in my funhouse of horrors, and I was glad I didn't have to explain.

Just like at the Kale ranch, the kitchen looked into the living room. The Christmas theme spilled over, but it wasn't the same Christmas.

The living room was quaint. The couch was outdated and the leather armchair had tears and stains on the armrests. A small tree was pressed up against the corner. Most of the ornaments were concentrated on the bottom half, because that's how tall I was at the time.

The warmth in my chest from the last two rooms faded as I looked closer at the living room. My eyes lingered the longest on the crackling fireplace. Hanging from the mantel was a stocking with my name on it.

It was the foster home that would've adopted me if they hadn't gotten pregnant with twins of their own and lost their jobs. Loraine and Evan were the first two people to want me, and then they didn't.

That definitely isn't it.

I looked back at the kitchen set for a Christmas morning feast.

That has to be the way out. Mrs. Kale's gift, the morning spent with a family, the feeling of finally finding a home. *That has to be it.*

My foot slid forward.

Don't make a decision before you know all of the cards you are playing with. Wiping the blood from my neck, I headed for the stairs.

I had never been to the second floor of the Kales' house. As I walked up the stairs, I felt like I was intruding on something private. I had to remind myself that I was in The Trial. This wasn't their real house.

On the second floor, I opened the door at the top of the stairs and balked. It was the rotunda of the highest floor in the North Tower. The window I had jumped out of was open, letting in a sharp mountain breeze. The house was so silent, I could just barely hear the rushing of the river below.

That room doesn't mean anything to me. I closed the door.

The room across the hall was Blake's bedroom, where he had taken me after Denny found out I had been hiding money to save up for a place of my own. The sheets were smudged with blood from my back. His window was open too, probably from when I had climbed out onto his roof.

Maybe that room?

I walked to the last door and immediately slammed it shut. It was my room on Haven Avenue. Piles of clothes littered the floor. On the bed was my light blue hoodie with fresh blood stains on the back. The window was open with the screen popped off. Fresh snowflakes danced and twirled into the room.

I'm never stepping foot in that cage again.

I limped back to the first floor and glanced through the broken window by the front door. I had forty-five minutes left. Pacing the hall, I ran over all the rooms in my head and repeated the riddle.

Hurry and choose the exit that means the most to you. Time is running short and you better not lose. For at the end of time's race, you will be stuck, and for the next Trial, you will not place.

The exit that means the most . . . the exit that means the most . . .

The kitchen was staged as the same morning where Mrs. Kale gave me the key to the ranch. It was the day I started associating the feeling of home with walls instead of a person, Blake. So far, that was the exit I was leaning toward.

But the gas station was where I left Kansas.

The North Tower was where I took my fate into my own hands for the first time.

But didn't someone say happy memories were better than anything else? Before I lost my nerve, I walked toward the kitchen and focused on the table of steaming food. I crossed my fingers and stepped into the room.

A gentle ring, almost like a wind chime on a back porch, dinged through the room.

"Incorrect," a calm, cool voice announced. "One try used. Two remaining."

What does that— The room exploded with fire.

I dove into the hallway, landing hard on my shoulder. The flames slammed against the threshold of the room and swirled up the ceiling, like it was being directed by an invisible force. Just as quickly as they had come, the flames were gone. The room was charred and smoking.

The last of Master Lenin's broken instructions finally made sense. I had three tries to figure out the exit of this house. And I only had two tries left.

I slapped my foot against the floor. "Dammit!"

"Don't get mad," I could practically hear Michael chiding me. *"You're wasting time. What are your options? Obviously, you missed something."*

I lay on the cold hardwood and crossed my one working arm over my face, and ran through the rooms again. The warmth from the flames was swiftly replaced by the merciless cold.

I need to see them again.

With a frustrated growl, I pushed myself to my feet and looked in every room again, hoping one of them would scream at me. None of them did. My exasperation grew each time I turned away from another room.

The exit that means the most to me? None of them did!

"What would Michael do?" I rolled my eyes. "For one, he wouldn't talk to himself."

I tried to conjure each room in my mind, but the ringing in my ear cut through my concentration. Then a thought hit me. Michael would look at ALL of his options.

I hobbled to the second floor and stopped in the hallway between the two bedrooms. A large ornate mirror was the only decoration on the plain wall.

With one arm, I hoisted it off its nail and let it fall to the ground with a crash. Glass shattered to every corner of the hallway. I winced as the sound joined the constant ringing.

Going to the now blank wall, I took out my wand. Not knowing what to do, I tried to hold it like a pen. It took some concentration to get my cold fingers to grip it.

Pulling on my magic, I almost sighed as a rush of warmth filled my chest. I pressed the tip of the wand to the wall. It sparked and burned the paint. That was the best sign I had seen all day.

Promptly, I wrote down all the rooms, the memories that went with them, and the people involved. I crossed off the kitchen. When I was done, I took a step back.

DENNY'S STUDY — PUNISHMENT AND SCARS
GAS STATION — LEAVING HELL, BLAKE
~~CHRISTMAS BREAKFAST — HOME~~
CHRISTMAS MORNING— BEING WANTED, LORAINE AND
    EVAN
MY HONDA — FREEDOM
NORTH TOWER — RICHARD AND BLAINE
MY PERSONAL ROOM IN HELL
BLAKE'S ROOM — MY ONLY FRIEND

With a quick glance out the window, I noted that I had thirty minutes. *Daniel wouldn't have taken this long.*

My knees almost gave out. I was suddenly breathless at the reminder that his blood was covering my hands.

Breathe. Just focus.

I looked back at the list, breathing deep. History overwhelmed me. To the naked eye, it looked like just a list. But in my mind, it was a tangled spider web of emotions. It was too much.

My cheeks puffed out with a slow exhale. *I have to cut it back or I'm going to get nowhere. Just make a move and cross something off.*

"Ok." Stepping back up to the wall, I crossed off a few rooms I knew for a fact wouldn't be the exit; Christmas morning, Denny's study, my room in Kansas, and the North Tower.

After that, only three rooms remained; Blake's room, the gas station, and the garage.

I left the list and carefully looked over those three rooms. I mentally crossed off Blake's room as a possibility. Compared to the remaining two rooms, it didn't make sense as a memory that meant the most. The time spent there was easy, but not memorable.

Downstairs, I stood in the hallway between the garage and the gas station. I shivered, wishing that more of these memories took place somewhere warmer.

The gas station was my greatest escape.

With that Honda, I wasn't a foster kid or an instrument of war. I was just Charlie.

Throwing caution to the wind, I stepped into the garage with the stolen car.

Ding.

"Incorrect. Try two has been used. One remaining."

57

The Exit that Means the Most

Magic vibrated from the walls seconds before fire blasted through the room.

It thrust me back, lifting my feet from the floor and tossing me from the room. I flew across the hall and slammed into the wall. The door closed with a bang.

Gasping, I cradled my side with my one good arm. The impact from the wall knocked the air out of my lungs and seemed to double the shrill in my ear. My eyes watered as I fought to catch my breath. At this point, there was more of me that was in pain than wasn't.

Breathing hard, I moved back up the stairs and aimed my wand at the garage on the list of options. Pissed off, I pulled on too much magic and blew a hole through the wall.

One try left and less than thirty minutes on the clock. I slid to the floor and looked at the remaining rooms. I went through them one by one.

Everything bad went back to the North Tower. My friend was murdered, nightmares plagued me every time I went to sleep, and I had scars from that night. Even my own memories were hidden from me because of it.

The gas station was the one place I had run away from the most. I had wasted so many bus tickets because I was too scared of the punishment that would follow if I didn't succeed.

Blake's room was where he took me away from Denny. It was the safest place in Kansas. We spent many summer days there, listening to music and just enjoying each other's company.

My room in Kansas was equivalent to a cellblock in hell.

I didn't even want to think of the study as a possibility.

And my first Christmas ended badly as well. Right when I thought life was looking up and that fate had dealt me a good card, I was ripped away and placed in Denny's house.

Those were my options. If I didn't know better, this house was set up for me to fail.

Ten minutes left on the clock.

I leaned my head against the wall. My whole body was shaking from the cold. I went over them again, searching for anything I might have missed.

Five minutes left.

I stood up and passed by Blake's room. His room was a mess like always. Various posters covered the navy walls. There were shelves of CDs and old records. The window looked across the street into mine . . .

Four minutes left. A thought hit me.

I went back to the North Tower. The window I jumped out of was wide open. The cold mountain air rushed through my hair and down the hall.

"Ok, ok." Slowly, pieces started to pull together. Maybe the room wasn't the exit. Maybe it was a pathway to the exit.

Spinning around, I bolted down the hall and skidded to a halt outside my old room on Haven Avenue.

The window was open.

The screen was popped out of the frame, leaning against the bed. Through the window, the overgrown tree wore a thick blanket of shimmering snowflakes. Across the street, Blake's house was decked out in Christmas lights.

Each room had one thing in common. All of the windows were open.

Two minutes left.

I'm such an idiot! The exit isn't a door. It's a window!

That window was the same one I climbed out of every time I went to the bus station to leave Kansas. It was the exit I knew would always be there. Every time I got into trouble, I promised myself that if it got too bad, I could always leave.

I backed up as much as the hallway would allow. Taking a deep breath, I took two running steps into the room. Fire erupted from the walls. I leapt onto the mattress as the wave of crimson flame rushed toward the center of the room. Bounding across the bed, I threw myself out the window.

I hit the ground with a thud. My bones slammed into each other. A groan rolled through my chest. Flipping onto my back, I looked up and saw the window hanging in the air. Next to it were other exits: doors, windows, gates, and even a hole in the ground.

I made it! I made it out!

But the clock was still counting down. I had one minute to cross the finish line.

Pushing myself to my feet, I spotted the finish line at the top of the hill. I could hardly breathe. I wasn't going to make it . . . if I ran.

Playing my final card, I pulled on my magic. It broke through my chest like a tidal wave of fire. Turning on my heel, I Ported over the finish line and fell to the ground just as the timer stopped.

"Congratulations, Contestants," Master Lenin declared. "You all have completed the Second Trial."

I grinned up at the sky. Using my good arm, I pushed myself to my feet and swayed as my head pulsed.

A flash of black popped in front of me.

I knew who it was before my eyes focused. I stumbled forward on my bruised ankle and threw my arm around Michael's neck. I melted against him. *I'm out. I made it.*

His arms wound around my waist, pulling me close. He said something, but I couldn't make it out over the ringing.

"What?"

Michael pulled back. He kept his hands on my waist as I started to sway. His smile of relief dissolved at the sight of me.

A little self-conscious, I tried to brush the hair out of my face. Michael caught my wrist before it neared my ear. Gently, he moved the blood-stiff lock from my neck. I winced as it tugged and peeled away from my tender, broken skin.

"I said 'well done'," he repeated a little louder, this time directing it to my left ear.

"No thanks to you," I said with a smile so he would know I was joking.

"Don't blame me. You were the one who took their sweet ass time."

"Like you could've done any better."

Michael shrugged one shoulder. "My dream house for sure would've been better. Yours sucked."

"It really did." My eyelids drooped as the adrenaline started to bleed out of my system. The air was warmer here, so I wasn't shivering. I just wanted to lie down.

Michael noticed. He noticed everything. His eyes moved back to the aching side of my skull. "Come on, Helen needs to take a look at you."

Nothing sounded better than being pumped full of potions and getting to sleep for the rest of the day.

Putting an arm around me to take weight off my ankle, Michael turned toward the other side of the field. Helen was waiting at the front of a black tent with gold lining.

I stopped.

Michael turned to me with a questioning eyebrow.

My eyes flew around looking for the medical tent with the crest of the University. On the opposite side of the field, I found it. In front, conversing with his Guardian, was Dmitri.

Every emotion I had locked up broke free, filling me with boiling rage. It was so intense that all of my injuries seemed to fade away.

In a heartbeat, I was beside Dmitri with my fist smashing into his jaw.

Magic surged through my ribcage. Before he could regain his balance, my foot slammed into his chest. He flew back, skidding across the grass.

I pulled one of Michael's knives from the new holster. Before I could step toward him, an Aquarius guard wrapped his arms around me, pinning my arms to my sides. I threw back my head into his nose.

He stumbled back, clutching his face. Magic burned in my fingers as I drove the knife into Dmitri's shoulder.

Exclamations and gasps came from the observing Masters and Contestants. But I barely heard them or paid them any mind.

Then I grabbed my wand.

Another guard Ported in front of me.

She grabbed my wrist and twisted my wand from my grasp. She spun me around, pulling me to her chest. Pinning my arms again, she lifted me off my feet.

"Let me go!" I yelled, kicking my legs out in all directions. Her hold was the equivalent to iron.

With bared teeth, Dmitri yanked the knife from his shoulder.

"You were supposed to come after me!" I lurched my shoulders, trying to throw the guard. "You said you were coming after *me!*"

Dmitri's lips pulled into a smile. "I missed."

I screamed, doing everything I could to get her off me. With one useless arm, there wasn't much I could do. But that didn't stop me from trying.

Michael yelled at her to release me. They argued over my head as she dragged me across the field, while her partner kept trying to move Michael out of the way. With each step, she pulled me farther and farther away from Dmitri.

She hauled me inside the Magisterium's medical tent just as I sank my teeth into the flesh of her thumb.

With a loud curse, she threw me to the ground. She pulled out her wand, and before I could get to my feet, she fired.

The ward struck me dead-center in the chest. Magic rolled through me, unwinding my coiled muscles and putting them to sleep. My aching body relaxed into the grass. The only thing I could do was breathe and blink.

Yelling, Michael shoved her out of the tent with so much force it looked like she flew.

Her cast had no effect on my magic. It flared through my chest, listening to my rage for Dmitri's head. It screamed through my veins, brightening the lights to match the afternoon sun. The glass doors of the medical cabinets cracked. Potions hissed and bubbled in their bottles.

Helen dropped to her knees beside me and stuck a needle into my arm. As the lavender potion drained into my blood, my magic cooled. The temperature of the tent dropped. My magic slid back into my core and remained still.

My mind didn't match. If I could open my mouth, I would be screaming. Silently, tears streamed across my temples and into my hair.

Helen gently levitated my limp body from the grass to a stretcher.

Michael turned away. Quickly, he ducked behind a cabinet of potions and retched into the grass.

"Master Kale!" Helen jumped toward him.

"I'm fine." He wiped his mouth with the back of his hand.

Helen hesitated, looking him over. Turning back to me, she filled another syringe and stuck it into my arm.

"What she did in that Trial . . ." Helen shook her head. "That has to have earned her a spot in the Top Seven."

"She just maimed another Contestant."

"I think they'll overlook it. I've never seen someone finish alone. She'll Ascend."

"I don't think that's a good thing," Michael said through clenched teeth. He refused to meet my gaze. "She'll have to go against Contestant Nineteen."

"From what I just saw, she can handle it." Helen stuck another syringe into my arm.

Michael shook his head. "She caught him by surprise. If it had been a fair fight, he would've killed her." He crossed his arms over his gut. "Have they recovered Contestant Phillips' body?"

I didn't think I could feel any more pain. Silent tears trickled from my eyes. I wish I had lost my hearing in both ears, then I wouldn't have heard that. I could have tricked myself into thinking they could have saved him.

Helen nodded. Her lips pressed tight. "I took him to the Magisterium. The knife went straight through his core. There was nothing anyone could've done to save him."

That should be me. He was aiming for me.

Michael turned away from me.

Helen bent beside my mangled ear. "This is a complete mess. I can repair the ear, no problem, but she won't regain all of her hearing. Master Lenin is calling it sabotage. Any idea who would do it?"

My earpiece was sabotaged? Was that why I couldn't hear Master Lenin's instructions in the house too?

Michael shook his head. "Anyone of the Next Fourteen could want her out of The Trial. That's not to mention the other Contestants who didn't Ascend, or someone outside The Trial who didn't want her to do well."

His dark eyes dipped down and met my gaze. He swallowed hard as more tears spilled down my cheeks.

The tent flap pushed forward as Master Lenin ducked inside.

Michael stepped toward him, putting himself between the School Master and me. Like he was protecting me from him. "Helen, it might be best if she's not awake for the remainder of the day."

Helen didn't question him.

Setting aside the healing potion, she opened a jar of black gel. Unscrewing the top, she took a deep breath and blew the fumes over my face.

The smell of mint swirled up my nose and I lost consciousness.

58

It Should've Been Me

When I opened my eyes, I forgot everything for a blissful second.
Just one.

I was warm, cradled in between heavy blankets. The quiet comfort of the Kale ranch surrounded me. In a blink, it was gone.

My skin ached with the memory of wounds. When I breathed, it was unhindered, but I kept expecting my ribs to whine from the impact of Dmitri's and Igorek's boots.

Daniel.

I pressed my eyes closed, but that only brought the bloody memory into sharper focus. My hands still held the feeling of his blood as I applied pressure to the wound. His brown eyes, matte and emotionless . . .

As my emotions flared, my magic rushed through my chest. Then my memories returned to Dmitri's smug face.

"I missed."

I pushed myself into the sitting position. The rustle of the sheets sounded muffled through my right ear, like it was coming from the next room over.

As I dropped my feet to the hardwood floor, the bathroom door swung open.

I looked up and met Michael's expectant gaze.

He looked as well as I felt. Dark circles hung beneath his eyes. The black locks of his hair were twisted and ruffled. His eyes cooled the longer he looked in mine. Despite the cheerful afternoon glow streaming through the windows, I had never felt colder.

"How long have I been asleep?" I asked, my voice just barely above a murmur.

"About twelve hours."

I nodded. "When is the Ascending Ceremony?"

"Seven." He pulled his phone from his back pocket and checked the time. When he didn't share that information with me, I pressed my hands into the mattress and pushed myself to my feet.

Michael jumped forward, tossing his phone onto the bed. His hands hovered by my sides, but I didn't sway. Surefooted, I walked around him and closed the bathroom door.

I gripped the edge of the counter, breathing slowly. The sedative Helen gave me . . . it made my head feel like it was underwater, like my whole body had been shocked by a bolt of electricity. I couldn't feel anything.

Numbly, I brushed the hair from my face and met the cold pair of eyes in the mirror. All of the blood and dirt from The Trial had been cleaned away. My hair looked like it was freshly brushed. I moved my hair away from my right ear expecting to see the jagged remains of cartilage and skin. But it was whole, as if nothing had happened. The ringing had stopped. With the slight loss of hearing on my right side, the world was so quiet.

I let my hair drop back and met the gaze of my reflection. There I found something new, evidence of the past day. Across my cheek, was a thin straight scar. It followed the edge of my cheekbone toward my ear.

My heart cracked and crumbled in my chest. Dmitri was aiming for my head when he missed . . . when his knife flew past me and into Daniel's chest.

Oh, God.

I bowed my head trying to breathe through the wave of nausea. But closing my eyes didn't help. I could still see Daniel's bloodless face, the trickle of blood from the corner of his mouth.

A light tap came from the door.

"Charlie, honey, can I come in?" Mrs. Kale called softly through the wood.

The door squealed as I pulled it open. When Mrs. Kale stepped in, she took one look at me and held out her arms.

A sob shook and shuddered through my shoulders. I wrapped my arms around myself, trying to keep my ribcage from completely coming apart.

Murmuring softly, Mrs. Kale gathered me to her chest and tucked my head under her chin. Her soft hands moved gently up and down my spine.

Not once, not for even one second, did her arms loosen. Not even when the lights over the sink flickered and glared as my magic throbbed with each sob.

I could feel every crack in my heart widen with each tear that soaked her shirt. As the cracks pulled away from each other, my knees weakened. I wasn't sure if I fell, that I would be able to push myself back up again.

I grabbed the grief and the horror pulsing through my ribcage and yanked it back. Pushing away from Mrs. Kale, I threw them in a box and slammed the lid. Sucking in a shaking breath, I brushed the tears from my face.

"I need to—" I hiccupped. "I need to get ready for the Ascending Ceremony."

"Oh, honey. I don't think—"

"I need to. I just need to move." My arms remained locked around my middle, trying to keep myself in one piece.

She nodded slowly. "Ok." Reaching into her back pocket, she pulled out a small black box. "Here are your gowns for the evening. Master Lenin sent them over . . . if you need anything . . ."

Wiping my nose, I took the box. I kept my eyes down until she left the bathroom. When the door closed behind her, I took two deep breaths, fortifying the hold on the torment seeping from my heart.

Popping the lid off the box, a stream of black fabric twisted and undulated along the bathroom wall. The dark cloud of fabric grew and settled into a line of black gowns.

Pulling the hospital clothes over my head, I grabbed the closest one and tugged it on. The full skirt billowed out from my waist in wisps of fabric that moved like smoke. The thin material clung to my chest, but left my arms bare.

I washed my face and put on enough makeup to hide the fact that I had been crying. I took the concealer Master Lenin gave me at the beginning of the summer and applied it to my demon scars. My fingers faltered over the newest line across my cheek.

Dropping my hand, I stared at my reflection. The black material of the dress made my hair look darker and my skin colder, like it was chiseled from marble.

I jerked away from the mirror before I could look at the scar again. I grabbed a pair of strappy shoes and moved out of the bathroom. As I sat on the bed, buckling the heels to my feet, Michael came back into the room.

He wore an all-black suit with a matching slim tie and shirt. His holster peeked beneath the folds of his jacket. The other suits had made him look handsome, but this one held him in a cold beauty. Maybe it was from the heartbroken look in his eye.

He looked me over, head to toe. He wasn't admiring the layers of the gown. His eyes bounced around, looking for the cracks I was so desperately trying to hold together.

"Are you ready?" he asked.

I nodded.

Stepping closer, he wrapped his calloused fingers around my wrist. Threading my arm through his, he Ported us to the front gate. Once we were on the other side, he Ported us to Greece.

Just like the last ceremony, there was a line of limos painted with Contestant numbers, this time in black. Michael quickly shuffled me inside. Neither of us spoke a word during the short, slow drive toward the Grecian theater.

When the limo stopped at the bottom of the red-carpeted stairs, Michael slipped out first and offered me his hand. The crowd cheered at the sight of the Master Hunter. Bright flashes reflected off his shoulders and the unruly mess of black hair.

With the crowd crying for his attention, I took his hand. The familiar feel of his fingers around mine was an anchor. I focused on the steady pressure of his hand instead of the sea of strangers.

Photographers called my name, demanding that I look at them, to smile, to answer questions.

"How was the Second Trial?"

"What did you face?"

"Do you think you'll Ascend to the Top Seven?"

"What happened to Contestant Phillips?"

Michael looped my arm through his and placed my hand on his forearm, but he didn't remove his hand. His strong fingers held my hand in place, keeping me beside him. Without giving the photographers and reporters any attention, Michael led me up the stairs into the auditorium. We had just enough time to find our seats in the front row.

Holding my breath, I prepared myself for the tidal wave of emotions when I saw Daniel's empty seat next to mine.

But the seat wasn't empty.

Clarence, dressed in all black, was quietly talking to his Guardian with the gelled blond hair.

I dropped into the seat meant for Michael, putting two seats of buffer between myself and Clarence. "What is he doing here?"

Michael followed my gaze down the line. The muscle in his jaw tensed as he sat down. "All Contestants, active or not, have to be here. If the judges didn't like either of the performances of the two Contestants that competed in the Second Trial, they can call on the third Contestant to move forward."

I turned my gaze away from him and made the mistake of looking farther down the front row.

I noticed Dmitri's blue hair first. My stomach lurched as if I were going to be sick. My gaze jumped around, finding Igorek next. He slouched low in his seat with one leg stretched before him; it was the same one the tree had bitten off. But it wasn't. The skin peeking under the cuff of his pants was stainless silver.

The lights flashed, signaling the ceremony was about to start. Lawrence walked up the stage as the crowd cheered.

"Good evening, ladies and gentlemen, Contestants and Guardians." The Master smiled coyly at the crowd. "Tonight is a very important night, one we have waited months for. Tonight, our Top Seven will be revealed.

"Once named, these students have the chance to change their lives. If they perform well, they'll earn a place to study under a Master. If their performance is extraordinary, our first place winner will earn a title of their own. Once called, their names will be written into history. The pressure will be great. You could win glory for your school and a title for your family. But if you lose, you won't be the same.

"I could go on and explain in depth the importance of the next Trial, but I can see you all are eager to find out who Ascended. Can I have all of the Contestants come up to the stage?"

My hands shook as I got to my feet. Michael stepped close, and together we walked up the tall steps. With each step, his shoulder brushed mine, reassuring my tangled nerves.

When we were all lined up, Lawrence continued. "When your name is called, step forward into the Top Seven. If you wish not to continue, please remain where you are and one of the other Contestants from your school will take your place.

"The judges carefully weighed the performances of both the First and Second Trials, looking for improvements. Did you exceed expectations? Did you fall short? Did you create more concerns than good impressions?"

As he spoke, a line of guards in bright red armor stationed themselves behind us.

"Those Ascending tonight showed the most promise and used both their skills and training to create a remarkable performance that embodied the core of their school." Lawrence turned from the podium to look down the line of Contestants. His bright blue eyes shone with excitement.

"In no particular order, the first Top Seven Contestant, from The Magical Academy of the Earth, for her ability to blend into her surroundings and for her hand-to-hand combat skills . . . Contestant Three, Tala Abalos."

The crowd roared. Tala wasted no time stepping forward.

The guards behind Lin immediately stepped closer, as if she might try jumping the other Contestant.

"Where is Malan?" I whispered to Michael. He had competed in the Second Trial. Lin hadn't Ascended to the second.

"He didn't make it out of the water."

"Next," Lawrence said once the noise calmed down. "From Aquarius: The Undersea School of Enchantments, for her use of her surroundings and expert wards . . . Contestant Six, Bailey Jones."

The ocean school Contestant stayed where she was, holding clenched fists. "Thank you, Master Hart, and thank you to the seven School Masters for this opportunity. But I must decline the invitation."

A murmur swept through the crowd. The School Masters all looked to Master Finch for his reaction, but he had none.

Lawrence turned his attention to Contestant Four, Amelia Markus. "As the only other Contestant from Aquarius, do you accept the spot in the Top Seven?"

Amelia stepped forward. "Yes, Master Hart, I do."

Lawrence nodded to her. "Welcome, Contestant Four, to the Top Seven." He turned back to the crowd. "From Lions of Magic, the man who placed for his strength and his cunning mind . . . Second Award Challenge Winner, Contestant Eight, Emeka Selasi."

As cheers filled the room, he stepped forward and bowed. Again, I noticed that the second Contestant wasn't the one who participated in the Second Trial. Aboiy should have been beside Emeka. Instead, it was Vienna.

"From The European Academy for Practical Magic, the Contestant Ascending on its behalf, for his courage and his quick thinking . . . First Award Challenge Winner, Contestant Twelve, Blake Johnson."

My head whipped around as Blake and Atlas strolled forward. That was another reason I needed to Ascend, to keep an eye on him.

My heart tripled its gait. My school was next. Michael stroked a finger along the palm of my hand in an attempt to calm me. It did nothing.

"From The Magisterium of Magic . . . for his agility and quick work of the First Trial, Contestant Fourteen, Clarence Hardy."

Everything slowed.

Lawrence's voice echoed Clarence's name over, and over, and over. Even then, I didn't believe what I heard until Contestant Fourteen stepped forward.

It felt wrong, all the way down into my bones.

It wasn't because I hadn't Ascended. I found that I didn't care about that or about earning a title. Those things didn't seem important anymore.

All I could think of was Daniel. The boy standing before the crowd, ready to face the next Trial, should have been Daniel. He was the smartest of all the Magisterium Contestants. He was gentle and kind. He would have made a great Master.

But it was Clarence. *Why pick a Contestant that only competed in one Trial?*

Then I remembered what Michael said after Emeka won the Second Award Challenge.

"Lawrence won't let me win."

I stepped forward.

The guard behind me grabbed my arm with a painful grip.

Clarence's Guardian, Brandon Moore, shot Michael a broad smirk of satisfaction before facing the front.

"Remove your hand or I'll remove it from your body," Michael growled at the guard.

After a beat, he did. Michael moved me so I was standing in front of him. If the guards on either side of us wanted to get to me, they would have to go through him.

"From The Serpentine School of Magic," Lawrence called, "for his cunning use of magic and wit . . . Contestant Seventeen, Thiago Luis."

Thiago nodded to Master Hart and joined the others at the front.

"From The University for Advanced Tactical Magic, for his skills in magic and weaponry . . . Contestant Nineteen, Dmitri Theodore."

Dmitri thrust his fist in the air. Igorek pulled him into a hug. Then Dmitri stepped forward into the Top Seven. He didn't even *look at me.* After everything, he didn't spare me a glance.

Because he won.

He got what he wanted. He went through The Trial, clearing the board of the most unpredictable players, so his road to a title would be smooth. He knew Clarence was the lesser Contestant. He won.

The son of a bitch warned me when I Ascended to the Second Trial that it would be my last. And now, Daniel was dead because I couldn't leave well enough alone. I provoked him for two months, and then made a fool of him at the start of The Trial.

Had I learned nothing from Denny? Actions breed scars and consequences.

With Dmitri moving forward, he drifted out of my reach. He would continue through The Trial and gain a Master's title—with who his father was, there was no way he wouldn't get one—I wouldn't be able to touch him. He'd become like a god.

Daniel's death would be a stepping stone.

And all I could do was watch.

The crowd cheered. The Top Seven bowed. Then the audience rose, clapping wildly, as the seven Contestants took it all in.

I turned to Michael. Just barely, I was able to choke out, "Take me home."

He didn't waste a second. He took my hands and Ported us off the stage. My ears rang in the silence with the lingering cheers.

With his hand still clutching mine, Michael shoved open the gate to the ranch and pulled me through. The ward flared bright gold as the gates closed, sealing us into the safety of the property.

Stumbling away from Michael, I fought to breathe. Hopelessness and failure crushed me. My hands couldn't stop shaking. My chest felt like it was about to break open. Grief crippled my body as the emotions I had sealed up broke free.

The pine trees groaned, swaying from my grief-stricken magic. Their dark green needles bleached to pale yellow, and rained around us like golden snow. With each struggling breath, my magic burned hotter, stronger, until I could see its golden light gathering in the tears below my eyes.

Michael was saying something I couldn't hear, or maybe couldn't comprehend.

I knew I was close to a flare. The unbearable pressure of my storming magic pressed against my ribcage, making it feel like I was going to explode. I had felt it so many times while I was on the run from Michael. But now, I found I didn't care if it tore me apart, if it meant I would stop feeling what I was feeling.

Michael took his wand and waved it over his head. A dome of magic surrounded us, cutting us off from the rest of the ranch. The trees stopped swaying and the fall of pine needles reduced.

Collapsing to my knees, magic blew from my chest. The snow melted as it slammed against the protective wall. Michael's ward kept the swirling storm of magic close.

With a sharp sting, I tried to pull my magic back. Pressing my forehead to the steaming dirt, I wrapped my arms tightly around myself, trying to quiet my magic. Sobs shook my shoulders. Hot tears dropped from my eyes, sizzling on the gravel road. I cried into the earth, gasping with sobs.

Michael dropped to his knees before me. He took my face in his hands and lifted my vacant gaze to his.

"I—I don't know what to do." A sob ripped from my chest. Magic darkened the ground beneath me. "Tell me what to do."

His jaw clenched. His silence was my answer. There was nothing I could do.

I did this. Michael told me getting close to Daniel would get him killed. I should have listened to him. *I should have left him alone.*

Every inch of my body screamed. It was as if my ribcage had been ripped out of my chest, leaving everything inside exposed and raw.

That pain spread like poison, but instead of going into my blood, it sank deep into my bones. Even my fingers felt like they ached with sorrow.

"I can't do this," I sobbed. "Make it stop. *Please.* Make it stop."

The muscle in his jaw pulsed. "Just breathe."

Shaking my head furiously, I pulled away from his hands. "You were right. I'll do nothing for your war but get you killed. I can't save you. Or anyone. Everything I touch dies. I can't even save the people I love when they're dying in my lap!"

His teeth were clenched so tight, there was no way he wasn't causing himself pain.

"I don't want to feel this. Make it stop." I reached under his jacket toward his holster.

His eyes widened. He grabbed my wrist before I touched the hilt of his wand. "No. I won't do that."

A burst of anger flared. How many times had this bastard threatened to kill me? And now, when I begged him to do what he'd wanted to do since we met, he wouldn't.

I shoved at his chest. "You want me to feel this, don't you? You're enjoying this!"

He captured my wrists before I could strike him again. "Don't put words in my mouth," he said gently.

I struggled against his hold, trying once more for his wand. I would have settled for one of his knives if I could manage it. Most of my strength had gone out with the flare, leaving my attempts frantic and pathetic.

Michael spun me around and caught me against his chest. He crossed my arms over my abdomen and held me tightly. I tried to break his hold, but fighting iron would have been easier. All I could do was weep.

"He missed," I cried. "It should've been me. *It should've been me.*"

I wept those four words over and over. And when I couldn't say them anymore, they echoed in my head. I gripped Michael's hands like they were the only things keeping me together.

He just sat there. He didn't say a word and he didn't move. He was still sitting there, in the cold, long after I lost my voice. He sat there until my eyes were unable to produce tears, and my eyelids were too heavy to stay up.

Numb and tired, I passed out.

And he continued to sit.

59

I Meant It

When I woke up, I squeezed my eyes tightly shut. If I never opened my eyes, maybe I could trick myself into thinking the night before was a nightmare, that the whole Trial was just a horrible nightmare.

I rolled over, pulling the covers closer. A gentle breath skimmed over my nose, across my cheek, and into my hair. A moment later, another followed.

I dared to open my eyes. On the same pillow, I was nose-to-nose with Michael.

He must have stayed close to make sure I didn't flare in my sleep. Not that I could blame him after last night . . . The Trial and Ascending Ceremony were fresh in my mind like an oozing wound.

I stared at him, taking in the angles of his face and the tousled fall of his hair. I had never seen him so relaxed. I had actually never seen him sleep. On most days, I was convinced he never did. Free from war, stress, and anger, he looked so different. Like he wasn't a Master Hunter, but just a man. Even his scar wasn't as noticeable in the soft morning glow.

Staring at his handsome face, I realized that now we both had scars on our cheeks. Reaching forward, I pinched a lock of his midnight-black hair between my fingers. *It's so soft.* For as sharp as his gaze, his appearance, and his words often were, this was a surprise. It almost made me want to run my fingers through the rest of it.

I snatched my hand back. Somehow, this was forbidden—that thought and this action. It warred with the Michael I met and the Michael I was beginning to know. In doing so, I caught sight of the tattoo around my wrist.

I had been so in-my-head that I didn't notice it had changed. It was now a dull grey instead of a rich black. In addition, there were five new images within the band.

Closest to my Contestant number was the first fear I faced in the First Trial; a belt coiled around itself. The end transformed into the next fear: the hand of a Dellamora. Its claws dug into the band of the tattoo making it look like it was trying to cut into my skin. Next to it was an empty space. I never faced my third fear, so there wouldn't be an image for it.

Next to the blank space was a diving board for the start of the Second Trial. Following it was a dryad tree with roots that looked like reaching hands. The final image was an open window for the exit that brought me to the finish line. After that, was more empty space. It must have been where the Third Trial would have gone . . . if I Ascended.

Rolling over, I pushed back the covers and sat up. I looked over my shoulder to see if I had disturbed Michael, but he continued to sleep.

Moving carefully and quietly, I went into the bathroom and closed the door behind me. My hair was a complete mess. Bobby pins and hairspray caused it to stick out awkwardly in mats. Makeup streaked down my cheeks. The dress was ruined by dirt and melted bits of metal. My fingers were bare; the metal splatters on the gown belonged to the melted remains of the sync ring. And the scar on my cheek . . .

My heart throbbed in my chest. My eyes were so sore, they stung when tears leaked from my overused tear ducts.

I didn't bother to wipe them from my cheeks. My bones ached as I removed the ruined gown. Hollow and exhausted, I staggered into the shower. When I got back to the room, Michael was still asleep.

Careful not to wake him, I crept to the closet. I pulled on my light blue hoodie and jeans. Slowly, to keep the door from creaking, I pushed it open and stepped into the hall.

Conversation halted as soon as I entered the kitchen.

Meg sat frozen at the table. Her hazel gaze kept jumping between looking me in the eye and the fresh scar on my cheek. Mrs. Kale stood before the stove, holding the door open.

"Morning," Meg said, breaking the spell. She readjusted her arms underneath Quinton and pulled him closer.

"Morning," my voice rasped between my lips. "Is there anything I can help with?"

"Yes." Mrs. Kale reached into the oven and pulled out a tin of fresh muffins. Bumping the door closed with her hip, she set the tin on the counter. "You can take these and put them on the table."

Grateful for something to do, I moved around her and grabbed the tin. Right beside it was the oven mitt she used.

I stopped and looked down. I was grasping the pan with my bare hands. Steam rose from where they made contact, but I felt no pain. Strong heat flowed into my hands, but, surprisingly, it didn't hurt.

I knew I was numb, but I didn't think I could be *that* numb. I set the tin down and turned my hands over. My fingertips weren't even pink.

My gaze dropped to the glowing stovetop. Tentatively, I reached toward it. Heat radiated from the glowing element and wrapped around my fingers. I laid my hand flush against the surface.

The intensity of the heat shocked me. I jerked my hand away. I waited for the accompanying sting, but there was nothing. I laid my hand back down. Nothing. My foggy mind refused to come up with an answer to explain it. I looked over my shoulder to see if anyone noticed, but the Kale ladies were preoccupied.

Removing my hand from the stove, I slipped on the bright red oven mitt and took the muffins to the table.

Before I could set them down, a door slammed against the wall.

"Mom!" Michael yelled down the hall. "Have you seen Charlie?" The edge of panic in his voice caught me by surprise.

"She's in here," she called.

No sooner had she said it than he burst into the kitchen. With ruffled hair and wrinkled dress clothes, he scanned the kitchen feverishly. He slumped against the wall when he saw me.

"I thought . . ." He shook his head and rubbed the sleep from his eyes. "Did you sleep alright?"

I shrugged, placing the muffins on the table.

He accepted my answer as it was. Straightening from the wall, he nodded to the food in front of me. "You should eat something. You haven't eaten since before The Trial."

I hadn't? I tried to remember what the last couple of days had been like. I couldn't even remember. But now that he said something, my stomach gurgled.

I sat next to Meg and put a muffin on my plate. My fingers couldn't tear the wrapper away fast enough. As soon as I devoured the whole thing, Mrs. Kale placed a full breakfast in front of me.

I mumbled my thanks as I dug into the warm eggs.

"Where's Dad and Zak?" Michael asked as he took the seat next to me.

"Your father's selling at an auction all day. Zak mentioned it was inventory day at the bar." Mrs. Kale set a glass of orange juice in front of me. "It's just us for the day."

The conversation lulled.

"You did really good. In The Trial," Meg blurted, filling the silence. "I've never seen a Contestant complete a Trial without help. And the way you Ported over the finish line—genius."

"Who taught you how to Port?" Mrs. Kale asked. "I thought they taught that during the Testing Year."

"I did," I mumbled.

"You taught yourself?" Michael's eyebrows shot skyward. "That kind of magic—It's not easy to master."

"I was motivated." I tried to smile, but the action felt unnatural. "I got some books from the library after I learned about the Achilles Heel." My fork stilled at my next thought. No longer hungry, I leaned back in my seat. "How was the rest of The Trial?"

No one answered right away.

"It was one of the more entertaining ones," Meg admitted.

Mrs. Kale sent her a stern look.

I turned to Michael. "How did Blake do?"

"Fantastic. Atlas taught him well."

"He finished fifth," Meg jumped in.

"Who crossed the finish line first?" Underneath the table, I crossed my fingers, hoping he wouldn't say one name.

"That guy who got the head start." Meg paused as she struggled to remember his name.

"Emeka Selasi," Michael supplied.

Meg nodded her thanks. "He completed The Trial so fast; he was able to watch everyone else finish theirs."

"How did—" I stopped myself. I was about to ask how Daniel performed. "What happened to Daniel?"

Michael dropped his gaze to his shoes. "They buried him this morning. Would you like to visit him?"

"No," I said quickly. I didn't need that image haunting my nightmares, too.

"You're welcome to hang around here." Mrs. Kale finally sat down and started to fill a plate for herself. "Megan and I were thinking of making a pie."

"Since you're not an active Contestant, you can have some." Meg shot Michael a daggered look, challenging him to contradict her.

"She has to be back at the Magisterium before dinner." Michael held up his hands to ward off the angry looks from his sister and mother. "Classes start tomorrow. You'll be finishing your Testing Year with the rest of your class."

My shoulders sagged with the news. I knew I would have to go back to the Magisterium, but I liked pretending I didn't have to.

"That'll be a breeze, compared to what you've already done," Mrs. Kale assured me with a warm smile. "Both Michael and Megan passed their Testing Years, I'm sure they would be more than willing to help if you need it."

Michael nodded. "Our nightly lessons will continue tonight at ten."

So that was it? Everything was just going to go back to normal? Before, I had a title to occupy my mind, but now . . .

I used my fork to kick crumbs around my plate. *I can't go back.* Even sitting at the table, my mind was still stuck in the aftermath of the Second Trial. I winced as I remembered the night before when I begged him to kill me.

"Can I talk to you for a minute?" I asked, rising to my feet. "On the porch?"

"Of course." Walking around the table, he led the way to the back deck and held the door open.

I stepped into the crisp air. A fresh layer of snow blanketed the yard and the tops of trees. A tired morning breeze drifted across the deck. Padding across the snow, I hopped onto the railing and waited for him to close the door.

"Um . . ." I cleared my throat. "About last night—"

"You don't have to say anything."

"I meant it, Michael."

His eyes snapped to my face.

"I'm tired." My throat nearly closed as all of the emotions from the day before swelled up inside of me. I continued in a whisper, "I'm so tired of surviving . . . I hate being the one left behind."

Exhaling slowly, he walked across the porch and leaned against the railing beside me. "I never understood why people fear death. Living is the worst kind of hell I've found. And believe me, I've searched."

My gaze lingered on his scar. How he had survived this long was beyond me. After everything he had gone through, he was still standing. Me? I had experienced a fraction of his suffering, and had begged to be put out of my misery.

"I'm not like you. I'm not strong enough to do what you want me to. With the war. I can't save people."

"You can't save everyone, that's true. But you can save some." He looked through the sliding door at his mother and sister at the breakfast table. Meg rolled her eyes, dropping her head against the back of the chair. Mrs. Kale swatted her shoulder.

"What about the ones you can't save?"

"You remember them." He pulled his gaze from the window to meet mine. "It's the only thing you can do. And as for you not being strong enough, I think you're plenty strong."

"Last night, I asked you to—" I winced.

"But you woke up this morning and you got out of bed. I'm not saying it'll get easier," he said gently, "or that you'll get over it. You'll just learn to live with it. There is incredible strength in that."

Michael spoke from the experience of living with hell in his veins, but I wasn't sure I wanted to gain that experience. My ribcage felt brittle, like a sharp intake of breath would explode my entire chest. I didn't want to learn how to function on shallow breaths to keep from shattering. I didn't want to get used to a world without Daniel . . . with the knowledge that he was dead because he liked me.

"I'm glad you're not in the Final Trial," Michael cleared his throat. "Seven Contestants go in, but seven never come out. And if you do make it out, you're haunted."

I wish I could agree with him. I just wished that Dmitri was also stuck in the limbo of not Ascending. Igorek was, but that didn't feel the same. I felt as if I had no direction.

"Just . . . keep breathing. That's all you have to do." He straightened and walked toward the door. "Come on, before you catch a cold." Once more he held the door for me.

Taking one last breath of cold air, I walked back into the house. Meg had already stacked all the plates and was moving them to the sink.

I helped clear the rest of the table. Mrs. Kale gave Michael eggs and toast before finishing her breakfast. As she ate, she murmured softly to her grandson.

When we got out the pie dishes, Michael disappeared to take a shower. When he reappeared, he was back in his usual dark-wash jeans and a simple black quarter-sleeve. Taking a cup of coffee, he sat silently at the table. Every time I glanced over, he was watching me.

While the peach-raspberry pie baked, I sat and listened to Mrs. Kale and Meg talk. I wanted to soak in the ease of the house for as long as I could. I tried to mentally prepare myself for what I was going to face, but the clock kept ticking away.

When the oven timer went off, Meg pulled out a tub of ice cream from the freezer. Mrs. Kale gave me a piece of the pie that was nearly a fourth of the dish. Meg wasn't shy in creating a small mountain of ice cream on top. Even Michael took his own healthy serving and dug in.

I ate as slowly as I could, hoping to delay our departure. But there was only so much I could do. When there was nothing but melted ice cream streaks on the plate, I had no excuse. It was time to go back.

Mrs. Kale gave me a long hug. She finished her goodbye with a kiss to the temple and a request that, if I needed anything, I would call her.

"See you later, Charlie." Meg waved from the sink. Soap suds coated her fingers and trickled down her elbow. "Don't be an ass, Michael."

"Have a great night too, Meg." He gave her a tight smile. With a hand on the small of my back, he guided me outside.

"Are you worried?" he asked as we stepped off the porch onto the gravel. "About the school year."

"I don't think so. Blending in is kind of my superpower." I tucked a stray wisp of hair behind my ear. "Do you think I should be worried?"

"I wouldn't say worried . . . just something to keep in mind. That

Russian kid, I wouldn't put it past him to try and rile you up. If he comes up to you—"

"I won't do anything stupid." *I don't have enough energy to do anything other than keep myself upright.*

"I don't know if that's even possible." He kept his expression deadpan, implying a joke.

I stuck my tongue out at him.

Reaching the gate, Michael held open the black iron and I stepped off the property. He reached under his jacket and took out a transporter. Taking my hand, he pulled on his magic and channeled it into the stone. In a flash, we Ported to the Magisterium.

When we appeared in the room surrounded by red bricks and leather couches, my mind whirled. It felt like a million years had passed since I had been in my apartment at the Magisterium. The room looked strange, dreamlike.

"Do you really think he'll try to come up to me?" I asked. *I don't know if I can face him.*

"Honestly, I think now that you're out of The Trial, he won't. He didn't want you in the Top Seven. He got his wish, so he should back off."

"I hate him." The words hissed out of the darkest part of me. My magic flared, heating my chest like a volcano. "After what he did, he should—"

"He'll get what's coming to him. Guys like him always do."

I exhaled, long and slow. Looking over his shoulder, I stared at the door leading to the rest of the school. That was that. Back to normal. Rolling back my shoulders, I headed for the door.

"Lessons tonight. Ten o'clock," he called after me. "Don't be late."

"I wouldn't dream of it." I stepped into the hall.

60

Red and Silver Thirteen

In the stairwell, the clatter of dinner chatter and the smell of beef stew rushed up to meet me.

With each descending staircase, my heartbeat increased. When I reached the main level, my hands were clenched so tightly I couldn't feel my fingers. The number of guards in black and gold were doubled on either side of the doors. In addition, they were on each landing.

At the threshold of the dining room, my gaze was drawn to the stage at the far back wall.

Behind the statue of Victor Haltland, was a long oak table with thick legs and ornate carvings on the side. Twenty-one chairs circled the massive piece of furniture. In those seats were the Top Seven, their Guardians, and their School Masters.

Like a magnet, my eyes slid toward the end of the table where Dmitri sat.

I had been so focused on what he would do when he saw me, that I hadn't considered what I would do when *I* saw *him*.

I thought back to the end of the Second Trial where I stabbed a knife into his shoulder. My hands were covered in Daniel's blood. My body ached with broken bones and the effects of magic. That was only two days ago, but it might as well have been seconds.

"I missed."

Something dark whispered from the back of my mind, telling me to grab my wand and fire, regardless of who sat around the Trial Contestant. I had the magic to make sure there were no survivors, even if my aim was off. It would be over just like that.

My hand dropped to my wand. The flames etched into the shaft warmed at my touch. Already, my magic pressed against my core, slowly bleeding into my chest.

My view of the head table was blocked.

Blinking furiously, I dropped my hand from my wand and focused on the student in front of me.

It was Nirean.

Wrapped around her left arm was a silver band with Daniel's Contestant number on it. Her eyes dropped to the scar on my cheek. And there her gaze remained.

I ducked my head, letting my hair fall in front of my face.

"Did you do it?"

"Did I do what?" My nails bit into my palms.

"Did you kill Daniel?"

My eyes snapped up from the floor. "Wha—" I shook my head. "N—no. God no."

She tilted her head back, looking at me over the ridge of her nose. "I've read about what happens in the Second Trial; Contestants take out their fellow schoolmate so they can Ascend. Daniel was my friend. So, I'm going to ask you again. Did you kill him?"

"Nirean, I would never hurt him. Dimitri—" His name turned sour in my mouth. "He came after us. He would've killed me too if his aim didn't suck."

She shook her head before I finished speaking. "That's not what Clarence is saying."

My eyes snapped toward the head table. The asshole sat in the seat meant for me, with his feet kicked up beside his plate. He sat with his back so straight, he might as well have been wearing a crown on top of his thick black hair.

"He said you asked Dmitri to take out the competition," Nirean huffed.

I jerked my gaze back to her. "I would never hurt Daniel. He was my—" *My almost.* "He was my friend, too."

Again, she shook her head. "Forgive me for not believing you."

"You're really going to trust *Clarence Hardy* over me? He wasn't even in the last Trial!"

"I've known Clarence for four years. And while he is an asshole, I know a hell of a lot more about him than I know about you." Her eyes dropped to my toes before slowly walking up my body. "I'm willing to bet that you're the kind of person willing to do anything to get what she wants. That's how you got into the Magisterium in the first place, right?"

She stepped closer. "Just know that when The Trial is over, and you're not protected by that tattoo of yours, we're going to get you back for what you did to Daniel."

Just as quickly as she arrived, she stalked back to her table. Everyone seated around it, Ace included, stared back at me with the same cold eyes. All of them wore a silver band around their arm.

I looked around the dining room and found the same look glaring back at me from the Magisterium students. Daniel's Contestant number was even worn by students from different classes and years.

My eyes darted back to the high table, to the boy sitting in my chair. *Why did everything I do have to come back and bite me in the ass?* I provoked Clarence at the Ascending Party and humiliated him in front of the entire school. Like all snakes, they were good at biding their time.

"Charlie!" Blake shoved away from the head table and ran down the stairs. He was dressed in the color of the Final Trial; black. The rich color contrasted with his olive skin, and made his candy apple green eyes practically glow.

His gait didn't slow until he slammed into me, pulling me tightly to his chest. I wrapped my arms around him and squeezed my eyes tightly shut. Just for a moment, the ache in my chest wasn't as sharp.

At least one person doesn't hate me.

"Bloody hell, where have you been?" Blake whispered harshly into my hair. "You disappeared. At the Ascending Ceremony, you came late, and then you left as soon as it was over."

"I needed some time."

"You should've called." When he pulled back his eyes dipped to the scar on my cheek. "If I had known what happened—if Atlas had told me, I would've been there. I could've—"

"No." Just the thought of Blake being on that cliff with Dmitri and Igorek made my spine stiffen with fear. Would Dmitri have thrown the knife at Blake instead of Daniel? My brain tortured me with images of Blake on his back with Dmitri's knife in his chest.

"I should've been there."

I shook my head. "The only reason I'm still alive is because he thought he killed me."

Anger darkened his cheeks. He took a moment to breathe before continuing. "I'm glad you're out of The Trial. You shouldn't have had to deal with any of it."

"And you should?"

"What I mean is, I'm glad you're out. You've been through enough."

He was referring to the scars across my back. They seemed so insignificant compared to the one on my cheek. "Is there any way . . . is there any way you can back out of the Final Trial?"

He shook his head. "There's no way Anna will compete. With Leon gone, I'm the only Contestant from my school that can play. If I leave the Academy without a Contestant, I'll be an outcast in every corner of the magic world."

Right. He has a future to worry about.

"Then promise me something," I gripped his hands. "Stay away from Dmitri."

"Like hell I will," Blake scoffed. "He tried to kill you."

"And he failed. That's punishment enough, believe me. If anything happens to you—" I gripped his hands tighter. "Please don't argue with me about this."

He saw something in my face, or rather on my face, that made his retorts stop behind his teeth.

"Promise me," I pressed.

With a tight jaw, he nodded.

I deflated with relief.

He noticed my reaction. "How are you? And please don't bullshit your way out of answering."

"I'm tired." I thought this answer was the simplest. But as soon as I said it, my eyes filled with tears. "I can't stop thinking about . . . I'm just tired."

Blake pulled me back to his chest and wrapped his arms firmly around me. Propping his chin on top of my head, he held me close as his black sweater absorbed my tears.

"You're ok," he said, stroking my hair. "You'll be ok."

A hole had been punched into my chest. With every breath, it ached.

Closing my eyes, I did my best to pull myself back together. Like Michael said, I needed to learn how to live with it.

"Are you hungry?"

I shook my head. Stepping back, I wiped my face dry with the sleeve of my hoodie. "I don't think I should be down here. Everyone thinks I killed Daniel."

"Not everyone." He put his arm over my shoulders. Keeping me close, he led me through the tables to where Cornelia sat.

As we got closer to the high table, my eyes strayed to the Contestant who took my place, and then to the Russian at the end.

Cornelia looked up from her plate and spotted me with Blake. Instantly she was on her feet and stepping out from the bench.

"Hey," she said softly. Her smile dimmed at the sight of my scarred face. "I didn't think you would be here until tomorrow."

I shrugged, not knowing what else to do. "Can I sit with you?"

"Of course." She dropped back to her seat.

As I sat, Blake took the spot beside me. He grabbed my hand under the table and gave it a gentle squeeze.

"Shouldn't you be up there?" I nodded to the head table.

He shrugged. "Probably, but the company is better right here."

A moment of silence followed.

Oh, God . . . did they think I had Daniel killed?

"I didn't do it," I blurted. "I didn't ask Dmitri to do anything. I was helping Daniel—he came out of nowhere. He was aiming for—"

"I know you would never hurt him," Cornelia jumped in. "I can't believe people are buying Clarence's story. I mean, come on. It's *Clarence*."

"Don't worry." Blake reached across the table and grabbed a roll of bread. "I'll personally make sure he gets last place."

"Blake—"

"I promised I wouldn't go near Dmitri. That wanker, however, is fair game." He looked over his shoulder at the head table. "Atlas has a tiff with his Guardian anyway, so it'll be fun for both of us."

"Hey! Now that you're out of The Trial, that means you'll be taking the Testing Year with me!" Cornelia literally bounced in her seat. "I've missed you so much."

Leaning into the table, she quickly gave me the rundown of what to expect. "At the end of each month, there are three exams. They stop classes the whole day for it. It's just you and the teacher in the room. After you're done, they'll give your evaluations to Master Lenin, who will send them to other Masters looking for apprentices. With all the training you got from the last two Trials, these will be nothing."

She rattled off the tests she had already taken and how she did. I tried to seem interested. I would laugh when Blake did and mirror his reactions. I didn't have enough energy to participate or care about the Testing Year.

Without realizing it, I turned to gaze around the room. I kicked myself when I realized I was looking for Daniel. My skin itched to be near him, to hold his hand. My ears strained for the undertones of his voice, as if he was just a table or two away chatting with one of his friends. I held my breath, doing my best to keep the tears from falling.

Dmitri's tall frame towered over the table as he rose from his seat. He casually knocked his cup over, causing the liquid to spill into Tala's lap. The large Contestant chuckled as he marched down the steps.

Cheese and rice. I didn't know if I wanted him to look at me or if I wanted him to pass by without a glance. I couldn't figure out what would be worse: his constant belligerent behavior, or him treating me like I didn't exist.

Dmitri was dressed head to toe in black, but one sleeve of his turtleneck was a bright red. Numbers two, seven, thirteen, and eighteen were embroidered down his arm in thick white stitching.

I glanced back at the high table. No one else was wearing red. I assumed the Magisterium students were wearing silver with Daniel's number because they all thought he should have Ascended.

"Why is he wearing red?" I blurted, unable to take my eyes off the sleeve.

Blake stopped mid-sentence to follow my gaze. He twisted around and stilled when he saw the object of my curiosity. He faced the table with a taunt expression. "You don't want to know. Anyway, I heard—"

"But I do." I cut him off. "Want to know."

Blake clenched his teeth and remained silent.

I looked at Cornelia, but she refused to look at me.

"Why is he wearing red?" I asked again.

Cornelia started slowly, "It's tradition—"

"A bloody stupid tradition," Blake snapped. "For their school, if you make a kill you're proud of, you wear red."

61
Motivational Red

My head whipped around to the retreating Contestant.

Two, seven, thirteen, and eighteen.

Red for a kill.

Michael said Malan, Contestant Two, didn't make it out of the water at the start of the Trial. Aboiy, Contestant Seven, was also not at the Ascending Ceremony. Dmitri killed them both?

"You mean—" I swallowed hard. "He's wearing red for Daniel?"

"Yes," Blake said stiffly.

My hands curled around the edge of my seat. He was celebrating the fact that he killed him.

The exhausted fog in my head evaporated as my magic slithered from my core. Everything I had felt in the Second Trial flooded through my body. However, this time I didn't crumble to the floor. Everything swirled together until it blurred into volcanic fury.

It roared through my bloodstream. My magic answered in response. The potent mixture pushed everything else out. All the pain I had felt earlier was gone.

My eyes snapped to the high table where Guardian Theodore sat. He turned to talk to the Guardian next to him. All the same numbers were painted proudly on his shoulder in red.

I grabbed that anger and stitched myself back together. I let it fill every crevice and crack in me. My eyes focused back on the retreating figure of Dmitri Theodore.

I could so easily picture myself following him out of the dining room. I would kick his legs out from under him. My fist would slam his head to the floor. I would curl my hands into his stupid blue hair before I snapped his neck.

No. Too quick. Too painless.

I would take my knife and slice his leg muscles so he couldn't walk. As he crawled across the floor, I would kick him onto his back. That's where I would open him up and—

A hand snagged my wrist. I was jerked out of my head and back to the dining room. Dmitri continued into the stairwell, completely unaware.

I was still at the table. On my feet, I straddled the bench like I was ready to act on my imagination. Blake held my wrist, unaware of the storm brewing beneath my skin.

"Charlie?" Blake asked slowly.

"I'll be right back." I twisted my wrist out of his grasp. Without removing my eyes from the doors, I made my way through the room. It was as if my body was pulled by a magnet.

I barely noticed as I left the dining room. The sounds of the dinner crowd melted behind me until all I could hear were Dmitri's climbing footsteps.

Rounding the clock tower, I took two stairs at a time. Just as my foot hit the first landing, a thread of gold wound around my ankle. Before I could react, my foot was pulled out from under me and I fell backward.

My back hit the black stone steps. I twisted, landing on my hip, then my shoulder, and then tumbled head over heels until I landed on my back in the middle of the stairwell. My lungs froze under the impact.

Gasping for breath, I rolled onto my stomach. Tears stung my eyes, from the fall and the lack of air. I struggled to get my hands and knees beneath me.

Footsteps came near me.

Panic seized my lungs. Dmitri must have been waiting for me.

I grabbed for my magic, but as I struggled to breathe, it did nothing but stir. Coughing and sputtering, I staggered to my feet. Whatever was going to happen, I was going to be standing.

But it wasn't Dmitri.

A Magisterium student I had only seen in passing stopped a few paces from me. Her expression was cold, and her eyes hard as stone. Around her arm was the same silver cuff with Daniel's Contestant number. In her hands was a large tin bucket.

It was then that I noticed none of the Magisterium guards were present.

A slosh of something wet hit my back seconds before she tossed the contents of her pail at me. A liquid as thick as melted honey and red as blood hit me square in the face. I was splashed from the right and left simultaneously, covering me from head to toe.

For as much as it looked like blood, it wasn't. The taste wasn't metallic. There was a strong flavor of soap and something chemical. I spit out a mouthful and gagged.

"Now you look like the murderer you are." She tossed the bucket at my feet.

Tears sprang to my eyes. My aching heart let out a scream that I barely kept contained. I opened my mouth to tell them it wasn't me, that I had nothing to do with his death; but the lump in my throat barely let me breathe, let alone speak.

"What's going on here?"

The girl before me bolted. Her companions scattered down different wings and out of sight.

"Charlie?" Helen stepped in front of me. "Oh, my goodness." Her wide eyes didn't know where to look.

I looked down at my hands. They were covered completely in the red paint. The image took me back to The Trial. I could feel the humid air along my skin, the hot earth beneath my feet, and the phantom pains of old wounds.

I scrubbed my hands against my pants. While they were covered too, I thought it would at least scrape some of it off. It didn't.

"It's not coming off," I whispered in a hoarse voice. "It's not coming off."

"Come here, honey." Helen helped me step out of the puddle and led me through the doors of the infirmary. She took me all the way back to her private quarters. She turned on her personal shower to help me wash off.

It took nearly half an hour to get all the paint off.

Dripping wet and scrubbed raw, I stepped out of the infirmary. My hands shook. The guards had returned to their posts around the empty stairwell. Judging by the low murmurs in the dining room, it was nearly vacant, too.

I thought about tomorrow. About what I would face. Would it be more paint? More cold looks and even colder shoulders? Worse, how many other students would accuse me of killing Daniel?

Instead of heading up the stairs, I went down. At the bottom, I walked up to Tessa Baker's desk.

"Contest—Miss Heart," she corrected. "How can I—"

"Is he in his office?"

"Yes, but he's asked not to be disturbed. Miss Heart!"

I was down the hall and closing in on his door before she could round her desk. Guarding the door were two guards in black and gold. When I drew near, they stepped closer, blocking the door.

"Please," my voice broke. "I need to talk to him."

"Miss Heart, I strongly suggest that you leave," said the man on the right.

"Please." I held up my hands. "I don't mean him any harm. I promise. I just need to—"

The door opened. "Miss Heart?"

The guards stepped to the side to reveal Master Lenin. "What are you doing here?"

I cleared the thickness from my throat. "Can I talk to you?"

"Of course." He stepped aside to let me into the room.

As soon as the door closed, I turned to him. "I was wondering if I could, uh . . . can I be expelled from the Magisterium?"

He acted as if I threw something at him. "Excuse me?"

"I don't need to be here anymore. I have a solid cover story for who I am. Anything I need to learn, I can get from textbooks and lessons with Michael."

"Miss Heart—"

"Michael and I can train longer if I'm not here! We can hone my skills. I can progress faster—"

"Miss Heart." He raised his hand in a halting gesture. "I'm not going to expel you. You're a Trial Contestant. That would draw too much attention."

"Then we make a cover story. I failed classes. I didn't uphold the core values of the school. We could even fake my death—"

"We're not going to do that."

"Please!" I clapped my hands over my mouth. I took a steadying deep breath. "I can't be here. Not after . . ."

Master Lenin sighed. "I am sorry for what you went through. There's a reason people call it the hardest way to a title. I spent over two centuries working to become a School Master. Even if The Trial got me there faster, I wouldn't trade a minute of it. The Trial is ruthless."

He crossed his arms. "I can't take you out of the Magisterium. There won't be anyone to watch over you. Master Kale's plate is going to be full with the Masters we gather from The Trial."

"Then leave me at the Kale ranch."

He shook his head. "I won't put them in that position again. They aren't babysitters. They're a grieving family."

But I'm a part of that, right? I thought about the key Mrs. Kale gave me for Christmas. Before I could protest, Master Lenin was speaking.

"You will join the rest of your class in the Testing Year."

"Master Lenin, please—"

"While you're not in The Trial, you can still learn and do great things. In fact, we're all counting on it. Now, if you'll excuse me," he walked around his desk, "you interrupted me earlier. And I have to get back to work." He picked up a stack of papers as if I had already left.

Numb, I walked out to the hall and closed the door behind me. I stood there in the quiet. It felt like the walls were closing around me. I was trapped again.

I had no title and no way to get one. I had no way out. No way to run. *How am I going to get out of this cage now?*

But I was too drained to think, and too tired to care. I tried to run before, and Blake got his finger cut off. I stayed, and Daniel died. I lost no matter what I did.

With nothing left to do, I turned on my heel and Ported up to my room.

62

Not Including the Knife

I didn't tell Michael about the incident on the stairs. I didn't think I could verbalize it even if I tried.

The next day, I kept my head low.

I didn't look at or speak to anyone. I kept my distance. My heart jumped whenever someone stepped in my direction. Everywhere I looked, I saw silver.

Moving through the breakfast buffet, I reached for the tongs to grab some bacon. A student on the other side of me swiped them from my fingers. After he served himself, he dropped the utensil on the floor and left. He wore a silver band.

Breathe. Keep moving.

Clutching my empty plate with white knuckles, I moved farther down the line. The pans holding cinnamon rolls were almost empty. A member of the cooking crew came over and removed the pan. When she came back, her eyes found mine. Instead of placing the full, steaming pan in front of me, she placed it on the far side by the plates. She met my gaze again before returning to the kitchen. On her arm was a silver thirteen.

My stomach grew heavy with knots. I set the empty plate down and ate chocolate covered raisins in my room.

The rest of the day wasn't any easier. The loyalty to Daniel went farther than the students and the cooking crew. The teachers took part in it too.

When I raised my hand in class, I wasn't called on. Even if I was the only one with the answer. I was overlooked, as if I wasn't there.

Mrs. Paylor was known for having cookies on her desk. Having not eaten anything for breakfast, I was looking forward to something to tide me over till lunch. But when I reached for a golden chocolate chip treat, the plate slid away from my fingers to the opposite end of her desk. I watched her pocket her wand.

I skipped lunch. When it was time for dinner, I was about to head up to my room to phone Mrs. Kale when I heard my name called.

"Charlie!" Blake waved at me from the front of the room where he sat with Cornelia.

My stomach hardened. I would have to go through the entire room. Not to mention that I would be closer to the stage. Luckily, neither Dmitri nor Igorek were there. At least I didn't have to see them.

Breathing slowly, I made my way past whispering tables and cold stares to the only friendly people in the school.

"Where have you been?" Blake asked once I got closer. "You vanished last night. I hardly saw you today."

Before I could answer, a burst of laughter rolled down from the table on the stage.

"Aye! Charlie!" Clarence turned his seat away and grinned down at me. "You've got something on your face." He gestured to his cheek with his little finger. "Oh, wait."

My new scar.

Blake stepped in front of me, blocking me from his view. "Oi. Lay off."

"I wasn't talkin' to you," Clarence said flippantly. "And you're in my way. I'm trying to thank her for keeping my spot in The Trial warm for me."

Anger rumbled in my chest like distant thunder. My magic churned in my core.

"Both of us know I've always been the only viable Magisterium Contestant. Phillips was too brainy. He couldn't even jump out of the way of a knife."

Rage, as deadly and furious as lightning cracked through my chest. No longer was I scared of buckets of paint or cold stares. My eyes zeroed in on the blabbering Contestant.

"The Common was going to die sooner or la—"

I Ported before I knew I had even pulled on my magic.

In a blink, I was in front of Clarence. I slammed my knee into his chest, pinning him in place. His chair rocked back on its hind legs and clanged against the table, silencing those seated around it.

My hands went for his throat. Using my thumbs, I arched his neck until I felt his bones resist.

Those around the table jumped to their feet. Some drew their wands. Others took it further and aimed them at me. The dining room hushed as all attention was directed to the high table. Guards rushed to the stage.

"Miss Heart." Master Finch rose from his seat. "Release Contestant Hardy this instant."

Eyes wide with shock, Brandon Moore was halfway out of his seat.

"Sit down." My eyes cut to his Guardian. "Or your Contestant won't have a head."

His cheeks flushed with anger as he lowered himself back into his seat. His rage made every muscle in his body tense. He held out his hand, wordlessly telling the guards to keep their distance.

"Clarence." My eyes snapped to the boy in my hands. "I've had two months of training that you haven't. And Michael Kale, *a Master Hunter*, taught me. I can kill you with ten different things on this table, *not* including the knife."

I arched his head further back. He gasped.

"You would be smart not to test me. I'm not a Contestant anymore, so I don't have to follow the same rules as you. You say *anything* about Daniel again, and I'll remove your head."

I stepped back, and Clarence fell on all fours, gasping.

Master Finch and Guardian Moore dove forward to check on the wheezing Contestant. I turned on my heel and shoved past the tense guards. Guardian Moore's hissed expletives shot through the silent room.

As I passed by crowded tables, I heard someone whisper, "I knew she killed Daniel."

I quickened my pace out of the dining room. If everyone thought I was a killer, then why not lean into it? Why not play the hand that fate dealt me?

What I told Clarence was true. Master Michael Kale trained me. He gave me the tools to be brutal and deadly. I was no longer tethered to the rules of The Trial. I could kill Dmitri. I could make him pay.

I planned to do just that.

63

Behind Every Monster

After my encounter with Clarence, people stayed out of arm's reach. Especially him.

Every time we passed in the halls, he'd shoot me a look of disdain before turning to his new group of fans. But that was all he did. The rest of the school continued to give me a cold shoulder. I felt the guard's eyes on me wherever I went.

But I wasn't bothered. Without people crowding around me, I could study Dmitri's movements. After a week, I had his routine down.

Dmitri was at breakfast by seven. That way he could have the most time to be seen, or torment other Contestants. He was off to class by eight, where he was always early, and the last to leave.

When he wasn't in class, he was at the Glasshouse surrounded by students. Then he was in the training room until curfew. On the weekends, he went home. All the while, Igorek followed him like a puppy. He was never alone.

But I was patient.

Every night I was transported to lessons with Michael. Thanks to The Trial, our lessons had become more brutal. At the beginning of the year, I would have protested. Now, I was eager. Everything he taught me brought me a step closer to Dmitri's combat level. If anything, I asked Michael for more.

"Right on time." Michael straightened from his spot on the wall.

I didn't respond. I tucked the transporter into my pocket. I already had my wand out, so we could start immediately.

Tonight, however, instead of barking instructions, he stood still. His eyes ran over my face, taking in the hard set of my jaw and the determination in my shoulders. His eyes finally settled on mine.

"Do I have something on my face?" I asked, shifting uncomfortably from foot to foot. His eyes followed the movement.

"No."

"Then why are you staring?"

"I'm thinking."

"Think somewhere else."

"I can't. You're what I'm thinking about." He sheathed his wand.

"Aren't you the one who's always complaining that I'm wasting time?" I rolled my wand between my hands. The designs in the wood glimmered as magic passed from my skin.

"Because usually you do." He walked over until he stood in front of me. Instead of his usual controlled expression, his gaze was gentle. "I know what you're feeling. I can see it in your face. You're angry."

My teeth clenched, caging my wild tongue. I just looked at him, hoping he would drop it.

"I know what it's like to be the reason someone you love dies. To have all the years they could have lived on your shoulders." His black eyes bored down into mine. "If you don't let it go, it will destroy you."

"That's funny coming from the man whose life mission is to destroy the man who killed his sister."

He nodded, unfazed by my direct response.

I could feel the time we were wasting as if it were tiny bugs eating at my skin. A frustrated breath hissed through my teeth. "I'm fine. Can we just get on with the lesson?"

"We're not having a lesson tonight."

"Oh, come on!" The lights flared. "*I'm fine.*"

"No, you're not." His tone was gentle. Again, his gaze held mine as if he could read my mind.

"Why do you care?" My voice bounced off the stone walls. "You're not fine and you're still fighting. If you want me to win your war, then teach me to fight. Teach me to win."

"You're not learning to win the war. You're learning to fight Dmitri Theodore."

"So?"

Instead of answering, he stared at me as if he could read even more than I was willing to admit to myself. Just when I thought I was going to explode, he held out his hand.

"Put your wand away. I want to show you something."

"I don't want to go anywhere. I want to do my job, unlike you."

Unprovoked, he said calmly, "You can stay here, or come with me. Either way, I'm not teaching you tonight."

A growl rumbled in my throat. I stood there, waiting for him to change his mind, but he continued to hold out his hand. He wasn't backing down. I could see it on his face.

"Fine," I spat. Roughly, I shoved my wand into the side pocket of my jeans. I willed my magic to still, and slapped my hand in his.

He turned on his heel and Ported us from the school. We appeared in a small meadow surrounded by a blue mountain range. An ocean of tall grass undulated around our hips from a lazy breeze. Proud evergreens towered around us. The deep blue sky stretched endlessly overhead.

Michael dropped my hand and moved around me.

I followed him with questions on the tip of my tongue. Walking through the tall grass, his confident strides grew shorter and shorter until he came to a stop. His shoulders were drawn so tight, a sledge hammer would've broken against his spine.

Before him was the cement foundation of a house, cracked and blackened. On the far side sat a lone chimney. While everything about the meadow was overgrown, nothing grew over the ruins.

"This used to be Lauren's house." His voice barely carried back to me. "This is where she was killed."

My anger immediately dropped to a simmer. A chill rolled over my skin. My eyes darted around the meadow looking for evidence of the horrors that took place here: bones, deep shadows, *something*. But the breeze was calm. Birds sang happily in the pines, and the sky remained cloudless. The only thing that appeared out of place was the remains of the house.

"I can remember everything about that night. I watch it nearly every time I sleep." He turned to me then.

His eyes were always dark and guarded. But when he turned to me this time, his gaze was so raw, it hurt to look at. It was the expression of a thousand held-back tears and countless sleepless nights. It was jagged as scar tissue, and just as painful as an open wound.

"I stood where you are now. Your father was about here." He pointed to the dirt beneath his boots.

I thought I was going to be sick. "Why are we here?"

"When you found Aanya Moose's body in front of the North Tower, do you know exactly where? Can you picture it right now?"

Of course. I could picture every splatter and drop of her blood on her sweater. The starkest memory was the tiny crack in her four-point diamond-shaped glasses.

"What about Phillips?"

I dropped my gaze to the ground. My anger returned with an explosion, scaring away the grass closest to me. My eyes squeezed shut. That only made the memory burn brighter behind my eyelids.

Michael turned around. The tall grass whispered around his legs as he came to stand in front of the charred, collapsed porch.

"When I got here, my sister, her husband Aaron, and their three-year-old son Lucas, were on their knees in a line." His eyes looked at the wood, as if he could see them. "Lauren invited me to dinner for our birthday. If I had come right over, like I told her I would, the outcome might have been different . . ." He trailed off, staring at the wood.

"Your father welcomed me by killing my nephew."

The air was knocked out of my lungs.

He faced me. "Lawrence didn't always hate those with less magic. It started after his brother died because a Deficient didn't have enough magic to save his life."

I blinked in shock. "You never told me he had a brother."

He nodded. "When you accept the invitation into the Hunter Guard, you get a death certificate. Legally you're dead. You're supposed to cut ties with all family. Marriages and children included. It allowed us to do what we needed in order to complete our assignments." He shook his head and got back on topic. "Jackson was younger but he matched Lawrence in status. But his heart was faulty. It didn't have the protective lining that all Users have; every time he used magic it hardened the walls of his heart. He was waiting for a heart transplant, but he needed a heart from a Royal and they don't die without extreme causes."

"What happened?"

"His heart started to fail and the doctor on call was a Deficient. The cast that could have saved his life called for more magic than the doctor had."

"Cheese and rice," I whispered.

"Avelyn and Charles, his parents, always loved Jackson more. I think it was because their attention was always on him, making sure he was comfortable and pain-free, that they forgot about their other son. After Jackson died, Avelyn and Charles killed themselves."

Bile rose up my throat. "Why are you telling me this?"

"Because you need to understand that behind every monster is a man. Lawrence grew up with me. He saw my family as his own. Yet, he tore us apart because I wouldn't back him. He believed he could save the world if he got rid of those who made it weak. When I didn't get on board, he punished me for it."

He spun away and walked a few feet past me. "I was thrown to the ground and held here." He pointed to the ground between his boots. "Lawrence asked me to join him. I told him no. He rewarded my answer by putting a hole in my brother-in-law's leg."

He closed his eyes as his face contorted with memories. "Lauren screamed for him to stop.

"Lawrence asked me again. He said, 'I want my closest friend by my side. We could be kings together. Think of all we could do, the worlds we could create.' I told him the world he envisioned wasn't the one I wanted to live in. So, he killed Aaron."

Darkness sank into his eyes. He breathed slowly, curling his hands into fighting fists. "I knew if I rejected his offer once more, he would kill Lauren. So, I agreed to fight with him . . . and she called me a fool." His lip twitched as a smile fought to control his lips. "Death was standing in front of her, and she still fought for her little brother to be good.

"But Lawrence knew my heart wasn't in it. I was only doing it to protect Lauren. That's when he killed her."

His eyes stayed on the steps for a long time. His breathing slowed to the point where his shoulders barely moved.

I didn't know what to do. If I went to him, would he recoil from me? I was the daughter of the man who made this beautiful place a graveyard.

"He was at the hospital when Lucas was born . . . he was the best man at my wedding. During school, people used to joke that we were the twins, not Lauren and I . . . but none of that mattered.

"When he set the house on fire, I lunged for him. I was drowning, which made me useless because his mind was clear. He was the perfect Hunter. I got this," he tapped the scar on his cheek, "somewhere in the middle of it. He thought he killed me—and he would have, if it hadn't been snowing that night. I was found nearly frozen. It was the only reason I didn't bleed out."

He turned from the skeleton of the house, meeting my gaze. His shoulders were set and his jaw was tight, and his eyes were so sad that my own heart ached in response.

"I've replayed that night over and over in my mind, feeding my anger. While my family grieved together and fell apart, I went to war.

"I let that night destroy me. Instead of being with my family, I went hunting. Anger became my life." A curt laugh burst from his mouth. "You know this because I took it out on you."

He stepped away from the house. Moving through the grass, he stopped in front of me. "I know what's going through your head. Your father walked the same path . . . so did I. But you are good. So good. But you won't be if you continue with the plan in your head. I know what darkness looks like, because I hunt it for a living and I see it eating away at you. Whatever you're thinking, it won't stop. There will always be one more thing you have to do, one more horrible act to make everything right. Don't let this destroy you."

"Are you going to follow your own advice? You're just going to let Lawrence live? You would let him go?" I snapped.

"If I do, people die," he said softly. "Before, I was just trying to kill him to settle the score. But now, he needs to be stopped to save people. Don't be like your father or me. Be better. Be stronger."

My breath shook. "I can't."

"You can. Just let this go."

"You didn't."

"And look at me." He held out his hand. "I'm hardly a man. Do you really want to be like me?"

I looked away from his honest eyes to my fidgeting hands. *Did I want to be like him?* If he had asked me five minutes ago, I would have said 'yes' because of the skills and merciless rage he had in his arsenal. But before that . . .

No. Darkness clung to the years I was in Kansas. I fought to be the person I was. I fought so hard to be good. I jolted with the realization that to kill monsters, I had been willing to become one.

My anger started to cool. Then fear took over. If I let go of my anger, would I shatter? I didn't want to fall apart again! I couldn't go through that again.

He tapped my chin so I would look at him. "Do what I didn't. Give yourself time to heal without the anger."

"What if I can't?"

"You can. I'll be here to help you."

My eyes landed on the blackened foundation behind him. Tears filled my eyes. "I'm so sorry."

He followed my gaze. "Me too."

His eyes stitched over the porch as if he could see more than the char and the grisly memories soaked into the wood. He stood so still; his mind was lost between two realities.

It was my turn to offer a way out. I took his hand, letting him know it was time to leave. He wrapped his fingers around mine, and gripped them tight. Taking a transporter stone from his pocket, he took us to the Magisterium apartment.

"You're free to do as you wish," he said. "Although, I would suggest using this time to sleep."

Sleep. It was a magical notion. "I like your suggestion."

"I thought you might." He went straight to the couch. Reaching underneath the dark leather, he pulled out a stack of blankets and his pillow.

"How come you never told me about Jackson?"

He paused in the middle of unfolding a blanket. "Because it's easier to fight a monster than a man twisted by grief." He draped the blanket across the cushions.

I used to think Michael was a monster. Now, I saw a man shattered by sorrow. Never in a million years did I think this man would ever save me. Yet, in the last few months he had done it more than once. On that night, he saved me from turning into the thing I feared most.

"Thank you," I said, before I realized my tongue had formed the words.

His eyebrows pulled together in question. "For what?"

How did you thank someone for saving you from yourself? The words themselves didn't even seem enough. Unable to articulate it, I shrugged.

"Goodnight, Charlie." He turned back to the couch.

"Night." I retreated to my room and softly closed the door behind me.

64

The Testing Year

Act normal.

Cheese and rice. I'm starting to think I never really knew what that meant.

In Kansas, my superpower was flying under the radar. I had gotten so good that a couple of my teachers forgot I was in their class.

I spent the better part of the morning chipping off the rust to fall back into my familiar role. Pulling my sweater over my faded Contestant tattoo, I kept my hair loose around my face. With my head down, I followed the stream of students to the fifth floor of the East Wing for Creature Studies.

Act normal.

Dmitri and Igorek sat in the front row, slouched low in their seats. Dmitri's long legs stretched out from under the desk. He laughed loudly at something Igorek said.

The sound put my teeth on edge. My hand itched for my wand at my hip. Anger bubbled in the pit of my stomach.

"Heal without the anger. Guys like him always get what's coming to them."

With Michael's voice in my head, I slowly expelled the breath I was holding and walked to where Blake and Cornelia were saving me a seat.

I sat down without grasping my wand. Instead, I took out my books. I gripped my pen with white knuckles and focused on the chalkboard. Unfortunately, that put Dmitri at the edge of my vision.

"Mornin'," Blake shifted his seat over to give me more room.

"Morning." I pulled my lips into what looked like a smile.

"We missed you at breakfast," Cornelia whispered around Blake.

"I slept through my alarm." In truth, I couldn't stomach the sight of Dmitri at the high table first thing in the morning. Not if I was going to try to be better.

Blake stretched his arm across the back of Cornelia's chair. "You missed all the excitement. Amelia nearly broke Tala's hand."

I pulled my eyes from the blackboard in surprise. "How'd she manage to do that?"

"She took the leg of her chair right out from under her. Tala went to brace her fall and landed wrong. Master Loran is pissed."

"Well, yeah," Cornelia said. "It's her casting hand."

"Is she ok?" I asked.

"She will be after a couple potions and a brace."

"That'll put her back in training." I chewed on the corner of my lip. "How much trouble is Amelia in?"

"She's denying she did anything." Blake shook his head. "If they prove it, I bet she'll be held back at the starting line."

Brandy Charles came in just as the clock announced the hour. Waving her wand over her head, the door slammed shut. Wrapped tightly in an emerald pencil skirt with a blush blouse, she strutted to the front of the room. The class quieted.

"Good morning," Brandy drawled. "We're going to close our discussion on Class A creatures in preparation for the Testing Year Exam next week. Unlike other teachers, I won't be opening office hours. If you have questions about the exam, you should've taken better notes."

I rested my chin on my palm. I wished I was surprised by her heartless speech, but it was Brandy.

"If you fail, it will be completely on you. Isn't that right, Miss Heart?" Her sapphire eyes locked on to mine across the room.

A rumble moved through the room as students shifted in their seats to look at me.

I blinked at her. "What?"

"As a discarded Contestant, you're used to failure. I thought you would be able to share something with the class to discourage them from following in your footsteps." Her deep red lips curled without teeth.

Dmitri's chuckle made my fingers curl into fists. I stopped breathing to keep my magic from playing with the lights.

"You would know more about that than I would, Miss Charles."

Blake cursed under his breath.

Brandy's sharp eyebrow lifted.

"Your Contestant was second string; she wasn't chosen for the Top Seven," I ticked them off on my fingers, "and you have a failed marriage. That's just three things I know about. I could ask your ex-husband for more. I'm sure Master Kale would be more than willing to give me a detailed list."

Blake choked.

"Master Kale was married?" Cornelia's mouth dropped open.

"Careful, Miss Heart," Brandy said. Her smile was frozen in place.

"Or what?" I tilted my head.

"You're excused for the day." She waved her long nails toward the door. "You can leave, or I can have you removed."

In her mind, this was worse than detention because I would be missing the remainder of this section. But she didn't know I had a secret weapon. She thought she was keeping information from me? Michael would just give it to me.

So, when I met her cold anger draped in a crimson sneer, I smiled. I stuffed my books back in my bag and pulled it over my shoulder.

"Master Kale is her ex?" Blake mumbled as I pushed myself to my feet.

I nodded. Not dropping my voice, I said for the room to hear, "I'll tell you at lunch how he made her a widow when he joined the Hunter Guard." Keeping my gaze locked ahead of me, I shoved my way out of the classroom.

My footsteps echoed in the vast, empty hallway. I quickly put some distance between me and Creature Studies in case Brandy came up with something worse than kicking me out.

Reaching the stairwell, I dug my phone from the bottom of my bag. Scrolling through the contacts, I selected the one titled 'JACKASS.'

"This is Kale." The phone rumbled as he moved it to his ear. He mumbled to someone on the other end.

"Am I interrupting?"

"No!" Surprise brightened his voice. "Not at all. What's up?"

"Your mom mentioned you got high marks on your Testing Year. I was wondering if you could help me."

"Sure. What are you doing right now?"

"Nothing actually."

"I'll meet you in your room in five."

My mouth opened to tell him we could do it later, but he ended the call.

Tucking the phone in my back pocket, I jogged up the spiraling staircases bathed in morning light.

When I stepped into my room, he was already there. A slight mist of sweat made his golden skin glisten. He had to have been in the middle of something.

I closed the door and slid the deadbolt in place. "You didn't have to drop what you were doing. This could have waited until tonight."

The leather of his jacket rumbled as he shrugged. "I wasn't doing anything important." He paused to read my face. "How are you?"

"Tired." I put my bag on the counter. "I share Creature Studies with Dmitri. So, I have to sit there and listen to Brandy rattle on about some mythical creature that isn't supposed to be real; meanwhile he sits in the front row and pretends like he didn't throw a knife at my face and kill my friend. All the while, the son of a bitch is wearing red because it's his school's twisted way of celebrating what he's done."

I roughly shoved my hair from one shoulder to the other. "On top of that, I'm overwhelmed. Everyone in my class has been learning different aspects of magic since they were in single digits, while I barely know what's going on."

"I can get Lenin to move you into another class," he said calmly.

"No, that's not why I—" I expelled a rough breath. "I'm just complaining because you're the only one who understands. I just needed to say it to get it out of my head."

Michael nodded, a slow single dip of his head. "Did you want me to do something about it?"

"No. What I want is to not fail my exams."

"Ok. What are you having trouble with?" Michael reached into my bag and started sorting my textbooks.

"All of it."

He gave me a dry look. "Lenin gave me access to your grades, so I know that's not true. Pinpoint it for me."

With a sigh, I leaned onto the counter on my forearms. "The formula for casting. There's math and angles—all of which I was terrible at in high school."

"You're in luck." Michael flipped open the textbook and thumbed through the pages. "In the training for the Hunter Guard, we were tested on accuracy distancing once a month. I was at the top of my class from start to finish."

"Your ego is truly amazing."

"Thank you." He located the chapter and briefly scanned the outlined lesson. "Ok." Michael clapped his hands and stepped away from the counter.

Reaching beneath his arm, he tugged his wand free from the holster strapped across his shoulders. With a gleaming arch of magic, he moved the furniture to the outskirts of the room.

"This is actually good for you to learn," he said, levitating the couch against the fireplace. "Wand technique is a fancy way of saying that you won't miss. If you get as good as me, which is doubtful—"

I tipped my head back and sighed at the ceiling.

"— you can hit a target from behind while looking someone in the eye."

That sounded useful and cool. I slid my wand free from the loops sewn into the side of my jeans.

"Of course, they won't teach you that in the classroom, so don't use that in your exam. That's more of a Hunter's trick." Michael stepped back up to the counter and turned the book to face me. "This equation tells you how to find the amount of magic you'll need to hit the target."

"I already know how to do that." I raised my wand and sent a burst of gold shooting across the room. The ward knocked a pillow over the armrest of the leather couch. A thin trail of smoke rose from where it hit the floor.

"You know how to hit something. This is teaching you how to do what you just did, without burning a hole through it."

Reaching into my bag once more, he pulled out a notebook and searched for a blank page.

"Ok." Michael grabbed a pen. "For the equation, you need the distance to the target and how fast magic travels." He glanced over his shoulder at the second decorative pillow on the couch. "I'd say the couch is . . . fifteen feet away."

"Cheese and rice, I already hate this."

"What is up with you and cheese and rice?" He set down the pen. "Is it a dish you make? Like, do you actually eat it?"

I bit back a smile. "It's an expression."

"Out of all the expressions, why would you choose that one?"

"Out of all the personalities, why would you choose yours?"

He reached across the counter and flicked the end of my nose.

"Hey!" I swatted his hand away.

Biting back his smile, Michael picked up the pen.

"Once you have the distance between the caster, you, and the target, you divide it by three." He scribbled it on the paper then flipped it around for me to see. "You take that number," he looped a circle around it, "and use it to determine the amount of magic needed to reach the target. Magic is measured on a scale of one to ten, like our statuses. Your answer here," he tapped the circled number, "will fit into that scale. If you use too little magic, the ward will dissolve before the target. If you use too much, you'll destroy it."

I studied the equation for a moment, twisting a lock of hair around my finger. "I don't remember you teaching me any of this." I picked up my wand and leveled it at the pillow.

"Because I wasn't looking for minimal impact." He cleared his throat. "Your judges will be looking for precision."

"Lucky me." I pulled on my magic. Warmth bled down my arm and filled the grooves in my wand with molten gold.

With a tight flourish, a spark zipped across the room and struck the center of the pillow. A curl of steam lifted from the cover, but it remained unscathed.

"Now, you do the work." He tossed me the pen. "Figure out the equation for one of the pillows on your bed."

Leaning my forearms against the counter, I tucked my hair behind my ears and got to work. Michael sat on the other side, silently watching.

It took three tries to get it right, much to the demise of my bedroom décor. Once I was able to only rearrange the wrinkles on the pillow cases, he had me stand beside my bed and knock books off the study shelves across the apartment. He wasn't concerned that I was breaking stuff. If anything, he got a little smirk every time I did.

"Your hour's up," Michael called into the living room. "You should head to your next class."

"Wait!" I skidded to a halt in the doorway. "Can you show me how you can hit someone from behind while you're in front of them?"

"That won't be covered on your exam."

"So? I want to see you do it. Unless you can't *actually* do it."

His eyes narrowed at my dare.

I grinned.

He picked up his wand from the counter. He stood the textbook on the edges of the hardcover and then retreated to the other side of the apartment.

The smug bastard didn't write down an equation or take a moment to think. He pulled on his magic and fired.

The golden orb arched over the counter with a small tail connecting the ward and his wand. Just as it was about to dip toward the far cabinets, he yanked his wand back, pulling on the thin string. The orb changed directions and knocked the textbook flat on its cover.

Cheese and rice.

"You *have* to teach me that tonight."

"Tonight, you'll be doing more equations." He tucked his wand back into his holster.

"Oh, come on—"

"You're going to be late for your next class."

Rolling my eyes, I collected my things and swung my bag over my shoulder. "Thanks for the help."

"Anytime."

I pulled open the door and hesitated in the doorway. My next class was History of Magic, which I shared with Igorek. I turned back to him with the corner of my lip between my teeth. "Can I ask you something?"

He nodded. "Of course."

"How do you face Lawrence, after what he did, and not kill him the second he walks into a room? How do you control yourself?"

The playful light in his eyes dimmed. With a heavy sigh, he dropped his gaze to the cuff of his jacket. "Control has very little to do with it. If I were to act on my impulse and attack, he'd deflect every ward or knife I threw to someone standing nearby. While his death would be worth it for me, it wouldn't be for anyone who just happened to be there."

I nodded slowly. I could picture it, me pulling my wand in the middle of Brandy's class and firing at the back of his skull. If the ward was rebuked, it could hit Blake or Cornelia. Then I would be doing exactly what he did to me in the Second Trial.

Seeing his blood wasn't worth that price, no matter how badly I wanted it. With those thoughts swirling through my head, I stepped into the hall.

Every time I thought of drawing my wand on Contestant Nineteen or

Contestant Twenty-One, I would look at those around me. No matter how hot my anger boiled, that thought kept my wand sheathed.

65

In a Moonlit Glade

A hand gripped my shoulder.

Ripped out of my nightmares, I sat up. The lights flickered with my heartbeat. As my breathing slowed, they went still, leaving the room dark as the rest of the night.

"You good?"

Pushing my hair out of my face, I turned to the man sitting beside me. "Yeah. I'm good."

Michael released my shoulder. His fingers trailed down my arm to the pulse in my wrist. When he confirmed it was slowing, he pulled his hand back.

Rising to his feet, he stepped back. "What was it this time?"

"I was drowning." Pulling my knees to my chest, I rested my chin in the crevice between them. The clock on the nightstand said it was just past two. "Did anything happen?"

He shook his head. "Just a light show."

My eyes darted around the room from one light fixture to the next. All the light bulbs were intact. He woke me up in time.

Sighing, I unwound my arms from around my legs. "Thank you." I grabbed the covers and pulled them up to my chin. With adrenaline still pumping through my body, I prepared for a long talk with myself to get back to sleep.

But Michael hadn't moved away from the bed.

"Do you want to go somewhere?" His voice was quiet and soft. Softer than I had ever heard it.

My eyes popped open. That was a question I had never heard him ask.

To be honest, he didn't ask very many questions. Lit only by the alarm clock, I saw that he was still dressed.

I snuck a glance through the door into the living room. The couch was free of blankets, meaning he hadn't gone to bed. And he was still wearing his leather jacket.

"I have Testing Year exams in the afternoon."

He bobbed his head in recognition. "I know."

There was something about his voice. Like he wanted to ask the question again, but didn't want to be rejected. But he still needed to know, and that kept him beside my bed in the middle of the night.

I wasn't going to sleep any time soon. I sat up and pushed off the covers. "Where are we going?"

Either the darkness was playing tricks on me or relief turned up the corners of his lips. "It's hard to explain."

I grabbed my hoodie at the end of my bed and tugged it over my head. "Alright, let me grab my shoes."

"You won't need them." He stepped up and grabbed my hand. With a sting of magic, we Ported out of the Magisterium.

My gaze was drawn upward. Bathed in the silver light of a full moon were trees as tall as skyscrapers. Their branches intertwined hundreds of feet above us.

I gasped when I realized the trunks were a dusty red. "Are we where I think we are?"

"The Redwood Forest," he confirmed as he guided me into a glade. He walked to the far side and settled against one of the massive tree trunks. I joined him. Even though frost outlined many of the leaves and the texture of the bark, I was surprised by how warm the soil was under my bare feet.

"Why are we here?" I whispered.

He checked his watch. "You'll see in a second."

Snuggling back against the tree, I crossed my arms in the pocket of my hoodie.

"Is this a new form of training?" I asked. "You're trying to get me used to sleeping in the woods?"

He shot me an amused smirk in the moonlight. "If this were a training session, I would've told you."

"Would you, though? This could be a test."

"Relax," he said. "There's no test or agenda."

"You could be lying."

"I haven't lied to you." He turned back to the glade. "Stop talking and watch."

Grumbling, I turned back to the trees in front of us. The full moon was doing its best to fight the shadows back. Most of them hid near the base of trees or large bushes.

Michael, of course, was as relaxed as a napping lion. He leaned against the tree with his arms crossed. His eyes carefully combed the forest floor.

Wrapping my arms around my legs, I rested my forehead against my knees. Staring at the dirt beneath my toes, I focused on the simple task of keeping my eyes open.

A jewel of silver sparkled through the dirt between my toes. Peering closer, my eyes focused on a hand no bigger than a pebble. At first, I thought my sleep-deprived mind was playing tricks on me.

The soil broke open as a tiny person crawled out of the ground. I jerked my foot back with a gasp of surprise.

Her hair and clothes undulated as she floated into the air. Flipping around, she reached into the dirt and tugged out a small green shoot from her hole. She straightened the plant, fanning out its tiny leaves before rising into the air.

She paid no attention to me. Flipping around, she went back to the ground and reached through the dirt again. Just like the first time, she pulled a tiny plant to the surface.

Michael nudged me and nodded to the glade.

Rising from the ground was a galaxy of tiny, glowing people. Each one unburied a new plant before hunting for more to unearth.

"What are they?" I breathed. I feared that if I talked above a whisper, I would scare them off.

"Sprites," Michael murmured back. "They only come out during the spring equinox to help new growth."

Three glowing sprites glided across the ground between us. After pulling up new shoots, they drifted into the air. Close up, I could just make out a humanlike face. They were so transparent, I could see their only organ; a light flickered in their chest where their heart was.

"How does a guy like you know about this?" I asked as the sprite passed in front of my face.

He turned to me with a raised eyebrow. "A guy like me?"

"You know what I mean." I stilled as the sprite slipped into my hair.

"Actually, I don't."

"These things aren't dangerous, are they?" My scalp prickled as the glowing creature moved between the locks.

"Explain your comment and I'll answer your question."

"Now isn't the time to be a smartass."

"Maybe not for you." He smirked.

"Michael!" I winced as the sprite tugged at my hair.

His smirk only grew.

"You're a Master Hunter. Your mind is supposed to be stuffed with blood, guts, and gore. A quiet night in a dark forest doesn't really seem like your thing." The sprite continued to tug at my hair. "Your turn."

"You just stereotyped me."

"There are things crawling in my hair. Can you please answer my question?"

"Sprites are harmless." Chuckling, he placed his fingertips underneath my chin and turned my face toward him. "They're just playing with your hair."

Relaxing, I turned back to the glade. The forest floor was now covered in fresh, new growth. The sprites moved farther out and up the trunks of the trees. Tiny mushrooms popped out of the bark.

"You didn't answer my question about how you know about this," I countered.

"You would've learned about them if you had been at the Magisterium a couple years ago." He watched a sprite dance across his palm. It took a lot of interest in the scar running down his thumb. "Lauren was entranced by the idea of them. So, every night on our birthday, she would drag me out of bed to watch this together." The sprite moved up his wrist and stopped on his forearm to examine another scar.

My head jerked toward him. The sprite yanked at my hair in annoyance. "Is today your birthday?"

After a pause, he nodded.

66

Raspberry Dark Chocolate

The sprite pressed her bright hands to the faded scar tissue on his arm.

"Were you going to mention it?" I asked.

"When you're a Royal, it's stupid to celebrate every birthday. You only do the big ones, or else they just become repetitive. And annoying." That was his way of saying he didn't want to celebrate. I couldn't blame him. After all, Lauren was killed on their birthday.

Is that why he wanted me to come? So he didn't have to be alone tonight?

I jumped to my feet. The sprite twirled out of my hair and rejoined the others on the ground. "I have an idea."

"Wouldn't that require you to think?"

I stuck my tongue out at him. "I'll be right back."

He was on his feet in an instant. The sprite flew away from him so fast it was a blur. "Where are you going?"

"That would defeat the purpose of a birthday surprise."

"Charlie . . ." The panic in his eyes dimmed with haunted memories. "Not today."

"You told me to let myself heal without anger. It's your turn."

His expression of hesitation didn't dissolve. "You'll come right back?"

"I promise."

The muscle in his jaw pulsed.

"Trust me." I took a small step back. When he didn't stop me, I pulled on my magic and Ported from the glade.

I could only think of one grocery store, and it was in Salina, Kansas. Ducking through the sliding glass doors, I pulled out my phone and sent a quick text to Meg. I knew she would be up with Quinton. She responded right as I got into the freezer aisle.

Quickly scanning the selection, I grabbed a container of raspberry dark chocolate ice cream. I was about to Port back to the glade when I remembered we needed spoons.

Without thinking, I Ported to a house not too far off on Haven Avenue. When I appeared in the kitchen of my old foster house, I was surprised by how apathetic I felt. I hadn't been here since Blake pulled me out over a year ago.

I gazed around the dull exterior. This place used to haunt me. Now it meant nothing.

I opened the silverware drawer and took two spoons. Pulling on my magic once more, I Ported back to the glade.

More sprites had woken up. The ground was almost completely covered by new growth. The air was fragrant with the smell of fresh earth and greens.

Michael was exactly where I left him. An obvious look of relief passed over his face as I came back to him.

I dropped back onto the dirt and patted the spot beside me. When he sat down, I offered him a spoon.

His eyes brightened when he saw the flavor on the carton. "How did you know this was my favorite?"

"Meg." Popping off the lid, I carved out a spoonful and held the utensil out to him. "Happy birthday, Michael and Lauren."

He dug out a scoop and clinked it against mine. I tossed my bite into my mouth. He hesitated only for a second before he did the same.

"How old are you turning?" I asked.

"Two hundred and nineteen."

He said that so casually.

I snuck a glance at him. It was so weird seeing him doing something so normal. Michael Kale eating ice cream was equal to a seal eating a hamburger. It was easier to picture him eating something dripping with blood.

"Do you really eat dragon hearts?"

He jerked his gaze from the ice cream to stare at me. Humor and confusion raised his eyebrows. "That's random."

"Blake said you eat a dragon heart once a year for their strength."

"Ah." A smile winked from the corner of his lips. "No, I don't. I was with a tribe of dragon hunters a while back . . . I think it was in New Zealand. It's tradition that when a dragon is killed, you eat its heart. I couldn't refuse when they offered me one. I'm not a fan of the texture. It's too chewy." He ate another scoop of ice cream. "Someone saw me eating it, and assumed it was my tradition."

"And you didn't correct it?"

"Why? I think it's hilarious." He grinned. "My favorite rumor is that I drink snake venom instead of liquor."

It wasn't hard to believe. "Did you really kill a hundred men by yourself?"

"No. Atlas was with me." He paused. "Now that I think about it, Atlas started that one."

"What about the one where you cut out one of your kidneys because it was failing?"

"That's true."

My spoon paused before my mouth. "You're kidding."

Sticking his spoon in his mouth, he pulled up the hem of his shirt exposing a thin, jagged scar under his ribs.

Dropping his shirt, he continued to carve away at the ice cream. "We were in the Swiss Alps when it started to go. We were tracking a group of Users who were burning cities of Regulars. It took nearly six months to find them. I didn't want to lose their trail."

"Couldn't you have used a potion or something?"

He smiled at my tone of horror. "In order to revive it, I would've had to go to a medical center, and that would've taken me out of the game for weeks."

"So, you just cut it out?"

He grimaced at the memory. "Sánchez helped. Surprisingly, it's not the grossest thing I've ever done."

"And Sánchez is . . ?"

"She's a Hunter on my team."

He never mentioned a woman before. Then again, he didn't really talk about being a Hunter.

I took another bite of ice cream. As it melted in my mouth, I asked, "Why did you become a Hunter?"

He stared down into the ice cream. "Normal life never called to me. My dad wanted me to run the ranch with him, but I wanted to do extraordinary things. I wanted to change the world."

"But why become a Hunter?"

"Back then, Guard was changing things. They were making plans to put all the monsters in cages. If they succeeded, the night would be safe. It would be the golden age of peace. I wanted to be a part of that."

He bent his head as he took another scoop of ice cream. Memories seemed to weigh on his shoulders.

Two more bites of ice cream followed in silence. "What's something about you that's not Hunter-related?"

He shot me a look. "You're full of questions tonight."

"You woke me up at two in the morning. You're obligated to answer."

"I woke you up so you wouldn't level the school."

"Just answer the question."

He chuckled. "I grew up on a ranch."

"Something I don't know, smartass."

"Like what?"

I thought for a second. There weren't many moments when he was willing to talk to me like this. I didn't want to waste what could be my only chance to learn something real about him.

"Something that makes you you."

With his eyes slightly narrowed, he dug through the vast storage of his mind. Eager to hear what he would say, I patiently ate ice cream.

"I don't like letting people down," he said after a while. "Although, in my line of work, it's inevitable. I'd do anything for my family . . . even if it hurts them." He offered me a soft smile. "It's my biggest weakness."

"I don't see that as a weakness."

"Oh, it is." His gaze dropped to the ice cream. "It isolates you."

"Well, I'm here. So, you're not totally isolated."

He met my gaze.

I smiled, a gentle upturn of the lips.

The chill in his eyes thawed, just a little. For a second, I thought he would smile, but something kept it from moving over his lips. He didn't respond and he didn't have to.

The reality was, while we were isolated from those we were fighting for, I would be by his side, and he would be by mine. That thought, almost comforting, made the oncoming war not look so bleak—whatever that looked like.

"When this war is over, you don't have to isolate yourself. In fact, that's my dying wish."

"You have to be dying to make one of those."

"Shut up. I'm serious." What came out of my mouth next surprised the hell out of me, but I meant every word. "You deserve better than this. Retire the leather jacket and go to a beach. At least one of us should get to live something that resembles a life."

"You can't save me, Charlie. This war will end me. I guarantee it."

"I don't believe that," I said firmly. "Do you promise that you'll try?"

His eyes flickered between mine, like he was trying to find something hidden behind them. I don't know what he was looking for or if he even found it. But whatever he saw made him give a tight nod in agreement.

I dug my spoon into the ice cream in victory. I savored the bite, letting it melt over my tongue.

His shoulders weren't as tense as when we arrived. He licked the back of his spoon. "Ok, I have a question. Where did you go on your summer vacation?"

"You really want to know?" I asked, watching his expression carefully.

"I do."

"You never asked before."

"I didn't care before."

A smile tugged at the corners of my lips. *But he does now.*

"Well, I stayed in Vegas for a month—"

"A month?" His eyes looked like they were about to pop out of his head. "You're kidding. I searched that place from the sewers to the highest floors! There's no way I missed you."

I smirked. *One point for Charlie.* "Blending in is my superpower, remember?"

He cursed, shaking his head in disbelief. "Ok, after you completely humiliated me in Vegas, where did you go?"

"I went over to the Grand Canyon and then up to Colorado to see the mountains. Those were amazing. I stayed there for a bit to save up money to go to Seattle. I stayed with Cornelia for a couple of weeks—"

He groaned. "Oh, come on. I checked there too."

"I exclusively Ported in and out of her house and stayed away from the windows. The rest you know."

Clearing his throat, he twirled the spoon through a melting pool in the corner of the carton. "I don't understand you. After everything you've been through, you can still laugh like you enjoy life."

"Are you saying you don't?" I ate another mouthful.

"Not like you. How do you do it?"

"Cold, hard denial."

A smile tickled the corner of his lips. "And I focus on my issues so much that I don't see anything else. We're pretty messed up, you and I."

He wasn't wrong. Then it dawned on me. "I think we finally found something we have in common."

He blinked in surprise. "I think we finally did."

I took a large scoop of the ice cream and held it out to him. "Cheers to that."

He clinked his spoon against mine and tossed the frozen treat into his mouth.

When the carton was nearly empty, and most of the sprites had gone back underground, Michael rose to his feet. He stuck the spoons in his back pocket and helped me to my feet.

With the help of a transporter, he Ported us back to the Magisterium. With heavy eyelids and full stomachs, we bid each other good morning and fell onto our separate beds.

For the first time since the Second Trial, my heart didn't hurt as much. Judging by how quickly he fell asleep, I don't think his did either.

67

An Eye for an Eye

Don't look.

My hands gripped the lunch tray. I kept my eyes on my destination. Our usual table near the front of the room was already occupied with my people.

Cornelia sat beside Blake. With sparkling eyes, she watched him prattle on with her chin propped on her fist. There was a slight flush in his cheeks.

Involuntarily, my eyes moved toward the front of the room.

Don't.

I shoved the screams of anger to the back of my head. If I didn't look at Contestant Nineteen, I could function like everything was ok.

I came to meals as late as possible, so I didn't see him for as long. Even then, I sat with my back to the stage. In class, I found a seat where he was out of my peripheral vision. I did everything to make sure I couldn't see his red sleeve.

With controlled breathing, I crossed the dining room. *You're ok.*

I stepped up to the table with a tight-lipped smile. "Hey."

"'Bout time you got here." Blake scooted closer to Cornelia, making room for me next to him. "You missed all the excitement."

Setting my tray on the table, I plopped down on the bench. I gave a quick scan of the back half of the room. Students were gesturing to the high table with animation. The volume was louder than usual.

"What did I miss?" I picked up my pulled pork sandwich, and sank my teeth into the soft bread. Tangy barbeque sauce ran down my chin.

"Tonight marks one month before the Final Trial," Blake announced. I couldn't tell if he was slowly dying after saying that out loud, or if he was genuinely cool with it.

I picked up my napkin and wiped my mouth. I forced myself to keep chewing even though my appetite died the moment he mentioned The Trial.

"That means tonight is the Viewing. The School Masters are releasing the first two full performances of the Top Seven to the public. They're going to be showing 'em to the whole school after dinner."

I forced myself to swallow. "Why would they do that?"

"It's supposed to level the playing field," Blake said as he munched on a french fry. "We get to watch the past performances of the other Top Seven Contestants to figure out their strengths and weaknesses."

"Plus, it gives us regular folk a chance to see why each Contestant was chosen for the Final Trial," Cornelia said. "We've been in the dark since the start of it. But now, we get to see everything in preparation for next month."

"They'll show all the performances?" I asked slowly.

Blake sipped his soda and shook his head. "No, just those in the Top Seven."

Panic coiled around my chest like an anaconda. The whole school would watch Dmitri's Second Trial, and everyone would see how Daniel was killed. That I had been the target all along, and he had missed. I might not have killed him, but he was dead because of me.

"They're showing them after dinner?"

Cornelia nodded. "I think they're going to move out all the tables and reconfigure the room."

"Are you going?" Blake asked stiffly.

She swallowed thickly. "Low Commons usually don't get seats for this kind of thing."

"Screw that. If you want to come, you can sit with me."

She shook her head. "I don't think I have the stomach for it. I was planning on skipping anyway."

"Lucky," Blake mumbled.

Cornelia smiled sadly at him. "I have to go and study. I'll see you two at dinner?"

After bidding us both goodbye, she waved her wand over her dirty dishes and sent them levitating to the other side of the room. Blake's eyes followed her all the way out of the dining room.

He caught me looking. "What?"

"If you stare at her any harder, she might burst into flames."

With a little smile, Blake crossed his arms on the table and rested his chin on them.

If he doesn't ask her out by the end of the school year, I might have to kick his ass.

"I've missed you," he said, breaking the silence at our table. "I've hardly seen you since the Ascending Ceremony. I'm always in training, and you're always studying for your Testing Year. I miss my best friend."

I pushed my lunch away. "I miss you too."

"I don't know if I can ask this . . . but would you join me for the Viewing?"

The bite of pulled pork in my stomach grew cold. I shook my head. "I can't—"

"I know it's dumb to ask, but I just . . . I'm going to sit beside Atlas as he points out the weaknesses in someone else's fears and memories, and I'm just afraid that I'll lose myself in it. I need someone to ground me." He lifted his head, but his arms remained tightly crossed. "Please? You've been through it. You know what it's like."

"Which is why I can't."

"Please, Charlie."

I gripped the bench to keep myself from twisting around to look at the high table. "Dmitri's Second Trial is where Daniel was killed."

"Bloody hell." Blake's gaze dropped to the scar on my cheek. "I wasn't thinking. I'm sorry."

"It's ok." I wanted him to believe that, so I picked up my cooling sandwich and took another bite.

With a slight tremor, he swiped at the clamminess on his forehead. "What if you just watched the First Trials? With Dmitri being the nineteenth Contestant, his will be shown last. You can leave before his Trial starts."

I opened my mouth to protest.

"Just the First Trials," he pleaded. "They're the worst of the lot. They deal with fear. I just—I just . . . You're right. You shouldn't be anywhere near this. I'm sorry, I'm not thinking clearly."

Seeing him so distressed made up my mind. "I'll stay with you."

His shoulders stilled, as if he wasn't breathing. "You will?"

Against everything in me, I nodded. "Just until Dmitri's." *I don't think I can survive that.*

He nodded fervently. "Of course. You can stay for however long or as little as you'd like." Scooting across the bench, he wrapped his arms around me. "Thank you."

I said nothing.

Clearing his throat, he picked up his forgotten sandwich. "You've got exams this afternoon, right?"

I nodded. "Creature Studies, Wand Form, and Accuracy Distancing."

He groaned. "Tough day."

"Speaking of." I looked at the clock over the dining room doors. "I've got to go."

"You just sat down."

"Miss Charles is making the exam first come, first served, and I have a feeling she's going to make me last."

Blake's teeth pulled back in a grimace. "Good luck."

"Thanks. I'll see you tonight." Pulling my bag over my shoulder, I left the packed dining room. Butterflies fluttered around my half-empty belly.

Just like I thought, Brandy made me the last student to take my exam, even though I was first to arrive. She took twice as long to reset the room. When she did call my name, her nails were a different shade of red, and the room smelled like fresh polish.

The moment I finished the exam, I sprinted to the other side of the school to take my exam on Wand Form.

And then finally, it was time for Accuracy Distancing.

My stomach growled as I dropped into one of the chairs lining the silent hallway. Only a few students dared to breach the quiet, and even then, I don't think they realized they were doing it. The kid on the other side of the hall mumbled magic equations to himself as he feverishly flipped through his notes.

"Charlie Heart."

I jumped at the sound of my name. Inhaled sharply, I hoped the extra oxygen would control the flare of magic in my chest. With shaking hands, I rose to my feet.

Mr. Hubert held open the door as I stepped into the room. All the chairs and tables had been removed. Without them, the room felt huge, like I was standing in the belly of a whale and the bare tiers were its ribs.

Levitating over each level was what looked like a stop sign. In the center of each red octagon was a number, one through ten. Before the teacher's desk was a tall table with a single sheet of paper and a yellow pencil.

"Whenever you're ready, Miss Heart." Mr. Hubert turned to his desk. Numerous clipboards, displayed in neat rows, covered the entire surface. Scanning through the alphabet, he found the one with my name and my fake status and faced me.

I set my bag down beside the door and walked over to the tall table. My fingers trembled as I picked up the pencil. On top of the page, it read: ACCURACY DISTANCING EXAM. Listed down the page, and onto the back side, were numbers that matched the targets in front of me.

You can do this.

Gripping the pencil, I looked at the first target. Quickly, I scrawled the equation Michael had shown me, taking the distance of the target and dividing it by the magical number. With the answer, I took my wand from the side of my jeans and stepped around the table.

Magic burned down my arm and into my palm. The crevices of my wand glowed and gleamed like embers. I aimed and fired. A small spark zipped across the short distance and struck the target in the center.

I glanced over my shoulder at Mr. Hubert. His pen bobbed furiously over the top of his clipboard.

With one small success under my belt, I retreated to the exam page and completed the equations for the remaining targets. One after the other, I fired.

When all of the floating targets were smoking, I handed my test paper to Mr. Hubert. He clipped the page to his board and, with a bright red marker, went down the line checking my math.

Finally, he nodded. "Well done, Miss Heart." Freeing the page from his clipboard, he handed me the exam results. "I'm giving you a nine out of ten because this answer is only partially correct." He tapped the third question. "You forgot the decimal."

"Thank you." I swiped the page from his hand and darted out the door. Feeling lighter than I had in days, I stepped into the East Tower and ducked under the stairs.

Reaching into my back pocket, I pulled out my phone and selected the contact labeled 'JACKASS.'

It rang twice.

"Hey," Michael said breathlessly. "How'd it go?"

"Accuracy Distancing can kiss my ass," I whispered excitedly. "I honestly thought I was going to blast a hole through the side of the school."

"That would've been eventful," he said with a smile in his voice. "What score did you get?"

"Nine out of ten. I missed a decimal on one, *but*!" I exclaimed. "I hit each target with the appropriate amount of magic."

"Are you sure you didn't get someone else's score? I would've put money on you getting a five, and that's a generous estimate."

"That would be a reflection of *your* skills as a teacher. But *I* am a stellar student."

Michael chuckled. "What are you doing to celebrate? I can pick up a pizza for dinner."

At the mention of dinner, my mood curdled. "Um . . . the Viewing is tonight. Blake asked me to join him."

The line went quiet. "Are you sure you want to do that?"

"Absolutely not." I squeezed my eyes shut. "But he needs me. I'll leave before Dmitri's performances."

"Do you think you'll be ok?"

No. "I'll be fine." I cleared my throat. "I'll see you tonight at ten for lessons."

"If you change your mind about the Viewing, let me know."

"I will. Don't die of boredom without me." Before I changed my mind, I hung up and stuffed the phone into my pocket.

Taking a deep breath, I held it until my lungs burned. When I finally released it, my whole body shook.

I can do this. For Blake.

Back on the main level, I stood at the threshold of the dining room. Just as Cornelia said, the room had been reconfigured.

All of the round tables had been removed. Cushioned chairs filled the large room in neat rows. At the far end, where the stage and head table usually sat, was a levitating pane of glass so large it almost touched each wall, the floor, and the ceiling. A stream of students flowed around me as they filled the rows of seats.

Move, Charlie.

But I couldn't. It was as if my feet had taken root. All I could do was stare at the pane of glass.

"Charlie!"

My gaze dropped to the crowded room. Blake had spotted me. He waved his hand over his head.

I stepped toward him. Then I took another step, and another. It felt as if I held my breath all the way to him.

"Hey." He seemed to visibly deflate. "You came."

He didn't think I would. "Of course." I looked around. "Where's Atlas?"

Blake sank into one of the padded chairs. "He said something came up. We'd debrief in the morning."

Overhead, the light flashed, not with my magic, but as a signal that the Viewing was about to start. With my stomach full of lead, I took the seat beside Blake.

Tessa Baker, Master Lenin's assistant, walked across the stage behind the large pane of glass. As the lights darkened, she drew a clear stone from the pocket of her trousers. She tossed it toward the center of the glass.

The stone struck, but the glass didn't crack. It absorbed the stone. Glowing bright gold, the whole screen glared. It was so bright, my eyes watered. As the screen slowly dimmed, words were left in its wake.

CONTESTANT THREE, TALA ABALOS.

I reached over the armrest and grabbed Blake's hand. My bones ached as he held mine with a white-knuckled grip.

I barely paid attention. My eyes stared without focus at the giant screen. I saw flashes of spiders the size of minivans, a creature with a ghostly countenance that crawled across ceilings, and family members with axes.

It was over in under thirty minutes, but it might as well have been thirty hours. There was no reprieve. At the end of Tala's Trial, Tessa Baker threw another stone up into the air.

CONTESTANT FOUR, AMELIA MARKUS.

Just keep breathing.

With each open door that appeared on the screen and the gaping darkness beyond, my skin jumped between hot and cold. I couldn't tell if it was my hand that was clammy or Blake's. He didn't move a muscle from the moment he took my hand.

CONTESTANT EIGHT, EMEKA SELASI.

At the first sound of a Dellamora scream, I was on my feet.

"Charlie?" Blake whispered after me, but I was already in the aisle. The horrors of the First Trial echoed around the room. Emeka's breathing sounded like storm gales, but not a sound came from the watching crowd. They were completely transfixed.

No one saw me run. My footsteps couldn't be heard over the sheer volume of the screen. Bursting out of the dining room, I nearly ran right into the clock tower.

Clutching the carved stone, I retched over the black stone. Nothing came up; I hadn't been able to eat dinner.

"Hello, little bird."

That voice brought an avalanche of goosebumps. I kept my gaze locked straight ahead, trying to convince myself that if I didn't see him, he wasn't there.

"How is the Viewing?" Dmitri stepped up beside me. "I'm surprised you're here. I thought you would . . ." He searched his mind for the English translation. "Cower like a dog."

From the corner of my eye, I could see his red sleeve. *Keep it together.* "I was invited."

"Invited," he mused. "Contestant Twelve did this, I assume."

My eyes snapped up to read his expression. He was staring into the dining room. On the screen, Emeka cast a ward of bright magic, which lit up the audience. I could make out Blake's grey beanie under Dmitri's gaze. My stomach dropped.

"I have been wanting to add more numbers to my arm." Dmitri stroked the red sleeve, moving over the white numbers.

His meaning slapped me across the face. The anger I had been trying to fight consumed me. I stepped forward with my hands clenched. "If you touch him—"

His gaze locked onto mine. "You can do nothing. I can add as many numbers as I want. I would collect them all if I could."

"Hey, break it up," a guard from beside the door called.

Dmitri paid him no mind. "I want Contestants Eight and Twelve." My fury nearly erupted. "And just so I can say that I killed two of the three Magisterium Contestants, fourteen." He pointed at Clarence lounging against a window on the side of the dining room. "My father would be proud, as would my king."

He bent down to my ear. "I would kill you, too." There was a smile in his voice. "But you're not an active Contestant. You're off-limits."

My heart frantically beat against my ribs. "If you touch Blake—"

"I do not care for your empty threats. You can do nothing . . . just like the Second Trial. You will watch."

At the mention of the Second Trial, my magic swirled furiously through my body.

The guard stepped between us, forcing us apart. "I said break it up."

Dmitri smiled at my reaction. "Enjoy the Viewing, little bird." Chuckling, he returned to his seat, and the guard returned to his post.

I stood there, glued to the floor for a completely different reason. My biggest fear bloomed in front of me.

I would watch the Final Trial as Dmitri cut down Contestant after Contestant.

And there would be nothing I could do.

My eyes flew over to Blake. He sat with his elbows on his knees. He bounced his foot anxiously as he stared at the screen. He was pale and clammy.

I would have to sit by and watch Dmitri take him away. I would be helpless.

Just like Moose.

Just like Daniel.

I ducked into the West Wing and dug my phone from my back pocket. Fumbling with the contacts, I called the one person who would know what to do.

It went straight to voicemail.

"This is Kale. Leave a message."

Beep.

"Michael." Tears filled my eyes. Taking a deep breath, I tried to keep them from clogging my throat. "Dmitri just came to me. He said he's going after Blake in the Final Trial." Closing my eyes, I whispered, "I need to know what to do. I can't—if something happens—I can't lose him. Please, I need—"

Loud footsteps echoed through the stairwell. Igorek made his way toward the stairs. The leg he lost in The Trial had been replaced by a steel replica. Not with hinges and screws, but a leg shaped completely out of enchanted metal with a kneecap, ankle, and thick thigh muscles.

I waited for Dmitri to follow. But he didn't.

My thundering panic paused. They never went anywhere without each other.

An idea, cold and slick with malice, snaked into my head. Goosebumps covered my arms.

I knew how to make sure Dmitri didn't go after Blake. An eye for an eye. But that was on the other side of a line I told myself not to cross. But if Dmitri killed Blake, I wouldn't survive.

I hung up the phone and tucked it back into my pocket. Anger bled into my muscles and strengthened my bones. I quickly made my way down the West Wing to avoid the guards seeing me. I ran up the tower to the top floor just in time to see Igorek head down the South Wing. I stayed hidden until I heard his door close.

Keeping away from the railing, I entered the South Wing and easily picked out which apartment was his. He had carved his Contestant number into the wood.

I don't remember walking down the hall. It felt as if I just appeared. I pounded my fist against the door.

"Who is it?" His voice came muffled through the wood.

"Housekeeping." I didn't recognize the smooth voice that passed my lips.

The door swung open. I stopped breathing as vengeance screamed through my veins. The last time we were face-to-face we were in the Second Trial. The dark part of my mind, the cold voice that demanded justice, took my moral compass and shoved it out of sight.

I planted my foot in Igorek's chest, shoving him deeper into the apartment. He dropped onto his back and skidded across the floor. I kicked the door shut behind me.

"What are you doing?" Pushing himself onto his elbows, Igorek tried to look brave by smiling at me.

"An eye for an eye."

His smile faltered. He struggled to get to his feet. His metal knee kept slipping against the hardwood.

Seeing him like that, vengeance crooned in my head. I stepped forward with my hands clenched tight.

68

Why Doesn't It Feel Like It?

Turning the handle, I stepped into my room.

"Hey." Michael rose from the couch. "I got your message."

The door clicked shut behind me. Stopping beside the kitchen counter, I set the knife down. Drawing my hand away, my fingertips streaked crimson across the countertop.

Where did I get the knife? It's not mine. Or one of Michael's.

Michael stared at the knife, frozen. Then his eyes snapped up, looking from the blood on my hands to the tear in my shirt collar. He tore apart my appearance looking for wounds or bruises.

When he found none, he locked eyes with me. "What did you do?"

"I stopped him." My voice sounded hollow. "I . . ." A slow breath escaped my lungs. "I made sure Dmitri won't go after Blake."

"What does that mean?"

The blood coating my fingers and hardening under my fingernails burned.

"Did you kill Dmitri Theodore?"

I shook my head. "He's at the Viewing."

"Then whose blood is this?" He pointed at the knife. "Charlie," he snapped, stepping closer. "*Whose blood is this?*"

"Igorek's." Saying his name out loud rocked me back on my heels. I looked at the blood painted across my skin.

"Holy shit." He shoved his hands into his hair. He didn't know where to look: the knife or my bloody hands. "What the hell were you thinking? I thought you dropped it."

A snarl rumbled deep in my chest. "Dropped it? Daniel was my—" I

470

took in a breath, stilling the tears rising in my eyes. *He wasn't yours. So, what was he?* "Dmitri walked right up to me and said to my face that he was going to kill my best friend. You can't expect me to *drop it.*"

"Charlie—"

"Isn't this what you've been training me for? For this . . . brutal kind of problem solving."

"This didn't solve anything!"

"Tell me. If Lawrence was standing *right here*, unarmed and on his knees, would you walk away or rip out his heart?" I hated that I asked, but we both knew the answer.

His mouth snapped shut. He didn't have to say anything. His eyes darkened to a shade beyond obsidian.

"Exactly. So, don't you dare tell me what to do when you would turn around and do the exact opposite."

"You won't like where this nightmare takes you."

"Why? Because I'll end up like you?"

Surprise hit him in the face.

I squeezed my eyes shut. The cold blood made my stomach roll. "Dmitri told me he would kill Blake because he knew I would have to sit behind a screen and just watch it happen. I couldn't just sit there knowing that. I saw a chance to finally save someone, so I took it."

"And it had nothing to do with you wanting to get back at him for what he did to Phillips?"

I opened my mouth to refute him, but I couldn't. A large part of me had gone to Igorek's room to protect Blake. But there was a small part that liked what it would do to Dmitri. He would feel the way I did after what happened to Daniel.

"I know what you're thinking better than anyone else," he said. "But just because you did it to protect someone, doesn't make what you did ok."

"I know." I looked up into his face. "I just didn't know what else to do. I can't lose him."

"Johnson is smart. He has Atlas backing him. Theodore would be a fool to go after him."

"You were my Guardian, and he went after me."

"He went after you because . . ." His eyes dropped to the scar on my cheek. He swiped the knife off the countertop and held it like the feeling of blood didn't bother him. "Take a shower and burn your clothes. You'll want to return to the dining room to your friend."

"Why?"

"You'll need an alibi for tomorrow." He shoved past me toward the door.

"Where are you going?"

"I'm going to stage Igorek's body. If Theodore's Guardian—a *School Master*—finds out you killed one of his students, he'll hit you with everything he's got. Depending on how big of a mess you made, I can make it look like his own son was ensuring his spot in the Top Seven."

"Why are you helping me?"

"I'm not. I'm cleaning up after you," he said tensely. "If you had waited until I got back, then I could've helped you."

"What would you have done?"

He stared forward, trying to find an answer. Finally, he shook his head. "I don't know." He yanked open the door. "But not this." Stepping into the hall, he slammed the door behind him.

Standing alone in the darkened room, the blood seemed to glow around my fingers. A dry heave rolled up my chest. The rancid blood turned my stomach to stone. I tried to breathe through my mouth, but then I could taste it.

I gagged again.

Running to the shower, I tore off my blood-splattered clothes and jumped under the hot spray. I scrubbed my skin until it was flushed and then dug under my nails. When the water ran clear and my skin ached, I dried off and dressed in sweats.

I gagged as I picked up the bloody clothes off the floor. The sounds Igorek made with each cut of the knife screamed through my head. Tossing the clothes into the fireplace, I turned to clean off the counter. I threw the bloody paper towels into the fire as well.

I stared into the flames until the evidence was ribbons of char.

I saved Blake.

Then why doesn't it feel like it?

My hands worried over each other like they were still searching for unwashed blood. Even though I had taken a shower, I felt grimy. Like there was a thick layer of grease covering my skin and dripping from my hair. My insides squirmed like they were transforming into maggots.

I saved Blake. I did it to keep him alive.

Then why does it feel like I traded my soul for it?

69

Wearing Red

For the first time, when I walked into the dining room, my eyes went straight for the head table without hesitation or dread. But now, I had to look past a new line of guards separating the stage from the rest of the room.

The table on display was in complete disarray with the news of a dead Contestant.

Not a single plate of food was touched. Chairs were pushed away from the table. Contestants and Guardians stood close to their School Masters in tight-lipped conversations.

Thiago lounged in his seat while his Guardian and School Master talked above him with frantic hand gestures. He watched the table warily, ignoring his breakfast. Tala and Emeka stood calmly, listening to their School Masters. On the opposite end of the table, Amelia dug her hands into her hair like she was seconds away from a panic attack.

Master Harlan was the only School Master who didn't seem bothered by the news. With a flippant hand gesture, he shrugged. *No big deal,* he seemed to say.

Atlas faced the room, his narrow hips leaning against the large table. His head was bent low toward his Contestant. His hand, tattooed with a curving spine, rested on the wand cinched low across his hips. Blake kept shooting glances over his shoulder at the dining room.

Guardian Moore stood over Clarence with the same cautious vigilance, while Clarence openly laughed at the distress of the surrounding Contestants. Master Lenin, shaking his head, descended from the stage.

Finally, my gaze turned to the far end of the table.

Dmitri sat stiffly in his seat. His muscles were tense like he was between jumping to his feet and marinating in shock. Anger and disbelief were etched into his face.

The coals in my chest ignited. The fire that drove me to Igorek's room licked up Dmitri's helplessness.

Guardian Theodore, flushed with anger, rose from his seat. Shoving his chair away from the table, he stormed down the steps, following Master Lenin from the room. He brushed past me without a glance.

Dmitri was exposed without his Guardian.

I pulled on my magic, letting it flood through me in a rushing wave of fire. Turning on my heel, I Ported onto the stage.

Amelia jumped when I suddenly appeared. Contestant Tala nearly spilled her drink. Blake's head snapped toward me.

Just before I could meet his gaze, I turned my back and leaned against the table toward Dmitri. "Morning."

"You don't belong here." Clarence's Guardian gave me only enough attention to show his displeasure. "Active Contestants only."

"I'm not here for you," I said over my shoulder without turning from Dmitri. "Igorek's dead."

"If you know what's good for you, you will leave." Dmitri crossed his arms. His eyes drilled into his uneaten breakfast. "Or I will throw you down the stairs."

"It almost sounds like you cared about him."

He bared his teeth. "What do you want?"

"I wanted to see how you were coping." My eyes dropped to his red sleeve. I remembered the first time I saw Dmitri's red sleeve: the rage, the horror. I wanted him to feel that.

I curled a lock of my hair around my finger. As I pulled it across my skin, I pushed magic into the hair. The lock bled a vibrant red, the same shade as his sleeve.

It took him only seconds to process what he saw.

His nostrils flared. He jerked to his feet, sending his chair flipping backward, clattering across the stage. The remaining Contestants turned their attention to us.

As soon as his feet were beneath him, he swung. Clumsy with rage, he threw his fist as hard as he could. Easily I ducked out of the way. With all his weight behind the swing, he threw himself down the stairs. He hit the bottom with a grunt. The guards jumped back in surprise.

Coolly, I walked down to meet him.

Dmitri jumped to his feet and grabbed me by the throat. He pulled me close, until we were almost nose-to-nose

"That is a proclamation of a kill," he snarled.

The emotions rolling off him fed the dragon inside me. I grinned up at him.

Breathing heavily, he shook his head. "Impossible. Igorek outweighed you in skill."

"I guess not." Magic surged down my arm as I grabbed his wrist. Fueled by my Royal status, I wrenched his grip from my throat.

He tried to grab me with his other hand, but I caught his wrist before he could. His arms shook as he used all his strength to fight my hold. But I had the higher status, more strength. My arms didn't budge.

"You can go after Blake," I hissed. "But that's only one piece of my heart. While you're locked in that Trial, I'll have access to everyone you've ever known."

"You don't know who's important to me."

"Are you sure? There's the obvious, your father. I'll start with him. Without a title, he's fair game, right?"

Fury roared across his face. A yell erupted from his mouth as he twisted out of my grip. He tore his wand from the holster at his side and pointed it at my face. Screaming, students jumped away, leaving a large circle around us.

The guards were no longer lining the stage. Now, they caged us in to protect the other students and School Masters.

A faint glow illuminated Dmitri's arm, and flowed toward his hand. Magic gleamed in his wand, shocking my forehead. I could see the ward swirling in his eyes. But my gaze never left his, daring him to try.

A wand crept into the edge of my vision and pressed against Dmitri's temple.

"Back the hell up," Blake said with a level tone. "Right now."

On the other side of Dmitri, Thiago was doing the same. His wand was bright with waiting magic.

Dmitri's eyes flickered toward the two Trial Contestants. He reminded me of a bull pinned tightly in a paddock.

The dining room doors burst open with a slam.

"Lower your wands this instant." Master Lenin's voice cracked across the room. Never had I heard his voice supported by so much power. Students cleared a path for the School Master.

"I'm not putting down my wand until this bastard does." Blake nodded his head toward Dmitri.

"Contestant Nineteen. Lower your wand." Master Lenin punctuated each word with a sharp commanding tone. "You will do so now, or you will be removed from The Trial."

"Dmitri. Do what he says," Guardian Theodore gruffly told his son. I didn't dare turn my eyes from the one holding a wand to my forehead to see where the two Masters stood.

"Your daddy gave you an order," Thiago taunted.

He never got to make the decision. With a flurry of leather and a flash of black, Atlas was beside him. His tattooed hands grabbed Dmitri's wrist and tucked it under his arm, pointing the wand at the floor.

Dmitri's ward blasted from the tip, cracking the black stone. The watching students screamed and jumped back.

Atlas twisted Dmitri's arm behind his back and wrenched the wand from his grip. Planting his boot against the base of his spine, he shoved him forward.

Contestant Nineteen spun toward the Hunter, eyes wide with fury.

Atlas met the heated look with a smirk. "Please, try something and make a fool of yourself. I dare you."

Master Lenin stepped between them and snatched the Contestant's wand from the Hunter.

"I want the four of you in my office right now." Master Lenin turned and addressed the whispering dining room. "The rest of you can finish your breakfast and make your way to class."

I followed Master Lenin toward the stairs. When I passed Guardian Theodore, his eyes landed on my hair. His nostrils flared.

As we exited the dining room, leaving behind the gawking, curious crowd of students, two sets of guards followed. Two stuck close to me and the other two walked with Dmitri.

Atlas fell in step with me. "Anything I should know about?" he mumbled.

I didn't answer.

"I can't help if you don't talk to me."

"What makes you think I need your help?"

"Other than the obvious?" He looked over his shoulder at the silent Russian duo stalking us down the stairs. "You've bitten off more than you can chew."

"Thanks for the heads up." I stepped in front of him and into Master Lenin's office.

70

Alibis and Lies

"Sit." Master Lenin stormed across the room and stopped behind his desk.

I took the seat closest to the door. I didn't take my eyes off the School Master as the others filed in. Blake and Thiago took the seats in the middle, leaving one seat on the other side of the room open for Dmitri.

Guardian Theodore joined the School Master behind the desk. His thick arms crossed over his chest, making his muscles bulge under his tight sweater. Thiago's Guardian and Atlas stood behind their Contestant's chairs while the guards fanned out behind us.

"Does anyone care to explain?" Master Lenin was too strung out to sit himself. Instead, he pushed aside his suit jacket and slid his hands into his pockets.

Dmitri didn't hesitate. "That Low Common bitch killed Igorek."

Atlas sucked in a breath through his teeth, hissing in disapproval.

Master Lenin's eyebrows shot toward his hairline. "That's quite the accusation."

"That's what I said." I leaned back, acting indifferent.

"Don't lie!" Dmitri yelled as he jumped to his feet. "She killed him! She said it!"

"Those words never came out of my mouth," I said dryly, meeting his glare.

His hands curled into fists when he realized I was right. "You little—"

"Contestant Theodore, sit down," Master Lenin snapped.

"I can help you if you're having trouble." Atlas patted the hilt of his wand.

A deep flush darkened Dmitri's face. Breathing hard, he dropped into the chair and buried his hands in his blue hair.

"Where were you last night?" Guardian Theodore watched me closely. His eyes lingered on my hands like he could see the blood.

"She wasn't at the Viewing," Dmitri blurted.

My stomach dropped.

"Contestant Theodore, when I want you to speak, I will ask you a direct question." Master Lenin turned to his Guardian. Despite being a good head shorter, Master Lenin didn't back down from the harsh glare. "Konstantin, let me—"

"Let her answer," Guardian Theodore interrupted. "That's the least this Common can do."

"She was with me." Blake's face contorted as loyalty and honesty raged against each other. "At the Viewing."

"I saw her leave," Dmitri snarled. "It was moments before Igorek left for the night."

"Where did you go?" Guardian Theodore stressed.

"The bathroom," I said flippantly. "I wasn't feeling well after watching some of the First Trials."

"Did anyone see you?"

"I did," Thiago said, raising his hand. "We chatted a bit by the bathrooms. I was lamenting that the Top Seven lacks any real personality." His Guardian bent to whisper in his ear. Thiago waved her away.

"What?" Dmitri turned in his seat to look at the other Guardian. "Speak!"

Thiago's Guardian spoke without missing a beat. "What he said is true."

Dmitri's face was bright red. "Liars. All of you!" He spun toward the Irish Hunter. "You can find the truth. You can see into their memories of that night."

My heart skipped.

Atlas shook his head. "Doing that would imply that I don't believe them."

"I thought Hunters were supposed to be impartial," Guardian Theodore spat.

Atlas swung his gaze toward the accusing Trial member. "You clearly don't know anything about me. I trust my Contestant to tell the truth."

Blake's gaze grew hard. His eyes looked more like foaming toxic waste than their usual cheerful green.

"Besides," Atlas continued. "After the Viewing last night, any student who was fond of Contestant Phillips has a motive to stab your pal to the wall."

Cheese and rice, that's what Michael did when he left my room last night. He stabbed Igorek to a wall?

"Present company included," Thiago said dully. "The only reason you're still alive is because of that tattoo."

"Are you saying you did it?" Guardian Theodore directed all his anger to Contestant Seventeen.

Thiago remained unfazed. "No, but I admire whoever did."

"There will be none of that," Master Lenin jumped in before someone started swinging. "Contestant Theodore, I understand that you're distraught after losing your friend, but that doesn't mean you can pull your wand on one of *my* students."

"My son makes a valid case, Henry." Guardian Theodore sneered down at me. "She is wearing red. That says she made a kill."

"That might be true at your school, but here it's just fashion," Master Lenin said. "She had it last year."

"She's had it for longer," Blake added stiffly. "We dyed it together when she was sixteen."

"Do you expect me to believe it's a coincidence she chose to dye it the day we learn one of my students was killed?" Guardian Theodore roared.

Master Lenin nodded. "Yes, I do."

Guilt slammed into my gut.

"Why are you so reluctant to question her?"

Master Lenin turned to face him head on. "Because she's not the one I want to question. We can discuss this later." Master Lenin turned to the three of us. "You are dismissed."

"She's not going anywhere." Guardian Theodore pointed at me with a beefy finger.

Master Lenin's lips thinned with irritation. "She's not a suspect here. Your son is."

His fellow Master balked in surprise.

"Mr. Len was found in his room, stabbed to the wall by one of your son's knives."

My eyebrows shot up. *That's a gruesome touch, Michael.*

Dmitri's face paled with a look of horror. "What?"

Guardian Theodore was equally wide-eyed. "He's the son of a School Master. He would not be so foolish."

"Well, obviously, someone was. A student has been killed in my school, and I intend to figure out who did it."

"I am his School Master. I will not tolerate—"

"Actually, you're not," Master Lenin raised his voice over the fuming man. "You revoked that title when you agreed to be his Guardian. And that's all you are for the moment." Without looking at us, Master Lenin went on, "The three of you are dismissed. Contestant Theodore, I was going to talk to you after breakfast, but since you're here, we might as well do it now. Guardian Theodore, you also may leave."

Dmitri turned his horrified gaze my way. The moment our eyes locked, his anger transformed into something else entirely. If I thought he was pissed before, now he had reached volcanic status.

I rose from my seat, tapping the skin beneath my eye. *An eye for an eye, asshole.* I spun toward the door before I could see his reaction. Blake didn't say anything or look at me as he stood. It was like he was trying to burn a hole in the floor.

Guardian Theodore began yelling as soon as we passed through the door. The three of us, followed by Atlas and Thiago's Guardian, walked in silence as his voice echoed after us.

When we reached the main staircase, Blake grabbed my arm. "Atlas, I'll see you tonight in the training room."

The Hunter looked between the two of us. His tattooed hand tapped the side of his thigh as his whiskey-colored eyes settled on me.

With a shrug, he stepped back toward the center of the school. "See you tonight." Pulling on his magic, he Ported. Thiago nodded to his Guardian, and she left too.

"I need to get to class." I stepped onto the first stair. "Unlike you guys, my grades are my main focus."

"Charlie, stop." Blake rocked his jaw from side to side as he carefully formulated his question. "Last night. When you left. Where did you go?"

Spinning on the stair, I faced him with a blank expression. "I went to throw up and take a shower."

Slowly, he started shaking his head. "Why do I have a feeling that you're lying to me?"

"Blake . . ." My stomach hardened. "Don't."

"I need to hear you say it." Closing his eyes, he said, "I just lied to two School Masters and my Guardian for you." When he opened his eyes, his gaze was heartbroken. "I want to know what for."

But I couldn't say it. I couldn't admit my darkest sin to my best friend. But the silence was just as loud as if I screamed my crime at the top of my lungs.

Blake stumbled back. "That asshole was right? You killed him?"

"Don't act so surprised." Thiago leaned casually against the railing. "The bastard was practically begging for it."

I rounded on the other Contestant. "Why are you here?" I snapped.

"Who bloody cares why he's here?" Blake's voice bounced across the black stone. "What happened? Did he go after you?"

My eyes narrowed at him. "You need to stay out of this. Both of you."

Thiago shook his head. "Whether you like it or not, we're a part of it now."

"This is between me and Dmitri."

"You can't seriously think you can do this alone," Thiago scoffed.

"I intend to."

"Bloody hell, Charlie." Blake looked like he was going to be sick. "What have you done?"

"As far as you know, nothing. And it will stay that way." Before they could protest further, I started up the stairs. With each step, regret knocked into my stomach like an iron fist.

When I stepped into my first class, whispers rolled through the room. In the front row, Emeka regarded me with cool, suspicious eyes. I took my usual seat and kept my eyes glued to the chalkboard.

A University student rose from the front row and lumbered up the steps. Her beady eyes latched onto me as she turned down the row and headed for the empty seat beside me.

I took my wand from the pocket along the side of my jeans and set it on the desk beside my textbooks.

Her gait slowed. She grabbed the back of a chair and dumped the student sitting in it on the floor. Shoving his books off the desk, she took his spot. The frazzled student collected his things and took the spot beside me.

When the class was over, I rose to my feet. The University student did the same.

Shit.

Pulling on my magic, I Ported to my next class. This was the pattern for the rest of the day. My nerves were strung as tight as barbed wire as I tracked each University student throughout each class. Porting in and out of the classrooms minimized my interactions with them, but I knew it was only a matter of time before one of them gathered enough courage to approach me even with my wand drawn.

At my last class of the day for the Laws and Boundaries of Magic, I stepped through the doorway and scanned the first row. It was the only class I shared with Dmitri that day. If anything was going to happen, it would be there.

But Dmitri's seat was empty.

Weird. I had never seen him miss a class.

As I sat down, I couldn't shake the feeling that something was wrong. I pulled out my books, looking around the room for the source of the uneasiness. I leaned back in my chair when it clicked. I was sandwiched between two empty seats. Blake wasn't here either.

My eyes snapped to the door. I tracked every student who came through. None of them sported a grey beanie. Nervousness attacked my gut. I barely had enough sanity to smile at Cornelia as she sat beside me.

Anna strutted into the room. When she saw me, her bright red lips stretched into a flirty smile. "There she is."

She walked up the stairs toward me. "The most talked about non-Contestant in the school." She leaned forward against the table. Catcalls echoed through the room. "So, did you do it? Did you kill him?"

"Anna," I said dryly. "A pleasure as always. How's your leg?" I asked, referring to the Second Trial when I stabbed her.

She ignored me. "Blink once if you did it and twice if you didn't."

I stared back.

"I think that means no." Cornelia pulled out her textbook and dropped it to the table with a *thump*.

"I wasn't talking to you," Anna said, giving Cornelia's status pin a mocking look.

"Don't be an ass." I took out my books. "Have you seen Blake?"

Anna sighed. "Do I look like his mother?"

I turned to Cornelia. "Have you?"

Shaking her head, her bright curls bounced around her shoulders. "Not since my last timeblock with Mr. Carter."

That was over an hour ago.

The teacher, Miss. Hoehn, got to the front of the classroom and waved her wand. As the door swung shut, she told everyone to take their seats.

Anna sighed dramatically and sat down.

I kept looking at the door, expecting Blake to bounce in with apologies. The deeper into class we got, the tighter the knot in my stomach clenched.

Where is he? Blake never missed a class.

Finally, the door opened.

My heart dropped. It wasn't Blake, but Master Lenin's secretary, Tessa Baker. Worry doused me like a cold bucket of water.

"My apologies, Miss Hoehn. Master Lenin wants Miss Clarkson and Miss Heart to meet him in the infirmary."

My heart stopped in my chest.

They wouldn't call Anna, a past European Academy Contestant, to the infirmary if something hadn't happened to the active Contestant.

Something had happened to Blake.

71

What Kind of Bullshit Logic is That?

Throwing open my bag, I shoved my books inside.

The large textbook snagged on the lip of the zipper and clattered to the floor. I cursed and picked it up, only to drop it again.

"I got it. Go." Cornelia grabbed my books and gave me a reassuring smile.

I didn't hesitate. I stood up and pushed past all the students in my way. I was in such a hurry, I almost tripped down the stairs.

Anna took her sweet time collecting her things. Meanwhile, my mind raced. If Dmitri touched him, I was going to peel the skin from his body. I didn't care who was around.

Anna finally got to her feet and made her way over. In her tall heels, she was slower than a dying turtle.

Screw this.

Shoving through the door, I sprinted down the hall and through the stairwell. I threw open the gold doors to the infirmary, praying to whoever was listening that Blake wasn't there.

My eyes flew around the room and landed on the only occupied bed. My heart squeezed painfully in my chest.

No. Please, no.

I skidded to a stop at the foot of the bed. The boy laying on his back was badly beaten. His face was swollen and bright purple. He was almost unrecognizable.

Anger poured through my veins with a new vengeance. I turned, intending to tear the school apart until I found Dmitri. But my attention snagged on Blake's sweater. On the left side was a gold compass with an owl perched on top. It was the insignia for The Magisterium of Magic.

I leaned closer to his face. Under the bruised and swollen skin, a smooth strip of skin split through one of his eyebrows. A scar.

Clarence?

As my anger cooled, the red in my vision cleared, allowing me to see there were other people in the room. Across from where Clarence laid unconscious, was Blake.

He sat with slouched shoulders as Helen carefully dabbed a potion on his bruising face. His suit was torn and stained with blood. One of his eyes was swollen shut. Gashes marred his cheeks and hands.

In front of him were Master Lenin and Master Harlan. My Master wasn't pleased that he was seeing me twice in one day. The other School Master nodded to me when he met my gaze.

Beside them were Atlas and Brandon Moore. Atlas, taking after Michael, kept his emotions on lockdown. He stared down at Blake as if he were a park bench. Brandon, on the other hand, looked like he was on the verge of flipping tables.

But I didn't care about any of them. I blinked and was in front of Blake. I didn't know if I ran over or if I Ported. "My God, Blake . . . what happened?"

"I got in a row with him." He jerked his blood-splattered hand toward Clarence.

"About what?" Blake hardly got into an argument with anyone, and when he did, he certainly didn't beat the shit out of them. He usually just fumed.

"Just Trial stuff. Nothing to worry your pretty head over." He gave me a crooked smile. His split lip gaped and leaked blood down his chin.

"It looks like you tried to kill each other."

"Nah. He couldn't hit hard enough for that."

"You son of a bitch." Guardian Moore jumped toward the Trial Contestant.

Before Atlas could move, Master Harlan slid between them.

"Remember your place, Guardian Moore," the School Master said stiffly.

"Wake him up, you little shit," Guardian Moore snapped over Master Harlan's shoulder.

Wake him up? Confused, I turned back to Blake. The golden doors opened, letting in Tessa Baker and Anna.

All the blood drained from Anna's face when she saw Blake. Her pale complexion made her bright lipstick look more orange than red. "What happened to you?"

"Apparently, he beat the hell out of Clarence," I said, crossing my arms.

Her perfectly sculpted eyebrows bolted under her bangs. "Contestant Fourteen? Why would you do that?"

He shrugged.

"You don't know?" Master Harlan spit out. "Damn you, Johnson. What are you playing at?"

"Nothing!" Blake was full-on glaring at the man. "He provoked me."

"You beat the shit out of him, and then put him into a magically in-duced coma," Atlas said dryly.

"He did more than that," Guardian Moore snarled. "My Contestant is unrecognizable."

"Blake. What did you do?" I asked.

He rolled his eyes like I was overreacting. "I made him take a nap. I don't see why everyone has their knickers in a twist."

"You're messing with The Trial. You put an active Contestant into an induced coma. This is the last time I will ask. If you do not undo this, I'll have you expelled," Master Harlan said.

Blake smirked. "Go right ahead. I bet the world would love to hear you expelled an active Contestant."

"Wake him up," Guardian Moore repeated harshly.

"I'll wake him up as soon as the Final Trial is over, or if I die, the en-chantment will break. He doesn't deserve to be in the Top Seven."

Guardian Moore stepped forward with fire in his eyes.

Atlas calmly took hold of his arm before he could take more than a step. "Please give me a reason to break your jaw."

Guardian Moore ripped his arm from Atlas's grasp. Crossing his arms, he continued to glare down at Blake. For a Hunter, his glare was lacking . . . but that was probably because I spent so much time with Michael.

Master Harlan turned to Atlas. "Will you convince him to give up this lunacy?"

Atlas shook his head, causing his earring to rock back and forth. "If he won't listen to two Masters, what makes you think he'll listen to me?"

"You're not even going to try?" Guardian Moore sputtered.

"This kid is as stubborn as my old man with a bottle of gin." Atlas shrugged. "He's made up his mind. I can't change it."

Master Lenin shook his head. "Then you leave me no choice but to expel you both from The Trial." He turned to Anna. "Miss Clarkson, will you take Contestant Johnson's place in the Top Seven?"

"Oh, hell no." Her heeled shoes clicked against the stone as she took a large step away from the bed. "I'm good with two Trials and a new tattoo."

"Miss Clarkson—"

"Oh, quit badgering her. She said no. Looks like you're stuck with me. Or you can continue without a Contestant for the Academy." Blake smirked. The smile instantly dropped when Helen smoothed the yellow potion over his cut cheek.

Anger tinted Master Lenin's cheeks. As his fingers kneaded his forehead, he slowly shook his head. Reluctantly, he conceded. "Fine. Then it seems I have no other choice. Since The Magisterium of Magic Contestant is unable to participate, and Mr. Phillips is no longer with us, Miss Heart will take Contestant Hardy's place in the Top Seven."

I spun around so fast, my feet almost slipped out beneath me. *Did I hear him right?* His expression was completely serious.

Atlas took out his phone and retreated from the bed. Turning his back to us, he quietly conversed with whoever was on the other line.

"What kind of bullshit logic is that?" Guardian Moore gasped.

"It's the rules," Master Harlan said slowly. "If, for any reason, the active Contestant is not fit to participate in an upcoming Trial, one of the remaining Contestants can be chosen to take their place."

"My Contestant could participate if someone punished this fucking Common and forced him to wake Clarence up," Guardian Moore fumed, gesturing briskly to Blake.

"And how would we do that?" Master Harlan asked. "That tattoo protects him from any of us touching him."

"For you, but not for me," Guardian Moore snarled.

I shifted closer to Blake.

"And by doing that, you would be breaking your contract. You would be thrown out of The Trial, as would your Contestant."

"If you forfeit, I'll wake him up right now," Blake offered.

Master Harlan cut to him with a look of silent fury. Very plainly, his expression told Blake to *shut up*.

Slowly, I turned to my best friend. "What the hell, Blake?"

"You started it," he said.

"She can't play," Guardian Moore pressed. "If you dug up Daniel Phillips' corpse, you would have a better performance."

"Show some goddamn respect," Master Harlan snapped.

"Who cares?" Guardian Moore responded with the same amount of venom. "He wasn't even your Contestant."

"He was my son," Master Harlan snarled. The lights of the infirmary shrunk as his anger grew. "Show some respect, or I'll strip you of every title you have."

Guardian Moore's cheeks grew brighter under the humiliation. I had never seen a Hunter showcase so much emotion.

"Miss Heart. I need an answer. Do you accept?"

I pulled my eyes from Blake to Master Lenin.

I nodded. "I do."

This wasn't about a title. This wasn't about running from Master Lenin and Michael. If I was in The Trial, I could personally make sure Dmitri never came within a mile of Blake. I wouldn't have to sit on the sidelines. I could protect him. I could save him.

"This is bullshit!" Guardian Moore turned on his heel. He kicked open the doors and stormed from the infirmary.

Master Lenin didn't even grace him with a glance. "I'll announce it to the rest of the school. You'll have to re-sign the Contestant Contract and reselect a Guardian." He shook his head. "Contestant Johnson, I really hope you know what you're doing."

He stormed from the room, followed by one royally pissed off Master Harlan. Their harsh, whispered conversation hissed back to us until the doors closed on them.

In their wake, Anna shook her head. "I don't know what you two are doing, but I don't want any part of it."

"Good." Blake stiffly nodded toward the hallway. "There's the door."

Without needing another invitation, her pointed shoes clicked loudly across the stone until the gold doors swung shut behind her.

Having finished his phone call, Atlas came back to his Contestant with crossed arms. "What's the verdict, Helen?"

"He'll live," she said tightly. "He'll be sore, but it shouldn't hinder him after a good night's sleep. I had to reset his nose and fuse a couple of his fingers back together."

"I guess it's a good thing I have one less finger. Less work for you," Blake chuckled weakly.

Helen, with lips pinched tight, kept dabbing his face with potions. "It's a miracle you didn't break anything important."

Atlas inspected Blake's injuries. Unwinding his arms, he smacked the back of Blake's head. "I see stupid shit every day, but this might top the list."

Blake clenched his jaw and stared at the floor.

"Bloody hell, mate. If you were going to beat the wanker, you should've punched him like I showed you. We'll have to lose a couple days of training to make sure your fingers heal properly."

"Guardian Atlas, I don't think that's what you should be reprimanding him on," Helen said with a cold tone of disapproval.

"Why? It was a brilliant move. It was reckless and about fifty kinds of stupid, but it was brilliant." His phone chimed in his pocket. Quickly glancing at the screen, he backed toward the doors. "Do I need to know anything or be scolded about anything else?"

Helen shook her head.

Atlas spun around and headed for the door. "I'm going to see what Lenin is saying to the school. Johnson, when you're all good, I'll see you in there."

As the doors closed behind him, Helen muttered, "Damn Hunters."

Without his Guardian present, Blake slouched forward. He closed his eyes for a brief moment, letting the full force of his pain roll through him.

"What were you thinking, Blake?" I asked quietly.

"Don't even start." He spat a wad of blood from his mouth. "It was the only thing I could think of that would keep you from getting yourself killed."

"I told you to stay out of it."

"Like hell I was just going to sit by. I heard a group of University students talking about how they were going to corner you tonight."

My stomach dropped at the thought.

"I should be asking you what *you* were thinking. Was this because of Daniel?"

My teeth ground together. I had kept the thoughts in my head for so long that, as the words came out of my mouth, it felt wrong. "It was at first, but then he threatened to kill you in the Final Trial."

He didn't seem nearly as concerned as he should have about that fact. "So you killed his best friend? You declared war on his entire school!"

"I can handle it."

He shook his head. "You're a Common, Charlie. They will crush you."

"Not anymore, thanks to you." My hands curled into fists. "I had everything under control."

He rolled his eyes. "What you were doing was a suicide mission. Once you're an active Contestant, that tattoo protects you from anyone outside The Trial. Dmitri can still try something, but at least it's not his whole goddamn school."

"I can—"

"If you say you can handle yourself one more time, I'm going to put my fist through a wall."

"Enough," Helen called over our arguing. She yanked off her gloves and tossed them into a nearby wastebasket. "Contestant Johnson, you can wash this off in three minutes. Miss Heart, you need to be in the dining room when Master Lenin makes the announcement of your reinstatement."

She collected the potion bottles on a tray and rose to her feet. "If I were either of you, I wouldn't repeat any of this conversation. I'll do my best to forget it." Taking her tray, she headed for the back office.

Blake and I regarded each other for a second. The only time I had seen his eyes that hard and that cold was when he was looking at my foster dad, Denny.

Shaking his head, he looked at the patch of black stone between his shoes.

I stormed out of the room. As I passed through the center of the school, under the gleaming staircases, I heard Master Lenin's voice boom through the doors. The guards watched me warily.

You can do this, I chanted, as I slipped into the dining room.

72

Welcome to the Top Seven

"Contestant Hardy is unable to participate in the Final Trial. That leaves one remaining Magisterium of Magic Contestant. Ah, there she is."

My heart seized when Master Lenin nodded to me from the stage. A rumble rolled through the room as every student twisted toward me. My hands trembled as I made my way around tables to the stage.

"Miss Heart has agreed to take Contestant Hardy's place in the Top Seven."

Yells of outrage erupted from the University students. Others were shaking their heads in disbelief. Overall, everyone was wondering what was going on. School Masters broke away from the high table.

"She cannot rejoin The Trial under these circumstances!" Master Aluna of Lions of Magic snapped, gesturing angrily toward me.

"Why not? I think it shows initiative and resourcefulness," Master Harlan replied.

"She *killed* another Contestant," Master Han of Serpentine stressed.

"So did Contestant Theodore," Master Harlan countered.

"She did it outside of The Trial."

"According to the evidence, Contestant Nineteen was the offender," Master Loran of the Magical Academy interjected.

"It was not my son!" Master Theodore's voice boomed around the room.

The School Masters weren't the only ones with things to say. As I walked through the crowded dining room, the mixture of whispers blended from astonished students.

"Did you hear what she did to Clarence?"

"He's barely hanging on."

"I had no idea she was so ruthless."

"The Trial always brings out the worst in its Contestants."

Dmitri blocked my way up the stairs. "You're not signing that contract. I will not allow you to pervert this Trial."

"You're doing that just fine on your own." I stepped onto the first stair.

He sprang forward faster than a bullet. But before he could move more than a few steps, two guards rushed up to intercept him. Each took an arm and pulled him up the stairs, away from me.

"Contestant Theodore!" Master Lenin gasped. "Control yourself! We have no choice but to accept Miss Heart back as a Contestant. Another outburst like that and I will remove you from The Trial."

"Release my son. Now!" Guardian Theodore bellowed at the guards. "Henry, when Master Hart hears about this—"

Master Lenin quickly shut him down. "He will have to deal with it. I'll admit, I don't like the way this turned out, but the Contestant Contract says, 'if *any* Contestant cannot participate, a remaining Contestant *must* be chosen.'" He took the contract out of his suit pocket and handed it to me. "So, Miss Heart will participate."

"As much as I hate to admit it, I agree with Master Theodore," Master Han asserted.

"Guardian Theodore," Master Lenin corrected firmly.

"Why can she not play?" Master Finch narrowed his eyes. "She is more capable than the other Contestant."

"This is no time to be childish." Master Loran walked over to Master Lenin and took the scroll from his grasp. "These rules have governed The Trial for centuries. We cannot break them. She plays."

Guardian Theodore sneered down at him. "Don't tell me what to do, Common."

I stepped around Guardian Theodore and took the scroll from Master Loran. I quickly pulled it open and grabbed the pen that rolled out of it. Before anyone could stop me, I slashed open the tip of my thumb and smeared a thick line of blood on the dotted line.

The tattoo on my wrist refilled to its original deep black. I was surprised to find I missed seeing it like that.

Guardian Theodore turned to Master Lenin. "Undo this. We cannot afford to put the likes of her in the Top Seven."

Master Lenin actually shrugged. "There is nothing I can do now. She plays."

Guardian Theodore dropped his voice, making his accent as harsh as sandpaper. "I hope you know you're sending her to a coffin. My son will kill her like he killed your other pathetic Contestant."

Anger moved me like a puppet. Before I could think, my fist connected with his nose. The bone gave way under my knuckles. Blood sprayed across my hand.

I moved to strike again, but a guard yanked me back. I twisted out of his grip, but found another guard in my way.

Guardian Theodore cursed in Russian. Blood sprayed from his nose. "I'll have your head for this!" Two guards stepped in front of him, just in case he tried.

If the guards weren't in my way, I would've been on top of him. "You can't touch me." I lifted my wrist, exposing my blackened tattoo.

He grinned. The blood colored his teeth with a yellow that unsettled my stomach. "Just wait. I always get what I want, and you're at the top of my list."

"Enough!" Master Lenin took in a sharp breath. "Guardian Theodore, control yourself, or I will remove you from The Trial staff and your son can choose another Guardian." Before the other man could retort, Master Lenin turned to me. "Contestant Heart, you may pick a Guardian—"

"I choose Master Kale," I said.

"And I accept."

I spun around and found my Master Hunter cutting through the center of the dining room. My stomach dropped at his expression. His eyes were the equivalent to steel as they bore into mine. With proud strides, he advanced toward the stage.

He's going to think I did this.

"Then welcome to the Top Seven, Contestant Heart," Master Lenin said with finality.

Outbursts of rage echoed through the room but I couldn't have cared less. I trotted down the stairs toward my Guardian.

When I approached, I held out my hand. "Pleasure to see you again, Master Kale."

He clasped my forearm harder than usual. "And you, Contestant Heart. If you don't mind, we have a lot to talk about."

"Lead the way."

With a stiff nod directed toward the Masters, he grabbed my arm and Ported us up to my room. Before I could take a breath, he spun me against the wall. My skull knocked into the bricks.

"*What the hell have you done?*" he yelled. "You couldn't just settle for what you did last night. You had to beat Clarence Hardy out of The Trial?"

"I didn't!"

"And why should I believe you? After what I saw last night, anything is possible!"

"Because I'm telling you I didn't!"

"And you expect me to believe that? Holy shit, Charlie, after *everything*, I'm finding it pretty damn hard to trust you."

I was surprised by the sting his words caused. Taking a deep breath, I took a moment to calm myself. The flickering lights settled a bit. "I'm not lying. You can ask Blake."

"How do I know you didn't ask Johnson to put Hardy into a coma?"

"You think I would ask my best friend to put himself in harm's way? Blake did that on his own."

Shaking his head, he started to look away but his gaze snagged on my red streak. He stepped back and cracked the muscles in his neck. "Johnson made the right call. Right now, that tattoo," he pointed to the fresh ink on my wrist, "is the only thing keeping you alive."

"I can take care of myself."

"Really? Theodore would've cornered you tonight or some other night when you were alone with a handful of his friends, and they would have torn you apart. And he would've gotten away with it. But now, the Contestant Contract stands between you two, and there's no way he'll jeopardize his standing with the Masters." His lips pulled away from his teeth. "Johnson saved your life. Until the Final Trial, anyway."

"He did it in the worst way possible."

"Only because you did the worst thing possible!" he barked.

"At least I didn't stab Igorek to the wall," I snapped, referring to how he staged Igorek's body with Dmitri's knife.

"No, you just slit his throat."

Silence flooded the room. His breathing was forced and deep with anger. He refused to look at me. Instead, his gaze was locked on my shoes.

Logical thought began to creep around the outskirts of my mind. For a split second, I started to process exactly what I had done. Just as my stomach started to churn, I quickly pushed it from my mind.

"So, what's next?"

He leaned against the back of the couch. "Your first two Trials will be released to the public. Since tomorrow is Saturday, you and I are going to sit down and watch the performances you missed while you ran around the school with a knife."

How does he make everything I do sound so childish without even trying?

"Next week, there's a party for the Top Seven. You can bring a date. Preferably a Royal."

My heart dipped. The person I instantly thought of was the one person who wasn't here.

"All the Masters will be there, so maybe you can make up for ditching them last time by playing nice. Lawrence will announce the theme of The Trial and the theme of the Award Challenge.

"From what I remember of the last Trial, they won't have training room separators. That means that while we're training, everyone can see what everyone else is learning. Pay attention and see what the other Contestants' strengths are.

"I can already tell you, the Aquarius Contestant is the weakest out of the seven, but that doesn't mean she's not dangerous." He crossed his arms and his jaw clenched.

Once more we were surrounded by silence. We held each other's gaze. I could practically see all the words he wanted to say fighting to escape his lips. He remained silent, however, looking at me as if he didn't know who I was.

A dull throb emanated from deep within my knuckles. My hand called for attention. I shot a quick glance at the throbbing appendage. My knuckles were bright red.

"How's your hand?" His voice had lost its edge. Now he just sounded exhausted.

I covered it from view. "I've had worse."

"You broke the bastard's nose."

"You saw?"

He nodded. "Atlas told me Lenin was reinstating you into The Trial. I knew shit was going to hit the fan, so I came as soon as I could." He paused. "Your punches have significantly improved."

"Thanks."

Looking away, he shoved a hand into one of the pockets of his jacket. He pulled out a purple jewelry box and wrenched it open.

"Here." With a flash of silver, he tossed something at me.

I caught it before it could hit me in the throat. Unwrapping my fingers, I found a silver ring. The band was made of three distinct strands braided around each other.

"It's another sync ring. Next time you think of slitting someone's throat, tap that to give me a heads-up," he snapped.

Biting the tip of my tongue, I worked the silver band around my thumb.

73

The Third Trial Party

After dinner, I dressed in all black.

My stomach was strung tight as I stepped into the training room. The walls that separated our individual rooms were gone, leaving the space open and exposed. No matter where anyone stood, they could see whatever or whoever they wanted.

Some Contestants were already there, depending on class schedules. Blake was warming up in his corner of the room. Atlas almost got decked because his eyes rested on me for too long.

The other Contestants did the same. Apprehension and interest narrowed their eyes as I left the doorway to join Michael.

Dmitri and Tala didn't look impressed in the least. In their eyes, I was a month behind in my training. Little did they know, I had been working every night.

As I stepped into my padded area, Michael didn't wait for me to draw another breath before he tossed me my wand. Then, we jumped in head-first.

Everything he taught me was for the purpose of inflicting harm. He told me to be harder and faster with each ward and punch. Nerves would've made my hands clumsy, but instinct kept me from showing it.

That was only half of my evening. The other half was scouting the competition. Every time I went for a sip of water or took a minute to breathe, I glanced around the room.

Atlas had transformed my best friend. The boy who once hated to hit anything was punching his way through sandbags. He handled his wand with the same grace and sharpness as his teacher.

Emeka was a different person with a weapon in his hand. Outside the training room, he was poised and collected. Here, he struck quickly and with force that sent a clap across the room.

The Aquarius Contestant, Amelia, was the weakest. She took too many breaks, and often didn't put enough force behind her strikes. However, that didn't mean she wasn't a threat. She could move without making a sound, and when she did use magic, it was simple but accurate.

Tala, from The Magical Academy of the Earth, had refined her movements. Like a spider, she drew you in only to cut you into pieces. It was enchanting and frightening all at once.

Thiago was always watching. Every time I glanced at his station, our eyes connected. I wondered if he trained at all or if he just stood there. The training I did witness consisted of blunt, short jabs. His movements were so subtle; it was like he hadn't moved until you found a dart in your neck.

Dmitri was the complete opposite. Constant shouts and clatter came from his corner of the room. His magic boomed and vibrated the floor. His muscles were exposed and gleaming with oil, so there was no way anyone could miss them. He was trying to scare, and it worked on some.

The next week flew by in an indistinguishable loop: meals, classes, heavy training, war lessons, and then sleep. Finally, the time for the final theme arrived.

"Are you good?" Michael stood in my doorway, dressed for the party. He wore an all black suit. Leather accented the collar of the jacket, the lip of the pocket square, and the cuffs of the sleeves. A slim tie hung down his chest. His rich black hair was combed and simply styled.

The hardness of his gaze, which he had whenever he looked at me these days, was accentuated by the sharp outfit.

"Yep." I turned back to the mirror so I wasn't staring. *Why am I blushing?* "Are you leaving already?"

His collar rustled as he nodded. "I have to pick up my date. So, I'll meet you there."

Another thing that was different about tonight was that we could bring a date.

"*Don't,*" he stressed, "be late."

I pinned a glittering earring in place. "Yes, because I'd hate to miss all the fun."

"I'm serious. Tonight is important. Since you missed the last chance to meet the Masters, you have a lot of catching up to do. Everyone else has already made acquaintances."

I almost tricked myself into forgetting that Daniel and I had ditched the last party. We were supposed to meet with Masters of all trades and convince them that, out of the two remaining Contestants, we were the ones worth voting on. Now it was just me.

"So, if you're late, I'll hunt you down and drag you through the door."

"I'll be there," I assured him, pinning the matching earring.

"I'll believe it when I see it." He tossed a transporter onto the bed. Pushing away from the door frame, he headed for the door. A fragrant trail of sage followed after him. With a rush of magic, the lights flickered as he Ported from the living room.

With him gone, I turned to get dressed.

I didn't need Meg's help to pick a gown for tonight. I knew what I wanted. The one I selected had tight sleeves and a neckline that dipped below my collarbones to drape from shoulder to shoulder. The bodice was fitted to my waist before it cascaded to the floor.

Diamonds sparkled across the midnight black fabric in the shape of roses in full bloom. The back neckline draped down and hovered above the small of my back. A thin piece of sheer fabric, embroidered with large black roses, covered my back, while still showcasing my scars.

I looked myself over in the mirror, making sure nothing was out of place. I curled my hair and clipped it in place over my shoulder with a pin in the shape of an arrow. My red streak snaked in and out of the long cascade.

Not wanting to give Michael another reason to be mad, I grabbed the transporter and Ported out of the Magisterium.

Thick, hot air washed over my skin. Camera flashes and shouts instantly filled the air. Screams and questions swam together in a sea of incoherent noise. Through the storm of lights, I could just make out an entrance.

Hosting the third and final theme party was Lions of Magic.

Set at the center of the Sahara Desert, the school didn't try to blend into its surroundings like the other schools. Instead, it stood proud with white, gleaming walls that reflected the sun. The outside was plain and smooth with oval-shaped windows. The entrance was a large archway protected by bronze doors. Lining the steps to the door were guards. Each wore armor that looked as if it was made of the sand around them.

Moving up the sandy stairs and through the arched doorway, I left the harsh heat behind. As the bronze doors closed behind me, the jarring cries from the demanding crowd were left outside. The pleasant sounds of a cello took their place.

Following the music, I walked down the white stone hallway to a dramatic staircase. The party sat below lined by trees. They were the same dryad trees from the Second Trial. Their gold branches stretched over the large room, blocking out the heat from the open ceiling. Unlike the ones in the Second Trial, they didn't move, and their leaves fluttered harmlessly to the floor.

A long bar with black stools was set up to the left of the room. Servers carried trays of tiny delicacies. Most of the attendees congregated on the outskirts of the room, around tall tables. The center was left open for the few dancing to the music.

The guards from Lions of Magic were stationed around the room. Their eyes constantly moved from one pairing to the next. There were others too. It looked as if each School Master was followed by guards dressed in their own school colors.

Nerves fluttered around my stomach. The men and women around the room were the most important individuals of the magical world. All of them were Royals, or High Commons with decades or centuries of knowledge.

My eyes sought out Michael. In the sea of black, it took me a moment to pick him out of the crowd. I actually found Atlas first. Standing in front of the smirking Hunter was a pair of taut shoulders I would know anywhere. Blake.

As I made my way down the stairs, my eyes swept over the room. I didn't know who I was looking for until I found them at the bar. Even dressed in an all-black tux, Dmitri had a bright red pocket square to declare his kills. Guardian Theodore grabbed his son's shoulder with a proud grip.

I almost tripped when I saw who they were talking to.

Lawrence Hart wore a red tux so dark it was almost black, with a matching vest and bowtie. He held his back straight with confidence. His hands rested lazily in his pockets, a perfect picture of calm and ease.

I wove my way toward Michael. The tension pooling in my stomach eased when I took the place beside the Master Hunter.

Atlas grinned across the black linen cocktail table. "Well, well, well. Look who decided to show."

"Right on time, Contestant Heart," Michael said.

"I told you I would be."

"Forgive me for being skeptical." Michael's dark eyes met mine, humor smoldering under the surface. But then he actually looked at me.

The moment I chose this dress, I knew what he would say. I expected him to comment on the fact it was backless or make fun of the sparkling jewels going against my superpower of blending in. I even came up with the perfect response, repeating his famous line, 'you assume I care what you think.'

I didn't expect silence.

His eyes followed the cascade of my hair and the bright red streak that ran through it to the sparkling material clinging to my shoulders. That led his gaze to my bare back. His eyes moved over the scars beneath the embroidered lace before rising to meet my gaze.

His lips parted and I could almost see the words resting on his tongue, waiting to be formed by his lips. Instead, the corners of those lips turned up in the most minute way. If I wasn't watching for his reaction, I would've missed it entirely.

In that gaze was neither judgment nor indifference. What looked back at me was something I rarely saw directed toward me. His steady gaze drew blood into my cheeks. It was one of those rare times his eyes were a rich, dark brown instead of their usual, soulless black. My skin warmed as his gentle gaze once more followed the hair over my shoulder.

His shoulders lowered as the breath slowly left his chest.

"Charlie." He broke the spell between us. Forcefully, he gestured to one of two women in front of him. "This is Renata Sánchez."

Reluctantly, I looked away feeling a little dazed.

Renata was a stunning Latina woman in a floor-length nude and sheer gown. Printed on the thin top layer was a black skeleton mimicking the body beneath it. The ribcage stretched around to her back where the spine followed the curve of her body. The hollow under the ribcage and above the pelvic bones was bare, offering a shadow of her belly button beneath it. Her thick black hair was braided from the crown of her head in a tight rope.

Inked into the skin of her thumb was a tattoo, a dart with a dripping red tip. She was a Hunter.

A hundred questions rushed to my mind. Before I could voice any of them, Michael was moving on to the next person in our party.

"And this is Master Stacie Mitchell," he said. "She's a Master of Communications."

The second woman looked like she would fall over if I breathed too hard in her direction; she was so gaunt, her bones were visible. Her black dress hung off her slouched shoulders like a curtain that had been blown away from a window.

I extended my hand toward the Master. "Pleasure to meet you."

She didn't take my hand. Her wide eyes looked me over with a harsh gaze. "I liked the other one better."

Atlas choked on his drink.

"Excuse me?"

"The other one. The boy. Clarence Hardy," Master Mitchell said slowly, like she was speaking to a five-year-old. "He was more capable than someone who couldn't finish their First Trial."

I dropped my hand. "Yeah, well, he was taken out behind a staircase. So, I don't know how capable he really is."

"He couldn't even throw a proper punch." Blake finished his drink in one swallow.

"Are you disagreeing with me?" Master Mitchell asked. Her cold eyes dared me to deny the accusation.

"Completely. Clarence is the laziest, most self-centered person I've ever met."

She scoffed at me and turned to Michael. "What a disappointment." She spun around, her black gown whirling about her ankles, and left.

74

The Master with the Blue-Green Gaze

"That . . ." Michael exhaled a long breath. "Wasn't as bad as I was expecting."

Atlas chuckled. "If you spat at her feet, it would've sent the same message."

"Nah, that's too straightforward for Charlie. She would probably trick her into a dark room and stab her to the wall," Blake said coldly. "Excuse me, I've left my date at the bar for too long." Brushing past his Guardian, Blake took off across the room. Cornelia sat awkwardly on a barstool in a stunning black lace gown.

"I see where all the fun has been." Renata Sánchez chuckled, low and smoky. Her deep-red lips curled while her heavy-lined eyes narrowed with fascination.

With a single fluid motion, she brushed the braid from her shoulder, then floated her hand down to the table to wrap around her glass of amber liquor. Her long fingers, painted red to match her lips, tapped the rim of her glass.

I quickly remembered my manners. Reaching around Michael, I offered her my hand.

"Hi, I'm Charlie." *Duh! Michael just introduced you!* Mentally I slapped myself.

"It's a pleasure." Her red-stained lips lifted as she gripped my forearm. "I've wanted to meet you for some time, but Kale insisted it was a bad idea."

"Anything involving Charlie is a bad idea." His smirk was playful.

Ignoring that, my eyes dropped to the ink on her hand. "Judging by your tattoo, I'm guessing you're a Hunter."

Renata nodded. "Correct."

"How many are on your team?"

"Four. Our last member—"

"Wentworth," Atlas supplied. "A real prick."

"He would've come, except he hates interacting with people."

"You say that like he can," Atlas added.

Renata gave another low laugh.

"What do your tattoos mean?" I asked.

Renata's eyebrow arched. "You ask a lot of questions."

"She hasn't even gotten started," Michael said.

Atlas braced his elbows against the tall table. "They represent our preferred method of killin'."

My eyes landed on the tattoo on the side of his neck. "A sword?"

He shrugged. "I like the way it separates the head from the body." The smile that pulled across his lips could've been Michael's. Cruel, brutal, and hungry.

I turned to Renata. "And you?"

"Darts."

Atlas groaned deep in his throat. "I love where you hide 'em."

I tried to keep my blush at bay. "What does the other guy have?"

"Went has a bottle of poison." Renata rolled her eyes over the rim of her glass. "A cowardly way to kill, if you ask me, but he swears poison is an art."

"A smelly art," Atlas grumbled.

I turned my curious gaze to the final Hunter in the circle. "What about you? I haven't seen your tattoo."

"That's because his isn't in a place easily seen." Renata's smoky eyes dipped to his chest like she could see through the fine material of his shirt to the scared skin beneath. I had seen hints of a tattoo coiling around his bicep, but I hadn't seen the full thing.

How has she seen . . . oh. My gaze flickered between the two Hunters. They moved around each other with an air of familiarity. He shifted forward, and she stepped closer. His eyes darted across the room to the man in red, and hers followed. Her gaze smoldered with the same embers of bloodlust.

In the nude skeleton dress, every man in the room was looking at her, hoping for a fleeting glance of her attention. But her gaze was only on one, the man standing beside me in the suit with leather accents.

An uneasy emotion filled my chest. I had a hard time naming it. I just knew that I didn't like what I was seeing.

"I prefer to use my hands," Michael answered coolly. Taking a sip of his drink, his eyes tracked Lawrence across the room.

"And that, Master Kale, is what sets you apart."

Our group turned to the new arrival.

Michael stepped forward with his hand extended. "Master LeOnie, it's good to see you again."

The woman grasping Michael's arm was the same one I had seen from afar at the start of each Trial; the same one that gave the cryptic nonsense before the Second Trial party.

Despite her wavy, flaming-red hair, she wore a satin pink dress. Her left eye was a deep blue and the right was a sparkling green. Those eyes stared unwaveringly at my Guardian. She was tall, a couple inches away from six feet, but that didn't stop her from wearing heels.

Her sharp eyes looked past him to me. "Contestant Heart, good to see you again. I've been waiting to meet you officially since your first performance."

"Really?" The word butted out of my mouth without permission.

Michael cleared his throat. "Charlie, this is Master Marigold LeOnie. She specializes in Strategic Foresight."

Taking the hint, I recalled my manners and offered my hand. "Pleasure to meet you."

She gripped my forearm tightly, like she was trying to feel the magic concealed by the beaded sleeve.

"I'm a bit fuzzy on Master titles. What is Strategic Foresight?" I asked, wrenching myself free from her grip.

"Based on who you are and previous decisions you've made, I can predict what move you'll make next."

"You're being modest, Master LeOnie," Renata said. "She can practically predict the future."

Master LeOnie shrugged at the compliment. "You're very kind, Hunter Sánchez."

"How do you Master in that?" I asked, a little starstruck.

"I created the title, actually. I started as a Hunter, went through the

Guard, and earned my Master title. But the bloody work wasn't for me. I loved the hunt, but not the close. So, I left the Guard and studied for years on the predictability of the mind. But my skills cannot be applied to the world's population as a whole; only a single person at a time. Which is why Master Hart has been courting me like his latest mistress."

Michael stilled like he always did when the war was brought into conversation. "Has he? I thought he'd be more subtle than that."

"Subtly isn't a word associated with war, Master Kale. If I can predict what move you'll make, how you'll spend your resources, and what you'll target, then Master Hart wants me whispering in his ear as soon as possible. You want the same."

"Master Lenin," Michael interjected. "He gives the orders."

Again, Master LeOnie's lips curled. "For now. Incentive is a mysterious thing. It rarely hits when you want, and when it does . . . well, it can get smoky." When Michael opened his mouth, she held up a silencing hand. She turned her intense gaze to me. "Contestant Heart. I'm going to grab a drink. Will you accompany me?"

"Oh." I looked at Michael.

Master LeOnie didn't give him time to respond. She threaded her arm through mine and pulled me away. Walking with matching steps, she led me around the perimeter of the dance floor.

"I rarely say this, so please take this as a compliment. You surprised me," Master LeOnie said. "Every time I thought I had all the information to make the correct prediction, you did the opposite."

"Not a lot of good has come of it."

"It got you here, didn't it?" She turned her steady blue-green gaze to the dance floor as we moved around the base of a tree. The Masters leaning against it regarded us with curious glances.

"I always thought these gatherings were fascinating." She looked around at the Masters conversing. "It's entertaining for someone in my profession to see how this unique combination of people stirs up trouble. Relationships are built and destroyed here. And I can see them all before they happen."

"Does that get tiring?"

Her bright red hair shimmered as she shook her head. "I enchanted my mind to not need to rest. I haven't slept in over a hundred years."

"Is that why you don't blink?"

Her eyes snapped to my face. "You're observant. That quality adds another variable, changing the direction of the choices I predicted for you this evening." She turned back to the room. "I never want to miss a detail, no matter how small. So, I use a potion that keeps my eyes moist."

That's creepy. "So how do you do it? Predict people's movements, I mean."

"It's the simple idea of addition. Four plus four equals eight." She pulled us to a stop. Her pale pink dress rustled softly as she turned us toward the far side of the room. "Guardian Theodore plus Basilisk Vodka equals him forgetting what's left of his manners."

At the bar, the Guardian's eyes were slightly glazed over. He wasn't drunk, but, judging by the number of empty glasses in front of him, he was well on his way. On the stool in front of him was the Master of Aquarius. Master Finch was grinding his teeth as Guardian Theodore laughed loudly in his face.

"When Guardian Theodore forgets his manners, he comments on Master Finch's impaired leg. When you add Guardian Theodore's slurred comments to Master Finch's infamous short temper, you get—"

Master Finch whacked his cane into Guardian Theodore's kneecap. The Russian was too tipsy to do two things at once: strangle the offending Master, and hold his throbbing appendage. As he clutched his bruised kneecap, Master Finch limped away, fuming.

"Bruises and a hangover." Master LeOnie continued toward the bar. She leaned against the dark wood and mumbled her drink order to the bartender. A glass of pink sparkling liquid was set in front of her.

"Be careful who sees your affections," I quoted her from months ago before another party. "Some will exploit it."

Daniel had stood beside me. And then, a week later, he died for standing beside me again.

She nodded. "You remember."

"I wish I had known what it meant."

"You didn't want to know. You just wanted to escape."

She wasn't wrong.

"Here's another equation." Picking up the delicate flute, she took a sip. "Master Hart and Master Kale haven't been in the same room for seventy years. When Master Kale joined The Trial to be a Guardian, that was the first time they looked into each other's eyes since battle lines were drawn." She turned, leaning her spine into the bar. She gestured with her glass toward my Guardian.

"Those two men want to see each other's blood. With that kind of tension, when you see Master Kale's tight grip on his glass, the way he's angled his body so Master Hart is always in his peripheral vision, and you add that to Master Hart's matching posture, and their wands both being close at hand, I can guarantee blood will be spilled by the end of the night."

My head snapped around to look at her. She said it so calmly, like giving a weather report.

"Don't all the people in this room change that result?" I asked. "Neither one would risk the future."

"Is that what you think this war is about?" she asked, looking at me with curious eyes. "For the future of society?"

"Well . . . yeah." What else would they be fighting for? Lawrence was fighting to have a world without low-status Users, and Master Lenin was fighting to protect the lives of innocent people. Master Lenin even said I was fighting to save future generations.

"Tonight, what were you told this event was for?"

My eyes narrowed at the topic change. "To meet Masters with the hope of getting apprenticeships after The Trial."

"If that were true, then why aren't Masters and Contestants interacting?"

That couldn't be true. I quickly located Blake on the other end of the bar. He was talking with animated gestures to Cornelia. Across the room, Thiago leaned against the wall with his eyes closed. Emeka was having a quiet conversation with his Guardian. Tala, Amelia, and Dmitri were all beside their School Masters.

All the other Masters were talking in tight groups with cautious eyes.

"This," Master LeOnie waved her arm toward the room and its richly dressed participants, "used to be for gathering apprentices. But that changed the moment Master Hart took control of The Trial. This is the one time, every fifty years, that all the Masters are in one place. Tonight is a competition for alliance. The Master with the most support wins.

"No. This isn't about something as simple as The Trial. This is about the war for legacy. It's about which king and his standards will reign."

Her words were like icicles dropping into my chest. "And who do you think that will be?"

"I told you, Contestant Heart, my skills cannot be applied to the world as a whole, but only to the actions of a single person." She pinched my red streak between her fingers and twisted it around her knuckles. Just as quickly, she released it. "I cannot tell you if there will be a reign of fire or a reign of Eden because it's not just two men fighting. They are dividing the world behind them."

"Then forget the rest of the world." I breathed slowly to keep my heart from racing. "Between Master Hart and Master Kale, who will win?"

She offered me another soft smile. "You ask a lot of questions. It's a quality I admire. If this were a normal Trial, I would offer you an apprenticeship."

That didn't answer my question. Gritting my teeth, I managed a weak, "Thank you."

"The thing about predicting people's movements is that there's rarely just one trajectory." She finished off her drink and set the empty glass on the bar top. "Until we meet again." With a low curtsy, she casually strolled to the other side of the room.

That whole conversation gave me a headache and half a heart attack. A shudder rolled down my spine at her prediction of tonight. I retreated to the far corner to my Guardian.

"Welcome back," Michael said when I rejoined the group of Hunters.

"Did LeOnie say anything interesting?" Atlas asked. His eyes followed the Master in pink as she walked up the stairs. "She's leaving early. You didn't offend her, did you?"

Shaking my head, I turned to Michael to tell him about our conversation. But something kept the words from leaving my mouth.

"She offered me an apprenticeship," I said instead.

Michael's eyes widened. "Really?"

"She liked that I asked questions."

"At least someone appreciates that." Michael smirked.

Atlas cursed. "We've got incoming."

Our party turned to see the only person walking toward us. It was Clarence's Guardian, Brandon Moore. He confidently strolled forward. His golden locks looked plastic, like a gold mold of hair was placed on top of his head.

"Can I kill him?" Renata pulled a dart out of nowhere and held it loosely between her fingers. Her eyes scanned over him like she was trying to find the most painful place to put it.

"If anyone is going to kill him, it's going to be me." Michael set his empty glass on a floating tray and turned toward the new arrival. He stepped forward, placing me slightly behind him.

The other Hunter stopped in front of our table. "Kale." The name slid out of his mouth, dripping with distaste. "I see you're still an alcoholic."

"You have that effect on people," Michael said dryly.

Brandon turned from Michael, dismissing him. "Ah, the rest of the Ponyboys."

"Boss," Atlas growled. "Permission to remind this sad son of a bitch why we're called the Four Horsemen."

Brandon went on as if Atlas hadn't spoken. His charming smile rested on Renata. "Lovely as always, Sánchez. Although not so lovely that I would miss you. Kale knew a thing or two back in the day when he dropped his trio to a duo. Master Hart and I have been functioning beautifully without you since your test with the barbed wire."

What did that mean?

Michael dropped his hand on top of Renata's, trapping the dart to the table.

When a couple seconds passed, he said, "You seem to have forgotten your manners, Kale. Aren't you going to introduce me to your friend? We never got the chance at the beginning of The Trial . . . or when she threatened to break my Contestant's neck."

"I would've introduced you, if you were worth the time it takes to say your name." Michael's smile resembled a hyena's.

Damn. And I thought he was heartless toward me last year.

Brandon's eyes tightened, but his smile remained. Reaching around my Guardian, he offered me his hand. "Brandon Moore, at your service."

I had no problem obviously ignoring the gesture. "You say that like it's supposed to mean something."

His lip twitched with annoyance as he dropped his neglected hand. "It should. Either you're poorly educated or ignorant."

I shrugged. "More like pleasantly unaware."

A smile laced with malice crossed his face. "I'm happy for you, Kale. You finally found someone as unpleasant as you."

"Why are you here?" Michael asked harshly.

Defiance sparkled behind Brandon's eyes. I had seen that look in some of the foster kids in Salina. It said they had a final card to play.

"Master Hart has requested that your Contestant meet him at the bar."

75

Master Lawrence Hart

Like, face-to-face?

Michael had gone completely still. The tension billowing off him was almost a palpable force.

"That's too bad. Charlie and I were just about to leave." Michael placed a hand on the small of my back.

"And miss hearing the theme of the Final Trial? I doubt that. Careful, Kale, your emotions are showing." Brandon's smile grew. "We don't want to keep him waiting."

I could practically hear Michael's teeth grind into each other as he moved to step around the cocktail table.

"Master Hart requested that she come alone." Brandon drank in Michael's distress. "With your inferior views, he didn't want things to get too heated with the world's finest around. I'm sure you can understand."

"I see his head is still firmly up his ass." Atlas pulled a cigarette from his suit jacket and placed it between his lips. When he took a deep breath, the end smoldered with live embers.

"Excuse me?" Brandon turned to the tattooed hunter.

"He means Lawrence is an idiot if he thinks I'm going to let him anywhere near my Contestant alone," Michael said sternly.

"You don't have a choice. See that large man in the armor beside my king?" Brandon pointed to the other side of the room.

In unison, the three Hunters and I looked at the stoic man in the deep red armor. In the warm, dim lighting of the party, his armor was almost black. His cool gaze scanned the room thoroughly; suspicion tightened the skin around his eyes.

"That's Steel. If you even move in Master Hart's direction, Steel will detain you in the most painful way. I'd hate for your Contestant to get caught in the middle of something." Brandon extended his hand toward me. "Come, Contestant Heart. Master Hart doesn't like to be kept waiting."

Michael looked like he was about to break him in half. "If you actually think I'm going to just sit here, I will personally rewire your brain for you. I'm quite fond of the feeling of blood on my hands, and it's been a while since they've been warmed by yours."

Brandon's smile only deepened. "I promise I'll return her. In what condition is completely up to her."

Michael stepped forward with eyes as black as coal.

"Michael." I grabbed his arm before he could leave my side. "Look at me."

With great effort, he turned his head, and then his eyes to me.

"I'll be fine." Silently I begged him to trust me. I knew if he came, or tried anything, Master LeOnie's prediction would come true. Blood would be shed.

Stay here and wait for me. Please.

His eyes ran over my face. The muscle in his jaw popped. He didn't look convinced. To be honest, I wasn't so sure either, but he nodded once, controlled and short.

Squaring my shoulders, I turned back to my escort. "Lead the way."

With a final smirk at Michael, Brandon looped my arm through his and pulled me across the room. With each step, my heart beat faster and faster. A slight tremor ran through my fingers.

I don't think I could have ever been prepared to reach the other side of the room. Even if that room was ten miles wide and I had a week to prepare, I wouldn't be ready.

When we were about ten feet from the bar, the large man in dark red armor stepped forward. "Good evening, Contestant Heart." He bowed his head.

I swallowed around my racing heart.

"I am going to need your wand and any weapons you have on you," he said smoothly. His deep voice was almost lost in the noise of the room.

I bent down and grabbed the hem of my dress. I pulled it up to my hip until the sheath was exposed on my thigh. I quickly removed my wand and slapped it into his hand.

"Thank you." My stomach twisted as he handed it to Brandon.

The smug bastard held it up to the light, admiring the carvings etched into the handle. "Fire, huh? You know, there's a wandmaker in the Alps who believes that these markings represent the core of who we are. This image," he ran his hands over my wand, "is tied directly to you. If I broke your wand right now, and you got a new one . . ." His hands tightened around the shaft.

I flinched forward but his fingers relaxed a second later.

"These markings would reappear just as they are now. New wand. Same look." His gaze returned to mine. "Interesting, huh? Most Users don't like to acknowledge this because it means magic is more out of our control than we realize."

"Let me guess," I said. "Your wand is as empty as your head?"

Steel chuckled.

Brandon glowered at the large man in armor. He slipped my wand into his coat pocket. My hands itched to have it clasped between them. "Cute. But you might want to keep that tongue of yours in check. The only reason I haven't smacked that mouth of yours is because my king ordered me not to harm you. Do you have any other weapons?"

"No."

"I find that hard to believe. I'm sure Kale has taught you how to tuck weapons in all kinds of places."

"Do you want to frisk me?"

"Well, now that you suggested—"

I held up my hand. "We're keeping Master Hart."

"It's my job to keep him safe." The grin that crossed Brandon's face made my stomach curl. "Put your hands on your head, and your legs shoulder-width apart."

White hot anger blew through my veins. Keeping the emotion off my face, I did what I was told.

His hands slid over my sides, touching more than they needed. My eyes met Michael's from across the room. The anger I saw there was ten times what I felt.

Steel dropped a hand to Brandon's shoulder, stilling his searching hands. "Master Hart is waiting."

Brandon shrugged off his large hand and pushed me toward the bar. "May I present Contestant Fifteen."

The man in the dark red tux slid off his stool to his full height to face me. Michael was tall, but Lawrence must have stood an inch or two above him. I felt Michael's height with every glare and abrasive word. But Lawrence's felt like a cold shadow. I felt small and insignificant standing in front of him.

"It's a pleasure to finally meet you." Lawrence Hart's voice was as smooth as melted caramel. Meeting him face-to-face was completely different than seeing him across a room.

Lawrence held out his hand, which was covered in a tight, black glove. The cuff of his jacket pulled away from his wrist. Burned into his skin were scars in the shape of fingers.

"I've met all the other Contestants but you."

I snapped myself out of my examination and quickly grasped his forearm. I was very thankful for the sleeve under his fingers as an added layer of protection.

"Thank you, Hunter Moore." He gestured to the stool next to his. "Please, have a seat, Contestant Heart."

As much as I disliked Brandon, I didn't want him to leave. I wasn't ready to be alone with Lawrence. With a bow, Brandon turned and left without another word. Steel turned his back and continued to watch the room.

I didn't breathe as I slid onto the stool and faced . . . *my father*.

Lawrence held a pleasant smile on his lips. "Can I interest you in a drink?"

"I don't eat or drink anything unless Master Kale gives it to me."

"Guardian Kale," he corrected. He glanced across the room to the man in question. "He has been and always will be the most careful man I know. He's quite brilliant." Lawrence smiled back at me. "You have nothing to fear here. Everything is perfectly safe."

My stomach churned. "I would rather not." My unsettled hands clasped each other tightly in my lap to keep still.

"Suit yourself." His eye contact didn't falter. "To my understanding, you've had quite the week. You were accused of killing a Contestant and then pulled back into my Trial. You have made quite the mess."

No signs of displeasure overcame his subtle smile. He raised his hand toward the bartender. Not six seconds had passed before an old-fashion was set in front of him.

He took the glass. His movements were so smooth the liquid hardly moved. Again, the scars of gripping fingers peeked out from their hiding place as he took a sip.

"I am curious. How did you get Contestant Johnson to take out Contestant Hardy?"

My heartbeat quickened. "You think I put him up to it?"

"Of course. Why else would he take out an obviously weaker Contestant? If he truly wanted to win, he would have let Contestant Hardy into The Trial knowing he could outperform him." He set the glass on the bar top. "So, how did you do it?"

His blue-grey eyes held mine with an intensity I had seen before. He was hunting for the truth with the intention of bestowing a punishment. Back in Kansas, that look was followed by a belt. I could only imagine what terrors would follow from Lawrence Hart.

"It was a mutual decision," I said, letting the lie slide easily off my tongue. "We figured if we went into the Final Trial together, we could help each other place higher."

"Interesting." Lawrence tapped a gloved finger to his lips. "I won't lie. It was a smart move, but you interfered with my agenda."

"Why does it matter so much if I'm in The Trial?"

"Because those who were originally chosen to participate are connected to key members of this world. They can show us what we were known for and can be known for again."

Master LeOnie's words came back to me. *This is a competition for alliance.*

"You are no one. According to your school records, you have no living parents, and little to no connections to the magical world. If I killed you right now, no one important would care."

My heart jumped. *Cheese and rice.*

Leaning against the countertop, his eyes flicked to my red streak. "So, tell me, darling, now that you've wiggled your way into my Trial, what do you hope to accomplish?"

I prayed I was the perfect picture to stiff indifference. "I believe that's between me and my Guardian."

"Try again." His gaze was intent.

I thought for a moment. "I want a title."

"There are easier ways to accomplish that."

"But this is the fastest."

"Are you short on time?"

"Aren't we all?"

He laughed, causing crinkles to appear next to his eyes. To my surprise, it was a warm, pleasant laugh. I was half expecting it to sound evil, like something straight out of a *Disney* movie. "That can't be it. Titles are motivating, true. I have two. The fire in your eyes says you hunger for something else."

Maybe that was true. I hadn't thought of earning a title since the beginning of the Second Trial. But I had already said too much. I had the impression that the man before me could take whatever I said and sharpen it against me.

"Be careful who sees your affections," Master LeOnie had said. *"Some will exploit it."*

"I'll keep that between me and my Guardian."

He took a sip of his drink. "Why did Michael agree to be your Guardian? Has he told you?"

"Maybe he liked my charm."

He chuckled. "I doubt that. Legends like Guardian Kale don't stick around unless something's in it for them."

"I'm nothing special. Trust me."

"Really? Because he seems to think otherwise. If he didn't, he wouldn't be wasting his time."

"You could ask him yourself." I gestured to where he stood. "I'm sure he would have a better reason than anything I'd come up with."

"I'm sure his answer would be amusing." Now he turned his attention to the man in question. He studied him carefully but with no emotion.

"He still has that nasty habit of clenching his teeth," Lawrence said coolly. "If he's not careful, he'll grind them to the bone. It's such a pity . . . we were brothers once. He has made us strangers."

A thousand things flooded to my mouth. Anger, disgust, and horror all begged to be voiced. Somehow, I kept all of that from leaving my lips.

With a sigh, he leaned back against the bar. "But that's what happens when two kings are trapped on one board. You cannot find a corner without hate. I do regret you being caught between us."

"You mean between you and Master Lenin?"

He huffed at the thought. "Henry Lenin is not a king. He's just another piece on the board. Although he likes to think otherwise. Kale is my opponent. Many view him as the other king in this damn war. In fact, he's the only one who doesn't."

"Why?" *Don't indulge him, Charlie.*

"Because he can't think past his anger. If he does win this war, people will expect him to be their leader, but he doesn't want to rule. All he wants is blood. Master Lenin has tried to step up, but no one accepts a child playing dress up."

My gaze traveled to the man in all black. I tried to picture him with a crown, but Lawrence was right. He was so focused that he didn't even act like another king . . . maybe that's why he took orders from Master Lenin, even though he was clearly the one in charge of the show.

"Your curiosity is pointless. He will never have to make the decision to rule."

The subject needed to change. Now. "Master Hart, I would rather talk about The Trial instead of my Guardian."

His eyes brightened. "Right you are. By the end of this evening, I will have talked to each Contestant. Since it is the Final Trial, I thought it best to tell you, personally, about the Award Challenge."

He set down his glass and turned to the person behind him. "My dear, hand me Contestant Heart's scroll."

My heart came to a complete stop when the woman behind him got to her feet. Brandy Charles smiled down at me as she curled her hand around his shoulder. She leaned into him, clearly familiar with the way her body fit against his. My mind went completely blank as I watched his hand curve around her waist.

Cheese and rice. She was with him? My mind raced a mile a minute. *Has she led him to the Kale Ranch? Oh, my God. Zak.*

I shot a glance toward Michael and saw he was already on his phone. I jerked my gaze back just in time to make eye contact with the Wicked Bitch of the West.

"Charlie." Her sneer deepened. "You look surprised."

"The scroll, my dear." Although his voice was calm, it held a certain edge, demanding obedience.

From the pocket of her emerald dress, she took out a black scroll and handed it to him. She placed her red lips on his cheek before she sauntered toward Brandon Moore.

Everything about her was draped with wealth. Diamonds the size of golf balls hung from her ears. The same gemstones cascaded down her spine, attached to the smoothest green silk, which clung to her dainty figure. Pinned in her halo of blonde curls was a comb of gems arranged to look like a bouquet of flowers.

Lawrence saw my gaze follow her across the room. "She's a lovely woman. You won't find another like her. She came up with the final Award Challenge."

That doesn't sound good.

He opened the scroll and slid it over to me. "Starting tomorrow, you will focus solely on the Final Trial. Sign here and you'll have officially graduated from The Magisterium of Magic."

That's not what I was expecting.

Slowly, I grabbed the pen. I scanned the scroll before writing my name across the bottom. And, just like that, I graduated.

"Now, for the Award Challenge." Lawrence took the scroll and placed it in his jacket. "It will span over a week. Starting tomorrow, each Top Seven Contestant will be assigned a day when they will battle their rival Guardians."

My stomach dropped to my toes.

"You won't have to face your own Guardian, but you'll have your plate full with the other six. If you don't show up on your day to compete, you'll be removed from The Trial."

The other six . . . meaning Guardian Theodore, Dmitri's father. My eyes seemed to move by themselves. I had no trouble picking the tall, bulky man out of the crowd.

"Guardian Theodore is to remain unharmed."

Anger and bloodlust answered without my permission. "That's not going to happen."

He tilted his head. "It will because I said so. He is a Master. You are a Common. You will do this. Just like all the other Contestants, you will forfeit the fight against him."

Yeah, and I'm going to turn into a toad at midnight. I quickly concealed my thoughts with a nod. "Of course, Master Hart. Is there anything else you wish to share with me?"

He didn't look satisfied with my answer, but he kept the conversation moving. "One more thing: the theme of the Final Trial. Your desires will become your fears."

"Did Brandy come up with that too?"

"No. I did." He got to his feet. "I'm worried Master Kale will make a fool of himself if I keep you any longer. You are dismissed. I will see you in the training room tomorrow."

Relief washed over me. I got to my feet and was about to walk away when he stopped me.

"Darling, find yourself a new Guardian." His cool blue-grey eyes slid toward the man in black across the room. "The survival rate around him is as low as the Titanic. And the rate of those who mess with my agenda is even lower. Get him out of my Trial."

'Or else' hung unspoken between us as he turned back to the bar.

76

Master LeOnie's Prediction

Adrenaline spiked through my body on the coattails of Lawrence's threat.

My hands shook as I spun around toward Cornelia and Blake. If Lawrence asked Blake about why he put Clarence into a coma, I needed him to say that I put him up to it. Lawrence was already not pleased that I was in his Trial. I didn't know how he would react once he found out I was a liar.

I hadn't walked a couple yards before Brandon snagged my elbow and spun me in the other direction.

"I'm supposed to return you to Kale."

"I can walk myself." I tried to yank free of his grip, but his fingers were locked around my arm.

"What kind of gentlemen would I be if I left you unescorted?"

"That's assuming that you are a gentleman." I yanked again. This time harder. The skin under his fingers started to bruise.

"With an accusation like that, now I have to prove it." He yanked me closer. "Dance with me."

I slammed on the brakes before I face-planted into his chest. "Let go."

"I insist."

"And you can shove it."

"Contestant Heart." He smirked. "Is that any way to talk to your superior? I'm a Royal. You're a Common."

"You assume that I give a damn about what status you have. I'm not in the mood, and I told you to let go." I tried to pull out of his grip again as my shoulder screamed in pain.

"Then get in the mood."

I seriously thought about taking my wand from his coat and stunning him in the face.

The familiar scent of ground sage brushed by my arm. Michael had stepped onto the dance floor.

Reaching forward, he grabbed Brandon's fingers and pried them off my arm. Then he took my hand and pulled me to his side.

"I said I would return her," Brandon said dryly.

Michael shrugged. "I'm an impatient man."

"I'm not done with her." Brandon moved to grab my arm again.

I had a feeling a game of Charlie-Tug-of-War was about to start.

Michael's hand tightened around mine. "Touch her again and I'll snap your spine." His famous, merciless smirk crossed his lips. "Your assistance is no longer required. You are dismissed."

A flush crept up Brandon's neck. He was about to leave when Michael grabbed his arm. Quick as a snake, Michael reached into his coat and pulled out my wand. Then he turned his back to the man, stuffing my wand in his jacket.

Brandon looked at Michael's back like he was seconds away from sticking a knife in it. A slow smile crept across his lips as he stepped away and moved back to his king.

Without a care in the world, Michael led me further onto the dance floor. He pulled me so close we could've held a piece of paper between us. He swayed easily to the mellow hum of the music.

Those closest to us on the dance floor shifted away. Everyone took a second or two from their conversations to look at us. They were as shocked as I was.

"People are staring." I sent a smile to a woman who was openly gaping.

"Let them." Spinning me around, he caught me against his chest. "You look shaken."

"I'm fine."

"I've seen a lot of bullshit in my days, but never a pile that big."

"Excuse me?"

"Look, it even talks." He smirked down at me.

Against my will, a smile emerged, but I sobered quickly. "Lawrence thinks I made Blake take out Clarence."

"Who cares what he thinks?"

"I told him I did."

He came to a complete stop. Shock settled on his face. But only for an instant, and then he stepped back into the rhythm of the music. Curses fell from his mouth like a rainstorm.

"Would it kill you to make my job easy?" His eyes quickly scanned the room. "Do you realize where the punishment is now going to fall?"

"Better me than Blake." I kicked myself as my hand trembled in his.

His hand tightened around mine. "Damn you, Charlie."

"Funny, I say the same thing about you all the time."

"This isn't a joke. Did he . . ." Self-control expanded his chest. "Did he threaten you?"

I glanced up, half-expecting him to be scanning the room for potential threats. I started when we made eye contact.

"Not outright."

Anger narrowed his eyes. I could almost feel its heat soak through his clothes. "That son of a—"

"I'm ok." I'm not sure if I said it to calm him or me. Either way, his anger was dialed down a notch, and my hands calmed.

Now that I had heard the theme of The Trial, we could leave. There was no reason to stay. If we left now, Master LeOnie's prediction would remain unfulfilled.

I slowly released my breath. My hand slid down his chest to feel his heart thumping against his ribs. His breath swept across my temple and his hand warmed my fingers. The past week dissolved from my mind with the constant, strong rhythm of his heart.

For the briefest moment, everything was ok. We were ok.

Over Michael's shoulder, my eyes landed on Lawrence. He was still at the bar talking with Brandon. The Hunter bowed to his king and moved through the crowd toward Brandy. When he reached her, he spoke low into her ear. Her eyes latched onto Michael's back.

Michael felt my muscles tighten. He pulled back just enough to look into my face. "What's wrong?"

Twisted pleasure lifted Brandy's lips as she removed the glittering clip from her hair. She ran her fingers over the jeweled surface, lengthening it into a short, narrow blade.

"I can guarantee blood will be spilled by the end of the night," Master

LeOnie's prediction whispered through my mind. *"Be careful who you show your affections to. People will exploit it."*

Without hesitation, she threw it right at Michael's back.

I Ported from Michael's arms.

In a blink, I was on the other side of him. My skirt flared around me. Magic roared down my arms—

My body jolted when the dagger struck my chest.

77

Oh, My God

Complete and utter terror parted Brandy's red-stained lips.

Someone screamed.

Brandy Ported from the party.

I looked down at the knife. My sternum cracked and gave way as the blade sank into the jeweled hilt. The sparkles on my gown turned red as blood poured down my front.

The hilt of the dagger was encrusted with chunky emeralds and thickly cut rubies. I would have thought it was beautiful if it wasn't stabbed between my lungs.

All feeling receded from my hands and feet. The world tilted as my knees gave out.

Michael barely had enough time to put his hand under my head before it hit the floor. He looked down at me with confusion. Then the glittering hilt caught his attention.

"Oh, my God." Fear whispered the words through unmoving lips.

Another scream broke through the room. The sharp sounds of terror popped the bubble of suspended time.

"I—I can't—" I gasped, "breathe."

Blood wet the corners of my mouth. I could taste it, sharp and metallic on my tongue. My burning lungs tried to expand to take in even a sip of air.

Michael's eyes flashed around the frantic crowd. Bodies blurred behind him as the party guests rushed for the exit.

"Mich—ael." Blood streamed out of my mouth. *You need to get out of here! Brandy. They're trying to kill you.*

Pain burst from the center of my chest as the shock drained from my body. With an iron grip, it locked onto my warning, keeping the words trapped in my throat.

My blurry gaze swung around the crowd looking for green silk.

"Hang on, Sunshine." Michael shoved his arms beneath me. He didn't have time or the right set of nerves to be gentle. "Hang on."

Fumbling in his pockets, he took out a transporter and Ported us under the bright infirmary lights at the Magisterium.

Across the room, a bulb burst in a shower of sparks. Another one quickly followed. The potions on the far side of the room rattled on their shelves.

Planting his feet firmly on the black stone floor, Michael hoisted me onto the nearest bed.

"Helen!" he yelled toward the back. Cupping his hands around the thin dagger, he pressed down with all his weight. "Helen!"

Under the pressure, the pain tripled in intensity. If I had enough oxygen, I would have screamed. My eyes clamped shut and my legs kicked weakly. My cold fingers slipped against his wrists, painting his skin with streaks of blood.

"I'm sorry. I have to apply pressure." He locked his elbows, keeping the force on my chest. Blood pumped through his fingers.

Helen appeared by his elbow. She flinched back as the light overhead exploded.

"Master Kale, I need you to put up a magic chamber, now," Helen barked. Another explosion of glass rained over them.

"I have to keep pressure," he snapped.

"Let me do that. If you don't put up that ward, she'll take out this whole wing before I can help her."

Gritting his teeth, he pulled his hands back. Helen's hands replaced his just as another pulse of blood flowed from the wound.

I groaned under the new weight. My lips moved with incoherent pleas.

Michael tore his wand from his jacket. Magic pulled Helen and my bed from the wall. Just as we came to a stop in the center of the room, he fired a ward toward the ceiling.

The cast exploded in the air. The firework of gold fell quickly to the earth, encasing our trio in a dome. As soon as it was anchored to the floor, the lights stopped exploding, but they didn't dim. They remained painfully bright. Above us, a chandelier rocked back and forth.

Michael was at Helen's side in a blink.

"I don't think the knife shattered her core." Helen's arms shook. "I think the tip of the knife broke through, but it's stopping her magic from spilling into her chest."

"What do you need me to do?" Michael yanked the suit jacket from his shoulders.

"Put your hands back here." She nodded toward her hands.

Michael slid his hands beneath Helen's and, once more, he locked his elbows.

I gripped his wrists. I wanted to beg for relief, just a bit less pressure so I could breathe. Even if it was just a sip. My fingers, clumsy and blood-slick, brushed against the jeweled hilt of the knife. The hem of my dress slipped over my knee. The heel of my shoe stabbed through the mattress.

Helen rapidly tried to wipe the blood from her hands. "I'm going to get my kit." She broke into a run through the wall of magic and returned with a cart of instruments and potions. With her hands now protected by gloves, she grabbed her wand and a syringe of bubbling green potion.

"On the count of three, take out the knife. One. Two."

Michael shifted his weight onto one hand and grabbed the hilt of the jeweled dagger with his other. His eyes met mine. "I'm sorry."

"Three."

In one clean move, Michael yanked the knife straight up.

I screamed.

Michael jumped in front of Helen, cloaking them both in a protective ward. Magic flared from my chest, tearing the magic chamber to shreds.

The walls shook.

The windows trembled and cracked.

The stone floor beneath me split down the length of the room and up the walls.

The chandeliers swung wildly, as if caught in the gale of a hurricane.

Then I passed out.

78

The Wound

A lingering taste of blood coated my tongue.

It felt like an elephant sat on my chest, crushing each rib. My lungs stung, as if I had breathed vapors of acid. My heart pulsed, sending surges of agony through every vein. The very things keeping me alive caused me the utmost agony.

I longed for unconsciousness. At least in sleep, no matter how restless, I would be numb to the war inside my chest.

It slowly dawned on me that I couldn't move. At first, I wondered if my limbs refused to obey because of their internal torture, but the more I concentrated, the more I realized they were being held in place.

Panic kicked my heartbeat against my chest with more fervor. *Why am I restrained?* Fragments of my last memory started to filter in.

The dagger . . . in my chest.

I could recall that much. I would never be able to forget that moment. *What happened after? Was Michael able to get me out? What if he was too late? The restraints . . . Did that mean Lawrence had me? If that were true, what happened to Michael? The blade was meant for him.*

Fear threw my eyes open. I willed as much strength as I could into my limbs. My wrists struggled against the restraints. I raised my head, searching for an exit or a shred of hope that this nightmare wasn't real.

Hands pressed my shoulders back into the pillows. The amount of pressure caused me to pause. It was firm enough to keep me in place, but not hard enough to cause bruises.

Blinking rapidly, my vision slowly came into focus. Two figures in black stood over me.

Atlas had a huge grin stretched across his face. "Damn girl, how many lives do you have?"

The man across from him grinned—or tried to. The smile looked painful, as if it would tear open the scar on his cheek. "I told you she'd make it," Michael said.

My eyes skimmed over him so fast they didn't notice anything. I tried to slow my panic in order to scan him for injuries. But he was the picture of health.

"Are you ok?" My imagination spun. Pictures of horror flew behind my eyes, each one worse than the last. "The knife was meant for you. Did they get you? What about Blake? Did everyone get out—"

"No one else was injured," he said curtly. Pulling his hands from my shoulder, he walked to the end of the bed.

I sucked in a deep breath as relief washed over me. But the action was cut short as pain rippled throughout my chest. Breathing ceased. My eyes squeezed shut, waiting for it to subside.

When I opened them again, the mood had changed. Atlas stood humorlessly. Helen fluttered about, putting potions in the IV bags that were connected to my veins. Michael stood with his back to me, every muscle rigid.

I didn't like being flat on my back. I was about to attempt sitting up, but I remembered the restraints. My wrists and ankles were cuffed to the railings. Thick straps kept my shoulders and hips firmly in place.

"Can I sit up?"

Helen and Atlas instantly jumped into motion. They moved to the headboard and fiddled around, murmuring soft instructions. Then, slower than cold molasses, the bed tilted forward.

The move upright caused something to shift in my chest. Something popped and readjusted. Muscles pulled and strained. A new fire lit inside the center of my chest.

When I was upright, Helen and Atlas moved around to undo the restraints. Once free, the first thing I did was move the hair from my face. My shoulders ached.

All the while, Michael stood with his back to me.

"Michael." He didn't turn. "Does your family know about Brandy?"

"My family isn't the one who took a knife to the chest." The lights shrunk from his harsh tone. "They're fine. Pissed, but fine." He rolled the tension out of his shoulders, and the lights went back to normal.

Almost reluctantly, he faced me. "How do you feel?"

"Like I swallowed acid." A tickle crept up my throat. Before I could stop it, a cough launched out of my mouth, splattering blood across the white sheets. "I'm going to kill her."

"Get in line," Michael growled. His eyes darted to my chest, and a fresh wave of rage washed over him.

The white hospital shirt had been cut down the middle below my collarbones to expose an angry wound. A small trickle of blood oozed down to my belly button. The rest of my chest was splashed with blues and purples. Every breath pulled in more pain and forced more blood out.

"Wow. That looks awesome." I wiped off the blood clinging to my lips. "Isn't the magic in this tattoo supposed to make it so that if someone throws a knife at me, it stabs them instead?"

"The wards only protect you from those outside of The Trial," Michael said stiffly. "Technically, Brandy is still in The Trial."

Right. That's why when Clarence slapped me, I felt it. God, I wish Brandy had just slapped me.

"Why would she attack you now? And in front of everyone."

"Because that would be the last public event where I didn't have a title," Michael said bitterly.

"And the last time she could kill you without consequences." *Shit.* "How bad is it?" I gestured to the wound.

"You're lucky to be alive," Helen said as she took out a fresh supply of bandages. "If you were an inch to the right or left, the knife would have hit your heart or your lung. If it went any deeper, your core would've shattered. I'm not even sure how you're still here."

I started to shift into a more comfortable position, but Helen's hand stopped me. "We just got that to stop bleeding. Please don't rip it open again."

The golden doors at the end of the room creaked open, drawing our party's attention. Both Hunters grabbed their wands. When Master Lenin stepped into the room, they relaxed.

I turned back to the nurse. "Again?"

"The dagger was soaked in magic." That statement was met by growls from the men in the room. "Thankfully, it wasn't in long enough to inject its full dose."

My head was too fuzzy for this conversation. "Can you talk to me like I'm a Regular?"

Helen gave me a sympathetic smile. "The magic on the dagger keeps the wound from closing."

I looked down. While it looked swollen, bruised, and flushed, it wasn't gaping. "It's closed now."

"It's not actually. The skin on either side of the wound is just pressed together. There's a mixture of potions and charms over the top that keep them like that. The magic in the dagger caused each side of the wound to act as if they were the same side of a magnet, pushing away from each other. No potion or magic can counteract it, meaning it will never heal." Helen nudged Atlas out of her way and took his spot beside me. "It will be a wound for the rest of your life."

I stared at her. The center of my chest suddenly felt brittle. If I breathed in too deeply, would the potions and charms split open? If I sneezed, would I start bleeding? *Cheese and fucking rice.*

Upon seeing the blood drain out of my face, Helen said, "Think of it as a victory tally." She wiped blood off the scar that Richard While gave me last year. At this rate, I would have as many scars in the front as I did in the back.

"If it makes you feel better, all the best women are covered in them." Atlas winked.

"Atlas." Michael didn't even look at him. "Go wait outside."

With one last smile in my direction, all humor followed the Irishman out of the room.

"You didn't have to do that," I said. "He was just trying to lighten the mood."

Michael gave no reply.

Master Lenin cleared his throat. Stepping up to the bed, he said gravely, "Contestant Heart, you have my deepest apology."

"You didn't throw the knife into my chest, so don't apologize for it." I winced as Helen wiped the skin too close to the wound. "Where's Brandy?"

"We don't know." Master Lenin kneaded his forehead. "Judging by her affiliation with Master Hart, I would assume he has her hidden somewhere out of reach."

Bummer. I'd really like to punch her in the face. My unused legs begged for my attention. I itched to stand or do something. "Can I stand?"

"No," all three, with variations of panic, shouted in unison.

"It'll tear open, honey."

"I don't think you're ready for that, Contestant Heart."

"Don't be stupid."

"I was just asking." *Jeeze.* That's when I noticed the sun was setting. Dread settled on my shoulders. "What day is it?"

I knew something was wrong the moment none of them answered. I looked from one to the other. Michael stared at the wall behind me. Helen was busy putting potions on the wound. Master Lenin kept glancing around the room.

"What day is it?"

Master Lenin finally cleared his throat. "Thursday."

I jerked upright.

"Honey, I need you to take it easy." Helen's eyes jumped between my face and the aching spot on my chest.

Michael stepped forward, unsure what to do.

"You kept me asleep for *four days?*"

"So you didn't get up and rip yourself in half," Helen said harshly, before she addressed the Master. "If she doesn't sit back, I will sedate her."

"Master Lenin, where is the Award Challenge?" Today was the fifth day . . . it was my day to compete. If I didn't show, I forfeited The Trial.

Michael knew exactly where my mind was going. He faced Master Lenin with his teeth bared. "Don't answer that." He turned back to me with a look so severe, I thought he might take my head off. "You're not going anywhere until we know for a fact you won't bleed out."

"It's my turn to participate! If I don't show up, they'll throw me out."

"That's a bit of a blessing now that I think of it. You need to rest before you kill yourself."

I slapped Helen's arm away. "Pity doesn't look good on you, Michael."

"And stupidity doesn't look good on you." He matched my temper easily. "Sit back. I'm not asking."

"No! I'm the Contestant. You're *my* Guardian, and I say let's go."

"So you can be taken down in the first round? Charlie, please." He stepped up to the end of the bed and gripped the rail as if to anchor himself to it. "If you enter that room, you could be killed."

For some reason, that wasn't on my list of things I needed to care about. "I can handle myself."

"If you were going against the Contestants, I would agree, but that's not the case. You'll be facing Guardians who have *decades,* if not centuries, of experience."

"If I die, you won't have to waste time with me anymore." I swung my feet to the floor.

The whole bed shook. The headboard slammed into the stone with a *crack.* The lights almost blinked out.

Michael's hands gripped the bedframe with white knuckles. Smoke curled from between his fingers.

"Do not make me beg." His words were slow and chosen carefully. "You're in this bed because of me." He looked up, finally meeting my gaze.

To everyone else, his normal expression of hardened anger was in place. But I saw the cracks. He asked me not to make him beg, but he already was.

"I jumped in front of that knife on my own," I said slowly.

"I never asked you to," he snapped. "I never—"

"Master LeOnie said blood would be spilled. I couldn't just stand there!"

"Fuck LeOnie, you should have!"

Those last three words bounced around the room.

Helen stopped trying to attend to the wound.

Master Lenin went completely still.

However, no one was as shocked or wide-eyed as I was.

"Let me make something very clear." Michael spoke in a voice so low, my ears strained to hear him. The cracks in his façade widened. "I thank you for saving my life, but that's all I'll do. You do not get to die for me. My life is not worth yours."

I looked at him. And I mean *really* looked at him.

Exhaustion clung to the edges of his eyes. He was still in his dress pants and shirt from the Trial party. Stubble shadowed his jaw. His hair was misplaced and ruffled. I had saved his life, and in return, he fought to keep me alive. By going to the Award Challenge, I was throwing all of that away.

Slowly, I nodded. "Ok."

He dropped his head with relief. With a deep breath, he straightened.

"You'll need to go to the Award Challenge and throw down a knife before each Guardian," Master Lenin spoke softly. He must have realized that World War III had just been avoided, and he didn't want to say anything that would put the option back on the table.

Michael nodded. "I'll go. I'll do it."

"Contestant Heart needs to be the one to do it." Master Lenin held up his hands to shield himself from Michael's glare. "It's the rules."

Curses rolled across his tongue. To my amazement, he swallowed them. "Fine. We can wheel you—"

Just the thought of being *wheeled* into the Award Challenge made my cheeks heat with humiliation. "If I'm going to do this, at least let me walk."

Michael nodded curtly. "Helen. Do you even have something that strong?"

"I can mix a few things together." She ran across the room to get what she needed.

"I'll inform Master Hart you're coming. That should buy you some time." Master Lenin quickly ducked out of the room.

Michael remained stoic at the end of my bed.

Within a few minutes, Helen had me drink from ten different bottles. Each one had a different taste and texture. Some were chunky, while others were as smooth as milk chocolate. Some tingled down my throat, while others made my toes itch.

"That's all I can do." She set the last empty vile next to the other nine. "Let's get you on your feet."

With Michael and Helen on either side of me, I placed my feet on the floor. They heaved me up, and then I was standing. I expected a head rush or to feel dizzy. Neither came. My chest throbbed, but it was manageable.

Releasing my hold on my human crutches, I took one step and then another. The wound remained closed. I had never felt so sure-footed. I almost wished I could drink that concoction of potions all the time.

I walked up to Michael and looped my arm through his. Not a second later, we left the Magisterium.

A shock jolted through my body as we Ported to the room where the second Award Challenge took place. I could so easily see Daniel leaning against the cement walls. His warm brown eyes, bright with the excitement of the afternoon.

Pulling my gaze from a moment in time, I followed Michael through the door and into the round room. Unlike the last time I was here, the floors were covered with thick padding. The black glass concealing the Masters and Guardians had been removed, leaving the Masters exposed. Above the audience, a large clock glowed bright red, casting a hellish halo over the Masters' heads.

As soon as we entered the room, a hush fell over the crowd.

Master LeOnie sat up against the wall. Her bright red hair made her easy to spot among the mass of Masters. When her blue-green gaze met mine, they sparkled with 'I told you so.'

Blake jumped to his feet, cutting her from view. His shoes squeaked across the matted floor as he ran toward me. "You look like shit."

My system was flooded with painkillers. I was so high, my drug-induced mind found that funny. "Thanks."

"What are you doing here?" He shot a scathing look up at Michael. "Can you even stand?"

"I'm fine."

"Contestant Heart," Lawrence's cool voice slid across the room.

Blake stepped out of the way, revealing the Master in red. Lawrence's indifferent gaze flickered to the wound peeking out of the draping neckline of my shirt.

"Master Lenin informed me of your condition," he continued. "How would you like to proceed?"

I opened my mouth. The words lined up on my tongue, ready to fill the silence. I would have said them . . . if I hadn't looked past Lawrence.

My eyes slid down the first row to where Dmitri sat. He gaped openly at the wound on my chest.

I quickly picked out the six Guardians I would have to face. I could picture myself standing before each one, forfeiting. Humiliation curled around me, making my cheeks pink. I would have to quit six times in front of Dmitri. And he knew it.

My response transformed on my tongue. "I'll play."

79

The Final Award Challenge

Michael stopped breathing beside me.

He turned his head just enough to look at me from the edge of his vision. His wide eyes screamed of worry and disbelief.

"Contestant Heart." Lawrence's eyes softened with pity. "You look like you can barely hold your own weight."

I didn't look away from Michael. I knew he could see the turmoil and the need in my eyes. He knew it well, because we bled the same way. I needed him to have my back on this.

Clenching his jaw, Michael faced my father. "She's fit to compete," Michael said tightly, like saying those words physically hurt him. "The Magisterium's physician released her."

He has my back. His words made my heart glow.

"You mean she's fit to lose," Dmitri muttered. His Guardian laughed beside him.

"I guess we'll see." Master Hart stepped back and faced the rest of the room. "Contestant Heart has chosen to compete. Guardians, please prepare yourselves. We'll start in five minutes."

As he walked back to his seat, Michael pulled me to the sidelines. "Start stretching. I'll be right back." He Ported out of the room.

I pulled my arms over my head. Pressure built up in my chest. With a small pop, a trickle of blood moved down to my belly button.

Oh, God. Breathing slowly, I continued to stretch out my back.

My eyes slid over the first row filled with Contestants and Guardians. The Trial pairs whispered together in tight groups. Most of the looks were filled with astonishment, with a thick layer of confusion. Blake bent over his knees, breathing slowly as he tried not to throw up.

At the very end of the row, there were no whispers or confused expressions. Dmitri and his father looked at me as if I were a wounded animal. Like predators drawn by the scent of blood, they were completely still. Waiting.

Michael reappeared moments later with a bag. He handed it to me and gestured to a changing room.

I quickly changed into the black workout gear. The traction in the shoes would stop a herd of elephants if they charged me, and the clothes were stretchy enough to give a good range of motion. But the best thing about the black gear was that no one could see the blood dripping down my chest.

When I returned to Michael, I had never seen his face so hard before.

"Michael," I dropped my gaze. "I'm sorry. I couldn't—"

"I know," he said briskly. "The point of this is for the other Contestants to see how you fight. Under normal circumstances, I would tell you to draw it out and not give anything away. But I want to get you out of here as quickly as possible so Helen can get more potions in you. Not all Guardians have combat experience. So you need to prioritize and conserve energy for those who do."

His dark eyes surveyed the row of Guardians. "Malik and Samuel will be easy. If you see an opening, take them down. Forfeit to Atlas. You're going to need everything you have for Shi, Breno, and Theodore."

Nodding, I pulled my hair into a ponytail.

He stepped closer. To everyone else, it looked like he was fixing my glove. He dropped his voice and, without moving his lips, said, "If you take a direct hit, your sternum will shatter, and there's no guarantee Helen can put it back together."

"Does everyone know about the wound?"

His eyes looked over my shoulder. Tightly, he nodded.

"Well, on the bright side, I know where everyone is going to aim."

He swallowed thickly. "Be careful."

A fresh wave of butterflies rushed into my stomach as I stepped toward the mat. With a deep breath, I took my place in the center of the room.

My eyes locked onto Guardian Theodore. The smile on his face blew on the fire in my chest. The shaking in my hands stilled.

"Since Contestant Heart was not here for the orientation, I will restate the rules," Lawrence said from his seat in the front row. "There will be no magic. Guardian Kale, take her wand."

I turned and handed it to him. Michael's jaw popped as he locked eyes with Lawrence. Reluctantly, he took it from me.

"You're allowed only a knife—if you choose. You have seven minutes for each round. If you're unable to pin a Guardian within the allotted time, it will be counted as a loss." Lawrence held my gaze. "The Contestant who pins the most Guardians in the fastest amount of time gets to choose which weapons are allowed in the Final Trial. The objective is not to kill the Guardian, but to incapacitate them. If you need it, your Guardian can administer a healing potion between each round." He gestured to a cart pushed against the wall beside Michael. On top of a black satin drape were seven syringes.

"Do you have any questions?" Lawrence asked.

I shook my head.

"Then we shall begin. Guardian Malik, from Lions of Magic, you're first."

A quiet applause fluttered politely around the room as he stepped onto the mat.

There was nothing extraordinary about him. He was as average as the word. I knew he wasn't a fighter by how soft his hands looked. Judging by how he held his right fist slightly behind his left, I guessed that was his dominant. Most of his weight was on his right leg as well. Michael was right. He would be easy.

Master Hart's voice whipped across the room. "Bow to your opponent, and the timer will begin."

I quickly dipped into a bow. When I straightened, another warm trickle of blood ran down my chest. *Shit.*

With a soft chime, the clock over the Masters started counting down.

Emeka's Guardian hesitated. That was his first mistake. His second mistake was taking his eyes off me so he could look at Michael to my left.

I lunged forward with my left fist. He easily moved out of the way.

I shoved my elbow into his ribs. He grunted as I heard a crack. I bent down and punched the side of his right knee. He tumbled onto his side. I jumped up and pressed my heel to his throat, pinning him on his back.

The bell sounded from all corners of the room. At first, no one knew what to do.

"She pinned him in ten seconds," Blake muttered.

I removed my heel and stepped back. The atmosphere had changed.

All eyes rested on me. For the first time since I entered The Trial, they were looking at me as if I could *do* something. It wasn't hearsay. I was a real Contestant for a title.

Unsure, the Masters clapped to congratulate me. All, except Master LeOnie. With a knowing smile, she nodded.

The other Guardians whispered fiercely to their Contestants. I shot a glance at Michael over my shoulder. His eyes shone with pride.

When Malik was off the mat, Lawrence called, "Guardian Connor Samuel, from Aquarius: The Undersea School of Enchantments. You're next."

As soon as he stood up, I knew this was going to be a very different match. The look on his face told me he wanted to win. I didn't have surprise on my side anymore. He positioned himself right where Malik had been. Then he flexed his muscles. *Cheese and rice, his arms are like trees.*

As soon the bell sounded, he jumped forward.

Yikes.

I leapt to the side and instinct caused me to stick out my foot. He tripped and face-planted into the mat. He instantly rolled to his feet and spun around like an angry bull.

"Unharnessed anger makes you stupid," Michael once said. *"Stupid gets you killed. There is nothing more humiliating than a stupid death. So don't be stupid."*

Guardian Samuel rushed forward again. Looking for a way to put him down quickly, I threw my knife at his leg. The blade sank into his thigh. With a shriek, he crumbled to his knees. I punched him in the temple, and he dropped like a rock.

The bell signaled the end of the match. I glanced at the clock. *Under a minute again.*

Next to my foot was a drop of blood. I looked at my shirt. The front glistened.

I walked toward Michael, who was calmly leaning against the wall. "I need a new shirt."

He surprised me by reaching into the bag beside him and taking out another black tee. "I thought that would be the case."

Keeping my back to the audience, I quickly tugged the wet shirt over my head.

Michael cursed at the sight of the blood-smudged bruises.

"Contestant Heart, are you ready?" Lawrence asked from his seat.

I pulled on the new shirt and spun around. "Yep." I walked back to my spot and waited for who was next.

"Guardian Shi, from The Magical Academy of the Earth."

A small man jumped to his feet and practically galloped onto the mat. As soon as the bell rang, he balanced on one foot, contorting into one hell of a karate pose. Then he did a freaking front flip, rolled, and came up swinging.

As sudden as a lightning strike, his hands hit the solar plexus just below my ribs. Before I could even curse, he whipped his leg into mine.

I crashed onto my side. Even with all the painkillers running through my veins, the impact made the wound shriek in agony. I braced my teeth against my own scream.

A cellphone shrilled through the silence.

Guardian Shi's head whipped toward the sound.

"Sorry." Michael quickly took out his phone and silenced the ringer.

The bell hadn't chimed yet. And my opponent was distracted.

I flung out my leg and knocked him to the ground. Before he could recover, I rolled on top of him and grabbed my knife. I latched onto his neck and poised my blade, ready to sink into his forehead.

The bell chimed. Defeat made him relax into the floor. I painfully rose to my feet. Already, I was feeling my energy start to leave me.

Maybe this wasn't such a good idea.

Shut up. You have three left. You can do this.

Shi pushed himself up, bowed, and went back to his seat.

I glanced over at Michael. All the time I had known him, I had never heard his phone make any noise. Ever so slightly, he winked.

The wonderful jackass made his phone go off on purpose.

Disappointment pressed Lawrence's lips together into a thin line. "Ladies and gentlemen, please silence all calling devices before we proceed. Guardian Arthur Atlas, from The European Academy for Practical Magic, you may step onto the mat."

The smug bastard jumped to his feet with a full-blown smile. Blake, on the other hand, looked terrified.

There was no way I was going to win this one. He was a Hunter, for crying out loud. My only experience with Hunters was Michael. Even on his easiest setting, he used me to wipe the floor.

"Charlie." Michael gestured for me to come to him.

Atlas took out a large knife and squatted over his heels. "Ready when you are, love."

I fought to keep myself upright. I leaned against the wall as Michael plucked a syringe off the cart beside him and bit off the cap with his teeth. Without much of a ceremony, he stabbed the needle into my leg.

"How do I forfeit this one without forfeiting the whole thing?" I asked, feeling the potion rush through my bloodstream and into my aching ribcage. Strength flowed back into my muscles.

"Throw down your knife. He'll know what to do."

I staggered back to the mat. Rising to his feet, Atlas was no longer smiling. Like he was unable to help himself, his eyes kept moving to the wound. He was trained to seek others' weaknesses, and he knew where mine was.

As soon as the bell chimed, I dropped my knife to the floor between us. The blade sank into the mat, holding it upright.

Atlas straightened from his fighting stance and put away his knife. The clock continued to count away our time.

In the training room, an hour felt like seven minutes. But on that mat, those minutes felt like hours. The potions in my blood made my head light. My eyelids begged to be let down. I couldn't tell if I was actually swaying or if my vision was playing with me.

Finally, the bell chimed, signaling the end of the seven-minute torture. With a wink, Atlas returned to the front row.

"Guardian Vanessa Breno, from The Serpentine School of Magic."

She walked onto the mat and didn't stop. The bell chimed, and she took out her knife, all the while walking toward me.

When she was within striking distance, I stepped forward and moved to punch her in the gut. My fist never landed.

She grabbed my hand, twisted it around my back, and used it to shove me forward.

I spun around and caught the knife coming toward my back. I tossed it aside and swung toward her head. She caught it before it made impact. She threw her other hand into my ribs.

The taste of blood was renewed in my mouth.

She shoved me back, planting her foot in my chest. I fell down screaming. Crippled by the pain that cracked through my chest, I didn't see the foot coming toward my face. I barely felt it above everything else.

I wrapped my arms around myself, hoping it would keep my sternum from shattering. Blood dripped onto the mat.

The sight of it made me go numb with anger. I struggled to push myself onto my hands and knees. Huffing in short breaths, I was somehow able to stand. Then I turned back to Guardian Breno.

My hands curled into fists. I stepped forward. Pain throbbed in my chest, but I kept going. I ducked under as she swung and dodged her other fist. I whipped my elbow into her face. Then I did the same with the other elbow. Blood sprayed from her nose.

Before she could gather her wits, I threw one punch after another, driving her across the entire mat. Gathering every ounce of strength I had left, I slammed my foot into her stomach.

She crashed into the wall so hard that blood marked where her head hit. She slumped to the floor and didn't move.

The bell chimed.

I spat a mouthful of blood at her boots. As I turned from the unconscious Guardian, my knee buckled. Michael was right there and caught me before I hit the mat.

"Back out now," he hissed. He stabbed a second syringe into the side of my leg. "You can't take another hit like that."

"I'm fine." I pushed away from him. The potion slipped around my ribs and erased the cracks. My nose ceased aching, and the blood flow slowed to a stop. The wound on my chest throbbed through the painkillers.

"I wasn't asking how you were." He dropped his chin so his words went straight to my ear. "He's a School Master, Charlie. He will kill you."

"Guardian Theodore, from The University for Advanced Tactical Magic, will be our final competitor this evening."

My eyes locked onto the end of the row as the School Master stood. With confident strides, he took his place on the mat. I never noticed before just how wide his shoulders were. Did he have to angle his body to get through doorways?

Anger rushed over the pain to the point where I couldn't feel anything but its burning intensity. I straightened to my full height with fire running through my veins.

"I got this."

80

One Last Guardian

Michael caught my elbow.

"Please don't tell me to back out," I whispered.

The muscle in his jaw pulsed. "Then fight like a rat bastard. Don't give him time to collect himself. Break anything you get your hands on. Put your whole status into your swings, because he's going to do the same. He will try to break you. So don't let him hit you." Reluctantly, he released my arm.

I turned to face the audience.

Lawrence caught my eye.

The look on his face could have matched Michael's. He barely jerked his head side-to-side, telling me to back out.

Yeah, well, screw you.

Taking my place at the center of the mat, I placed my feet hip-width apart and lifted my fists in front of my face. In my mind, it was just him and me.

Surprise lifted Guardian Theodore's eyebrows up his forehead. Twisted amusement curled his lips as he matched my stance.

My eyes moved intentionally over his body, taking note that his left foot was forward and his right fist was held just a little higher. His fists were calloused and scarred from experience. I paused at the pin stuck through the collar of his shirt, declaring his magic status.

He was a Royal Eight. While he outranked me in title and experience, I had the upper hand when it came to magic. I was a Royal Nine.

"With your magic status, you're at the top of the food chain," Michael once told me.

When the bell rang, Guardian Theodore beckoned me with two fingers.

I dropped my arms and rushed him.

His fist swung powerfully toward my head. At the last second, I leapt to the right. Planting my foot against the wall, I pushed myself into the air and smashed my fist into his face with the full force of my status behind it.

When both feet hit the ground, I spun around, whipping my elbow across his nose. The observing Masters gasped as blood arched high into the air.

I hooked my leg around his and pulled it out from under him. He crashed to his knees seconds before I slammed my fist into his face again. He landed on his back with a loud thud.

I drew my knife.

Curses flew out of his mouth, spraying the mat with blood. He rolled to his feet and grabbed the weapon on his hip, which looked more like a small machete than a knife.

He slashed forward. I barely ducked out of the way. The tip of the knife slashed across my collarbone.

"Guardian Kale. Stay where you are," Lawrence barked across the room.

My eyes snapped away from the Russian in front of me. Michael had taken a step onto the mat. His jaw was clenched tight as he stood, helplessly watching. Then panic took over his gaze.

My stomach dropped. I had just turned my back to a man with a small machete.

I turned around just in time to get a foot to the chest. I landed hard on my back. A hoarse cry squeezed through my clenched teeth as I grabbed my chest. Blood seeped through my fingers and onto the mat.

"Stay down, girl." Guardian Theodore's shadow fell over me seconds before he fisted a handful of my hair. My red streak streamed through his fingers. His knife flashed downward as if to cut it from my head.

I slapped my hand over my discarded knife. *Like hell.*

I slashed the blade across his calf, severing his muscles. Releasing my hair, he fell to his knees again. Flipping the knife around, I slapped the handle across his face. This time, when he landed on his back, I jumped on top of him.

All my rage forced a scream out of my throat.

I stabbed the knife toward his face.

Control gripped my hand, embedding the blade into the mat beside his eye.

The bell chimed for the final time.

Gasping through the tightness in my chest, I pried my hands from the handle. I pushed myself to my feet and stumbled away. If I didn't, I would have taken the knife from the floor and put it where it belonged.

The room had gone completely silent.

I spat blood out of my mouth, not taking my eyes off the man on the floor. Forcing myself to look away, I stumbled toward my Guardian.

Michael jumped away from the wall, audibly exhaling relief. Then his eyes flashed over my shoulder.

Through the exhaustion oppressing my mind, I realized what was happening. I forgot the most important rule in combat: never turn your back to your opponent unless he isn't breathing.

I just humiliated one of the most powerful men in the world, and then turned my back to him. Everything stilled around me. I didn't even breathe as I watched Michael's eyes widen.

I whirled around, my hair momentarily blocking my view. Guardian Theodore was on his feet, and his fist was raised.

But I had nothing left to give.

There was a flash of black and a rustle of leather. Darkness pressed in from every corner of the room as Michael Ported between us. There was the sound of bone snapping and a body hitting the floor.

With a single punch, Michael had thrown the School Master to the ground. With half-closed eyes, Guardian Theodore's broken jaw hung open.

Anger poured off Michael in waves that were almost tangible. The lights were so dim that half the audience was concealed in shadow.

Lawrence's eyes bore into mine, but I felt no fear. Not standing behind Michael Kale. I was under his protection, and the whole room knew it.

"Lawrence," Michael growled. "I believe that concluded the Award Challenge for my Contestant. We're leaving." That last part was punctuated with sharp edges. Even if Lawrence had something else, Michael was leaving, with or without permission.

My Master Hunter collected the duffle bag and took me by the arm. Gently, he led me from the room. As soon as the doors closed behind us, we Ported to the ranch. At the top of the hill, my knees gave out, and I crumbled in the middle of the yard.

Michael ran onto the porch long enough to bang his fist against the door. "Mom!"

He Ported back to me and dropped to his knees. "You're insane. You know that? You're completely insane." He smoothed the bloody hair away from my neck and took my pulse. He didn't look happy about what he found.

"I had to—" My response was cut short by a mouthful of blood that decided to come up my throat. "You broke his jaw."

"I should have broken his spine."

Mrs. Kale burst out of the door. My eyelids won their battle and slid closed. My forehead dropped to his shoulder.

"Call Helen," was the last thing I heard.

Gravity shifted. The temperature changed. I really didn't care what was going on. The only thing I cared about was the soft bed under me. Then, I was finally able to surrender to my exhaustion.

81

We're Friends?

"Take as deep of a breath as you can."

My ribs groaned. The wound in the middle of my chest ached deeply.

"Is that as deep as you can go?" Helen asked. She shifted the stethoscope across my back. "Can you try again?"

I nodded. Sitting up straighter, I pulled in as much air as my lungs could hold. The tender skin holding the wound together stretched uncomfortably, and my sternum groaned again.

"Good." She peeked over my shoulder to make sure my chest hadn't ripped open. "Good!"

"The potions are holding," Mrs. Kale noted with relief.

"It appears so." Helen draped her stethoscope around her neck. "I'll leave you with some topical potions for the wound itself in case it starts to bleed. But no more cocktails to keep you together."

My shoulders sagged forward. "Can I lie back?"

"Yep. I'm done."

As Helen got to her feet, Mrs. Kale helped ease me back into the pillows. Once she collected all her equipment, she turned to Mrs. Kale. "If you need anything, call me. Day or night."

"Thank you, Helen." Mrs. Kale squeezed her hand.

"Thanks, Helen." I managed a weak wave.

With a tender smile, Helen left the room. A few moments later, we heard the front door close.

"I can't imagine what would've happened if that knife hit Michael . . ." Mrs. Kale said quietly. "You saved my son. I'll never be able to repay you for that."

"You really shouldn't thank me. I hate him almost every day."

"Almost every day?" Michael shuffled into the room. "I must be slipping."

"Hey, baby. Welcome back." Mrs. Kale's eyes ran over him, looking for new injuries. When she found none, she asked, "Can I get you anything?"

He shook his head as he tugged off his jacket. "I'm good. Thank you. How is she?"

"The wound has remained closed for a full forty-eight hours, and Helen gave her a thumbs-up." Mrs. Kale turned to me. "If you're up to it, I have one more test before I give you the all clear."

I shrugged. The movement was small enough not to aggravate the wound. "Sure."

Walking back to my bedside, she sat on the mattress and lifted my wand from the side table. She turned it around, offering me the hilt. "I just need you to pull on your magic."

My eyes turned to Michael. His relief over the wound staying closed was completely gone.

I took the wand from her grasp. With the pain already weighing on my ribcage, I braced myself for what might come. Taking a deep breath, I pulled on my magic.

It awoke with a long yawn, filling my chest with warmth. It rolled down my arm to fill my wand. I thought the wound would burn or groan. Instead, it felt molten, like it was swirling around the barely held-together wound, looking patiently for an escape.

"That's fine," Mrs. Kale said, placing her hand on mine.

I released my magic and set my cold wand on the nightstand. Mrs. Kale stretched the collar of my shirt down over the wound. Michael and Mrs. Kale watched expectantly.

When the skin didn't burst open, Mrs. Kale sat back with a smile. "Any pain?"

I shook my head.

"Good." Michael rubbed a hand over his face and managed a smile in her direction.

Mrs. Kale smoothed the hair away from his forehead. She rose on her tiptoes and placed a kiss on his cheek. Then she left the room. As soon as the door closed behind her, he sat beside me and leaned against the head-board.

"How was the final round of the Award Challenge?" I asked, shifting over to give him more space. "Did you kick Dmitri's ass?"

"Of course."

I grinned, knowing that while everyone else's Guardian had fallen to the mat one way or another—except Atlas—mine stood undefeated. "I wish I could've seen it."

"It wasn't much of a fight. I could've done it with one hand tied behind my back."

"Did they announce the winner?"

Michael nodded. "It was Contestant Nineteen."

Figures. "Has he chosen what weapons we can bring into the Final Trial?"

"Each Contestant can bring their favored weapon in addition to their wand."

"That's surprisingly nice of him." I expected him to say we couldn't bring in anything.

"Oh, it wasn't. He said it didn't matter what weapon you brought in; he will defeat you. This at least makes it interesting."

"What a cocky asshole."

Michael made a noise of agreement.

I thought for a moment. "I can bring those knives we practice with. I'm not completely terrible with them."

He shook his head. "You would have to be close to your opponent. I would prefer you have something that gives you more room to maneuver."

"Like a javelin?" I laughed at the thought of running around with something taller than I was.

"God, no. You'd end up stabbing yourself." He dragged his hands through his hair. This only made it even more unkempt than before. "I think I might have something." He swung his legs over the mattress and rose to his feet. "I'll be right back."

"Do we have to do this now?"

"I'll be quick," he called just before the bedroom door shut behind him.

Sighing, I relaxed into the pillows and waited for him to come back. I'm not sure how long he was gone. My eyes slid shut, and sleep fell over me.

I jerked awake when the door bumped into the wall as he strolled back toward me.

"Can you stand?"

I groaned. "Do I have to?"

"This will be quick. I promise." He offered me his hand.

I took a few seconds to prepare myself. Michael patiently waited with his hand outstretched. With a deep breath, I grabbed his hand. Squeezing my eyes tight, I pulled myself into the upright position.

Pain whipped around my chest. I breathed slowly through my nose. Only when the pain subsided to a dull torture did I finally open my eyes.

"Sorry." My hand was wrapped around his like a viper.

He gripped my fingers before I could pull away. "You're doing good. Take your time."

Before I could talk myself out of it, I pulled myself to my feet. His strong hand rested on my waist to keep me from swaying.

"Are you ok?"

I nodded. "I'm fine."

"Does anything—"

I smiled. "This is as good as it's going to get."

He glared at the patch of gauze peeking over the collar of my shirt.

"What did you get me?" I asked, pulling the collar higher.

Reaching into his back pocket, he took out a bundle of black silk and parted it to reveal the weapon.

It was the size and shape of a long TV remote, but with no buttons. Its surface was a flawless, smooth silver. It was so perfect, I could see my reflection.

"Thanks . . ." I said slowly, taking it from his palm. "You shouldn't have?"

Amusement gleamed in his eyes as he repositioned it in my hands. Taking my thumb, he pressed the end. From the opposite end, a blade shot out. If Michael's hands hadn't been around mine, I would've dropped it.

The four-foot blade had a dramatic curve on one side, while the other was straight. The metal reflected everything perfectly, just like the handle. The edge looked sharp enough it could cut through an entire cow in one motion.

"What is it?" My voice dropped into a whisper of wonder.

"An enchanted switchblade. It will only open for you. If anyone else tries, the enchantments will sear their hands." He moved my hands, one underneath the other, around the pommel.

My brain was unable to distinguish it from my arm. It was so natural to hold. And light. "This is mine?"

"It is now." He positioned my arms so I held it just above my belly button. "You're going to hold it here. With your left hand, use your pinky and middle finger for support." His foot nudged my left one back. "Just like with a wand, keep your dominant foot forward and your body angled." He stepped back, taking his hands with him.

"What's it made of? It hardly weighs anything."

"Dragon stone. It's the bone found in dragon wings. It's very brittle until enchanted. Then, it's the second strongest substance on earth."

Removing my eyes from the single most beautiful thing I owned, which wasn't saying a lot, I looked at the person who gave it to me. "Thank you."

He nodded with a smile that was barely visible.

Shifting my grip, I moved it through the air. Using too much momentum, the edge dipped toward Michael's neck.

"Hey!" He jumped back. "Let's learn how to use it before you move it like that."

"Sorry." Color rose to my cheeks. "How do I make the blade go back in?"

"Push the button again." He gestured to the opposite end.

Carefully removing one hand from the hilt, I pressed the button. The blade slid back into the handle with a quick, clear sound. Michael took it from me before I accidentally reopened it.

"Where did you get that?"

"When I was given the title of Master Hunter, the Master of the Guard gave it to me. But I've never used it. Just wasn't my sort of weapon. It decorated my desk." He tossed it onto the bed.

"You had a desk?"

"Back when the Guard was running, I had an office."

I couldn't even picture him behind a desk, let alone trapped in an *office*.

"We can work on using it tonight," he said.

"In the meantime, can I sit back down?"

"Of course." He jumped forward, ready to help me.

I pushed away his offered hands and eased myself back onto the bed. Holding my breath, I leaned back until my spine was resting against the headboard. Michael hovered beside me until I was comfortable. With his jaw clenched, he sat by my feet.

"How are you feeling?" he murmured.

"Like I was hit by a train." The corner of my lips tipped up when I heard the rumble from his chest.

"That's an improvement. Most people would have compared it to having a plane fly into them." A crooked smile formed on his lips.

"What's the worst injury you've ever had?"

"Hmm." He stared at the headboard through half-closed eyes. "I broke my back once."

"What?" I leaned forward and winced at the flare in my chest. "How can you break your back and still kick my ass?"

"You say that like it's hard to kick your ass."

I stuck my tongue out at him.

"I have two magically enhanced plates keeping my spine together. The magic also makes sure I'm able to walk." He lifted his left leg. "But I can't feel anything past my knee."

"What happened?"

"Your father and I were hunting a man who had completed the demon transformation. When we caught him, he was a Celestial Eleven."

"Cheese and rice," I muttered. "I've never heard anyone mention Celestial as a status before."

"Most Users don't believe they ever existed. They're kind of like the Greek and Roman gods of User mythology. Anyway, his status was just a guess. When a demon dies, it's impossible to tell anything from an autopsy because of how decayed the body is. During the encounter, he threw me from a rooftop. I lost my grip on my wand, so I couldn't buffer the landing."

I winced. "How far was the drop?"

"Twelve stories, maybe."

"How are you not dead?"

"Users are more resilient, remember? I fractured my skull, broke my spine in two places, and shattered my ribcage. My shoulders and hips had to be remodeled."

I tried to picture what that would've been like. "I take one knife to the chest and I don't want to move ever again. While you broke nearly everything, and you probably didn't even say 'ouch.'"

"Trust me, I said a lot of other things."

My eyes fell to his leg. "You really can't feel anything in your left leg?"

He nodded. "Atlas put a knife in the back of my calf once to see how long it would take for me to notice."

"You're kidding."

"Nope. If it hadn't bled so much, I don't think I would've noticed."

"That man is insane."

"You don't even know the half of it." His humor evaporated when he looked at the gauze peeking from my shirt.

"I've been meaning to ask you." He took a deep breath and slowly released it. "Why did you jump in front of that knife?"

"The last thing I needed was for my Guardian to die. Can you imagine having to find a new one this late in the game?" I scoffed. "Talk about a nightmare."

He didn't respond to my joke. His gaze remained cool and intent. "Why, Charlie? I should be the last person you would do that for."

I had wondered when he was going to ask. I kept replaying that moment at the party. One minute we were dancing, and the next I was behind him with a knife flying toward my chest.

"I guess it's a really dramatic way of saying I have your back, too."

His eyes locked onto mine and for a while, he didn't say anything.

"Thank you." The words were so soft they melted into the stillness of the room. "But promise me you'll never do it again."

"I can't do that."

"Well, I can't have you like this because of me again." He gestured to my prone body.

"So, you want me to just stand by when death is heading toward you?"

"Yes."

"Then, you're an idiot." I crossed my arms over my chest. "Why are you so convinced that you don't deserve someone else's protection? You're the one who's always running around trying to make sure everyone else is safe."

"I've done things—" He wrestled with the words in his mouth. Fighting them back, he said instead, "I've done things to people that, when my time comes, I don't want anyone to stand in the way."

"I don't believe that."

"I'm not asking you to. I'm asking you not to put your life in front of mine."

"Well, too bad."

"Charlie—"

"Shut up." I rolled my eyes. "What kind of friend would I be if I watched you get stabbed when I knew there was something I could do to stop it?"

He stared at me, taken aback. "We're friends?"

Cheese and rice, I did say that. "Maybe . . . I don't know. It depends on the day. And what mood I'm in. And how much of a jackass you are."

His mouth twitched, just barely. The movement was so small, and the room was so dim, I almost thought I imagined it.

"If friendship makes you uncomfortable," I said slowly, "I can insult every aspect of your being until we hate each other again."

"No," he chuckled. "Being friends is . . . fine. I surprisingly don't hate the idea. I mean, it doesn't make me gag."

"Oh, come on," I laughed.

"Just don't ask me to give you a back massage or tell me about your feelings. There are limits to this thing." He gestured with two fingers between us.

"Don't be ridiculous." I rolled my eyes. "You don't have any feelings, so you wouldn't be able to relate anyway."

Matching my grin, our laughter made the room feel warm, like it didn't reek of potions and the undertone of blood. It was one of the rare moments when I didn't feel the constant ache in my chest.

Accidentally, his gaze dropped to his watch. His humor left him with a sigh. "We should get you back to the Magisterium."

"Do we have to?" I had fallen in love with the secluded, relaxed nature of the ranch. No one expected anything from me.

"Lenin said as soon as my mother and Helen gave you the green light, that you had to return."

I sighed. "And orders are orders."

With tight lips, he nodded. "You can rest a bit longer. I'll gather your things and we'll leave after dinner."

Arguing about it would be a waste of energy that I didn't have. I closed my eyes and let exhaustion take me as Michael silently moved about the room.

82

Illusions

Over an hour later, Michael tapped my shoulder.

Helping me sit up, he handed me a tall glass of bright pink liquid. I chugged the entire thing. As all pain receded from my body, Michael grabbed my hand and led me outside.

We arrived at the Magisterium just as dinner was being put away. As soon as we appeared, the student chatter changed in pitch. Murmurs of shock and whispers of excitement swept through the room. The Contestants at the high table stopped their conversations to turn.

"Charlie!" Cornelia burst through the crowd and threw her slender arms around my neck.

Michael dropped my bag and quickly yanked her back. He exhaled when he saw I wasn't in any pain. Turning to my friend, he said, "Miss Montgomery, please don't break her before she breaks herself."

Cornelia leapt back. "I'm so sorry."

"You're fine." I waved off her apology. "I'm so numb, you could shoot me in the back and I wouldn't feel it."

Michael rubbed his eyes. "For the love of God, let's not test that."

"I agree."

A touch of warmth sparked in my chest at that voice.

I spun around just as Blake stepped up to me. His eyes weren't steel-coated with disappointment. Relieved, he wrapped his arms around my shoulders and held me like I was made of brittle glass.

"You're a bloody fool," he muttered into my hair.

"I've been called worse." I blinked back the moisture building behind my eyes and pulled back. "Are you alright?"

"I should be asking you that. I didn't take a knife to the chest."

I waved him off. "I'm fine."

Michael tapped my arm. "I'm going to take your things to your room. Can I speak to you for a moment, Contestant Johnson?"

Blake's eyes widened. He shot me a slightly panicked look before nodding. "Yes, sir."

Michael stepped back, and as soon as they were out of eavesdropping distance, he started speaking with a stern expression.

"About time you came back! I was thinking I lost my bet." Thiago bounded down the stairs from the high table. His eyes lingered on my chest, looking for the wound.

"What bet?" I turned away from Blake and Michael.

"There was a wager among the Top Seven on how long you would survive."

"Oh, nice. What did you bet?"

"I bet that you would make it. If I won, I could choose any Contestant I wanted, and they wouldn't be able to practice with their selected weapon for a week. The Russian bet the same, only he said you wouldn't make it two days."

"No surprise there." I glanced at the high table and saw Dmitri studying me, looking to see how the wound affected my movements. I crossed my arms over my chest, determined not to show any discomfort.

"Thanks to your stubborn will to live, the Russian can't touch his weapon for a week." Thiago grinned.

"Where have you been?" Cornelia asked. "I kept checking the news for updates on your condition, but they said you hadn't checked in anywhere."

"Guardian Kale knows a couple places off the grid." I looked at Michael. He was still with Blake, but this time the roles were reversed. Blake was the one with his arms crossed as he sternly addressed the Master Hunter.

"I don't understand how you could take a knife to the chest and still pin almost every Guardian in under a minute." Again, Thiago looked at the wound.

I gripped my shoulders hoping to hide my Achilles Heel from his invasive eyes.

Cornelia nodded with wide eyes. "It was incredible."

"Or a trick." Emeka had left the high table to stand beside Thiago. He, too, looked me over, but with intense scrutiny. "You gave everyone the illusion that you were weak. That's how you were able to do it."

"As soon as she knocked your Guardian on his ass, I think everyone knew what they were getting into," Thiago chuckled.

Cornelia snorted and quickly covered her mouth.

Emeka's face flushed. He stepped menacingly close. "I will not be laughed at by a Low Common."

I stepped in front of her. "Touch her, and I'll show you how easy it was to throw your Guardian on his ass."

"She barely has enough magic to be worth her place in this school. She does not deserve your protection."

"And you barely have enough of a soul to be called human, but I still dragged you through the First Trial." I forced myself to hold his gaze without blinking. "You were talking to me, so talk to me."

He shook his head. "You set the whole thing up. The attack at the party. The wound. None of it's real."

"You're kidding," I snapped, not believing what I was hearing.

He shrugged off my sarcasm. "You manipulated your way into the Top Seven. Why wouldn't you do this to win?"

"That's funny coming from the guy who couldn't even finish the First Trial by himself." Thiago grinned.

Emeka inhaled, ready to reprimand his fellow competitor, but as soon as Blake stepped into the circle, his mouth clicked shut.

"What did he want?" I asked, nodding to Michael's retreating figure.

"He wanted me to make sure you stayed out of trouble." Blake's eyes raked over Emeka. "What are you doing here?" From Blake's tone, he wasn't really looking for an answer. He just wanted him to leave.

Emeka's eyes dropped to my chest, looking to see past my protective arms and sweater. With a shake of his head, he retreated back to his dinner at the high table.

"Pompous ass," Blake muttered. "Did he tell you he thinks you and Guardian Kale planned the whole thing at the party?"

I nodded with an eye-roll. "It's a good theory. It almost makes me wish I was that smart."

"Don't be ridiculous." Blake shuddered. "We should get to the training room."

"That's my clue." Cornelia squeezed my hand and gave Blake a quick hug. "I'll see you guys at breakfast tomorrow." Spinning around, she headed back to her dinner.

"Are you ok to join us?" Blake asked, as the three of us moved out of the dining room.

"I'm fine. This thing," I tapped the bandage on my chest, "has ten different potions on it. The only way it's going to rip open is if it takes a direct hit. I can do a cartwheel to prove it."

"No!" He grabbed my arm before I could raise them above my head. "I'll take your word for it."

"I don't break easy, remember?" I laughed. "If Guardian Kale didn't think I could come back to school, I'd be staring at a ceiling right now, surrounded by scented candles and flowers."

"Did he have you at a hospital, or a spa?" Thiago asked, amused.

"I'm not concerned with what Guardian Kale thinks," Blake said harshly. "He only wants you to do well in The Trial so you can add points to his side of things. He's the reason you had a knife in your chest in the first place."

I stopped dead in my tracks. The other two turned to face me. Thiago was watching my expression with amusement. Blake knew he said something wrong, but he didn't take it back.

"I jumped in front of that knife because he's my friend, and his life is worth saving," I said sternly.

"You jumped in front of it?" He exhaled sharply. "Holy shit, Charlie. He's a Master Hunter. Master Hunters don't have friends. Do you even know what he had to do to get that title?"

"You don't know what he's done. For me or—"

"Oh, come on! He protects you because you're a pawn in his game against Master Hart."

Shock shot through my chest. I opened my mouth, wanting to refute him, but there was nothing to say, because that's exactly why I was brought into their war. But Michael and I had moved past that. Right?

"You might want to dial it back a few notches." Thiago's eyes darted around to make sure no one was listening closely. "Remember who you're talking about."

"I know exactly who I'm talking about," Blake continued. "You were hurt because you were with him. You should never have been anywhere near that knife."

Shaking my head, I stepped back. "Where is this coming from?"

"I saw what Denny did to you. I don't want this guy to do the same."

"You have no idea what you're talking about. He's not Denny. He's good. Just, shut up." I stormed down to the training area, leaving before he could retort. Anger burned in my chest, causing the lights to shudder as I passed.

When I stepped onto the training mat, Michael's eyes looked up at the flickering lights. "Are you alright?" he asked, as I grabbed my training clothes.

"I'm fine." I slammed the stall door and pulled on my training gear. I took a moment, pressing my forehead to the door, to breathe. Once I was sure my magic wouldn't break something, I returned to Michael.

Blake was across the room with Atlas. When Blake's eyes met mine, my eyes narrowed.

"Are you alright?" Michael asked again, following the dark look to the other side of the training room.

"I said I'm fine," I snapped. Taking a deep breath, I stamped down my irritation. In its place, my head swam. "Actually, I'm a bit light-headed."

His eyes focused on the hidden wound. "We don't have to train today."

"I don't think we can afford any more breaks."

He knew I was right, but that didn't mean either of us liked it. He paused to replace his wand in the holster under his arm.

"Then we're going to train in a way that won't make you exert yourself so much."

"How does that make any sense?"

He smirked. "Trust me. Take a seat."

I gratefully dropped onto the bench that outlined the room.

"It's a shame you weren't able to grow up in our educational system. Everything magic has to offer is nothing short of . . . magical," he said with a light chuckle. "To become a Hunter, I had to pass each Testing Year at each of the Seven Great Schools. By doing that, I learned there's so much more to magic than just waving your wand around. Some of it can be used for trickery."

"Like card tricks?"

He shrugged. "They follow the same idea of making someone think you're doing one thing, only to surprise them with something else." Michael took a scrap of paper from his pocket.

Magic flowed over the surface, changing it into a black playing card. He spun the King of Spades through his fingers, and flicked it around his shoulders to catch it in his other hand. He brushed the card against the tip of my nose and when I refocused, it was the Queen of Hearts.

A smile tugged at his lips. "Would you like a challenge?"

Curiosity flowed through my veins. "You know I would."

He smoothed his hands over the card, making it vanish. "An illusion is something few Users can accomplish because it requires a high status. An illusion creates a magical projection around you that tricks people into seeing whatever you want them to see, without seeing you."

My eyes widened. "Can you do it?"

He almost looked offended. "Of course. It's one of my best tricks. The key is to keep everyone distracted, so they can't see what's really going on. That way, your enemy will think you're standing in front of them . . ."

He pinched the card between his fingers. With a flick of his wrist, he shot it toward my face. A hand reached around from behind me and snagged it from the air an inch from my nose.

". . . when you're really behind them."

I almost fell off the bench as he chuckled low in my ear. Jumping to my feet, I spun around and found him comfortably leaning against the wall.

I looked back to where he had been playing with the card. He didn't Port. There was no Porting circle burned into the padded floor, and there was no way he could have moved that fast.

I turned back to him, grinning like a fool. "You *have* to teach me how to do that."

"I will. But it'll be difficult, and the chances of you succeeding are slim. This is an advanced magical technique."

"Yeah, yeah. What do I have to do?"

"Pull on your magic."

My magic was already roaring through me, ready for his next instruction.

"You're going to push your magic onto your skin. You'll direct it over your body to create an exact mold. Every hair, wrinkle, and dimple needs to be saturated, or your illusion will look like Swiss cheese."

Taking a deep breath, I forced my magic up and through my skin. To my surprise, it was a lot easier than I expected. The magic itched and burned as it flowed over my body. "What's next?"

"This is the hard part. You're going to step out of the magical mold without disturbing it."

"How do I do that?"

"Anchor the mold to the floor and then detach it from your skin. Think of it like peeling dried glue from your body. Don't actually peel it," he said when I reached toward my arm. "Think, and let your magic do what it's told."

I closed my eyes and pictured the magic slowly lifting from my skin. I winced when I felt it tear around my elbow. When I thought I had the majority of it off, I inched back, feeling the burning mold pull away.

Michael burst out laughing.

I opened my eyes and saw a monster. It definitely was me. It had the general shape of my body, hair color, and my clothes. But unlike Michael's, my creation had one leg, two and a half eyes, and so many holes it looked like someone had taken a machine gun to it. Along every tear, golden magic sparkled.

"You're such a gentleman." Sarcasm poured off my words.

He sucked in a big breath, probably with the intention to snap back, but it came whooping out in another round of laughter. He drew all eyes toward our corner of the training room as my creation toppled over and dissolved into the floor.

"It wasn't *that* funny."

Unable to form words, he nodded, still laughing so hard that tears glistened in the corners of his eyes. The sounds of unbridled joy coming from him caused me to smile too. But my pride refused to let me laugh with him.

Finally catching his breath, he said, "It really wasn't that bad of an attempt. I just wasn't expecting that."

"What did I do wrong?"

"Beginner's mistake. The layer of magic you put on was uneven, and you were too clumsy taking it off. It took me months to be able to do it perfectly. Now." He sat down with an amused smile. "Do it again."

On my second try, I forgot the head.

Every time I tried to make a mold, something was missing, or it was riddled with holes.

Every once in a while, Michael glanced over my shoulder. One time I followed his gaze, and saw a few Guardians watching intently. The Aquarius Guardian was trying to teach his Contestant the same thing. Atlas just laughed.

After my fifth try, he rose to his feet. "It's time to call it a night."

I looked at the clock. We had barely been there an hour. "We just got started."

"If we aren't careful, you could run out of magic." He sent a pointed look to the number on my chest. I had totally forgotten that I was parading around as a Common Six. Someone with that magic status wouldn't be able to use that much magic consistently without running out.

I nodded, starting to feel the potions wearing off. Exhaustion, physical and magical, forced a yawn from my mouth.

Collecting my things, Michael ushered me toward the door and up seven flights of stairs to the apartment level. In my room, I collapsed onto my mattress and was out before Michael closed the front door.

83

The Top Seven's Choice

"Charlie! Come on!" Michael hollered from the living room.

Stumbling over a pile of dirty clothes, I tripped right into the wall. Biting back an array of four-letter words, I yanked open the door.

"What?" I snapped, flicking the hair out of my face.

"We need to get going. Have you seen my jacket?"

"No." Turning back to my room, I grabbed my shoes and tripped over the same pile of clothes. "It wouldn't be in here."

Leaning against the doorframe, he released a heavy sigh. "That means I left it at the ranch. We'll need to leave now if we want to be on time."

"Do you need it?" I sat on my bed and began untangling the laces.

"It's my leather jacket." He said it like that explained everything.

Hiding my smile, I tapped my wand against the laces. As I stood up, they pulled together in perfect bows. "We better get going then," I said, threading my arm through his.

Porting from the Magisterium, we appeared outside the gate guarding the property and climbed the hill to the ranch house.

"I'll be quick." Michael pushed open the door. The aroma of sweet blueberries rushed onto the porch.

If he thought I was going to stay out here after smelling that, then he was out of his damn mind.

Pushing past him, I went straight into the kitchen. Mrs. Kale was just closing the oven door. In her hands was a casserole dish filled with French bread. Chunks of cream cheese and blueberries were piled on top, making my mouth water.

"Well, hello!" Mrs. Kale set the dish on the table. "I wasn't expecting you today."

"Michael forgot his jacket." I couldn't take my eyes off the steaming breakfast. "What's that?"

"Only the best damn breakfast ever." Meg turned in her seat with a smile. Quinton cooed in her arms.

"Breakfast?" I laughed. "It's noon."

Meg shrugged. "Breakfast is a state of mind and an all-day pleasure."

Michael popped into the kitchen with his jacket in hand. "Alright we should get . . . is that blueberry french toast?"

Instead of answering, Mrs. Kale returned to the stove. Collecting a saucepan, she placed it on the table beside the sweet breakfast dish. Lifting the lid, a cloud of steam twisted and curled into the air. Inside, still bubbling, was a thick, purple syrup.

Meg took out her wand and flicked it toward the fridge. The doors swung open, releasing a can of whipped cream. It flew across the kitchen and landed next to the sauce.

Michael was as transfixed as I was by the display on the table. Meg's smile only grew as the silence lengthened.

"Do you want some?" Mrs. Kale asked, barely keeping a straight face. "Your father and brother are in town getting a new horse, so there's plenty to go around."

"We need to get going." Michael took a step back into the hall, but his eyes never left the table.

"We can be a little late." I forced my gaze from the table. "Right?"

Michael checked his watch. "We really can't be late today."

"You can't tell me that whatever Trial thing you're going to is more important than this." Meg took her wand out of the knot on top of her head. A bead of gold darted into the casserole and cut out a large chunk. It levitated out of the pan and onto the plate before her. With another flick of her wand, dollops of blueberry sauce splashed over the top. Lastly, she levitated the whipped cream bottle to release a mountain of sweet cream on top.

Cheese and rice. My stomach rumbled as my mouth became a waterfall.

Michael shook his head. "We're presenting which weapon Charlie's taking into the Final Trial to all the Masters."

That would've been nice to know. "Do we need to get it from the training room?"

Michael shook his head. "I have it. After that, we're going to Founder's Hall."

The mood of the room changed, not dramatically, but enough for me to notice. Mrs. Kale bowed her head. Meg stared at Michael with an intense, unblinking gaze.

"I've always wanted to go," Meg said softly. "You're lucky. They don't let in just anyone."

"What is it?" I asked.

When Michael spoke, it was with an air of reverence. "It's where Masters, Trial Winners, Hunters, our most influential leaders, and the most heroic Users are buried."

Oh. That was the last thing I was expecting.

"It's been a while since you've been there," Mrs. Kale noted.

Michael nodded. Memories pulled at the corners of his lips. "The last time was to visit Arwin."

Meg lowered her wand. "Has it really been that long?"

Michael nodded.

"Well, I think it's good that you're going. I've often wondered, with how things are going, if Lawrence would destroy it." Mrs. Kale sat beside Meg and took Quinton from her so she could eat.

Michael shook his head. "History is too important to him."

Meg scooped whipped cream into her mouth to keep herself from replying.

Michael stepped back toward the door. "We should get going. Enjoy your late breakfast."

"Can I at least pack some up for you?" Mrs. Kale added in a rush. "You can pick it up later."

He smiled softly. "Fine."

"I'll pack some for you too, Charlie." Before he could change his mind, she jumped to her feet and placed Quinton in his arms. She rushed into the kitchen to collect some Tupperware containers.

"Thank you!" I fought back a yawn. I looked over and met Michael's appraising gaze.

"Mom, do you have any Adraffeen?"

"In my bathroom. Why?" Mrs. Kale followed his gaze. "Oh. Meg, can you grab it?"

Meg stuffed her mouth with a large bite of cream cheese and blueberries. Chewing, she marched up the stairs and came back with a tall black bottle. She unscrewed the cap and poured a yellow potion into it. Then she handed it to me. She quickly returned to her breakfast.

I brought the cap to my face and sniffed. I jerked away from the potent smell with a crinkled nose. "Is this alcohol?"

Michael chuckled. "No. You're stupid enough when you're sober." He smirked. "It'll help you wake up. Lenin won't be happy if his Top Seven Contestant looks like she just rolled out of bed."

He had a point.

I tossed the yellow liquid into my mouth. My entire face scrunched up as it slid down my throat. It was like I put a whole lemon in my mouth and started chewing. As soon as it hit my stomach, the exhaustion haunting me ran off. I stood up straight, my mind cleared, and my eyelids didn't feel as heavy.

He plucked the cap from my hand and set it on the table. "See you later, Mom."

I followed Michael from the house and back down the road. When the gate was closed behind us, he took the transporter from his pocket. Taking his hand, we Ported to the training room.

Almost everyone was already in the training room when we arrived. The School Masters were in a tight circle on the far side of the room. The rest of the Masters lined the walls in low conversation and scrutinizing glances.

Master LeOnie, wearing the same soft pink, met my gaze. She nodded once, acknowledging me. I couldn't bring myself to do the same.

She knew what was going to happen at the party. Yet, she didn't do anything to stop it. The wound at the center of my chest pulsed painfully.

I turned from her and scanned the group of Guardians and Contestants. Thiago and his Guardian were never on time, so naturally, he wasn't among the group. Blake was on the other side of the circle with Atlas. Before we made eye contact, I looked away.

"What's up with you and Johnson?" Michael muttered, following my gaze.

"Nothing." I caught Michael's 'that's bullshit' look from the corner of my eye. "He's just being an idiot."

"About what?"

"Nothing."

He gave me the same look again, but I didn't continue. Blake would come around, and I wanted him to be in Michael's good graces when he did.

"Welcome, Contestants!" Master Lenin called from the front of the room. "You have an exciting afternoon ahead of you. As you were told, we will be visiting one of the most important places magic has created: Founder's Hall."

I tilted my head toward Michael. Just above a whisper, I asked, "Where's Master Hart?" My eyes scanned the room, but I didn't spot his usual red suit among the crowd. This seemed important enough for him to accompany us.

"I don't know." The crease between his eyes told me we shared the same thought.

"You'll get to see where all the previous Trial Winners have been laid to rest," Master Lenin continued. "Before we begin, let me remind you that today marks three weeks before the Final Trial."

An explosion of butterflies erupted in my stomach. *Cheese and rice, that's so close.*

"I have been impressed with your diligence in the training room. I look forward to watching how each of you perform." Master Lenin shifted his hands into his pockets. "Third Challenge Winner, Contestant Dmitri Theodore chose what you all will bring into the Final Trial: the weapon of your choice and your wand. You have had some time to select your preferred weapon. Now you will share it with the rest of the Top Seven.

"Second Challenge Winner, Contestant Emeka Selasi. What is your weapon?"

Our group turned as Emeka stepped forward. In his grasp was a spear.

Dmitri snorted and whispered in his father's ear. Both sneered at the other Contestant.

I didn't know what they were laughing at. The weapon had a sharpened animal tooth on both ends. The weathered, stained shaft told of the battles it had been in. The way Emeka held it, I could tell they were old friends.

Master Lenin nodded. "Wise choice. Contestant Amelia Markus, please present to the group."

Contestant Four stepped forward with a trident, a real, honest-to-god trident. The weapon shined like it had just been polished. It was large, with a lot of curves and sharp edges.

Again, a burst of mockery came from Contestant Nineteen. Even Michael shot a look of displeasure their way.

Michael bent down. His warm breath tickled my ear. "It's too bulky. I bet she loses it within the first five minutes."

"Contestant Tala Abalos, what have you chosen?"

In her hands were two knives that reminded me of pitchforks, except the middle prong was the longest. The handles were short, barely extending past her palm. The blades were thin and narrow.

"Sia." Master Lenin said the word with admiration. "A hard weapon to use well. Good luck. First Challenge Winner, Contestant Blake Johnson, present."

I wasn't surprised to see him pull a stainless-steel, compound bow from his shoulder. It was modest, undecorated, and slim. It only had the essential pieces and nothing more.

Back in Kansas, we had spent many summer afternoons in his backyard with that bow. I would lounge in the grass, in charge of the radio, as he shot targets across the yard. He rarely missed.

My teeth were put on edge when the Russians rolled their eyes and their shoulders shook with muffled laughter.

"Contestant Charlie Heart. What have you chosen?"

Michael reached under his jacket and pulled the weapon from his holster. When I took it from him, the metal warmed, ready for action.

Atlas's eyes widened at the sight of it. The Masters started whispering feverishly to each other. Guardians pulled their Contestants close for hurried conversations.

I looked down at the weapon. I wasn't holding it upside down. So, why did it get such a reaction?

"What is that?" the Aquarius Contestant, Amelia, asked.

"It's an enchanted switchblade. A Master's weapon," Atlas explained. That comment caused people to look more closely.

"She probably does not know how to use it. Do you hope to hit people over the head?" Dmitri called with a chuckle.

I hit the button against my hip. Those standing between us jumped out of the way as the blade shot out toward his neck.

"I won't hit you over the head." I dragged the edge across his cheek, removing the thin layer of whiskers. "I'll remove it."

"Thank you, Contestant Heart." Master Lenin's tone implied I needed to put it away.

I ignored the disappointment in Master Lenin's voice. I was enjoying the bald spot on Dmitri's cheek too much. I wish I had taken a lock of his stupid blue hair, too. With a smile, I pressed the button and the blade retracted.

"Contestant Thiago Luis. Present."

He held up three darts. Each identical to the one next to it. Just looking at them made my insides curl.

"And our final member, Third Challenge Winner, Contestant Dmitri Theodore."

He took his weapon from his father's hands. Boldly, he stepped forward with the weapon proudly displayed in his grasp.

Masters shifted around each other to get a better look. Contestants looked at the weapon with awe. Michael, on the other hand, barely hid his eye roll.

It was a double sided axe. On one side was a wide blade that could probably slice through stone like cheese. The opposite end was the hook of a pickaxe. The weapon screamed with fatal possibilities.

"Ah. The weapon from the past Winner, Victor Haltland." Master Lenin glanced at Guardian Theodore, who beamed with pride.

"Some think, if you use the previous winner's weapon, it will grant you favor with the judges," Michael whispered. "I think it's stupid."

I nodded in agreement.

"Well done, Contestants," Master Lenin called across the room. "I look forward to seeing how you incorporate them into your performances.

"Now it is time for the main event. You may stay at Founder's Hall for as long as you wish. The afternoon is yours.

"When you get there, the staff has requested you leave your wand, any other weapons, and shoes at the door." He paused. "Where you are about to go is sacred ground. Please show respect to those who influenced our world the most." Master Lenin bowed his head. "Guardians, you know where to go. Have a great day."

One by one, members of our group began Porting from the room.

84

Founder's Hall

Michael grabbed my hand. Before I could draw another breath, we Ported from one chilly location to the next.

I looked around and saw we were standing in a place I had only seen in movies. Atop a great many white stone steps sat the Lincoln Memorial in Washington D.C.

I spun around, soaking in the landscape. Thousands of people milled around. The noon sun blazed gloriously over the long Reflecting Pool. A couple of the cherry blossom trees were trying to get rid of their last few bouquets of soft pink petals.

Amelia shoved her shoulder into mine as she made her way up the stairs to the memorial.

Glaring at her retreating figure, I asked, "What are we doing here?"

"Founder's Hall was created by Lincoln." Michael's eyes were also narrowed at Contestant Four's back.

"Lincoln was a User?"

He nodded. "He spent the majority of his youth searching where figures of our history were buried so he could bring them here. He was one of the most accomplished low Magic Users in history."

"What was his status?"

"Deficient Three."

We stepped into the shade of the memorial. Abraham Lincoln, with back straight and eyes forward, captured the attention of the plaza.

I had been soaking in the magical world for so long, I forgot anything existed outside of it. Standing in a place built by Regulars, and surrounded by Regulars, felt almost unnatural.

Following the group, we rounded the statue to the left where Master

Lenin waited. Once everyone was there, we followed the School Master over the restricted rope and through a wall of concealing magic. It glided over my skin, itching and burning.

Invisible to the Regulars milling around the memorial, Master Lenin took his wand from his tan suit jacket and tapped the base of the statue twice. Color bled into the white stone. Vibrant panes of colorful stained glass twisted and assembled into an arched doorway.

Master Lenin pushed open the doors and waved for us to go through. A broad staircase twisted down into the earth below the statue. I trailed my hands along the spotless walls as I followed Michael.

At the bottom was a small foyer with a stunning crystal chandelier. There were no decorations, except for the doors at the end of the room, which were twice the size of the set on the side of the statue above.

Between us and those huge doors were fourteen guards in white armor, one for each member of The Trial. Each of them held a tray before them. Michael led me to a pair and began removing his weapons.

He removed his wand and the four knives in his holster. I thought he would stop there, but he added two more knives from the cuffs of his sleeves.

Cheese and rice. Sometimes I forgot just how truly terrifying he was.

I placed my wand and switchblade on the tray. Then I unzipped my boots and placed them on the tray as well.

Once everyone had removed their shoes and weapons, the doors opened.

The foyer opened up to a massive hall. Everything was white, from the shiny floors to the hundred foot ceilings. Eight crystal chandeliers the size of a grand piano hung in a row. Spaced evenly down the hall were five sets of tall double doors with a description above each: Heroes, Historians, Masters, Hunters, and Trial Winners.

The most impressive thing about the hall was the statues. All around the room they occupied the space between the doorways. The men and women depicted in marble stood with regal postures, their arms raised over their heads with palms flush on the ceiling.

"Who are they?" I whispered, gazing up at the towering, proud figures.

"The first School Masters." Michael pointed to the closest marble giant. "Antonio Esperenzo. Guinevere Stamos. Harvey Charles Lenin. Adelaide Montenegro. Vladimir Theodore. Jamieson Apollo. Prescott Sue."

"Lenin? Theodore?"

He nodded. "Their ancestors. Sometimes being a School Master runs in the family."

At the center of the hall was a life-size statue of Abraham Lincoln himself, with his broad hat and wingtip shoes. The statue appeared so realistic; it was as if Lincoln himself stood there, painted white. Clasped in his hands before him was his actual wand.

Behind the statue was a stained-glass mural. The brightly colored glass portrayed a man with the same top hat standing before the stained-glass doors of Founder's Hall. With his wand pointed at the doors, the mural froze the moment in time when he created the hall.

On the other side of the colorful glass was his coffin, made of the same glittering granite. Carved into the sides, with remarkable detail, were images depicting his life.

"Every resting place has the life story carved around the coffin. The stained glass," Michael pointed to the mural, "memorializes their greatest accomplishment."

It was the single, most-magnificent piece of art I had ever seen. Slowly, I walked around, looking at each side of the coffin, absorbing each intricate carving. After a few moments, I realized how quiet it was.

The main hall was empty. Everyone had moved on, passing the Heroes' and Historians' Halls. Embarrassment showed on my cheeks as I peeked over at Michael.

He was the most impatient man in the entire world, yet he didn't usher me to follow the others. Standing calmly beside me, his shoulders were relaxed, and his hands rested in his pockets.

Turning from the Lincoln statue, I quickly followed the others. At the end of the corridor, with the biggest set of doors, was the Masters' Wing. Flanking it were the Trial Winners' and Hunters' Wings.

Through the crystal doors, the Top Seven and their Guardians moved around the long hall of Trial Winners. Stopping under the last glittering chandelier, my gaze moved to the other side of the foyer.

Spinning around, I pushed against the glass doors. Soundlessly, they swung open into the Hunters' Wing.

Lining the walls were more white statues of men and women. Each was poised with their hands clasped before them, with their gaze forward and proud. At the bottom, their name, birth date, and death date were etched. Draped over the white stone was an article of black clothing.

One statue had fingerless gloves. Another had a vest lined with slots for daggers. It was their signature-clothing piece, like Michael's leather jacket or Atlas's trench coat.

Like the ones in the main entrance, behind each statue was a stained-glass mural and a coffin. There wasn't one floor of Hunters. Above me, floor after floor rose high up to a ceiling too far to see.

I slowly turned, taking it all in, and found that Michael wasn't beside me. He stood at the mouth of the hall, his toes just behind the threshold.

With his hands in his pockets, he looked around the first floor, then to the next, and the next. But he didn't move into the wing.

When his gaze met mine, it was like he had forgotten I was there. Taking a deep breath, he stepped into the room and walked to meet me.

"I thought there would be more black." Even though my voice was quiet, it echoed toward the ceiling.

"This is the only time a Hunter wears white."

"Did you know any of them?" I asked, gesturing to the room.

He nodded. "Some. Hunters aren't expected to live long. Well, long by Regulars' standards. But by magical ones, not so much."

Walking further into the hall, he stopped in front of a Hunter with black spurs on his boots. His nameplate read Master Don Frank. "He was a legend when I was in the Guard. He was the longest living Master Hunter. He was killed when I was a fourth of the way through my training."

"What happened to him?"

"He had a bit of a drinking problem, from what I can recall. He got so drunk one night, he couldn't defend himself against a kid fresh out of the University." Returning his hands to his pockets, he continued deeper inside

Falling into step with him, I asked, "How come some of them say Hunter and some of them say Master Hunter?" I remembered Moose telling me the difference, but that was a while ago.

"Back then, there was a chain of command. Hunter—like Atlas—then Master Hunter—me—and then *the* Master Hunter who gave out all the assignments." Michael paused for a moment. "You should meet someone." Without another word, he took off down the hall.

At the end was a huge, stained-glass pane with THE HUNTER'S OATH written from floor to ceiling. Most of the fragments surrounding the words were colored different shades of red. In each shard was an iridescent face of those in coffins around the room.

In front of the stained-glass pane was a coffin. This one wasn't just made of white granite. Gold and pearls outlined the lifelike images carved into the sides. The statue in front of it had no signature black clothing.

The man's strong face watched the room without worry or expectation. His hands were clasped before him and between them was his wand.

"Master Hunter Arwin," I read. "Who was he?"

"My boss. When you finished training, he decided if you got to be a Hunter, which trio you would serve on, and which Master Hunter you would work for. If you were good enough, he'd petition the School Masters to give you a title and a hunting trio of your own."

I recalled that Michael was a part of the *Four* Horsemen. "Don't you have four people on your team?"

"It was me, Atlas, and Went at the beginning. Sánchez joined us later. She actually worked for Lawrence and Brandon Moore."

My head whipped toward him. "No way."

Michael nodded. "Moore was an idiot back then too."

I looked up into the face of Master Hunter Arwin. I tried to picture what he looked like in real life, but no matter how hard I tried, he remained a colorless statue. "Did you know him well?"

Michael didn't answer right away. "I liked to think he was my friend, but Master Hunters live the oath for so long that there's not a lot left in them that makes them human." He pointed to the wall of red stained-glass behind the statue.

In elegant strokes, it read:

With this oath, I hand over my life and everything attached. I reject my family and the responsibilities they hold for me, holding only the name they gave me. With this oath, I become one of the dead, the forgotten, the unwelcomed. With this oath, I stand outside the laws of heaven and hell.

I will not seek any future of my own interests.

I will not rest nor indulge in the pleasures of life until my task is complete and I rest in stone.

I will produce no children, for I will take the lives of many children.

I will have no love, for I will take the lives of many loved ones.

I will fight for those who cower behind me.

I will respect those who stand with me.

I will guard the backs of those who stand in front of me, and I will show no mercy to those who stand against me.

With this oath, I will sin to condemn those who have sinned. They may burn me in hell's fires, and drown me in heaven's tears, but I will not stray from this oath.

With this vow, I become a Hunter of darkness.

My stomach churned. Now I know why he thought this war would take him, why he thought he would be alone when his time came. His oath demanded everything for the greater good, even if he was damned in the process. His title held so much more weight now. And to think, not that long ago, I thought he just hunted animals. I was such an idiot.

"Did you swear that, too?" I asked.

He nodded. "Every Hunter does when they're chosen."

"Is that when you get your death certificate, too?"

He nodded, looking at the grave with an expression of pure serenity. I had never seen him so calm, even when he was sleeping. He looked weightless, like nothing existed outside those white walls.

"I've never seen you like this."

His eyes never left the tomb. "Like what?"

"Calm. Like you don't have a war to win."

He stared blankly at the coffin in front of him. A minute or two passed before he broke the silence. "This will be my resting place . . . if the war turns our way. That, or my body will be displayed under Lawrence's boots. He has a thing for trophies. But I hope I'll end up here."

That was the most human thing I had ever heard him say. I wanted that. The peace that soothed his smoldering soul.

"Can I ask you something?"

He nodded.

"I'm guessing I won't end up in a place like this, but when this war ends . . . can you put me somewhere that's as peaceful as you look here?"

His eyes snapped away from the memorial. Shock raised his eyebrows. "What makes you think I'll consider that?"

I smiled up at him. "Because you're a good man."

He huffed. "I'm not a good man. That oath describes the kind of man that I am, and the unforgivable things I'm required to do."

"That's not what I've seen."

He shook his head, looking back at the memorial in front of him.

"Or maybe because I'm your friend?"

He winced ever so slightly. After a moment, he finally answered my question. "You have my word."

I turned back to the coffin and tried to imagine if I was put to rest in a place like this. What would be on the side of my white box? What single moment would be put in colored glass behind me?

Michael took in a deep breath and stepped away from Master Hunter Arwin. "Come on. You should see the Trial Winners."

I wanted to go up to every floor and look into the face of every Hunter. I wanted to hear Michael talk about what this part of his life was like. But the look on his face said he didn't want to be in here anymore.

So I nodded and followed him down the hall. Just once, I glanced back at the man frozen in stone.

"How did Master Hunter Arwin die?"

Michael stiffened, and the air around him grew cold. The muscle in his jaw pulsed with memories. "Lawrence. It was the night he killed Lauren. He killed everyone in the Guard, including Master Hunter Arwin. It was his way of moving into a new era for his kingdom, making Hunters a thing of the past. Lawrence, Moore, Sánchez, Atlas, Went, and myself are the only ones left."

His words knocked against the walls of the silent wing. The eyes of the statues followed us as we passed. Moose told me one day that all the Hunters disappeared, leaving the Four Horsemen, and a couple that were loyal to Lawrence, alive. She had wondered what happened to the rest of the Hunter Guard. And now I knew.

For the first time, the anger in my chest wasn't for Dmitri.

Stepping into the main hall, Michael grabbed the doors, but he paused before closing them. His eyes wandered over the people who only lived in memories. The fire in my chest intensified.

Michael pulled the doors closed. Silently, he walked across the hall to where the rest of the Contestants were.

The statues in front of these coffins now held the weapon they used to win their Trial. The moment of their victory was painted vibrantly on the glass behind them.

We walked silently past each . . . and that's when I noticed that every previous Trial Winner was dead. When we reached the end of the section, a statue of Victor Haltland stood. Every single Winner was here, except Lawrence Hart.

"Why are they all dead?" I asked, keeping my voice low. Other Contestants wandered around the hall in hushed pairs.

"It's called the Winner's Curse. Each Contestant copes with it differently, but it always ends the same. The Trial kills you, or your memories of The Trial do."

"Except for Lawrence."

He shook his head. "What he did to get to the finish line drove him to join the Hunter Guard, so he did die in a way."

I looked up at Victor Haltland. His broad face held the same bitter determination as his hand that gripped a replica of the axe Dmitri claimed to take into the Final Trial.

Behind the statue, in brilliant color, was a picture of him using his axe to push himself to his feet. Carved into the sides of his coffin were depictions of him training others back at his school. There weren't many images. The date at the foot of his statue confirmed he hadn't lived a long life.

I opened my mouth to tell Michael I wanted to see his Trial when we got back to the Magisterium, but the request never left my mouth.

The sounds of feet marching down the hall cut through the hushed conversations around the room. The chandeliers rattled overhead. A scream rolled down the hallway before being cut short. A guard's body flew past the door and slammed against the wall. It crumpled to the ground in a heap of broken bones.

Michael took a cautious step forward, placing me behind him, as the footsteps grew louder.

Shadows swept over the floor seconds before a group of masked Users flooded the room. Raising their wands, they fired.

85

Get Her Out of Here

Michael shoved me behind a coffin.

The first ward hit the granite beside me. Michael threw himself across my body just as debris exploded around us. The air heated as magic tore through it. The ground shook. Glass shattered and clattered to the floor.

Michael hauled me to my feet and shoved me toward the back of the room. He whipped us around the last coffin and pushed me to the floor. He crouched in front of me on the balls of his feet.

More sounds of catastrophe blasted down the hall.

"Who are they?" I asked. Every cell in my body was alive. Magic stirred restlessly in my chest. If only I had my wand.

"Someone who wants to screw with The Trial." He peered around the corner. "They're attacking Guardians." Michael put his fingers into his mouth. A whistle cut through the explosion. "We need to get out of here."

"Can't we Port?"

He shook his head. "There's an enchantment over the Hall, so no one can grab something and leave with it. The only way out," he nodded toward the battle raging through the room, "is through the front door."

Now it was my turn to curse. That would mean we would have to go through the Users in the masks. We were unarmed and without shoes.

A flash of black joined us behind the coffin. A scream jumped into my mouth.

"Ello, love." Atlas dropped beside his boss with a wink. "This is surprising. Here I was, thinking we were going to have a boring afternoon."

"One could hope." Michael faced his fellow Hunter. "Do you have a way out?"

"Of course." Atlas shifted near the edge of the coffin. He pointed across the room of flying debris and blood splatters toward a small hallway. "That's used by the cleaning crew. It goes straight to the main lobby, and then to the surface."

"Where's Blake?" My stomach dropped when another blast of magic rocked the room. "Oh, God—" Michael pinned me down before I could stand up to look for him.

"Relax," Atlas yelled over another blast. "He's already heading up those stairs with Thiago."

"You left him alone with that weirdo?"

"Give me some credit. I taught the kid how to defend himself. It's that other bloke you should be worried about."

I knew Blake was smart. Having him state the obvious did nothing to loosen the tight grip of fear on my throat.

"Are you sure that way is safe?" Michael flinched toward me as another blast threw chunks of marble at us.

"I checked it out myself."

Michael nodded. "Then get her out of here."

"What?" I jerked my focus to him. His face was mere inches from mine. Specks of plaster dusted his face like white freckles. There were even some on his eyelashes.

"I'll meet you at the Magisterium," Michael told him.

"What are you going to do?" Atlas directed his question to Michael as he shifted toward me.

"I'm going to make a few introductions." Michael nudged me toward the other Hunter. "I'll make sure you get to the hallway. Stay with her, and keep her safe."

Atlas held his eyes with a steel gaze. The obvious dislike for the order made the muscle in his jaw pop, but he didn't verbalize it.

"I got this," Michael said.

As Atlas grabbed my arm, it finally clicked. Michael wasn't coming with us.

Atlas pulled me away from Michael as the Master Hunter darted into the open. Golf ball-size chunks of marble rocketed across the floor. More magic spilled into the air. I couldn't tell if it was from the fight around the corner, or if it was coming from me.

Pushing me in front of him, Atlas guided me across the room. Dust filled the air like a thick cloud. Magic flashed. The majestic memorials were reduced to broken statues and empty window frames. Blood was smeared and speckled every few steps. Gagging, I stepped over a severed ear.

Atlas looped an arm around my waist and jerked us behind the remains of a Contestant's statue. A ward exploded into the figure seconds later. I peeked out and instantly located Michael.

He stood in the middle of the hall, proving why he was still alive in this war.

He stalked forward without taking cover. The masked men scurried for shelter, but they were like ants trying to hide from a boot.

He must have taken a wand from one of the fallen. He slashed the weapon up. The ward he fired ripped the other man in half. His blood splashed against the white stone and intertwined with the colored glass on the floor. An orb of gold slammed into Michael's arm, but he continued like nothing happened.

He shot two wards back to back, casting a man into a statue and then exploding it. The wand in his hand was aglow with magic, and his eyes filled with intent to kill.

Atlas roughly shoved me forward. I tripped over a slab of granite. Blood dripped down my knee. He lifted me up and threw me into the hallway.

"We can't leave him!"

He gripped my shoulders to keep me from going back. "He can take care of himself—"

I threw my fist into his stomach, causing him to double over in shock. Just as I was about to round the corner, he looped an arm around my neck and twisted me back to where I was.

"We need to get out of here. Now." His tone sounded remarkably like Michael's. "He can handle himself. Trust me. You haven't seen him hunt."

The glimpse of Michael stalking forward and ripping a man in half sent chills down my spine. That should have reassured me, but I couldn't shake my panic. "We can't leave him."

"I have my orders." The bastard then *threw me over his shoulder.* My screams of fury couldn't be distinguished from the mess behind us.

Atlas flew down the hall and turned into the main lobby. With a curse, he spun around and placed my feet on the ground. Quick as a snake, he grabbed a shard of glass from the floor and lunged forward. A masked User fell to the floor, blood spraying out of their neck.

Atlas propelled me toward the exit. Four men rapidly descended upon us. He scooped up his wand from the weapon containers and turned to fire.

I stumbled toward the cache and frantically searched for my wand.

I glanced over my shoulder. Atlas was taking on the four of them at the same time. He was brilliant, blocking and casting simultaneously.

I located my switchblade first.

I spun around just as one of the assailants broke away. I struck the button, releasing the blade, as the masked man raised his wand. I threw the switchblade as hard as I could. It cut through the air and slammed into his chest, throwing him back.

Turning back to the containers of weapons, I finally found my wand.

Magic flooded down my arm like lava. The fire designs on my wand glowed. I whipped my wand over my head. An arch of magic slammed into the ceiling.

The granite cracked, crumbled, and then fell. Screams escaped the masks of the four Users as the sky rained down on them. They were covered in stone within seconds. Blood spilled out from under the boulders.

Atlas pushed me up the stairs and threw open the doors. Sunshine poured through the memorial. It looked too cheerful, too normal for what was happening underneath our feet.

I spun back toward the entrance. The sight of blood was seared into my eyes. All I could think of was that Michael was somewhere down there, bleeding.

"Don't make a scene, love." Atlas threw an arm around my shoulders and casually stepped out from under the barrier of magic.

Regulars gasped as two people, covered in dust and speckled with blood, popped out of nowhere. I didn't care if I made a scene or not. I didn't care if random strangers thought I was crazy.

I struggled against Atlas. I cursed. I twisted. The buttons on his shirt cuff dug into my skin. I slammed my elbows and fists into any part that I could reach. I dug my heels into the floor.

But he wasn't slowed by any of it. He nodded in apology to a frightened couple as we passed out of the memorial. Once outside, he struggled to grab a transporter from his pocket and Ported us off the street.

Just as my feet touched down in my room at the Magisterium, I sank my teeth into his forearm.

86

I've Got Your Back and You've Got Mine

"Bloody hell!" He jumped back. "Get a grip."

"You left him!" I picked up a pillow and hurled it at him.

"Oi!" He jumped out of the way. "If anyone can handle themselves, it's him."

"You don't know that. We have to go back."

"I have my orders to stay here and make sure you're not targeted."

I gritted my teeth to the point where I wondered if they were cracking. The lights flashed like fireworks.

Atlas glanced at the light show. He took a deep breath, and when he spoke, his voice was smooth and calming. "He's exactly where he's supposed to be."

"He could be dead!"

"He's fulfilling his oath."

Ice water poured through my veins as the words filled my mind. *With this oath, I hand over my life and everything attached.*

Shattered glass. Splattered blood. Broken statues. The scene in the Trial Winners' Wing flooded my mind. Michael, surrounded by chaos. I couldn't kick the fear that as soon as we left, Michael was on the floor without a wand. He taught me that any battle can turn on a dime.

"He's exactly where he's supposed to be," Atlas said again, drawing me out of my head.

"Then go back and help him. I'm fine."

He was shaking his head before I finished. "My orders are to stay here until he comes back."

"And if he doesn't?"

"He will." He nodded to the blood dripping from my knee. "You're bleeding on the carpet. You should get cleaned up." Leaving the doorway, he dropped onto the couch. He rolled his sleeve up to his elbow.

I was familiar with the tattoos on the back of his hands: a heart and a curving spine. I didn't realize he had more. His arm was completely covered. Barely any of his skin showed through the black ink.

Within the collage were images of organs. Most of them were detached skulls. There was a heart on the inside of his elbow, and a pair of lungs on the inside of his wrist. Stamped into the center of each was a letter.

Atlas placed the tip of his wand to a bare spot on his arm. The rings around his wand glowed as black ink darkened his skin. The slope of a neck solidified, and a shard of glass stabbed through the image.

Cheese and rice . . . was every tattoo for someone he killed?

As the tattoo settled, the skin around it puffed up and blushed a sore red.

"Does it hurt?" I asked as he pressed his wand to his skin again.

He didn't look up. "I'm used to it."

The only thing that made a sound was the clock on the mantel.

"Does it bother you . . . killing people?" I asked.

He didn't answer right away, which wasn't like the flirtatious Atlas I knew. When he did answer, his voice was low. "Yes."

"Then, why do you do it?"

"Because I have a gift." A humorless chuckle shook his shoulders. "A twisted gift, but it's all I've got." He rolled down his sleeve and leaned back into the couch. "I took the same oath Kale did. I will fight to uphold it." He rubbed his arm where the new tattoos rested. "You should really stop bleeding all over the carpet. It's a bitch to get out if it dries."

He leaned his head back against the couch and closed his eyes. All the while, his fingers moved in circles around his new tattoo. I looked to the door. Even though his eyes were closed, I knew he would beat me there if I tried to leave. Wanting to give him some privacy anyway, I retreated to my room.

I caught a glimpse of myself in the mirror hanging from my closet door. I really was a mess. My black clothes were different shades of grey from the dust and debris. The leggings were ripped and crusted with dried blood.

After closing the bathroom door behind me, I pulled the ruined garments over my head. I stopped at the sight of the scar under my heart, my first victory tally from Richard While. I untangled my wand from my clothes and pulled on my magic.

Remembering what Atlas had done, I pressed the tip of my wand right under the scar. I pictured what I wanted and forced magic from my wand. The magic sank into my skin and burned. Slowly, a picture started to form, a letter 'I' with a knife stabbed through the center.

My victory tally for Igorek.

The image looked foreign on my body. The scar over it was a bit lighter than my skin tone, so it was easy to overlook. But the black tattoo stood out as if it were a neon sign.

Bile rose up my throat. If I let my mind wander long enough, I could feel Igorek's blood under my fingernails and between my fingers. Quickly, I jumped into the shower before those memories could make me sick.

After a quick shower, I pulled on my light blue hoodie and stepped back into my room. Crossing the room to my dresser, I picked up the brush from the top.

The front door clicked closed.

Leaning onto one leg, I peeked into the living room. It was empty.

Tossing the brush aside, I ran to the front door and slowly eased it open. Peeking into the hall, I watched Atlas head for the stairwell.

He's heading to the infirmary. He has to be.

Pulling the door closed behind me, I crept down the spiraling staircases to the main floor. Atlas moved across the rotunda to the infirmary, just like I had suspected. He slipped through the heavy doors, not bothering to latch them.

Creeping down the last few stairs, I pressed myself up against the door and peeked into the room. I pressed a hand to my mouth when I saw him.

Michael sat on one of the infirmary beds with his elbows braced against his knees. His head hung low. He was breathing, but that was the only thing to celebrate.

Blood dribbled from his temple. Helen stood behind him removing glass from his back. The left side of his ribcage was an ugly dark purple. His right bicep had matching bruises. In his hands, was my switchblade.

On his left arm, I saw the tattoo I had seen hints of for the last year.

A black king cobra coiled around his bicep. The snake wound around his shoulder and hissed from his pec. Atop its head was a glittering crown. Its mouth was open, exposing its fangs with fury. An arrow cut through its skull and out of its mouth.

Around the tattoo, it seemed that, every few inches, there was a different scar. Each one looked more painful than the last. A thin one draped over his collarbone. Another twisted around to his back. Small star-like shapes peppered his ribs.

At the center of his abdomen were two thin scars right next to each other. They were stab wounds. Thanks to The Trial, I knew what those looked like. The right one sliced upward like the knife had been yanked toward his heart. My chest ached just looking at them.

His oath whispered back to me. *I will sin to condemn those who have sinned.*

"You should've called me back," Atlas spat.

"You were needed where you were." The sound of Michael's voice made it worse. It was quiet, borderline weak. I had never heard him like that.

"Then you should've called Sánchez or Went. Hell! You could've called your brother. Literally anyone was better than no one."

"I had it under control."

"Yeah. I can see that," Atlas scoffed. "There were at least ten different ways you could've handled that. Literally ten. I counted."

Michael hissed as Helen tugged a shard of glass from his back. "How's Charlie?"

"She's fine. She's in the shower." He paused. "Your girl bit me."

Michael looked up, confusion pulling at his eyebrows. A horrid purple bruise painted his cheek. One of his eyes was bloodshot. "She . . . bit you?"

"She didn't take kindly to the idea of leaving you. I think she even cracked one of my ribs." Atlas rubbed the side I had thrown my elbow into. "Be prepared for fire when you see her."

"I expect nothing less." Michael straightened his spine as Helen yanked something out of his back. His lips pulled away from his teeth at the pain.

I clasped my hands tightly over my mouth. *Oh, God.*

"You should've seen her," Atlas continued. "When she got her wand, she saved my neck."

"I was about to ask." Michael ran his hands over my switchblade. "I found this sticking out of one of them."

"She threw it like a javelin."

"Huh. We'll have to practice that."

I rolled my eyes. He was bleeding all over the place, Helen was pulling glass out of him, and he was thinking of training. Typical.

"She might be ready to fight for the Heel."

My stomach dropped. *Did that mean I'd have to go to the front?* I had seen movies that took place on the front lines. The screams, blood, and torture—I could barely sit through them. And those didn't involve magic. I knew this was what I was found for. Literally, it was my only purpose for living, but that didn't stop the flood of terror at the thought.

"No." Michael kept his eyes on the switchblade. "She's only been in the magical world for a year."

"From what I saw, I think she could handle herself." Atlas counted off with his fingers, "She's intuitive, quick, and smart. I'd trust her to watch my back."

Michael thought for a moment as he ran his hands over my switchblade. Exhaustion sighed out of him. "I don't like the idea of taking someone so young to the front."

"Neither do I, but I don't think you'll find a better time. It's best to see what she can actually do rather than assume and end up putting her in a place she's not prepared for."

Michael gave him a bloody smile. "I like it when you try to sound smart."

"I am, despite what you think. I've kept you alive this long, haven't I? That's harder than this whole sodding war."

Michael managed a weak chuckle. "Point taken."

"How did you get like this?" Atlas waved his hand at the bloody mess smeared across Michael's body.

Collecting the blood in his mouth, Michael spat it onto the floor. "One of them was parading as one of the wounded. When I went to help, he took me by surprise."

"There are two things I never thought I'd hear. You, helping someone, and the word surprise."

Michael remained silent. He continued to run his hands over my switchblade.

"Do you know who was behind it? Since you took this fight from me, I call the one where we find these bastards and take 'em out."

Michael shook his head. "Sorry. This assignment goes to Went and Sánchez. You've got The Trial to focus on."

"Oh, come on. I can multitask."

Michael gave him a dry look. His bloodshot gaze silenced the tattooed Hunter.

"At least tell me you got something useful from 'em."

"No. They didn't have any tattoos or colors."

"But?"

"But, I noticed some people missing from our party. They were attacking Guardians. I'm thinking a School Master or two hoped to alter The Trial by taking out the Guardians of the Contestants that were stronger than theirs."

"No one's done that in years."

"My guess is that they're getting desperate. During the theme party, Lawrence told Charlie that he's basically giving first place to anyone who can help him with the war."

Helen shook her head. Stepping back, she washed her hands in a bowl on the bedside table. Pulling on bright blue surgical gloves, she gathered sewing equipment and healing potions.

"What do you want me to tell Went and Sánchez?"

Michael gritted his teeth as Helen pinched his skin together and threaded a needle through it. "Look at Theodore. I'm sure he's pissed for what I did to his son during the Award Challenge. Spend some time sniffing around Han and Loran. Just because their Guardians were killed in this mess doesn't mean they weren't behind it."

Two Guardians were killed? Cheese and rice.

Atlas shifted like he was ready to jump right to work. "Want me to watch Hart's kid until you're done?"

"No. She's safe where she is."

Without another word, Atlas Ported. As soon as he was gone, Michael slumped forward with an exasperated sigh.

"Michael Kale, you're the dumbest man I've ever met," Helen remarked sharply from behind him. "If I collected all the sutures I've used to stitch you up over the years, I could put together a blanket that would cover the world twice."

"That wouldn't help with global warming," he mumbled to the stone floor.

Helen shook her head, fighting a smile. "Why are you so convinced that you have to do everything alone?"

"I had it handled."

"This wound to your lower back says otherwise." Silence filled the infirmary as she continued to stitch his shoulder back together.

He didn't wince at the pull of her fingers. He didn't move as she turned her attention to another wound. He just sat there, hunched over his knees, running his hands over my switchblade. A lock of bloody hair fell forward, but he didn't move it.

Unable to look at him any longer, I went back to my room. Too worked up, I paced the length of the apartment.

A while later, the door slowly opened and Michael limped into the room. He looked a bit better since the infirmary. The bruising on his face was now red instead of deep purple. Helen's potions must have started kicking in.

Easing the door shut, he halted when he saw me.

"Hey," he said, his voice hoarse.

I crossed my arms over my chest. "You're an idiot."

He shrugged and winced at the careless movement. "I've been called worse."

"I didn't jump in front of a knife for you just so you could turn around and throw yourself in front of another one."

A sigh left his lungs. It sounded as exhausted as he looked. "It's my job, Charlie."

"I don't care. You were alone. That was foolish and reckless."

He blinked, looking taken aback by my words. "It's my oath. My life means nothing if I—"

All around the room, the lights brightened. I stepped forward with my magic hot, matching my temper. "Don't you dare say that. I almost died for you. Don't discredit that, or this scar was for nothing."

His mouth clicked shut. For the first time, Michael Kale was speechless.

"Why did you force me to leave? I could've helped."

He didn't answer.

"Michael." I snapped. "Why?"

He rolled the words around his tongue for a few seconds before answering. When he did, his voice was quiet. "I couldn't have you jumping in front of me again."

"That's what I'm here for—"

He opened his mouth to protest, so I raised my voice.

"—to help you, and you won't even let me!"

"This was different." Covering his mouth with the back of his hand, he coughed. Pain contorted his face from the movement. Quickly, he crossed his arms, trying to hide the blood splattered across his knuckles.

"How? We're in this together, right? I've got your back and you've got mine."

"Yes, but—"

"Then that means we fight together." My bones ached as I looked at the bruises across his cheek and neck. I hated seeing him so battered and broken. He was supposed to be unshakable. "Ok?"

He just looked at me. An irritated red surrounded one of his pupils, making them appear an extreme dark brown that I rarely saw.

Finally, he nodded. "Ok."

"Good." I'm not sure what I won, but I knew I had. "I'll take the couch tonight."

His shoulders sagged with gratitude. He reached toward his jacket to take it off, but he grimaced. More color leached out of his cheeks.

"Let me." Walking around him, I stood on my tiptoes and carefully peeled his leather jacket down his arms. Up this close, I never noticed how many places the leather was stitched or patched. Once his hands were free, I carefully folded the worn garment and draped it over a stool at the kitchen counter.

I reached for the strap of his holster. His hand came up and took my elbow, wordlessly telling me to stop.

I looked up into his bruised face, to his bloodshot gaze. His pupils were dilated. His hand trembled ever so slightly against my arm. I remembered how I felt after the First Trial: jumpy, shaken, paranoid. Was he feeling the same?

"You're safe," I mumbled. With gentle fingers, I pulled the strap over his shoulder, causing the knives to clink softly. When he didn't stop me, I pulled the holster farther down.

With his hand still on my elbow, I moved in front of him and reached for the strap on his other shoulder. Standing so close, his warm breath played with my hair. Carefully moving the strap over his tender skin, I brought it to rest in the crook of his elbow.

Taking his hand from my arm, I pulled it free from the holster. Moving around him, I did the same, until I had the whole thing off. I draped it across his jacket.

Still holding his hand, I led him into my room. Taking out my wand, I waved it over the bed, causing the covers to pull back. Stiffly, he lowered himself to the mattress.

Before he could lay down, I dropped to my knees and pulled at his boots. One after the other, I tugged them off his feet. Shards of stained glass and pebbles of marble sprinkled out of his socks.

Standing back up, I helped him lay back into the pillows. His breath hitched when his back touched the mattress. With shallow breaths, he shifted into a comfortable position. He was asleep before I tugged the covers over him.

87

The University

Michael was still asleep when I left for breakfast.

The dining room was alive with conversation. For once, it seemed everyone, regardless of status, shared the same thought.

The attack at Founder's Hall was the most disastrous thing to have happened in years. Students, teachers, Contestants, Guardians, and Masters were outraged. The crowning jewel of the magical world was invaded and shattered.

After the attack on the Guardians, the high table was almost empty. The only Contestant who wasn't afraid to be front and center was Dmitri.

The arrogant bastard ate his breakfast without his Guardian to watch his back. Lounging in his seat, he ate with his heels kicked up on the table. His mocking gaze followed the frantic students as they scurried from one table to the next.

Rolling my eyes, I grabbed two plates and collected a breakfast big enough for two.

Dmitri saw me just as I was heading toward the doors. He lifted his glass with a mocking sneer. I set down one of the plates long enough to raise my middle finger in response.

Bounding up the stairs, I got to my apartment and kicked the door shut. After I set the plates on the kitchen counter, I peeked into the bedroom and found Michael in the exact position I left him.

Uneasiness settled into my stomach. I stood in front of him, fiddling with the hem of my hoodie. Hesitantly, I reached forward and placed two fingers against his neck. I expected him to flinch from my touch like he always did because of my status. But he didn't move.

His skin was hot to the touch, like gripping a mug of freshly poured coffee. *Fever?* His heartbeat was unhurried, and thankfully strong.

Spinning around, I rushed past the plates of breakfast and back down the stairs. Instead of going to the dining room, I turned into the infirmary.

Before I could push the doors, they swung open. Thiago stopped when he saw me.

"Good morning," he drawled with a smile. "I would hold the door for you, but I'm an arm short."

Sure enough, one of his arms was caught in a sling across his chest.

"What happened?" I asked.

"My Guardian shoved me behind a statue, and I caught a ward with my elbow. The tendons in my arm had to be reattached." He rolled his shoulder. "Thus, the sling."

I remembered what Michael said last night. "I heard about your Guardian. I'm sorry."

He shrugged. "It's an occupational hazard. My School Master gave me a list of replacements when I woke up this morning. I'm headed to my school to pick a new one now. What are you doing here?"

I knew I couldn't tell him that my Guardian had been passed out for over twelve hours. I wasn't about to tell him I was out and about without backup.

"I hit my head yesterday. I'm hoping Helen has something to clear it up."

"If you get the chance, sneak a bottle of the bubbling pink potion. It'll clear your head of pain and thoughts for six hours." Thiago moved to hold the door open for me. "You'll giggle for thirty minutes straight, but you won't be in any pain."

"Thanks for the tip." I moved around him and toward Helen at the end of the wing. I kept my steps slow until I heard the door close behind me. Then I was across the room in a blink.

"Charlie! Good morning." Helen turned with a smile, but it faltered when she saw me. "Is everything alright?"

"It's, uh." I glanced around and stepped closer. "Michael hasn't moved since he came in last night."

"That's not uncommon after what he went through yesterday." Moving to the back wall, she grabbed two tiny bottles, one white and one green. With a hand on my shoulder, we went up the stairs to my apartment.

In my bedroom, she sat on the edge of my bed and placed her fingers on his neck.

She took out the bottle filled with the milky liquid and filled a syringe halfway before sticking the needle in the side of his neck. With a new needle, she squeezed in two drops of the green potion.

Helen rubbed his shoulders until his eyelids fluttered. He mumbled something as he rolled onto his side. His lips pulled away from his teeth in pain, but his eyelids remained closed.

That must have meant something good because Helen rose to her feet. "I gave him something to help his muscles relax. He was hit by a lot of magic yesterday. Pure magic kills live tissue. If treated early enough, it can be revived, but it takes time and energy. So, just let him sleep."

With a smile, she squeezed my shoulder. As she headed for the door, she said, "When he wakes up, just make sure he gets some food."

A sigh of relief rushed from my lungs. "Thanks, Helen."

When she softly closed the door behind her, silence was the only thing to keep me company. I went back to my room and stood in the doorway. My fingers fiddled with the hem of my hoodie; I didn't know what to do.

He just looked so . . . broken and weak. I had almost believed his leather jacket was impenetrable, that mountains would break under his fists. But seeing him there, bruised and healing, reminded me he wasn't actually Hades. He was just a man. A very mortal man.

With an uneasy stomach, I ate breakfast alone. Trying to get my mind off the man in the other room, I pushed the furniture against the walls and practiced illusions until I was lightheaded.

After lunch, I sat beside my bed, leaning against the bedside table. I closed my eyes for a moment and drifted off.

I woke up as Michael was struggling to his feet.

"Hey!" Still half-asleep, I struggled to my feet and almost knocked the lamp off the nightstand. "How are you feeling?"

"Sore." He braced his hands on the mattress and moved to stand.

"Don't be an idiot." I placed my hands on his shoulders before he could get too far off the mattress. "What do you need?"

He sagged back down. "Water would be nice."

"Yeah, of course." I Ported into the kitchen and grabbed a water bottle from the mini-fridge. I Ported back, took off the lid, and handed it to him.

"You didn't have to Port." He accepted the bottle and raised it to his lips. "I could've waited an extra twenty seconds."

A flush heated my cheeks. "You're welcome."

The corner of his mouth curled. "Thank you."

As he drained the bottle, I walked to the kitchen and grabbed the cold breakfast. "Helen said you should eat something."

Setting the empty bottle aside, he accepted the plate onto his lap. Using his fingers, he picked at the food.

Despite the healing potions, his bruises had gotten darker. Half of his face was now painted a stormy red. The color highlighted his collarbones and ran under his shirt. I remembered how his ribcage looked the night before. I could only imagine how bad it looked now.

As I settled onto the bed beside him, I didn't know we would be setting the pattern for the next few weeks.

We had all of our meals sent to my room. We continued to train in our designated training area, but we never stayed longer than we had to. Partly because Michael was on high alert, the benefit of the doubt wasn't something he believed in. And partly because he was still healing, so he slept most of the time outside the training room.

During training, he was a bit slower, but that didn't mean he lacked potent accuracy. He had dueled with death, he was exhausted, and he could still throw me on my back with one hand.

Time rolled by with increasing speed, and before I knew it, we were a week away from the Final Trial.

"Are you ready?" Michael asked, clutching his own bag by his side. His face was finally clear of bruises.

"Nope."

With an apologetic look, he held out his hand regardless. I placed mine in his, and he Ported us from the Magisterium. I expected snow and wind to assault us from every angle, but the day was bright and sunny. The air was crisp, just a couple degrees above a good frost.

Thin clouds lingered above sharp pine trees. The ground, yellow with sleeping grass, curved and dipped along a mountain range. Behind us, tall mountain peaks shot toward the sky. Snow hugged the sloping sides with gleaming brilliance. Draped across the valley was a solid wall of ice. The glacier competed with the sky for the most dazzling shade of blue.

Carved into the mighty ice face was a set of doors, framed with flaming torches, the entrance to The University for Advanced Tactical Magic.

Michael started toward the doors.

With a sigh, I followed after him.

As we drew closer, the towering doors of ice swung open. The ice grated against the stone with a sound that put my teeth on edge.

Guardian Theodore, flanked by two guards in red and black armor, stepped out to meet us. "Guardian Kale." He nodded. "Contestant Heart, the University welcomes you." He stepped aside, sweeping his arm in invitation.

Stepping over the threshold felt like stepping into a lion's den.

"Thank you for having us," Michael said tightly.

Guardian Theodore nodded, but offered no reply. Neither of them looked even close to happy about being in the same room. The steel in the Russian's eyes said that if it weren't for The Trial, Michael would be dead. Michael returned the look with just as much brutality, but with a smirk.

The front foyer was made of ice: the floors, the walls, and the doors. Rugs of dark animal hides were the only things to contrast the light blue walls. Huge black iron chandeliers hung from the high ceilings, so no corner was left darkened.

The guards pulled the doors closed behind us. As soon as they shut, the foyer flooded with activity. Servants took our coats and bags. Snow was dusted from our shoes, and in the span of ten seconds, they were gone.

While the two ex-Masters continued to mentally tear each other apart, my gaze drifted around the foyer. Intricate battle scenes were carved into the icy walls. Magic highlighted the art with different colors.

Guardian Theodore caught me eyeing the scenes. "They are stories of User victories. You will find them in every area where the school gathers regularly."

"They're . . . very well done." I tried to keep the disgust out of my voice. The picture in front of me was of a beheading.

"Of course." He turned to lead us further into the school with his guards close behind. "We expect excellence in everything."

As we followed, the Russian Master eagerly boasted about every statue and mural we passed.

"This one you will recognize. Hercules." If it was even possible, his chest puffed out even more. "He killed many monsters in his time. He was taught within these walls."

"Hercules," I repeated dumbly. "I thought he was a myth."

Guardian Theodore smirked at my ignorance. Stepping closer to the ice wall, he pointed to the top of the mural. "He was one of the last descendants of the Celestials." Under his meaty finger was Zeus. The image depicted the man with broad shoulders and a long, flowing beard. In his hand was a jagged bolt of lightning. His eyes were solid gold.

"If Celestials were so powerful," I asked, "how did they die out?"

"Anything can be killed. You just need the correct tools." Guardian Theodore's icy stare swung toward Michael. "Take a Hunter for example. One of the most brutally equipped Users, yet if you dangle the correct bait and exhaust him just enough, you can kill even a Master Hunter."

Michael met his stare with an indifferent expression.

Guardian Theodore turned back to me. A satisfied grin stretched across his face. "Celestials were killed for their power. Then their legacy was diluted by low status Users. Come. I will show you more since it seems your education is lacking."

When he turned his back, I whipped toward Michael with wide eyes. "Hercules?"

Michael nodded. "From what I heard, he was a total dick."

Shaking my head, I continued after the Trial Guardian. My mind spun through my ancient history classes from Kansas. *How many historical heroes were Users?*

Loving the sound of his own voice, Guardian Theodore talked for the better part of an hour. I'm pretty sure he took the scenic route, showing us the most elaborate carvings and statues. All the while, he bragged about the Users that were taught here. Michael looked bored the entire time.

Finally, we reached our destination: the Contestants' quarters.

It was much like the rest of the castle; the walls were made of pale-blue ice and intricately carved. There were two fireplaces in the common room with a dark wooden table in the center for meals.

Spaced around the edge of the room were seven doors, each stamped with one of the Top Seven's Contestant numbers. My room was thankfully sandwiched between allies, Blake and Thiago.

Guardian Theodore led us across the common room to the door with the number fifteen.

Inside, was another fireplace. All of the furniture was covered in thick furs of different colors. The four-poster bed had blackout curtains draping elegantly to the floor. Layers of animal furs were piled generously on the mattress. The windows proudly displayed the grand landscape of jagged mountains and pines.

"You may eat with the other Contestants or food can be brought to you here." Guardian Theodore gestured with upright palms. "Pick your preference. All you have to do is let my staff know, and they will accommodate you."

Michael nodded. "Thank you."

"The training room is at the end of the hall. The medical wing is down that hall and to the left." He smirked. "I thought you would like to be close."

Was that a threat?

"Good. I'll be sure to direct your son there when the chance arises," Michael said with a perfectly straight face.

I pressed my lips together to keep from smiling.

Guardian Theodore narrowed his eyes. "I was thinking of you since you were in that attack a few weeks ago. You look so pale."

The muscle in Michael's jaw popped. His hands clenched into fists at his sides.

I stepped between the two. Looking over my shoulder at the rival Guardian, I put on my best smile. "Not as pale as your son will look when he loses."

The Trial Guardian snorted. "You speak like that is a possibility." Rolling his eyes, he headed for the door. "If you need anything, my staff is here to serve you. I'll see you both in the training room." He departed with a smile that had all the cruelty and coldness he could gather.

Michael quickly crossed the room, closed the door, and locked it. He glared at the lock for a few seconds. I trusted it about as much as he did.

The fire crackled and fizzed in the silence. I had been deliberately trying not to process the fact I was in the heart of the enemy territory. But in the silence, there was nothing else to think about.

My hand tightened around the wand at my side. It comforted me, having it close, but that was all it did. I didn't trust anything. Would the ceiling collapse? Did any of the locks work? If I slept on the bed, would the furs strangle me?

Michael must have sensed my uneasiness or he wanted to comfort himself because he began checking the room. He peered in every closet and tested every lock. He ran his fingers along the walls and tapped his wand against a couple. He found nothing.

That only fed my suspicion.

Seven days flew by, and before I knew it, the Final Trial was knocking on my door. The tension lingering around the Contestants rose like a flash flood.

I found myself in two places: the training room, or our apartment. We had our food brought to us. Michael tasted everything for poison. He only told me not to eat one thing and that was because it was disgusting. Both of us thought it was a goat stomach.

The day before The Trial, my stomach felt as if it were twisted into six different knots. I hadn't eaten much that day, which Michael didn't like. But what little I had eaten was threatening to charge back up my throat.

I tried taking a nap, but all I could do was stare at the canopy over the bed.

Michael tapped on the door as he eased it open. I knew what he was going to say before he opened his mouth.

"I'm heading out. The Guardians are getting briefed on the Field."

Pushing myself upright, I curled my legs under me. "When will you be back?"

"About an hour. If Atlas doesn't crack any jokes or ask stupid questions, it might be sooner."

I must've made a face because Michael straightened from the doorframe and came to stand in front of me. "How about this? I'll leave a transporter here, and you can head to the ranch. I'll meet you there for dinner. I think I heard Mom say something about a caramel apple pie."

My lungs released the air they had been holding. "I can do that." I nodded and dropped my eyes back to the furs. I couldn't watch him leave. I didn't know if my nerves could handle it.

The ring around my thumb buzzed twice. *You ok?*

My eyes jumped up to meet his. With a soft smile, I tapped my sync ring twice. *Ok.*

With a reassuring smile, he closed the door behind him.

I took a long drag of chilly air through my nose. Flopping onto my back, I set an alarm to wake me up. Closing my eyes, I hoped my mind would let me take a small nap.

I didn't get a chance to hear my alarm. A knock woke me up before it went off.

Rolling over, I ignored it.

They knocked again.

I pushed myself into the sitting position with a spike of fear. Michael would just walk in. Was it Atlas? It was a stretch to think it was Blake. We hadn't spoken since our dispute after the theme party.

Apprehension filled my gut as I grabbed for my wand. I slowly padded across the fur-covered floor to the iron door as another knock came.

I slid back the lock and opened it just wide enough to peek through. Shock made me lose my grip on the door.

"Contestant Heart." It was the tall man in the dark red armor. The same one who accompanied Lawrence everywhere, almost as if he were his red shadow. He bowed stiffly at the waist. "My name is Jeffery Steel. I'm in the employment of Master Hart."

My eyes darted over his shoulder and down the hall. The Master in red was nowhere to be seen.

"I remember." Behind the door, I started tapping my sync ring.

"Master Hart has requested to meet with you."

My eyes bulged. "Now?"

He nodded.

My throat went dry. I tapped the ring faster. "I'll be right out." I had difficulty forming words. I moved to close the door, but Steel stepped forward with clear intentions. He would wait peacefully as long as he could see me.

Michael. I need Michael.

With my heart knocking into my ribs, I retreated into the room. His heavy footsteps followed me.

Trying to appear nonchalant, I grabbed my cellphone. My hands shook as the phone rang for 'JACKASS.'

"This is Kale. Leave a message." The sound of his voice caused me to jump and almost trip into the dresser. There was a beep and recorded silence.

I glanced over my shoulder. The armored man stood stoically beside the door. His eyes were fixed solely on me.

I quickly turned my back. "Hey, it's Charlie—"

"Contestant Heart." Steel stepped away from the door. "He doesn't like to be kept waiting."

I nodded. Turning back, I said into the phone, "Where are you? I need you to come back. As soon as you get this." I hung up and tossed the phone on the bed.

I slipped my wand under my sleeve. Clenching my shivering hands, I followed Steel into the hall. I walked slowly, tapping the sync ring, and hoping Michael would ride in and save the day.

He didn't.

Our footsteps echoed down the icy hallway. Once we reached the front door, Steel extended his hand, palm up. Against every instinct in my body, I placed my hand in his. He Ported us from the ice castle.

88

No Better than I

A warm breeze greeted me with a gentle embrace. We reappeared on a mountain top with a royal blue sky stretched above us, and no clouds to rival it in either direction.

Steel stepped around me, pulling my attention from the scenery of lush palm branches and leafy trees. Following the man in dark red armor, my mouth fell open.

Nestled on the side of this tropical mountainside was a mansion that looked like something out of a fairy tale.

A thirty-foot crystal doorway stood in front of me, with beautifully decorated pillars holding up a high ceiling. The entire front of the building was made of glass, letting light filter into the castle made of brilliant white stone. My eyes stung as the sunlight boldly reflected from it.

Guards in matching red armor opened the crystal doors as we approached. The castle was so quiet that my boots clicked loudly against the shiny floors. At first, I thought the floor was reflecting the sunlight, but then I saw that they were made of solid gold. The bright reflection cast ribbons of light that played over Steel's armor.

Men and women glided down the halls. Draped in expensive fabrics and glimmering jewels, they looked like they had stepped off the red carpet only moments earlier.

My escort led me down the brightly lit hallway to a pair of doors made completely of rubies. The sunlight reflected off the jewels in fractured slivers of light, painting the walls and floor with hues of sunset colors. If that wasn't impressive, the room they guarded outdid them easily.

The ballroom curved up to a glass ceiling. Large beams crisscrossed from one wall to the other, holding up the giant panes. Gold leaf covered the thick beams, reflecting the bright ocean sun around the room.

At the front, a platform of five steps held a single throne. Gold and marble—no, it was too colorful for that. Opal, maybe? Sitting on the red cushion was a crown.

Hands grasped and twisted around each other to make the band. Two hands held the centerpiece, a stunning ruby in the shape of a human heart.

"Contestant Heart."

My escorts halted.

I jerked my gaze from the crown to its owner. Lawrence Hart walked toward me with a casual air about him. Everywhere else I had seen him, he stood with regal politeness. Here, he was comfortable. He wasn't even wearing a tie.

He nodded to the man beside me. "Thank you, Steel."

The large man bowed to his king before walking back to the doors. I found that I didn't want him to go. I didn't want to be alone with my father.

Lawrence's cool blue-grey gaze locked on to mine. "I'm glad you came." He gestured for me to walk in front of him toward a set of French doors.

"I was surprised by your invitation." Following his direction, I stepped onto a shaded balcony. The golden railing twisted and curved protectively around the perimeter. At the center was a small table with two chairs.

"I would have had you come sooner, but as we gear up for the Final Trial, I find that my time is not my own." Lawrence stepped up to the railing, into the sunlight.

"Why am I here?"

"You're not one to indulge in pleasantries, I see." He turned toward me with an easy smile. "With the Final Trial approaching, I wanted to meet with the Top Seven one last time."

Tentatively, I stepped up beside him. As I looked over the railing, my attention was drawn downward. A few stories below, the ground sparkled. At first, I thought the patio was made of gold as well. But patios don't have eyes.

A dragon, the size of a semi-truck, was curled up on the lawn. It was smooth as molten gold, no spikes or jutting scales. Its angular head was lizard-like with frills plumed around its neck. Around each limb was a thick shackle tethered to the ground with a mighty spike.

"I never took you as one to keep pets," I said, unable to take my eyes off of it.

"She's a relic from a different era. When I was just a Hunter, I was assigned to kill her. She had killed hundreds of Regulars for sport." Clasping his hands together, he leaned his elbows against the railing. "She fought hard and killed my whole Hunting trio. When I finally cornered her, I couldn't do it."

"So you kept her as a pet instead?"

"She reminds me of the world I'm fighting for." He turned and pulled a chair away from the table. "Have a seat." It wasn't a request.

I lowered myself into the chair. I fought to hide the storm of emotions I was carrying.

The small smile on his face said he wasn't fooled.

He moved around the table and carefully removed his suit jacket. He folded it neatly and laid it across the back of his seat. As he sat, I noticed again the scars encircling his wrists.

"Michael—"

"Guardian Kale is of no concern right now."

"He won't be happy I'm here."

A smile lifted his lips. "Is that statement supposed to mean something? He's as dangerous as a scorpion in a bottle. Although, he likes to pretend otherwise."

We obviously saw him differently.

"You're smart, Contestant Heart. The fact you're in the Top Seven is evidence of that, but you have made one mistake."

I laced my hands together to keep from shaking. "Is this about Michael again?"

He cocked his head to the left. "You know your error. Your misplaced trust in him. I've seen you. He has your loyalty. Are you sure he's worth it?"

"Of course," I said without hesitation.

Shaking his head, Lawrence leaned back against his seat. "I've known Michael nearly my whole life. When he gets a goal into his head, it doesn't matter what or who is standing in his way. He'll do anything to get it done."

"I don't know what I hate more," I said dryly. "Men who are selfish, or men who don't say what they want."

"My point, darling," he leaned forward, "is that you have placed your trust with the wrong king. He fights for a world that will never be strong enough to thrive. I fight for a better world."

"Making the world a better place and wiping out a portion of the population are two different things."

"I disagree. I think they are the same. If we continue the way we have been, there will be no more Royals. Deficients have diluted the potency of magic in our blood for generations. Royals used to dominate the earth. Now, there are only a handful left. With time, there won't be any. This world needs change." A small smile touched his lips. "I'm just the man who's finally doing something about it."

"Just because one Deficient failed to save your brother doesn't mean all of them have to forfeit the right to live."

Lawrence's spine jerked straight. Just barely, the lights flickered.

"Michael told you about Jackson?" he asked slowly.

Gripping my wand under the table, I nodded. "Yes, he did."

"Did he tell you that the doctor watched my brother die? He didn't call for anyone. He just stood there watching his heart fail."

"That was just one. That doesn't mean all of them are the same."

His lips curled without humor. "That doctor was responsible for the death of six other Royals. Deficients assisting the Hunter Guard got three of my trios killed due to their lack of experience. Across the globe, they stand by and watch fellow Users die because they physically cannot help. They feed off the blood and sweat from other statuses, because with their inadequate power, that's all they can do. Getting rid of them makes us, as a species, stronger."

Taking a deep breath, he turned his chilly gaze to the view. "I did not bring you here to talk about my past. I have a proposition for you."

My shoulders tensed.

"I was impressed by what I saw at the third Award Challenge. You're a natural with violence. After this Trial, your education will make you a strong player in this war." He tilted his head in confidence. "And I want you at my side."

Oh, shit. I tucked the hair dancing on the lazy breeze behind my ear.

"I already told you that each Contestant in the Top Seven was selected because of their connections to powerful members of our world. While you have none, your skill set, with a bit more refining, will come in handy. I see the possibility for greatness in you. All you need are the tools."

I shook my head. "But I'm a Common Six. Isn't that below your standard?"

"If your status is paired with a Master's title, it will more than make up for it."

My heart skipped a little. *Can he give me a title?* The whisper of freedom stoked a longing in my chest. With a title, I would be untouchable, free from anyone's expectations and will. I would be in charge of my own life.

Remember what Lawrence has done. A title isn't worth the cost.

I shook my head again. "I chose Michael, and I'm sticking by my decision."

"Sooner or later, he'll remind you who he really is. As one of the Horsemen, he prefers shadows and the stench of death too much to stay away for too long."

I pushed my chair back from the table. "You don't know what you're talking about. And I'd like to leave."

"Are you truly that loyal to him?"

"I think that's a dumb question seeing as I took a knife for him."

"And what has he done with that? Has he offered you anything in return for your wand? Has he even asked?"

I wanted to give him seven different reasons and then tell him where to shove them. But Michael never asked me to fight for him. He blackmailed me to be on his side. Blake was missing a finger because of it.

"He has my back," I told him. "And I have his. Nothing you offer is going to compare to that."

"Do you really want to ally yourself with a man nicknamed after Hades or Death of the Four Horsemen."

"Your nickname is Lucifer."

A chuckle shook his shoulders. "Touché."

"It doesn't matter who offered me what. I don't want to fight any war."

"Neither do I."

My eyes narrowed. "You started one."

"Michael started it by opposing me. I intended for him to help create a better world. War was never a part of my plan."

"And yet, here we are talking about my loyalty."

"Yes. Here we are." He opened his hands, gesturing to the balcony. "And you still haven't told me what Guardian Kale has offered for your loyalty."

"Nothing. I just chose him."

His head tilted once more. His gaze washed over my face, seeing more than I wanted him to, despite my best efforts to keep my emotions hidden.

"You are nothing to him. He won't even own the side he's on. He lets Lenin stumble around acting like he's calling all the shots. If that's not true, please, speak up."

I so desperately wanted to, but I had seen it play out every time Michael and Master Lenin were in the same room. The School Master gave the orders, while Michael took them without question.

Get a grip, Charlie! He's trying to get into your head.

"I know the look in your eyes, half-scared and wary, but hardened by the will to live. In my experience, the scars on your back are from someone trying to beat something out of you. Whatever it was, they didn't succeed."

He leaned his elbows onto the table. "I know your kind. You have always cowered underneath a raised fist, waiting for it to fall. With me, you won't have to wait. You'll be the one standing with raised fists. No one would challenge you. You would be a queen in the sight of everyone in my new world. All of this could be yours." He gestured to the grounds over the railing.

I looked into his eyes, the same color as mine, with a longing that stilled my breath. His pretty words danced through my head. What would it be like to never be in pain, to never feel the icy grip of fear, to just soak in the pleasures of life without the looming feeling of consequences?

I wanted that so badly. To never be bruised or broken? I couldn't even imagine what that would be like. Most of my life, I had spent healing. I always thought things like that weren't meant for stray dogs like me, a kid thrown out with the trash.

"I created this Trial to find the best magic," Lawrence continued, "and to remind our world of the power we used to possess. A time is coming when I will ask for loyalty. And I want you to choose the correct side."

"I have your back," Michael's words whispered in the back of my mind.

I once thought home was something unattainable, yet Michael had given that to me. I thought I was weak and powerless, until he put a wand in my hand. I thought 'ally' was a word exclusively associated with fairytales, but I had found that in Michael; I had his back, and he had mine.

But if I said that, would Lawrence kill me on the spot?

I thought it best to lie.

"Thank you for the offer." I got to my feet. "I'll need to think about it."

His face settled back to its calm demeanor, but I saw through it. In the steel of the blues of his eyes and the controlled nature of his breathing, something dangerous lurked beneath. I made my escape toward the throne room.

"You should know that the man you so desperately cling to is no better than I," he called after me.

I stopped. My temper bubbled up my throat. "Michael didn't kill a sister in front of her twin, along with her son and husband. Michael didn't kill the Hunter Guard. Michael didn't—"

"Michael Kale is a Master of his craft. He's a Hunter, a Master Hunter, and that's all he'll ever be. He's so covered in darkness, he sees things that are in the dark as if they are light."

"What the hell is that supposed to mean?"

He smiled like he just won . . . and that scared me. "A man who kills an innocent boy to get rid of a distraction seems like something I would do, doesn't it?"

"What are you talking about?"

"A blind man could see Daniel Phillips' affection for you. When most students are chosen for The Trial, they know they might become one of the damned. Instead, he smiled when your name was called after his."

Pain sliced through my chest. My heart ached with memories.

"Michael saw you as a way into my Trial, a way to influence the other Masters and School Masters to his side. Take a girl from nothing and make her a Master, a *Cinderella* story. But you were distracted. You would've thrown everything away if you could protect him. So, he had Contestant Phillips stabbed through the heart."

"*I* got myself into this Trial," I breathed, barely containing the urge to yell. "And Daniel was killed by a stupid boy who will pay for his actions."

"Yes, a boy did put the knife in his chest . . . but who told him to do it?"

"Dmitri was aiming for *me*."

"Are you sure?" Lawrence rose to his feet. He leaned closer and tapped his gloved finger against the scar on my cheek. "His knife flew right by you, and hit Contestant Phillips square in the chest. That doesn't sound like he missed. That sounds like he hit his mark exactly."

I stared up at him. The scar on my cheek tingled.

"Indulge me in my line of thinking," he said coolly. "If Contestant Theodore were aiming for your friend, what would he gain from killing the young man? Think before you speak."

My mind spun. Dmitri told me that the First Trial weeded out the weak. Then in the Second Trial, he was going to go after the stronger Contestants. That's why he killed Aboiy and Malan. With them gone, the Final Trial would lean in his favor.

"You are weak, all brain, no strength," Dmitri said to Daniel. "Going against you would be like taking candy from children." He looked at me. "After watching your performance, I found you disappointing. Too emotional."

"Judging by that description, I don't sound like much of a threat," I said dryly.

"You aren't, but your Guardian is."

By killing Daniel, it meant either Clarence or I would join the Top Seven. He wanted the Final Trial to be easy. *What would Dmitri gain from killing Daniel?*

"Nothing," I said. "He would gain nothing."

"Correct. But Michael on the other hand . . . he would have your attention brought back around. He would get you into the Final Trial. He hasn't done anything for anyone but himself in decades. What makes you think he would change for you?"

I shook my head, stumbling away from him. "You're wrong. He would never do that. He said—"

"Think, darling, truly think. It's all lies." His eyes locked onto mine.

Against my will, my brain thumbed through my memories looking for evidence. It landed on one moment I should have questioned, but faith and trust told me not to.

Michael took exactly one step in my direction before Master Lenin waved him over.

They shared a brief conversation. Michael's shoulders tensed. Master Lenin's lips were pressed tightly together as he beckoned Dmitri over. Master Lenin made quick work of scolding the Contestant before moving upstairs.

Before Dmitri could step away, Michael grabbed his arm.

I almost laughed at Michael's expression. Was he seriously threatening him?

Michael waited for Dmitri to nod, then he headed toward me. Dmitri whistled for Igorek's attention. The pair huddled together in a tight conversation. Igorek grinned.

"Making new friends?" I asked when Michael got close enough.

"The opposite, actually."

"Contestant Heart." Lawrence drew my attention back to him. "Do you see where I'm going with this? Michael had your friend killed."

89
Ask

The air rushed from my lungs as if a wrecking ball slammed into my stomach.

"You're wrong." As the words left my mouth, I wasn't sure I believed them. Lawrence's sweet, calm words slithered through my mind like a sickening perfume that clung to every memory, tainting it.

Was he right? Did Michael . . .

Lawrence collected his suit jacket. "Ask Michael yourself. If he's the man I think he is, he'll tell you the truth." He strolled across the terrace but paused in the entryway. "This war will end one way, and that is in my favor. I've been planning this for a long time. I'm ten steps ahead and I still have cards up my sleeve.

"Anyone who follows the Achilles Heel is doomed. Are you sure his side is the right side to be on? I would hate to see you, and the potential you possess, go down with him. I'll see you tomorrow at the Trial Field, darling."

As he returned to his castle, I gripped the back of the closest chair, trying to catch my breath. *Oh, my God . . . Michael . . .*

Stop! I took a deep breath. *He wouldn't do that.*

Yes, he would.

Shut up! He's changed! He has my back—

He threatened to kill Blake. What would stop him from actually killing someone? Nothing! I saw how he acted at Founder's Hall, how he walked boldly through the room, firing cast after cast. He didn't flinch, not once. Not even when he cast a man to stone and broke him to pieces.

I wildly shook my head, trying to clear it. With all of my strength, I held together the remaining pieces of my sanity and loyalty.

Lawrence was trying to throw off my confidence for tomorrow. He didn't want Michael to succeed. This was just his ploy to ensure what he wanted came to pass.

I loosened my fingers from the chair one by one. Trying to keep my breathing even and my magic calm, I found Steel waiting in the doorway. Without a word, he led me from the castle back to the University.

Back in my room, I rushed toward the bed. With fluttering hands, I rummaged through the fur covers for my cellphone. There were no missed calls or messages. I selected his contact, but my thumb hovered over the call button.

Did he . . . ? As the question bounced around my skull, I tossed the phone onto the bed and dug my hands into my hair. *I'm being ridiculous. I'll ask him and he'll deny it.*

When the transporter chirped, my nerves were strung tighter than a bowstring. The butterflies had left my stomach and were running loose through my body. All around the apartment, the lights pulsed with my pounding heartbeat.

I stared at the glowing transporter as it *beeped* and *beeped.*

Knock it off! I snapped. *Don't let Lawrence get into your head.*

Even though I knew what he was doing, what he was trying to do, it took me five minutes to grab the transporter. It burned against my palm as it ripped me away from the walls of ice. I reappeared right outside the ranch gates. Using the key Mrs. Kale gave me, I opened them and started up the drive.

"Charlie!" Meg yanked me into a hug as soon as I entered the kitchen. "Perfect timing. Dad is just taking the steaks off the grill."

"You're late."

My heart leapt and then somersaulted. There he was. Michael leaned back against the counter with Quinton swaddled in his arms.

Words clogged my throat. My breath stalled like a failing car. Dressed in all black, he stood out dramatically against the cabinets. Had he always looked so out of place? Or was it just because Lawrence had knocked me off balance with a few well-crafted lies?

"Can you put this on the table?" Mrs. Kale thrust a basket of bread in my arms. "I hope you're hungry. We're celebrating your final moment in this Trial with a feast fit for a winner," she sang as she returned to the stove.

"Seriously," Meg said. "The steaks she bought are the size of large cats."

Zak grimaced. "Not the greatest comparison."

Quinton squawked and stirred in Michael's arms.

"Mommy's coming!" Meg rushed over and scooped him from her brother's arms. She peppered his tiny face with kisses.

"You ready for tomorrow?" Zak pulled out his seat and sat down. His hand clenched and unclenched around his glass of water. "You know what they say, seven go in, but seven don't come out."

"Oh, come on!" Michael exclaimed. "Not cool, man."

"Zak!" Meg gasped.

"She does *not* need to hear that right now," Mrs. Kale scolded from the stove.

I glanced at Michael. The question rolled around my mouth, but my lips refused to release it.

"What? It's not like she hasn't heard it before. I'm betting on you." Zak took a slow, savoring sip of his water. He was probably imagining that it was a chilled beer.

"Don't be rude." Mrs. Kale set a steaming plate of baked potatoes in front of him.

"Steaks are ready!" Mr. Kale announced as he pulled the sliding glass door closed behind him. The platter in his arms was weighed down with what looked like a fourth of a cow. The hearty aroma of grilled beef and peppery spices curled through the air. The enticing smell only made my twisted stomach knot tighter.

"Come sit down." Mrs. Kale nudged me toward the table as she walked by with a platter of green beans.

With nerves running rampant through my body, I placed the basket of bread on the table and sank into my seat. Every cell in my body was focused on the man in black beside me.

I don't know why I was so nervous. All I had to do was ask. I knew the answer . . . I was just worried how he was going to react to the question. Yeah, that was it. I cursed Lawrence. He and his stupid lies made my stomach squirm.

"Ask him yourself. If he's the man I think he is, he'll tell you," Lawrence said.

"So, what's the game plan for tomorrow?" Zak asked, pulling the bread basket toward his plate.

Michael arched one of his eyebrows.

"For Charlie. What words of wisdom did you give her for the Final Trial?" Zak snickered. "Please tell me you gave her a rallying speech."

"I don't know if Michael is capable of that." Meg grinned.

Michael chuckled. "I don't have anything to say to her."

"Oh, come on. You're not even going to tell her 'go get it, kid'?" Zak asked.

Michael shook his head. "Charlie will go into The Trial and do what Charlie does, which is usually unhinged and completely unpredictable. But it's a hundred percent Charlie." He looked at me with a small smile. "She's gotten this far because of herself. I had nothing to do with it. So, I'm just going to let her be her, and pray I don't have a heart attack."

A round of easy laughter moved around the table.

Meg lifted her glass. "I'll drink to that."

I couldn't take it anymore. Gripping the table, I closed my eyes and blurted, "I met with Lawrence today."

Every glass froze in midair. All eyes swung toward me.

Michael set his glass down so quickly, it nearly sloshed all over his plate. Emotions raged across his face in a swirl of concern and apprehension. "You did what? Did he try anything?" His hands clenched into fists, dimming the lights. "If he did, I swear to God, I'll break him at every joint."

The knots in my stomach twisted tighter. For a moment I thought I was going to throw up. I shook my head. "No. He just wanted to talk."

"You should've called me." He yanked the phone from his pocket and cursed. "The stupid thing died." His fingers were also bare. "And I left my sync ring. What the hell did he want?"

How can I phrase this without setting him off? My eyes involuntarily dropped to the knife resting beside his hand. Even though it was a step up from a butter knife, I knew how easily he could make it into a weapon of mass destruction.

My courage tried to wiggle from my hands, but I gripped it tighter. Shifting in my seat, I turned to face him head-on, needing to see every reaction on his face.

"He told me I was loyal to the wrong king. He asked me to fight for him." I rushed on before he could react. "I told him to shove it, in a respectful sort of way. I think."

Michael visibly relaxed into the back of his chair. For a moment, I thought he was going to sink right through to the floor. A shadow of a smile formed around his lips.

"I bet you did," he chuckled. "I would've paid money to see that."

"Seriously." Zak looked at me with a new level of respect. "Did the old bastard tilt his head like a confused dog?"

"Good one." Michael tried to grin, but the nerves over my statement were still too fresh in his system.

A round of laughter bounced around the table. Meg went back to feeding Quinton. Mr. Kale started the task of eating his portion of the cow.

"Was that all?" Michael asked once the laughter had settled. "Once you dumped him like a prom date, I doubt he hung around for much longer."

I wanted to shake my head. I wanted to say, *"Nope, that's all. I just wanted you to know."*

But I didn't lie. I didn't want to.

"He said something else." I looked into his obsidian eyes. In this lighting, surrounded by his family and under the house he grew up in, the darkness of his gaze wasn't as harsh. I could almost make out rich, dark browns as the overhead light lit his face.

Those eyes belonged to my mentor and my friend. I trusted him. He had my back and my loyalty. I had his back and I liked to think he was true to me too. Holding on to that, I released the question eating away at my insides.

"He said you had Daniel killed."

Zak choked, snorting water on his plate.

Meg shot me a look of mixed disgust and shock. Without words, she asked, "He said my brother did what?"

Mrs. Kale rolled her eyes at her baked potato. Shaking her head, she cut into the steaming vegetable.

Mr. Kale continued to chew his monstrous steak without missing a beat.

All of this was background noise. My eyes were focused on the man in front of me. The last Kale member didn't react at all. He stared back, unmoving as a shadow.

When he spoke, his voice was void of all inflection. "What did he say exactly?"

A coldness settled into my chest. "That you told Dmitri to kill Daniel."

"That man never ceases to amaze me with the stupid shit that leaves his mouth," Meg laughed.

"Megan." Mrs. Kale shot her a disapproving look across the table.

Why isn't he denying it? The fractured pieces of my heart ached with his silence, but I refused to let my brain get ahead of itself.

"Did you?" I asked.

He continued to look at me. Every tick of the clock chipped away at the confidence I had built in him over the last few months. But I refused to let it crumble.

Michael had my back. I had his. Any minute now, he was going to open his mouth and go hoarse with laughter.

Silence hushed the table. Even Quinton settled down. Food was neglected once more as all eyes moved to the Master Hunter at the head of the table.

"For crying out loud," Mrs. Kale blurted. "Just answer the question."

Still, he didn't say anything.

"Michael," I breathed. "Did you ask Dmitri to kill Daniel?"

Finally, he flinched. The movement was so small. If I weren't facing him, I would have missed the tick of his left eye, like the scar on his cheek flared with an unexpected burst of pain.

"No."

I almost passed out. I didn't realize I had been holding my breath. Hearing him deny it caused all the air to rush out of my lungs. I could have melted to the floor. I was so relieved. The corner of my lips lifted—

"Lenin did."

90

Now I Am

The silence that followed was deafening.

His answer bounced around my skull, growing louder and louder with each pass.

"Oh, my God." Meg covered her mouth like she was going to be sick.

"No." Mrs. Kale's hands shook so hard she knocked her glass to the floor. The dark wine spilled unnoticed across the hardwood. "Master Lenin would never do that."

Unable to blink or look away, I just stared at him. "I don't understand."

Michael worked his jaw back and forth. "Lenin feared you were distracted. After the First Trial, he doubted your ability to put your feelings aside to do what needed to be done. After you rushed in to save Selasi, he thought you would do the same for Phillips. He told Theodore—I was ordered—" He rubbed a hand over his face. "I was ordered to stand by."

"Ordered," I breathed, feeling sick. "Master Lenin—" I squeezed my eyes shut, trying to block out his expression.

His eyes were wide with growing panic as he fought to articulate his actions. His expression was so sincere.

"But you tried to save him," Zak said slowly. "When he was falling over the cliff, you told Charlie how to save him."

Michael didn't look away from me. "Lenin gave the order, and I tried to undo it. But then Theodore came, and there was nothing I could do."

The agony of the Second Trial gushed from the pieces of my shattered heart, filling my chest and pushing against my eyes. All around the kitchen and the living room, the lights brightened until there were no shadows. The walls of the house groaned as the floorboards creaked beneath my chair. I struggled to breathe as my magic stretched the confines of my ribcage.

"What have you done?" Meg twisted in her seat, pulling Quinton away from Michael, shielding him with her body.

"I am trying to secure a future for you and your son. I didn't know Lenin was going to do that." The muscles in his jaw pulsed, as if his own words made him sick.

"He was a kid—" Zak started. Unable to finish, he leaned away from his steak.

I couldn't take it anymore. Stumbling to my feet, I pushed away from the table. Pictures around the room cracked and then shattered, sprinkling glass to the floor. Water and wine boiled in their glasses. Lights flickered throughout the house.

Bile rose in my throat as I stumbled away from the table. Tears blurred my vision. Unable to see or breathe, I fled the kitchen. The house moaned beneath my footsteps. Hairline cracks split through the paint as I rushed for the front door.

"Charlie, let me explain." A chair scraped away from the table as heavy boots pounded after me.

Gasping for air, I staggered out to the yard. Magic boiled through my chest, burning brighter and hotter with every step.

He let me believe it was Dmitri and Igorek . . . that meant . . . I killed Igorek for nothing. I gagged over the gravel.

Michael touched my shoulder, turning me to face him. "Charlie—"

My hand struck his face. Caught off guard, he stumbled to keep his balance.

Breathing hard, I backed out of his grip. Anger exploded through my chest as I stared at him.

This was the man who sent me into The Trial, oblivious of the pain I would endure. He held me as my heart crumbled in my chest. He helped me pick up the pieces after grief tore me apart. I took a knife for him.

The disbelief shaking my body gave way to an anger so strong, words could not articulate it. It burned sharper and hotter than the magic raging in my chest.

I struck him again.

He didn't flinch or try to stop me. When my hand struck his cheek, he closed his eyes as he struggled to keep himself upright. But he didn't move, even as the pain burned red across his face.

Legend says the Four Horsemen only bring desolation. The very name told me what he was capable of, yet I focused on the hope that he was a good man. I wanted so badly for him to be good. For once I wanted to put my trust in someone good.

Tears spilled down my cheeks. The pressure in my ribcage was so tight I couldn't breathe. Molten magic spilled through my chest. The never-healing wound stung as my magic rolled down my shoulders. A sob broke through as my magic collected in my hands, glowing around the bones.

On either side of the gravel road, the thin pine trees moaned and swayed without a breeze. The needles of the nearest branches turned brittle and brown. They rained around us like dead snow.

"Why? Why would you do this to me?" I screamed. "You held me together and when I talked about my anger, you just stood there and did *nothing!*"

I hit him again.

Michael fell to his knees, but the pressure didn't defuse. If anything, it got sharper. His cheek darkened as bruises curved with his jaw and spread up toward his hairline.

"I wanted to tell you." Struggling to his feet, he stepped away from me, the ground scorched black beneath my feet. "It killed me every time I didn't, but I—"

I clapped my hands over my ears. "Stop. Just stop!" I doubled over as my sobs threatened to bring me to my knees. "I hate you. *I hate you!*"

My voice bounced from one side of the drive to the other as if the dying evergreens threw my hateful words at Michael's feet. The driveway brightened as more magic filled my hands.

"Why?" I sobbed. "Just tell me why."

Through clenched teeth, he said, "I didn't know he was going to ask Dmitri to do that."

"You could have stopped him."

"I had orders not to."

"You could have said no!"

"My oath—"

"Your oath died with the rest of the Hunters! You're an idiot if you think Master Lenin's in charge of anything. *You're* the king of the Achilles Heel. This was *your* choice."

He opened his mouth to refute me, but there was nothing to say. Because I was right.

"I killed Igorek, because I wanted to hurt Dmitri like he hurt me. But it was you. All along it was you." My words came out choked and broken. "You broke me. You made me like you!"

He hadn't flinched when I hit him, but he flinched now.

"Your biggest mistake was not *trusting me*. I've done nothing but have your back, but you kept treating me like I was your enemy. Well, now I am." I dug the key from my pocket and tossed it at his feet. I pushed him out of my way and headed toward the gate.

"No." He captured my wrists. "I'm fighting a war. We're outnumbered and without any advantages. Lenin was protecting our chances."

"You sound just like him." I struggled against his hold. The harsh winter air froze the tears to my cheeks. "A life isn't a pawn for war strategy. I thought you knew that after what Lawrence did to Lauren."

He recoiled from me. "Charlie, please."

"Let me go," I pleaded. "Please, let me go." In vain, I tried to twist my wrists from his locked fingers.

"You can't leave like this. You're too close to a flare." The glow in my hands brightened. "Your wound—you could—"

I threw all my weight backward, but his grip remained.

"I said, let me go!" I planted my hands on his chest and shoved. Magic flared down my arms, lighting the driveway. Instead of flaring out of my chest like it did with my nightmares, it went in a single direction. Straight into Michael's chest.

His fingers slipped from around my wrists as he flew back into the night. Meg screamed from the front porch.

I fled down the driveway. I braced my hands against the gates and pushed, but they didn't budge. The key Mrs. Kale gave me to the gate was in the front yard. Golden magic crackled from the gates, streaking high into the sky. I needed something of the Kales' to open them.

Desperately, I Ported back into the house to Michael's bedroom. Mr. and Mrs. Kale were yelling. Something crashed upstairs.

I grabbed one of Michael's shirts from the closet and Ported back to the gate. Pressing it against the seam, I shoved them open and stepped off the property. I dropped the shirt and Ported.

91

Past the Boundaries of Reason

I reappeared back at the University.

In the silence of the room, the cosmic anger swirling through my chest started to still. I tried to hold on to it, but it retreated from my fingers as I collapsed against the door and fell to the floor.

In its absence, the pieces of my fractured heart pulsed and ached, making it hard to breathe. I hugged my knees to my chest to keep my insides from shattering. It didn't matter how tight I held myself, I continued to fall apart.

Through my tears, my kaleidoscope vision showed that my hands held the remnants of my glowing magic. Unwinding them from around my legs, I held them in front of me.

My wand was in my room. Yet, I had thrown Michael across the yard as if I had it in my hands.

On the other side of the room, on the coffee table was the transporter to the Magisterium. Tentatively, I opened my hand. Magic concentrated in my palm and pooled between my fingers. It slithered across the room, lifting the magical object from the table and pulling it into my palm.

Michael said I couldn't do magic without a wand . . . What else did he lie about?

I have to get out of here. Jumping to my feet, I ran into my room. The lights flashed brightly as I passed. Tearing open my duffle bag, I threw what little I had inside.

I can't run.

If Michael were smart, and I knew he was, he would be thinking of ways to get me back under his thumb. He probably thought I was too unstable and needed to be brought around before I exposed him. The only way to do that was to get to Blake.

"Be careful who sees your affections," Master LeOnie's words came back to me. *"Some will exploit it."*

He already threatened Blake once. Master Lenin said the next time I left it wouldn't be a finger that would be removed, it would be his head.

Thankfully, Blake had the protection of The Trial with the tattoo around his wrist. But he was only an active Contestant for the next twenty-four hours. And Michael wasn't a patient man. Who was to say that he would even wait for him to cross the finish line, and then do the same thing to him as he did to Daniel?

He would probably have Atlas sabotage his performance, letting The Trial kill my best friend.

I couldn't let that happen. I had to see him get out . . . plus, if I wanted to live, I needed to cross the finish line too. Or else the tattoo would poison me.

Knowing Michael, he'd probably take me out of The Trial and make me watch as Atlas got Blake killed.

The only way he could get me out of The Trial was if Clarence woke up. Then, he would continue in my place, and Dmitri would go after Blake. I couldn't let that happen. I wasn't going to let another person be taken away from me.

I pushed the grief from my mind. My aching heart was forced to the background as anger controlled my body. I wiped my face dry. Then I forced magic into the transporter.

I Ported to the center of The Magisterium of Magic beside the clock tower. Loud voices and clinking silverware flooded out of the dining room. Students from all seven schools milled around the hall. A few moved toward the staircases, ready for bed.

Crossing the guarded rotunda, I headed for the infirmary.

The guards on either side of the doors stepped into my path.

"No one enters without—"

"I have a note from Guardian Kale," I interrupted. I took out a folded piece of paper from my back pocket. What it was, I had no clue. But they didn't know that. "He sent me to get a potion to help me sleep tonight. I need to see Helen."

"No one enters," the guard repeated a bit more forcefully, "without written approval from Master Lenin."

Shit.

"Fine," I shoved the paper in my pocket. "Then I'll have Guardian Kale come down himself."

Both guards flinched. The quiet one immediately grabbed the door and opened it for me. I stepped inside and let the doors close behind me before the other one could object.

Strolling across the long room, I found Clarence in the same bed he had been in for the last month. Unlike the last time I saw him, he was fully healed. If I didn't know any better, I would have thought he was taking a nap.

"Charlie!" Helen stepped out of the back room with a smile. "I wasn't expecting you." Her eyes looked around the room. "Where's Guardian Kale?"

"Busy." The voice that left my mouth was not mine. It was as cold and sharp as broken ice.

"I'm surprised he let you out of his sight this close to the Final Trial." Her eyebrows pulled together with worry when I didn't respond. "Is there something I can help you with?"

She wasn't going to let me out of this room with Clarence. My gaze moved over her shoulder to the wall of potions. One bottle, near the middle, caught my attention. I knew the black potion was used to make people sleep.

Magic slid from my fingertips and removed the cork. A few drops rose from the bottle and glided toward me.

"Charlie?" Helen stepped forward. "Are you alright?"

My eyes snapped back to her face. She didn't see the potion go into her nose. Her eyes widened in panic when she recognized the smell of mint. Before she could utter a cry, her eyes rolled back into her head and her knees gave out.

My magic caught her before she hit the floor. I levitated her to a nearby bed and turned back to Clarence.

I grabbed the end of his bed but paused. Around my wrist was the bracelet Master Lenin used to track me. I gripped the bracelet and drew magic to my palm. The bright golden glow melted the silver chain from my wrist.

Free from their tracking, I gripped the bed and Ported him from the infirmary.

We reappeared in Kansas, just outside the coffee shop I used to work at. The spring air was sharp with an incoming frost. My teeth chattered as I levitated the bed inside the storage container behind the coffee shop. Then I melted the doors closed.

Now that I had Clarence, my mind turned to Blake. We weren't on the best of terms at the moment. I wasn't even sure he would let me watch over him through The Trial, or if The Trial would even put us in the same space.

Desperation made me think far and wide, past the boundaries of reason. Dark memories, full of candles and moonlight, floated from the back of my mind.

Last year, Richard While performed dark magic, a binding curse, in the North Tower. I remembered candles, blood, and a small leather-bound book. Anything that happened to me also happened to Mr. While.

If I could take all of Blake's injuries . . . he would survive The Trial. Whatever Michael ordered Atlas to do would backfire by injuring their golden goose.

But that book was gone . . . or was it?

If my memory served me right, Michael gave the book to Master Lenin while I was still in the infirmary. And where would Master Lenin keep books only he had access to?

The Records Room.

I used the transporter to Port back to the Magisterium. To avoid Master Lenin's gatekeeper, Tessa Baker, I Ported in front of the door right across from Master Lenin's office.

I gripped the handle and pushed magic into my hands. My fingers glowed like they were illuminated with fire. The handle snapped off and the door swung open.

A barrier of magic filled the doorframe. Waves of heat rolled off it in a warning. I pulled on my magic and pressed my hands to the barrier. My arms went numb as the magic fought me.

Grabbing more magic, I pushed harder. The protection ward bent around my hands. I put my whole weight into it and the seal tore. The magic dissolved from the doorframe, leaving it empty.

Boldly, I stepped over the threshold.

Rows of thirty-foot shelves rose toward a chandelier-lit ceiling. There were four distinct sections, leaving the center of the room open. The school crest was carved into the floor beneath the largest chandelier in the center.

The shelves closest to the doors housed the school records, while the remaining shelves contained student records.

I walked over to the death records and scanned the shelf. I looked over nearly the whole collection before a strip of faded leather caught my eye on the bottom shelf; Richard While's magical book of horrors.

Dropping to my knees, I pulled the small book onto my lap. My skin crawled from just touching the cover. I quickly flipped through the pages, not really sure what I was looking for. Toward the end, I stopped. The title read *Consumer*. On the bottom of the page was a compass.

Bingo.

The ingredients weren't something I could stop by Walmart for. Helen's cabinets however . . . I Ported to the infirmary. Helen softly snored as I advanced toward the shelves of potions lining the back wall.

Checking the list, I found three red nightshade buds, two dried hemlock leaves, one sliver of mandrake root, a vial of tiger snake venom, four crows-blood candles, and two binding coins. Grabbing a pillow off a nearby bed, I pulled the pillowcase off and dropped the ingredients inside. Once I had everything, I Ported to the top of the North Tower.

At the beginning of the year, Master Lenin said they had cleaned and repaired it. I hadn't wanted to confirm that. After Moose died in front of the tower door, it wasn't a place I willingly sought out.

All the ash and char had been removed from the black stone walls. The bright lantern hanging from the ceiling gleamed across the reflective stone. The wall of glass was clear, allowing it to let in streams of fading daylight.

Tipping over the pillowcase, I dumped the contents onto the floor. I flipped the book open to the binding curse and read the first line.

LIGHT THE BLOOD CANDLES FROM NORTH, WEST, SOUTH, to EAST. MIX THE BLOOD OF THE PERSON YOU WISH TO LINK WITH THE VENOM.

I cursed. I needed blood from Blake.

I grabbed the transporter and Ported back to my room at the University. The cold room of ice was still dark, which meant Michael hadn't come back.

Good.

I slipped through the iron door in the common area toward the door marked *Twelve.* I stopped with my hand on the handle.

Am I really going to do this?

I had already done something terrible. What was one more? I was willing to do anything to keep Blake safe.

I released a bit of magic into the door. The lock slid back and the door swung open. Despite being barely past eight, the room was dark and quiet.

My eyes flew around the apartment that was set up exactly like mine. Two rooms mirrored each other on either side of the living room; one room was Blake's and the other belonged to Atlas. Picking one at random, I quietly padded toward it. I slowly pushed open the heavy door.

On his stomach, shirtless, was Atlas. The low light of the bedside alarm clock caught the curve of his shoulders and the tattoos covering his skin.

Wrong room.

I noiselessly pulled the door closed. Once it was latched, I turned toward the other door and rammed into the Hunter.

Atlas's eyes widened in shock. He took a step back and lowered the knife he had aimed at my neck. "Bloody hell, love." He scrubbed a hand over his face, wiping the sleep from his gaze. "Is everything alright?"

"I had a bad dream about Blake," I lied. "I wanted to see if he was alright."

Atlas yawned. "He's fine. He's down the hall if you really want to check." He moved past me to his bed. "Just close the door when you leave."

"I will." I waited until he was back in his room before I moved toward Blake's.

This time, when I opened the door, I wasn't as quiet. Blake had slept through a tornado once. Me tiptoeing into the room wouldn't even register for him.

Blake was sprawled across the mattress. His hair jutted out at random angles. A soft snore was the only sound in the room.

I moved over to the side of the bed. Gently, I pulled his arm to hang over the edge. I paused when I saw it was his hand that only had four fingers. My anger came back as I stared at the lonely knuckle.

I grabbed the cup on his bedside table. Taking out my earring, I pressed the sharp edge to the inside of his wrist, making a small prick.

His breathing hitched. Reaching over, he scratched his wrist, smearing a little blood over his skin. But he didn't wake.

I collected enough blood to cover the bottom of the glass. Once I had what I needed, I ran my thumb over the cut and let my magic seal it closed.

I placed his arm the way it was before. Then I covered him with the fur comforter and pressed a kiss to his forehead. *Please let this work.*

I quickly left the room and used the transporter to go back to the North Tower. I read over the first line in the instructions and added a drop of the venom to Blake's blood. Then I read on.

BOIL THE BLOOD OVER A FIRE OF NIGHTSHADE BUDS, HEMLOCK LEAVES, AND MANDRAKE ROOT.

I gathered the herbs on the floor. With a snap of my fingers, they burst into flames. Curling my legs beneath me, I levitated the glass over the flames. Soon, the blood started to boil. The metallic stench made me gag.

MIX THE ASHES INTO THE BOILING BLOOD.

I blew out the remaining fire and levitated the scalding ashes into the glass.

COAT ONE COIN WITH THE BLOOD OF THE CONSUMER. FUSE WITH MAGIC. KEEP THE OTHER COIN CLEAN.

That would be me.

My hands shook as I grabbed one of the coins. I dug the point of my earring into the pad of my thumb and pressed the coin into the blood that welled up.

DROP BOTH COINS INTO THE MIXTURE. MIX SEVEN TIMES CLOCK-WISE.

I grabbed the other coin with my clean hand and dropped it into the glass. My blood-covered coin quickly followed, and I stirred.

Pour mixture into a compass rose. The directions must be true.

I plucked the glass from the air as I got to my feet. Before my mind could take me on a stroll down Memory Lane, I tipped the glass and poured the mixture onto the floor.

I started with the North, dribbling the mixture in a straight line until it reached the South. I repeated this from West to East. When I was done, only the coins remained in the glass.

Melt the coins into one. To remain linked, keep it on your person. The link can be destroyed with fire, or by breaking the binding coin.

I tipped the glass over my hand and caught the coins. I pressed them together and tugged sharply on my magic. It rolled down my arm and pooled around the coins. I squeezed until the blood was burnt and only one coin remained.

My head went light. My vision clouded. Grasping the coin, I fell to my knees. I gulped in air, but it didn't make a difference. I was out cold.

92

A Card to Play

When I opened my eyes, a high-arching ceiling loomed over me. The black stone glared brightly with sunlight. My gaze followed the sunbeams to the windows of the tower and found the sun just peeking over the horizon.

I closed my eyes, just for a second. When I opened them, I found the sun had left the horizon and was shining on the tower with its full strength.

Wait. That meant I was late—The Trial.

"Dammit!" I staggered to my feet. Blood rushed to my head, almost blacking out my vision.

I needed to get to the Trial Field, but I had no idea where that was. Michael would have Ported us there, or he would have left a transporter for me in my room at the University. But I couldn't go back there. Michael could be waiting for me.

How am I going to get to the Trial Field?

I pulled out my phone to text Blake. *But then Atlas would know, and he probably already has orders against me. Who else would have a way there?*

I got another idea.

Pulling on my magic, I Ported to the center of the school beside the clock tower. I grabbed onto one of the faces in the carved artwork as my vision tilted.

I took a few deep breaths until my head wasn't spinning. I followed the staircase down to the teachers' level. At the bottom of the stairs was Master Lenin's assistant, Tessa Baker.

"Miss Baker!" I stepped off the last step and rushed to her desk.

She startled around. "Contestant Heart. You shouldn't be here."

"I lost my transporter," I blurted. "And my phone is dead, so I can't get a hold of Master Lenin or Guardian Kale. I need to get to the Field."

"You caught me just in time. I was just about to head that way." She grabbed her purse off the desk and rooted through the contents. "You can use this one. If you see Master Lenin, tell him I'm five minutes out." She set the transporter in front of me.

Before she could turn back to her task, I snatched the transporter off the desk and thrust magic into the black stone. I vanished from The Magisterium of Magic.

"Contestant Heart!"

Flashes blinded me as photographers yelled for my attention. Screams of excitement attacked my ears. My name resounded and blended from hundreds of different voices.

"Contestant Heart has finally arrived at the Trial Field . . ."

"The other Top Seven Contestants have been warming up for hours . . ."

"It appears that Guardian Kale isn't with her . . ."

Before me was a stadium twice the size of ones used for pro football. The rumble of a crowd rose over the tall walls, spilling to the surrounding steps below.

That's right. Anyone can watch this Trial, not just Masters.

Barriers lined the stairs, holding back a crowd of flashing cameras and reporters yelling questions. Draped from the top of the stadium were thirty-foot banners of the Top Seven with their Guardians behind them.

The poster for The Magisterium of Magic glimmered with a lining of gold. I looked strong. Guardian Kale stood protectively at my shoulder with his hands in his pockets. We looked impressive and deadly.

I pulled my gaze from the poster before I got to his black eyes. Clenching my hands around my burning magic, I bounded up the red-carpeted stairs toward the main door.

A large man dressed in bright red armor stepped forward before I could touch the door.

"Identification, please."

I tugged up my sleeve and offered him my tattoo. He touched the tip of his wand to the center. Magic rolled over the black ink, authenticating it.

"Where is your Guardian?" the guard asked.

"Don't know, don't care."

Surprise moved across his face. "You cannot enter the Trial Field without him."

I ground my teeth together. "I'm a Contestant."

He nodded. "I have orders that Guardians and Contestants must enter together. That way, the tattoos verify each other."

"Well, my Guardian isn't coming, so you don't need to authenticate his tattoo."

"Your tattoo has his initials around it." He gestured to the bands caging the icons and Contestant number. "With those, you can't enter without him."

"Then I don't want him as my Guardian."

His eyes widened again. Leaning forward, he whispered, "Do you know what you're saying? You wish to reject Guardian Kale?"

"Yes."

As soon as the word left my mouth, my tattoo glowed. The bands repeating Michael's initials dissolved from my skin. And just like that, he was no longer my Guardian.

The red guard stepped back. With a bow, he opened the doors into the stadium.

Grey walls stretched into twisting hallways. Food carts smelling of frying oil, and drink carts offering beer and other fizzing drinks lined the wall separating the main lobby from the stadium. Every hundred feet or so was a stand of t-shirts, hoodies, and ball caps. They came in the colors of the Seven Great Schools with the corresponding number of the Top Seven.

This close to the start of the Final Trial, people were getting last-minute snacks and Trial paraphernalia. The sea of Trial staff and excited onlookers hurriedly moved around.

"Excuse me," I stopped a staff member. "Where can I find my room?"

"Contestant Heart!" The small girl dipped into a hurried bow. "I can show you. Please, follow me." Quick on her feet, she spun around and started down the hall.

Blinking the exhaustion from my eyes, I followed her to an elevator. Practically twitching with excitement, she led me inside and pressed the button for the lowest floor. I leaned my head against the wall, fighting off the drowsy effects of casting the binding curse.

"Charlie!" Blake ran across the room as the doors opened. "Bloody hell, where've you been? We were supposed to be here four hours ago."

"I slept in." My eyes were still having trouble focusing. The staff member hadn't left yet. "Can I have a bottle of Adraffeen sent to my room?"

"Yes, miss." She bowed at the waist and ran off.

My heart seized as a figure in black stepped up beside Blake. "I expected you to be the first ones here," Atlas said.

I stepped away from the Hunter. My skin crawled just looking at him. *Did he know, too?*

"You look downright awful, love." Concern pulled at his handsome face. "Where's Kale?" He looked at the elevators like they would open again.

"He's not coming." I looked past them and saw a door marked with my Contestant number. I stepped around the pair toward it.

"What do you mean he's not coming?" Blake asked slowly.

Atlas grabbed my wrist and jerked me around. He pulled my sleeve from my tattoo, exposing it for the whole room. Fists hitting sandbags, weapons clattering into each other—all of it stopped.

"What's going on?" A rocket launching would've been quiet compared to Atlas's voice. "Where the bloody hell is Kale?"

I yanked out of his grasp. "Ask him." I stepped toward my room.

"I asked you." His fingers curled around my elbow.

I shoved him back. I just meant to get his hand off of me, but I forgot one of the most potent effects of a high magic status in Royals. It made us strong.

Atlas flew back into the wall. A crack shot through the cement from the impact. The lights flared. The one over his head burst in a shower of sparks and glass.

I reined my magic back into my chest, stilling the lights. "Don't touch me."

Blake stepped back. His eyes flickered between my face and my hands. His own were slightly raised by his sides, like he thought I was going to strike him.

The shattered remains of my heart crumbled further.

Keeping my breathing slow to placate my magic, I yanked open the door marked for Contestant Fifteen and slammed it closed behind me.

The room was painted black, from the floor to the ceiling. Even the tile floor was a mosaic of obsidian shards. The only thing before the wall of glass, separating me and the Trial Field was a black leather couch set. On the glass coffee table was a briefcase with my Contestant number painted in white.

My shoes squeaked as I crossed the room. Popping open the case, I scooped the clothes from the main compartment. Tucked into the top were two glass jars, each with an earpiece inside.

Dropping the clothes to the table, I tugged the jars from the protective foam and bashed them into the floor. Glass shot under the couch as I crushed each earpiece under my heel.

"Contestants." Master Lenin's voice filled the space. "We will begin in ten minutes. You may converse with your Guardian on the lawn before they head to their observation rooms."

I scooped up the clothes once more and stepped into the bathroom. They were the same as the last Trial, only this time they were black, from the leather jacket and tank top to the combat boots.

I once thought the color was powerful, dangerous by association, untouchable and ruthless. The dark color made my eyes look more grey than blue, and the scar on my cheek appeared sharper. Just like Michael's. I shuddered at the thought.

Back in the main room, a bottle of Adraffeen waited beside the open briefcase. With eager fingers, I twisted open the cap and took a large gulp. My teeth ached at the sharp taste of lemon.

Immediately, my eyelids lightened and exhaustion left my bones. For the first time that morning, I was able to think clearly.

Setting the bottle aside, I took the three-piece holster from the briefcase. I thought about leaving it. Michael had it made for me, and I wanted nothing from him.

But I needed all the help I could get. With my teeth clenched tight, I strapped the holster around each leg and cinched it around my waist. I sheathed my wand and found one last thing in the briefcase.

The switchblade Michael had given me. The stainless-steel was a bright contrast to the all-black interior of the case.

I thought about leaving it, one last middle finger to Michael. But the metal warmed in my hands as I picked it up, almost as if it were letting me know it was happy to see me, to be used, that it was on my side.

"Always have more than one weapon on you," Michael's voice said from the back of my mind. *"You never want to be caught empty-handed."*

Gritting my teeth against the voice, I clipped it to the holster.

"Contestants," Master Lenin announced, "it's time to line up. Please step onto the Field and find your starting plate."

Rounding the coffee table, I stepped through the glass. A blast of incoherent chatter rushed at me. All around the stadium, the seats were filled with a mess of colors and cheering Users. Some waved flags with a crest of a great school. Others had a cutout of a Contestant's face on a stick.

So many eyes should have made me nervous, but my gaze lifted to the top of the stadium where a familiar terrace stood, protecting the viewing Masters.

Directly over the Contestant holding rooms was the same black glass that housed the Guardians. Of the seven blocks, six were lit from within, offering hints of the Guardians caged inside. The one where Michael would be was the only one still dark. It felt strange not to hear him breathing in my ear.

My attention was drawn to the black glass housing the judges. Above them was a box just for the School Masters and Lawrence.

I jerked my eyes away before I saw Lawrence's face. I didn't want to see the horrible '*I told you so*' expression he had to be wearing.

My nails dug into my palms as I walked across the short grass and stepped onto my starting plate. Before me, on the other side of the Field, were seven doors. The School Masters must have wanted blood because they put my door right beside Dmitri's.

I glanced at the line of Contestants. All the Guardians had escorted their Contestants to their starting plate. Each pair looked down the line at the empty space beside me.

The murmurs from the crowd hushed with disbelief.

"Pst," Thiago called, a few paces away. "What are you doing?"

My fingers ached as I coiled them tighter. I struggled to take in a deep breath; the tightness of the new jacket kept the breath shallow. I jerked it from my shoulders.

With my tattoo now in full view, an uneasy, almost angry, murmur ran over the crowd. One sound stood out.

Dmitri hooted with laughter, deep and menacing. "Little bird, do you want to die?"

I cut my eyes to my opponent. Contestant Nineteen looked truly frightening in his hard leather top and fitted pants. His double-sided axe was strapped to his back. Painted in red, down his chest, were the numbers of the Contestants he had killed. My eyes lingered on the number thirteen, Daniel's number.

"Welcome, Contestants!" The crowd cheered upon hearing Master Lenin's voice boom across the stadium. "Guardians, please make your way to your observation boxes."

One by one, each Guardian Ported from the lawn. Atlas lingered the longest, trying to meet my gaze, but I kept looking forward at my door. Finally, he Ported from the grass too.

"In a moment, you will enter the final test of The Master's Trial. Your desires will be waiting for you. Your fears will be waiting for you. You have your weapons, and you have the skills. Use them wisely. Contestants . . ."

I glanced at my opponents. They were crouched, ready to spring forward. All but one.

Dmitri wasn't looking at the door.

He was looking at me.

Without breaking eye contact, he pulled the axe free from his back and into his eager hands.

"He outmatches you in skill," Michael's voice whispered from a memory.

That may have been the case, but I had a card to play that would level the field. I was a Royal Nine.

I dropped my wand onto the grass next to my rejected jacket. I stood tall, matching his posture. Magic poured from my core, spilling through my body.

The crowd slid forward with anticipation for the obvious clash.

The silence in my ears was deafening.

"You may begin."

93

The Final Trial

Contestants leapt forward.

Five ran for their doors.

Dmitri sprang from his black marble slab.

I Ported next to him and tripped him to his knees.

His axe sprang from his hands as he barely kept his face from hitting the dirt. I Ported in front of him and kicked him in the face. The magic racing through my blood lent me the strength to flip him onto his back.

I could have ended it right there. All I had to do was open my switchblade and remove his head. But I didn't. I stepped back.

"I know he put you up to it. My quarrel isn't with you," I said. "I'll give you a chance to walk away."

He pushed himself to his elbows. Blood leaked from his nose and over his lips. "You think I did it because he asked? Little bird, I did it because I wanted to." He pushed himself to his feet and spat the blood from his mouth.

"This," he pounded his fist against the bright red thirteen, "is a victory of war. And now, without your Guardian watching over you, you'll be my next."

He swung, knocking his fist into my ribs like a torpedo. The air rocketed from my lungs. His fist landed again. Pain shot through my ribcage.

Just barely over the roar of the crowd, I could hear the Russian shouting in his earpiece. He aimed his fist for the wound on my chest.

Pure panic took over. I grabbed his wrist, jerked it over my shoulder and slammed my other fist into his elbow. It popped. I twisted his broken arm behind his back, and jerked it from the socket. Then, I let him fall to the grass.

Anger contorted his face as he looked up at me for a second time. As he muttered something in Russian, I remembered there were technically three people in this fight; with his Guardian giving him instructions, he had the upper hand.

Dmitri clambered to his feet and rushed me. Magic burned in my chest and rushed down my arm. I ducked his swing and barely missed the other. Golden magic spilled through my fingers, gathering in my palm.

I planted my hand on Dmitri's chest. My magic sank through his shirt and circled his heart. The magic mimicked my fingers as I squeezed.

The crowd murmured, confused.

Stumbling back, the blood drained from Dmitri's face. He dropped to his knees, gasping for air.

Pushing the hair from my face, I stooped over him and took the wand from his belt. He was so weak all he could do was reach toward me with limp fingers.

Stepping out of his reach, I ran my fingers over its rough wood. The designs looked like someone had taken a knife to it and started hacking.

How appropriate. I snapped it against my knee. The crowd gasped. He weakly reached toward me as I threw the splintered pieces into the grass.

Kneeling beside him, I pressed his face into the dirt and pulled out his earpiece. I pushed magic through my fingers, frying the magical object with a bright spark.

Pain erupted from my side. Warmth soaked my shirt. I cried out and fell to my knees. Stunned, I looked at the blood glistening from my side.

Another flash of pain sliced across my shoulder. *What the*—My heart dropped. *The binding curse—Blake!*

My eyes flew to his door, green with a white frame. He was behind it with the remaining five Contestants. Whatever was happening behind those doors, blood was being spilled.

My concentration lingered on the sudden wounds for too long. I realized the lack of magic in my chest too late. I spun around to Dmitri, but he was gone.

Dmitri scrambled over to the only weapon he had left. Struggling to his feet, he scooped up his axe. Like a starving animal, Dmitri's eyes locked on to the fresh blood dribbling through my fingers.

Without breaking stride, the muscles in his arms rippled as he hurled the axe with all his strength.

Gritting my teeth, I got to my feet just in time. With a wave of my hand, his axe swerved to the side.

The crowd screamed, not in excitement, but in astonishment. I had deflected the axe without a wand.

Just as the weapon slammed into the grass, Dmitri's shoulder rammed into my stomach.

My feet left the ground. The air was punched out of my lungs as my back flattened against the earth. My ribs groaned. I couldn't tell if I felt something crack, or if it was just the shock from the impact. The wound in my chest howled as his weight pinned me to the grass.

He pulled back the fist of his good arm and aimed for my cheek. This was not the first time I had been on my back with a fist aimed at my face. However, this was the first time I could do something about it.

I twisted my hips and rolled on top of him. His blue hair fanned out over the green lawn. Magic flared through my chest, surging down my arms. As it pooled brightly in my hands, the grass beneath me scorched to black.

Bracing my hands on his chest, I shifted forward. Glowing brightly, my hand slid effortlessly through his skin and between the ribs, melting the cartilage as I pressed further. The furious magic in my fingers popped his lungs as I grasped his heart.

"You took mine," I said, as cold and harsh as I felt. "So I'm taking yours."

Wrenching my arm back, I yanked his heart from his chest. Blood poured down my arm and dripped from my elbow. The muscle pulsed weakly before going motionless in my hand.

Dmitri relaxed beneath me. His dark blue eyes stared upward with a lifeless glaze. The crowd went ballistic. The cries of distress from the stands were deafening.

A howl of rage broke through the noise.

I whirled toward the sound.

Guardian Theodore was no longer in his box. He sprinted across the grass toward me. He stooped, scooping the battle axe from the ground. Swinging the weapon over his head, he hurled it with all his might.

I dropped Dmitri's heart. With bloody fingers, I reached for the axe hurtling toward me. The handle slammed soundly into my palm. Using its momentum, I spun a full circle and sent it flying back to the Guardian.

The axe struck his chest with enough force to knock him off his feet. He flew into the glass wall of the arena. The windows cracked on impact, but didn't give way. Guardian Theodore slumped to the ground.

Mayhem broke out. Masters were up and out of their seats, running for the exits as I faced the stands.

I met Lawrence's gaze. The heat in his stare told me he was pissed. If only I cared.

Turning away, I reached for my wand on the ground. I stared down at the black wood lying on a bed of emerald grass.

Magic still gleamed underneath the skin of my bloody fingers, warm and bright, like molten sunshine.

I didn't need it. Maybe it was another way Master Lenin and Michael tried to control me.

Turning my back to the wand etched with swirls of fire, I started toward the black door with the gold frame.

Waving magic over my head, the remaining doors erupted into a whirl of splinters. I passed through mine just before it joined the storm. The door crumbled behind me as soon as it clicked closed. There was an air of finality as the shards fell to the ground.

94

You'll Have to Prove It

Sunlight streamed boldly from a cloudless sky.

It held nothing back as it unleashed its full force of scorching heat. Dry, compacted dirt stretched in front of me. It was a stark contrast to the perfectly manicured lawn I left behind.

Directly in front of me was a city. The skyscrapers were splashed with sand, like a dust storm had just blown through. The streets were wider than usual, and empty of streetlights, cars, or any kind of vegetation. Dunes crisscrossed over the street.

There was no cover. If I wanted to hide, I had to run a block and turn down the street or go into one of the buildings. The School Masters had thrown all seven Contestants into one place with hardly any cover, so we would have to meet each other. Violently.

"Seven go in, but seven never come out," I muttered, and I finally understood why.

You're wasting time.

I took only a couple of steps before I had to stop, as my head swam. It was easier to use magic without a wand. But without it, I used more, and it was less controlled. I could already feel the lack of energy, the lack of heat, coming from my chest.

I'd have to be more careful, or else I would find myself in a situation where I had no magic to draw from.

Giving my magic a break, I took the switchblade from my belt and hit the button. The blade answered and sprang out. I started forward.

A few yards ahead, something sparkled in the sand.

Creeping closer, I saw a silver rod sticking out of a small dune. I kicked it from the pile. A silver arrow rolled into the sunlight.

I forgot about everything: the heat, my side, and the blood on my hands. The only one who came into The Trial with an arrow was Blake.

I dropped into a crouch. My eyes ran over the sand. Footsteps, slashes, and dips told of a fight that allowed two people to leave. I couldn't tell if they left as friends or if they were chasing each other.

I broke into a run, adding my footprints to those already there. I went a few blocks before the silence was shattered with a yell.

I slid around a corner. The sand took my traction, but I was able to catch myself before I fell to the ground.

At the end of the street, Emeka battled with a stunning woman. Covered in the same sand that coated the city was Vienna, the second Contestant from Lions of Magic. What she was doing here, or how she got here was beyond me. A grunt drew my attention to the closer battle.

Blake was on his back, but he was alive. His assailant raised her switchblade above her head with perfect form. With everything her muscles could muster, she swung the blade toward his neck.

I Ported next to him just in time to knock her back. She recovered quickly and made me her next target. Our switchblades clanged together. My heart about popped in my chest when I focused on the face behind the weapon.

It was mine.

I blinked to confirm what I was seeing. The girl in front of me wore a light blue hoodie and ripped jeans. A red lock of hair mingled with her dark brown hair. The only thing that was different was the amount of sand that covered every inch of her.

Getting over my shock, I shoved her back and aimed to take her head from her shoulders. She was ready for me. Every strike I directed her way, she was waiting for. It was like fighting a mirror.

"Charlie, duck!" Blake yelled from behind me.

I threw myself to the ground just as an arrow zipped past my ear. The arrow plunged into the sand-Charlie's chest. Another quickly followed, implanting in her forehead. She fell back, and as soon as she hit the ground, she dissolved into sand.

My aching rib pressed against my lung, restricting my airflow. Gulping down fresh oxygen, I pushed myself up to my hands and knees. Weariness started to weigh on me.

Feet scuffled through the dirt seconds before I heard the sound of a bow being drawn. I was relieved to see Blake. He was covered in sweat and his eyes were crazed, but he was fine . . . he was also aiming a notched arrow at me.

"It's me." A cough wheezed out of my lungs as I forced myself to my feet.

He didn't relax his weapon.

"Blake." My eyes darted to Emeka. He had survived his fight and was now holding his spear, ready to throw at me.

I glanced over my shoulder, expecting to see someone behind me, but there wasn't anyone. They were aiming at me.

I raised my hands. "I'm not going to hurt you."

"I don't know that." Blake's fingers flexed around the shaft of his bow. "Atlas said you just killed Dmitri and threw an axe at a School Master. I don't trust you."

"Neither do I," Emeka agreed.

Pain shot through my chest and it had nothing to do with the wounds marking my skin. "Blake, I would never hurt you—"

"I'm not so sure anymore. You killed *two* people. Hell, maybe three!"

"Put the bow down and I'll explain."

"You can't talk your way out of this." He shifted his grip on his weapon. The acute tip of his arrow gleamed in the sunlight. "What happened to you? The Charlie I knew would never—"

"The Charlie you knew was scared of her own shadow. She let people put scar after scar on her back." My voice whipped across the street as magic flared dangerously in my chest. "Dmitri was going to come after you. I was protecting you. Doesn't that mean something?"

"Yeah, it means you're like him." Frustration growled up his throat. "How can you justify something like that? I told you what being around that man would do to you."

He lowered his weapon. "No, I will not watch myself. That man is poison," he said to Atlas. "Don't make me take you out of my ear." It seemed the Hunter heeded Blake's warning because Blake pointed the arrow back at my chest. "I don't know who you are anymore."

"What do you want me to say, Blake? You were right. I picked the wrong Guardian." I gestured to the arrow. "Will you put that away?"

"Don't you dare," Emeka snapped at him. "How long are we safe? Until she decides she doesn't need us?"

"I don't need *you*," I snapped. When neither of them moved, I pulled on my magic. It wrapped around their weapons and tugged them out of their grasp. I caught Emeka's spear in one hand and Blake's bow in the other. My fingers smudged Dmitri's blood on the shiny surface.

I promptly threw them down to the sand. "Blake, I've always had your back. I'm not here to hurt you. I'm here to get you out." I looked at Emeka. "Shouldn't you be running off by now? Or have you finally come to terms with the fact that you can't finish a Trial on your own?"

Emeka reached for his wand.

Magic pooled in my palms. "Go ahead. I dare you."

He hesitated.

Blake flinched, reaching toward his earpiece. "Atlas?"

My mood darkened at the mention of the Hunter.

Blake's eyes widened. He glanced at me before taking a step back. "I need a sec." He retreated down the street. With nervous energy, he conversed with his Guardian out of earshot.

I wondered what Atlas was telling him.

Emeka held my gaze. "What's your angle? Why reject your Guardian?"

"I didn't need him." Gritting my teeth, I pressed my hand to my side. I did my best to keep the pain from showing on my face.

"You remember who you're talking about, right?"

I nodded once. "Hard to forget a jackass like Michael."

"He's a Master Hunter."

"Both things can be true."

He muttered something to his Guardian. "You think you'll get higher marks by finishing The Trial alone. That's it, isn't it?"

I rolled my eyes. "Please, shut up."

Blake spun around and came back toward us. He walked past me, to the pile of sand which held two of his arrows. "What am I looking for?"

He was still talking to his Guardian.

Bending down, he took a pinch of sand and placed it on his palm. He brought it to his nose and sniffed. "It smells bitter." He took another whiff. "Like burned herbs."

I stooped beside him and pinched some sand into my palm. It tickled with magic as I brought it to my nose. The moment I inhaled, my eyes watered from the bitterness of the scent.

Blake flinched. Reluctantly, he tossed the sand into his mouth. He ran it over his tongue a couple times before spitting it out. "Tastes like blood."

I decided to take his word for it.

His lips parted. "You're joking."

After a couple seconds, I piped up. "Are you going to share with the rest of us?"

"Mas—" He winced and cleared his throat. "Atlas says it's a blood enchantment."

"What does that do?"

"It evokes the theme of The Trial; our desires will become our fears. Anything we want, while in this Trial, will rise up from the sand." Emeka kicked a small pile at his feet. "And try to kill us."

Dusting my hands clean, I rose to my feet. "Anything? So, like if I wanted a glass of water—"

A slight gurgling noise came up from our feet. The ground trembled right before it cracked open. We dove out of the way, just in time for a geyser to erupt from the asphalt.

The water curved unnaturally and headed directly for me.

I threw up my hands and braced for impact . . . that never came. Peeking out from my shielding hands, I found the geyser frozen solid.

Breathing hard, Blake lowered his wand. "*Yes,* like if you wanted a glass of water."

Cheese and rice. "My bad."

"We should get moving before she does anything else stupid." Emeka grabbed his spear from the sand. "Let's go, Johnson."

My eyes narrowed at Emeka. All Trial long, he was very adamant that he could complete this Trial by himself. So, why was he keeping Blake close? Hell would buy heaters before I left Blake alone with him.

"I'm coming too," I said, stepping forward.

Emeka jerked around. "No. We just said that we don't trust you."

I shrugged. "You know what they say. Keep your enemies closer than your friends."

Irritation twitched through his nose. With a roll of his eyes, he turned. Over his shoulder, he said to Blake, "If you can't kill her, put an arrow through her leg and let's get out of here."

My heart soared when my best friend shook his head. "She's coming with us."

Emeka flipped around. "You're kidding."

"I wish I was." Blake's eyes moved over me like I was concealing something deadly. His gaze lingered on my bloody hands. "Atlas says three sets of eyes are better than one. I agree."

"The only reason she'll be watching our backs is to put her blade through them."

My eyes narrowed at Contestant Eight. "If I wanted to kill either of you, I would've let the sand people do it."

He gathered the spit in his mouth and spat it at my shoes. Muttering to his Guardian, he started down the street.

"He's right, you know," Blake muttered, picking up his bow and arrows. "I don't trust you."

My heart sank to my toes. "I'm not your enemy, Blake."

"You'll have to prove it." Without another word, he started after the other Contestant.

95

In the Dark

No one spoke.

The city was so quiet, I could hear the sand grinding beneath our shoes. Blake's arrows clinked together with each step. Emeka's spear hissed across the sand between his footsteps.

The sun beat down on us with a merciless, scorching heat. Blisters were beginning to bubble on the back of Blake's neck. Eventually, Blake put his bow across his shoulders, and Emeka rested his spear against his back.

Out of nowhere, Emeka and Blake slowed. They pulled out their weapons and cautiously turned the corner. Michael taught me never to put my weapon away, so I was already ready.

Wrapping both hands around the handle of my switchblade, I rounded the corner of the skyscraper. I came to a stop beside Blake.

Blocking the street was a collapsed building. Drywall was stacked and cracked under the pressure of the fallen skyscraper. Fractured glass littered the ground. The hollow windows showed only a few feet into the building before the shadows took over.

"That looks like fun," I said.

Blake shot me a weird look. "Atlas said the same thing."

"Hunters." Emeka spat into the sand.

"Is there a way around it?" I asked.

Blake shook his head. "It goes all the way around the center of the city."

"Like it's guarding something?"

By the looks of it, Blake and Emeka thought the same thing.

The door.

Our way out.

I stepped toward the darkness, without fear of the shadows.

Blake stopped me with a hand on my arm. "Hold on. We don't know what's in there."

"There's only one way to find out." I sheathed my switchblade and grabbed a chunk of plaster. When it didn't crumble in my hand, I began to climb the debris.

With looks of unease, both Contestants followed.

The merciless sun heated the side of the building, making it uncomfortable under my fingers and palms. Just like the time I laid my hand on Mrs. Kale's glowing stovetop, the heat didn't do anything other than flush my skin. Every once in a while, a curse rose from Emeka or Blake climbing behind me.

My arms started to shake the higher we climbed. Maybe the School Masters wanted us to go over the entire building.

Reaching above me, my hand hit open air. Clutching the ledge, I dragged myself up and over the edge.

It was where a section of windows used to be. Now it just gaped open, a hallway spilling over with a darkness so thick it hid everything from view. Above it was smooth with no handholds. The only way forward was through.

At the mouth of the darkened hallway, I waited for the others to join me. My eyes tried to pierce the darkness in vain. Magic flooded down my arm, into my hand, and then flowed from my fingertips. It collected into a small orb above my head.

"How are you doing that?" Blake asked, pulling himself onto the ledge. His eyes darted between the thick darkness to the light. Emeka was a couple seconds behind him.

I shrugged. "It's just like using a wand."

"I've never seen that kind of magic," Emeka commented, rising to his feet. "Not from a Common Six." By his tone, that was supposed to be an insult.

"I'm not a Common Six." I turned to their startled gazes. "I'm a Royal Nine."

Blake snorted. "Yeah, right." His eyes jumped between the orb of magic above us and my glowing hands. His humor faded. "You're serious?"

I nodded.

Emeka stepped back, examining me as if I were a new threat. His heel slipped over the edge. He leaned forward in time to prevent a freefall.

Blake's mouth dropped open. "Why the bloody hell would you lie about that?"

"Commons get less attention."

"But—"

"We should get moving. Since you're the one with the most magic, you go first." Emeka nodded his chin first to me and then to the darkness in front of us.

Blake's smile dropped into a stony glare. "I think you should go first, mate. Since you're the one with all the bright ideas."

"She's a Royal," Emeka stressed. "That puts her at the top of the food chain. Most creatures will smell her and back off."

"You're forgetting that we're in the bloody Master's Trial. I doubt the School Masters would choose anything so easily swayed."

I put my hand on his arm, stopping whatever was lined up next on his tongue. "I'll go first."

Blake tore his eyes from the other Contestant and gave me a once over. "You're bleeding."

I shrugged. The action pulled at the split skin over my ribs, lacing the wound with fire and fresh blood. "I'm fine. He's an ass," I cut my eyes to Emeka, "but he's right."

"Charlie—"

I spun toward the mouth of the hallway and tugged the switchblade from my holster. I hit the button against my hip and stepped into the shattered building. The magical orb floated over my head. Blake was a step behind me. I hated having Emeka at my back, but the darkness in front of us I hated more.

Goosebumps prickled over my arms as the temperature dropped dramatically with each step. Since the building was on its side, we were walking on the walls. Every so often, we would step over a doorway.

Cheese and rice. I clenched my hands around the handle of the switchblade, to keep them from shaking.

These shadows were unlike any I had ever seen. They were so thick, the magical light barely cut through them.

We stepped over light fixtures and moved around broken furniture. The doors above us were mostly closed. We peeked into the devastated rooms below us to ensure they were empty.

Soon all sunlight fell behind us. The walls and cracked ceiling became our only surroundings.

Slowly, the air grew damp, and with it came the pungent smell of raw meat. The chill of the building created clouds from our breath. After what seemed like an eternity in silence, we came to a branch in the hallway. We could either descend or climb.

"Up or down?" I whispered. I wasn't asking the Contestants, but their Guardians.

"Down," Emeka and Blake said in unison.

"How far is the drop?" I refused to turn my back to the void. I strained my eyes for any movement. My nerves didn't settle when I found nothing. If anything, that pulled them tighter.

"Fifty feet," Emeka answered.

"Is it too high to jump?" Blake asked, staring into the darkness. In the silence, I heard Atlas answer him.

"Well?" I asked.

Blake shook his head.

I remembered Michael's story of how he fell and broke his back. And that was in broad daylight. Who knows what was waiting for us below?

"We could levitate down," I suggested.

Blake looked around our group. "Does everyone have enough magic for that?"

"She does." Emeka gestured toward me with his spear.

"She can't do all of us."

"She's a Royal Nine. Of course she can."

Reluctantly, Blake turned to me. "How are you feeling? Are you up for it?"

I nodded. "I'll go down first so I know how much magic to use."

"No." Emeka stepped forward. "You'll leave us here."

"I guess you'll have to trust me not to." Pulling on my magic, I faced the void. Magic slithered down my arms and through my fingertips.

Cheese and rice, Michael and I never practiced anything like this.

You don't need him. You taught yourself to Port. You can figure out how to levitate yourself.

I created a disk of magic over the open air. Carefully, I stepped one foot onto it and then the other. I wobbled a little, but I was upright.

Thank God.

Slowly, I lowered myself into the darkness.

"Leave the light," Emeka whispered harshly when the orb began to descend with me.

Clenching my teeth around my temper, I left it with them. The shadows eagerly embraced me, swallowing me like the ocean tide. I stopped breathing altogether when I was completely submerged. My imagination sent my hands shaking.

The thick darkness hid everything. If it weren't for the cool air passing through my hair, I wouldn't be able to tell I was moving at all. Surrounded by silence, I found myself missing the sound of Michael's voice in my ear.

My feet slammed into the surface below. A scream startled in my throat at the sudden change. I clapped a hand over my mouth before I could release the sound.

Doing my best to breathe through my panic, I removed the magic from my feet. My shoe squished into the floor.

I turned my gaze to the light above me. Raising my voice as loud as I dared, I whispered, "Who's next?"

Blake moved to step out, but Emeka halted him with a hand on his shoulder. Before my friend could voice objections, Emeka stepped over the edge.

I considered letting him drop. But him hitting the ground would have made too much noise. Instead, I let him fall for a foot or two before wrapping his shoes in magic. Just to piss him off, I left the light with Blake.

Just before the shadows engulfed him, Emeka paled with horror. I also may have let him fall a little faster than I did when I lowered myself.

In a matter of seconds, his deep, slightly panicked breathing drew closer.

"You're almost to the bottom," I warned him with a whisper. When I heard the butt of his spear knock into the floor, I released my magic. His heavy boots stomped into an unseen puddle.

I turned my gaze up to where Blake stood. "Last call for the levitation express."

"Can you be any louder?" Emeka hissed.

I didn't bother responding. As Blake stepped out, magic flew from my palms and pooled beneath his feet. Carefully and slowly, I lowered him to me. The orb of light followed after him.

The light shocked my eyes as he came down the corridor. Blinking rapidly, I didn't dare turn away in case I dropped him.

As the light descended, it caught the reflection of the puddle at our feet. Color started to appear on the walls. I couldn't tell if it was from the intensity of the light, but it looked as vibrant as blood.

Blake slid past a smudged handprint. He jerked out his wand just as his feet touched the floor. Following his gaze, I stumbled back against the wall, unable to take my eyes from the scene before me.

The wall beneath our feet was soaked in blood. The crimson tide collected around our shoes and in the creases around door frames and corners. Smudged handprints dragged across the walls toward the doorways above us. Despite all of this, the hallway was empty of bodies.

Blake was the first one to move, although it wasn't a confident step. His wand trembled in his white-knuckled grasp. When neither Emeka nor I moved, he looked over his shoulder. "Come on."

I just stared at him.

"Do you want to stay here?"

No, but I didn't want to walk through it either. Swallowing down the fear in my throat, I stepped forward. Gore bubbled up from under my shoe.

"Don't make the light too bright," Blake whispered when I added more magic to the orb. "We don't want it to attract anything."

"Actually, you should make it brighter." Emeka hadn't taken his eyes off the shadows ahead of us. "The light might scare it away."

Blake and I stopped midstride. At the same time, we asked, "It?"

Emeka gripped his spear, the point extended toward the shadows. "It's just a hunch."

"Which is?" My eyes darted to a creaking door above us.

He paused, like if he said it out loud, it would make it real. "It could be a caligo."

Blake tilted his head toward his earpiece with a frown. "That bad, huh?" he asked Atlas.

Emeka nodded. "They're creatures that used to be Users, miners, actually. A group of them got trapped so deep in the earth that they forgot what light looked like. Their magic absorbed the darkness, transforming them into shadows."

"Lovely," I muttered.

"They don't need to eat because shadows exist wherever light is absent. They kill only because they like the taste."

In silence, the three of us stared at the blood-soaked floor.

"Maybe it's not a caligo," I offered. "Maybe all of this is just to freak us out."

"Let's hope. In the meantime," Emeka nodded his head toward the floating golden orb, "keep that light bright. It could be the only thing keeping them back."

Magic flooded from my core, doubling the brightness of the orb. The light stretched down the hallway, giving us a few more paces of visibility. Whatever terrors lurked just on the other side remained still, waiting.

I shifted closer to Blake. Gripping my switchblade, I slowly moved across the saturated surface. Thankfully, Blake didn't move away. Even Emeka stayed close.

Moving as a unit, we crept down the hall. Each footstep sloshed the gore covering the floor. Blake put a hand on his quiver to keep the arrows from clinking against each other.

Most of the doors were closed, and we moved past them without much of a glance. But the ones that were open gaped with darkness. Blake aimed his wand into the shadows while Emeka stepped over. Then, when Emeka was aiming down into the gaping darkness, Blake ushered me to step over. When all three of us were on the other side, we continued.

Far ahead, a series of clicks and rattles quietly trickled down the hall.

Our pace slowed. Without anywhere else to go, we pushed forward.

The sound grew louder.

And louder.

The glowing orb pulsed with my heartbeat as we walked by each bloody handprint. Finally, through the dim light, we found the cause. The door handle of a closed office was moving.

"Charlie?"

I startled away from the door. My head whipped around to look at Blake. He met my panicked gaze with one of his own.

"Charlie?"

Blake's voice was calling my name, but his lips weren't moving.

"Caligo," Emeka breathed.

A whimper escaped through the door as fingernails grated against the wood. The door handle shook with more fervor.

Emeka swallowed thickly. "More light."

The orb brightened to fill the hall. As soon as the light hit the door, the rattling stopped. Ahead, something shrunk back around the corner.

Blake, pale as a ghost, nudged me forward. As soon as the door was concealed with a shadow, the handle began to shake. Once more, the creature whimpered my name.

As we drew closer, Blake pulled me behind him and jumped around the corner with his wand raised. He motioned Emeka and I forward. Barely breathing, we kept walking.

"Blake!" a panicked voice cried as something slammed into the door over our heads. Instead of whimpering, the caligo wailed. "Blake, help me, please!"

Blake stumbled back just as the door handle beneath us rattled. A strong voice called for Emeka.

Further up, fingernails cut away at the wooden doors in a chorus of horror. From every closed room of the long hall, voices from family members and friends begged us to let them out. I recognized the sound of Blake's mother and even Cornelia. Meg pleaded for my help.

Emeka broke into a run, no longer caring about the noise he made or the thick shadows around us.

"Go." Blake shoved me forward. With each hurried step, we splashed through the thick blood. We barely slowed to jump over the light fixtures and doorways.

Hearing our urgency, the doors shook harder. Cracks split the wood. The drywall fractured. The cries turned into screams. Darkness pooled just outside the limits of the light.

A couch with torn cushions and bloodied stuffing sat cockeyed across the hallway. Right in our way.

Blake fired a blast of magic over my shoulder, snapping the couch in half, clearing the hall. The top, however, fell backward and crashed through one of the closed doors.

The moment the light fell over the doorway, an inky mass hissed back into the deepest corners of the room. One after the other, we jumped over the doorway without pause. But the second the golden light left the door-way . . .

Just over our racing heartbeats and splashing footsteps, we heard the distinct sound of a handle unlatching and the whine of a door hinge swinging open.

The chill that shot down my spine would've made glaciers feel pleasantly warm.

Farther down the hall, another door unlatched.

And then another.

And another.

Running faster, we splashed across the floor to another bend in the hallway, leading farther down into the building. As we rounded the corner, sunlight spread across the floor.

There was no patience for levitation. Emeka shoved me out of the way and jumped down the hallway. Blake and I did the same before Emeka landed. Pain rocketed up my legs upon impact.

Stumbling into a run, we charged toward the sunlit exit. Behind us, doors burst open. I threw a glance over my shoulder but saw nothing. The thick darkness hid everything.

Bursting from the building, I doubled over my knees, sucking wind so fast, my lungs didn't have time to register it. The golden orb evaporated as I squinted against the brightness of the outdoors.

Emeka screamed.

I spun around and met his wide-eyed stare.

A caligo, a faceless iridescent figure, had Emeka by the neck. Without a sound, it dragged him back into the building. Emeka's spear clattered to the ground as his screams faded into the vastness of the shadows.

96

A Little Honesty

Blake looped his arms around my waist and threw me down to the street.

I fell to my knees. Still in the shadows of the neighboring building, Blake scooped me up from the sand and pushed me forward.

The shadows around our feet darkened. A hand shot from the inky blackness and wrapped around Blake's ankle. His face hit the dirt. Gravel cut into his chin as the shadows drug him backward.

My chin burned. Magic flooded my hands. Throwing my arms forward, fire plumed from my fingertips, engulfing the street, scorching the sand to glass, and blasting against the surrounding buildings.

The shadows shrieked. Blake's backward slide stopped. Scrambling to his feet, he ran for the sunlight.

I pulled the flames into a tidal wave, driving the shadows back toward the darkened corridor. Slowly, I backed up to where Blake stood in the sunlight. The faceless creatures retreated to their lair as the fire brightened.

When I stepped into the warm sunshine, I cut off the flow of magic. In a whoosh, the fire spun out, leaving the ground charred and steaming.

The shadows remained motionless.

My ears rang with silence.

I stepped toward the building with my magic at the ready.

Blake snagged my arm before I could leave the sunlight. "You can't go back in there."

"We can't just leave him!"

"Do you really think he survived that?"

I looked back at the silent darkness shrouding the insides of the building.

The cries of the caligo still rang in my ears. If what Emeka said was true, those creatures killed him the moment he was submerged in shadows.

"Can Atlas see him?"

Blake shook his head. "Guardians can't see anything other than their own Contestants this time."

"Dammit!" I yanked free from his grip and thrust my hands into my hair.

"Yeah, I know," he snapped at his Guardian. "Just give us a damn minute to breathe."

"There has to be something we can do." I paced in front of the shadows.

"There isn't." Once more, he grabbed my arm, but this time his grip was gentle. "Unless you want to run through there looking for his body. If those things even left one."

He was right. Drowning in defeat, I spun around, putting my back to the terrible shadows.

"Come on, we need to get away from here." Blake pulled me away from the fallen building. In the silence of the street, I heard Atlas murmuring instructions.

Blake ushered me down five blocks before he finally stopped. The pace he set quickened my breathing, as if the excitement in the darkness hadn't made it fast enough. Breathing deep was painful, thanks to the aching ribs pressing on my lungs.

Stopping in an alley, I leaned heavily against the cool stone siding of an ice cream store. I clutched my side. My shirt was damp with fresh blood.

Blake wiped the sweat from his brow. He barely nodded to whatever his Guardian was saying. "Can I see your wounds?"

I waved him off. "I'm fine."

"Sure. Because that's what normal breathing sounds like." He paused, letting my strained breathing fill the silence. Stepping forward, he grabbed the bottom of my shirt.

I grabbed his wrist. "I said I'm fine."

"You don't trust me?"

"I trust you with my life. It's the man in your ear I don't trust."

"Then trust me." Slowly, he twisted his wrist from my grasp and lifted my blood-stiff shirt above the wounds.

His face contorted with a mix of sympathy and anger. "Bloody hell, Charlie . . . what happened?"

My eyes dipped to the slash in his shirt, the one that matched the wound over my ribs. The skin peeking through was smooth and unscathed. "I got it at the start of The Trial."

"Well, it's a mess." He leaned closer to the wound. Underneath the slash, from my underarm to belly button, was a blanket of blues. "A damn mess."

He pulled his wand into his hands. "I'm going to illuminate your bones, so Atlas can see how bad it is . . . be patient with me. This is the first time I've done something like this."

Trust him, I chanted on a loop as his wand drew closer to my bruised skin. I sucked in a deep breath when he made contact.

His magic surged through my chest. I braced for it to burn, but a pleasant warmth flowed over my bones. The closest thing I could compare it to was standing under a showerhead after a cold day. But the feeling was concentrated in my ribcage.

Each bone glowed under my skin, just like the ones in my hands when I was about to use magic. Over the collar of the tank top, under the never-closing scar, the cracks in my sternum didn't glow with the rest of the bones. The place where the knife almost shattered it was clearly evident.

Blake hissed, drawing my attention to the bones directly under the infuriated wound. He confirmed what I was seeing. "You have two broken ribs."

"So that's why it hurts when I laugh." I mustered a weak smile for him.

The corners of his lips lifted, but that's all he would allow. I gratefully slumped against the wall when he removed his wand from my skin.

He brought his hand to his earpiece. "Is there something I can do so she's not breathing like that?" He winced. "Can I numb it?"

Judging by the way he cursed, the answer was no.

Blake made quick work of shrugging out of his jacket. "You'll want to roll this up and put it between your teeth." He repositioned himself on his knees and pointed his wand at the first fractured rib.

I crammed the jacket between my teeth and hugged the remaining fabric to my chest. With eyes squeezed tight, I breathed slowly through my nose.

I expected him to count down, but he didn't. With two quick sparks per fracture, my ribs popped back into place and fused. My teeth cut through the fabric of his jacket. Tears gathered in my eyes.

When the magic faded, the pain went with it. I sucked in a sharp breath and found that I could breathe deeper and easier.

Blake gently tugged the jacket from my mouth. "You good?"

I nodded, breathing deeply through my nose. Quickly, I wiped the moisture from my eyes.

"Atlas says you're welcome." Blake stepped back and replaced his wand at his hip. He stood there, watching me for a second. To my surprise, he reached up and removed his earpiece. "Why'd you kill Dmitri?"

I tugged my shirt back over my side. "Can we leave things the way they are?" I pushed away from the wall and started down the street. "I don't want you to hate me more than you already do."

"You're my best friend, Charlie. Hating you is in the fine print," he called after me.

I stopped, staring at the barren landscape of the dusty city. Sand shifted around my shoes.

"All I'm asking for is a little honesty."

My hand cradled my side. With the binding curse, I had given him everything. But if he asked a question tied to a horrible answer, could I say it, knowing I would destroy this tender truce between us? I could lie, but that was all I did. My hair color was even a lie. I didn't want to do that to him.

So I faced him. "Ask and I'll answer."

He didn't right away. With a contemplative silence, he fiddled with his earpiece. "Those scars, the demon scars. How'd you get 'em?"

"Would you believe me if I told you I cut myself shaving?" I asked, craving one of his crooked smiles.

There was no smile. He wasn't even amused.

"My curiosity got me into a situation where a demon tried to steal my magic."

"And that's the reason why you hide your real status?"

I shrugged. "It's one of them."

He looked down at his earpiece. "Why did you reject Master Kale?"

I knew he was going to ask. If I were in his shoes, I would want to know too. But I had no idea how to even phrase it. My mind battled against reality, holding onto the moments when Michael's eyes were a dark, rich brown and his lips curled with smiles instead of smirks. Soft moments when the weight of the world wasn't pressing on his shoulders. When he called me Sunshine.

But reality, cold, hard, and relentless, drove back those memories. It illuminated the calculating steadiness in his gaze and the manipulative way he strung his words together. He had reeled me in close so I couldn't see what he was doing behind my back.

"Did he do something?" he prompted. "You were his number one fan not two days ago."

"You were right about him," the words fell softly from my lips. "He doesn't know the difference between good and evil anymore." I dropped my gaze to my fiddling hands. "He's the reason Dmitri killed Daniel."

Blake went still in front of me. "Oh, my God, Charlie . . ."

Another wave of sorrow swept through my chest. I squeezed my eyes tight, hoping it would fight the onslaught of memories from the Second Trial: Daniel joking with me right before Dmitri arrived, blood trickling from the corner of his mouth, his body slipping over the edge to the water below.

"Why?" Blake shook his head, trying to dislodge the shock from his skull. "He didn't pose a threat to you Ascending."

"He said Master Lenin gave the order, but I don't know how much of that I believe." I swiped at the tear trying to roll down my cheek.

Blake dragged his hands through his tight curls. "I hoped you were right about him. I really did."

So did I.

"Is there anything else?"

"My name's not Charlie."

His eyes looked like they were about to pop with shock. "What—"

"I'm kidding." I met his scowl with a smile.

Humor drained from me with my next thought. "Dmitri told me he was going to add your number to his arm. I did what I did to keep you safe. I've had too many people taken from me."

"That's not going to happen," he assured me. "The devil himself would have to drag me away."

That's what I'm afraid of.

"Promise me we'll do this together." He stepped closer. "No more running behind each other's backs. Promise me that you'll trust me."

"I can do that."

Blake popped his earpiece back in place. "Then let's get out of here."

My gaze drifted toward the earpiece peeking from his ear canal. "Can I speak to your Guardian for a second?"

Blake's eyes narrowed. Just barely, I could hear Atlas voicing his objections. "You're not going to break it, are you?"

I shook my head. "I won't. I promise."

Fighting his reluctance, Blake reached into his ear and tugged it free. Then he held it out to me.

With a reassuring smile, I took it and turned my back to him. Taking a few steps away, I pressed the earpiece in place and shuddered as it expanded.

"So, now you want to talk to me?" Atlas asked dryly. "You weren't very talkative this morning."

"I had a lot on my mind."

"Like premeditated murder?"

"If I wanted a lecture, I would've kept Master Kale as my Guardian." I glanced over my shoulder to make sure Blake was far enough away. "I know Master Kale is your boss. I don't know if he gave you an order to lock me in here, but, if he did, I want you to keep Blake out of it. Do everything you can to get him out."

"Of course I will. It's my bloody job. I don't half-ass anything."

I wish that put my mind at ease, but Hunters lied.

"Good. Because if Blake doesn't make it out of here in anything less than perfect condition, I will hunt you down and kill you."

Atlas burst out laughing. I flinched at the volume of it. "I'm a Hunter, love. That's impossible."

"Yeah. And so is doing magic without a wand."

He wasn't laughing anymore.

"Get him out. If you think what I've done was awful, you've only seen me when I'm protecting myself. Neither of us knows what I'll do when I'm angry." I ripped the earpiece from my ear and stalked back to Blake.

Blake popped his earpiece back in. "Do I get to know what you two were being so secretive about?" Atlas jumped right in with an answer, causing Blake's eyebrows to spike up. "You're threatening Hunters now? Is that smart?"

"Probably not." I wiggled my finger in my ear, trying to get rid of the tingling feeling the earpiece left behind. "But I've never been described as smart."

I started down the street. For the first time since I had entered The Trial, for a brief, fleeting moment, I thought we would be ok.

That got me daydreaming. All I wanted was a nice, quiet walk to the door and a hot shower. No sooner had the thought crossed my mind than the air grew warm with magic.

I hit the button on my switchblade. The blade extended with a sharp, metallic ring. Blake went still beside me. His eyes scanned the street, looking for what caused the reaction.

At first, I thought exhaustion was making the ground fuzzy. I tried to blink away what I was seeing, but my vision didn't clear.

The sand slid from under our shoes, down from buildings, off our clothes, and into piles. The more sand that was added, the taller the pile grew.

"Run!" Blake yelled.

<h1 style="text-align:center">97</h1>

Your Desires Will Become Your Fears

With matching strides, we charged down the street, leaping over the growing, moving heaps.

The sand rose to my right and took on the form of my foster dad, Denny. He reached forward with a meaty fist. I swiped my blade through his neck. He quickly dissolved back to the ground.

A hand shot out of the earth and wrapped around my ankle. I fell hard against the asphalt. I flipped onto my back, slicing my switchblade as I went. The blade cut through a sand version of Blake. He broke apart, drenching me in grit. Spitting it from my mouth, I jumped back to my feet.

An arrow whizzed across the street and landed in the forehead of a kid I had seen from Blake's school. Blake didn't watch his friend fall to the ground. He notched another arrow and let it fly.

From the corner of my eye came a glint of steel. I whirled around and my blade connected with another. Bubblegum-pink nails gripped the hilt. Cornelia grinned before trying to hack me into pieces.

I forced myself to look past the face that belonged to one of my closest friends. My attachment to her forced my blows to lack strength, and my aim to waver. Her sword sliced across my collarbone.

The pain sharpened my focus, drawing my attention to the sand that covered her. I sliced through her midsection, dissolving her back to the ground. Not giving myself time to process, I turned back to the intersection.

My blade cut through Ace and Nirean. My throat was tight with tears as one after the other fell. Meg was the hardest, not only because her brother was a Hunter who obviously passed on a few of his tricks to her, but because every time my blade cut into her—the very one her brother gave me—an image of her son flashed through my mind.

She's not real. This isn't the real Meg.

I kicked her away, but was too slow raising my blade. Her weapon, a wood-chopping axe, arched above her head before falling toward my own.

Something flashed in the corner of my eye. An arrow rocketed by my nose and punched Meg in the chest. She burst against the wall like a water balloon.

The intersection went quiet. Except for me and Blake, who gasped for air. I didn't feel any new injuries, so I knew Blake was alright.

I stared at the sand, feeling like I was going to throw up, or cry, or both. I knew it wasn't Meg, but I couldn't stop seeing the arrow hit her. *Holy shit.* Tears gathered in my eyes. A sob built in my throat.

"What . . ." Blake bent over with his hands on his knees, ". . . the hell . . . was that? They . . . came out of bloody nowhere!"

I dragged a hand across my damp forehead. *Shit.* "It was me."

Panting, Blake shot me an inquisitive look.

"When we were walking, I wished for an easy walk to the door." I gulped down air. "Your desires will become your fears."

A chuckle rumbled down the street.

Blake and I spun around, weapons raised. Thiago stood across the street, leaning his shoulder casually against the closest building. Ignoring our raised weapons, he remained relaxed.

"Were you just standing there?" My switchblade shook as I fought to catch my breath.

"Yep." Thiago rolled his eyes at our appalled expressions. "You should take that as a compliment. I knew you had it under control."

"Yeah, because everyone bleeds when they have it under control."

Thiago smirked with one eyebrow cocked. "I've seen you take a knife to the chest. I think you can handle a scratch."

Sucking in a deep breath, my eyes darted around the intersection. With the sand people gone, we were the only three standing. Without Blake, I had no idea where to go next. I fought the urge to touch the ear that would have held an earpiece.

"Where did you come from?" I asked.

"The door."

My ears perked up. "*The* door?"

Thiago nodded. "It's a couple blocks that way." He pointed to the street on my right.

"Yeah, and I'm a bloody unicorn," Blake snorted. "If the door was that close, you wouldn't be here."

"Haven't you been paying attention?" Pushing off from the wall, Thiago strolled into the street with his hands in his pockets. "Nothing is ever simple in the Final Trial." He passed right by me and kept walking down the street he indicated.

I stepped to follow, but Blake moved in front of me.

"You're not seriously going to follow him?" Blake muttered.

"Is Atlas telling you to go the other direction?"

He nodded.

Hitting my switchblade against my hip, the blade retracted with a clear, metallic zing. Smirking at Blake, knowing his Guardian could see, I moved around him and followed after Thiago.

Blake hesitated only for a moment. He replied sharply to Atlas before jogging after me.

For two blocks, we walked in silence. Blake and I flanked the new arrival, keeping a couple paces behind him. Thiago strolled down the middle of the street without a care in the world.

Finally, Thiago slowed to a stop. Flattening his back against a glass skyscraper, he edged his way to the corner. Coming to a stop, he motioned with two fingers for me to look around the corner.

Trading places with him, I scooted along the slick glass and peered around. The alley opened up into a large plaza. Right in the center was a single white door.

Relief flooded through my body, filling me from my head to my toes. That was the way out. On the other side of that door, all of this would be over. Blake would be safe.

But just like Thiago said, nothing in the Final Trial was ever simple. Between our unlikely trio and the door cars were strewn about, like they had been abandoned in a hurry. Doors were flung open. A couple of them were even upside down, charred with the memory of fire. Wandering aimlessly around the cars were hundreds of sand people.

Blake shoved Thiago back and leaned over my shoulder. "Damn."

"Now you see my dilemma," Thiago said quietly.

"Have you tried anything?" I asked, unable to look away from the door.

A laugh shook his shoulders. "I'd be an idiot if I tried anything alone."

"So you were just waiting for us?" Blake's hand twitched toward his wand.

"Calm down, Brit," Thiago said sardonically. "I was waiting for someone to test the waters first."

"You mean no one's gone for the door yet?" My gaze swept over the plaza. Even though a horde of sand people milled about, the sand covering the plaza was undisturbed.

"Nope. Tala is six blocks that way," Thiago jerked his thumb over his shoulder. "Last I saw, Amelia was drawing stupid ass strategies in the sand over there." He pointed to a tiny alley opposite us.

"What's everyone waiting for?"

"The way I figured it, this is the final test." Thiago leaned against the cool glass. "This is the last chance we have to prove ourselves to the Masters. Once we're through that door, this is over."

"Huh." Blake examined the other Contestant with narrowed eyes. "I had no idea you weren't an idiot."

Thiago smirked. "It's a secret I like to keep hidden, or else people might start expecting things. So," he nodded his head toward the door, "got any suggestions?"

"You think we're going to help you?" Blake shook his head with a laugh. "I take back what I said."

"You'll need all the help you can get to make it to the door."

Blake opened his mouth, probably with something smartass to say. But Thiago was right, we needed all the help we could get. The School Masters expected us to do this alone, to fight against each other. But I was in the kind of mood to piss off as many of them as possible.

"First things first," I shot Blake a silencing look. "We need to take precautions."

Thiago gave Blake a shameless grin. With a look of victory, he turned back to me. "Such as?"

"We need to keep our minds empty. Don't think about anyone or anything, or it's going to pop out of the sand. I don't know about you, but I've had enough of killing everyone I know. Just focus on the door."

"Just focus on the door," Thiago echoed with a nod. "Got it."

Blake's face paled as his mouth fell open. His eyes slid closed as a single word fell from his lips. "Damn."

Cold water poured through my veins. "What?"

A roar tore through the silence. The ground trembled with the tremendous noise. The sand scuttled across the asphalt as another shriek rang through the city.

Thiago and I turned to Blake. In unison we hissed, "What did you do?!"

"I'm sorry!" With clammy palms, he pulled out his wand. "You told me not to, but my brain jumped anyway—dammit!"

"What did you think of?"

He gulped. "A dragon."

98

From the Shadows

Another roar echoed across the sky.

A rush of wind blew by the mouth of our alley; on it was the smell of smoke. The ground shook, and glass shattered. Once more I peered into the plaza, only this time I was afraid of what I would find.

Struggling up from the ground was Blake's dragon. Spikes jutted from the back of its head, across the spine, and down to the tail. Two more spikes pierced through its eyes, making me wonder if it could see. It was pale in color, matching the beige sand covering everything. As more sand pulled toward the mighty beast, two wings arched over its head.

The sand people scurried away. Its giant foot shot forward, smashing those closest beneath its claws.

"I don't think we have much time to plan anything," I said as the sand people drew closer.

Blake came to stand beside me. He was so close, I could hear Atlas barking orders in his ear. "We need a distraction over there." He pointed around the corner to the right side of the square. "If we can draw the sand people out of the way, we can sprint to the door."

"What about the dragon?"

"A distraction should work for that guy too. Hopefully."

"I'll go." Looking at the opposite side of the plaza, I scouted a shorter building. "If I set that building on fire, I think it'll do the trick."

"Why do you get to be the bait?" Blake narrowed his eyes. "You have a wound—"

"Which is fine."

"I can be the distraction and loop around to the door," Blake said.

"Over my dead body," I snapped. "If I go, I can Port as soon as you guys are close to the door."

"How much magic do you have left? Atlas told me about how much you used at the start and that had to have used a lot." When I was too slow to contradict him, he pressed on. "I'll run around, make a bunch of noise, and double back when I see an opening."

"He's right," Thiago said before I could add anything else. "You've used enough magic. You need to get through the door."

I bristled at those words. "Like hell—"

"I'll be the distraction," Thiago stated calmly.

"I can Port."

"So can I," Thiago said.

I blinked in surprise.

"What?" Thiago laughed at my expression. "Did you think you were special? After I saw what you did in the Second Trial, I had my Guardian teach me. I'm not as good as you, but I can get by."

"How do we know you'll actually create the distraction and not head for the door yourself?" Blake demanded.

"You don't. So, I guess you'll just have to trust me." Thiago grinned. "Sounds like fun, huh? Catch you on the other side of the door." With a wink, Thiago ran down the alley and out of sight.

"Come on." Blake retreated from the plaza. "Atlas says there's a better vantage point a couple blocks away."

We made the short trip to where Atlas directed Blake. The alley was much smaller, only ten feet wide.

I crept to the mouth of it and pressed my back to the wall. The cars were thinner from this spot. However, the amount of sand people were not. If anything, their numbers had doubled.

Blake's dragon climbed up the highest skyscraper. Its claws, the size of tree trunks, cut easily through the side of the building until it reached the top. Pulling itself up, it sat on the roof. The windows below cracked and exploded under its weight, raining glass down below. Then the beast went still.

"Why are there spikes in its eyes?" I whispered to Blake.

He shrugged. "Beats me. Probably a twist of The Trial."

I don't like the sound of that.

Blake stepped back from the mouth of the alley and retreated a few paces. He sighed, "If Thiago does manage to distract the sand people, we'll use the cars for cover. I think that should get us pretty close. Then we run like hell." Quietly, he muttered to his Guardian.

My eyes darted through the plaza, mapping out which cars would give us the most direct route. We could sprint for the light blue minivan with the crushed hood and then bolt to the grey Honda a few paces away. The next few cars were lacking doors, so I didn't know how much cover they would provide. Maybe that was where we started running like hell.

"Have you seen any of the others?" Blake muttered to Atlas. He grunted with displeasure. "Hopefully, they'll have their hands full with—"

A sharp prick popped under my jaw. Keeping my eyes on the door, I itched the patch right over my pulse. My fingers came away wet. I jerked my hand back and found blood on my fingertips.

"Charlie?" Blake said from behind me.

I spun around and almost dropped my switchblade.

Emeka held the tip of his spear to Blake's neck. Half of his head was drenched in blood; his left ear was missing, leaving a gaping hole in the side of his head. Underneath his shredded clothes, his skin was marred with claw marks. His hand trembled as it gripped the sharp weapon. Insanity brightened his eyes.

"What are you doing?" I asked slowly, eyeing the blade close to my friend's jugular.

"What I have always been doing," Emeka growled. "Getting myself to the finish line."

"Do you have to do it with your spear at his throat?"

"Yes. If I don't, you'll leave me behind. Again."

"We didn't think you were alive, mate." Blake kept his voice calm.

"Did you even stop to check?" Emeka snapped, jerking his spear closer to Blake's neck. I tried not to flinch as a prick of pain stung my neck.

"Would you?" Blake countered.

"Of course not. I was only with you so you could get me to the door."

"Your Master was right. Maybe you can't finish a Trial without someone's help." I slid my foot forward, hoping he wouldn't notice.

His eyes shot to my feet. "I will kill him."

Blake clenched his teeth as the spearhead pressed closer to his neck. The same spot on my neck felt the cold sharpness of the blade.

Think, Charlie, think! There has to be some way out of this. Every idea that came to my mind had one end result: me dead on the ground leaving Blake to the mercy of Contestant Eight.

I moved my foot back. *There has to be something I can do . . .* Against my will, my mind ran over lessons with Michael.

Emeka glanced over my shoulder. Hunger widened his eyes as he stared at the door. "So, what was your plan? How were you going to get through the sand people?"

"You're under the illusion that I . . ." I stopped. The idea that popped into my head almost made me dizzy. "That I'm going to tell you anything."

Illusions.

Trying to hide the fact I was drawing up a battle plan, I smiled. "In case you're confused, I'm not. Not until you let him go."

Carefully, I pulled on my magic and let it leak over my skin. A shiver rolled up my spine as it burned over every inch, engulfing me from head to toe.

"Then you're mistaken as well," Emeka snarled. "He's the only thing keeping you in check. You either tell me, or I slice him open right here."

Blake's eyes widened.

At that moment, I was completely covered in magic. Carefully and methodically, I started to peel the mold from my body. The last time I did this, it didn't work. Last time, my best friend's life wasn't on the line.

"His blood will attract the dragon, and while that beast is licking up the remains of your friend, I'll be running to the door."

Blake swallowed thickly around the knife. In response, the skin on my neck stung.

Emeka pressed the spearhead closer to Blake's pulse. "So, what was the plan?"

The mold was completely detached. Somehow, I had managed not to rip anything too noticeable, only a spot under my arm and the backs of my knees. I took a deep breath and stepped back. The mold held and remained standing.

I took the switchblade from my belt and walked around the mold. Emeka's eyes didn't leave the magical cast.

"Our plan," I said slowly, as I moved around him, "was to use a distraction. But you won't get to see it. You should've run to the door yourself."

I slammed the hilt of the switchblade against his skull. Knocked out cold, he tipped forward. His spear slipped from his hand, the sharp edge sliced Blake's skin, and clattered to the ground.

Blake whirled around, clutching his neck. Instead, it was my neck that held the small incision; a trickle of blood ran to meet the collar of my shirt.

"What the hell?" Blake whispered. His eyes were locked on the cut across my neck.

I cut off the flow of magic and the illusion crumbled to the ground. The gold magic melted without a trace. Lightheadedness fluttered around my skull, causing my vision to double. Breathing slowly, I fought it back.

"How . . . how did you . . ." He pointed to the wound. "That should be . . ." His hand cupped the side of his neck.

"It's a binding curse." I wiped the blood from my neck with the back of my hand. "Whatever happens to you, transfers to me."

"What?" His eyes bulged.

"I meant what I said. I'm not going to let anything take you from me. So I made sure of it."

He shook his head, unable to process. "Bloody hell, Charlie—" His head snapped toward his earpiece. In the same moment, he looked up toward the unblemished blue sky.

He crossed the space between us in a second. Just as he grabbed me by the shoulders, the buildings on either side of us exploded.

Glass shot across the alley like a volley of arrows. Rooftop stone and plaster stormed down on our hiding place below. Blake's dragon straddled the alley. The two spikes jutting out from its eye sockets glowed brightly as it lowered its head toward us.

Blake's hands tightened around me, keeping me still.

99

The Distraction

The beast's head barely fit between the two buildings.

The spikes jutting out from its jaw scraped across the stone as it dipped its nose toward the sand. With a whoosh of hot air, it sniffed the ground . . . right where my illusion dissolved. The spikes in its eyes glowed brighter.

It might not have been able to see worth a damn, but it sure as hell could sense magic.

Its giant head snapped up. The spikes grated across the siding as its unseeing eyes looked our way.

Blake's fingers painfully pressed into my shoulders.

The dragon swung its head forward and stopped within inches of me. Its nostrils flared. Hot, stale breath flipped my hair off my shoulders. There was no doubt it could sense the magic coating my skin. Suddenly, I wasn't so proud of my illusion.

The dragon opened its mouth. The air rushed in around us, moving down its glowing throat. Then, fire erupted from its mighty jaws.

I threw my arms around Blake and Ported.

We appeared in the alley we first met Thiago in a couple blocks over. The dragon roared into the sky, shaking the ground.

The sand people, drawn by the agitated dragon's cry, sprinted across the plaza. Away from us.

"I guess that's our distraction! Let's go!" I pulled him into the plaza.

"The binding curse—" Blake yelled after me, "that's why, when I fell and hit my chin, yours was the one to bleed." Taking out his wand, he blasted two sand people to pieces. "That slash on your ribs. That was from the beginning of The Trial when Tala threw a knife at me, wasn't it?"

"We can have this conversation later!" Magic blasted from my hands. Cars and sand people were thrown back like rag dolls.

Sensing fresh magic, the dragon leapt into the sky, thrusting its wings toward the ground. The scorching gust of wind berated us with sand. The giant creature banked, stretching its wings wide.

"All this time, I thought Master Kale hurt you. Instead, it was me." Blake grabbed my arm and spun me around to face him. "I do not want to live at the expense of your life. Break the damn curse."

I shook my head. "Once we cross the finish line."

"Do it now!"

The dragon flipped backward and pivoted. Pulling its wings close to its body, it dove toward us. Opening its mouth, a geyser of red flame fell from the sky.

I pushed Blake behind me. Magic raced down my arms and into my raised palms. I had no idea what I was doing. I just thrust it forward in an arch.

The dragon flames collided with the golden dome. My shoulders ached under the pressure as I struggled to keep it up. My skin flushed and burned with the heat of the fire, but the flames rolled harmlessly around us.

The dragon swooped overhead. Crossing the plaza, it banked again and turned back toward us. This time, its clawed feet were extended.

"Dammit, Charlie!" Blake yanked me toward the door. "Stop doing that! I won't be able to live with myself if I'm the reason you die."

"And you think I will if I don't do everything I can to keep you alive? You're my only family."

The dragon destroyed our diversion. Like moths drawn to the flame, the sand people rushed us. Screams and cries for blood were overpowering. They clamored over cars, shoving each other out of the way.

Grabbing Blake's arm, I turned and Ported to the door. I shoved it open and we dove over the threshold into a field of golden wheat.

In front of us, the field sloped upward. At the top was a white ribbon of magic hovering a few feet off the ground. Behind it was a set of stands crowded with cheering Users.

The finish line.

Blake and I sprinted up the hill. The tall wheat bowed around us as we raced forward, toward safety, toward the end of this nightmare.

Behind us, the dragon roared. The ground shook with the mighty sound. I slowed and then stopped. Breathing hard, I spun around. The door was still open. Loose sand shifted over the threshold and curled in the air.

Thiago was still in there.

The crowd erupted in cheers. Turning back around, Blake had just broken the finish line. The white ribbon glowed bright gold in celebration. Atlas Ported beside him and threw his arms around his Contestant, slapping him on the back.

I turned my gaze back down the hill. *Thiago would've used the diversion, right?* I thought back to the horde of sand people running chaotically around the plaza.

Come on, Thiago. Come on.

As more time slipped by, I realized we had doomed him. Or, more specifically, I had doomed him. Creating the illusion had summoned the dragon, and Thiago's plan had been null and void. I had stranded him in there.

"Charlie!" Breaking away from Atlas, Blake dove forward, but the finish line solidified, locking him on the other side. "What are you doing?"

I tore my gaze from the door, hating the way he was looking at me. "Thiago should be right behind us."

"I'm sure he is. Come on, love." Atlas waved for me to come closer. "He's a smart kid. He'll make it out on his own."

He wasn't in the position to make promises. Seven went into the Final Trial, but seven never came out.

Shaking my head, I stepped back toward the door. "I'll be right back."

"No!" Blake yelled.

I spun around, a mess of tangled hair clotted with blood flew around me. I charged back down the hill, and before I lost my nerve, I burst through the door.

Another roar shredded the air. The dragon landed on top of a building. Its gnarly arm reached between two structures, trying to get a hold of a Contestant.

There you are.

The dragon roared in frustration.

Sitting back, it raised its head into the sky. The beast no longer had a lower jaw. Someone had been busy entertaining the creature.

As the dragon took a deep breath, its belly glowed hot. Positioning its head over the alley, fire blew from its throat.

I Ported in front of the prone figure of Thiago. Raising my hands, I threw magic into the flames. The dragon blaze parted around my hands and slammed into the surroundings walls.

Thiago uncurled his arms from around his head. As he watched the flames dance harmlessly around him, he threw back his head and laughed.

The dragon fire paused only long enough for the beast to draw in another breath.

Thiago jumped to his feet and together we ran from the charred alley.

The blind dragon blasted the ground again. The wave of flames gushed out of the alley, taking the last of the sand people with it.

Its giant head swung our way. Without the lower half of its jaw, fire dribbled from the tunnel of its throat and sizzled against the sand. With each step, the ground shook beneath its clawed feet.

Thiago and I slowly backed away from the blind creature. Both of us were breathing hard, covered in sweat. Unfortunately, with each step, we were moving away from the door.

"Got any ideas?" I whispered.

"Yeah, actually." Thiago nodded his head toward the plaza. "Can you levitate one of those cars?"

I nodded. "What did you want me to do with it?"

"Throw it at its head."

"Ok. And what happens after that?"

"I think I'm just going to wing it." He twirled his wand across his palm. "Go!"

Magic flooded from my hands once more. Twin golden veins yanked an SUV from the sandy street and shot it at the growling dragon.

Its head snapped toward the sudden burst of magic just as the hood of the SUV crashed between its eyes. Metal shrieked and tore as the car crumbled against the beast's tough skin.

The dragon stumbled under the impact. Its massive shoulder slammed into a nearby coffee shop, decimating it.

Thiago threw a magic lasso around a streetlight and slung it into the sky. Just as the dragon got its huge feet back under him, the light pole flipped in the air and fell back to earth.

Thiago's magic latched on again, but this time he yanked the streetlight down. It looked like an arrow streaking through the air. With a final flash, it broke through the back of the dragon's head and drove into the ground.

Immediately, the fire in the beast's chest blinked out, leaving it cold and colorless. The beast slammed to the ground with a thud that caused the surrounding structures to shiver. Slowly, the tip of its nose began to dissolve. As the head melted, the rest of the body followed suit, returning to giant hills of sand.

"Nicely done." I swiped the sweat from my forehead.

"I know." Thiago grinned. Spinning on his heel, he ran back to the main plaza.

As we raced back to the door, I pushed ahead while Thiago glanced behind him. Before I could do the same, he tackled me to the ground. My head cracked against the concrete. For a moment, I couldn't see through the pain.

Thiago pushed himself off me, but stayed crouching. In the siding of a car, where my back would have been, was a sai.

Contestant Tala Abalos was close.

Painfully pushing myself to my knees, I peered under the car. I couldn't see her feet. "Where is she?"

"Five cars that way." He pointed toward the door.

In other words, she was in our way.

"Wanna split up?" I rose enough to look through the window. With the sand coating the glass, I couldn't see much but vague outlines. "I'll take right. You take left?"

He gave me a wary look. "Splitting up would be, in my humble opinion, the dumbest thing we could do."

"Then what would you suggest, smartass?"

He rose until he could peek over the roof of a yellow taxi. "I think if we keep low, we can pass without another encounter."

"Sounds good to me."

Dropping back to a crouch, he grinned. "Then let's go."

Keeping low, we moved around the taxi, pausing only to make sure the way was clear. With light feet, we crept from one car to the next; our heads on a constant swivel, looking for the remaining Contestants.

Five cars passed.

And then ten.

Bang!

Both of us froze. Metal striking metal came from our left. I gripped my switchblade and jumped onto the balls of my feet.

I looked over the hood and saw Contestant Four, Amelia, wielding her trident. Her movements were clumsy and unpracticed. Her opponent was Contestant Three, Tala, with her sai. Their fight was pushing them toward us.

I tapped Thiago's shoulder and dropped to my belly. Sand grated and scraped my skin as I dragged myself under the nearest car. Thiago did the same.

One of the fighting Contestants slammed into the hood above me. Their feet sent sand into my face. The trident clanged to the ground seconds before its owner fell next to it.

Amelia barely got out a cry before Tala's blade entered her chest. Weakly, Amelia reached for her weapon . . . and her eyes landed on me. They widened as blood gurgled from her mouth. With one last cough, her body stilled.

Tala removed her blade, chattering briskly to her Guardian in Tagalog.

I shifted the hold on my switchblade, ready to strike anything that came near me. Tala's feet moved around another car and out of view. A couple seconds later, I heard the door shut.

Using the door handle, Thiago pulled himself out from under the car. He bent down and helped me to my feet.

"Is everyone else through?" Thiago whispered.

I shook my head. "Unless you saw Emeka."

"I haven't seen him since the start. Are you sure he's still alive?"

"Unfortunately." I pointed to the far side of the plaza. "Last time I saw him was over there. Hopefully, he's still unconscious."

"You should've just killed him." He moved forward at a crouch, with his head on a swivel.

Since the dragon fell, nothing else moved. There were no more sand people walking around. Everything was quiet. So quiet that with each footstep, we could hear the sand grind under our shoes.

We heard Emeka before we saw him. His gasping breaths echoed from one car to the next. There was a limp in his step that dragged through the sand.

Thiago and I dropped lower.

"Where is he?" I breathed.

With a grim look, Thiago pointed ahead.

Shit. He was between us and the door.

Thiago took one of the darts from his belt. Rising slowly, he peered over the hood of a car. He dropped back down. Taking two short breaths, he quickly rose and threw the dart. He crouched down as it hit a car. The sound echoed around the plaza.

"Who's there?" Emeka rasped. "Show yourself."

Thiago gestured to the right. Moving slowly and quietly, we crept forward.

"I know you're there!" he yelled.

Moving around a few cars, I spied the door through a shattered windshield. My heart skipped. We were so close.

"If you don't show yourself, I'm going to break the door in half!"

Thiago and I went completely still.

"Can he do that?" Thiago murmured.

I thought back to the start of The Trial. With a wave of magic, I had reduced the doors to a flurry of splinters. They could be harmed. But there was no way Emeka would damage the only way out of The Trial.

Before I could answer, there was a flash of gold, and a crack.

My heart jumped into my throat. Rising on my tiptoes, I peered through the cracked windshield.

"He took off a chunk of the top," I said, completely appalled.

Thiago cursed.

100

The Door

"Show yourself!" Emeka screamed.

Thiago jumped to his feet with his hands raised. "Dude, calm down."

"Are you the only one left?" Emeka's voice shook.

Thiago nodded, taking a step away from me.

"What are you doing?" I hissed.

"What was that?" I heard Emeka limp closer. His injured leg hissed through the sand. "I heard someone."

"Shit," Thiago mumbled without moving his lips.

"You said you're the only one left." Emeka's voice rose with his growing hysteria. "But I heard someone. I did. I heard a whisper."

"You're closer to the door," Thiago said evenly. "Just go through, man."

"No! Is someone else with you? I swear I will break this door—"

With a curse, I rose to my feet.

Emeka's eyes widened. Blood covered the side of his head from where I hit him. One of his eyes was starting to swell. He raised his wand and fired.

I dragged Thiago to the ground just as the ward crashed into the car beside me. It rocked onto its side, smoking, and with a molten hole in the side.

The car that hid us from Emeka's gaze shot toward us. I rolled out of the way just in time. The hood clipped Thiago's shoulder and dragged him backward. Tipping over, it crashed onto his arm.

Thiago screamed. He spewed dozens of foul curses as blood dribbled to the sand.

Without the cover of the car, we were exposed. Emeka rushed toward us, stumbling and half-crazed.

I looped my magic around a minivan and yanked it into his path, just as he fired. His ward sliced the car in half. It gave me just enough time to get back on my feet.

Emeka staggered through the blazing halves of the car. I remembered the first time I saw him in class. He was put together and levelheaded. The Contestant in front of me was wild. The look on his face said he was seconds away from breaking.

He aimed his glowing wand at my chest. "The winner's title is mine."

I watched the magic bloom out of the tip of his wand and streak toward me. Hadn't he told me once that I drew people close only to break them? He was so close. Why not push him just a little further?

Pulling on my magic, I deflected his ward to the side. "And the door is mine. *I want nothing more.*"

As soon as I uttered the words, the sand at our feet rattled. Metal shrieked against the asphalt as the cars between us and the door slid away.

Rising from the sand in their place were dozens upon dozens of white doors. As they surrounded the original, the cracked frame mended, making it appear whole and indistinguishable from the replicas.

And then they began to move. Like a shuffle of cards, the doors wove in and around each other. All the while rotating in a large circle around me and Contestant Eight.

Emeka raged, turning round and round as he tried to spot the original door. He groped at one of the door handles. As soon as it opened, it dissolved back into sand.

"You know what else I want?" I yelled at him. "Good weather."

Immediately, the sky darkened. Thunder rumbled and the clouds churned like ocean waves. The hairs on my arms rose seconds before lightning flashed. The bolt struck the space between us. Wind tore through the plaza, creating an abrasive gale of sand.

The doors circled us, round and round. The effect was dizzying, but I refused to look away from Emeka.

"I want—"

"Shut up!" he roared, firing at me.

I jumped to the side. One of the circling doors clipped my shoulder, throwing me off balance. Another gold orb flew toward me.

Lightning crackled from the clouds. As the bolt raced down to smite me, I heard Michael's voice. *"Energy attracts energy."*

Time seemed to slow. I pulled on my magic and forced it into the raw electricity. Gritting my teeth, I changed its trajectory and shot it toward Emeka.

With a flick of his wand, the bolt shot over his shoulder. The side of his face steamed and blistered. Screaming, he fired ward after ward at me. I countered each with a cast of my own. But he had more experience. He was faster and more brutal.

When the sky unleashed another bolt, I pulled it to me and poured as much magic as I could get away with into it. It glowed white-hot as it streaked toward him.

This time, he was prepared. He not only deflected it, but he reflected it back to me.

I jumped out of the way, landing on my side. The blur of magic slammed into the line of doors behind me, reducing them to sand. The booming thunder rattled my whole skeleton. My ears filled with a sharp ringing.

Gasping on the ground, the world spun around me. I couldn't tell if it was the doors circling me, or if the lightning bolt had induced vertigo.

Desperately, Emeka opened door after door. Each slipped through his fingers as they dissolved into sand. He screamed in rage. The sound was lost over the teeming sky.

Waving his wand over his head, a rush of gold magic blasted against the rotating doors. My heart jumped into my throat as they all dissipated.

All except for one. The door slowed and came to a stop back at the center of the plaza.

Emeka scrambled forward. Yanking it open, he threw himself through to the other side. Half-running, half-limping he made his way up the hill toward the finish line.

Lying on my back, I gasped for air. Above me, the thunderclouds broke up. Blue sky peeked through the mess of rumbling purples. As the wind came to a rest, the sun once more poured over the plaza.

"That . . . was insane," Thiago said weakly.

Through a wave of nausea, I somehow got to my feet and staggered over to him. "I honestly forgot you were still here."

"Yeah, that showed," he panted. His arm was still pinned. His face was nearly white, and his lips were almost blue.

"It's bad, huh?" He stared up at me, shivering.

There was so much blood around him. "Can your Guardian use your Save and help get you out?"

He shook his head. "No Save for the Final Trial. Remember?"

Right. "Ok. That just means we'll have to be quick." Taking out my switchblade, I released the blade and cut off his pant leg.

"W—what are you doing?"

"Trying to keep you from bleeding out." I tugged the scrap over his foot and moved up to his bleeding shoulder. My fingers shook as I tied it around his wound. I knotted it as tight as I could, despite Thiago's groans.

Not giving him any time to brace or waste, I grabbed the roof of the car and lifted it. A part of me thought it wouldn't work, but the Royal in me moved the car off his arm. As he cursed up another storm, I pushed the car over enough so it wasn't on him and dropped it back to the sand. I tried not to look at the mangled mess of blood and splintered bone.

"Why the fuck wouldn't you give a warning?" he spat.

"Because I didn't want to count down." I grabbed his good arm and pulled him up to his feet. "I'm really ready to get out of here."

Together, we stumbled across the sand to the only standing door. I kept my mind empty just in case one final thing sprang up out of the sand. I didn't think I had enough energy to fight something else. I wasn't sure I had enough energy to make it back up the hill to the finish line.

Breathing heavily, Thiago grabbed the door handle. His bloody fingers streaked the white wood. When he pushed it open, he let out a little, choked cry. Clearing his throat, he steadied himself against the doorframe. Then he stepped over.

I released a long, slow breath. It felt like I had been holding it ever since the night before. I stepped forward to cross the threshold. My leg halted like I had walked into glass.

My heart jumped in my throat. *No.*

Thiago turned, just a foot away. "What?"

I stepped forward again, but received the same result. *No.*

He reached to pull me through, but his hand met the same resistance. His expression mirrored the same horror blooming in my chest.

No!

Magic flared from the door, throwing me back into The Trial. I slammed into an overturned car. My head snapped back, and the world went black before I hit the ground.

101

The Final Desire

A chill crept into my chest and attacked my ribs with a *crack*.

I jerked upright with a scream. The taste of sweet peaches coated the back of my throat.

I yanked up my shirt. The mess of bruises faded under the layer of dried blood. The chill sealed the scratch on my shoulder. A hoarse cry snuck from my mouth as another rib snapped into place.

"Dammit," someone said behind me. "I knew I forgot something."

The plaza stretched around me. It was scattered with smoldering cars and rubble. I was still in The Trial, and someone had just healed me. But there was no one left . . . all the Contestants had crossed the finish line.

I placed a hand on my belt. All of my weapons were gone, confirming the person behind me was not friendly.

Calling my magic, I jumped to my feet. It blasted to my hands, ready to consume and destroy. But instead, it slammed against my fingertips, scalding my hands. With a cry, I quickly cut the flow of magic, shaking the pain from my fingers.

What the hell?

"I may have forgotten the numbing agent, but I didn't forget the ingredient that blocks magic." Michael stood between me and the door.

I stumbled away from him.

Except it wasn't Michael. Everything from his dark-wash jeans, black Henley shirt, and leather jacket was the same. It was the vacancy in his eyes and the sand covering him head to toe that was the difference.

He raised a single eyebrow. "Surprised?"

"You could say that."

His gaze slid over me, lingering briefly on my injuries. "Finish this." He offered me the bottle of healing potion. "You can finish it yourself, or I can cut you open and pour it into you, which would defeat the purpose of the healing potion."

I took the bottle, knowing he meant every word. "Why heal me? I was done." Against every logical cell in my brain, I tipped the rest of the thick potion into my mouth. As it tingled down my throat, strength returned to my muscles. Even the ringing in my ears quieted.

He embodied the definition of casual as he stuck his hands into his pockets. "Orders. You dying from your own foolish actions is anticlimactic. But, having the man you jumped in front of a knife to save be the one that kills you . . . that's iconic."

My eyes snapped to the door. My mind raced for any possible exit, or a way to at least wound him enough to get there.

Each scenario ended with me dead. Because this was Master Michael Kale. He and Atlas killed a hundred men, just the two of them. He was calculating, skilled with violence, and brutal in every sense of the word. To put it plainly, I had no chance.

"You don't have to do this." Even as I said it, I knew it wouldn't make a difference. The Michael I knew had no empathy. The Trial version would be no different.

"Orders are orders."

"You could let me go."

Shaking his head, he stepped forward. "I'll make it quick. But that's all I can do." Reaching under his jacket, he pulled one of the four knives from his holster. The blade was small, with an angular tip.

"Close your eyes." He flipped the blade across his fingers.

His empty eyes remained locked on mine. From the first time I met Michael, there was always something in his gaze, a burning hatred or frigid bitterness. The man before me was emotionless; he didn't care. Orders were orders.

If there were a way out of this, I had to take him by surprise. Unfortunately, Hunters are trained to never be surprised. I would have to draw him close. But that was like pulling a starving tiger into my lap.

But what other choice did I have?

My eyes fluttered closed.

Cold, gentle hands, familiar hands, turned me around. How many times had those same hands helped me to my feet? How many times had they soothed my injuries?

Leather crinkled as he looped his arm around my neck and pulled my back against him. The chest against my spine was as hot as the sun-scorched sand under my shoes, but he had no heartbeat.

His other arm whispered by my shoulder, bringing the knife over my heart. I squeezed my eyes tighter.

There was a rustle as the knife descended.

My hand snapped away from my side and latched around his wrist. The point of the knife hovered above my chest.

I threw my other elbow into his nose. The blow stunned him, loosening his grip around my neck. Twisting the knife from his hand, I spun around and clocked him over the head with the hilt.

He moved as if the blow didn't faze him. He swept my legs out from under me, throwing me onto my back. The back of my skull cracked against the asphalt. Sand ground into my hair, and my vision faded for just a moment.

His boot collided with my ribs. The newly healed fractures groaned under the impact. I opened my mouth, gasping, but my lungs refused to expand. He slammed his foot into the same spot. A crack forced a hoarse cry up my throat.

I scrambled to my feet and launched myself at his middle. He anchored his feet, and, using my momentum, twisted and tossed me away. When my side hit the cement, a series of cracks rippled through my chest.

I barely kept the scream behind my clenched teeth.

Over my raspy breathing, I heard him stalking closer. His footsteps stopped. His foot lifted from the sand and arched backward.

I rolled and swept my legs under his. He fell onto his shoulder with a grunt. Wheezing, I dragged myself through the sand. *I just need to get closer to the door.*

His hand wrapped around my ankle and jerked me back. My cheek dragged across the ground. Broken glass sliced into my hand as I reached out for anything to help.

I grasped a large shard and thrust it behind me. It slammed into his side. I snapped the glass in two, leaving the end embedded. Then I slammed a new shard between his ribs.

With a growl, he grabbed a handful of my hair and slammed my forehead into the concrete. Pain split through my head, dulling my thinking.

Almost out of reflex, I threw my elbow back. It smashed into the bridge of his nose with a crack.

I dragged myself out from under him and rolled onto my back. I expected him to dissolve into sand. Blood dribbled over his lips and off his chin. It dripped from the wound on his side.

I looked down at my hand, finding it covered in blood. He was a sand person . . . he shouldn't be bleeding.

Dragging myself over to a demolished car, I grabbed the door handle. My arms shook as I pulled myself up. The two blows to my head still echoed, causing my vision to double. With shallow breaths, from my once-healed and now broken-again ribs, I moved to the other side of the car. It wasn't much, but at least something was between us.

Showing no signs of pain, Michael watched me. Blood pooled around the sole of his boot. Reaching under his jacket, he took out a large knife with a clean, sweeping edge.

"It takes more energy to swing and miss than it does to swing and hit," Michael's voice coached from the back of my mind.

Without being hindered by his wounds, Michael stalked around the car with quick strides. Raising the blade over his head, he swiped toward my neck. I ducked and grabbed another shard of glass from the ground, stabbing it into his leg.

I straightened, taking the glass with me, and arching it toward his neck. He grabbed my forearm and dropped his arm onto my elbow. The jarring pain caused me to drop my only weapon.

Flipping the knife around, he thrust it toward my chest.

I spun out of his grip and bent backwards to avoid his next attack. The tip of his blade sliced across my collarbone. No matter how fast I was, he was faster. Within minutes, I was covered in cuts.

Then he flipped the knife and smacked me over the head, sending me back to the ground. Black dots filled my vision.

He kicked me onto my back. Instead of planting the knife in my heart, he pressed his boot to the wound on my chest.

No! I wrapped my hands around his foot. My arms shook as I tried to lift it away from my Achilles' Heel. Leaning forward, he applied more weight.

My knuckles lowered until they pressed into the tender skin. My injured sternum screamed under the pressure.

"Stop," I gasped. "Please."

He continued to stare down at me with vacant eyes as the vulnerable skin split open. Blood drained from the opening and slid over my neck to the ground.

Magic swirled angrily through my chest and into my hands. They glowed with desperation. While my magic couldn't leave my hands, heat billowed off my fingers in ferocious plumes. The material of his boots melted in my grasp.

He yanked his foot back.

Air rushed into my lungs. Stiffly, I rolled onto my side. I reached under the car and yanked out a metal rod. Using it to push myself to my feet, the metal burned red hot under my glowing fingers.

I whipped the burning metal across his face. The blow threw him to his knees. Raising the bar over my head, I slammed it on top of his spine. The glowing rod melted through his shirt and scalded his sandy skin. I raised it again.

He caught it before it could strike his face. The rod burned into his flesh, sizzling and blistering his palm to a dark red. He showed no pain as he wrenched it from my grasp. Then he turned it on me.

When I hit the ground, my eyes wouldn't focus. Before me was a mess of sand and steel. Blood trickled from the impact of the pipe, sliding like hot lava into my hair and pooling beneath my head.

I was losing blood. I was losing ground to the door, and I was losing strength.

I was just *losing*.

With blind fingers, I reached forward, groping through the sand as a last-ditch effort of survival. Something sparkled in the edge of my vision.

My numb, bloody fingers wrapped around the glittering object. The smooth metal warmed in greeting against my palm.

Recognition sparked in the back of my mind. *My switchblade.*

Michael grabbed a handful of my bloody, tangled hair. Yanking me from the sand, he pulled me against him.

Just as he gathered the strength to snap my neck, I slammed the switchblade into my gut and pressed the button.

The blade shot out, slicing through my abdomen and up into his chest. His body jerked.

His hands stilled.

Blood flowed over the handle, dribbling over my fingers before it dripped to the ground. Was it mine, or his?

I hit the button again, retracting the blade. He crumpled to the earth behind me. I collapsed to my knees. Doubling over, I braced my hands against the sand and watched blood flow around me.

My arm buckled, dropping me to the ground. My vision darkened. I didn't have the strength to fight it anymore. *Cheese and rice, did I even want to?* I was so tired.

The pain faded, as did the feeling of the sun beating down on my skin. My breaths were no longer shallow. Just for a moment, I wasn't tired anymore.

And then, something happened that I didn't expect.

I woke up.

102
Waking Up

The moment I realized I was conscious was one of the biggest surprises of my life. I couldn't remember why I felt that way. I just knew I shouldn't be awake.

My heavy eyelids reluctantly lifted. I blinked, confused at what I was seeing. The light above me was refracted, like I was underwater. With another blink, the world slowly started to solidify. The fog encapsulating my brain dissolved, making me aware of the cool liquid I was submerged in.

The potion slipped past my lips and easily into my lungs without so much as a tickle. I could breathe. Turning my head, I pushed my floating hair out of the way to see the black walls of the Magisterium infirmary around me.

Slowly, everything came flooding back. Dmitri. The Trial. The door closing me in. Michael . . .

How did I get here? I had lost consciousness in The Trial. There was no way I could have made it to the finish line.

I lifted my hand and saw my Trial tattoo had changed. Next to the window from the Second Trial, were three new images.

The first was of a two-sided axe, mimicking the weapon Dmitri brought into the Final Trial. The second image was a silhouette, with a matching image stepping out from behind it for the illusion I used to save Blake from Emeka. The third and final image was of a heart. A switchblade sliced through one side, and emerged out the other.

If it changed, then I for sure crossed the finish line. But I couldn't have made it out of The Trial. Not with the wounds I had.

Reaching out of the liquid, I grabbed the edges of the tank and sat up.

The thick potion pulled back my hair and glided over my skin, back down into the tank.

I pulled in a shallow breath. The air met the potion in my lungs and choked me. Doubling over, I coughed so hard, my chest ached. Mouthfuls of potion came up my throat.

Helen seemed to appear out of nowhere. Yanking her wand from her cardigan, she hit the call button on the wall beside her. With a flurry of magic, the glass box dissolved. The blue potion fled down the drain in the middle of the room, lowering me to the mattress underneath.

"It's almost out." She grabbed a towel from under the bed and draped it over my shoulders.

I sucked in a final deep breath, and coughed, like I was trying to expel my lungs from my body. The healing potion dribbled down my chin, splattering the soaking sheet beneath me.

When the coughing stopped, Helen asked, "How are you feeling?"

"Fuzzy." My voice was steady, but slow, like my tongue was half asleep.

"That's common after you've been in a submersion tank. Your motor skills should come back within the hour." Her bright eyes flickered to the vital monitors behind the bed. "You were a challenging puzzle to put back together. I doubted we would be able to do it."

I looked over my body, checking for bruises or bandages. When I found none, I pulled the damp shirt away from my chest. The wound over my sternum was the same furious red it had always been, but it wasn't bleeding.

"It's a miracle that even closed," Helen said. "The wound had been open for nearly an hour by the time I got your ribcage back together. Plus, with the amount of magic you used—"

"Do you have any more nourishing potions? Or is this it? Went was asking for some." Atlas stepped out of Helen's office with a jar clasped in his tattooed hand. When he spotted me, his boots squeaked as he stopped suddenly.

"You look better since the last time I saw you," Atlas said indifferently.

I couldn't stomach his cool gaze, so I looked down at the damp sheets. My weak fingers could barely hold the towel as I moved it over my face. Dropping it to my lap, my eyes landed on the demon scars defacing my palms and wrists.

A memory broke through the fog of my mind. "Is Blake alright?"

Helen took a stethoscope from around her neck and put it in her ears. "He was in perfect health when he crossed the line. As far as if he's alright, well, I think he's rather angry with you."

"Try blisteringly pissed," Atlas muttered.

I didn't much care. If he was angry, he was alive. That's all I wanted.

Helen placed the stethoscope to my back and listened intently. Satisfied with what she heard, she stood, draping the stethoscope over her neck. With light feet, she retreated to the far side of the room to the wall of potions.

My eyes turned back to the Hunter. His whiskey-colored gaze bounced around my body, where memories of fists and wounds ached.

Helen returned to the bed with a mug of bubblegum-pink potion. The thick liquid fizzed around the edges, releasing small clouds of steam over the rim.

She took my hands and wrapped them around the mug. Once she was sure I wouldn't drop it, she nudged it toward my lips. I took a sip. Light notes of pepper, strawberries, and vinegar rolled over my tongue.

"Miss Heart, you took a patient of mine," Helen said gently. "Where is Clarence Hardy?"

My heart pinched in my chest. The light above my head pulsed. "He's behind a coffee shop in Salina, Kansas. I put him in the storage unit."

"Is he alive?"

I hated that she had to ask. My hand slid up my side to the victory tallies beneath my heart. I nodded.

Helen stepped back from the bed. "Drink that slowly. I'll be right back." Taking a deep breath, she pulled on her magic.

"Helen."

She paused.

Unable to meet her kind gaze, I watched the potion fizz. "I'm sorry. For knocking you out."

"We all do crazy things for the people we love. I can't judge you for that." She turned on her heel and Ported from the infirmary.

Silence violently beat against my eardrums. Raising the mug to my lips, I sipped at the pink potion.

It was weird to be in the infirmary without Michael. From day one, after the bus crash, he had always been there. I expected to look over my shoulder and see him standing there with his arms crossed and a glare.

I wondered if he had watched the Final Trial. As soon as the thought crossed my mind, I mentally kicked myself. He wouldn't waste the time.

"You're really good, you know that?"

I blinked at the Hunter.

Atlas tossed the jar from one palm to the next. "With the whole helpless bit. I've seen a lot of liars in my day, but none as polished as you. Everyone really underestimates you . . . but I guess that's the point, right? You distract them, draw them close, and then break them. Brilliant trick. I've known Hunters who took decades to master it."

"Why are you here?" I asked, dropping my gaze. "Is Michael too much of a coward to face me himself?"

Helen Ported back into the room before he could formulate a response. Tightly gripped in her hands was the missing infirmary bed. On it, Clarence snored softly. Helen stood, breathing hard, and brushed a sweaty lock of hair from her forehead.

Atlas quickly crossed the room to help her. Mumbling in soft voices, they hooked Clarence up to a monitor like mine and connected a couple potion bags to his arms.

I watched carefully, hoping that my game of hide-and-seek didn't injure the jerk. I hated Clarence, don't get me wrong. But I didn't want him dead.

Helen and Atlas moved without urgency. Their whispered conversation was low and easy. Taking that as a good sign, I lifted the steaming potion to my lips and took another sip.

The gold infirmary doors creaked open.

I jumped to my feet, or tried to. My knees nearly buckled. The mug slipped from my fingers and shattered against the black stone. Hot potion splattered across my bare feet.

"No." I backed away from the man entering the room. "You stay the hell away from me."

Master Lenin slowed to a stop. Perplexed, his eyebrows pulled together.

Helen rushed forward and poured more potion into a mug. As soon as the thick liquid filled the cup, it began to steam.

Meanwhile, Atlas watched the School Master through narrowed eyes.

"Miss Heart—" Master Lenin stepped forward.

I held up my hand between us. Magic swirled around his feet, locking him into place.

"Amazing," he marveled, staring at the gold around his feet. "Master Kale forgot to mention it."

"Did he also forget to mention that I met with Lawrence before The Trial?" I took another step away from him. "He said Michael told Dmitri to kill Daniel."

"You cannot believe everything Master—"

"Everyone heard Kale say you gave the order." Then Atlas added through his teeth, "Sir."

Master Lenin nodded slowly. "I am trying desperately to secure a positive outcome of this war. Mr. Phillips was only going to get in the way of that. He was collateral damage. Unfortunate. But necessary—"

"Shut up," I snapped. Magic flared from my hands, itching to circle his throat.

"You would've done the same in my shoes." Master Lenin's voice was as smooth as cream cheese frosting. If anything, that aggravated me further.

"No. I'd never kill an innocent boy just to punish someone for being *distracted.*"

"Isn't that what you did to Mr. Igorek Len? You killed him for Mr. Theodore's attention and punishment."

My magic faltered. "I—I did it to protect Blake."

"And I did it to protect the rest of the population." Master Lenin went on before I could respond. "Miss Heart, we told you at the beginning of the school year that this war will be horrific if we don't have your magic. Your crush on Mr. Phillips was only going to distract you from the work we need you—"

Magic surged down my arms. Flying from my fingers, it streaked through the room like spears of golden light. Master Lenin drew his wand from his suit jacket, and with an elegant whirl, dissolved them.

"It's beyond me why Master Kale insisted on being in Hunter Atlas's observation box," he said tensely. "If he knew how hateful you are, I wonder if he would've just left you in The Trial to die."

103

I Didn't Know

My fury stilled. "What do you mean Michael was in Atlas's box?"

"Master Lenin, this conversation can wait," Helen said softly. "I haven't done my full exam yet."

"Master Kale broke in," he continued, as if she hadn't spoken. "He proceeded to give instructions to his fellow Hunter, which helped you and Mr. Johnson through The Trial. He even went into The Trial and got you over the finish line, despite his injuries."

My heart tripped. "What injuries?"

Master Lenin huffed in disbelief. "Do you really not know? Apparently, you sent a direct blast of magic into his chest. Isn't that right, Hunter Atlas?"

"No, I—" My last moment at the ranch came screaming to the front of my mind.

Magic flared from my hands, shooting into his chest. I thought the blast had just removed his hands from my arms. That night was so muddled that I couldn't remember if I felt his fingers go lax as he flew back into the night.

"Remind me, Hunter Atlas, how long did it take Hunter Wentworth to get his heart beating again?"

Atlas didn't take his eyes off the School Master, meeting the other man's gaze coldly. "Eight minutes."

Those two words punched the air out of my lungs. *Holy shit.*

"And what of his other injuries?"

"Over half of his ribs were broken. His liver and pancreas failed. Most of the tissue in his lungs was dead," Atlas said briskly.

Master Lenin turned his gaze to me. "It took his team the better part of nine hours to get him breathing right."

I turned to my only ally in the room. "Is it true?"

Reluctantly, Helen nodded. "I was unconscious, so I wasn't aware of the situation until after The Trial."

She was unconscious because of me. My stomach dropped.

Master Lenin reassured Helen, "Even if you were aware, he refused medical attention. Which came to no surprise. He thinks he's immortal."

"But he's ok?" My hands gripped each other like I was praying.

"He would've been fine. He's had greater injuries. But at the end of The Trial, when Hunter Atlas went to meet Mr. Johnson at the finish line, Master Kale went to your observation box to see you through to the end. Master Hart was waiting for him."

My eyes snapped back to his face. His expression was genuine.

"Master Hart completed a binding curse."

My whole body went cold. I stopped breathing.

Then, Master Lenin confirmed the nightmare growing in my mind. "The version of Master Kale you faced in The Trial was bound to the real one."

That's why the sand version bled instead of losing sand.

Bile rose in my throat as images of the injuries I inflicted swirled through my mind. I stabbed him twice in the gut and once in the leg. I thought of the horrible sounds the red-hot pipe made as it connected with his flesh. And then my switchblade—

Oh, God.

My hands clutched the skin where the weapon had cut its way into his chest. The enchanted blade had hacked through bone and tissue. The end of The Trial was foggy with pain, but I remembered how motionless he was behind me. How glad I was that he had stopped moving.

"Did I kill him?" I whispered.

"Isn't that what you wanted?" Atlas asked, watching me closely.

"No! He was holding my arms—I just wanted him to let me go. I didn't know I could do magic without—" I faced Atlas. "I swear I didn't know."

In true Hunter fashion, his expression gave nothing away. My heart split right down the middle with my next thought.

If Atlas is here, does that mean that Michael was . . . "Did I kill him?"

"No." Atlas shook his head. "It would take more than the likes of you to do Kale in."

Relief surged through my broken body and around my fractured heart.

The sudden rush weakened my knees. I gripped the bedframe to keep myself upright, ignoring his obvious insult.

"W—why would he do that? Why would he come back and do all of that?"

"Beats me," Master Lenin said harshly.

"I think you can go," Atlas told him. He nodded to the doors.

"You should," Helen agreed firmly.

Master Lenin huffed. Reaching into his pocket, he tossed a keychain onto the bed beside me. "The transporter will take you to a safe house. The key will allow you through the front door."

He turned his gaze to Helen, lifting his chin as if everything was as it should be. "As soon as she is fit, make her leave. She is no longer welcome in my school." Master Lenin turned toward the doors with stiff shoulders.

In the silence of his departure, I lowered myself to the bed. I stared at the black stone between my feet.

"I don't get it," I mumbled. "Why would he come back? Why would he help me? He had no oath. The Guardian Contract was void after I rejected him—"

"He didn't do it out of obligation." Atlas combed his hands through his thick black hair.

"Then why?"

He shrugged. "You'll have to ask him." Turning away from me, he stepped toward the door.

"Wait!" I flinched as his harsh gaze came back to me. "How . . . how is he?"

"He's healing," the Hunter said simply. "I know you don't care, but you should know that Lenin gave the order. And yes, Kale stood by knowing what was going to happen, but he did try to save your Daniel, if you re-member."

Of course I remembered. He gave me the instruction to cut the dryad tree that would send its roots after me to keep us from falling over the cliff. A moment later, Dmitri came charging through the treeline with his knife drawn.

"Kale did nothing, and while that doesn't excuse his actions, it shouldn't condemn him either. He's a good man, the best I've ever known. Don't write him off entirely." Nodding his head to Helen, he Ported from the room, leaving a bright Porting circle smoldering in the black stone.

In the silence, Helen handed me another mug filled with the steaming pink potion. She dragged a stool out from under the bed and sat in front of me.

I barely blinked as she drew blood and checked my motor skills. I did what she asked, but I couldn't lift my gaze from the floor. Every once in a while, she nudged the mug toward my lips until it was empty.

"Helen . . ." I wasn't even sure what I wanted to say. An apology? An excuse? "I didn't know."

"I know, honey." Unwrapping the blood pressure cuff from my arm, she gathered the keychain and pressed it into my hand. Without another word, she began cleaning up.

"As soon as she is fit, make her leave. She is no longer welcome in my school."

With no reason to stay, I pushed magic into the transporter and left. The air around me was cold. The medical clothes I wore were still damp with potions, so the cool air covered my body in goosebumps.

Before me, surrounded by proud maples and an untamed lawn, was a mansion. It was plain in color and decoration. It seemed that whoever lived here didn't care enough to take care of it, or they were never around to do so.

Barefoot, I walked across the concrete sidewalk, cracked from weeds and time, to the porch. Unlocking the double front doors, they swung open with a high-pitched squeak. Another sign of abandonment.

Three chandeliers burst with light, illuminating a grand ballroom with exposed wooden beams. Across the empty room was a wall of glass overlooking golden hills and a pond.

The front doors swung shut with a boom. The sound ricocheted down the halls before fading into a lonely silence. Shivering, I followed the long hallway to my left. My footsteps barely made a sound.

I found a fully stocked kitchen and a staircase. Upstairs opened up to a sitting area with a TV. Following the hallway to the back, I found a bed draped in dark green sheets and what few belongings I had at the Magisterium.

My breath came out in a rush. I truly was no longer welcome at The Magisterium of Magic.

I padded across the carpet, past the private balcony, into a large bath-room. Unlike the rest of the house, there was a smell that clung to the air. It was faint. Someone had stayed here, but it was some time ago.

I struggled out of the potion-soaked shirt, peeling it away from my body. My heart froze when I saw my reflection.

I had a new scar from my belly button to the underside of my arm. Now I would never forget what I did to keep Blake alive.

Everywhere Michael's knife had split my skin in The Trial, there was a new scar to document it: my collarbone, shoulder, and ribs. I knew there was another one running along the top of my thigh.

I gingerly touched the thin scar on my abdomen. Pain sliced through my torso, like the blade was cutting to the other side. Memories rang through my ears in haunting echoes of Michael's ragged breaths.

But, he's fine. He's alive.

Clinging to that thought, I took the fastest shower of my life. When I was dried and dressed, I stared at my red streak. Just for a moment, I thought about ripping it out. Swallowing the impulse, I stepped back into the bedroom.

I was met by silence.

Something needed to break it. I couldn't remember the last time I had been alone. For the last year, there was always a man in black by my side.

Quickly, I crossed the room and turned on the TV. The blast of noise cut through the eerie silence, but my relief was short-lived.

". . . this afternoon. The head physician at The Magisterium of Magic reports that Contestant Heart will have no deficits from being submerged in a healing potion. With a couple days of rest, she will make a full recovery.

"I wish I could say the same about Master Michael Kale. The last time we saw him was at the finish line."

A video of Michael popped up beside the reporter.

With a hoarse cry, I rushed to the TV.

Bruises colored the entire left side of his face, highlighting his cheekbone, jaw, and temple in a storm of purples so dark it could only be replicated by thunderclouds. His left eye was bloodshot. Peeking over the collar of his black t-shirt were the same horrific and fatal plum bruises. He was covered in blood. His hair was matted with it. With each breath, it trickled down his chin. His shirt glistened with it.

In The Trial, he collapsed to his knees beside me. His bloody fingers searched for my pulse. His lips moved with words I couldn't hear over the reporter. With trembling hands, he pulled me into his arms and struggled to his feet.

As he stumbled back to the door, I read his lips. *I'm sorry. I'm sorry.*

I rushed to the bathroom. The fizzing potion Helen gave me rushed up my throat. I retched over the toilet as the reporter continued in the other room.

"No reports of the Master Hunter have been given by any hospitals. The Magisterium's physician commented that he is being taken care of, although she did not divulge a location."

I sobbed over the bowl. Images of him broken, bloody, and weak played through my mind.

"Many people are still reeling over the final test of The Master's Trial. I, for one, am completely shocked to see Masters behave this way. These Users are supposed to be exemplary, the ones we look up to. Instead, Guardian Theodore enters the Trial Field to extract vengeance for his son. He, of all people, should know the devastating nature of this Trial. If you ask me, Master Theodore should be facing serious consequences for his actions, instead of just a damaged shoulder."

So, Master Theodore was still alive . . . I didn't know how I felt about that. Wiping my mouth with the back of my hand, I rose on shaky legs.

"Then there's Master Hart. This man has been advocating for strength and unity for over seventy years. He demonstrated the exact opposite. Sealing a Contestant inside a Trial, using dark magic on another *Master*, and then using that same magic to further interfere with The Master's Trial. Master Hart has lost some serious support by messing with one of our oldest traditions."

I peeked out of the bathroom. On the screen was a picture of a white room with a large glass desk at the center, with a keyboard and a large orb on top. The far side of the room, from wall to wall, ceiling to floor, was a screen that showed inside The Trial.

So, that's where Michael was for each Trial.

Lawrence stood behind the desk meant for Michael. His displeasure was evident. And my Hunter was bound to a chair, slumped forward with hooded eyes. A large puddle of crimson glistened underneath him.

"The real star of this whole mess, and I think everyone will agree was Master Kale. He had no legal obligation toward Contestant Heart, yet he broke nearly every rule to get her across the finish line safely. This is something we have not seen from Master Kale in a very long time.

"If what the Magisterium's physician said was true, I hope to see Master Kale healed and well at the Naming Ceremony. In the meantime, Master Hart needs to comment on his behavior."

When the reporter moved on to the details of the Naming Ceremony, I stared blankly at the screen. Even though he was no longer pictured, I could still see him, broken and bruised, bleeding and waning.

I sank to the floor, pulling my knees to my chest. I clasped my hands over the scar that lined up with the one aimed to kill him.

He went through all of that for me, to get me out. I almost killed him, and despite all the pain I caused, he came back. He carried me over the finish line.

I should be happy to never see him again.

I shouldn't care about him.

But I did. I really, really did.

104

The Placing Ceremony

The doorbell rang.

Numb, I stood and padded down the stairs. For a brief second, I wondered if it was him. I paused in front of the door. I didn't know if I could face him.

Biting my lip, I pulled open the door just a little and found no one. There was a floating white garment bag with a box beside it.

Stepping onto the porch, I peered around to see if there was any evidence of who had left it. There was nothing.

I opened the box first. Inside was a letter, a transporter, and a bottle of Adraffeen.

Contestant Heart,

The Naming Ceremony marks the end of The Master's Trial. Tonight, the places awarded by the judges to the Top Seven will be announced.

Please wear the selected gown. White is the color of Trial Winners.

The ceremony starts promptly at seven. Please arrive early to be escorted to your designated area before the ceremony begins.

Master H. Lenin.

I looked at the garment bag. *White, the color of Trial Winners.*

I pulled down the zipper to reveal the dress underneath. It was sophisticated, with a tight sash around the waist, and a long train. The high neck and long sleeves would hide almost every one of my new scars. The satin gleamed in the sun like a fine opal.

Pulling it off the hanger, I let the smooth fabric slip through my fingers. *How could they expect me to wear such a pure color? After everything I did?* Finally, I fully understood why Hunters wore only black.

I could still feel it all. The gore and blood from Dmitri's chest under my fingernails. The grit of sand and the burning sun lingered on the back of my neck. The weight and pressure of Michael's boot against my chest . . . his hot blood soaking through the back of my shirt.

The fabric bunched as my fingers curled into fists. I tore the gown in half. Pulling at the seams, the sleeve tore away. I shredded the bodice and threw it across the room.

Breathing hard, I looked at the scraps. It felt good to destroy something that belonged to The Trial.

Then I turned my gaze to the discarded letter. *Shit.*

I thought about calling Cornelia for something to wear, but that would mean I would have to see her. She had watched the Final Trial. She saw every horrible thing. I couldn't stand to see her disgust too.

I took a deep breath and pulled my temper back. When it was a low simmer, I gathered the white scraps. With magic glowing in my fingers, I did the best I could to put something together that resembled a dress.

The end product reflected how I felt. The skirt was split and frayed, every edge raw and unraveling. I could only get one sleeve back on. The bodice had charred under my fingertips, leaving a hole in the side.

I struggled into the ruined garment. If I cared, I would have been embarrassed or nervous to be seen in something like this. But I didn't. I just wanted it to be over.

Half-assed, I bunched my hair at the back of my neck. My red streak threaded in and out of the mess. At the bottom of my bag was the jar of concealer Mrs. Kale made for my scars and the potion to hide my magic.

As I met the raw gaze of my reflection, I took in the haunted stare and thought it looked best with the scars. I didn't want to look unassuming anymore. I wanted the scars to let everyone know that all I did was break things. So I left them bare. For the first time, I didn't hide a single one.

The transporter glowed yellow and chirped right at six-thirty. I grabbed the stone and Ported into a long, grey hallway. The clamor of thousands of feet and excited voices startled magic into my hands. I pulled it back before the lights could react.

A stagehand with a headset waved me over. "Stand in order of your Contestant number," he barked before rushing off to another task.

Turning the corner, my heart seized. The remainder of the Top Seven were lined up in front of me.

Master Lenin moved back and forth between the Contestants, telling them to stand straight or fix their clothes. When he saw me, his eyes widened at the tattered dress. With lips pressed tight with disapproval, he waved me to stand between Contestant Twelve and Contestant Seventeen.

My eyes met Blake's.

He broke away from the line and rushed to me. He wrapped his arms securely around my shoulders. Words rumbled from his chest, but I couldn't hear them beyond his hug.

Squeezing my eyes shut, I clung to him. Tears spilled silently down my cheeks. *We're ok. We made it out.*

When he pulled back, his watery eyes scanned my face. On the shoulder of his white jacket were two mascara smudges.

Wiping the tears from my cheeks, he shook his head. "I haven't seen you since—" He shuddered. "How are you?"

"I'm all shiny and new."

He wasn't amused. "You know what I mean."

Unable to keep my smile up, my eyes dropped to the floor. "I'm alive."

All the ways I had kept myself alive during The Trial started to creep into my mind like leaking water. "How are you?" When I looked into his face, my chest throbbed.

The makeup on his face barely hid the red rimming his eyes. At a glance, he looked fit to charm his way around a room. Up close, he was on the edge of breaking, just like me.

"I'm alive."

"Good to see you, Charlie," Thiago said from behind me. He was dressed in all white as well. Even the sling cradling his arm was white.

"Good to see you, too," I said and meant it. Stepping back from Blake, I pulled him into a hug.

Clearing his throat, he shifted his weight from one foot to the other. "Thanks for coming back for me."

"Get ready!" Master Lenin called from the stage doors. "When your name is called, go to the stage. You'll have a chair waiting for you with your number on it. I'll see you up there." He passed through the doors, and a wave of applause flooded the hall after him.

Blake led me toward the line where Atlas held his spot. The Irish Hunter caught my gaze and held it. Seeing him reminded me of my lack of company. Quickly, I looked away.

Over his shoulder, I met Emeka's gaze. Magic trickled to my fingers. *That son of a—*

Blake stepped to the side, blocking my view. "When this is over, do you want to go someplace to watch a movie? I can get hot chocolate. It'll be like the old days."

"I'd love to." That was an understatement. I would have sold my soul for just an hour of what it was like in those days. I never thought I would miss Kansas.

Blake squeezed my hand and faced the doors.

My eyes scanned the hall and the people milling around. I realized then what I was doing. I was looking for Michael.

He wouldn't miss this . . . right? I held on to that hope with both hands. *I just want a glimpse. Just so I know he's ok.*

Master Lenin's voice blared down the hallway from unseen speakers. I watched as Tala, dressed in shocking white, straightened and passed through the doors with her Guardian.

Then, Emeka and his Guardian.

A few moments later, Blake and Atlas did the same.

"From The Magisterium of Magic, Contestant Fifteen, Charlie Heart."

When I stepped into the room, lights blared from the high ceiling. Cameras flashed from every angle. Keeping my eyes forward, I walked to the stage.

There were seven unassuming thrones, one for each Contestant. Behind each, to the right, was the School Master. On the left, was a place for the chosen Guardian. Behind the far throne for Dmitri, there was only one person, Master Theodore.

His nostrils flared upon seeing me.

As I reached the stairs, Master Lenin extended his hand to help me up. Gathering the torn skirt, I ignored his hand and headed for the throne next to Blake's. I faced the audience, acutely aware of the empty place to my left.

In the front row, I was surprised not to see Lawrence. Maybe he was keeping a low profile after The Trial. It had to be killing him, staying away from the completion of his plan. That thought brought me a little solace.

My eyes combed the rest of the section. With any flash of black, my heart seized, and just as quickly, would drop further down my chest. No matter how many times hope lifted its weak head, it was beaten back down. The black never belonged to Michael. But that didn't stop me from searching.

"Welcome, ladies and gentlemen, to the final act of our Trial," Master Lenin began as the crowd quieted. "It has been quite a journey to get to this moment. We started with twenty-one Contestants with no idea who would make it here. These Top Seven Contestants rose through the ranks with their wit, their gut, and their magic use, separating themselves from the others in their school."

Master Lenin took a scroll from his jacket. "The decision of who did the best was not an easy one. Each Contestant was weighed against all the others. The judges scrutinized and criticized each performance down to the very second. What decisions did they make? What cast did they choose? Did they risk enough? Did they do enough?" Master Lenin turned to the scroll in his hands. "Contestants, please stand."

Tala, Emeka, Blake, Thiago, and I rose in unison.

When everyone was standing, Master Lenin opened the scroll.

"In seventh place, the judges have chosen . . ." Master Lenin paused, reread the first line, and then looked up at the crowd. "The Magisterium of Magic, Charlie Heart."

"What?" Blake blurted.

My Contestant tattoo glowed brightly, changing it for the final time. The symbols that represented the First Trial brightened to gold, the Second Trial images glinted with silver, and the Final Trial images remained black. A new white band twisted and swirled around the tattoo, mimicking the arches of a dainty crown.

The shocked crowd devolved into a sea of confused whispers. Several Masters rose to their feet, as if it were some kind of joke.

"How does that make any bloody sense?" Blake asked incredulously.

"Easy, mate," Atlas murmured.

Blake's eyes flashed my way. "There's no way—you did the whole thing without a Guardian."

I took his hand. "It's fine."

"Like hell it is—"

"Ladies and gentlemen," Master Lenin called over the noise. "Please, let us continue. For sixth place, the judges chose . . . The European Academy for Practical Magic, Blake Johnson."

Blake choked beside me. What started as an uneasy murmur at the first proclamation, now sounded like a hive of bees. More Masters were on their feet. A few even tried to move up the stairs, but Master Lenin's guard kept them from advancing.

Atlas jerked around to look at the School Master standing behind him. "What's going on, mate?"

"I have no idea," Master Harlan said. His gaze remained locked on Master Lenin.

With flushed cheeks, the Master of the Magisterium lifted the scroll once more.

"In fifth place," he called over the noise, "Aquarius: The Undersea School of Enchantments, Amelia Markus."

"She didn't even cross the finish line!" someone yelled from the crowd.

Trying to keep up appearances, Amelia's Guardian bowed and stepped away from the empty throne. Master Finch looked at Master Lenin confused.

"Fourth place is given to The Serpentine School of Magic, Thiago Luis."

Thiago's bewildered gaze flashed down the line to meet mine. His whole body jolted as his School Master gripped his shoulder with pride.

"Third place is awarded to . . . The Magical Academy of the Earth, Tala Abalos."

Tala turned to her Guardian with an extended hand. The two clasped forearms. Turning to Master Loran, the pair bowed respectfully.

"In second place, the judges chose . . ." Master Lenin shook his head. "Dmitri Konstantin Theodore from The University for Advanced Tactical Magic."

"He never made it off the Field!" someone bellowed.

Master Theodore bowed from the stage, as if the noise of the room were celebrating his son. He turned ever so slightly to catch my eye. A wide grin stretched over his face, victorious.

Master Lenin had to raise his voice over the crowd as they shouted their questions at the announcing Master. Outraged and perplexed, every occupied seat seemed to be asking the same question, the very one Blake had uttered at the start of the ceremony.

"That means, in first place, for the first time, from Lions of Magic, Emeka Selasi is our Trial Winner!"

The spotlights locked onto the last standing Trial Contestant. While Master Lenin praised the new Trial Winner over the rumbling crowd, my eyes slid closed.

105

When You Sleep

It's over.

"In a month's time, we will crown our winner with his own Master title. I will see you all at the Crowning Ceremony."

Outraged and confused, the crowd grew louder. Masters tried to push by Master Lenin's guard. The onlookers flooded out of the stadium.

Blake grabbed my hand. He said something that was lost in the commotion of the room and gestured to the side door.

An escape. Anxiety drained out of me.

Catching Thiago's eye, Blake waved him over. Together, the three of us, dressed in white, crossed the stage and passed through the side door. My soul begged for peace and quiet.

As soon as we stepped through the door, another crowd greeted us. Reporters with bright lights pressed close, each yelling their own questions.

"What happened in there?"

"How do you feel about your placement?"

"What are your thoughts on a Contestant who never made it to the finish line getting second?"

"Are you going to appeal your placement?"

Over the crowd, I saw Amelia's Guardian, held by two burly men being wrestled into a vehicle. The School Master of Aquarius looked on with a stony expression.

"Where do you want to go?" Blake shouted in my ear.

Pulling my eyes from the crowd, I handed him the transporter for the safe house. Blake handed it to Atlas, who Ported us away from the torrent of questions.

The silent house greeted us with deep evening shadows. The air was sleepy with fog and tired crickets. It was a stark contrast to the buzz of the charged crowd.

"What the hell was that?" Blake snapped, whirling on his Guardian.

"You know as much as I do." Atlas's tone was odd, as he surveyed the sleepy mansion behind us. He recognized it.

"You have to have a guess," Thiago said. "I did pretty well in the Final Trial—if I do say so myself—but there's no way anyone thought I did better than a Royal Nine who finished The Trial without a Guardian or a wand."

"I was backed by Master Lenin and Master Kale." I faced the house to hide the grimace from saying his name. "There's no way Lawrence would have let me get anything other than last."

"The panel of judges are kept from everyone, so they can't be corrupted," Atlas argued. "Masters included."

"There has to be something we can do," Blake said, tugging off his white tie. "If we talk to Master Lenin—he hosted the bloody thing, maybe we can—"

"It's done," I said firmly. "I'm done. I just want to move forward." I nodded toward the mansion. "What is this place?"

Atlas was slow to answer. He shifted from one foot to the other, as if the answer wasn't a simple one. "Somewhere safe."

"It's kind of creepy for a safe house," Thiago muttered as he walked up the porch.

Stepping into the lonely darkness of the house, I kicked off my shoes.

"Where were they taking Amelia's Guardian?" I asked, turning toward the stoic Hunter.

"Probably his grave." He unbuttoned the collar from around his neck. "If your Contestant doesn't get the ranking your School Master wanted, you're as good as dead. Tomorrow, the only Guardians who'll be alive are the ones smart enough to find a rock to hide under."

"Are you going to be alright?" Blake asked Atlas with a look of concern.

Atlas gave us a cruel smile. "You have to ask? They'd be fools to come after me." He turned to the surrounding house. "Are you planning on staying here?"

Blake nodded. "If Charlie's ok with it."

"You can stay for as long as you want," I said numbly.

Atlas didn't look thrilled. "What about your parents? I'm sure they want to see you."

Blake shook his head. "I can't . . . stay in my childhood bedroom. Not after everything. I'll call them later. Maybe see them in the morning."

Atlas shrugged. "That's your call. I'll have your stuff sent over." He headed back to the porch.

"Atlas, wait!" I ran after him. Stopping in the doorway, I struggled to find the words I wanted to say. "How is he?"

The Hunter shrugged. "I'm on my way to see him. You're not the only one he's been avoiding."

"But he's ok?"

"He's been through worse." With nothing else to say, he Ported out of the evening light, leaving only a shimmering gold circle to tell me that he had been there.

Emotion rushed up my throat and pressed against my eyes. Turning away from the empty sidewalk, I stepped back into the mansion where Blake and Thiago waited.

"You better not have been lying about that hot chocolate," I said with a weak laugh. Brushing past both of them, I headed down the hall.

"I never joke about hot chocolate." Blake fell in step with me. "Do you want some, Thiago?"

"Are you sure there's any food here?" Thiago looked around the room. "This place looks abandoned."

"There's a kitchen, last opening on the right." I gestured down the hall. "It was stocked when I got here."

"Does it have any alcohol?" Thiago asked, heading toward the kitchen. Maybe it was the light, or how fast he moved, but I could've sworn his hands were shaking.

"You're welcome to check." I had a feeling he wouldn't find any. "I'm going to go change," I told Blake as I turned to leave.

"Hey." Blake grabbed my hand, stopping me. "That placement was shitty. You were brilliant, and you should—"

"I was terrible." I shook my head when he started to refute me. "Please, let it go. I got out. I'm done."

I felt him watch me all the way up the stairs. When I stepped into the bedroom, a tear slipped down my cheek. Breathing slowly through my mouth, I tried to keep the rest of them behind my eyes.

Closing myself in the bathroom, I pressed my back against the door. My chest ached, but not from the permanent wound. This was deeper. It throbbed in every rib and down each vertebra.

It was silent in that bathroom. I couldn't hear anything: not my heartbeat or my breathing. Nothing.

I was alone.

Throughout the whole year, and The Trial, someone was always with me. When I entered The Trial, Blake was there. In the First Trial, Emeka was there. In the second, it was Daniel. And then after Daniel, there was . . . Michael.

No. He was there from the beginning. Even though he didn't want to be, when I got myself into The Trial, Michael was with me from day one.

Then I went into the Third Trial by myself. I chose that.

And now, I was alone.

But then, why does this feel so different from the Third Trial?

Because I wasn't alone then. Not really.

Michael was in Blake's ear. Going through the building of caligo, he was the one who taught me to levitate. When I was fighting the sand people, I used the switchblade he gave me. Even in the Second Trial, when my earpiece broke, I could hear him in my head telling me what to do. When Daniel was falling, Michael told me how to save him.

It all came back to Michael. And he was gone. Because of me.

I pushed away from the door and shed the white gown. I quickly dressed in the comfiest clothes I could find and pulled my light blue hoodie on top. I thought the familiar garment would bring me some comfort since it was from simpler times. But it felt like it belonged to someone else.

I couldn't stand to be alone any longer. I rushed to find Blake and Thiago. I found them in the living room.

Thiago was slouched low in a recliner with his bare feet kicked up on the coffee table. Pinched between his fingers was a rolled cigarette, but the smoke smelled of salt and ocean storms.

Blake was on the couch with three mugs of steaming hot chocolate in front of him. He stared intently at the TV, flipping through the channels so fast, I wondered if he saw anything.

I settled into the space between them and grabbed a large mug of hot chocolate. I cradled it to my chest, enjoying the warmth.

Thiago took in a long drag and blew the aqua and lavender smoke toward the ceiling.

"Is that mermaid reed?" Blake paused from his intent TV search.

Thiago nodded. "Want some? It's the good stuff from the Indian Gulf." Reaching around me, he handed the joint to Blake.

To my surprise, Blake took it. His cheeks sunk in as he breathed deeply. Closing his eyes, he held it for a beat and then exhaled slow.

"You're right," he handed it back. "That is good."

"Do you want some?" Thiago asked, holding it out to me. "It'll help."

My eyes leapt from the smoking cigarette to his questioning gaze. "With what?"

"Whatever's going on in your head."

I opened my mouth to ask just how he knew, but I saw it was leaking through the cracks in his mind too. The nightmares of The Trial. Every horrible thing we faced or did.

I put the joint between my lips and breathed in slowly, not knowing what to expect. I thought it would burn, like my magic did whenever I pulled it from my core. Instead, the smoke was cool and slid easily into my lungs. It tasted of salt and seaweed.

The smoke seemed to go right to my head. It swirled around and clogged my ears, like I was underwater. The tension in my shoulders loosened. The pain pulsing through my ribcage dulled to a steady pressure.

I exhaled a cloud of blue smoke and handed the joint back to Thiago. Leaning back into the couch, I washed the salty taste away with a large mouthful of melted marshmallows.

"How many rooms does this place have?" Thiago mumbled.

I shrugged. "I'm not really sure. Why, you want one?"

"If you don't mind."

I thought back to what Blake told Atlas. "*I can't. Not after everything.*"

"I don't mind at all. Take whatever you want."

Blake settled on a medical drama to watch, and promptly fell asleep. Thiago settled back, content and smoking. I'm sure neither of us watched the show. I wasn't even looking at the screen. I stared at the wall beside the TV, cradling my steaming hot chocolate between my palms.

Not long after Thiago finished his smoke, he too drifted off.

The mermaid reed had dulled the pain to something that was manageable. My eyelids drooped. The underwater weightlessness in my skull spread through the rest of my body. I didn't even realize I lost consciousness.

I awoke with a jolt.

A cry rang in my ears. I thought it was the echo from a dream. But as my eyes adjusted, I saw the lights were flashing with the frantic beat of my heart.

I sat up, trying to blink the sleepy fog from my mind. I couldn't remember where I was.

Turning my head, I found Thiago standing, with the recliner between us. Breathing hard, he didn't look away from me.

"Blake, are you alright?" he asked breathlessly.

I followed his gaze to where Blake stood, a few paces away. The TV flashed with static. The lamp was smoking. The drywall was cracked. The coffee table was overturned at his feet. He clutched his red, blistering hand.

My heart skipped. "Oh, my God." I stumbled to my feet. "Blake, what happened?"

"You wouldn't wake up," he mumbled.

Recognition sent me cold. I feel asleep. And I flared. I hurt him.

"I'm so sorry. I didn't mean—" I stepped toward him, not sure what I was going to do. My magic was still glowing hot in my hands.

I pulled my magic back to my core. The room darkened as the TV turned off, and the flickering lights settled.

"Is magic supposed to do that while you sleep?" Thiago asked in a small voice.

"Royal problems, I guess," Blake laughed weakly.

"I didn't mean to—" I swallowed thickly. "I would never hurt you."

"I know, I know." He cradled his hand to his chest. "It's not that bad. Really."

"We could just call Hunter Atlas," Thiago said. "I'm sure he can help."

And once he sees that I hurt Blake, he'll take him away . . . Should Blake even be here?

"It's really not bad. It just needs to be run under some cold water." He gave me a tight smile and left the room.

"So, uh." Thiago gestured to the cracked TV screen. "Does that happen every time you sleep?"

I wanted to say no. But that was before the Final Trial. Before, nightmares were on and off, and then I had Michael to wake me up. I knew he could handle my magic flares. I couldn't live with myself if I hurt Blake or Thiago.

"I'm so sorry." I bolted from the room. Across the mansion, I closed myself in the darkness of my room.

I blinked—and I saw Michael with my blade sticking through his chest.

I heard the sound of the blade sliding free, piercing skin, and cracking through bone.

Fumbling through the darkness, I found the dresser. On top was the bottle of Adraffeen Master Lenin sent before the ceremony.

My hands shook as I twisted off the cap. The strong smell of lemon drifted up my nose as I took a sip. As soon as it hit my stomach, sleep fled. Strength returned to my muscles, and my eyes focused.

Hiding the bottle in the dresser, I sat on the edge of my mattress. Cradling my knees to my chest, I stared at the wall until the sun came up.

106

Milkshakes and French Fries

I never gave much thought to what life would be like after The Trial.

At the start, I assumed I would get a title and get the hell out of Dodge. And then, somewhere along the way, that changed. I thought I would return to the ranch for another summer filled with Mrs. Kale's cooking, Meg's quick remarks, and training.

But that wasn't an option anymore. I doubted I was even welcome. All of the progress I had made was gone in a blinding flash of magic and the slide of a switchblade. If I'd known when the last hug from Mrs. Kale was, I would have held on a little longer.

Since I had graduated from the Magisterium, there were no more classes. I would never have to step foot in that black stone castle again. Night lessons with Michael were discontinued. I kept waiting for my transporter to beep, signaling a return to a bit of normalcy. But it never did. It sat on my bedside table as a paperweight.

Weeks passed in limbo.

With no one to direct each waking moment, I created my own schedule. As the sun started to rise, I would run around the property until the light left the horizon and I couldn't breathe.

Blake was up by then, filling the house with music. Sometimes Thiago joined us for breakfast. Other times, it was a couple days before we saw him. Neither Blake nor I asked where he went. Dealing with his demons was his business.

Some afternoons, a transporter was delivered with detailed instructions from one of the School Masters. While there were no more required training, Award Challenges, or parties, there were still Trial events. Interviews, photo shoots, poster signings—whatever they wanted us for, we were there. But not for a moment longer.

When we got back to the neglected mansion, we would sit in front of the TV with hot chocolate and mermaid reed.

Blake had always liked music. But for the past few weeks, he had something playing constantly. At first, I thought he was listening, but he wasn't. It was just to cover up the silence. If there was more than a minute of silence, he would turn on the radio. If I left the room, it was only a matter of time before he followed.

When Thiago was here, he turned on every light and every lamp in the whole house. One time I caught him moving furniture to diffuse the shadows underneath. It made me think of the darkness with the caligo. So, I made sure the lights were bright, and shadows were scarce.

At the end of the day, when Blake and Thiago were asleep, I would take a sip of the Adraffeen and stare at the ceiling until the sky began to brighten. Then the routine would start all over. I had my Winner's Curse and they had theirs.

Finally, the Crowning Ceremony was a week away. After Emeka got his title, all of this would be over. No more interviews. No more photos. I could pretend like it never happened.

After my run, I jogged into the safe house. Judging by the silence, Blake was out. Since the lights were off, Thiago was gone, too. Panting and covered in sweat, I jogged up the stairs and found Atlas sitting on the couch.

Shock rushed through me. He never came unless he had to, and he certainly didn't come when Blake wasn't around.

"Morning." I panted as I made my way into the kitchen. I tried to appear nonchalant, but I was on edge. *Why is he here?*

He stared at me for a couple of seconds, which wasn't like him. He always had a snide remark to pair with some nickname.

"Actually, you're wrong." He glanced at his watch. "It's noon, love."
Ah, there it is.

"I must have slept in this morning." I avoided his gaze as I pulled a water bottle from the fridge. "Can I help you with something?"

"I'm here to take you to lunch."

"No thanks." I popped off the cap and stared at the water inside. My stomach churned.

"It's not with me," he said calmly. "Blake arranged it."

"Oh." My mood instantly brightened. "Great. I'll take a shower really quick." Setting down the water, I headed for the bathroom.

"How are you?"

The tone of his voice threw me off. I snuck a glance and found he was watching me closely. It was a look I had never seen on his face before.

"Fine," I said slowly.

"How are your nightmares?"

Michael told him about those? "I'm managing." It wasn't a lie. I rubbed my dry eyes. "I'll be right out."

Quickly, I ducked into my room. I washed the morning run from my skin and dressed in the mandatory all-white. Just in case, I took out the bottle of Adraffeen and took a sip. The potion started to work as I replaced it in its hiding place.

When I stepped back into the living room, Atlas rose to his feet and offered his arm. The lack of sarcasm piqued my attention again.

"Are you ok?" I asked as I looped my arm through his.

"Of course."

"Wait, no 'I'm not ok, I'm sexy' jokes?" I shot him a smirk.

"I thought that went without saying." He matched my smirk and Ported out of the mansion.

We reappeared in the startling sunlight. The sudden brightness caused my eyes to slam closed. Blinking rapidly, I forced them to adjust. In front of us was an open restaurant beside the ocean. With minimum walls, it gave a fantastic view of the waves from any table.

A real smile stretched across my lips at Blake, sitting at a corner table. Pulling my arm from Atlas's, I started toward my friend.

"Will you be alright?" Atlas asked. "I know being separated from me for long periods of time can be difficult."

I stuck my tongue out at him. Spinning around, I wove through the tables. My smile only grew when I saw Thiago sitting beside him. My steps faltered when I saw Cornelia was with them in a pink dress.

Before I could retreat, she looked up and saw me. "Charlie!" She waved.

People started to turn and look.

With fidgeting hands, I closed the space between us. "Hey, Cornelia. I didn't know you were going to be here."

"You wouldn't know because we haven't talked in a month." She gave me a stiff hug before sitting down.

The comment stung. But she wasn't wrong.

"You'd think without training for The Trial that we'd have more free time," Thiago jumped in to help me. "I feel like I have less time now than I did last month."

She hummed in the back of her throat, but made no comment. Threading her fingers through Blake's, she took a sip of her lemon water.

"Since when do we go out to lunch?" I asked with a weak laugh.

"Cornelia suggested it," Blake said. "Apparently, this place is known for their milkshakes."

She nodded eagerly. "The best one is the rainbow shake. Each layer is a different flavor, and it changes as you drink it."

My stomach rolled.

"The burgers are really good, too. My favorite is the one topped with onion rings and barbecue sauce."

I breathed slowly through my nose. Turning to Blake, I cleared my throat. "Since when do you send Atlas to come get me?"

"We were together this morning when Cornelia called," he said flippantly. "He offered, since you don't answer your phone. Your eyes are doing that thing again."

Curiosity pulled at Cornelia's expression. "Me?"

Blake picked up his mug of tea and shook his head. "Charlie. Her eyelids try to copy hummingbird wings sometimes."

"The wind is blowing," I stated matter-of-factly. "It's drying out my eyes." It wasn't true. I had noticed my eyes were getting drier. Maybe from the Adraffeen.

Blake gazed at Thiago over the rim of his cup.

Needing the subject to change, I turned to Thiago. "What have you been up to this morning? You were gone when I came in."

"I went to Serpentine to speak with Master Han. A lot of Masters have contacted me with apprentice opportunities. I wanted to get his opinion about which ones are worth considering."

"Do any of them sound interesting?" Cornelia asked, sipping her water.

"A couple. Some of them I've never heard of." He fiddled with the knife beside his plate. "I don't even know if I want to apprentice under someone. At least not yet."

A waiter came by with a tray of milkshakes. He set a large glass right in front of me. Layers of different colors were skewered by a straw in the shape of a cloud.

"Oh, I didn't order anything." I looked around the table as he continued to pass out milkshakes. "Did you order already?"

Thiago shook his head.

"These are from the owner. They're on the house for Trial Contestants." He bowed awkwardly, still holding the tray, and quickly darted back to the kitchen.

My stomach twisted into knots at the sight of the spirally whipped cream in front of me.

"The Trial has so many perks." Cornelia picked up her glass.

Blake smiled weakly.

She held her milkshake out over the center of the table. "Congratulations on crossing the finish line and for placing. I hope The Trial continues to enrich your life. It is an honor to know you all."

"That's very kind," Blake said tenderly. "Thank you." He clinked his milkshake against hers. Thiago did the same, and then I followed.

Thiago stuck a spoon into his milkshake and scooped it into his mouth.

"You're supposed to use the straw," Cornelia laughed, taking her first sip.

Thiago shook his head. "I don't get a brain freeze this way."

"Is that a real thing?" Blake looked torn between using the straw and picking up his spoon.

Thiago shrugged. "It helps me."

"Is something wrong with your shake?" Cornelia asked. All eyes turned to me and my untouched glass.

"No! It's fine." I smiled reassuringly.

"You haven't tasted it."

"Oh." *Shit.* "I'm not that hungry. I had breakfast less than an hour ago," I lied.

"Didn't you use to say that you had a second stomach for desserts?" Blake laughed. Forgoing the spoon idea, he took a large gulp from the twisted straw. "Wow, that's good."

If I didn't eat, they would know something was up. Another wave of queasiness swirled around my stomach.

Swallowing hard, I picked up the milkshake. I almost gagged as the first flavor of cake batter hit my tongue. I forced myself to swallow. As soon as it hit my stomach, it rolled.

Focusing on my breathing, I pushed through. As the conversation progressed, I kept up the act of being happy and hungry, both of which were lies.

By some miracle, I finished half of the milkshake. My stomach gurgled, threatening to flip inside out.

I excused myself from the table and walked to the bathroom. As soon as I was out of their sight, I ran. I made it just in time to lock the door and fall to my knees.

When every last milkshake layer was out of my stomach, I stopped retching. On shaky legs, I moved away from the toilet and leaned against the cold wall.

The Adraffeen is making you sick. I tried to ignore the voice in the back of my head, but it had been getting louder recently. I could handle the side-effects as long as it meant I didn't dream.

I took a moment to collect myself. I cleaned up and rinsed out my mouth. Replacing my smile, I went back to the table. The kitchen had brought out a platter of sweet potato fries.

"Look what they gave us!" Blake was almost glowing; he was so excited. "You *have* to try them." He scooped some onto another plate and set it in front of me. Grabbing a couple, he shoved them into his mouth.

Just the sound of his teeth crunching through the crispy fries made me gag. I covered it with a fake cough. Keeping up the lie, I nibbled on a couple. Before I swallowed, I spit them into a napkin. I dropped a couple to the floor to make it look like I ate more. But it wasn't enough, they were noticing.

"Is not eating a Royal thing?" Cornelia asked, eyeing my plate. "I remember you eating a ton at the Magisterium, or was that a part of your lie?"

I dropped the fry I was fake-eating. Her tone was pleasant, but there was hardness in her gaze. *She's mad that I lied about my status.* She was lying about hers as well, as a Deficient Three, but she raised her status out of necessity. I lowered mine.

"I'm just not hungry," I replied evenly. "After breakfast and this huge shake—"

"Why did you lie about your status?" she butt in.

"That's Charlie for you," Blake chuckled. "Some people work their whole lives to stay out of the shadows, while Charlie works just as hard to stay in them."

"But you're a Royal Nine," she stressed. "You shouldn't have to hide in the shadows. Most people would lean into it."

"And most people would like to have it for themselves," I said, a bit harsher than I meant. "I'm sorry I lied to you. Really, I am."

"So, why did you?"

For some reason, I was still loyal enough to the Heel not to tell their secret about finding me. So I crafted something that was half-lie, half-true. "A demon tried to steal my magic. I lied, so it wouldn't happen again."

Her sapphire eyes dropped to the scar on my neck.

I cleared my throat. "I think I've been up for too long. I'm going to head back and take a nap. Thanks for the invite to lunch. Although I'm not sure milkshakes and fries is a lunch," I laughed forcefully, hoping it would lighten the mood. "It was good to see you, Cornelia."

"Yeah, you too."

I quickly turned from the table and headed for the beach. *I think I have successfully ruined all of my relationships.*

I breathed deeply of the ocean air, trying to keep my emotions from forming tears. Every person I had met at the Magisterium was either dead, or not talking to me anymore.

I took the transporter from my pocket and pushed magic into the orb. But I didn't appear at the safe house like I was expecting.

Instead, I was in the Magisterium infirmary.

I looked down at the transporter. It was enchanted to only take me to one location, the mansion. I didn't think magical objects could malfunction . . . unless this wasn't the transporter I had when I left the house. *Did Atlas switch them?*

"Hello, Miss Heart."

I turned to see Master Lenin, with Helen.

107

The Winner's Curse

"What's going on?" I asked warily.

Atlas Ported beside me. In his hand was my bottle of Adraffeen. Quickly he walked over to Helen, and handed it to her.

Anger sparked in my chest. "Are you just searching my stuff now?"

"So, you admit that you've been taking this?" Helen held up the half-empty bottle.

"Yeah." I shrugged. "I've had a couple sips here and there."

"That's not what your eyes say," Helen said sternly. "Your pupils are enlarged, and the corners of your eyes are yellow. How long have you been taking this?"

Shit. My hands fidgeted around each other. "I don't see what the problem is."

"This." Helen held up the bottle. "This is the problem. You've lost weight and muscle mass. Now I asked you a question. How long have you been taking this?"

Helen had never been anything other than warm and sweet toward me. The sharpness of her tone caught me by surprise.

"A month."

Atlas let out a low whistle.

Helen drew closer and peered into my eyes. "Are your eyes dry?"

I nodded.

"When was the last time you ate something?"

"I just had a milkshake and some fries—"

She raised her voice to cut me off, "And kept it down."

Abashed, I cleared my throat. "Maybe last week."

Helen sighed. "Why didn't you say something?"

I put on a smile. "I don't understand what the big deal is. I'm fine. Master LeOnie hasn't slept in over a hundred years."

"She consulted dozens of doctors and Masters before placing those enchantments on herself. You are misusing a potion that is not meant to be used this regularly," Helen barked. "I didn't work so hard to keep you alive, only to have you throw it away."

"Miss Heart." Master Lenin stepped closer. "You will let Helen put you to sleep, and that will be the end of—" He stopped when the lights flickered.

A cold sweat broke over my body. My hands shook so hard, I felt it in my shoulders. "No. Anything but that."

"It's the only way to undo what you've started," Helen said with a huff.

"You don't understand—I can't go to sleep," I repeated.

"You have to be exhausted."

"Of course I am." My voice cracked. Tears gathered in the corners of my eyes. I was so tired, I felt the exhaustion in every one of my bones. Most days, I couldn't think. Breathing even required concentration. "But I can't go to sleep. Every time I close my eyes, I see—" The lights flared. I dug my hands into my hair as my heartbeat increased. "I can't."

"You've been through enough." Atlas stepped away from the door. "Let us help you."

Anger ignited in my chest. A light bulb burst behind me. "I don't need help." I turned back to Helen and Master Lenin. "I'm fine."

"Miss Heart, you will let Helen do this." Steel coated Master Lenin's voice, as if he thought that would work on me.

"You lost the right to tell me what to do the moment you gave the order to kill Daniel." Spinning on my heel, I started toward the doors. "I'm leaving."

Atlas stepped forward with his tattooed hands reaching for me. As his fingers neared my arm, I felt the shadows of my nightmares hovering around the edge of my mind, waiting to consume me.

My heart skipped. My magic responded to my fear without permission. It surged from my core, knocking him back before he could touch me. His head struck the stone wall, and he slumped to the floor.

Oh, my God.

"You're unstable," Master Lenin called from the center of the room. "If you continue, you will hurt someone."

"Just leave me alone!" I screamed. The beds nearest me skidded away, knocking over stools and bedside tables.

Master Lenin stepped forward and raised his wand. With a wave of my hand, I knocked him across the room. I turned sharply on my heel, trying to Port. Instead of leaving, I just spun around. He must have cast something, so I couldn't leave.

An arm looped around my neck. A leather jacket crinkled against my back as a hand tilted my head to the side while the other sank a needle into my neck.

"No!" I screamed.

Terror filled my veins. My magic flared from my fingers. Just before I could direct the golden flow, it slipped away. My magic eased back up my arms and over my shoulders.

"Please, don't," I choked. My fingers clawed uselessly at the leather sleeve. "I have to stay awake. I don't want to see him," I sobbed. "I don't want to kill him again . . ." My head rolled back, dropping against my captor's shoulder. "Please keep me awake . . . Please."

No one moved to help me. Helen turned her face away; her cheeks glistened.

My knees gave out. I gripped the leather arm holding me. Black dots filled my vision. I forced my eyes wide, hoping it would keep me awake.

But my heartbeat slowed. My grip loosened, one finger at a time. My eyelids betrayed me and began to droop. When they finally closed, my hands fell to my sides.

The man behind me gingerly lifted me off my feet, holding me close to his chest. Gently, he placed me on the nearest bed. Seconds after his arms left, I felt another needle enter my skin.

Through my muddled mind, I heard Master Lenin say, "Thank—"

"Don't," a rough voice answered. The rest of his reply faded as I lost consciousness and descended into nightmares.

I woke up curled into a tight ball. The sheets were tangled around me, keeping out the cold air.

I pushed myself upright and looked around the room. Helen was asleep in the chair next to me. There was another empty chair beside hers, but there were no signs of who had been sitting there.

On the bedside table was a glass of water. My arm felt like it weighed twenty pounds as I reached for the glass. Too weak to hold it, the glass slipped from my fingers and fell back to the table. It tipped and sloshed water all over the floor.

Helen was awake instantly. After blinking the sleep from her eyes, they focused on me. I expected the same fury to return, but her eyes were soft. "Hey . . . how do you feel?"

"Tired." My throat was raw, like I had a cold.

"You look better." With a flick of her wand, the mess rose from the floor and went down the drain in the middle of the room. She grabbed a new cup and filled it only halfway.

She helped me sit up fully. Then, taking my hands, she wrapped them around the glass. Once she was certain I wouldn't drop it, she sat back down.

I sipped the water. No nausea came when it hit my stomach. Instead, an intense thirst overcame me. I drained the entire glass in seconds.

After I finished my third glass, I asked, "Did I hurt anyone?" I didn't recall dreaming, but my mind felt raw. If my magic flared because I was jumping from a tower, I could only imagine what would happen after three Trials.

She shook her head. "No . . . but you screamed a lot."

I winced. Guilt stirred in my gut. "I'm sorry. About the Adraffeen."

She settled back in her chair with a sigh. "Everyone deals with the Winner's Curse differently . . . I'm just glad we caught you in time. You have no idea how many children I've watched damage themselves beyond repair."

Getting back to her feet, she Ported from the room and appeared a moment later with a tray full of food. I ate slowly. Not used to food, my stomach cramped as if it wasn't sure it liked the weight.

When I had eaten as much as I could, I asked, "Is Atlas alright?"

Helen nodded. "He only got a headache."

I didn't think I could hate myself any more than I already did. Michael was right all along. I was unstable.

Helen moved the food aside and helped me to my feet. She told me to walk up and down the room. She let me stop only when she was satisfied.

Once her examination of my eyes was complete, she called for my ride to take me back to the neglected mansion.

Blake Ported into the room five minutes later. Wearing baggy pants and a large hoodie, he was dressed just the way I wanted to be.

When he saw me, he smiled, "Hey, you."

Shame heated my cheeks. I examined the nail polish chipping from my fingers. *He must think I'm an idiot.*

"How is she?" he asked, coming to stand beside me.

"She'll be fine once she gets back on a proper sleep schedule. Can I count on you to make sure she rests and eats?"

"Of course."

"Good. I'll come by in a couple days to make sure she isn't trying anything."

"You mean you're going to check to make sure I'm not lying anymore." I peeked up at them through my hair.

Helen placed a comforting hand on my shoulder. "This will get easier. You just have to give it enough time." With a gentle squeeze, she stepped back.

Blake took my hand and pulled me up from the bed. He wrapped his arm around my shoulders and used a transporter to Port back to the mansion.

It was sprinkling. The tiny raindrops barely made a sound as they dripped onto the sidewalk. Each one that landed on my skin felt like a pinprick of ice.

In the early hours of the night, the bare house was hardly visible. Keeping his arm around me, Blake and I walked in silence up to the front porch.

"I'm sorry," I said before he could unlock the front door. "I hate how meaningless those words sound because I've said them so many times, especially in the last month. But I really am." A tear slid down my cheek.

Blake sighed. "Come here." He pulled me into a hug and rested his chin on the top of my head. "I hate seeing you like this."

I held my breath, fighting back a flood of tears building behind my eyes. I was so tired of apologizing. I was so tired of being tired.

Unwinding his arms from around me, Blake unlocked the door and took me inside. "We promised each other that we would do this together. No more hiding things from each other."

I nodded. "It's just . . . every time I close my eyes . . . I'm scared I'll see my switchblade in Michael's chest. Or maybe there won't be anything at all, and it will be darkness that screams."

"They're just nightmares," Blake said, walking up the stairs. "They can't hurt you. And even if they could, you're a damn Royal. They're the ones that should be scared."

His attempt to make me laugh only brought on a wary smile. "I have magic flares when I sleep."

"I know that—"

"You don't know how bad they can get. I nearly set a ranch on fire." My heart dropped even further when I remembered the ranch, and that I would never be welcomed back. "I didn't want to hurt you while I slept."

"Well, that's not going to happen." Taking my hand, he led me up the stairs to my room.

Instantly, I noticed something was different. The ceiling, once painted a plain white, was now glossy and black. There was also something else . . . a rich, earthy scent lingering in the air, too faint to name.

Blake pointed to the black ceiling. "It glows when it detects magic. It should be bright enough to wake you up."

"Where did it come from?" I climbed onto the bed and ran my fingers along the glossy surface. The glass prickled with magic.

"Master Kale installed it."

I froze. My eyes darted around the room, looking for proof. "He was here?"

"Yeah. He left when I got the call to pick you up."

He left as soon as he knew I was coming back. I lowered myself to the mattress.

Blake shuffled his feet against the carpet. "Can I get you anything?"

I shook my head. "I'm just going to try to get some sleep."

"That sounds like a good idea." He kicked off his shoes and settled down beside me. "Do you mind if I watch some TV?"

I shook my head. I rolled over, placing my back to him. For a long while, I watched the raindrops race down the sliding glass doors. Every once in a while, they would absorb the light of the room before disappearing back into the night.

108

In White

I woke up alone.

It was a common occurrence since my mornings had become everyone else's afternoons. Sunlight filtered through the sliding glass doors, streaming across the room. You would have thought the bright light would've woken me up long before it reached the bedsheets. But, after not sleeping for an entire month, very little woke me up.

I laid there, curled on my side, watching a lazy breeze jump from tree to tree in the unkempt yard.

Silence curled through the room. It sat in the armchair by the dresser and stood in the darkened bathroom. The thick quietness held the windows closed, blocking out the laughing wind and lively birds.

The sheets whispered around my hips as I rolled my back to the window. A faint glow pulled my eyes toward the black glass ceiling. Gold sparkled through the tiles, brightening the room.

Closing my eyes, I took a deep breath and soothed my magic back into my core. The room dimmed behind my eyelids, but I didn't open them.

I didn't want to see what I did to the room during the night while my mind ran wild with magic. The lingering wisps of smoke told me enough.

A light tap came from the door. The handle rattled and turned before the door squeaked open.

I lay still, hoping Blake or Thiago would think I was asleep. I wasn't in the mood to pretend that everything was ok.

Shoes padded across the carpet.

"Are you sure we should wake her?" Cornelia whispered from the doorway.

"I don't think the Masters would take kindly to her missing tonight," Blake said quietly.

"Can we let her sleep a little longer? It doesn't start until seven."

His clothes rustled as he sat on the bed. "She has a habit of being late."

His hand hesitated over my shoulder before settling his fingers on my skin. Gently, he jostled my shoulder. "Hey, Charlie. You need to wake up."

I took a deep breath, savoring the darkness behind my eyelids, free of pity and fragile conversations, and the nightmare side effects. Faking drowsiness, I blinked once and then twice before looking up at my best friend.

A small smile pulled at his lips. His candy green eyes searched my face for triggers or signs that I was about to break again.

Rubbing my eyes, I pretended to look around the room. "What time is it?"

"Just a little after five."

I turned back to Blake before I looked at Cornelia. *Did he tell her?*

My heart sank at the sight of him. He was dressed in an all-white, three-piece suit. The sharp color contrasted with his olive skin, making his eyes look brighter, with more jeweled tones. His hair was freshly cut, short on the sides with some height up top. Looking at him like that, it made my soul ache for when his eyes were drowsy, and his ears were tucked under his grey, fraying beanie.

"Why are you all dressed up?" Pushing myself up onto my elbows, I scooted back against the headboard.

"The Crowning Ceremony is tonight." He looked over his shoulder for help.

Cornelia stepped away from the door, grinning brightly. "Which is why I am here! Right now, you look like you have a hangover, and you need to look like a Trial Winner."

I tried not to wince at her statement.

"There are three racks of gorgeous dresses downstairs. But first," she gave my hair a pointed look, "you need a shower."

"I was going to order pizza," Blake chimed in. "I figured you should eat something before heading over."

"You don't need to babysit me." I tried to reassure him with a smile, but I couldn't make it look more than a sad attempt.

"I know. I just want to help you take care of yourself."

What he didn't say escaped through his gaze anyway. *Since you won't do it by yourself.*

Leaning forward, I grabbed his hand and squeezed. "Thank you." Kicking off the covers, I dropped my feet to the floor. "What kind of pizza are you going to get?"

"I was thinking pineapple and ham, for sure." He looked over his shoulder at Cornelia. "Did you want anything?"

"I'd love sausage and black olive."

He faced me. "Any preferences?"

I shook my head. "Both sound good."

Keeping my eyes on the carpet, I ducked into the bathroom. Just before I closed the door, I caught Cornelia moving closer to Blake. Their murmured conversation didn't make it to my ears. Lifting his hand from his lap, Blake intertwined his fingers with hers.

Easing the door closed, I pulled my light blue hoodie over my head. The black victory tally on my rib drew my attention to the mirror. I stared at the small image, a capital 'I' with a knife piercing it. My gaze wandered to the empty skin beneath it.

The lights shuddered as I pulled on my magic. Pressing my index finger under Igorek's tally, I pushed the magic from my skin.

The flurry of gold sank into my skin, causing me to hiss through my teeth. Pins and needles blackened my skin, following the image in my head. When I pulled my hand back, a dripping letter 'D' glowed faintly beneath it. The scar running from my belly button to under my arm cut the new image in two.

I stared at the two victory tallies, no longer feeling proud to wear them. In fact, my stomach twisted with nausea at the sight of them. Hopefully, with them on my skin, they would keep me from adding a third.

I took my time in the shower, savoring the moments away from Blake's watchful gaze, and Cornelia's wounded friendship. Wrapping tightly in a towel, I blow-dried my hair before stepping back into the room.

The warm scent of melted cheese and roasted garlic assaulted my stomach as soon as I opened the door. My stomach growled, demanding to make up for lost time.

Cornelia had made the bed, so there was a flat surface to display the boxes of pizza. When she saw me in the doorway, she jumped to her feet. A slice of sausage and black olive was already half-eaten in her hand.

"About time!" Setting down her pizza, she rushed over and grabbed my hand. "I've been dying to go through these with you." Her blonde curls bounced around her shoulders as she pulled me from the room and down to the ballroom.

Just as she said, there were three long lines of dresses, two running along opposite walls, and one down the center of the room.

"You could have just picked something," I said, stopping on the last stair. "I really don't care."

"I can't just *pick something*. Whatever you wear tonight will be immortalized in history books." Her eyes glittered with excitement as she ran her hands over the fine fabrics, a collage of textures and materials. "This feels important."

Biting the tip of my tongue to keep my thoughts to myself, I started on the far line of gowns. My eyes got lost in all the white. My fingers itched to tear them apart.

Cornelia kept me on track, asking what fit I liked.

"Did you want lacy or plain?"

"What about buttons?"

"Sleeves or sleeveless?"

I shrugged my shoulders to each question. I would have gone in the towel I was wearing if it meant I could get the evening over quicker.

"What about this one?" she asked, holding up a gown made of layers of thin fabric. As she pulled it free from the line, the material shimmered and floated with each minute movement.

I shook my head. It looked too delicate, like an actual princess should wear it. Not someone who knew what a beating heart felt like in her palm.

My hands involuntarily clenched at the thought. Magic sparked through my fingers, charring the unfortunate gown in my fist. Clumps of burnt fabric drifted to the floor.

Unwinding my fingers, I moved farther down the line. A glimmer caught my attention. Quickly moving away from the ruined gown, I grabbed the hanger and pulled the dress into the open.

"Hey," I inclined my head to where Cornelia browsed. "What do you think of this one?"

Standing on her tiptoes, she looked over the rack. She smiled. "I think it's perfect." Dropping a look at her watch, she clapped her hands together. "Let's hurry up and get you into it. You've got an hour before you need to be there."

Draping the gown between my arms, I followed her back up the stairs. Sitting me down, she put me close to the pizza box and took out her wand.

I ate as she cast my hair into tight curls. Her nimble fingers twisted them up into a collection at the base of my head. Then, she wove my red streak in and out of the masterpiece.

Her easy, carefree conversation tricked me into thinking this was just for the Valentine's Day party, that Moose and Daniel were waiting for us in the dining room by the chocolate fountain. Just for a split second, I believed it.

When my makeup was done, and I had taken care of half of the pizza by myself, Blake poked his head into the room.

"I'm going to meet up with Atlas. I'll see you there."

I waved from the bed.

Cornelia looked like she wanted to say something to him, but she just smiled. His candy green eyes warmed, taking in her jovial expression. Seeming to know what she was thinking, he nodded and ducked out of the room.

"And you can get dressed." Stepping in front of me, she admired her handiwork. She nodded, granting her approval as she slid her wand into the loops on the outside of her jeans.

Licking the last bit of marinara sauce from my fingers, I grabbed the dress and stepped into the bathroom.

It was different from anything I had worn. For one, it was two pieces. A sloping neckline fell off my shoulders. The sleeves were long and fitted to my arms. The hem of the top consisted of a silk ribbon that hugged my chest just under my breasts.

The skirt, with a matching white ribbon, began over my belly button. The skin between the two pieces exposed my waist, all the way to my back, highlighting my scars and victory tallies.

The skirt was covered in diamonds. It draped elegantly to the floor and trailed a couple feet behind me in pleated layers. It even had pockets.

Stepping back into the bedroom, my hands fidgeted in front of me. "Well? How do I look?"

Cornelia beamed. "Like a force to be reckoned with."

"I sure don't feel like it," I grumbled to myself.

Cornelia crushed me into a hug. Her vanilla perfume curled around me, calming my nerves just as much as her arms did.

"You can do this," she said. Pulling back with watery eyes, she smiled.

Picking up the transporter from the bed, I pulled on my magic. With one last smile at Cornelia, I Ported from the neglected mansion.

In a single moment, all the warmth in my body was sucked out. Biting back curses, my eyes flew around the darkened rooftop. I was on an island taken up entirely by a building of white stone.

The lake surrounding the island was covered with chunks of ice. They reflected the silver moonlight, making the surface look like a pattern of lace.

Old Porting circles covered the rooftop in empty, black, overlapping rings. At the center, leading below, was a staircase. Lining the roof's edge were guards dressed in white armor.

The one closest to the stairs stepped toward me. "Welcome to Masters' Square. Invitation, please."

"I, uh . . ." Looking over my shoulder and slowly turning about, I saw that I was completely surrounded.

The guard's eyes dropped to my wrist. His eyebrows rose with recognition. "Forgive me, Miss Heart." He stepped away from the stairs and bowed at the waist. "Enjoy your evening."

My hands shook as I stepped toward the stairs. Keeping as much distance as I could between us, I grabbed the icy railing and descended the stairs.

The tight passage twisted and opened up to a flight of grand white marble stairs. The sharp icy air stayed above as I stepped into the party.

The high ceiling was draped with glittering white fabric. Seven chandeliers gathered the fabric before releasing it to drape to the next one. When it reached the wall, it pooled onto the shimmering white floor. The impressive room was decorated with gold and vases of the most magnificent flowers I had ever seen.

The party guests themselves were dressed almost as well as the room. Different shades of white were draped across women in the latest fashion.

At the center of the room stood Lawrence. He, too, wore a bright white suit with a bow tie. After seeing him in red for the past year, to see him in another color was hard on my eyes.

He stood with his guard, Steel, and no one else. Everyone else stood a few feet away from the pair. The circle around him wasn't large, but it was enough to be obvious; no Master was talking to him.

Taking a deep breath, I pulled my spine straight. Donning a look of cool indifference, I ignored the turning heads and made my way down the last few stairs.

"Miss Heart." Master LeOnie slipped around a group of chatting Masters. Her loose-fitting gown was a light shade of pink. The color was so faint, it could have passed as white if she weren't surrounded by the color.

She bowed her head to me. "I was hoping to catch you before I left."

"Before you left?" I glanced at the large grandfather clock across the room. "Nothing's happened yet."

"Nothing will happen that I haven't already foreseen."

I guess that was a perk of predicting the future. You could leave social events early.

"If Master Hart weren't pulling the string of the whole Trial, your performance would've earned you first place." She took a sip of her bubbling pink liquor. "But I think you will be pleased with the ceremony this evening."

"I doubt that."

She smiled softly. "Your performance cemented my reasons to take you on as an apprentice. Does that sound like something you would be interested in?"

If Michael were here, I would have looked at him for the correct answer. I thought I would be at the ranch for the summer, training for the war. But with Michael avoiding me, I wasn't so sure what my future was going to look like.

"You don't have to answer now. Your answer might be irrelevant by the end of the night anyway."

"What do you mean?" The last time she said something like that, I took a knife to the chest.

She dismissed my apprehension with a wave. "It's nothing you should worry about because it's nothing you can prevent. This evening is a cross-roads."

"You think Master Hart is going to make a move?"

"I think he will tie up loose ends." She finished off her glass and placed it on a passing floating tray. "I know this Trial was challenging for you, especially with what you learned about Master Kale."

"If I had your title, I would've seen it coming."

"No. I think you would still be blinded by hope. And if this last Trial proved anything, it's that there is good in even the darkest of men, and evil in the hearts of every king." Stepping closer, she took my hand in hers. She barely flinched from the burn of my magic. "Miss Heart, you need to decide which legacy you want to see stretch into history.

"I cannot tell you what to do. I predict the future, not alter it. I can only hope that you make the right decision and choose the correct king. This world needs change and you, like everyone in this room, get to decide what that will look like."

I didn't want that kind of pressure. I never wanted any of this. For a moment, I caught myself thinking about Salina, Kansas. The solution back then was to run. Was that the same solution here? Could I disappear and leave all of this behind?

"My hope is that you will give your loyalty to the king you truly want to see rule, and not to spite the other."

I shook my head. "It's not that black and white."

"Things rarely are."

Releasing my hand, Master LeOnie leaned back. Her blue-green gaze swept over the room like she too was searching for the man in black.

Her unblinking eyes returned to me. "Please remember what I said. Good luck." Dropping into a low curtsy, she strolled across the room and up the stairs.

109

Crowns and Medals

The grandfather clock chimed with a deep bellow.

The sound cut through the conversations of the room, silencing them as Master Lenin strolled up to the stairs.

"Can I have the Top Seven join me on stage?" he called from the front.

The room fell quiet with anticipation as Emeka, Blake, Thiago, Tala, and I untangled ourselves from the crowd and walked up the stairs. We were directed to stop a few steps below the Master and were sorted in the order we were placed.

"Good evening, Masters," Master Lenin said with an easy smile. "Tonight is the final event of The Master's Trial. Tonight, we celebrate our winner and the remaining Contestants. Tonight, we crown our schools' finest and award them with the status of a Master.

"After much conversation, the other School Masters and I have decided to do something a little different. For the first time, all surviving Contestants will be rewarded with a title."

The watching Masters mumbled among themselves. A thrill ran up my spine. *A title. I'm getting a title.*

"The Contestants who were killed in The Trial will not be receiving a title. It doesn't matter how they died; The Trial won. Their families will only be receiving medals tonight."

"The awards, please." Master Lenin beckoned someone offstage. The School Masters lined up behind him on the right. Each School Master had a glossy white pillow held in front of them.

I shifted my gaze over my shoulder to Master Theodore. His bloodthirsty stare was already fixated on me. He held the pillow in one hand. His other arm, the one that took the axe, was limp at his side.

"For the past month, we spent many late nights determining the perfect title for each Contestant. The title had to embody what was accomplished and learned in The Trial. It had to be unique to their skill set and victories. Contestants," he turned to us, "these titles will shape your future.

"For Charlie Heart, our seventh place, we created a new title due to her unique circumstances. In our history, never has there been a User who could perform magic without a wand. For that, we have titled her the Master of Handling Magic. Her technique and precision could be compared to any Master Ward Caster."

Master Lenin turned and reached out his hands. A white pillow was given to him. On it was a thin and delicate crown made of a shiny white metal. Decorating the band were seven jewels.

Master Lenin explained to the room, "These seven jewels represent each school you went against. The main one," he gestured to a black diamond, "is for the school you represented."

Up close, I could identify which stone was for which school: yellow for Lions of Magic, a pale pink for The Magical Academy of the Earth, an amber stone for The Serpentine School of Magic, light blue for Aquarius: The Undersea School of Enchantments, an emerald for The European Academy for Practical Magic, and a ruby for The University for Advanced Tactical Magic. In the center was the biggest of the bunch, a black diamond for The Magisterium of Magic.

Master Lenin carefully lifted the crown and placed it on my head. My shoulders tensed, fearing it would slip off if I breathed wrong.

"Congratulations, Master Heart." Master Lenin dipped into a bow and faced the crowd.

Master Heart. The name sent a chill down my spine.

"For our sixth place, Blake Johnson, we chose to name the Master of Execution. Every plan he devised with his Guardian, he completed successfully. Every cast of magic and task put before him, he went above and beyond to achieve his goals."

I twisted around and offered him a small high five. Almost giggling with happiness, he high-fived me back.

The room grew louder as Master Harlan descended toward his student with a crown. The thin band fit Blake's head perfectly. Short in height it was also a stunning white.

Master Harlan bowed to Blake. When he straightened, he pulled him into a hug before returning to the crowd.

"For our fifth place, Amelia Markus, we have this medal to celebrate her extraordinary skills in illusions, charms, and trickery. To accept her award is her School Master, Master Harley Finch."

Master Finch stepped forward, accompanied by his cane. On the decorated pillow was a small medal that was too far for me to see the details. With the pillow supported in one hand, he bowed and hobbled off the stage as the room applauded.

"We award our fourth place, Thiago Luis, with the title Master of Impossibilities. He conquered his fears without using his wand. He killed a dragon with a limited magic status. Most would think that impossible, but not this Master."

Master Markus Han walked toward his Contestant. Upon the pillow was a crown with the matching jewels. Holding the amber stone at the center was a double-headed snake.

"For Tala Abalos, our Trial's third place, we award you the title of the Master of Blades. Coming into The Trial, you showed skill with weapons. You then honed that skill until you outranked all of the other Contestants. Congratulations."

As the room clapped, Master Loran stepped down to his Contestant with his pillow. This crown was much bigger. Seven large spikes rose up from the band, each holding the jewels of the school. The large pink stone sat in a setting that matched the school insignia, a lotus flower in full bloom. Once the crown was in place, they bowed to each other, and her Master left the stage.

"For Dmitri Theodore our second place, we have this medal," Master Lenin gestured to the pillow held by the School Master. "Nearly every battle he went into, he demonstrated clear strategic forethought and quick follow-through. Here to accept his award is his father and School Master, Konstantin Theodore."

The Russian bowed to the man in white and descended from the stage. When he stood back in the crowd, he turned his icy glare to me. The material of the pillow bunched under his white-knuckled grip. The opal medal, glittering with red jewels, slid off-center.

"Finally, we crown our Trial Winner. He receives a title and his school receives the declaration of the best school out of the Seven Great Schools until the next Trial. In each Trial, he twisted every situation to come out victorious. For that, he is titled the Master of Wit."

The room erupted. Cameras flashed as his name echoed around the room. Master Aluna strolled down the stairs with pride on her face. As she passed me, I could feel her smugness.

The pillow clasped between her hands was bigger than the last two. The crown stood taller and, if it was possible, it shined brighter. The jewels were the size of eggs, cut and fashioned into the shape of each school crest.

As Master Aluna placed the magnificent crown on his head, Emeka's eyes gleamed. He scanned the room, soaking in the admiration.

"When you wear these," Master Lenin addressed the Top Seven, "you represent your year of training and hard work. You display your courage and your strength. You express the blood, sweat, and magic you poured out. You demonstrate your power and the magic you possess. You have mastered yourself in the face of fear, the impossible, and even death. You are true Masters now."

Master Lenin bowed. Like a ripple in a pond, the audience followed. When he straightened, he clapped, and soon the whole room was doing the same.

"This night is yours. Drink! Eat! Celebrate a marvelous Trial. Well done to all of you." Master Lenin started another round of applause. The music started once again, pulling people back to the dance floor and laughter back to the room.

Blake was immediately pulled into a conversation with his School Master and Atlas. Master Lenin turned toward me.

Quickly spinning in the other direction, I ran right into Emeka. My hands curled into fists.

"Congratulations," Emeka said smoothly. "Considering how you blundered at the beginning, for you to end up with a title is a great achievement."

"You're welcome for getting first."

"Why should I thank you?"

"Because if it weren't for me, you would still be in the First Trial, acting as a Dellamora's chew toy. You're here because of me." He opened his mouth and I could see the bullshit moving up his throat. "If you say what I think you're going to say, you won't have a heart, and I'll have ruined this dress."

A slow arrogant smile pulled at his lips. "I'm a Master now. You can't touch me."

"If you think I give a shit about rules, you haven't been paying attention." Stepping forward, I placed my hand on his chest. My eyes never left his as my fingers glowed with magic.

"If you ever speak to me again," I said, replicating the smile he had earlier, "I will make whatever the caligo did to you look like a daydream."

Emeka went completely motionless under the threat. I could feel his heart racing under my fingertips.

Dropping my hand, I bowed my head. "Goodbye, Master Selasi."

110

With an E

Gathering my skirt, I descended into the crowd.

Snaking my way through, I moved to the outskirts of the room where a row of French doors let the cold air in. I slipped out onto the balcony and gripped the cold handrail. Facing the patchwork of moonlit ice, I breathed in the tranquility of the shadows.

I have a title.

After wanting one for so long, it didn't feel real.

It didn't feel like I deserved it.

How I earned it . . . the weight of those actions . . . would follow me every time someone spoke my name.

I wish they hadn't given it to me.

How I longed for the innocence I had before I entered The Trial. To be just Charlie didn't seem so bad now. Master Heart, it made me sound like the man I fought so hard to not be like. Maybe we were more alike than I wanted to admit. So many months ago, Michael had said it didn't matter how far the apple fell if it grew from a poisonous tree. Maybe he was right after all.

A whirl of cold wind ruffled my skirt, causing the diamonds to clink against the white tile. The crown sitting on my dark brown curls was starting to make my head ache.

"Miss Heart, you need to decide which legacy you want to see stretch into history."

I squeezed my eyes shut so hard they began to water. The cold railing groaned under my clenched fingers. I didn't want to choose a side. I didn't want to fight anymore.

"Master Heart. With an E."

I jerked around. Lawrence stood in the doorway. The light of the party cast an angelic glow on his head of golden curls, and the shoulders of his white suit.

"Hello, Master Hart," I said dryly. "How's exile going?"

He cocked his head. "Exile?"

I nodded back to the crowded room. "I didn't see many people willing to talk to you."

His expression grew tight, but his smile remained in place, although forced.

"Can you feel remorse?" I asked. "For locking me in The Trial, or using a binding curse on Master Kale. Are you capable of that?"

"Do you regret pulling out Contestant Theodore's heart?" he countered.

"How could I not?"

He hummed low in his throat, unconvinced. "With practice and age, you will get over that." He offered me one of two glasses of wine, coaxing me back into the room. "I came to toast you on your new status. Master Heart . . . it has a nice ring to it." His smile grew. "It's quite the achievement. One worthy of a toast."

I took the wine just to have something to do with my hands. "That's going to take a lot to get used to."

"The toast, or the title?" he asked, amused.

"The title." I swirled the wine around the glass.

"You earned it." He clinked his glass against mine and raised it to his lips. He paused. "Please, drink."

"Why? You tried to kill me once already."

"That makes you even more impressive. I was a Master Hunter once, and we were trained to be successful. Yet, you dodged my best efforts. You showed your worth, so you have nothing to worry about from me."

Someone bumped me from behind. Wine sloshed over the rim and splattered on the floor. Surprisingly, none hit the white dress.

"You never made a toast." I stepped back from the puddle and looked up at him.

He gave me a questioning look.

"It isn't a toast unless someone says something."

"You are quite right." He lifted his glass. "What would you like to toast to?"

I raised my glass next to his. "You're the one who wanted it."

"How about this?" He looked me right in the eyes. "May forgotten memories come to light, and old friends come back to our hearts. May fortune and luck smile upon you. May this war be won and over."

I clinked my glass against his, hoping it would bring our time together to an end.

"You never answered my question," he said before putting the rim to his lips. "The one I asked before the Final Trial."

Dread filled my stomach. I lowered the glass before I took a drink. "You mean the one where I fight for you?"

"Precisely. I think now would be the best time to answer since Master Kale is no longer in the picture."

My heart throbbed. "Because of you."

He sipped his wine. "And because of you."

He's not wrong. "Do you even still want me? I have a habit of going against orders."

He nodded. "Obedience can be learned. And magic like yours cannot be ignored. I do think we would work well together. That is, after we get to know one another. You could live at my palace and get a taste of the life you would have, if you want."

With a light hand on my shoulder, he turned me to face the party. "Every room will look like this in my new world." He gestured to the expensively decorated people and walls. "Achilles Heel thinks they're doing the same, but they're fighting for a dying age. But you can be at peace. The man who gave you the scars on your back will not exist, and no one will rise to take his place in my new order.

"Will you leave with me?" He nodded to the stairs. "I have a room ready for you. If you fear being alone, a couple of your fellow Contestants will be there as well. If you're not convinced, I can show you my plans." He smiled. "I'm confident you won't be able to resist."

My gaze slid over his shoulder. I met Master Lenin's tight-lipped expression. *You're a weapon to him, nothing more.*

My eyes shifted and found the only person wearing black. There was a tightness in Atlas's jaw that I knew all too well. Even if I wanted to fight with Achilles Heel, I wouldn't be welcomed by all. Not after what I had done to their king.

And the truth was . . . there was nothing keeping me with them.

I could leave all of this, the Heel and Lawrence. With my title, they could do nothing to stop me. Lawrence could shove it, and I was about to tell him just that when the volume of the party changed.

Quickly, it dipped into whispers and shocked gasps. People turned to the staircase. Noticing the change immediately, Lawrence looked over his shoulder.

Following his gaze, my lips parted. Air rushed into my lungs.

He stood at the top of the stairs in a perfectly fitted three-piece suit, as black as midnight. While the look was impressive, what stood out was the neatly folded pocket square—a startling white. His sharp, dark eyes scanned the room.

Then, Michael Kale looked at me.

111

A Memory Catcher

The wine glass slipped from my fingers and shattered at my feet.

He's here.

Michael broke eye contact when he reached the bottom of the stairs. His attention flicked to the man in front of me. Before fury could consume his face, Michael looked away. He nodded, acknowledging those who bowed to him, and started through the parting crowd.

I tried to remind myself to breathe. I could hardly recall the motions to make myself blink.

My eyes ran hungrily over him, re-memorizing him. The curve of his jaw, the slope of his nose, the sharpness of his scar; all of it was so familiar, but so different now. My memories of him were haunted with bruises of stormy blues and split skin. But he was here, and he was whole.

Lawrence put an arm between us as my foot slid forward. "You'll ruin your gown, darling."

I tore my eyes from the Master Hunter to the puddle of wine on the floor. I stepped back to collect myself.

He's here.

My gaze returned to him. Nonchalantly, he clasped Master Lenin's forearm and nodded to those in the Master's company. As a pleasant conversation started, he looked over his shoulder back to me, not the man I stood next to.

I didn't give a shit about staining the dress. I went right through the puddle toward Michael. My heart hammered harder against my ribs with each step.

Excusing himself from his company, Michael walked to meet me.

When we met in the middle of the room, my mind went completely blank. The most intelligent thing my brain could come up with was a breath-less, "Hi."

"Hi." He bent into a low bow. When he straightened, his eyes flickered to the crown on my head.

Tongue-tied, all I could do was stare, soaking in his dark eyes. My breath hitched when I didn't find any hatred there.

"Master Kale, I didn't think you would come." Lawrence stepped up to my shoulder. The motion did not go unnoticed by Michael, whose jaw clenched in response. "Master Heart and I were just about to toast. Would you care to join us?"

Reluctantly, Michael turned his gaze to the man next to me. The familiar spark of fury darkened his eyes. "I'd rather roll in mud than drink with you."

"You wound me, Master Kale." An edge rimmed Lawrence's tone.

"If I wanted to wound you, Lawrence, I would have my hands inside you as I deboned you like a fish."

Cheese and rice. I missed this cruel man.

"I came to speak to Charlie." When Michael's eyes found mine, they were hesitant. "If she would allow me a moment of her time."

My mind was still reeling because he was here, and now, he had used *my* name and not the last name he gave me. My eyes flickered between his, hoping to find a hint, or even a shred of evidence as to what his intentions were. Why would he want to talk to me? After everything I did.

"Charlie?"

I blinked. "Yes, of course. Sorry. I—"

"There's no need for that." His smile was one of cautious optimism. "I would like to talk in private, if that's no trouble."

For fear of saying a third stupid thing, I just nodded.

"Lawrence, please excuse us." And just like that, without even looking at him, Michael dismissed one of the most powerful men in the world.

My heart threatened to beat out of my chest as Michael placed his cal-loused and scarred hand on the small of my back. He held my gaze for a beat more before guiding me deeper into the room.

Michael politely nodded to those who addressed us, but he didn't stop. He took me to the outskirts of the crowd, to one of the doors lining the room, and ushered me inside.

With the door shut, the sounds of the party fell into the background of muffled voices and a humming piano tune. His hand left my back as he stepped deeper into the well-furnished office. Taking a deep breath, he faced me. A clock by the door ticked awkwardly, telling us how much time we were wasting.

"Lawrence called you Master Heart," he said, cutting through the quiet of the room. "Does that mean you got a title?"

I nodded. "They gave everyone a title."

"I guess that was to make up for the shitty placement this year. What title did they award you?"

"Master of Handling Magic." I held up my hands and wiggled my fingers. "Not the most creative, if you ask me."

"You have to give them some credit. You presented them with something they've never seen before." The corner of his lips lifted into a crooked grin.

My heart ached at the sight. It was an expression I never thought I would see again. I blinked, and that moment at the ranch flashed behind my eyelids, my hands glowing, my magic hitting his chest.

The warm lighting of the office made his eyes look a deep dark brown, as rich as dark chocolate, instead of the black I was accustomed to.

"You deserve it," he said, nodding.

I tilted my head. "Do you really believe that?"

With the title, Michael and I were on the same level, but I had never felt more distance between us. A title meant he had no hold over me. I could leave and never look back, and there was nothing he could do about it. That thought used to bring me hope. Now, I just felt tired.

"I do. I really do. You deserve all the freedom it allows." He let his gaze fall from mine, taking his time to take me in. His dark eyes followed the cascading fabric of the gown before stalling on the strip of skin between the two pieces. The victory tallies burned under his gaze.

"You're missing one."

My gaze snapped to the section of skin in question. I had one for Dmitri and one for Igorek.

"May I?" He reached under his jacket and pulled his wand from his holster.

He stepped close and placed one hand on my hip to keep me steady. I held perfectly still, in case he pulled away. He touched the tip of his wand to the skin under the tally for Dmitri. Magic filled the smooth surface of his wand before bleeding into my skin. My jaw locked as it stung.

A black M stained the empty skin on my torso, matching the size and look of the tallies above it. An image of my switchblade stabbed through the center.

"You deserve this as well." His quiet words played with the curls framing my face. "Master Hunters are supposed to be untouchable. You fought well and beat thousands of years of Hunter training."

Finally, I gathered my courage to speak. "Why are you here?" I met his gaze. "I didn't think you would come."

He pulled his hands from my body, leaving my skin cold. "Honestly, I wasn't planning on it." He sheathed his wand and leaned back against the desk.

"Why did you? You've avoided me everywhere else."

"I wanted to see you." He said it so simply. Like it shouldn't have sent a shock rocketing through my system.

"It's not like you didn't know where I was," I sputtered.

His head bobbed in agreement. "My time has been occupied. After the Final Trial, Masters have been coming forward in support of the Heel. No one can get behind a Master who tried to kill one of his own with dark magic." He lowered his gaze to his shoes. "And I wasn't sure you wanted to see me."

My stomach twisted with images that I almost killed myself to avoid: him blood-soaked, broken, and almost lifeless.

Propelled forward, I crossed the room and flicked aside his tie. My stomach was in knots with apprehension as I made fast work of the buttons on his shirt.

"Charlie." He grabbed my wrists. "Don't."

I looked up into his face. "I need to see."

Reluctantly, he released me.

Finishing with the buttons, I pulled his shirt away, and there it was. Just below his left pec, under the head of his snake tattoo was a thin scar. So easily, my mind conjured images of my switchblade cutting through his ribcage.

But that wasn't all. Below, on the right side of his ribcage, were two jagged lines from when I shoved glass into his side. Near the center of his chest, intermixed with old battle wounds were faint scorch marks in the shape of thin fingers. I aligned my palms with the marks. My hands matched perfectly.

I jerked back so fast, the crown slipped from my head and rolled across the room. "I'm sorry—that night—I didn't mean to hurt you. If I'd known—I almost killed you." Taking another large step away from him, I wrapped my arms tightly around my stomach. "I should be the last person you want to see. So, why are you here?"

Usually, he would've matched my tone. Instead, he kept his voice low, almost soothing. "I came to congratulate you."

"You could've sent a card."

Nodding, his fingers worked the two halves of his shirt back together. "I also wanted to give you something."

I wasn't expecting that.

When his shirt was buttoned up and his tie hung neatly once more, he reached into his pocket. When his hand came back into view, it held a small black velvet box.

Michael didn't give people things. In all the time I knew him, he only gave insults and injuries, or instruments to destroy, and I had given those things right back. Anything else was out of character, or it went against the nature he had developed in the Hunter Guard.

"I promise it won't explode," he said when I just stared at it without moving.

Not really knowing what it could be, I plucked it from his hand and pushed up the lid with my thumb.

Hanging from a delicate chain was a silver rectangle no bigger than my thumb. Around its edges was a plain golden frame. It looked like a mirror that would hang in a dollhouse.

"What is it?"

"A memory catcher," Michael explained. "Some Regulars believe dream catchers filter out bad dreams. This one actually does. It's an enchanted mirror made in pairs. As long as you wear it, you'll only have good dreams. You shouldn't ever have to taste Adraffeen again."

Embarrassment rushed to my cheeks, burning them bright pink. *Of course he knows about that.*

"That's not all." Stepping closer, he took the box from my palm and removed the necklace. He placed the delicate chain around my neck and then set the charm on my palm. "When you grab the corners like this," he used one of my hands to pinch the corner on the top right and the other on the bottom left, "and pull." He moved them away from each other. The charm expanded to the size of a book. "It grows to any size you wish. You can even change the look of the frame."

"What does it do?" I asked, completely astonished.

"Think of a memory. Then touch the surface and it will appear for you. I know memories can be the worst form of torture. So, I thought you would want to keep your good memories close."

The reflective surface rippled under my fingertip. I waited with hungry eyes as colors mixed and lines constructed an image. When it stilled, Daniel smiled up at me.

112

Murmured Oaths

A deep ache began to rise through my ribcage.

It was hard not to think of alternate versions of tonight. If I had never competed, if Daniel never took a knife meant for me, would he have been the one crowned with a title?

Michael went still. His shoulders were tense, anticipating a lightning strike of anger.

"You broke me." The shattered words came straight from the gaping hole in my heart. I shrunk the charm and dropped it from my palm. It snagged on the chain and thumped against my chest.

I looked up into his face, expecting to see his typical blank Hunter expression. But his dark eyes were raw, waiting for me to make the first move.

"Why did you do it?"

"Anything I say, you won't like," he said softly.

"Answer anyway."

Refusing to break eye contact, he took a shuddering breath. "Obedience has been my second nature for over a hundred years. I knew it was wrong, but I told myself it was an order. But you were right. I have more control than I thought."

"So, you let me think it was Dmitri?" My chest had been frozen with numbness for the past month. Now it warmed with anger.

"I wanted to tell you, but things were good. We were friends," he reasoned. "I didn't want it to end."

"You were the one who ended it," I exclaimed.

"Do you really think I took pleasure in watching an innocent kid die? Do you truly think that lowly of me?"

His dark eyes moved over my face. I had no doubt he saw it all: the sickness in my throat, the torment behind my eyes, and the distrust guarding what was left of my heart. In his eyes, there was a hint of longing, like he was searching for something that used to be there.

He clenched his jaw and dropped his gaze. "I didn't come here to argue with you. I hope I didn't ruin your evening." With a hand on his stomach, he bent at the waist. "Congratulations on the new title and completing The Trial, Master Heart. May fortune favor you."

Refusing to look at me, his shoulder brushed mine as he walked toward the door.

Deep down, I knew if he left, I would never see him again. Not like this. Not with his heart on his sleeve. I shouldn't have cared, but dammit, I did.

"Lawrence talked to me tonight." I turned to find him motionless in front of the door, his hand gripping the knob.

His grip tightened, causing the metal to groan and distort beneath his fingers. "I saw."

"He told me why he should be king. He gave me his reasons for why I should follow him. So, tell me, why should I follow you? Why should I help you rule?"

A harsh laugh chuckled from deep in his throat. Shaking his head, he turned to face me. "I'm not going to bribe you, Charlie."

"That's not what I meant—"

"That's what he's doing," he said firmly. "That's what he always does. He dresses up horrible situations like they're mannequins. He once told me that slaughtering families of Deficients was pest control. You want honesty? Here it is."

He flung out his arms like he was throwing the word at me. "I have nothing to give you. I have no fancy future for you to dream of. I can't promise luxury or rest. I can't even promise to keep you safe." His eyes trailed along the scar on my cheek. "I let people down. That's what I do. Which is why I don't want to be king. I'd do a piss-poor job of it."

"You can't seriously believe that. Do you see the way people react when you walk into a room? If you walked out to that party right now and asked those people to fight for you, they would drop everything."

"You think I don't know that?" A brief moment of fear strangled his breathing. "If I went out there and asked for their wands, half of them would be dead by the end of the year. Do you know what I thought when I first saw you?"

I balked at the sudden subject change. "I can imagine."

"You'd probably be wrong . . . it was in Kansas, the night before you got on the bus. You were sitting on your roof, watching the snow fall." The corner of his lip twitched at the memory. "You were innocent, free of this mess, and untainted by me. I hated you, not just because of your bloodline, but because every time I looked at you, you were a constant reminder I was failing.

"I failed to protect my sister. I failed to protect my Master Hunter. Anything Lawrence threw at me was a punishment I gladly accepted for that. This is my war and my burden. When I looked at you, all I saw was another person who would die for it. I have too many lives painted on my hands because I can't kill the man who used to be my best friend. And I didn't want to add you to that list."

Ever since I had entered the magical world, I had heard the Heel was few in numbers. But it never seemed to bother Michael, only Master Lenin. Now I knew why. He wanted Lawrence's attention directed solely on him. He wanted the brunt of it.

"I won't ask anyone to join this." He waved his hand toward the door and the crowd behind it.

"You can't do it alone, either."

"I'm used to it. It's an occupational hazard."

"It shouldn't have to be. You were meant to be more than just under Master Lenin's chain of command. There are so many people who want to stand beside you, if you would just ask."

As the words left my mouth, I realized what I was really saying. I wanted him to ask me. I didn't know what my answer would be. There was a wound on my heart that throbbed every time our eyes met, and I didn't know if that would ever go away.

At the start of this, he pressured me to his side with a threat hanging over Blake's head. I was never given the choice to stand beside him.

But I wanted him to ask.

I wanted him to give me the choice.

He stilled at my words, reading me better than a favorite book. Emotions swirled through his gaze like an early morning fog. Hope. Guilt. Aspiration. Doubt.

"I hunt darkness," he began slowly. "I have for over a hundred years, and that killed something inside me. People think I'm a monster, and most of the time, I believe them. I've done things that make me no better than the things I hunt. I've been broken for so long that I've forgotten what it's like to not be wounded.

"I don't have a plan for what it will be like if the Heel wins this war, but I do know it has nothing to do with killing those with less magic. It has nothing to do with deciding who is worthy of the right to live."

His gaze cooled. When he spoke again, his words were low, almost breathless. "I will fight for life, regardless of magical status. I will fight for what's right . . . and I want to do it with you.

"When I'm with you . . . I feel like the man I used to be. I started thinking like him, acting like him. For a man like me, that's nothing short of a miracle." His eyes moved over my cheek and paused on the scar he might as well have put there. "I'm not asking you to forget. I'm not even asking you to forgive me. All I ask is that you give me a chance to be better."

"I did give you a chance. And then you sent me into the Second Trial."

He flinched back, the steady light building in his gaze snuffed out. For a moment, I worried that had silenced him.

But he wasn't done.

Reaching under his jacket, he pulled a knife from his holster and grabbed my hand. Before I could object, he had my fingers wrapped around the hilt and the blade pointed at his heart.

"I swear this to you. You have my hands, my magic, and my loyalty. With this oath, I hand over my life—"

I tried to jerk my hand away. "Michael, you can't just—"

"I've thought about this. Thoroughly. This makes sense. This feels right. Let me finish. Please."

He tightened his hold. "This oath will obey no other. I will fight for those who cower behind me. I will respect those who stand beside me. I will guard the backs of those who stand in front of me, and I will show no mercy to those who stand against me. I won't raise a hand against you, or another innocent. I give you control over this knife, so if my actions do not reflect these words, you can use it and silence me forever. The magic of my bones binds these words to your will." His eyes bore into mine. "Do you accept my oath of loyalty?"

Too shocked to do anything else, I nodded.

His fingers relaxed around mine, lowering the blade. With his other hand, he continued to hold mine. He gazed boldly into my eyes. That look of longing returned as he searched my face.

"Will you fight with me?" he asked quietly. "None of this makes sense without you. I know you, and I know you'll fight for others, just like you did in The Trial, no matter who's against you. You give me hope that we can do this. But if you want to be with Lawrence," he looked pained, "I'll let you go. You can use this knife and end it right here. I won't force you any longer. You have my word."

I stared, unable to think. My skin tingled under his calloused fingers. The weight of his pledge rested on my shoulders and filled the air like smoke. The Michael I knew would never say something so unguarded, but then again, maybe this wasn't the Michael I knew.

The door flew open and slammed against the wall. Atlas burst into the room.

Michael and I turned with matching looks of hostility. Any objections died in our throats when we took one look at the Irishman in black. His eyes held a wildness only brought on by panic.

With the door open, a wave of uneasy murmuring came from the main room.

"It's Lawrence," Atlas panted. "He's addressing the room. I think he's about to ask the Masters to choose sides."

Michael stepped toward him, but paused, just for a second. He looked at me just long enough to commit the moment to memory.

Was this the last time we would look at each other without weapons drawn?

The softness in Michael's face was gone in a blink. He dropped my hands; his fingers left mine cold. Turning his back to me, he stepped into the hall.

113

Between Two Kings

"Some of you know my story."

Lawrence stood on the stairs with his hands clasped behind him. The glimmering chandeliers cast his golden curls in a halo of heavenly light. Gone was the charming man with a pleasant demeanor. The man addressing the room was about to draw battle lines, and he held the gravity of that decision with taut shoulders. He was a king, demanding his throne.

His guards, dressed in crimson, lined the room with wands drawn. Steel stood with them.

"I'm the last of my bloodline," Lawrence said. "A Deficient Three brought a family of Royals to ruin because he was given more than he could handle. I watched the same thing happen countless times while I was in the Hunter Guard. Low status Users are parasites on our society.

"They feed off of our hard work and magic and give nothing back in return," Lawrence stressed. "When they need to step up, all they can do is stand by and watch. When they fail, they drag us down with them. The thing about parasites is that they can be eliminated."

Lawrence's cool gaze moved from one captivated Master to the next.

"What I ask from you, our world's finest, is to stand by me. We were once on the brink of a golden age of peace. We can find our way back, but this time we can enter it strong. We do that by ridding ourselves of those who pollute our statuses and those who feed off our efforts. With our combined magic and support, we can redesign the world to what it should be. No Deficients and no Regulars. We can recreate Eden, but this time to last."

The crowd was drunk on his words. Men nodded. Women smiled with a hunger for that to be reality. Others looked around with unease.

"With me as your king—"

"You're not a king." The interruption was soft and hesitant.

The euphoric haze around the room burst. Heads whipped around, looking for the source of the voice. The crowd parted, revealing the man in a black suit with a white pocket square.

Michael stood with his hands clenched tightly at his sides.

I, along with everyone else, gaped at the Master Hunter. Out of everyone, he was the last person I thought would speak up. Master Lenin, sure. But Michael? He couldn't even think of leading the war without gasping for air.

Lawrence's eyes locked onto him with an intensity that could be felt across the entire room.

"You're a Hunter," Michael continued. "Loyal to no nation or title—"

"The Hunter Guard is dead."

Michael shook his head. "You took an oath to protect life, no matter what form it took. Not decide it."

"This is me protecting life."

"It's genocide."

"Empires are built with bones and blood. History taught us that."

"You always did beat around the bush."

"And you always acted like you were better than me, better than our founders. At least I don't reject the traditions that define our kind." Lawrence shook his head.

"Tell me, were there any judges for this Trial? Or was it just you, pulling the strings?" Michael's voice grew louder, more confident as he spoke. "I don't know how else a Contestant can go through the Final Trial without a Guardian and get seventh, while a kid who didn't even make it to his door got second."

The crowd's attention shifted back to the Master on the stage. Michael had a point.

Michael tilted his head in question. "I thought you wanted to preserve the strengths and the traditions of our founders. Yet last month, you used a binding curse to try and kill me, a Master and a Royal, at that. And that's not the first time you've killed a Master."

Michael's words electrified the room. Those who were swooning from Lawrence's promises moments earlier were now stiff with anger.

"You know what they say," Lawrence said just above a growl. "Sometimes healthy tissue has to be cut out along with the diseased."

Michael shook his head. "No one's buying that. You saw an opportunity to dominate the board and you took it, despite the rules. Who says you won't sacrifice any of these Masters to forward your game? What oaths will you break when it suits you?"

Lawrence was smart not to say anything. If he tried to defend himself, nothing he said would stand up because Michael was living proof that he killed Masters, the very beings he told everyone were untouchable.

"What do you have to offer?" A Master across the room asked.

Michael shifted nervously from one foot to the other. For so long, he had avoided that question.

"I cannot promise you Eden," he said to the room, "or that no blood will be spilled. But I believe everyone should have the right to live, no matter what status they have. Any blood that will be spilled will be freely given to remove him from his self-proclaimed throne." A fire danced in his eyes as he pointed to Lawrence.

"Do not forget that Master Kale was the one who brought us so close to that golden age of peace so many years ago," Master Lenin spoke up from the far side of the room. "He caught the deadliest Users. He brought some of the world's deadliest creatures to extinction. All to protect the citizens of the magical world. If anyone can bring us to that golden age again, it would be the Prince of Peace."

The crowd murmured among themselves as long-forgotten memories came back. Some looked at the man in black with new eyes.

I couldn't help but look at him, too. I had never heard him called the Prince of Peace. It was hard to think that title belonged to him when scars covered the majority of his body. But if I had learned anything this past year, it was that there was so much I didn't know about Michael Kale.

"Prince of Peace?" Lawrence laughed. "That man died. That man," he pointed at Michael, "is called Hades. He may have brought us to the golden age once, but let's not forget that he also started this war. He drew first blood, killing my Hunting Trio, a sacred group."

"No." Michael shook his head. "You did, when you killed six families of Deficients and eliminated the Hunter Guard and its leader, Master Hunter Arwin."

Some people gasped throughout the crowd. Beside me, I heard a Master whisper, "I thought the Guard just disbanded. Master Hart killed them all?"

"What do you know about anything?" Lawrence sneered at Michael. "You're a relic from a deceased era. Do you really think you can rule?"

Michael hesitated. "I don't know, but I do know it shouldn't be you."

"You can't even say the words. Because of that, you'll never be king." Lawrence returned his gaze to the room. "I'm asking for your loyalty." Lawrence stretched out his hands. "Come and pledge yourself to me. Before everyone here, accept me as your king. Then we can get started on strengthening and purifying our world." His cold eyes combed over the crowd. "Who will join me?"

No one dared to breathe.

Everyone stood motionless, waiting for someone to make the first move.

Atlas stepped forward, but only to move closer to Michael. Lawrence was neither surprised nor annoyed.

Master Han slid through the crowd. Upon reaching the stairs, he held his wand toward his fellow Master. Dropping to one knee, he said, "You have my title and my wand, my Lord."

Lawrence grinned. "Welcome, my friend."

Master Finch shook his head. "You're mad."

"You refuse to serve?" Lawrence tilted his head. Once, I thought it was a small movement, and now, it reminded me of a predator staring down its prey.

"You're not my king." Limping across the room, Master Finch bent as much as his bum knee would allow in front of Michael. "You have my title and my wand."

Michael bowed to him with his jaw clenched tight.

"Masters!" Lawrence called from the stage. "Where do you place your loyalty? Which future do you choose?" His eyes landed on me.

Right. Now that we have titles, he's talking to us too.

Emeka stepped forward. With his crown gleaming, he walked across the room and bent before Lawrence. "My title and wand, my Lord."

Tala was the second to move, with Master Loran quickly behind her. Tension hung in the air like thick smoke. It filled my lungs and crawled over my skin with every person that bowed.

Masters of all different trades offered their wands. A Master of Combat bowed before Michael. A Master of Ward Casting pledged her loyalty to Lawrence. A Master of Weapons quickly followed.

Master Lenin and Master Harlan offered their wands to Michael. Thiago walked across the whole room to bow before him too.

"Master Heart," Lawrence called from the stage. He held out his hand. "Join me."

I was still frozen in front of the office. The intimate conversation behind the closed door cooled in my memory as I gazed up at Lawrence Hart.

My magic stirred in my chest, offering me a third option. *Run,* it seemed to whisper.

My thoughts bounced between the two kings: one dressed in white and the other in black. One was decorated with scars and the other with jewels. One king promised I would never see blood. The other couldn't promise me anything.

I turned my eyes from Lawrence's inviting hand to the man who stood silently watching me. He didn't offer me his hand.

"Charlie." My name fell softly from Michael's lips. "Go where you wish. I won't hold it against you."

Michael hardly showed any emotion, and that's what I was used to. The man addressing me now wasn't concealing anything. He didn't beg or invite me forward, but his heart bled through his gaze all the same.

I could run. I could vanish off the face of the earth and let them battle it out like I had planned. But the familiar drum to *run* wasn't there. I hadn't heard it in a long time.

My head clearly knew which choice had the best outcome, the best survival rate, and the most comfort. Standing in that room, surrounded by extravagant flowers and white drapes, it was effortless to imagine the life Lawrence described: never being hungry or cold, anything I wanted at the snap of my fingers. I wouldn't be able to recall what worry felt like. I never wanted to fight. In Eden, I wouldn't have to.

What I couldn't imagine in that fantasy was the hollowness in my chest or the twist in my stomach. I was feeling it at that moment every time I thought of stepping forward. Every cell in my body screamed against the logical decision my mind tried to raise.

Because I wasn't loyal to him. I wanted nothing to do with his cause. My loyalty and my heart rested with another. And it had for some time.

I moved forward; the clicking from my shoes pierced the stillness of the room. Turning my back to one king, I faced the other.

"I would offer you my wand, but since I can do magic without it . . ." Turning my palms to the ceiling, I lowered myself into a curtsy. "If you'll have me, my magic and title are yours."

Blake broke through the crowd and bowed beside me. "You have mine, too."

Michael smiled—a full, drunk-on-relief smile. Bending at the waist, he bowed to us. When we were all standing, he said, "I would be honored to serve alongside you both."

His eyes didn't leave mine as I stepped forward and took the place beside him.

Overwhelmed, he took my hand. His calloused fingers wrapped around mine and gripped them just as tightly as I held his.

"How disappointing." The coldness in Lawrence's voice caused the room to feel like the frozen water outside. He turned, and over his shoulder, he said three words.

"Kill them all."

The Masters before him didn't miss a beat. They drew their wands. Golden magic flared through the air.

I stepped forward from the line of Achilles Heel.

Magic flooded through my veins. The bones in my arms glowed as it swarmed to my fingers. The glittering chandeliers brightened as the smaller lights around the room popped into showers of sparks. Fire roared across the walls. Answering my call, it crashed toward the charging party like a tsunami.

Lawrence turned. The flames glinted in his cold eyes. He saw he was about to lose.

He took his wand from his coat and fired at the ceiling. Quicker than anyone could react, it shattered.

I turned my palms skyward. The fire disappeared with a mighty whoosh, leaving the air cold and dry. Magic blasted up, covering the broken ceiling. The weight of it pressed against my shoulders. My knees almost buckled.

"Go!" Michael yelled, waving his arm toward the new members of the Heel. "Get out of here!"

With the command from their king fresh in the air, the Heel Ported in batches. Some hesitated when they saw their king made no move to follow.

My arms shook. The ceiling began to lower. Gritting my teeth, I forced more magic through my hands, trying to raise it back up.

Lawrence's men rushed up the stairs, fleeing in a stampede of chaos. The ones too far from the stairs Ported.

But there was one very angry Master who broke free from the crowd. Master Theodore, baring his teeth like a wild animal, shoved another Master out of his way. The poor woman was trampled beneath the exiting masses.

Master Theodore's arm trembled as he aimed his glowing wand at my chest.

Michael tackled me, knocking me out of the way. As my feet left the ground, my grip on my magic slipped.

We slammed into the tile. With a mountainous roar, debris fell around us.

114

You'll See, Darling

When I came to, my head ached sharply. The right side of my face was hot and sticky with blood.

Blinking my eyes into focus, a wand manifested in front of my face. I flinched back with my heart in my throat.

As my vision sharpened, I saw no magic smoldering in the etched designs of the shaft. Following the wand up to the owner, I found him on the ground with glassy eyes.

I propped myself onto my elbow. Chunks of debris slid off me and clattered to the floor. Clenching my teeth, I fought the groan climbing up my throat.

That's when I realized how quiet it was. Holding my aching head, I looked around the once magnificent room. Without the bright chandeliers, the only light came from the moon, and she was reluctant to show more than necessary.

Struggling to my knees, I looked around for any familiar faces. Then I saw Michael a few feet away, pinned under a block of the ceiling.

Shaking with relief, I pulled myself across the floor toward him, glass cutting into my palms.

"Michael," I whispered, shaking his shoulders. His head rolled limply to the side. Sharply, I patted his cheek, leaving a smudge of blood on his face. "Michael."

His eyes jerked open. He lurched upright, ready to attack anything that moved. His efforts ended with him nearly head-butting the rock pinning his leg. Cursing, he fell back with a groan.

"You're pinned."

"I noticed." Squeezing his eyes shut, he took a couple deep breaths. "Are you alright?"

"I'm ok." My head throbbed, demanding my attention. There was a sharp pain in my side, but I ignored that as well. "Can you feel your legs?"

He nodded. "But I'm not feeling anything good." Opening his eyes, he looked at me upside down. Gently, he touched my forehead. "Your head is bleeding."

To illustrate his words, a trickle ran down my face and dripped onto my hand. "It's just a scratch." My aching head called me a liar. "If I levitate this, can you pull yourself out?"

Breathing heavily, he nodded.

Pulling on my magic, my hands glowed once again. Placing them under the ledge, I pushed.

Michael cried out. "Stop, stop, stop!"

Quickly, I cut the flow of magic. My hands fluttered uselessly around him.

"I take it back," he gasped. "My leg is crushed."

"Wimp. You've had worse."

He chuckled, but it was strained. "That doesn't mean it doesn't suck." He grabbed my hand and closed his eyes. "Give me a second and we'll try again."

My leg jerked out from under me, causing me to drop to my elbow.

"Charlie?" Michael twisted to look behind me.

Disoriented, I struggled to get my knees back under me.

He yanked his hand from mine and reached for his wand. Out of reach by a foot, he snapped, "Charlie. My wand."

The pain in my head was so sharp, I could hardly see. Through my fuzzy vision, I was able to make out the shape of his wand to my left. I reached for it.

"Charlie!"

Magic burned around my ankle, jerking me away from him. He snagged my hand, stopping me only momentarily.

Our hands, slick with blood, clasped around each other, and then slipped.

Dragged through the debris, I was jerked into the air. I slammed against someone and, through my fogged mind, I heard Michael yelling. Arms wrapped around me before magic filled the air.

I was Ported from the ruined building.

We Ported once, twice, and then a third time. Just when I thought my head was going to break, my captor tossed me to the floor, nowhere near the Crowning Ceremony or Michael.

I held out my blood-slick hands, but they did nothing to keep my head from bouncing against the floor. My eyes refused to focus on anything farther than five feet. Fear chased my heart around my chest.

Shiny shoes stopped at the edge of my vision.

Clarence Hardy crouched in front of me. "You don't look so good." Gone was his black hair and charming country accent. In their place were blond locks and sophistication. His split eyebrow looked out of place. "Did you miss me?"

I tried to push myself away from him, but my arms were weak. Keeping my eyes open was even a struggle.

"I hope you liked my presents. The Dellamora and the mice were fun. Sabotaging your earpiece was my favorite. I thought you would back out of The Trial, but you were always so stubborn."

Shock blew through my mind. "That . . . was you?"

"Of course. Who else did you think it was? That's right. You didn't think." He chuckled. "If only you played along." The smug look on his face contorted with annoyance. "You put Johnson up to taking me out of The Trial. I'd love to punish you myself, but all in good time."

"Why?" I asked. "Why did you do it?"

"It's obvious," he said harshly. "I had orders from my king."

"Don't be rude, my son." Lawrence came to stand behind him and peered down at me. The bastard's white suit didn't have a single wrinkle or speck of blood on it. "Get her into the chair. I'd like to get this started." He turned and walked out of my view.

Clarence grinned. Through my fogged mind, he reminded me of a crocodile. As he straightened, hands grabbed me from behind and jerked me to my feet.

I think I passed out; the pain in my head overcame all my senses. When it died down, I was on my back in a reclining chair. Silver cuffs were strapped around my wrists and ankles, anchoring me in place.

Lawrence stood silently in front of me. He took his time removing his jacket and neatly folding it. When he had his sleeves rolled up, he took out his wand. Dragging over a stool, he sat beside my head.

"What are you going to do?" My voice was barely audible.

"You'll see, darling."

He touched his wand to my forehead. With a glaring bright light, heat blew from the tip, and tore through my skull.

END OF BOOK TWO

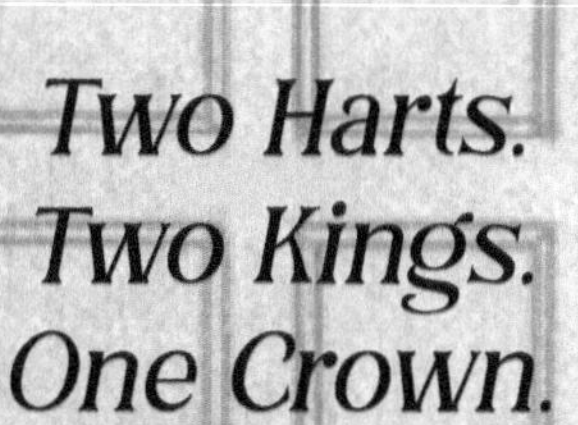

Acknowledgements

First, I'd like to thank you, the person holding this book at this exact moment, reading these exact words.

Thank you for continuing this story. I know how few hours there are in a day, so it means the world that you would spend what little you have with these characters and their story. I can't believe I get to do this, and that I get to share it with you. You have no idea how much joy the thought of you with this book brings me. You make my day, my month, my year, my whole life. I could say thank you a thousand times, and it will never do what I feel justice.

This book is a work of so many minds. Out of all of the books in this series, this is the one I spent the most time editing and reworking. There were so many people who influenced the twists and turns or helped me expand upon what I started with when I was sixteen.

First, Jonathan and Matthew. Thank you for your help coming up with the names for the Seven Great Schools. The group chat we had was the first time I had someone else take this little world of mine seriously. For the first time, it didn't feel so small. Plus as a homeschooler, you made the names sound so much cooler than I could have ever come up with alone. (The European Academy was originally Rolling Hills High. *cringe*)

Patricia, thank you for taking a chance on me, a complete stranger, and my writing so many years ago. You were the first person to say they liked my voice as a writer. You were also the first person to tell me that my story had kept them up past their bed time. Oh, what a feeling! After all of these years, I still remember your kindness and the helpful critiques you offered, and I will forevermore.

To Laurel, Jess, Paolo, Megan F., and Kim, I owe you so much. You helped weed out the melodramatic bits, the cringe, and unearthed the soul of this story. Through texts, phone calls, long winded emails or lunch dates, you were always there to hear me out. You helped me layer the pieces to make the horrifying, painful, and wonderful plot that it is today. I am so proud of this story and the growth of its cast, and it wouldn't be this way without you. Thank you from the bottom of my tender, dark, and twisty heart.

Thank you, Jodi Keller at NY Book Editors, for ripping my heart out, making me lose the will to live and write, but also giving me a golden nugget of an idea that made me SO excited to write it that I barely slept for a week. You are ruthless, but you are good.

Emily Snyder and Natalia Junqueira, thank you for making this book look like a real book! From cover design to the interior details, it completely surpassed all of my expectations. Thank you for giving my story a face.

Mom, I was so nervous to share this story with you to edit. You were my teacher for so many years, I didn't want to disappoint you. This was a part of myself that I didn't know if you would understand. But getting your notes and perspective has been one of the greatest parts of this process. I am so thankful for all the work you poured into me and this story. I love this book so much for all of the people it brought me closer to, and now you're one of them. Thank you for being a part of my team and constantly being in my corner.

Last by not least, my sister Meg. You changed my life, and I don't think you know it. You were the first person to hand me a fantasy book. You ignited the theater in my mind. You lit the fire that churned out idea after idea after idea that then led to a foster kid in Kansas and the magical, brutal journey she would go on. I don't think I ever told you that. I am forever grateful for the gift you have given me (my wallet hates you for all of the books I buy, but my soul loves you). You are the best older sister, and no one can tell me otherwise. Thank you for being you.

With much love,
M

Photo by *Laurel Anne Creative*

Michelle lives in Colorado Springs, Colorado, covered in cat hair and always with a cup of tea in hand. When she's not writing, she's either daydreaming up the next scene or sketching something from her world.

Connect with me
Instagram | @michellenhagood
Series Updates and Fangirl Fuel | @_theroyaltrilogy_
Website | www.michellenhagood.com

www.ingramcontent.com/pod-product-compliance
Lightning Source LLC
Chambersburg PA
CBHW031227310726
48971CB00004B/913